1864

An Alternate History

James Cupelli

Copyright © 2006 by James Cupelli

Edited by Vicki Allen and Heather Mic Murphy

ISBN 0-7414-3082-7

Published by:

PUBLISHING.COM

*1094 New DeHaven Street, Suite 100
West Conshohocken, PA 19428-2713
Info@buybooksontheweb.com
www.buybooksontheweb.com
Toll-free (877) BUY BOOK
Local Phone (610) 941-9999
Fax (610) 941-9959*

Printed in the United States of America

Printed on Recycled Paper

Published July 2006

A note from the author regarding the use of italics

I chose to use italics in this book as a means to help the reader clearly identify the difference between past and present. I fully understood that the frequent use of italics to represent recollections of the generals would slow the early part of the novel. I still felt this labor a necessity. The recollections are meant to allow the reader to fully understand how past events could have motivated each general's decision-making process.

I had read several books on Civil War battles, and was left by many of them, wondering why a general made certain decisions that seemed painfully obvious to an outsider. It was not until I read Shelby Foote's The Civil War A Narrative that I was able to understand significantly more. Mr. Foote's very comprehensive account of the epic war put much into context.

I felt that the history leading to the events in this book was necessary in order for one to fully understand what might have motivated the decisions of those involved. Thus, allowing the reader a glimpse at what might have caused the debacle that sealed the doom for the South's last great campaign of the Civil War.

On War

With the exception of Robert E. Lee's actions in this story, the events that you read concerning the Confederate march to Spring Hill. are for the most part historically accurate. This is in fact, the story of John Bell Hood's bold and tragic offensive into Tennessee.

This Spring Hill is his second chance.

The dialogue between those involved in this book was derived from conjectures taken from a myriad of Civil War literature, including biographies, autobiographies, letters and personal accounts by those involved. There are also several direct quotes that were used to ensure that the alternate history would read as real as fiction would allow.

<u>Thanks</u>

To my wife, Heather, who unselfishly gave up five of the most laborious years of our life in order for me to comprise this history, and then weave it into a very realistic what could have been.

To Robert and Ann Cupelli, parents who never doubted anything I set my mind to.

To Peter Negri, my father-in-law, for sitting in the car next to me on all our Civil War trips, and allowing me to argue with myself over and over and over again.

Most importantly, to those that served during the Civil War, to the families they left behind, and to those who keep their memories alive today.

Lee's Situation

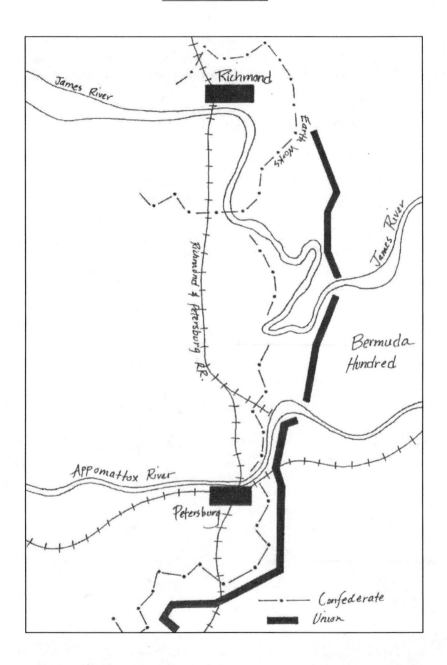

Chapter I

November 17 1864

Virginia

A cold wind crept through the long abandoned home and wrapped itself around the shadows of two strong men. The older man stood in the middle of the room like an ancient gnarled oak. His body bent and worn, but his foundation securely rooted in the soil of Virginia. The younger man was in many ways a seed from that same tree. He turned his back for a moment, to stare into the darkness that awaited them both outside the window. The hour was rapidly approaching midnight, and it seemed to be getting colder. That darn bitter wind refused to remain outside, as it cut through the cracks of the shanty like an unstoppable deluge, much like the Federal juggernaut that had pushed and cornered this once valiant and optimistic, overachieving and yet tatterdemalion army.

The gray haired man rubbed his hands to keep warm, while his younger general thoughtfully danced calloused fingers through his thick brown beard. The younger man kept his eyes intent on the trenches that formed their last line of defense. He knew that the better days were gone. It was only a matter of time, until the war of attrition ended the Confederacy.

The older man broke his trance.

"Well my war horse, I hope you have a good reason for persisting on meeting me here at this time."

General James Longstreet always felt a touch of pride when General Lee referred to him, as his war-horse. It had strong connotations. However, now was not the time for such feelings. He looked into the eyes of his commanding general, and said a small prayer, that maybe this time he would listen.

"General Lee, we have no chance, here." That was how he said it. He ended his statement with the word *here*. He was hoping that if he let Lee figure this out on his own, that it would seem like Lee's plan. That was the key. Longstreet realized only now the mistake he made at Gettysburg when he tried to offer Lee sound advice. He had not given Lee the chance to form a conclusion on his own, and so Lee must have thought that he meant to override his command.

That could not happen again.

General Lee was a good Christian, but he was also a proud man. No one knew that more than Longstreet. Lee appeared benevolent and humble to all, and he was. However, he was also very proud of his army's unperceivable victories over superior forces. No matter how hard Lee tried to repress his pride, for the Lord considered it a sin, Longstreet knew it was there, existing just a few layers beneath his skin. Lee's pride was the driving force of this army. It was really all that they had left to fight for. Lee had to know this, had to feel proud of his accomplishments. He deserved to be. Yet, Longstreet felt a wrenching rage in the pit of his stomach because of this pride that Lee had in himself and in his army. This unwelcome nausea was caused by the three-day event that had occurred during the summer of '63 at Gettysburg.

After an extremely successful first day offensive in Penn-sylvania, the Southern army had an opportunity to side step the Federal army and get between them and their capital. Wasn't that the reason for the offensive in the first place, to outmaneuver the enemy, draw them into the open, find good ground, dig in and let them attack? Longstreet had shown Lee how well such tactics had worked back at Fredericksburg, where the Federals, with superior numbers, were massacred trying to take a well-fortified position. How had such an intelligent man not seen this, seven months later, when the tables were turned?

Pride. That was how.

When it was clear that the Yankees were not intending to attack at Gettysburg, he practically begged Lee to leave them on the defensive, and simply move around them to threaten Washing-ton. This would have forced the enemy to abandon their defenses and attack us instead of us attacking them. That was the key to winning a war where your opponent had the upper hand in numbers. The set up was there, practically handed to them. They were given a golden opportunity to cut off the Federal army from its capital. Longstreet could imagine hearing the Northern politicians angrily yelling their complaints and fears at the President. They would have cajoled Lincoln into having the Northern army attack before Washington fell to the rebels. The result would have been another slaughter like the one the Yanks suffered at Fredericksburg. Longstreet fully understood that, and he expected Lee to as well.

2

Unfortunately Lee would attack. The more Longstreet thought about it now, the more it caused the pain in his side to threaten to rip through his soul. How could an army, without its cavalry and thus not knowing the exact position or size of its enemy, go on the offensive over open ground, against a well-fortified position?

Again it was pride. Pride enhanced by Lee's prior victory at Chancellorsville.

It was shortly after the defensive victory at Fredericksburg, when Longstreet's corps was sent south of Richmond to forage for much needed supplies as well as to contest the Federal forces that were threatening the coast. Thus, he was not present for Lee's greatest triumph. Incredibly, Lee had done the impossible against an army that doubled his in size. While the Federals were pressing Lee at Fredericksburg, Union General Fighting Joe Hooker detached more than half his force, numbering more than Lee's whole army, into the Confederate rear. Lee was now faced with two armies pressing against him, one from each side. Audaciously, he decided to leave a small force to contest the Federal crossing at Fredericksburg, hoping that their recent failure to cross the river would prevent another attempt. This allowed him to send the bulk of his command to face General Hooker's force of eighty thousand.

Several factors had allowed his plan to succeed, the primary one being General Hooker's inability to command. The failure of the fifty thousand Yanks left back at Fredericksburg to speedily and decisively shatter the twelve thousand Confederates that opposed them, allowed Lee to concentrate the majority of his army on Hooker's advance. Still, the Southern army was well outnumbered and should have hoped for a stalemate at best.

Longstreet doubted whether anyone involved at the battle of Chancellorsville truly believed that the outcome would result in a Confederate victory... except perhaps for 'Stonewall' Jackson. The unorthodox Southern commander consistently led his corps in tactics that were unforeseeable to both the enemy and even many on his own side.

Jackson was a firm believer in the offensive. He had a concept of how a smaller force could defeat a larger one. It required hitting it in its flank. It was like taking a ten-foot stick and placing it against a five-foot stick. Obviously if the ten foot stick hit the five foot stick head on, its sheer size would crush the

3

smaller one. Yet, as Jackson dogmatically believed, if you took the five-foot stick away from the front of the ten-foot stick, and placed it across the top of the bigger stick, you would make a letter 'T'. Now the smaller stick was much bigger than that portion of the larger stick that it faced. That was how you had to hit a superior force. Hit and never stop until it was entirely defeated. In that, Jackson was a genius.

At Chancellorsville, Jackson had a plan that called for yet another split of the Lee's army. He would march thirty thousand of Lee's fifty thousand soldiers around the Federal flank, as if they were retreating. Once out of the enemy's view, Jackson would then turn his men and redirect their marching columns so that they would position themselves upon the exposed Yankee flank. Once in place, they would emerge from the woods and hit the Yanks head on. Lee's twenty thousand were to hold Hooker's whole entire army in place as Stonewall completed his maneuver.

Longstreet still felt the same about the plan now as he did then. It was ludicrous. Had he been there, he knew that he would have done all that he could to dissuade Lee from listening to Jackson. How could you split an army in the face of an advancing force, which doubled your own? Hooker should have crushed Lee, then turned on Jackson. That was what most of the Federal commanders had wanted. Yet because of Hooker's sudden panic, it didn't happen that way. Once again, the Federal command failed its soldiers. But Longstreet knew that it was more than just their failure in command, it was their fear of Robert E. Lee. Hooker had simply halted all movement. He must have needed time to contemplate Lee's strategy. The rebels should have retreated, how could they not? Hooker had succeeded in getting his army across the fords in Lee's rear and now appeared to have the rebels squeezed on both sides .He must have known that his army was much larger than Lee's. Yet, he couldn't come up with an answer that would explain Lee's audacity to turn his back upon Fredericksburg, and meet him upon the battlefield at Chancellorsville. Perhaps Hooker thought that Longstreet's corps had returned from below Richmond?

Longstreet wondered if he would ever fully understand what caused Hooker to deviate from his well thought-out plan. The only answer that made any sense was one of intimidation.

Hooker may have thought that if Lee had chosen to face him at Chancellorsville, well then it was because Lee wanted it to be so. *It probably frightened Hooker terribly when he realized that Lee had somehow managed to steal the initiative from him, and was probably getting ready to expose the Federal army for splitting up from the rest of the force at Fredericksburg. The poor fool must have thought that his only hope lay in sitting tight, and getting out of this trap as quickly and safely as he could.*

He ordered General Howard to guard the extreme right flank of the Federal army. Unfortunately, Howard was not absorbed in the exaggerated fears of his commander and only kept a part of his men on guard. The rest of his corps was behaving more like they were on a picnic than fighting in a war. They apparently had bought into Stonewall's ruse, believing Jackson and his men were falling back to go after the Federal cavalry raiding to the south. That tragic assumption was Howard's folly. A good commander should never allow such assumptions to be confused with reality. Howard should have known of Jackson's reputation for tenacity. No matter how many reports claimed that the rebels were in retreat, Jackson would never have fallen back.

The result was a complete surprise attack on the Federal flank. Jackson and his thirty thousand screaming soldiers exploded from the woods like terror itself. Howard's men were caught completely by surprise. They did not even feign an attempt to stop the attack. Rather, they did all that they could to get up and run. Their momentum created a domino effect, as other Federal regiments down the line were compelled to take flight with them.

The Yanks fighting Lee were bewildered when they witnessed what was transpiring on their right flank. The whole Federal line collapsed. The two things that saved their army from total destruction, was the tragic shooting of Jackson by his own men, and the late arrival of Federal soldiers who had finally succeeded in crossing the Rappahannock River at Fredericksburg.

Upon hearing that a large enemy force was moving through Fredericksburg, Lee chose to once again split his army. He left a contingent of his command to hold Hooker in place, while detaching enough soldiers to face the new threat coming from the east. The Yankees coming from Fredericksburg reacted much like Hooker had. They feared that they were exposed to the Confederates, and rather than face certain destruction, decided against staying for the battle. In the end, the Federals managed to retreat both of their armies from the south side of the Rappahannock... over one hundred thousand Yanks running from under fifty thousand Southerners.

Virginia was free again.

Lee was proud of his men and the victory, but sorrowed by the loss of Jackson. If Lee had to describe his relationship with Jackson and Longstreet, it may be one of the sword and shield. Where Longstreet was like his shield, repelling the masses of troops thrown at him, Jackson was his slashing sword. This army would sorely miss Thomas Jackson. However, Lee had to move on. He still had his men, and his faith in God. He believed that God had shown by this victory that the South could not lose. How else could an army ill supplied defeat a force better equipped, and twice its own size?

Thus, the important lessons learned from the defensive fighting at Fredericksburg were vanquished from Lee's stratagem at Chancellorsville. All because of a Union general that lost his nerve and a Southern general who credited the miracle to God.

It would be this conviction, in his men, and in his Lord, that would later allow Lee to give the command that would send his army into the jowls of death on Cemetery Ridge at the battle of Gettysburg. Those battles now seemed so long ago, and Longstreet knew that he could not allow for past lesson's to repeat again... not now and not ever.

Lee broke Longstreet's thoughts with a deep sigh. "I know that we have no chance here," he said. "That is what I fear as well, though I wish it were otherwise. We have met every advance by General Grant and repulsed each and every one of them. Yet, our forces are not numerous enough to allow for any counter attack. Grant knows this, as do we. So why are we discussing this at this hour General?"

"Sir, it's just that there must be something that can be done."

"Without more men, we are limited in our options. Even our defensive capabilities are faltering. Our poor men sleep in frozen trenches with a handful of ammunition per day. We lack sufficient food to feed them, and those that do get fed are forced to consume what is unfit for the worst creature on God's good earth. Grant has the ability to just throw his masses at us, knowing eventually we must break somewhere. And we will General. We will."

Longstreet's spirits lifted at what Lee had last said. The

old fox was learning. Until recently, the results of attrition were not comprehensible to a greater part of the Southern command. Longstreet had tried explaining that with the North's vast reservoir of manpower, they could afford numerous Fredericksburgs, and still win the war.

This was his chance.

"And now I hear Sherman has left Atlanta with his army and is heading east," Longstreet said.

Lee raised his sunken head and looked deep into his general's eyes. Longstreet couldn't tell if Lee was disappointed when he said that he now understood why he was still awake at such a late hour. "You want to go west again?"

Longstreet did not know how to answer his commander. He looked at Lee, and methodically removed a cigar from his coat pocket and lit it. The small fiery glow flowed from his side to his face like a purposeful firefly. He had to be very careful at this critical juncture. The entire Confederacy depended upon it.

"Sir, how do you feel about our chances out west?" Longstreet very purposely answered Lee's question with another question.

Lee put his hands in his pockets, and paced the room. Longstreet could tell that Lee was struggling internally for an answer. Lee walked over to the hearth and put another log onto the dying fire. He rubbed his hands in front of the warm flames, and then pulled up a chair. He motioned for Longstreet to do the same.

"Atlanta has fallen," was all Lee said.

"And how do you feel about General Hood's performance at Atlanta?"

Lee gave a Longstreet a very quizzical look. "We both know that General Hood is a good man."

"No question about it sir, I am not here to question his capabilities."

Lee went on as if he hadn't heard Longstreet's interjection. "He has served me as a fine commander at every level that he has attained. He was remarkable at Gaines' Mill. McClellan's troops really had us tied up at that hill, until Hood and his Texans charged through their relentless hailstorm of fury to shatter their position. Pure and gallant heroism."

Longstreet saw Lee's eyes gaze towards some window into the past. He needed to draw him back. "I remember that well sir."

"So many nights I reflect on that, and wished Picket, Pettigrew and Trimble had possessed at least some part of that Texan fury."

Another reference to Gettysburg. Longstreet again had to hold his tongue. There was no comparison of Gaines' Mill to Cemetery Ridge. Whereas an isolated corps of Yanks defended Gaines' Mill, Cemetery Ridge had the advantage of being defended and supported by their entire army. Attacking the former was tough, but possible, attacking the latter was suicide. When Lee had ordered the fifteen thousand soldiers of Picket, Trimble and Pettigrew to assault the Union center at Gettysburg, Longstreet could only shake his head in denial. His only comment had been that he did not believe that any fifteen thousand soldiers ever arrayed for battle could take that position.

"Yet I always feared Hood's ability when he was promoted to commander in chief in place of Johnston," Lee continued. "How I greatly admired his ferocious offensives when he was my divisional commander. He could afford to take such chances then. But when you lead an entire army like that, one that can not be reinforced, and you continually throw all of your men into battle after battle..."

"Your army bleeds itself to death," Longstreet finished the sentence.

Lee stared at the flames, and continued. "Still, who could blame Hood for his actions and their results. He was promoted practically in mid battle. I doubt he even knew where Johnston had all of his divisions positioned. On top of that, our government had done everything they could to order him to attack. That was why Johnston was removed, he kept giving ground."

"Yes, but a pity for his removal. He kept the army together."

Lee turned his face from the fire, and focused on Longstreet. His tone was like a reprimanding father, "General, you were offered a chance to take command of that army, were you not?"

"I was sir."

"And did you not refuse it?"

"Sir I did. And I would refuse it again."

For the first time, Robert E. Lee had a face of unabashed perplexity. He thought he knew where Longstreet was going with this. Even before Gettysburg, Longstreet had lobbied for the transfer of troops to the west. He got his wish after the loss of Gettysburg. Longstreet took two of his divisions to reinforce General Bragg in Northern Georgia. The result was an astounding success, as Longstreet's troops smashed the Federal right flank at Chickamauga, and sent the Yanks scampering back to Chattanooga. However, the success was not followed up, and the North was able to reinforce their beleaguered army. The Union army was then able to attack the Confederates and drive their army south into Georgia. The defeat cost Bragg his command of the Army of Tennessee and led to the promotion of General Joseph E. Johnston.

Lee knew that Johnston was rewarded the position mainly because others like Longstreet refused it. Longstreet had written him a letter detailing how the Army of Tennessee had lost its only chance when it failed to defeat the demoralized Federal army at Chattanooga. Longstreet had been very clear when he said that the fate of the Army of Tennessee was a hopeless one, and that he did not want to command a force he felt was destined to fail. The question was, why was he alluding to the West now?

"General, if you did not want to take command, then why are you bringing this up now. Didn't you yourself say the situation was hopeless?"

Longstreet was eager to voice his concerns, hoping his plans would unfold before Lee with as much clarity and precision as they had for him. "Sir, that situation has changed."

Lee nodded for him to continue.

"Sherman is sending more than half his army east, probably all the way to the Atlantic Coast. He will be utterly unopposed." Longstreet became voracious, leaning closer to Lee to emphasize his absoluteness as to what he was going to say next. "Sir, we cannot stop him."

Lee broke his momentum, "Sherman does appear to be heading east, and you are correct, we cannot stop him. And I also cannot afford to let you take troops west again. We do not have the reserves. General you know this."

Longstreet went to take Lee's hands in his own, forgetting that his right arm existed for show only. The useless limb hung limp from its socket, a constant reminder of the bullet that passed through his neck and crashed into his shoulder during the battle in the Wilderness. It had only happened this past May, and so he had not fully come to terms with life without the full use of his arm.

The bullet had been fired by one of his own men, on a field not far from where Jackson was tragically fired upon by his own soldiers. Ironically, Longstreet was forced to suffer the same fate. 'All the more reason why we must learn from our mistakes,' he thought.

"I do not want to send any troops west sir," he said. Lee smiled and seemed a bit relieved by Longstreet's acceptance of the current situation. "General Lee, I only want to send you."

If Longstreet thought Lee looked bewildered before, he was beyond words for this. He felt Lee's hand slipping from his own, but he did not let go. For a moment he thought he saw the same doubtful look in Lee's eyes as he did back at Gettysburg.

Longstreet waited for Lee to take in what he had just said. He did not want to push too hard. Lee gently pulled away from his war-horse and stood up under obvious anguish. He rested his tired hands on the backside of his hips and walked over to the table. Longstreet turned his head to follow.

"I have been asked that before, by yourself included, and my answer now is the same as it was then. I will not leave my Virginia," said Lee. "I was also offered command of the Union forces when this war first began, and I turned that down as well, for the same reason. General Longstreet, I will not leave these good men to defend Virginia without me. We have been through far too much for me to leave them in the hands of another. Especially when they need me the most."

"General, the best chance these men have is for a decisive victory in the West, and right now there is a darn good opportunity for just that," Longstreet said. He couldn't discern if Lee was willing to listen to give him the benefit of the doubt, or if he was letting him speak just so he could get to bed. He hoped for the former.

"Sir, you know that my sources have always given me near accurate information. Well, it stands to reason that Sherman is heading this way with over sixty thousand men, and that leaves about that much left behind to face Hood's army of thirty thousand. Now here is where I feel that this plan can work. The sixty thousand or so facing Hood are divided between Schofield's command at Pulaski and Thomas' at Nashville. There are also a few rivers in between them, which would hinder those forces from consolidating. Sir, I believe Sherman has made a huge mistake heading east. I do not think that our army has ever had such favorable odds as we have now. If we can catch Schofield off guard, we would be at even numbers with the Yanks. Heck, that is all we ever asked for. If we defeat Schofield, then all that is left is Thomas. If he is beaten, then I can assure you that Tennessee will be ours. Sherman will have to turn back. Think of what this will do for the Union's morale. One hundred and twenty thousand Yanks take Atlanta, and a month later, the whole west falls to fewer than thirty thousand Confederates. All the while Sherman is on some massive raid through land that has little strategic importance."

"If Sherman is truly headed this way," said Lee.

Longstreet smiled inside. Lee's words meant that he was at least interested in his plan. He answered, "Sir, I hear Northern papers are quoting him as saying that he wants to march to the sea, to bring the war to the heart of our homeland. Our own General Wheeler has been confirming this for the past few days. He has begged every commanding general for any men that can be spared. Sir, make no mistake, Sherman is moving east."

"If we are to believe their presses," Lee said. He ignored Longstreet's comments about General Wheeler. "In any event, I have been with President Davis and he has informed me that Hood is already planning an offensive very similar to the one that you propose. Why do you feel so strongly that I need to go and do what Hood is planning?"

"Because we must win General. We must win. This is our best chance, and you are our best commander. Leaving you trapped here, with the ability to do nothing but wait to receive another attack or flanking maneuver from Grant is a waste of our greatest asset. Hood has had control of that army since Atlanta. He has shredded it by attacking an army that more than doubled his own. Our leaders have chastised Johnston for falling back from northern Georgia, but they haven't given him credit for inflicting twice as many casualties as he himself has suffered. All the while Johnston was falling back, he avoided becoming outflanked, and thus kept the army together. Hood on the other hand, in making desperate attacks, has lost over sixteen thousand men, not to mention the city of Atlanta.

And what did that cost Sherman, a few thousand men? We admonished Johnston for falling back from Atlanta, and instead we allowed Hood to just give it to the Federals, along with sixteen thousand men from the Army of Tennessee. That is a lot of Southern boys to lose to the enemy. You and I both know that we cannot afford such losses. If we had let Johnston fall back, at least there would still be an army left to oppose Sherman."

"General, I see your point, but let me remind you that we are not here to speak ill of General Hood."

"Yes sir, that was not my intent. I was only trying to make it clear why we need you out west. You won't fail. And more importantly, think of what that would do for morale. Morale on both sides. Sir, can you imagine our boys out there waking up one fine cold morning, and seeing you. You know that they would do anything for you. You tell them that they have even odds, man for man against the Yanks, you tell them that, and that they must win against Schofield, sir I honestly believe they will win on will alone. And think of them Yankees. When they hear that General Lee is out west, why there's no telling what they would do. Do you think Schofield is willing to stand up to you? I tell you what they'll do sir. Why, when they hear good old Robert E. Lee is facing them, they'll freeze in their tracks. Freeze just like Fighting Joe Hooker did last year at Chancellorsville."

Longstreet had to silently pat his own shoulder. The reference to Chancellorsville was not planned, but seemed to fit perfectly with his current argument. He hoped that the mention of the battle would spark the fire in Lee's furnace. That battle was Lee's greatest glory. He whipped a force more than twice his size. If he had had one more day, he knew Lee felt that he could have destroyed the whole Union army. Now he dangled that carrot in front of Lee. He offered him his one more day. One more chance to take the offense and relive his glory. The question was would Lee bite?

General Lee smiled and let out a laugh like a father amused when his son is trying to impress him. "That is a grand plan, General, but I could not leave my Virginia. But I do believe that your plan, which is much like Hood's, can work. Perhaps we can think of someone else to lead it, perhaps even you."

Longstreet was shaking his head from side to side before Lee even finished speaking. He faced the window and pointed into the distance.

"Sir, this is my type of fight. I told you at Fredericksburg to stick me behind a solid wall, on good ground and I could repel any attack the Yankees could mount. Well if it is all right with you, I'd rather do just that. You are the master at attacking. Besides, I think we both know how President Davis feels about me. He was not very enthusiastic about me taking command of that army when I was given the chance. I think that he was glad that I turned it down. There are very few men in this army whom Davis would allow total control like that, you being the best suited."

Longstreet stared into the burning embers for a few moments before continuing. "I would also like to point out that General Grant was reluctant to head east, and look at all that he has done for their army. He has transformed them into a relentless fighting army. He did what six commanders could not do. He has changed the look of this struggle. Might you not have a greater effect by taking command out West? Wasn't it you who wrote a letter to Hood himself, stating that the army would go anywhere and do anything if properly led?"

Lee smiled, wondering again how Longstreet attained such accurate information. Longstreet judged the grin differently. He thought that perhaps Lee was finally beginning to understand. The old fox was rubbing his head methodically. Longstreet was hoping that Lee's pride would take over and let him see that victory was possible out west. If he did, he would have to go, the situation here in Virginia was too obvious. Time was working against them. With their backs pinned to Richmond and Petersburg, their initiative was gone. Heck, even if they weren't pinned down, the size and the condition of this army could never go on the attack against the hordes of Yanks waiting for them. These were desperate times, and James Longstreet knew that something, anything had to happen fast, before the doors closed on the Confederacy forever.

"General," Lee said. "Who would command here if I were to leave?"

Longstreet had his answer ready, obviously having rehearsed this meeting and anticipated all of his commanders concerns. "General Joseph Johnston, sir."

Lee nodded his head in agreement with his general. "Yes, General Johnston could defend Virginia. But, the harder task would be convincing President Davis to allow such a promotion. Johnston was removed because of his constant retreats from the enemy. Yet, that considered, perhaps it would not be too hard to convince the president after all. Johnston could not retreat with this army even if he wanted to. We are already pressed with our backs to the capitol, there is nowhere else for him to go. Perhaps

Johnston would be the best man suited for such a task, he has proven his defensive capabilities in his strategic withdrawals from Sherman."

"The same reasons why he was removed from command," Longstreet said. "Maybe now our *Presid*...excuse me, our politicians will see the folly of their ways. Johnston kept the Army of Tennessee together by defending, while Hood has all but shattered it in attacking."

Lee began to walk towards the door, signaling the end of the conversation.

"General, I will think on this and have your answer in the morning."

Longstreet was all too familiar with those foreboding words of dismissal. Lee had said the same thing to him the night before the Confederate disaster at Cemetery Ridge. Feeling inauspiciousness creep within him like thousands of tiny crawling maggots, he desperately pulled Lee back by the shoulder. "Sir, what ever you decide, I will stand by you. Your old war-horse forever. But sir, I must stress one immensely important aspect of this plan. No one must know about your travel west, if you should choose to go. Surprise is our only ally at this point. That, ...and you is all that we have left."

Lee took his general's hand from his shoulder and held it firmly. He looked as if he was about to say something, but the moment passed. He turned back to leave the cold shanty, and said only, "I will think on this General, and you shall have my answer in the morning."

Robert E. Lee left Longstreet in the weathered home, and stepped out into the cold. He had much to contemplate upon, on this already short night. Could he actually leave his Virginia? He pulled his collar up over his neck to avoid catching the clasping grasps of the cold biting wind. As he turned up the path that led to his headquarters, he felt a bounce in his step. He could see the light from the fireplace through the windows. It would be warm in there. Then he looked back east, to the lines of trenches in the distance. Those poor men were freezing tonight. Unfair, it was all so unfair. As he turned to continue to his headquarters, he saw a soldier sleeping against a tree. The man was obviously wounded in a skirmish earlier today. Yet, even in his weakened sleep state, the soldier made his best effort to stand and salute Lee as the general passed him. Lee saw the grim determination of the South in the soldier's eyes. But he also knew that that facade was masking the pain and cold that now dwelled inside him. The soldier was making his best effort not to show that to the general. Lee was proud of that. He saluted the soldier, and proceeded on to his headquarters. He stopped after several steps, and returned to the man who had not realized Lee had come back. Lee placed a hand on his shoulder, and wiped his brow.

"Thank you sir," was all the soldier could say.

Lee smiled and turned back towards his headquarters. He wiped a tear from his cheek. That man wants to thank me, he thought. Thank me for what, for allowing him to freeze, or allowing him to starve? I should be thanking him. No General Longstreet, I cannot leave these proud men. What kind of thanks would that be? They are depending upon me, and I must be here with them. Win or lose, my commitment is with these proud boys.

The general nodded to the officers at his door. Their blank looks an obvious indication that they had forgotten that Lee even left several hours earlier. Lee closed the door to the cold and pulled his chair and blanket closer to the fire. He thought about his bed, but there was too much on his mind. He began rocking to and fro, back and forth, the motion of which, reminded him of the constant attack and retreat of the North.

Back and forth for over three years, to and fro....

Chapter II
Later that night

Lee awoke in the night still feeling very much tired. By the look of the fire, he must not have slept for too long. He wished he could easily fall back to sleep, yet knew that he would not. Frustrated, Lee stood up and grabbed the poker, and began to stir the logs within the fireplace. There was too much to think about. Longstreet did have a convincing argument. He just wished there was someone else who could lead that attack. Hood was out west now, and he knew Hood to be an excellent soldier. However, recent news of the disaster around Atlanta confirmed that Hood would not prove to be the effective commander as hoped by many in Richmond.

When Johnston had command, he was lambasted for constantly retreating. Johnston's refusal to give battle led to Hood's promotion and with it, the promise to have the Army of Tennessee on the attack. Hood was true to his word, but with disastrous results. Instead of forcing the Federals back over the Chattahoochee, Hood had launched several offensives that did nothing but consume the ranks of his army. The end result was that there were insufficient men left in his command. Hood was forced to vacate Atlanta, much like Johnston had wanted to. The difference was that Johnston's retreat was planned, and would have kept an army alive to impede Sherman's advance.

Still, Lee could not concede that Hood was to blame. General Hood had performed admirably at every juncture of his military career. He could not help but think positively when he thought of the giant Texan. Lee had to laugh at his own reference to Hood as a Texan. The man was from Kentucky, but he became famous and revered for his leadership of his Texan brigade. Surely the man who led such fierce soldiers had to be a Texan at heart, even if he was from the state of Kentucky.

Thoughts of him quickly brought back memories of the South's better days. The battles seemed to juxtapose, and melt together as he recalled each in turn. Specifically, there was the breaking of McClellan's siege of Richmond, Second Bull Run, Fredericksburg, Antietam, Chancellorsville, Gettysburg, and the recent battles in the Wilderness and Spotsylvania. In all of those battles, Lee's army had more than held its own while inflicting heavy casualties upon the enemy. But it was those last two battles that caused Lee to realize just how much this war had changed.

Up until the Wilderness and Spotsylvania, all of Grant's predecessors would march to the field of battle, for the most part suffer a defeat, and then retire to lick their wounds before deciding where and how to come after Lee again at a later date. That was not the case with Grant. Grant mostly lost the battles but kept advancing anyway. He had the reinforcements to do so.

All of the lessons learned at the academy, all of the studying of Napoleon's tactics and strategies, it all meant nothing if an enemy could just keep coming. That was what Lee had to face. For the most part, he won the battles, but was losing the war. Grant would line his army up in direct confrontation with Lee, and if he could not win by attacking, he would just move around the rebel flank. Time and time again, Lee had to rapidly march his command in order to arrive at the next position before Grant. And each time, the same result would occur. Grant, disappointed that Lee had beaten him to position, would form ranks and attack, only to be repulsed with heavy losses. And amazingly, the defeat did little to deter Grant, for he understood that Lee did not have the manpower to conduct a serious counter attack. Owning the initiative, Grant would attack until he realized he could not budge the Confederates, and then he would march around Lee's flank to force him out of position.

What angered Lee the most was that he knew he could do nothing but wait for Grant's maneuver and then react to it. Sadly, like a surreal premonition, he knew the eventual result. In time, his army would be pinned down around Richmond and Petersburg, as was the case now. There would be no more retreating. Grant had him where he wanted him, and would keep attacking, until somewhere, someone on his line would allow the breakthrough that would end the war for Southern independence.

Still, Lee could not think to leave his men here while he left for Alabama to lead the South's last hope. He looked around his room as if the answer to his problems lay somewhere yet searched. He felt a warm smile soften his face as he realized he would not find what he was seeking on any unread dispatch.

Lee stood from his chair and walked over to the bed. Very carefully and deliberately, he dropped to his knees, and clasped his hands in prayer. Resting his elbows on the bed, he prayed to God for some guidance. This was not his first time in prayer, nor would it be his last. Lee strongly believed in the hand of God. He attributed all of the South's success to the Almighty. That could be the only explanation for such immeasurable victories. He knew that only God could guide him now. As much as his men loved him and looked to him for leadership, Lee knew that he was but a sheep in the Lord's flock. 'Please God, only show me the surest answer to this our darkest plight.' He knelt in prayer for several minutes. Upon finishing, Lee crawled back into the bed, and slept in the comfort of his Lord...

$$* \quad * \quad * \quad * \quad * \quad * \quad * \quad *$$

On that same night, far away in Northern Alabama, General Hood was also having difficulty trying to sleep. He had spent the past few hours lying in his bed in a quiet, yet disturbed contemplation. His soft blue eyes stared into the dark emptiness of the room. 'This must be what my soul resembles,' he thought.

If the Confederacy could be personified as a wounded soldier, Hood was the apotheosis of its character. He was a fierce fighter, extremely strong willed, and yet damaged beyond repair. He had lost the use of his left arm at Gettysburg. Lost, making an attack he did not want to make. Perhaps that was what hurt most about it. It was not that he could not use his arm, it was more that every time he went to raise it and failed, he was reminded of the missed opportunity in Pennsylvania. Hood was never one to back down from glory, and if it meant a loss of a limb, then so be it. The important thing was achieving victory. But to lose his arm in an attack that he did not want to make seemed unfair.

As he lay there in the mists of his reflections, Hood subconsciously lifted an arm that couldn't move and went to rub an ankle that was not there. Half asleep, half-awake, the general let out a laugh. He had lost his right leg at the battle of Chickamauga. The loss of his leg had been by far a harder ordeal to cope with physically, than the loss of his arm.

Always one to lead his men into battle, Hood had done so again at Chickamauga. He could still remember the pain as the bullet hit and shattered his bone a few inches below the hip. The disbelief of the wound consumed him, as he lay upon the earth, listening to the battle rage. The sound of his men getting fainter as they charged into the distance, spoke of their victory. He was found soon after and brought to a doctor. The leg had to be amputated in order to save his life. And yet he could accept that fate with much more understanding than he could the loss of his arm. At the least his leg wound came at the cost of a great victory. Next to his valiant charge at Gaines' Mill, Chickamauga was perhaps his greatest day of heroism.

The victory at Chickamauga helped offset a horrible summer for the Confederates. July 3 and July 4 1863, could very well be the days that some historian would look back on and claim 'thus ended the Confederacy'. First Vicksburg, the South's western bastion, had succumbed to a Federal siege, no doubt because of General Joseph Johnston's inability to bring his army against Grant's rear and help relieve the pressure from General Pemberton's beleaguered command. Those poor boys held out as long as they could without food, ammo or supplies. Over thirty thousand soldiers removed from the war effort without getting their chance to bite back.

And only a day later, the world would learn that General Lee had failed in his offensive to gain the initiative in the East. The defeat at Gettysburg would be devastating. Many Southerners feared that double defeat would ensure that Britain and France would not intervene in the war.

Yes, those two losses could very well be the days that marked the beginning of the end for Dixie. That was unless something could be done. And if there was someone who was going to do it, Hood wanted to guarantee that it was to be him.

The South would have its chance just a few months later in North Georgia, near a river called Chickamauga. Named by the Indians, it translated to 'river of blood', and on September 19 and 20, it would live up to that name. At the time, Hood was under the command of General James Longstreet. His former commander had advocated a plan to send his divisions west to assist Bragg in defeating the Union army under the command of General Rosencrans. If the maneuver was successful, it would give the Southerners close to even numbers with their enemy.

The result was an immeasurable success. While Bragg pinned the Federals on their left flank, Longstreet's men stormed the Union right, where miscommunication had caused a gaping *hole near the center of their line. Such was the spot where fate had placed Hood's attack. The whole Federal line crumbled, causing a mass retreat to Chattanooga. Hood was wounded in this attack, and his only regret was not being active enough to convince Bragg to follow up the attack and crush the Federal Army at Chatta-nooga. Instead, while Hood was healing, Bragg decided to siege Chattanooga. Fortunately for the Yanks, they had Grant and not Johnston coming to their aid. Grant's arrival, coupled with the North's ability to rapidly send troops to Chattanooga, helped turn the tide. The Federals were able to break from their siege and send the Confederates scampering back south into the mountains of Georgia. The Federal victory eventually cost Bragg his command. In the restructuring of Southern command, Hood was promoted to lieutenant general within the Army of Tennessee, and found himself under the command of General Joseph Johnston.*

'What a wasted time that was,' Hood thought. Johnston's legacy was to leave behind an army that was unable to assume the offensive.

Hood rubbed a perspired hand through his hair as he lay in bitter contemplation. He wanted nothing more but to sleep this night, yet the past kept haunting him. He tried shifting his position in bed, but that failed to bring the comfort he sought. Hesitantly, for he knew that it could backfire, he reflected upon images of his love Sally Buchanan Preston. Buck, as she was called by those who knew her, was perhaps the only person who could make Hood hesitant in his actions. In fact, he admittedly surrendered to her upon first laying his eyes on her. That brought a smile to his tired lips.

The ranks upon ranks of Yankees could never force him to throw in the white flag, but Buck, oh Buck, he would give up in a heartbeat to her demands. And that was the secret that crippled Hood most. How could a man of his stature and command be respected if he could not even control the love of this one woman? A woman that was so beautiful, and yet so mean. A woman whose blooming red lips could so easily curl into mordant cynicism, like they did the night he overheard her choice of horrible words to describe his love for her.

He was in Richmond during the winter of 1863, recover-ing from the loss of his leg at Chickamauga. Yet, all was not melancholy. It seemed that the whole city was held in captivation by his presence, welcoming him as a hero returned. This allowed Hood to enter certain privileged social circles that he may not have been in otherwise. He knew that the men would welcome him openly, even without his leg. It was the women that worried him. They would not be as understanding. Realizing this, Hood had a plan to help alter his appearance. It may have cost him over five-thousand-dollars, but the cork leg that was smuggled in from France, was worth every cent. It would never perform like his real leg, but aesthetically, he was able to put on pants, and walk with a limp into his new social life.

Hood, in an effort to the make the most of his situation, used this brief respite to further his relationship with Sally Preston. Admittedly, he adored her like a lovesick schoolboy. While gazing into her blue eyes, he could honestly feel his legs buckle. It was during a dinner one night, when he carefully broached the topic of marriage with her. Buck smiled, not with the warmth of a person considering the other's feelings, but rather the way a condescending parent would smile at a child when the child claimed he wanted sweets for dinner. Buck removed her hand from his and simply said that there was no hope for love.

Hood gripped his pillow with his good hand, and refused to shed a tear at that hurtful memory, but at least he was no longer thinking about the war. The more important matter was that it did not take Buck long to finally come to her senses and have a change of heart. It wasn't even a month later, when she had changed her mind and accepted a proposal from him during a most romantic carriage ride. That's how fast things could change in love.

Hood needed to remember that in his current situation. Things change, and so can the direction of this war.

Hood carefully awoke at the sound of a skirmisher's rifle blasting into the night. He tried to regain his sleep, but the effort was futile. He thought about getting up to question the shot, but it was obviously unimportant. Otherwise, his room would have been bombarded with subordinates needing commands, like dogs needing the guidance of a leash. Yet, what difference would that make? They never followed his orders anyway. No matter what plan he would set into motion, it would somehow become bungled on the field of battle. Bungled orders had plagued him ever since he became the commander of the Army of Tennessee. Never before were his orders so misconstrued as at the gates of Atlanta. As hard as he tried to suppress it from his mind, Atlanta consumed his soul like a dark and suffocating blanket.

More shots rang out in the night threatening to wake the many tired soldiers huddled against the cold, but Hood continued to disregard them. Sporadic gunfire was not uncommon in the night. Still, the noise was not helping his insomnia. Hood thought of getting out of bed so that he could put some warm fluid into his body. Unfortunately, the chill in the air and the amount of labor it took to get up with the use of only two of four limbs far out-weighed any desire he could muster for a late night beverage.

Instead, he reached over to the table by the side of the bed and swallowed a hearty throat full of his laudanum. His doctor had prescribed the syrupy liquid to help calm his nerves. The effect of the opium-derived elixir was a magnificent wonder to him. In just a few moments, his mood would shift from depressed hopeless-ness to one of euphoria. Knowing that he needed to pass the time until the medicine took its effect, Hood continued with his recollections of Atlanta. There was something absolutely cathartic whenever he became consumed in his dwellings of that part of his very recent past.

He obtained the command of the Army of Tennessee when General Joseph Johnston was relieved of command. Admittedly, it was not the most auspicious time for a change in command, but Jefferson Davis was tired of Johnston's strategic retreats. Instead of keeping the Federal army out of North Georgia, Johnston had fallen back repeatedly until his army was encamped in Atlanta.

And Atlanta could not fall to the enemy.

Not only did the city have vital railroad connections to the rest of the Confederacy, it was also a major supply depot, as well as the symbol of Southern might. Yet, here was Johnston, falling back to Atlanta, without seriously engaging the Union army. Amazingly, Johnston advocated falling back further, and simply giving Atlanta to the enemy. President Davis could not let that happen, and thus Johnston was removed from command and replaced with Hood.

For any commander, no matter how much military acu-men he may possess, the acquisition of this position was nothing more than a prophetic damnation. Hood was charged with defending Atlanta against an enemy that outnumbered him two to one. In addition to this, Hood did not even know the whereabouts of many of his divisions. And if all that was not enough, there were the egos of his subordinates who felt chagrined at not getting the promotion over Hood.

Hood and his Christian beliefs may have felt some slight guilt about the latter. He was after all, part of the blame for the other generals' ill feelings concerning the promotion. Jefferson Davis' original intent sent General Bragg west to review the situation with Johnston and if necessary, have Johnston replaced with Hood's peer, General Hardee. Unbeknownst to President Davis, Hardee never stood a chance of receiving that promotion.

Festering grudges plagued the Confederate command like maggots devouring rotten flesh, and so Bragg had not forgiven Hardee for his is open criticism following the defeat at Chatta-nooga.

Hood fully understood this opportunity and used it to seize the initiative. He helped convince Bragg that if Hardee were given command of the army, he would no doubt follow Johnston's course and fall back from Atlanta. Bragg, seeing a chance to avenge his pride, chose to endorse Hood, instead of Hardee, as Johnston's successor.

Hood did feel some responsibility for this, though he would admit it to no one. Yet, he had done it for the good of the Confederacy. He knew that in order to ensure that this army fell back no more, he would have to take command of it himself. That he did. And true to his word, the Army of Tennessee stopped giving ground. In fact, it roared back at the approaching Federals, like a wounded lion protecting its young.

Hood's main objective in defending Atlanta was keeping its railroads free from Federal interference. Atlanta, via rail, held vital links both east and west of the Confederacy. On July 18, 1864 Sherman's Army threatened the Georgia railroad east of the city. The loss of that line would prevent any chance of Robert E. Lee sending Hood reinforcements from the eastern theater. Hood had to do something to prevent this. He had the bulk of his army facing this threat, as two Federal corps, commanded by Schofield and McPherson, approached from Decatur. That was when Hood saw a tremendous opportunity handed to him, one that appeared to be Jackson like in its potential for a complete victory.

North of the city lay Peachtree Creek, a natural barrier

that offered the South their last best defense for Atlanta. Sherman was not coming at Hood simply from Decatur, he also had Thomas single corps crossing the creek north of the city. Thomas would converge on Atlanta simultaneously with Schofield and McPherson's arrival from the east. Sherman indeed had enough men to launch a multi offensive attack against a beleaguered enemy. Yet his plan had two faults... and both potentially fatal.

The first was that Hood was not like Johnston. The flank attack from the east would not force Hood out of Atlanta. Even if Hood thought of retreating, he could not. There was no option here, but to fight. The second mistake Sherman had made was that Thomas, although heading for the same objective as Schofield and McPherson, was several miles from the rest of the army. This gave Hood a tremendous opportunity. He knew that the Federal army was larger than his own, but with Thomas's corps isolated, he could greatly increase his over all odds. If he could detain Schofield and McPherson long enough, Hood could use the bulk of his army, under the command of Hardee and Stewart, to squash Thomas against the river, then turn his attention to face the two Federal corps approaching from the east.

The location of Peachtree Creek was never so valued as it was that day for Hood's strategic masterpiece. Even though it was hard for an army to cross a large body of water, it was even harder to fight with it against your back. If routed, there was no means of escape. An army could be forced to capitulate under such circumstances, or even better, be utterly annihilated. Hood hoped for the latter.

Once Thomas was destroyed, the victorious Confederate Army could then turn and outflank the other two approaching Yankee corps from the east. He could use Cheatham's command to hinder their advance until Hardee and Stewart were finished with Thomas. With the consolidation of his three corps, Hood could then go on the offensive and drive the Yankees away from their vital supply lines and into the jowls of destruction.

As Hood lay in his bed contemplating, he could still feel the tingles of a stupendous victory course through his body like the feel of Buck Preston sitting near him on a carriage ride.

His plan had been so simple, but God, how his command-ers failed him and ruined his enormous opportunity. Cheatham's corps was bolstered by the Georgia State militia and by Wheeler's cavalry. There should have been no trouble detaining the corps of General Schofield and McPherson. The main objective of the plan fell upon the shoulders of Hardee and Stewart and their ability to launch the attack meant to crush Thomas.

At the time, Hood did not question Hardee's capabilities to lead the attack, but only now, months later, did he realize that mistake. Hardee had lost his promotion to Hood. Of course there would be some resentment there, but Hood did not think that Hardee could harbor such malcontent as to risk the survival of the Confederacy? Yet, there was no other explanation for the disaster that ensued.

The attack was slated to begin on July 20 at 1:00 p.m. However, reports soon arrived warning him that the enemy approaching from the east was more numerous than originally anticipated. In order to hold them off so that an attack could be made against Thomas, more men would be needed under Cheatham's command.

Hood tried to slam his fist now as he did then. But like that day when the news arrived, his useless arm hung limp. It was unable to obey his commands, much like his generals who served him. He had to smile at the irony. His arm, an extension of his self, could not respond to his commands, much like his generals, the extension of his military prowess, would not respond to his very clear and precise orders. Orders that could and should have changed the fate of his beloved Confederacy.

The reports of the approaching Federals left Hood with no choice. His entire plan hinged upon the detention of Schofield and McPherson until Thomas could be destroyed. If Schofield and McPherson were allowed to push back the roadblock in their path, the divisions assaulting Thomas would find themselves in dire jeopardy. They would be forced to fight Thomas from the front and the newly arrived Federals from the rear.

With no supply of reserves available, Hood had to order Cheatham to shift his corps one mile towards the south, preventing McPherson's corps from overlapping his right. Cheatham, not one experienced with such large-scale maneuvers in the face of the enemy, moved his divisions two miles farther than anticipated. They had to be realigned and reorganized.

This blunder cost the Confederates some very valuable time. The attack originally slated for 1:00 was delayed for nearly three hours. Hardee blamed this delay on the shift of Cheatham's corps to his right. Hood could not believe that this simple maneuver took so much time to complete. He wished he could have been there to make them boys move with vigor. Yet, wasn't that how Robert E. Lee commanded, tell your generals what you wanted done and trust them to do it?

When Lee gave an order to Jackson, it was obeyed. There were no excuses allowed, and any initial failures were to be tolerated until a victory could be achieved. Hood expected the same. He felt that if he could emulate the way Lee commanded, he could not possibly fail. Hood had always looked up to Lee, ever since his days at West Point. And though he felt that he learned much during his service under Lee, those lessons failed him at Atlanta.

However, he did not attribute that failure to himself, instead he placed the blame where it duly deserved to be, on the man who preceded his command of this army... that damned Johnston. This army had learned nothing from his command except pessimism. Johnston's constant tactics of retreat were now the only maneuvers that the Army of Tennessee knew how to execute. Hood would have to find a way to show these boys how to grit their damned teeth and charge. They only needed to experience that intense adrenaline rush once, and the need to do it again would be all too compelling. Hood would have to think on that again later, his memories of the first day of battle around Atlanta were too overwhelming.

Hood tried to think of what, if anything, he should have done differently up to this point. The attack was delayed, but the troops were shifted. There was still time for the complete victory that he sought. If only Hardee…

Just then Hardee's snug face superimposed itself over his recollections like an enticing demon. Hood didn't know what to believe concerning Hardee's inaction that day. Reports told that Hardee became confused as to his objective due to the shifting of Cheatham's corps. Hardee's plan was to move forward towards Thomas, while keeping in contact with Cheatham on his right, and Stewart on his left. However, when Cheatham began shifting some of his divisions to meet his new threat, he broke contact with

Hardee's right. This caused an immediate disorganization in command. Hardee did not stop his attack, but it was delayed, and not committed with its full strength. Hardee argued that Cheatham caused the delay, and blamed the attack's lack of enthusiasm on General Stewart. Stewart's men jumped into the attack too early and were not in echelon as ordered, Hardee claimed.

Hood could still hear the words of his un-contrite general as if they were being whispered in his ear now, 'I had an ill-advised attack on my left and a widening gap to my right. There is only so far my men can be expected to stretch.' All Hood could think about, was why didn't Hardee just send a dispatch to explain his dilemma?

"Because the damn jealous fool held a grudge," Hood answered himself out loud.

The halfhearted attack from Hardee, coupled with Stewart's virtually unsupported attack resulted in a loss for the Confederates. The three-hour delay in the attack allowed Thomas to cross the river with all of his men and artillery. With quick fortification, Thomas easily held his ground, while the two Federal corps from the east threatened to overrun the rebels in their path. Hood had to call off the attack and retire his forces back to a line that was much closer to the city.

As much as the tired general tried to keep reflecting on his ill fortunes, the lids of his eyes felt as if they were trying to support two of the heaviest cannon balls. Engrossed in his catharsis, and his heart racing from the euphoria caused by his medicine, the troubled John Bell Hood finally fell asleep.

Chapter III
November 18
Florence, Alabama

General Hood chose to have his breakfast outside amongst his staff commanders. By joining several tents together, the loyal Captain Wigfall had constructed a makeshift pavilion. The woven apparatus was large enough to cover a rather large company of men.

As Hood made his way through the pavilion, he was thankful that he felt in better spirits. He had expected to have a rough morning due to his troubled sleep. Surprisingly, he felt very rejuvenated. He eagerly greeted his corps commanders, Cheatham, S.D. Lee and Stewart, as well as several other subordinates, including the tough Irishman Patrick Cleburne.

"This weather is terrible. Can it get any colder or wetter? And what was all that skirmish fire last night?" asked Hood.

Cheatham was rubbing his cold hands together, trying to warm them against his cup of so-called coffee. Judging by his rosy cheeks, Cheatham probably had more then just coffee in his mug.

"Sir, you would think in this weather that the Yanks would just let us be at night," he said. "Our boys encountered a small detachment of Yankee skirmishers, probably trying to spy upon our current situation. We scattered them away, and managed to capture two and kill three of them. And boy, one of them fellows is a real upstart. We got his name as John Murphy. You know how feisty those Irish can be. And this one is as pure Irish as they come, red hair, freckles and all."

Despite the cold and dreariness of the morning, all of them found the mirth to share a hearty laugh at the expense of one of their own with Irish blood, Patrick Cleburne. Cleburne donned a sarcastic grin as he rose from the table. He very deliberately put on his coat and then turned towards the flap of the tent. He lifted it open, and for a second Cheatham thought he had seriously offended the Irish commander. Even though Cheatham was of higher rank, he did not want to draw the ire of Patrick Cleburne. There were not many who did.

Cleburne faced the opening of the tent, and felt the cold

rain mist against his head. He also heard the ubiquitous tapping of the rain upon the overhead tarp of the tent. He turned back towards the room full of commanders and walked over to Cheatham. The men gathered in the room were still, waiting for something to happen. The unnatural stale silence contained within the tent was made more threatening by the pelting rain coming from outside. The sonorous pitter-patter resounded like bullets thudding into a dead man's chest. Cleburne leaned over and pinched Cheatham's stomach.

"Perhaps if ye Southerners had more Irish blood in ye, and less lard, we may have won this thing a long time ago."

He then tipped his hat and vacated the tent to the applause and excited laughter of the men in the room. Cheatham took a hard swallow at the contents of his mug, and kept the cup in front of his face. It was a bad attempt to hide his chagrin.

"He doesn't know what he is talking about, I am as fit as can be, and will never allow my self to gain excessive weight."

Hood let the laughter subside as well as the redness on the face of Cheatham. He waited for his officers to finish their meals, then asked everyone to leave, except for his three corps commanders.

"Gentleman, we must discuss this current situation. What have we of General Sherman's army?"

General S.D. Lee put down his mug of coffee and spoke first. "Sir, by all reports, he is estimated at sixty thousand strong, and still moving farther east from Atlanta. As far as his influence on our current situation, he has none. He is too far away, and would take days to get to us."

Hood was pleased with that. He wanted to fight Sherman again, but not yet. Not until he could even the odds, then he would meet his adversary on any battlefield and give him the whippin' of a lifetime…

"And what of Schofield's position, is it the same?"

This time it was Stewart who was eager to furnish an answer. "Schofield still has his troops deployed at Pulaski. By all reports, his numbers are very close to ours."

Hood was further pleased with this news. There was one last piece to be provided, and he turned to Cheatham for the answer. Cheatham had anticipated the question before it was formed on his commander's lips. "Thomas is still in Nashville, gathering reinforcements."

Hood took a moment to gaze into the eyes of each of his generals. "Gentleman, you can see the situation before you clearer than anything we have faced in the war to date. Sherman, it appears, doesn't think that we are worthy enough of his attention. He is heading east. We need to draw him back. If not, General Lee will have more than he can handle. That great man has done enough for our army, and we need to give him one back. Adding to this, Schofield and Thomas are separated. Any commander can see the blunder in this, and fortunately, we know that the Yankees don't have any commanders. We need to defeat Schofield before Thomas can reinforce him."

Hood called for an adjutant to enter the tent. The young man was soaked from head to foot, but made an obvious effort to keep the contents under his tattered coat dry. He gave the map to Hood, and was dismissed. Hood opened the map on the table, as the generals cleared away the remains of breakfast. He opened the map, which looked like it was drawn only moments ago.

He pointed to Columbia, Tennessee. "This is where we must go." Columbia was situated at the halfway point between Pulaski and Nashville. It rested on a river that divided Tennessee at that point almost in half. In effect it divided the two Federal armies.

"We have to beat Schofield to that point," he continued. "As you can see, Schofield has the shorter route, but we hold the initiative. He doesn't yet understand our objective. We must beat him to the punch. The Duck River will prevent Thomas from descending on our rear from Nashville." Hood emphatically stomped the index finger of his good hand on the river. "This river is the key to the race against Schofield. At all costs, we must get there first." He looked to his commanders for understanding, and they all were studying the map and nodding their heads.

"This weather and the conditions of the roads won't make this an easy race," said S.D. Lee.

"No, it won't be easy General," said Hood, "but it will be an even race. Schofield will have to contend with the same conditions."

"What if Schofield doesn't follow us as we hope. What if he picks another path to unite with Thomas?" added Stewart.

Hood glared at the map. The hue of face clearly showed that he was hit with a question he did not anticipate. Part of him felt compelled to scold Stewart for questioning his judgment, but he knew better than that. Stewart was correct, there was a chance

Hood's Situation

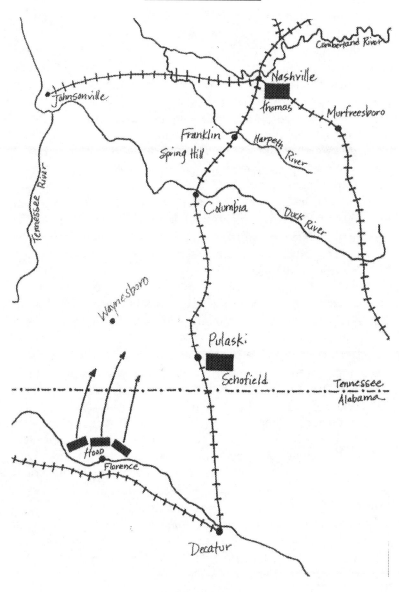

that Schofield would not move as they expected, and Hood needed to show these men that he had an answer for any intangible circumstance.

Hood kept his focus locked upon the map, both for an answer, and to avoid the eyes that stared at him in silence. It was his method to stall for time, hoping that he could somehow find the solution to this question. He tried thinking of how General Lee would handle such a crisis, but found it hard to concentrate with the annoying repetitiveness of the rain pelting the tent from above. The silence was becoming threateningly uncomfortable, until he found the answer upon the map. Schofield really only had two choices to join Thomas. He would either have to cross the river at some other point, or move east around the river, past Murfreesboro. Either option suited Hood just fine.

"Stewart, your question is a superb one. However, Schofield will not have many options. If he chooses to avoid the bridges at Columbia, and seek another crossing, then we must be ready to block that path as well. If we are ahead of him, we need to be alert as to his moves. If we can beat him to Columbia, we can intercept him anywhere. His other option is to move east of the river and come north through Murfreesboro. And if he chooses that route, we will have to continue north and defeat Thomas first, so that we may then descend upon Schofield."

Hood had been so dogmatic about his plan, his three commanders were hesitant to voice their concerns. There were still several flaws to this offensive, especially in the event that Schofield did not march towards Columbia. Stewart wanted to know what they would do if Thomas didn't sit still at Nashville? What if he left the city to consolidate with Schofield near Murfreesboro? Worse, what if Schofield let Hood get to Columbia, so that he could slip to the south and cut the Confederates from their own supply lines while Thomas descended from Nashville? Then Hood would be the one trapped.

Hood continued to look at the map, obviously content in his own mastery of his plan. Stewart reluctantly chose not to voice his concerns. He quietly hoped Schofield did as they expected. A staff officer entered the tent with some warm coffee, and then quickly departed. The commanders, taking a break from the seriousness of the situation, sat back and warmed their insides.

Their break did not last very long. Captain Wigfall purposefully walked thought the flaps of the meeting and hesitantly handed Hood an envelope. Hood very nonchalantly regarded the parcel. He thanked Wigfall with a nod of his head and then tossed the letter upon the table without reading it. The other generals took notice of his actions.

"Brent again?" Cheatham asked.

Hood nodded his confirmation.

George W. Brent was General Beuaregard's assistant adjutant general. Beauregard had recently been given command of the newly formed Military Division of the West. This fancy title enabled Beauregard to have the final say over all operations that concerned both, General Taylor's department of Alabama, Mississippi and Louisiana, as well as Hood's Army of Tennessee.

Hood did not like that.

He did not like having to get approval from a man that was not in the field of battle. He was the commander here, and this was his army. Adding to this resentment was the fact that he and Beauregard had been at a silent war with each other since Hood ordered his army to vacate northern Georgia.

It felt like a lifetime ago, and not a month, when Hood's army was situated in the mountains of north Georgia. The Confederates had been outmaneuvered from Atlanta and were forced to give the city up to the Yanks. Rather than flee away from the enemy, Hood chose to remain close to Sherman by moving around his flank into his rear. It was his intention to harass the Federal supply line and cause Sherman to abandon Atlanta or risk his army to a logistical disaster. What Hood truly hoped for was that the Yankees would come after him. Sherman would have to weaken his force in order to garrison Atlanta. This would help to even the numerical odds in the eventual battle between the two armies.

Unfortunately, Sherman would not take the bait.

Hood did have initial success as he wrecked railroads and captured isolated Federal garrisons. However, when Sherman brought his superior army to battle, Hood chose to have his smaller, more mobile army scamper off. Sherman must have clearly understood Hood's intent. He knew that his army was too large a force to waste its time and efforts in an attempt to capture Hood's smaller command. But what else could he do? Surprisingly, his decision was one that no one could have foreseen.

Sherman left half of his army in Georgia, still twice the

size of Hood's, and led the rest of his command east towards the Carolina's. The fiery red headed Northern commander wanted to make it his priority to wreck the Southern morale by taking the war into the heart of their homeland.

Hood was incredulous at Sherman's decision, still doubting the reports until this very day. He realized that he did not have the army to match up against Sherman's, but he did not want to submit the initiative. That was all he had left. He resolved to let Sherman go and to continue with his plan to cut the Federal supply line. If he were successful, Sherman's army would find themselves hungry very soon, and too far away to do anything about it. Their morale would weaken, causing soldiers to wither from the ranks in dissension.

With much enthusiasm, Hood left the mountains of north Georgia and headed for Gadsden, Alabama. From there he planned to move north and cross the Tennessee River to get in Sherman's rear. It was at Gadsden, on the 21st of October, that he started this 'war' with general Beauregard.

After dining with Beauregard, Hood had disclosed his masterful plan that would gain him occupation of Sherman's rear. It was also at this time that Hood decided on a much more alluring objective. He not only wanted to cut Sherman from his supply base in Nashville, he wanted to occupy the Tennessee capitol himself. Hood was convinced that such a victory would rally the good men of Tennessee, and allow his own ranks to swell. From there, he could turn his army loose into the undefended state of Ohio, or better yet, turn east and march to the aid of Robert E. Lee.

Beauregard appeared skeptical, and his complaints concerning the plan were condescending, but in the end accepted Hood's strategy...with certain modifications. He told Hood that his cavalry commander, Joseph Wheeler, could not join him on his raid. Wheeler would be needed to detain Sherman's eastern advance.

Hood was enraged.

First, he had called his campaign for Southern victory a raid, and then he stole one of his favorite generals, one whose skill in leading a cavalry was unsurpassed. Hood took this as a direct insult. Obviously, Beauregard could not comprehend the magnitude of his plan. If allowed to defeat Schofield, there would be no need to worry about Sherman's advance. The Union commander would be forced to back track and deal with Hood.

Hood asked Beauregard how he proposed for the attack to proceed if he had no cavalry? Beauregard informed him that he would appropriate the services of Nathan Bedford Forrest and his thirty five hundred troopers.

Hood found himself at a loss for words. Though Forrest was a revered cavalry commander, he was no Joseph Wheeler. And Forrest's ability to command a campaign had not been proven. At best, Hood felt that Forrest was an exceptional raider who lacked a formal military education.

Hood soon further fuelled the flames of animosity on the 23rd, when his plans for crossing the Tennessee were altered. He chose not to cross the river until he was linked with Forrest's cavalry, which had not arrived yet from the west. Hood didn't feel the need to inform Beauregard. First and foremost, this was his army not Beuaregard's. Secondly, it was Beauregard who chose to take Wheeler and replace him with Forrest. If his newly appointed cavalry commander was not present for the crossing into Tennessee, why should Hood be held accountable?

Instead, he continued moving west and south of the river. On the 26th, his army encamped just a few miles outside of Decatur, Alabama. It would be another day before Beauregard could catch up with Hood and demand a meeting.

Hood remembered his anger at being chastised by Beauregard for not sending him reports to keep him informed. Beauregard also was belligerent in pointing out that Hood's current course had him over a hundred miles from the railroad that was supplying Sherman. When he tried to protest, Beauregard cut him off, fuming that his movement thus far had done nothing except alert Schofield and Thomas of his intentions, which had probably enabled the Union command to prepare a defense. Hood recalled uttering the words to Beauregard that he would later regret... that Decatur would be where his army would cross the Tennessee.

The next day, Hood's scouts reported that Decatur was too heavily defended to risk an attack. Beauregard had been correct, the Federals had moved quickly to impede Hood's advance. Realizing that speed and surprise were the keys to his campaign, Hood would not risk a prolonged engagement against the entrenched enemy. The attack at Decatur was called off, and with no other choice, Hood continued farther west.

Besides needing a location to cross the Tennessee, another problem that was plaguing his command was his dwindling supplies. Reports were stating that he was running low on the necessary provisions needed to feed his army during their operations in Tennessee. And his problems did not end there. His amount of barefoot marching regiments was growing. As the leader of this army, Hood knew that he had to be the one to take command of these debilitating issues.

Hood studied the maps, and found that there was a solution for him. Twenty-four miles to the west was Tuscumbia. Tuscumbia offered a favorable place to cross the river, as well as proximity to Cherokee Station, the eastern terminus of a railroad that could supply his army. Also, by moving farther west, he would be accelerating his consolidation with Forrest's command.

On October 30, Hood occupied Tuscumbia, and sent troops over the Tennessee into Florence. But just as it appeared as if he finally had his pieces ready to perform the checkmate over the Federal command, Hood's situation took a turn for the worse.

Cherokee Station could not be used to supply his army.

His staff despondently reported that the railroad was in wretched condition and the ability to transport supplies would take longer than anticipated. Much longer... for adding to the problem of the faulty railway, was the flooded river. Abundant rain had raised water levels, causing a deluge into the surrounding areas. The part of the rail that connected Cherokee to Tuscumbia was now submerged under the same waters that prevented him from crossing into Tennessee. And no matter how much faith he had in his engineers, they could not repair a railroad that was as drowned as his own spirit.

Hood's reaction was furious. Why was every plan that he conceived subject to such intangible defeat? What did the Tennessee River have against him? Was he not here to set it free from the Yankees? Why did these unforeseen things keep occurring to him?

It was then that the first of many envelopes would arrive from Beuaregard's assistant adjutant George W. Brent. Brent had all but ordered Hood to summarize his every move since his departure from Jonesborough, Georgia to his present location in Tuscumbia, Alabama. As Hood began to crush the letter in his hand, a sudden twist of extreme pain shuddered through his nerves and his joints. The pain was so intense, that he collapsed beside his desk. Assistants rushed in to aid the fallen General. The doctors called it Rheumatism, but Hood personified it as Beauregard. He was ordered to remain in bed for the next few days.

He would reply to Brent's letter several days later. Apathetically, he informed Beauregard that he was not feeling well, but planned to cross the Tennessee on November 5. Another letter came from Brent on November 4, repeating the instruction to summarize his actions since leaving Jonesborough, Georgia.

Again Hood ignored the request to furnish a summary of his operations. Instead he wrote that it was not possible to furnish any plans for his future operations, since so much depended on the movements of his enemy. Hood deliberately changed the impetus of the letter as a message to the lower ranking Banks. He would no longer answer to anyone.

This was his army.

It was not Brent, but Beauregard who returned the arrogance to Hood tenfold. On November 11th, six days past the date Hood said he would cross the Tennessee, Beauregard had gone over Hood's head and ordered General Stewart, who reported directly to Hood, to conduct a grand review with his command. Stewart, idly waiting orders to cross the river, had no other responsibilities and since no new orders had come from Hood, he performed the review for Beauregard.

Hood learned of the parade on the morning of its occurrence. Trying to hide his chagrin, he wrote a letter to Beauregard asking how someone so familiar with army regulations could supersede the chain of command and not ask his permission to perform such a review. Hood wittingly added the question as to whether such a review might not alert the enemy to the size and position of his army?

Like dueling siblings, Beauregard quickly wrote back stating that he thought it was Stewart's role to report the request for review. Beauregard also wrote, with much condescension, that if he thought the Federal army did not know his size and location by now, he was sadly mistaken. Beauregard ended the letter with the finality as to who was indeed the commander of this army. He concluded by saying that as soon as circumstance permitted, he would also review Cheatham and Lee's corps.

When Hood had read the last line, he felt the onslaught of pressure upon his nerves. He remembered having to fight the urge to collapse for a second time, as he had to seat himself with *clenched teeth upon the bed. 'Who does he think he is?' he thought.*

Without wasting any more time, Hood finally crossed the Tennessee River with his army and occupied Florence. Ironically, the maneuver was done more to get away from Beauregard than it was to get to the Yankees.

Before departing, Hood made it a point to ensure that Beauregard was not informed of the crossing.

Since then, there had been no direct communication with General Beauregard except for the continuous arrival of envelopes that Hood refused to open. The latest of which was the one that had arrived this morning and had interrupted the breakfast with his commanders.

Escaping from his recollections, Hood looked up at his generals, and told them to be ready for his command to begin the march north. His military offensive was to commence today. He then departed from the table and dismissed himself from the tent.

The other generals watched him with apprehension. They knew of his recent fights with Beauregard, as well as his physical condition due to his handicaps and the rheumatism. However, they could not pity him. He was their leader. His ability to command was the difference between life and death for themselves, their troops, and their nation. The three generals raised their cups in silent understanding, and followed Hood into the cold rain.

*   *   *   *   *   *   *   *

John Murphy was considered by many to be one tough Irishmen. He sat huddled in the cold, making a strong effort not to show his discomfort with the weather. Last night, he and a small unit of skirmishes where sent to monitor the movements of Hood's army. They were only supposed to watch, but a fellow soldier became hotheaded and fired at a rebel patrolman.

The rebel was hit, and fell like a sack of potatoes, but the shooting was senseless. They were not supposed to engage the enemy. Their monitoring of Hood's force was to be secretive. The Union high command wanted to make Hood believe that he held the initiative.

Now some dumb American had jeopardized that. John

would have to find a way to make amends. He was not fighting in this war for the sport of it. He had escaped from a harsh life in Ireland, and was now struggling in America to help his family survive. And if it meant that he needed to risk his life and become a soldier, than so be it. America symbolized freedom, a freedom he had never known before. That was what had gotten him through his struggles in the new country, a belief that his reward would be paid when his children were older. They, unlike he, would live in a world where all men were equal.

John Murphy would not allow Southern upstarts to ruin that.

When this war broke out, he readily enlisted and thus far felt that he had performed admirably in all his duties. But now that was all taken from him, all because of some soldier's heated temper for battle. A member of his own army had helped to remove him from the war effort. And that was a fact that was not easy for him to accept.

John had his chance to escape last night, but someone was needed to hold off the rebel pursuit. John tried to form a strategic withdrawal through the forest, but the majority of the men ignored his pleas and chose flight instead. In the end, only eight men would brave the confrontation. Five of those men were now dead, and the other three, himself included, had surrendered.

Now they were being held captive by men more concerned about the inclement weather, than they were with guard duty. John raised his head as one of his captors approached. He stoically accepted the offer of water with a casual nod of the head.

He would eventually escape, that he knew. However, when that time came, John wanted to be able to return with some piece of information that would greatly aid the Federal army... something that would ensure that these Southerners would never end the dream of America's democracy.

Chapter IV
November 18
Outside of Florence

General Nathan Bedford Forrest rode through his camp like a man possessed. If the vicious rumors held in the North were accurate, then on this day he would more than exceed those expectations. The Yanks often referred to him as the devil himself. Ironically, the self-made Southern general held a strong resemblance to many of the connotations of the evil one. Forrest's strong jaw supported the thick goatee frequently depicted in many satanic illustrations. Some could argue that Forrest lacked the horns, pitchfork and tail needed to complete the entire transformation. However, some of his own men might say that his saber was his pitchfork, and the tail... well he had one when he was mounted. As for the horns, there was still an arguable debate as to whether or not they were carefully hidden beneath his full head of hair.

If one of his men had asked him today if he was possessed, the general could easily have answered with the glowing ire flickering within his eyes. Forrest was hungry for battle. The ice-cold rain that left the majority of his men huddling in tattered blankets had absolutely no effect on him. This in turn had an immediate effect on his men. How could they freeze and be so bothered by the cold, when their commander paid it no heed?

That was the influence of Nathan Bedford Forrest. He was a commander that men felt compelled to follow. Some would say that he led through fear. They would be correct. Forrest's men could not make mistakes, could not give up any position, and they could not lose. If they did any of the above, they would have to answer to Forrest. And that was the one thing they would not do.

And now Forrest had to set those expectations with the two new divisions that were added to his command. They were Jackson's troopers, left behind by Wheeler before he departed to go after Sherman. Jackson's troopers were not exactly jubilant with the news that their new commander was Forrest. They made purposeful arrangements to avoid fraternizing with Forrest's critter crew... as they were called.

Forrest sensed this obvious prejudice upon his arrival in

Hood's camp on November the 14th. The awkwardness had lasted since, but today it had to end. Today was supposed to be the start of Hood's invasion into Tennessee. That was his homeland. It didn't take a military genius to discern that the success or failure of this offensive would seal the fate of the Confederacy. The quick capture of Nashville offered the South's best chance for recruiting the men of Tennessee, as well securing a base for a future invasion into Kentucky, leaving Sherman no choice but to abandon his march through Georgia, and return to face an empowered Confederate army.

However, if Hood failed, Sherman would march unopposed east and there was no telling the havoc he could create through an undefended country. Forrest knew that his offensive must be quick and concise. There could be no other way. In order for the army to achieve such a success, there needed to be a sense of urgency and a sense of brotherhood. Watching the two cavalries operate to this point was like trying to mix oil and vinegar. He knew that now was the time for these men to understand what was meant by brotherhood. Once he could get past that, imparting a sense of urgency would be easy.

Forrest directed his horse into the middle of the camp. He was directly in between many of Jackson's mounted men as well as those of his own. He called a few officers from both commands and told them to have all the men surround him in the next ten minutes.

Forrest's men all reported in less then five minutes, while Jackson's took the full ten, and added an additional fifteen. Forrest did not like their lack of haste. He gripped his reins in anger, but knew enough not to let it show. He needed these men on his side.

While waiting for the final drips of Jackson's men to gather around the now large circle, he noticed several Union prisoners in the background. They were loading supplies into wagons. Forrest motioned for one of his officers.

"Sir, I know not why those prisoners are present at the front of this army and not at the rear, but I want them out of here at once."

The officer looked startled, as if to say it wasn't by his orders that they were here. "Yes sir, but we were instructed to use them to help load the supply wagons, being we are so short on that kind of personnel."

The officer's tone indicated that he thought his answer

was sufficient and justified. That was until he noticed Forrest loosen his grip on the reins, only to readjust them with a tighter noose upon his collar.

"There are at least five thousand men gathered around us at this moment. Do you not think we have enough men to load our own supplies?"

Forrest leaned over his horse and pulled the soldier even closer. With one hand he forcefully retained the grip on the officer's collar, while the other dug an extended index finger into the man's sunken chest.

"I will personally get off my horse and lead us in the loading of supplies if need be. However, there will not be Union men at the vanguard of my army. Not now, not ever. Is that understood?"

The shaken officer nodded and almost fell to the ground when Forrest released him. The officer mounted his steed and quickly trotted to the rear. Forrest watched as the shaken officer gave his best efforts to gather the prisoners and herd them back towards Florence.

By this time, all of the cavalry in Hood's army was gathered around him. Forrest took deliberate time directing his purposeful stare in a circular taunt. An ominous silence settled upon the conglomeration, as the cold rain started again. Many men began buttoning their top buttons, or pulling on worn blankets. Forrest purposely unbuttoned his coat. They were not here to complain about the weather.

Forrest's men were the first to settle down and accept the rain. Jackson's men were not to be outdone and did the same. Forrest was gleaming on the inside. This was the start he was looking for. With affirmation and with pride, Forrest raised his voice with complete disregard of the cold rain.

"Since I rode into this camp, I have sensed a disliking for me and my boys."

Jackson's troops remained uncomfortably silent. Instead of agreeing with their new commander's assessment, they chose to turn their heads down at such a direct confrontation. That was good. It showed Forrest that for all their boisterous jabber, they still held respect for his authority.

"You may have heard some things about me that don't suit you. And that's fine. I can't change what you heard. But my men will tell you, I'll lead you to victory. That's what I want to do for you now, lead this Army of Tennessee to victory. We are going to march today to face the Union army. They have also heard things about me that don't suit them. That's fine too. However, they have more of a reason not to like what they have heard about me. You see, today, I am going to kill them Yankees."

This brought a few hearty cheers and applause from the men gathered. Several from Jackson's troopers.

"You on the other hand, I ask you to join with my boys and help me kill some of them Yankees. Will you join me in that?"

Now the cheer rose to an outright ovation. Many of Jackson's men had seen Forrest ride through the camp, but had never heard him speak. All they knew of him was what they had heard passed through a long and tangled grapevine. Hearing him speak to them in person had a very humanizing effect. Forrest waited for the cheers to subside before continuing.

"Well, soldiers, I came here not so much for you to join me, but for me to join you. I'm going to show you the way into Tennessee. My conscripts are going, and I know Hood's veterans can go. I started this with three hundred and fifty men. I have thirty five hundred conscripts now. And when we move out as one, there will be over five thousand of us. Since May I have fought in every county in West Tennessee. I fought in the streets of Memphis, and the women ran out in their nightclothes to see us, and they will do it again in Nashville. I have fought a battle every twenty-five days. I have seen the Mississippi run with blood for two hundred yards, and I'm going to see it again. I've captured seventy eight pieces of artillery and sixteen thousand Yankees, and buried twenty five hundred of them."

Once again the more than five thousand present let out a howl into the rain. The twenty five hundred under Jackson may have even been the louder.

"Now I ask you boys. Will you take me? Will you let my conscripts join and increase the ranks of this cavalry? Then lets kill some Yankees and get their infestation out of my beloved Tennessee."

Forrest puffed his chest in the pride he now felt. It was exactly the inspiration he needed for the next confrontation he was faced with. He started moving through the crowd as they parted for him, and headed to Florence. He had an unscheduled meeting with John Bell Hood.

*   *   *   *   *   *   *   *

He had to lower his hat to protect his face from the increasing intensity of the downpour. Forrest observed how much his horse sank into the earth with each passing step. It would be hell trying to move this army north. The roads were in no condition to tolerate the passing of an army forty thousand strong. Yet, it must be done.

So must his meeting with Hood be done. There was a lot on Forrest's mind since receiving the order to join with Hood. At the time he was conducting some very successful raids in western Tennessee. He was having such a threatening effect on Sherman's rear that Sherman decided to dispatch General George Thomas' army of thirty thousand from Atlanta back to Nashville. In effect, what Sherman was saying by such a defensive maneuver was that he held more respect and fear for Forrest's thirty five hundred raiders, than that of Hood's army of forty thousand.

Forrest accepted that with pride. He only wished those in Richmond could do the same.

Forrest had risen through the ranks of the Confederacy by his brave and heroic deeds. His promotions were not granted because of whom he knew or who his father was, but for what he accomplished on the field of battle. Some thought the stories of his success to be exaggerated. Yet, if one was unsure of his savagely tenacious skills as a fighter, one only needed to examine the circumstances that caused his wounding at the battle of Shiloh in 1862.

However, the more battles he won, the more clear it became that his lack of Southern nobility was a detriment. He soon learned that if he wanted to supply and recruit for his own cavalry, than he better do it himself because Richmond would not assist him. And what hurt his pride most was the unsaid reason why. His victories were applauded as successful raids and nothing more.

Undaunted, Forrest would rely on those same skills that had gotten him where he was today. And those skills were his ability to not just fight a battle, but to find any means necessary to win it.

Win it, like he had to do now with the commander in chief, General John Bell Hood. He wasn't sure if he liked this man, and he needed to be sure before he led this army into the

Armageddon that he was hoping for.

Forrest had been in Hood's camp for four days, but had not chosen to address the issues that bothered him as of yet. Those issues began festering in early November. It was bad enough, that for all of his success against the Union army, for all of the printed fears that the Union army had of him, his own commanders saw him as a great raider, but nothing more.

'How could they be so blind?' he often thought. Could a raider accomplish what he had recently done in Johnsonville, Tennessee? Do what he did, with thirty five hundred men who supplied themselves? General Bragg sure couldn't.

Yet he was just a raider.

Nonetheless, in late October, this raider had set off to cripple Sherman's supply line in western Tennessee… and he enjoyed nothing but success.

Forrest first attacked Fort Heiman, one of the northern-most supply depots for Sherman's army. He set up artillery to blockade any movement of supply ships along the Tennessee River. On October 29, he struck. An unsuspecting Federal steam ship towing two barges appeared on the river, and Forrest's artillery pounded them into submission. The steamship was forced to the eastern bank, and her crew routed into the surrounding woods. Forrest's men looted the ships for some much-needed supplies. Forrest had to retreat when Union gunboats arrived on the scene. However, the retreat did not indicate a loss. Forrest had deprived the Union of three ships and supplies while re-supplying his own men with the spoils. He was not here to fight the Yankee navy. Though he would get a chance for that soon enough.

Forrest retired down river, and struck the Union navy again the next day. This time, he had even greater success. His artillery had helped to shell a steamboat, two transports, two barges, and a gunboat. The steamship was so damaged it barely crawled away to safety. The Confederate artillery took care not to let the other ships escape their wrath so easily. The onslaught lasted nearly six hours, Forrest thought for sure that Union reinforcements would arrive at any moment, but none came.

When the battle died down, the barges and one of the transports were destroyed. The Confederates boarded the captured gunship, as well as the surviving transport, and raised the proud flag of the Confederacy. Not only did Forrest recruit, supply and lead his own army, but he now found a way to form his own navy.

Yet, he was a raider and nothing more....

Forrest re-supplied his army with the captured loot, and on November 1, sailed down river towards Johnsonville. Forrest's makeshift navy never made it by boat. More Union gunboats finally arrived, and Forrest wisely gave up his mini armada. Outnumbered in ships, and not being a real navy, Forrest abandoned the fight and the boats, and took to the land with his troops.

Though he had accomplished much, Nathan Bedford Forrest had only just begun.

On November 4, he set his sights on the Federal supply depot across the river at Johnsonville. What he saw was a prime opportunity to punish the Federal supply line. The bank was crowded with wharves that docked both transports and gunboats, and close by there was an immense warehouse stocked full with Union surplus. The bank itself, along with the wharves was also overcrowded with Yankees moving supplies. It seemed that all you had to do was shoot a cannon, and you would hit something. With so many targets, a blind man would find it impossible to miss.

The only obstacle opposing him was the Union fort strategically positioned on a high hill, where it was ready to defend the wharf. Forrest also knew that this garrison was probably alerted to his presence. They were most likely ready for his attack. The problem was, they were not ready for the attack that Forrest had in mind.

He was not going to lead his men in one of their famed cavalry charges against the enemy. Instead, he was going to leave this to the artillery. After all, they had performed so well along this river already, showing what damage they could inflict if given the chance. Forrest was all too eager to give them that chance again.

From behind the concealment of the thick forest, and overlooking the supplies across the river, Forrest and his men carefully placed his artillery where it could inflict the most damage. When all was in place and ready, Forrest gave the word.

To the unsuspecting Union soldiers loading the supplies, two o'clock was the hour that hell erupted on earth. Ten guns, from across the river bellowed in unison like a ravenous behemoth. The shells shattered Union boats, exploding boilers and maiming scores of men. The scene looked like a page from Revelations. The boats were scorching in flames as men jumped from the sinking ships into the water. Adding to this chaos was a thick smoke that choked the air and helped spread panic among the Yankees left scrambling for cover.

His artillery crew were eager to hit the Union supplies, especially the huge warehouse, but Forrest made sure that their destruction stayed on the boats so that they could not sail out to offer his men battle. Their barrage became so accurate and intense that the Federals feared a Confederate attack was imminent. They reacted by blowing up the rest of their ships, to ensure they were not captured, and routed from the hell fire.

With the threat of the Union gunboats gone, Forrest very gleefully allowed his men to finish destroying everything on the bank. By nightfall, Johnsonville was a burning hell. The flames roared high into the night, with several million dollars of Union supplies consumed in its heat. In one week, Forrest's thirty five hundred men had caused more fear and hurt upon the Union army in the West then any army commanded by Beauregard, Johnston's, Bragg, and even Hood.

And what thanks did he receive? How did the Confederate high command show its appreciation?

The reward for his heroics would come in the form of a letter from General Hood. It had read, "When can I expect you here or when can I hear from you? I am waiting on you."

It was as if all Forrest had accomplished meant nothing, as if he were playing around while the real army needed him.

Forrest's insides were boiling now as they did when he had first read that letter. He knew that he couldn't let his feelings fester internally like this. Sooner or later, his control would slip and he would wind up landing his knuckles across Hood's lower jaw. It didn't matter that the man had only the use of one leg and one arm, Forrest would tie one arm around his back, tie one leg to a stake and even offer to blindfold himself if that was what it took to offer Hood a fair fight.

Forrest's led his mount into Florence searching for General Hood, yet when he arrived, all he saw was a lethargically moving army. This was supposed to be the day of the march north, spirits were supposed to be high, yet this weather dampened more than just the road. Forrest began to search the area for a sergeant to be reprimanded when he heard a name that he recognized.

"General Cleburne, sir," a sergeant was yelling.

Forrest trotted ahead to confront the sergeant. If he could find Cleburne, then he could find Hood. He rode up behind the man. When he was about to question the man concerning Cleburne's location, he saw the General several yards ahead of him. With the other officer still yelling for Cleburne, Forrest continued to gallop, until he caught up with the much-famed Irish General.

"General Cleburne," Forrest said.

Cleburne finished giving an order to his adjutant before looking up at the man on the horse. He also noticed a small entourage of mounted officers behind the general.

"General Forrest. Glad to see you and your staff."

The two shook hands as Forrest stepped down form his horse. Forrest had not noticed that his staff had trailed him, nor did he care. He led Cleburne off the path as units began marching along the muddied trail in the direction of Tennessee.

"How goes the front?" asked Cleburne.

"We are ready to move out, elements of our leading brigade have already departed. Spirits are high and eager."

"I wish they were a little brighter here, but this weather is having a damaging effect on morale."

"General Cleburne, sir," a voice called. It was the sergeant that Forrest passed on the road. Forrest turned towards the soldier with an agitated stare. A stare that was colder and harder than any rain his cold bones had felt thus far.

"Um, sir, I…it can wait."

The sergeant backed away from Forrest and Cleburne, returning from whence he came. Cleburne turned to Forrest with a quizzical shrug, not realizing what had caused the officer's reticence.

"General, I would love to talk more with you, but the urgency at hand requires I return to the front as soon as possible. I came to have a word with General Hood. Might you know where I can find him?"

Cleburne, also eager to get back with his men, and lead them north, pointed farther down the road towards a rather large pavilion.

"I just left General Hood moments ago. We had breakfast

over in that tent. When I left, he was with Generals Lee, Cheatham, and Stewart. I would guess they were finalizing plans before the march north."

"Thank you sir, I must take my departure from you now".

Forrest sat upon his horse and headed in the direction of the tent. He could see Cheatham, Lee and Stewart departing from the area and heading their separate ways. He looked at them with a frown chiseled across his face. Once again he had been slighted. Hood organizes one last council before the offensive, and doesn't feel the need to include his cavalry commander?

Taking his gaze from the three generals, he could see Hood in the distance. Hood was farther ahead, going towards his headquarters.

Forrest slowed his canter. He needed to somehow assuage his ill temper before he confronted Hood. He told his staff to remain behind, inhaled the November air, and then steered his horse towards Hood.

Unfortunately, the more Forrest tried to calm himself, the more upset he became. He began second guessing himself. Perhaps he should have confronted Hood the day his cavalry arrived in Florence, four days ago? He at least should have brought up his frustration concerning the order he received while conducting operations in Tennessee. What soothed his temper then was a second letter received from Hood, informing him that he would have the command of the entire cavalry as the Army of Tennessee went on the offensive. Delighted as he was, Forrest knew that he should have taken care of old business before moving forward. He wrongfully hoped that the promotion and responsibilities given to him would offset Hood's derogatory telegram he received while in Johnsonville. And it did, the problem was the damage to his pride was not forgiven, it was only submerged under his newly appointed title.

That would prove to be a dangerous place, because instead of alleviating his problem, Forrest put it in the one place it would grow and fester, a place so far inside it rested between his heart and soul. It would be a place ill suited to contain the cankerous sore, as Forrest would later find out when he was approached by one of Hood's officers.

It was a skinny little man with trembling hands that had handed Forrest his orders. Forrest took only a few seconds to read the letter before crumbling it up and throwing it back in the officer's face.

Hood had appropriated Forrest's supply wagons and mules for the immediate use of his own army.

Forrest had been so insulted that he chose to ignore the command. The next day, Major A.L. Landis of Hood's headquarters confronted him.

Landis approached Forrest with stern confidence, making an obvious attempt to show that he would not be intimidated. He boldly asked Forrest why he had not sent over his mules?

Forrest had regarded Landis with disgust. It wasn't that he did not want to turn over his mules, it was the principal. His mules were his, and not the property of the Confederate army. Why should he have to supply an army that refused to supply his cavalry when the roles were reversed? And because the army could never find the means to supply his troopers, Forrest had been forced to find his own supplies... and not just mules. Every thing his cavalry now possessed was earned the hard way... through the spoils of war, and the courtesy of dead Yankees.

But a price had also been paid in the blood of hundreds of dead Southerners, which would no longer occupy a saddle within his force.

Those brave boys died for him, and for the opportunity to capture vital supplies needed to sustain his cavalry. And now, the army that couldn't spare to supply his three thousand troops was not even asking, but ordering to take its supplies to help their thousands.

Never.

Forrest walked up to Landis, and brought his face to within one inch of the Major's. The breath they shared was inhaled almost entirely by Forrest.

"Go back to your quarters, and don't you come here again or send anybody here again about mules. The order will not be obeyed; and moreover, if the quartermaster bothers me any further about his matter, I'll come down to his office, tie his long legs into a double bowknot around his neck, and choke him to death with his own shins. I whipped the enemy and captured every mule wagon and ambulance in my command; I have not made a requisition on the government for anything of the kind for two years, and...my teams will go as they are or not at all."

Forrest's tone was cemented with belligerence, backing

Landis until the Major slipped and fell in a soup of very thick mud.
Landis quickly stood up, and fumed back to headquarters. Forrest
hadn't heard from him or Hood since then.

As he rode up to the hobbling Hood, Forrest tried for one last time to calm himself before the confrontation. His contempt needed to be soothed and cleared before this campaign could begin.

"General Hood, a moment if your time," he said.

"Major General Forrest, you missed breakfast."

"I did not get the invitation."

"My apologies. Please leave your horse and step inside for some warm coffee."

"I did not know that there was any coffee left in the South," Forrest replied. He then handed his horse to a soldier standing outside of Hood's headquarters. As they walked in, Landis happened to be walking out. Forrest gave him a look, which caused the officer to drop his head while exiting the room.

'Sir, I need a moment alone with you."

Hood looked at Forrest and the men in his room. "Of course, please sit down." He then dismissed the officers until they were alone. "Although I must admit, I would feel more comfortable with you at the head of this army, and not with me here."

Forrest had no interest in discerning if Hood was trying to make a joke. He chose to get right to the point.

"General, before we begin, I need to be sure that we are in this together."

"Of course we are. I would not have appointed you my commander of all the cavalry if I did not."

"No you would not have. But you also would not have if you still had Wheeler at your disposal."

Hood did not answer.

"General, I am here because I did not like the tone of your telegram that I received while at Johnsonville. I am also here because your quartermaster ordered to appropriate my mules."

"Please calm down Nathan. I hope I can call you Nathan behind these closed doors. I am sorry if my courier sounded demeaning, but I have been harassed by General Beauregard, and all of Richmond for that matter, to get this offensive moving as soon as possible. I could not do so without you. The anger that you may have felt from my order was not meant to be for you."

Forrest seemed interested. He wanted so much to defeat the Yankees, he was eager for anything that would calm the volatile temper that was now directed at General Hood.

"As long as that is an honest answer, I will accept it. But what of your quartermaster? Surely the command came from you?"

Hood had to be careful here. Part of him understood Forrest's dogmatic ire. It was not too long ago when he had his own captured ambulances being ordered from him. It was during a march into Maryland when Major General Evans demanded that Hood's spoils be turned over to his North Carolina troops. Hood was so absolute in his reluctance that he soon found himself under arrest. His own recollection of such an ordeal allowed him to concede somewhat, but more importantly he understood he would greatly need Forrest's services in the days ahead.

"General…Nathan…I made a mistake."

That was all he said. Maybe it was the laudanum that he was on since he woke up, perhaps it was his fatigue with the situation and he just wanted to get this army moving, but that was his answer.

Forrest had heard much about the fighting ability of Sam Hood. He was ready for an all out duel in these headquarters. The simplicity of his contrite answer caught Forrest completely off guard… and that was no easy task to accomplish. Forrest felt all the tension in his nerves subside in an instant. He took the mug of coffee offered from Hood and accepted it, like he accepted Hood's answer.

"What has been said here General Hood, will stay between us."

He shook Hood's hand and went to depart from the room. As he approached the door, he turned once more.

"I will be proud to lead this army into Hell. And I promise that I will personally lead it out, with the devil himself at the end of my saber."

*   *   *   *   *   *   *   *

As Hood watched his cavalry commander exit his headquarters, he tried to imagine what General Forrest would look like when riding out of hell… at the end of a saber.

Chapter V
That same day... far away Virginia.

Lee sat on Traveler in clear view of the enemy across the open field. He had no fear. He rode his horse around the wooded clearing to an opening that allowed him to see his objective. The Federal army was in occupation of a very long stretch of land that was anchored on both ends by hills. They had picked a very strong position.

All previous attempts to take those anchored hills had failed, but Lee strongly believed that one solid push against their center would cause the entire Yankee position to crumble. Artillery exploded around him, rocking the earth's soil, but he did not notice.

That center must be taken.

Longstreet approached from behind and put a gentle hand upon his shoulder.

"General, the wall is behind us, come with me."

Longstreet was trying to lead him back behind the trees. Lee looked and saw the low-lying wall that offered his own men a solid defense. Lee removed the general's hand from his shoulder. There was no going back.

He smiled at Longstreet, and told him to let the boys begin the attack. Longstreet shook his head in disbelief. He begged Lee to reconsider, there was no way that center could be taken. Lee told him that it had to be taken. The war would end today. God has willed it thus, and thus it shall be. He heard the thunderous approach of his attacking force and told the general to step aside.

"Watch my dear sir, and see how a position is taken."

Out from behind the woods, and stepping into the clearing was a magnificent display of Southern might. Row after row of Confederate soldiers lined up and prepared to walk down the valley of death with undaunted alacrity. Lee stared at the men in disbelief. This was not Pickett's division. Lee felt his insides bursting with hope. It was the Stonewall brigade in all its glory. How could that be? This unit had been severely dwindling since its glory days. Yet here it was, ready to serve Lee one last time.

The men of the Stonewall brigade stood statuesque as the

Federal cannon fire crashed into them. Lee saw the cannon balls exploding into his lines, but when the smoke cleared, there wasn't a single casualty. This was the invincible army he had trusted and loved.

Lee smiled harder, and put his hand on Longstreet and told him condescendingly, to go behind his little wall. Longstreet walked off with his head bent to the ground. Lee turned to personally lead the brigade over the open ground, but had to stop when he heard a shout beckoning from behind.

He turned to watch the units part to let a man riding on horseback enter. The scene was biblical, as if Moses was stepping through the Red Sea. This was surely another sign from God, that there would be a victory this day.

As the man moved closer, Lee felt the warm tears run down his cheek. It was his beloved General Thomas Jackson. How could this be? He was told Jackson was dead. Yet here he was approaching him.

At the same moment of Lee's recognition of the rider, it was if the Federal army also realized his identity. Canon after canon fired from the Union lines, with each shell whistling directly towards Jackson. And explosion after explosion, each shell struck his sturdy general, until the air was choked with so much gray smoke and ash. When the bombardment ceased, there was an anxious silence.

When the air cleared, Jackson stood in front of Lee and saluted. Lee jumped from his mount like a schoolboy to hug his long lost son.

"I will take that center for you sir," was all Jackson said.

Jackson stepped back onto his horse and began moving towards the enemy. His brigade followed. Lee watched the troops advance. The combined sounds of their stomping mixed with the bellowing of the Federal guns sounded like a cacophony conducted in hell. Yet for all their firepower, the Union guns were ineffective. Lee watched the Confederate battle flags mow through a fence that blocked their approach. They reformed and picked up their cadence as they approached the Federal lines. Then, as Lee had predicted, they hit the Federal lines and caused it to buckle.

Several independent struggles raged all along the center. There was one particular angle to the left that seamed to sway between the armies. Lee watched it all with knowing anticipation.

His victory was to be today.

Union guns were captured and being turned on the routed Yankee army. The flags of Stonewall's brigade were waiving defiantly on the hill. The Confederates had taken the center.

Lee watched as Jackson's army reformed by a cluster of trees behind the Union lines. He knew his general was already making plans to turn on the isolated Federal flanks. J.E.B. Stuart was probably already in the Federal rear rounding up the fleeing bluecoats.

This was the victory Lee knew he would receive today. He looked though his seeing glasses to get a better view of the hill, and he saw Stonewall Jackson standing on the ridge and waving back to him. He was bidding Lee to bring the reserves forward to join him. Lee saw his mouth moving, and even heard the words, yet they didn't exactly sound like Jackson's.

"General Lee sir, this is what you asked for. It is time to get going."

Lee felt the slow shake, and opened his eyes. He saw Taylor standing above him, gingerly shaking him to help him awake. Lee had to orient himself. Where was he? Why was Taylor standing above him, in his military gear, when the war was over?

Then the melancholy hit. He realized he was still in his headquarters. Jackson was dead, there was no victory. 'Oh, it had been so real.'

Taylor walked to the table, and set a small breakfast for Lee.

"Sorry I had to wake you sir. You looked as if you were having a pleasant rest. But you did instruct me to awaken you at this time."

It was still dark outside, but Lee did ask to be up. There was no time these days for sleep. He made a mental note to inform Longstreet that any future meetings were to be conducted at a much earlier hour.

He thanked Taylor for his meal, and sat down to fill his stomach. He said a small prayer to the Lord, and thanked him for his breakfast and more importantly for his dream. Though waking to the dream had been a bitter cruelty, Lee felt it must have been a sign that victory was near.

Taylor left him alone to his meal, which made Lee thankful. That was the one officer who always knew what was best for him. Lee sat and ate methodically, pausing to listen to the mysterious silence of the predawn. It was too quiet. Lee would often sit on mornings like this, reflecting on matters of the past, and how he could benefit his future situation. And each morning those reflections were always interrupted by his expectations of hearing the bellowing guns of Grant's artillery signaling the launch of the predawn assault that would finally crush his dilapidated army. Lee didn't know what his adversary was waiting for. For whatever reason, Grant was acting more like McClellan, and for that he was grateful. But for how long? Lee knew that as each day passed, his army dwindled that much more. What was he to do?

He tried to concentrate on his breakfast, hoping that for a brief few moments, he could take his mind off of the war. Unfortunately, each swallow of his meal, along with the accompanying sip of coffee, stabbed into his heart like the cold steal of a bayonet. How could he sit in his warm room, and enjoy a hot meal, while those men out there who put it on the line for him, sat in those cold muddied trenches eating whatever morsels they were lucky enough to find?

With that thought, he stood up and brushed the crumbs from the table into his palm, and chose to eat them too, rather then waste anything. It was for principle alone. He would not waste food, while others starved for him.

Lee washed his face, put on his coat and hat, and stepped outside into the morning's chill. He had a very direct purpose this morning. He needed to inform Longstreet that he could not leave his men here to die. However, he did feel that Longstreet's plan was a sound one. And the general was correct, it would take someone other than Hood to pull it off. Hood was a good man, but he was not the person best qualified for such a dire task. Lee would offer that to Longstreet or even suggest giving the command back to Johnston.

Lee saluted the waking officers who were posted outside his door, and stepped onto the cold hardened path. He pulled his collar up to cover his throat from the chill, and started towards the place where Longstreet was probably still sleeping.

As he turned up the road, he remembered the wounded soldier from the night before, and decided to pay the man a visit. He wanted to tell him to return to his headquarters for a much-deserved meal. Lee whished he had the means to do that for all his men. He would gladly exchange his role as this army's commander in chief, if he could just feed his men for the duration of the war.

It was still dark, and finding the man was not an easy task. Lee searched quietly, not wanting to startle him if he was still asleep. Lee finally saw the silhouette of the man, resting with his back to the tree. He walked over, and put a warm hand to his cold head. Lee bent down to wake him, gently nudging his head, much like Taylor had done to him earlier. The only difference here was that this man did not move. Lee inched closer to see the dead eyes staring back at him. Lee slowly closed them. There would be another mother deprived of her son because of this war. More tears back home.

Lee kissed the man on the head and said a prayer to God, asking that this soldier's sins be forgiven so that he would be accepted into His immortal kingdom. Lee saluted the man and returned to the road.

'You arrogant fool', he said to himself. You would rather sit here with these men, and allow them to freeze and starve, than leave. All because this is your homeland, your Virginia. How proud is that, and do the proud not get smitten? Lord please forgive me. I have asked for a sign and there can be none clearer than this. The only way for me to save these men, is for me to leave them. Your wisdom strikes us in the most peculiar ways.

Lee's sudden awakening fueled his already deep faith. God had shown him what would happen if he stood here waiting for some miracle. Waiting for Jackson to come back from the dead, like Jesus himself. That was not going to happen. The Lord helps those who help themselves. Suddenly, Longstreet's plan made more sense.

It was time to lead an army on the attack, and not wait to embrace one.

Why had he spent so much time at the Academy studying men like Clausewitz if he was not going to use their lessons when it was practical to do so? The defensive strategy without an active purpose, a plan to take the offensive at some point, was self-contradictory both in strategy and in tactics. To just sit here in trenches and wait for the enemy to attack was the very inaction that Clausewitz had warned against.

Lee thought of the west, he thought of what Longstreet had said about the situation at hand. There would be equal numbers between the opponents. A victory there would force Lincoln to remove some pressure on his lines in the east, in order to help the west. That he was sure of. Lincoln had done as much after the victory at Chattanooga. Panic had seized Washington that summer, as Union brigades were rushed to the west as fast at those trains could carry them.

Lee walked towards Longstreet with an impatient determination. He could not help but begin to feel very sorry for General Thomas and General Schofield.

*   *   *   *   *   *   *   *

Longstreet was not asleep. He was inside of his tent with a few members of his staff. They were deep in some conversation about their current position, and a possible surprise attack on an exposed Union flank. Longstreet was arguing something concerning the Union reserves quickly plugging the breakthrough, and then they would be the ones exposed.

Longstreet was the first to see Lee come through the tent flap. He quickly dismissed his staff and offered the general a seat. Lee sat, not like a man suffering from four years of lamentation, but like a schoolboy anxious for ring of the dismissal bell.

Longstreet offered Lee a cup of hot coffee. As he poured the mug, he noticed the dawn beginning to break.

"I hope you slept well?" he said.

Lee took the cup and drank a warm sip.

"General, from now on, we shall not meet at such a time, when hardworking men like ourselves should be asleep."

Longstreet agreed. He tried not to act impatient with his commander, but he wanted to know Lee's decision. He took a moment to study the man before him. Lee sat cross-legged, sipping his coffee, and perhaps hiding a grin beneath his old gray beard. Longstreet did not want to become hopeful. He could not risk the let down. However, this man before him now did not possess the same demeanor that he did that dreadful morning back in July when he announced that he would charge the center at Gettysburg. That man seemed determined, and yet doubtful of his own decision. The Lee that sat across from him now was not doubtful. He was anxious. Very anxious.

"Well general," Lee said, "I have given your plan much consideration. I have prayed to God all night that he might show me the correct path. This is not an easy decision for me. If I go out West, as you say, I risk the Army of Northern Virginia, at its most needed time. These men have fought for me, they have bled for me, and they have died for me. But most of all, they have won for me. General, they can win again."

Listening to Lee talk of this army winning again was like swallowing a thousand bumblebees. He felt them swarm in his stomach, and he had to fight the urge to be sick. It was beginning to sound like it was going to be the suicide of Gettysburg all over again. How could he be so foolish and think that Lee would come here to tell him otherwise? He thought of offering his resignation right there, but before he could, Lee continued.

"However, this time, these men need me to win for them. I need to sacrifice. The Lord has shown this to me through the Bible. There is hope in sacrifice. I cannot stay here while these men freeze to death at my doorstep, while I sleep under warm comfort. They are starving, hoping for supplies and reinforcements that we both know are not coming."

"I came here to tell you that I am going to Richmond to see President Davis. God willing he will accept this proposal, and agree to send me west. This army is now yours to command."

Longstreet was stunned. He had not expected this. He stood up and grabbed for Lee's hand. The smile that spread across his face was infectious. They both shared a moment. A feeling of hope had entered this tent, one that had not been with this army for a very long time. It was an auspicious beginning.

"Remember sir," Longstreet said. "This must all remain a secret. No one but us must know of your departure, and no one but a select few must know of your trip west. Just remember how easily word leaked to the North when my corps was sent west. That must not happen again. Besides, it should be easier to keep this a secret, you being one man missing, as opposed to when my whole army left."

"General, I will promise to keep this a secret, and I will also promise to convince President Davis to allow for my departure. However, I must be honest about one thing. I have to tell the President that this plan was mine. He will not accept it coming from anyone but myself. I hope you can understand this?"

"Of course. I did not think on this for my own personal gain. What of Johnston?"

"I will also convince the president to give him this command again, at least until my victorious return. And I will be sure to stress the part about being victorious."

Lee and Longstreet shook hands again and embraced before departing. Lee handed his mug back to Longstreet, who took it and placed it on the table. As Lee turned to leave the tent, he had one more thing to say to his beloved general.

"I want you to understand it has taken a lot for me to accept this plan. I have also made many promises to you. I ask of one promise in return."

"Anything, just say the word."

"When I return from the west, I expect the Army of Northern Virginia to be here and to be ready for its final battle."

Longstreet's grin was full of arrogant cockiness. There was a gleam in his eye like the one he had on the hills of Fredericksburg.

"Oh they will be ready General, that I can assure you." As Longstreet reassured his commander, he couldn't help but remember a particular letter that Lee had sent to him while he was away in Tennessee. The irony was overwhelming. "General perhaps you have heard this before, but this time, please allow me to be the one delivering the message. Lee, finish the work before you and return to me. I want you badly and you cannot get back too soon. Do not let Sherman capture you and I will endeavor to hold Grant till you return." With a wide smile upon his face, he saluted Lee and watched the general leave his tent to head for Richmond.

Now it was Longstreet's turn to be the anxious schoolboy, and he cherished the moment.

Chapter VI
November 19
Richmond, Virginia

Lee rode through the streets of Richmond in the back of a closed carriage. This was once one of the proudest cities in the South. Its citizens would tell you that this city would stand against Northern tyranny for any amount of time. That was what they would say. But one carriage ride through this city would tell you something different.

Lee saw it in the face of every person he passed. It was despair. There was a severe shortage of food, clothes, money and supplies. It was not much different than what his men were facing in the trenches. The only difference here was that these people were not being fired upon. As the carriage turned down a narrow street, Lee couldn't help but think that if something did not change soon, those bullets would soon reside here as well.

The carriage was forced to stop due to a commotion caused by a large gathering of people. Lee peered out and saw a large line of people massed outside of a bakery shop. Apparently, the shop owner had tried to close his shop, claiming that he was out of bread to sell. That did not go over well with the people. They were mostly mothers, with several children clinging to their sides. They were screaming and pleading for food. One woman, just hugged her little boy and cried, as she told him there would be no food for them again.

"Why God, why does this happen?" Lee said slightly above a whisper. "I do not mean to question your ways, but must we suffer at home as well as on the battlefield?" It was a question that Lee knew would remain unanswered.

By the time Lee's carriage had entered the scene, the line that had formed at the baker's door had filtered out into the street. Some of the pedestrians began tossing rocks at the shopkeeper's windows. The crash of glass startled the horses teamed on Lee's carriage.

Lee tried to remain in the carriage. The whole scene had made no sense. Why were these people taking out their aggression on their fellow man? It was not Christian. More now than ever, we need to treat our neighbors as we would have them treat us. Lee again looked out of his window, and noticed that some of the people began heading towards him. They were screaming obscenities about how the rich could ride in their carriages and eat, while their husbands were taken away to fight and die while they starved.

Lee's driver, a man named Bill Carroll, opened the front screen that separated him from Lee.

"Sir, I think that this may get out of hand. Please try to stay in the carriage."

Bill reached down by his feet and produced a shotgun. He began waving it at the approaching mob. The result was not what he had hoped for. Lee could have told him that. The ploy may have worked under different circumstances, with different people. However, these individuals had nothing to lose. Everything had been taken away from them. By the looks of most of them, if they did not have food soon, their lives would be gone as well.

The crowd began throwing rocks at the carriage. Lee heard several of the stones thud upon the outside of his shelter. It was ironic, that for all his fighting in the war thus far, his most serious brush with danger was in his own city amongst his own people. This could not go on.

Lee opened the carriage door and covered his face as he stepped out to face the mob. There was a moment of hesitation, as the gathering of people waited to see who came out from the carriage. One older man threw a rock that narrowly missed Lee.

"What is wrong with you, that is General Robert E. Lee," Bill yelled into the mob. Again, the mention of the name caused another hesitation in the crowd. Then one by one, the mob recognized Lee by his white beard and hair. In that moment of recognition they became ashamed.

"My good people," Lee said. "I assure you, if the owner of this shop had any bread left he would give it to you, as would I. Your brave men of the Confederate army are right now fighting and starving so that you may remain free. When I return to the front, how do you think they would respond if I were to tell them what I saw on this day?"

There were cries of humiliation from the crowd. Lee just stared at them with patience.

"More importantly, how do you think our heavenly Father feels when He looks down and sees this? Please try to remain patient. I know you are all cold, hungry and tired. We all are." Lee had to swallow hard at his next sentence. It was his faith in God that allowed him to utter the words he fought desperately to believe. "You will have food again soon. We will beat the Northern forces, and end this strife soon enough. Now go back to your homes and pray. God will provide. He always does. Remember that."

Bill Carroll watched the crowd disperse and did not know if it was Lee's speech or Lee's presence that had produced such an effect. Whichever it was, it was not long after Lee stepped back into the carriage, that the street was cleared.

Bill was able to continue towards the White House, relieved that he did not have to use his shotgun. He gripped the reins and began to move forward, when he noticed the shopkeeper running across the street towards him. Bill quickly and discreetly dropped his hand to the shotgun and waited.

"Good Sir," the baker said, as he looked back over his shoulder. "I only wanted to thank you for saving my store, and I wanted to give the General this."

He produced from under his apron, several loaves of hard bread. Bill was as nervous to see the bread, as the baker was to show it. If any of the departing crowd saw the loaves, there was no telling the magnitude of the riot that might ensue.

"Are you crazy sir?" he said.

The baker snatched the bread back and scampered to the side of the carriage. He knocked on the door. Lee slid the shade to see who it was, and judging by the attire of the individual, guessed it was the baker.

"General Lee, three of my finest loaves for you sir."

General Lee looked at the bread as he opened the door. "You had these three loaves of bread left and you closed your store?"

The baker was taken back by Lee's obvious disappointment. "Sir, it is just that I only had these three loaves, and you saw how many people were gathered here."

"Did our Lord Jesus not feed the masses with just a few loaves of bread and fish?" Lee replied.

The baker stood speechless as Lee took the loaves from him and told Bill Carroll to continue. Lee put the bread beside him, as the carriage rolled up the street.

It was a long time before the baker moved from the middle of the road.

*   *   *   *   *   *   *   *

Lee looked out the window with a desperate determination. Then he saw what he searched for. He told Bill to turn down the next street. Bill was concerned, knowing that it was in the opposite direction of the capital. When he steered the carriage and made a right turn, he understood. Lee told Bill to stop for a moment.

Most men would not do anything to delay a meeting with the President. Lee was not like most men. Bill watched with a warm smile upon his face, as Lee caught up to the woman. He knew instantly that it was the woman that they had seen outside of the bakery, the one that held her boy and cried knowing that they would go hungry for another night. As Bill watched the tears of joy cascade upon the woman's face as Lee gave her the bread, he now understood what made this man something special on the battlefield. The woman and the boy both gratefully hugged the pious general. Lee patted the lad on the top of the head before he returned to the carriage.

"Let's see the President now," was all he said.

Bill helped Lee back inside the carriage and closed the door. "God bless you sir," he said.

As the door closed behind Lee, he sat back in his seat, and slumped a little. He thought of the starving mob outside of the bakery. He thought of his starving men in the field Lee brought his head down upon trembling hands, as he heard Bill say God bless you.

All he could think of was, 'for what?'

*   *   *   *   *   *   *   *

Lee waited in President Davis' office. He heard the President talking to his secretary in the next room. The words came muffled through the door, but he clearly heard the statement. 'not to be disturbed.' The doors across from Lee opened, and Jefferson Davis entered the room. For all the stress Lee felt these past few years, it paled in comparison to the wraith that sat across from him. Davis looked like a man who had not slept in months. His eyes hung over his cheeks like a man that was constantly sad. The President tried to hide it, but to Lee the façade was poor. Davis looked as if he had been eating, drinking, bathing and living in all the comforts of despair.

Davis shook Lee's hand, and forced a smile upon his wrinkled face.

"Robert, it is good to see you."

Lee smiled and returned the greeting. President Davis motioned for Lee to sit opposite his desk, and called his servant to bring them cool refreshments. A black man entered the room and placed a pitcher and two glasses on the President's desk. Upon resting the tray, he methodically retired from the room, closing the doors behind him.

Davis poured drinks into both glasses, and heartily swallowed the contents of his own. Without any segue he placed his glass down, and opened the conversation.

"General, what brings you from the battlefield?"

"My men are ill equipped and they are starving."

Davis leaned back from Lee. The topic was an obvious open sore with no remedy to heal it. Lee's words were like salt to the wound.

"I have done all that I can, I have sent all that I can. I had always hoped that the Europeans would break the Northern blockade. I had no concept of how suffocating such naval tactics could be."

Lee was sympathetic towards Davis. He knew that his President was not like the baker in town. If Davis had anything to give Lee, he knew it would have been given. And that was the point. There was nothing left to give to his Army of Northern Virginia.

"And men. Are there any additional troops that I can expect?"

Lee knew the answer to his question. But he had to ask. He had to let Davis speak the answers, confirming the hopelessness of the situation that they now faced.

"We are doing what we can to raise more men, but the bigger problem is not the recruiting, it is the absentees. If only half our absent soldiers would return to duty, we could raise an army as large as yours. But that is a forlorn hope."

Lee sat in silence, letting the lackadaisical tone of the President's response speak for itself.

"How does General Hood fare in the West?" Lee asked.

This question sparked a hint of hope in the Presidents

eyes. Good. That meant that even he realized that their last best chance resided in Tennessee.

"Hood is now planning to gain Sherman's rear. He has an opportunity for some great accomplishments. Hood may reverse this tide yet".

Lee noted the stress that Davis put on the word 'yet.' Davis' choices for commanders in the West had made him look the cuckold too many times. It was Davis who was dogmatic about Bragg keeping his command. The President was able to silence his critics when Bragg had the Federal army starving in Chattanooga. Unfortunately, his elation was short lived, as his proud head was forced to sink in shame when the besieged Federal army emerged from their containment and swept away Bragg's ill positioned army. Swept them away with as much difficulty as when the wind scatters the autumn leaves.

Joseph Johnston replaced Bragg, and though he would not take the offensive against the Federals, he kept their progress in check by constantly impeding their path. Unfortunately, that was not good enough for Davis, who wanted the Federals destroyed. Either he did not understand, or he did not care... either way he refused to acknowledge that the Federals severely outnumbered the Confederates in manpower. Belligerent and dogmatic, he removed Johnston from command of the Army of Tennessee and replaced him with John Bell Hood.

To this point, it was another decision turned disastrous. Hood attacked with all the fury and might that Davis expected. But he also attacked with an army that was inferior in numbers, just as Johnston had warned. The result was the loss of a lot of Southern soldiers, as well as Atlanta and for all intents and purposes the state of Georgia.

"Do you believe that Hood can accomplish what you ask?"

"Robert, I do not know. If you asked me that when I first met him, when I saw him while he was recovering here a few years ago, I would have said yes. I would have staked everything on it. He was a giant proud man. I remember him fondly, sitting on the sofa, his head held high, without a concern for the loss of his leg. I told him that I was sorry for his loss, and do you know what he told me? He said that he was the one who was sorry. He wished that the Federals were defeated in total at Chickamauga. He was sorry that they were allowed to escape. It did not take much more than that to convince me that he was a man deserving of promotion. When I did so, he stood proudly and shook my hand with the strength of a mountain. He told me that he was thankful, and that if I ever took command of this army on the battlefield and led the way forward, he would follow me to the death. I admired that in him. That is the morale that we need."

"And now?"

"Now? Now, I hear too many things. Hood has lost Atlanta, and yet General Bragg and Governor Harris of Tennessee sing his praises. They say he has had a significant effect on raising the spirits of the men and making them believe in themselves. Others say differently. Beauregard is constantly complaining that Hood does not keep him informed. Hood was supposed to be in Sherman's rear already. I just hope he knows what he is doing. A victory out there, one of substance, would have dramatic effects for this country. We just need a victory in battle again... another Fredericksburg or better yet, a victory like we had in northern Georgia, when Longstreet helped Bragg rout the Yankees."

Lee was not used to the President questioning his own decisions. This was a rare moment, and Lee wanted Davis to continue.

"Do I think Hood is the right man for the job, you ask," Davis continued. "Sometimes I lie in bed and I think of many things. I wonder if I made the right decision in placing Hood in command over Hardee. Perhaps it should be Hood in Charleston right now. Do you know what hurts the most? When I made my last trip out west, to survey the situation first hand, I rode amongst our soldiers, and they cheered. Only, they were not cheering for me, or for my decision to put Hood in command. They cheered for that scoundrel Johnston. They begged me to put that man back in command. Do they not know, do they not realize that their defeated condition is his fault?"

Lee wanted to defend Johnston, but he did not come here to argue with the President. And experience had taught him that you did not want to argue with Davis. To be an effective commander in this army, you needed to appear docile and full of alacrity for anything that Davis had to say. To oppose his way of thinking was a sure way to lose his favor, and find yourself transferred to a lesser role in the army. Lee had seen that happen too many times and thought better than to challenge the President.

"I am sure that the soldiers did not mean you any disrespect, they are demoralized by recent failures. They do not see Johnston's retreat from Sherman as a loss, they see it as a tactical move that saved them from suffering high amounts of casualties. In retrospect, they do not understand that General Hood's attacks were designed to save the Confederacy, they only see that they have lost a great many men. They simply associate the days serving under General Johnston with far fewer casualties, as compared to their service under Hood."

Davis looked quizzically at Lee, and finally nodded his head in consent.

"Perhaps... perhaps."

Davis refilled his glass, and offered more to Lee. Lee declined, having only sipped his drink once.

"General, what is the real reason for your visit here?"

Lee smiled at Davis, "Is there nothing that can be concealed from you?"

"Shouldn't the President be astute to such things?"

Lee nodded, and raised his glass. Anticipating his time to speak, his second sip lasted much longer than the first.

"President, the situation that we face in the east is futile. It is as I feared when I warned of the consequences of Grant's army crossing the James. We are besieged, it is only a matter of time."

"Robert, I understand the situation. I have tried, I am still trying to get us more men, but it is a battle far worse than the one you face in the field. Our own governors and politicians argue against any conscription. Conscriptions go against state's rights, they claim. How can we ask our government to demand conscripts from the states? If we allowed this, we would become the same as the adversary that we are facing."

"Sir, I know this. But there must be some way to make them understand. If we fall on the field, then the government they are trying so adamantly to protect will also fall."

Davis turned his eyes down and watched his fingers waltz between both hands. "Robert, I am trying."

"My men have no food, they are shoeless and shelter-less. Christmas is not far off and there is no chance of even the briefest of furloughs for my men. I am asked not only to face the Federal army, but also to keep disheartened men in the ranks. Sir, the rate of stragglers alone, will be the defeat of my army, not General Grant."

Davis realized that Lee was not here to voice his complaints without reason. He was not that type of man. Lee was not telling him of his desperate situation in admittance of defeat. If he knew that men and supplies were scarce, then there was something else he must want. He looked into Lee's eyes with a stare that indicated it was time to cut to the chase.

"Robert, what is it you want?"

"I have come to ask your permission to allow me to take command of General Hood's forces in the west."

Several moments of silence ensued.

"You have had that permission since the last time I requested it. In fact, I believe that it was offered in this very same room. Only when I asked it, you very diplomatically skirted the question. Tell me what has brought on this change of mind?"

Lee was relieved. He wasn't sure how Davis was going to respond to this, but at this point he seemed acquiescent. He had been offered this position before, and had turned it down.

"The circumstances at this time are different. We were not in such desperate times back then."

"Are you saying, that there is a chance that you were wrong in not taking that position a year ago, when I had all but begged you to take it, and ease my mind in the west?"

Lee's first reaction was to lash out, and defend himself from such a brash statement. However, his belief in his faith, taught him patience and forgiveness.

"I have only performed and acted as I thought best for our country."

"Your country, or your Virginia?"

Lee dropped his head, and remained silent.

"What do you believe that you can do out there now, that could not have been done a year ago?"

Lee's head snapped back to attention.

"Win."

Lee refilled the President's glass a third time. He wanted his last word to penetrate any judgments that Davis might feel towards him at this moment.

"We have an excellent chance before us in the west. It is apparent that there is no more that I can do here. General Early's offensive against their capital was almost triumphant beyond all expectations, but it has ended in the worst of failures. There are no more choices. Our supplies are all but gone, and there are no more men to be had. There is nothing left we can do, but wait. We must wait until the enemy brings enough to finish us off. And that, my dear President, is exactly how we will win the war in the west, and save ourselves in the east."

Davis was captured. He beckoned Lee to continue.

"Grant cannot attack us at this time and win. He has tried several times and his casualties are too high. However, he knows that we are too weakened to attack him. It is only a matter of time, until our dwindling numbers are so much reduced that an attack is possible. He can quicken this process, and bring much relief to their President, if he can get a force large enough into our rear. We are already too stretched out to defend against such a move. At this time, Sherman has over sixty thousand men marching through our heartland. It is undoubtedly his intention to come from behind our entrenchments in order to combine with Grant and crush us in between their hammer and anvil.

"This move, designed to end our hopes of independence, is also our last greatest hope. The Federal offensive has left roughly sixty thousand men to face Hood's thirty thousand in Tennessee. Remarkably, those sixty thousand Yankees are divided under two commanders, and they are unconsolidated, and miles from one another. General Hood has a chance to face either half of this army on equal terms. A victory over one half would put the forces in the west on equal terms. A victory over the other half would send the North into turmoil."

Davis was agreeing before Lee could finish.

"They will flock to you Robert. With our flags raised high over the Nashville capitol, the people of Tennessee will flock to our colors. We could increase our numbers by twenty, no, thirty thousand."

"And we know what Lincoln would do," Davis continued. "His own politicians will force him to protect the west. Like they did every time we had a threat in the Shenandoah valley."

"And that would mean that he would have to pull forces from the east, thus relieving the pressure on this front," said Lee. "All that we need is secrecy in my departure. Grant cannot know that I am no longer here. We will also need the forces defending Petersburg and Richmond to hold out until we can achieve our victory."

"If Richmond, or Petersburg were to fall in your absence, do not stop for a moment and think that a strong willed nation can not survive. All we need is our people to keep hope and remain strong in their will to resist the enemy. If we have that, then Richmond, or no Richmond, we will still be here for your triumphant return."

"I have but one question Robert."

Lee knew the question, and was afraid to answer.

"Who will lead this army until your return?" Davis asked.

Lee looked as confident and as sure as he possibly could. "I assure you that for this position, there is no greater person to lead this army until my return, than General Johnston."

Davis tried his hardest to suppress the look of anger upon his brow. If it were a poker game, he would have lost his hand.

"Of all the men at your disposal, your best suggestion is Johnston?"

"Sir, I am only confident in him because of the situation at hand. His role is simply to defend Richmond and Petersburg until my return. We once joked that all Johnston knew how to do was retreat in the face of the enemy claiming that he needed more men. Remember when it was said if we gave Johnston Florida to defend, he would fall back to Cuba?"

"And this is the man you suggest to lead the Army of Northern Virginia?"

"Sir, for all intents and purposes, the present position of the Army of Northern Virginia is Cuba. Johnston has nowhere else to fall back to. I will talk to him. He and Longstreet have similar tactics when it comes to the defensive. Remember Fredericksburg. With the two of them here, Grant will have several Fredericksburgs if he were to risk an attack that he is not ready for."

"My heart is against giving this command back to Johnston, but I will trust you Robert. I will promote Johnston first thing tomorrow."

"I would suggest against that. This must be all done in secret. No one but a select few can know that I am gone and Johnston has command. We will say that I am sick and confined to my headquarters. Johnston can command from there, conveying his orders through Taylor and Longstreet."

"How will you get west?"

"I will take the rail as far as I can, then a select escort from Hampton's Cavalry will be guide from there."

"When will you depart?"

"I will finalize that once Johnston arrives. I would like it to be as soon as possible. Every day counts," Lee said.

"Then we are done General. Expect Joseph Johnston's arrival soon."

Davis stood up and shook Lee's hand. "This will remain a secret. Once your victory is attained, the Southern spirit will soar to such heights, that the world must take notice."

*   *   *   *   *   *   *   *

As Lee left the White House, he had a tough time with the thoughts of leaving his wife Mary behind. He somehow wanted to get word to them concerning his departure, but knew that the severity of his secret superseded even the bonds to his family. She would have to think that he were sick, just as every one else. The thoughts of her worried face threatened to tear his heart from his chest.

Bill Carroll held the carriage door open long enough for Lee to get comfortably inside, and then returned to his drivers seat. The sadness that radiated from Lee's posture had a discomforting effect upon his own mood.

Bill had thought that his life was a troubled one, but after spending this day escorting Lee through Richmond, he was able to utter a small prayer of thanks.

"At least I am not wearing that man's boots."

Chapter VII
Nashville, Tennessee
Still the 19th

Dressed in all the fine accoutrements the Federal army had to offer, General George H. Thomas dwelled in a fine dining room at the Saint Cloud Hotel. His towering six-foot frame was considered large by any standard, but not even his own size could support the augmented hyperbole that was attached to his name following the battle at Chickamauga. Since then, many of his own officers asked from what granite his body was made? It was at the battle of Chickamauga that his generalship saved the life of the Federal army, and because of it, Thomas was soon to be ordained the 'Rock of Chickamauga.'

Thomas, with a delicateness that belied his size, poked a tiny silver fork into his meal, placing the last bit of meat into his mouth. He gingerly put his eating utensils down, and then slid them to the end of the grand dining table. He marveled at the workmanship of the wood, it was a solid sturdy piece, but it was the staining that made it magnificent. It had enough color to send the hue into a deep cherry colored frenzy, but not too much to hide the swirls and dancing of the wood's grain. The swirls were like clouds, and depending on the mood he was in, could transform into the very shapes that resembled the darkest issues that lay rooted deep within his subconscious.

Right now, the swirls in the grain were spinning an inferno.

Thomas rested with his elbows upon the table, allowing his head to fall into their embrace. There was just so much to do... To put off thinking for a moment, he scratched his thick beard, and rubbed his deep brow. The brief respite allowed Thomas to remember that one of his staff members had brought him the maps that he requested before dinner. He got up and retrieved them from the bureau on the far side of the room. He found the one he wanted most, and placed it upon the table.

Tennessee was opened before him.

"Now I am to save us again," he grumbled.

If Thomas was not bursting with enthusiasm for his current objective, it was for good reason. He felt slighted in the worst way. When this war began, Thomas had chosen to fight for the side that he believed in. That was the North. The only problem with that decision was that his proud family was from the South. They were Virginians, and there was no greater insult to them, than their son choosing to take arms against his home state. From that fateful day forward, he was their son no longer. The decision demanded a lot of fortitude, but he held to his beliefs. In the beginning, there were many Northerners who still questioned his loyalty. He left a family who disowned him for an army that did not trust him.

Yet he persevered.

He fought bravely in all his engagements, but it was the battle at Chickamauga that had made him most famous. It was perhaps two days of the most consistent and savage fighting that this war had seen yet. And it was Thomas that bore the brunt of it.

At the time, General Rosencrans led the Union army of the Cumberland. Unfortunately, Rosencrans had been pushed and cajoled into movement by the decision-makers in Washington. Why is it that those that are farthest from the battle think they know best regarding how a battle should be fought? Rosencrans' superiors did not care about logistics, nor any other matters that were a concern for those actually fighting the battle. They only wanted to hear that the Federal army was in motion and in pursuit of the enemy.

Thus Rosencrans found his army in an exposed position west of the Chickamauga creek in late September 1863. And yet, even though Rosencrans was not enthusiastic to be so far into the enemy's heartland, his soldiers were. The recent news of the rebel defeat at Gettysburg had the morale of his army soaring. Following these reports were the headlines taken from the newspapers back East. The bold black ink was the harbinger of the wars end. The rebellion was almost crushed. Chief of Staff Henry Halleck shared the sentiment of the presses. From his neat little office in the capitol, he commanded Rosencrans to make the final push that would crush the Confederate war effort.

Thomas occupied the left flank of the army that stretched for over four miles along the Lafayette road. By all reports, they had the rebel army outnumbered. Thomas' men began the assault against a Confederate brigade opposite him. Surprisingly they *were repulsed. More surprisingly was that the rebels began a counterattack. Thomas was able to repulse their effort and then counter with his own. That began the singsong struggle that would last throughout the remainder of the day. Thomas' corps and the rebels fought a series of battles along this front, ending with no significant gains for either combatant.*

Rosencrans held a council that night and expressed his concern that Thomas would be attacked again in the morning. He ordered his men to prepare for the assault by building earthworks during the night. Rosencrans prudence had paid off, for as the day began, the Army of Tennessee once again attacked Thomas' corps.

Rosencrans began issuing orders to send reserves to Thomas' aid.

In the chaos of the battle, the shifting of troops had left an opening in the Federal line below Thomas' command. Any break in the defensive line against an advancing enemy was always a serious misfortune with catastrophic implications. But, never so much as it had been on that day. Confederate General James Longstreet had arrived in full force the night before, bringing with him his two divisions, virtually another army. The disparity in arms was now leveled, and as fortune would have it, Longstreet's attack struck the point where the Federals had a gap in their line.

The result was not a rout of the Federal right, but an all out stampede. The whole Federal army withered away under Longstreet's attack. With Longstreet advancing from the left, and Bragg concentrating on the right, it was soon to be one of the most absolute victories of the war. A third of the Federal army was disorganized, scattered and racing for Chattanooga. Those that were left behind were quickly dissolving, leaving Thomas' corps virtually alone and delegated with the task of bringing the advancing rebel army to a halt.

Thomas, fully understanding the disaster at hand, knew that he had to give the rest of his army time to escape. He had to disengage from Bragg at his front, and reorganize his line so as to face Longstreet approaching from the south. Simply put, his men had to sacrifice themselves and hold off Bragg to the east, and Longstreet from the South. If they did not, the Federal army of the Cumberland would cease to exist.

Once again Thomas persevered.

Though Longstreet had smashed the Federal army, they themselves were exhausted and disorganized. Their subsequent attacks were not fully concentrated. Bragg's men were also tired, having been engaged in battle for the past two days. If pure exhaustion was not enough to hamper any further damage caused by the enemy, the timely arrival of Granger's reserve corps ensured that Thomas would be able to defend against the rebel offensive. At the end of the day, the casualties had been high, but the Federal army had escaped. Appreciation and recognition went deservingly to General George Thomas, the Rock of Chickamauga.

Remarkably, the enemy had not followed up their attack the next day. Instead they settled around Chattanooga in an attempted siege. For the Union army, it was Vicksburg in reverse. The soldiers had to subsist on reduced rations until relief could be provided. Fortunately, the Union had been quicker to respond to this plight than the Confederate's had been in their similar situation at Vicksburg. Thomas was ordered to replace General Rosencrans until Grant could arrive from the West. All that was asked of Thomas was that he hold until Grant and reinforcements could arrive.

In the face of starvation and despair, Thomas again persevered.

General Grant arrived, shook his hand, commended him for his heroic work, and then began to immediately reorganize his command. Thomas felt slighted. He did not need Grant to take command of the offensive. The reinforcements would have been just fine.

Food was still a problem though. Even if Federal troops were en route to the besieged city, they would only starve when they got there. Something had to be done. Thomas studied maps with his chief engineer, who discovered a route that could be used to get food into the city. It was a success. Cartons of food started pouring in for the famished troops and the 'Cracker line' was opened. And it was Grant who was given the acclaim and considered a hero.

Thomas had to chew on his share of crackers and swallow their jagged edges with his pride. It was he who kept the army together, he who held out during the siege, a chief engineer that found the route to get food into the city, and yet the papers chose to exalt Grant.

As the Federal reinforcements arrived, it became apparent that Thomas was not going to be Grant's chosen commander for the offensive. Grant had a stronger affection for General Sherman. Thomas' slide down the totem pole had been a harsh one.

Thomas' fears became a reality when Grant revealed his plan to break the siege of Chattanooga. Grant wanted Hooker to attack the left flank of the rebel line anchored at Lookout Mountain. Thomas would do nothing but put on a show of force against Bragg's center. This would help to keep the main portion of the Rebel line in place at Missionary Ridge, while the beloved Sherman crossed the Tennessee River to the north, and attacked the right flank of the enemy.

With this plan, Thomas would have no chance to strike the enemy. This was an insult. If any troops deserved to be leading this attack, it was his. They were the men whose honor was crushed on the fields of Chickamauga.

Thomas accepted the plan with a poker face of gritted teeth.

Sherman's attack had struck the right flank of the rebel line, but was seriously repulsed. Hooker succeeded taking Lookout Mountain, however, that put his troops too far south of the main battlefield. If Bragg chose, he could concentrate a massive counterattack against Sherman to the north, and crush him. Fortunately for Grant, Bragg had sent Longstreet's troops north against Burnside in Knoxville. Had Bragg had those troops at that point, Thomas may never have had his vindication.

Once again, it was Thomas who turned the tide of battle. His troops stormed forward without any official orders. Grant was fuming at the attack. Thomas would not forget the look on his face as he paced amongst his staff demanding to know who had ordered those men forward.

Thomas watched, internally cheering his men on. They stormed the rebel line and shattered it.

And you came here to show us how to fight, he had thought. With the rebel center obliterated, their whole army caved in. It was the fitting revenge for the insult at Chickamauga. The Confederates were in full flight back into Georgia. Thomas had won the day, and yet the newspapers continued to praise Grant as the hero.

The rock had to endure.

Thomas continued to serve under this pretense, until Grant received notice that he had been promoted to commander and chief of the entire Union army. Before he could leave

Tennessee, he had to promote someone in his place. Thomas had little doubts as to who that would be. There was no question that he knew that he deserved it, he had proved himself time and time again. It was just that there was a brotherhood between Grant, Sherman, and the army that came with him from Vicksburg.

Sherman was given command, despite being Thomas' junior in rank. Thomas, the man who turned his back on his family in Virginia to serve for the North, was slighted once again.

Thomas found it hard to pull away and escape his bewildered trance. He stood up, stretching his powerful arms high over his head. It is not good to let such anger dwell in your soul, he thought. He did not want to remain bitter, he only wanted what he deserved. And he did not deserve this new situation. After the fall of Atlanta, Sherman had decided to march east, instead of chasing Hood's army and finishing it off. Sherman departed with half of the army, and left the other half scattered throughout Georgia and Tennessee.

Hood's consolidated force was at present larger then the scattered force under Thomas' command. Did no one realize the potential for disaster except he?

Once again, it was Thomas who was called upon to save the army. Sherman had sent him to Nashville a few months ago to quell the threat that Nathan Bedford Forrest's cavalry imposed. Hood, Sherman had said, was not to be a concern.

At that time, Thomas' situation was not such a desperate one. He sent troops after Forrest, but the elusive rebel cavalry had escaped. When the threat of Hood's' army emerged in Northern Alabama, Thomas was told simply to stop any advance that they tried to make. In the event that Hood followed Sherman east, like Sherman expected him to do, Thomas was told to pursue. This would trap the rebel army between Thomas and Sherman. The only problem with these orders was that Hood's intentions were not as Sherman had suspected. Instead of following Sherman east, Hood like Thomas, saw the Federal vulnerability in Tennessee and with it the potential for Southern gain.

Hood was soon reported to be advancing west looking for a place to cross to the north side of the Tennessee... and Thomas knew all to well what that would mean, and he also knew that his command was not prepared for the eventual confrontation. But that did not stop him from reacting quickly. Brigadier General

Edward Hatch's Cavalry had been en route to join Sherman on his march east. Thomas sent orders that called him back to Tennessee. He needed the cavalry as the eyes and ears for his army and it would be Hatch's task to report any movements conducted by Hood. It did not take Hatch long to give the report that Thomas was looking for. A brief skirmish a few weeks ago had rewarded the Federal high command with a loose-lipped Southern prisoner.

The captured rebel confirmed that Hood was marching north, and what was worse was that Forrest was en route to join him. If Thomas needed any more assurances, it came a few days later, when he learned Cheatham had crossed the Tennessee. Right behind that news, was a report given by an escaped Federal prisoner. The soldier was a lieutenant from the 2nd Michigan cavalry. He added that he witnessed over seven hundred supply wagons en route behind Cheatham's advance.

And so it was confirmed that Hood was coming for him.

Thomas still sat deep within his fog of incredulity. The roads were so devastated by the cold rain, it seemed impossible for an army to be on the advance. Yet he had his reports, he had the words of rebel prisoners, as well as his own men who had escaped being prisoners themselves. Earlier today, it was reported that Hatch was engaged with Forrest's cavalry, and Hatch was being pushed back.

Thomas' choices at present were quite simple. If he was to face Hood, he had to gather his forces. His biggest conglomeration was with Schofield at Pulaski. Based on Schofield's current position and Hood's reported march west of that, he had no other options but to call Schofield back to Columbia. He could not allow Schofield's command to be cut off.

Thomas, glad that his aggression was finally focused on the rebels and not his pride, began writing his orders. Schofield must fall back at once from Pulaski with great speed. He also prepared a telegram to send to Halleck in Washington. Thomas thought that this must have been the same pressure that Rosencrans was under when he had command. He knew that the right thing to do was to pull back and regroup. Unfortunately, he also knew that Halleck and Grant would see that as a retreat, and a loss to the enemy.

And yet, if Thomas was confident about anything in this war, it was that he did not care what anyone thought. What mattered most was that he had to persevere.

November 21
Pulaski, Tennessee

The morning was colder than usual. A chilling wind crept into the Federal camp and stung the soldiers with an icy frost. Those that braved the cold were soon to be greeted with a squalling snowfall. The wind seemed to be angered that the snow dared to share its space. With all of its might, it tried to force the snow out of its presence. The result was a fierce and frenzied snowfall with winds that threatened to tear down the sturdiest of tents.

Still, many of the Federal soldiers were content. They huddled next to their fires and played card games as they reminisced about the war. They felt that they could allow themselves such idle time, since for all intents and purposes, their part in this war was over.

They were not sure exactly what duty was left for them to perform. They had been ordered to fortify Pulaski against an attack, and that they did. But an attack from whom? Sherman had destroyed Hood's army. Hadn't he? Sherman must have thought as much when he took half of the army with him when he headed east in an effort to consolidate with Grant. Those left behind were pleased. The west had been liberated, Atlanta had fallen, and now there was nothing left to do but wait until Lee's army was destroyed. And by the recent newspaper reports, that was soon to happen.

So what was a little snow, as compared to the other boys who were marching all the way to the Atlantic?

That was the prominent attitude of Schofield's forces until very recently. Like the sparks of a brush fire, the rumor mill had swept from tent to tent across the ten thousand-man army posted in Pulaski. Hood was not destroyed, but was on the move again. They knew what that meant. The next battle fought with the enemy would not be like any of the more recent ones. With Sherman no longer at Atlanta, the disparity in numbers between the two armies began to level out. Many wondered if these latest rumors would mean that Sherman was coming back?

There were some soldiers who were not as worried, thinking this developing threat to be a bit apocryphal. "Just look outside of your tent," they would say, "and see the savage snowstorm, feel it shake your tent with its icy wind, not to mention the thick cold mud that make the roads uneven and nearly impossible to traverse." There was no way an army could be mobilized under such inclement conditions. The veterans of this campaign could remember the rebel dead around Atlanta, several of which where dressed in tattered apparel that did not include the luxury of any sort of shoes. How could such an ill-equipped force tread north into the cold?

It was that rationale that allowed the Union army at Pulaski to welcome winter with open arms. The snow was indeed cold and bothersome, and yet it was also a friend. Seeing the white fall from the sky was proof enough that there was no need to concern them with any rebel threat. If anything were to happen, it would be when the weather cleared.

Yet as the more worried soldiers consoled themselves with constant peaks outside of their tent flaps, an alarming sight passed through the snow. Officers were being summoned to General Schofield's headquarters. By the haste in their step, they knew that something had their commander worried.

A long and ominous silence settled over Pulaski, as the soldiers fed their fears into the rumor mill.

*   *   *   *   *   *   *   *

General John M. Schofield stood against the window at his headquarters in Pulaski. He methodically rubbed the top brass button on his military jacket, as he observed his army spread out before him.

They will never be ready to march out of here, he thought. The Federal army lay bivouacked in and around Pulaski like a slumbering bear. They were content to let the winter put them in a sojourn of hibernation. It would be hard to get them moving. Like a muscle that needed to perform first thing on a cold morning, without properly stretching, it could easily be torn apart. Schofield faced that irony with deep consternation.

The telegrams and couriers had been coming in and going out with much more frequency these last few days. At first they concerned two independent concerns, Forrest and Hood. However, the more recent reports indicated that those concerns were no longer acting independently. Forrest was now with Hood and apparently leading his army into Tennessee. When these reports were first brought to his attention, Schofield was convinced that Forrest was only conducting another raid. Like his men, he was sure that the foul weather would hamper any actions by Hood's army, and so he did not react with prudence.

Schofield scratched his pale forehead, and looked through the latest dispatches that were set before him. They were from general Hatch. The one he held now was delivered yesterday. It reported that the rebel infantry was fourteen miles north of Florence, with a host of over ten thousand cavalry proceeding their way. Schofield shuffled the paper behind his latest telegram. This one had come from General Thomas in Nashville.

It contained a more detailed report of the enemy's location. General Stephen D. Lee's corps was twenty miles from Florence approaching Lawrenceburg. General Cheathem was on a parallel road towards Waynesboro. There was a reported thirty to thirty five thousand infantry between them. Thomas must have excellent sources to report such detail, he thought.

Thomas' message ended with a direct quote from General Hatch, 'There is no doubt of their advance.' Schofield could not misconstrue what Thomas meant.

Schofield swallowed hard. Until now, he was confident that this was only another of Forrest's raids, but now he knew that he had been wrong. What was worse than having ensured Thomas that he needn't worry, was that his lack of concern left his army unprepared to move against the enemy. Thus by his inaction, Schofield had yielded Hood the initiative.

Schofield called for a staff officer and informed him to gather all of his generals and their senior officers. The officer noted Schofield's tone, and what it implied. He did not stop to don a coat as he raced from the headquarters with several other staff members trailing close behind. Schofield walked to the window, and watched them run with reckless abandon into the cold wet afternoon. He nodded, hoping that his army would move with the same sense of urgency.

Schofield opened his map, and noted the position of his men around Pulaski, and compared it to the position of Hood's army as reported in the dispatches. They were almost parallel. Then it struck Schofield like a cannon ball above the shoulders and between the ears. He started placing coins on his position, the position of the rebel army, and the position of Thomas. Then he saw the Duck River, and almost lost his breakfast.

Hood and Schofield were on the same side of the Duck. Thomas was across it. If Hood beat him in a race to that river, he could have the rebel army in a position to face Schofield alone. Schofield would be trapped.

There was a knock at the door, and a member from his staff arrived with the latest telegram from Thomas. Schofield, revealing too much of his new found apprehension, snapped the letter from his officer's hand and read it.

"General Schofield... without hesitation, you must immediately vacate your current position and fall back to Columbia." He did not have to read any further. Schofield dismissed the officer and waited for his generals to arrive. This time tomorrow, his army had better be moving towards Columbia with great haste.

Schofield again found himself rubbing his top brass button, this time so hard that it almost fell off. "Hood, you damned fool," he smirked. "To think, it was I who encouraged you to stay in the army back when you had so many demerits and demotions from being absent. What a fool was I? And now, because of my divine intervention, the young officer who was to fail out of the United States Army, now stands to destroy it."

*   *   *   *   *   *   *   *

Nashville, Tennessee

Thomas stood atop the highest structure in Nashville, and raised his field glasses towards the south. He knew it was fruitless, but he was hoping to see Schofield's corps.

"Nothing," he muttered to himself.

"Sir, you have just sent the telegram," Wilson said.

Thomas was angered, his statement being rhetorical. However, what angered him more was the situation with his new chief of cavalry Major General James H. Wilson. Wilson was sent west in late October to rebuild Sherman's cavalry. His task was supposed to be completed weeks ago. It was not, and was now presently leaving Thomas' army in a very precarious position.

"When can your horse soldiers be made available? Hatch alone can not stop Hood's advance, and we must detain him long enough, until we can consolidate our forces with General Schofield."

"General, we have the men ready, but there are no horses. And the guns are still en route from New York, they have not arrived as of yet."

Thomas remained calm. He would need Wilson in the days ahead. He looked through the field glasses again, in the direction of the reported rebel army. Still nothing. Without removing the glasses, he continued to ask the questions that kept him in a pessimistic mood.

"Has there been any word from the sixteenth corps?"

"Major General A. J. Smith is en route with ten thousand soldiers."

"General Wilson, please inform me of what I do not know. They were supposed to be here a month ago."

Wilson tactfully accepted the derogatory statement. Different Generals liked their food served on different plates. Some wanted small servings carefully fed to them bite by bite, but Thomas was not one of those. Simply serve him the whole meal on one massive plate and then allow him to digest it on his own.

"General Rosencrans is crediting the weather for Smith's delay. The roads are far too difficult to traverse."

Wilson knew he hade made a mistake, before he finished the sentence. He was only reporting what Rosencrans had said and not his own opinion. Unfortunately, Rosencrans was not the one present for Thomas' rebuttal.

"The roads are in no condition to travel?" Thomas said. "Well, will someone tell that to Sam Hood. You get a message back to Rosencrans, and to Smith. They had better find a way to hasten those soldiers. I don't care what condition the roads are in. I don't care how cold the weather gets. Do they not understand the peril we are now in? Schofield is in a race for the Duck River. If he gets cut off, we are going to need a force here to save him. As of this moment, I have twenty five thousand men ready to face a rebel army estimated at thirty five thousand. Thanks to a depletion in horses, and late arrival of guns from New York, we have three thousand cavalry facing Forrest's ten thousand."

Thomas took a moment to calm himself before continuing. "General Wilson, I apologize for being brash, but I need you to understand the severity of the situation. I need you to get a cavalry together somehow, and detain Hood's march."

Wilson saluted Thomas. "Sir, I will depart at once and assume command of the cavalry in the field. My adjutant will stay behind and see that the munitions arrive, and that my cavalry is properly equipped."

"Thank you sir. And general, one more thing... the next time Rosencrans feeds you anything about how difficult it is to travel in these wintry conditions, please inform him that if he thinks the march here is too difficult, wait till his soldiers arrive and have to face Hood's army alone ... because by the time they get here my army will have ceased to exist."

Chapter VIII
Still the 21st and into the 22
Waynesboro Road, Tennessee

General Hood rode amongst Cheatham's Corps on the road towards Waynesboro. If the biting wind was a nuisance to him, he did not show it. Hood was too busy trying to keep his pride bursting from nostalgic enthusiasm. For the first time, in a long time, he was able to watch his army march forward and towards the enemy.

If this cold wintry weather meant to hinder his triumphant return into Tennessee, it had failed. The November temperatures actually assisted rather than hampered his army. It was in fact so cold, that the weather helped to harden the muddied earth. This allowed his men to walk tall and proud, upon a ground as solid as they were. Spirits could not have been higher.

Alongside Hood rode Cheatham and Cleburne, their respective staff's snaking several yards behind. Cheatham was commenting upon the crude sign that they encountered upon stepping onto Tennessee soil. It read, 'Tennessee, a grave or a free home.' The soldiers had raised their caps and given the rebel yell as they marched past it. Hood grinned. In so few words, that sign perfectly described the confrontation that he was hoping for. They were going to liberate their state from Northern aggression, or die trying.

Suddenly, the column was halted.

"Sir, wait here and I will see why we are delayed," Cleburne said.

Hood waited with Cheatham. He did not think that there was much to fear from the enemy. Forrest was ahead of them, and reportedly sweeping the Yankee cavalry before him. Still, he listened for the sound of musket fire, but none came.

He could see the troops parting before him as Cleburne returned with a man on horseback.

"General Hood sir," Cleburne said. "I present you with the honorable Isham Harris, the rightful governor of Tennessee."

The Confederate troops that heard the introduction raised their hats and howled.

"General Hood," Harris said, "I have been exiled from my post for some time now. Nothing has lifted my spirits as when I was told that you were marching back home. Tennessee welcomes you, I welcome you. This is a proud day for us all."

Hood felt Cheatham pat him on the back with excitement. Hood offered his hand to the governor, and Harris eagerly embraced it. Hood held him tightly, as he turned to the soldiers present.

"Governor Harris, this is a proud day, now made prouder by your presence among us. We are here to liberate Tennessee. We are marching today to redeem, by these soldiers' valor, one of the fairest portions of the Confederacy. This can only be achieved by battle and by victory. These men before are such harbingers".

The rebel yell that followed Hood's speech was tumultuous. If will alone could win a war, there would not be an army strong enough at the moment to face the Army of Tennessee.

Cleburne waited for the ovation to subside and then resumed the march. He instructed his officers to get the static columns moving forward. He then steered his own mount to the side of the road to make room for the governor as he heard Hood ask Harris if he would join them for a while.

"I would be most honored," the governor replied.

"How are the good people of Tennessee?" Hood asked.

"They await such a glorious return general. If you do not mind sir, perhaps you can share with me your plans for victory?"

Hood slowed the pace of his mount. He saw no harm in telling Harris his objective. It being repeated may even serve to ensure that Cheatham understood it completely. At the very least, and more selfishly, it might help to relieve a good amount of internal stress. Ever since they crossed the Tennessee/Alabama border, his impatience to embrace the enemy was sickening. All he could think of was combat situations, and how he would react in them. A myriad of scenarios were juxtaposed in his mind, giving him a constant headache. Talking to Harris could relieve a lot of that.

"Governor, this is General Cheatham. These are his corps that you are riding with. Already ahead of us is General Stephen Lee and his command. My other corps, under General Stewart is marching parallel to us, along the Lawrenceburg road. Forrest's cavalry is protecting our march by covering our lead and flank. Our plan is rather simple. We are to converge behind Schofield's forces at Pulaski. This will divide the Union forces in half, with the Duck River as a natural barrier between them."

Harris was visibly excited. "And then what?" The question was not meant to be a hard one, but the look on Hood's face was clearly one of puzzlement.

"Governor, that is why you must trust such military matters to those with proper rank. Now if you will excuse me, I must attend to a certain matter. Cheatham, if you will, please attend to the governor's every needs."

Hood turned his horse towards the rear, and rode for his supply wagon.

The governor was surprised with Hood's abrupt departure. He looked to Cheatham, but the general only shrugged.

    *   *   *   *   *   *   *   *

As Hood rode towards the rear, he felt his horse sinking into the earth. He looked down, and realized a new dilemma. The ground, once frozen hard, was softening under the footfall of his passing army. The light snow that was settling had a moistening affect. The troops that were passing now were creating a thick and sucking mud for those yet to come up. Already there was an artillery battery with its wheels covered with the dark wet earth. Several men were trying to pry it in motion, but had little success. 'This will greatly hinder the advance,' he thought.

Why do these mishaps keep befalling me? Hood felt the slow wave coming on. It struck his chest, causing his heart to race. The spell had a funny effect, for even in this cold weather, it made him break out in such a profound sweat. Hood could not tell what caused it. He had been fine for a few days. He thought that this new offensive had cured him. But during his conversation with the governor, it had returned.

Hood found his wagon and he instructed a staff officer to retrieve a small wooden case from within. Hood waited until it was secure in his grasp and then rode off into the woods. Once alone, he snapped the case open, and removed the glass bottle. He quickly took several gulps of his laudanum and awaited its affect. Within moments he felt the calming of his nerves. He replaced the bottle within the case and returned it to his wagon. Once again his troubled spirits were calmed.

Opium had such an effect.

"The governor wants to know what I will do once I am between Schofield and Thomas," he said to his horse as he patted its head. He knew all too well that he needed to have that answer himself, but for the moment he had none. And so what if he did not have it yet, there was still time. Hood felt a wave of nausea attempt to consume him, as if it were the chimes of some internal clock threatening to expose him. This problem he did have an answer for, in fact the remedy was an easy one.

A second sip of the elixir quickly shattered his panic like he would eventually do to the Yankees before him.

*   *   *   *   *   *   *   *

November 22

The road flowed before them, showing the path that led into Waynesboro, Tennessee. The Confederate cavalry had dismounted a few moments ago. The lead elements had come to a complete halt due to a volley of fire from well-entrenched Federal cavalry. The 7th Alabama cavalry was becoming accustomed to this new type of mounted warfare. Their general, Nathan Bedford Forrest, had done much to show them the best means to counter an entrenched enemy. The glorified charges from the days of Napoleon were no longer practical. In fact, they had become devastatingly obsolete. Accuracy, coupled with the rate of fire that modern weapons possessed, had a "de-saddling effect" on a charging cavalry.

Forrest was quick to realize this. Most other commanders were beginning to believe that since the charge was no longer effective, then the cavalry could not be used as an offensive weapon anymore. But unlike other commanders, Forrest possessed an uncanny ability to adapt.

He used his horses as a means to rush his troops to the battlefield. Once there, they would dismount and perform like infantry. The concept was revolutionary. It worked so efficiently, that in several instances attacking Federal forces were known to have halted in their tracks, hesitating due to the sudden appearance of 'rebel infantry.'

The 7th Alabama began to deploy along the road, taking

cover behind their surroundings. Several yards ahead, lay the bodies of three of their men. Several newly dropped tree limbs blocked the path past the fallen soldiers. Behind that screen, lay the Federal force. The Union troops kept up a steady barrage of fire, keeping the Confederates ducking for cover.

Colonel Edmund Rucker knelt behind his horse as he tried to ascertain the current situation. Up until now, he had been enjoying the rare luxury of outnumbering the enemy, and his brigade had been taking full advantage of that, driving the Federal cavalry farther and farther north. That was until now. This obstacle before him represented his first real challenge during this campaign. Hundreds of Yankee troopers stood to block this road and prevent the advance of his command.

Rucker could not let that happen. This whole offensive depended upon their ability to slip behind Schofield's rear at Pulaski and cut his command off from Nashville. It fell upon Rucker and the rest of the Confederate cavalry to clear these roads so that the infantry would be able to march unobstructed and allowed to reach their position before Schofield could realize his peril and escape.

Being held up here was not helping that plan.

More companies of his command were arriving from the south, with the infantry not far behind. Rucker understood the longer that he was detained upon the road, the greater the chances of his command causing the massive bottleneck that would force Hood's offensive to come to a complete halt. There was no way that Rucker was going to have that happen and have to admit this defeat to his commander Forrest.

Rucker called for one of his couriers.

"Ride and find Chalmers. Tell him we are currently held up and forced to dismount due to a strong position occupied by the enemy. There seem to be several hundred Federal cavalry in my front."

"Yes sir."

Rucker watched as a few of his men flanked to the right of the road. More Federal shots cracked into the air, and another one of his men fell hard. The 7th Alabama was not moving. It is too cold for this, he thought. A tingling sensation had begun to course through his fingertips. Blowing on the exposed flesh did little to keep his digits from turning blue. He wondered if he could even fire his pistol with his frozen fingers. Rucker allowed himself to cover behind their surroundings. Several yards ahead, lay the bodies of three of their men. Several newly dropped tree limbs blocked the path past the fallen soldiers. Behind that screen, lay the Federal force. The Union troops kept up a steady barrage of fire, keeping the Confederates ducking for cover.

Colonel Edmund Rucker knelt behind his horse as he tried to ascertain the current situation. Up until now, he had been enjoying the rare luxury of outnumbering the enemy, and his brigade had been taking full advantage of that, driving the Federal cavalry farther and farther north. That was until now. This obstacle before him represented his first real challenge during this campaign. Hundreds of Yankee troopers stood to block this road and prevent the advance of his command.

Rucker could not let that happen. This whole offensive depended upon their ability to slip behind Schofield's rear at Pulaski and cut his command off from Nashville. It fell upon Rucker and the rest of the Confederate cavalry to clear these roads so that the infantry would be able to march unobstructed and allowed to reach their position before Schofield could realize his peril and escape.

Being held up here was not helping that plan.

More companies of his command were arriving from the south, with the infantry not far behind. Rucker understood the longer that he was detained upon the road, the greater the chances of his command causing the massive bottleneck that would force Hood's offensive to come to a complete halt. There was no way that Rucker was going to have that happen and have to admit this defeat to his commander Forrest.

Rucker called for one of his couriers.

"Ride and find Chalmers. Tell him we are currently held up and forced to dismount due to a strong position occupied by the enemy. There seem to be several hundred Federal cavalry in my front."

"Yes sir."

Rucker watched as a few of his men flanked to the right of the road. More Federal shots cracked into the air, and another one of his men fell hard. The 7th Alabama was not moving. It is too cold for this, he thought. A tingling sensation had begun to course through his fingertips. Blowing on the exposed flesh did little t keep his digits from turning blue. He wondered if he could ev fire his pistol with his frozen fingers. Rucker allowed himsel

"General Hood," Harris said, "I have been exiled from my post for some time now. Nothing has lifted my spirits as when I was told that you were marching back home. Tennessee welcomes you, I welcome you. This is a proud day for us all."

Hood felt Cheatham pat him on the back with excitement. Hood offered his hand to the governor, and Harris eagerly embraced it. Hood held him tightly, as he turned to the soldiers present.

"Governor Harris, this is a proud day, now made prouder by your presence among us. We are here to liberate Tennessee. We are marching today to redeem, by these soldiers' valor, one of the fairest portions of the Confederacy. This can only be achieved by battle and by victory. These men before are such harbingers".

The rebel yell that followed Hood's speech was tumultuous. If will alone could win a war, there would not be an army strong enough at the moment to face the Army of Tennessee.

Cleburne waited for the ovation to subside and then resumed the march. He instructed his officers to get the static columns moving forward. He then steered his own mount to the side of the road to make room for the governor as he heard Hood ask Harris if he would join them for a while.

"I would be most honored," the governor replied.

"How are the good people of Tennessee?" Hood asked.

"They await such a glorious return general. If you do not mind sir, perhaps you can share with me your plans for victory?"

Hood slowed the pace of his mount. He saw no harm in telling Harris his objective. It being repeated may even serve to ensure that Cheatham understood it completely. At the very least, and more selfishly, it might help to relieve a good amount of internal stress. Ever since they crossed the Tennessee/Alabama border, his impatience to embrace the enemy was sickening. All he could think of was combat situations, and how he would react in them. A myriad of scenarios were juxtaposed in his mind, giving him a constant headache. Talking to Harris could relieve a lot of that.

"Governor, this is General Cheatham. These are his corps that you are riding with. Already ahead of us is General Stephen Lee and his command. My other corps, under General Stewart is marching parallel to us, along the Lawrenceburg road. Forrest's cavalry is protecting our march by covering our lead and flank. Our plan is rather simple. We are to converge behind Schofield's forces at Pulaski. This will divide the Union forces in half, with the Duck River as a natural barrier between them."

Harris was visibly excited. "And then what?" The question was not meant to be a hard one, but the look on Hood's face was clearly one of puzzlement.

"Governor, that is why you must trust such military matters to those with proper rank. Now if you will excuse me, I must attend to a certain matter. Cheatham, if you will, please attend to the governor's every needs."

Hood turned his horse towards the rear, and rode for his supply wagon.

The governor was surprised with Hood's abrupt departure. He looked to Cheatham, but the general only shrugged.

*   *   *   *   *   *   *   *

As Hood rode towards the rear, he felt his horse sinking into the earth. He looked down, and realized a new dilemma. The ground, once frozen hard, was softening under the footfall of his passing army. The light snow that was settling had a moistening affect. The troops that were passing now were creating a thick and sucking mud for those yet to come up. Already there was an artillery battery with its wheels covered with the dark wet earth. Several men were trying to pry it in motion, but had little success. 'This will greatly hinder the advance,' he thought.

Why do these mishaps keep befalling me? Hood felt the slow wave coming on. It struck his chest, causing his heart to race. The spell had a funny effect, for even in this cold weather, it made him break out in such a profound sweat. Hood could not tell what caused it. He had been fine for a few days. He thought that this new offensive had cured him. But during his conversation with the governor, it had returned.

Hood found his wagon and he instructed a staff officer to retrieve a small wooden case from within. Hood waited until it was secure in his grasp and then rode off into the woods. Once alone, he snapped the case open, and removed the glass bottle. He quickly took several gulps of his laudanum and awaited its affect. Within moments he felt the calming of his nerves. He replaced the bottle within the case and returned it to his wagon. Once again his troubled spirits were calmed.

Opium had such an effect.

"The governor wants to know what I will do once I am between Schofield and Thomas," he said to his horse as he patted its head. He knew all too well that he needed to have that answer himself, but for the moment he had none. And so what if he did not have it yet, there was still time. Hood felt a wave of nausea attempt to consume him, as if it were the chimes of some internal clock threatening to expose him. This problem he did have an answer for, in fact the remedy was an easy one.

A second sip of the elixir quickly shattered his panic like he would eventually do to the Yankees before him.

*   *   *   *   *   *   *   *

November 22

The road flowed before them, showing the path that into Waynesboro, Tennessee. The Confederate cavalry dismounted a few moments ago. The lead elements had come complete halt due to a volley of fire from well-entrenched Fed cavalry. The 7th Alabama cavalry was becoming accustome this new type of mounted warfare. Their general, Nathan Bed Forrest, had done much to show them the best means to count entrenched enemy. The glorified charges from the day Napoleon were no longer practical. In fact, they had bec devastatingly obsolete. Accuracy, coupled with the rate of fire modern weapons possessed, had a "de-saddling effect" charging cavalry.

Forrest was quick to realize this. Most other comma were beginning to believe that since the charge was no l effective, then the cavalry could not be used as an offe weapon anymore. But unlike other commanders, Forrest poss an uncanny ability to adapt.

He used his horses as a means to rush his troops to th tlefield. Once there, they would dismount and perform infantry. The concept was revolutionary. It worked so effic that in several instances attacking Federal forces were kno have halted in their tracks, hesitating due to the sudden appe of 'rebel infantry.'

The 7th Alabama began to deploy along the road,

become so engrossed with his frigid condition, that he did not notice that it had become suddenly quiet.

No more shots clamored through the air. Cautiously, the 7th Alabama peered ahead. It was ominously still. The men that had earlier set off to flank the road, called out from up ahead.

"It is all clear, they are gone."

Rucker was dubious. He mounted his horse, and led his troops forward.

"Why would so many soldiers simply disengage from such a formidable position?"

One of his officers rode past him, carefully studying the earth works.

"A better question sir," he said, "is how did so many men disengage?"

Rucker had no answer. He looked into the woods along both sides of the road. There was no enemy present. He gave the command to continue forward, then returned down the road as General Chalmers approached.

*   *   *   *   *   *   *   *

The sun was setting at the conclusion of a cold day's march. The Confederate cavalry was making excellent progress along both the Waynsboro and the Lawrenceburg roads. To this point, the presence of the Federal cavalry was likened to nothing more than a swarm of annoying mosquitoes. Whenever the Yankees tried to offer some form of resistance, Forrest's Cavalry would easily swat them away.

Thanks to the efficiency of the cavalry, the Confederate infantry was able to march unhindered along the Waynesboro road and were now approximately fourteen miles outside of the city that held the road's name. With the setting sun, the troops went into bivouac. Several campfires lit the night, and the mood continued to be one of elation. The soldiers of Hood's army once again felt alive.

The retreat from Northern Georgia and the loss of Atlanta was now far behind them. Not even the cold mattered, nor the hunger that they had learned to live with. Rather they were inconveniences that were used like coal to burn deep in each man's personal furnace. It was what fueled their animosity. Each step forward, brought them one day closer to bellowing their internal hatred at the Federal forces that occupied this part of their beloved Confederacy. The price to pay now was worth the reward to be received later.

Most of the fires were congregated in close proximity to each other. However, there was one larger fire that had a little more space between it and the others. That was due to respect. Huddled around the fire, and fueling their appetites, was the high command of General Cheatham's Corps.

"A good days marching," Cheatham said to Hood. "We should be arriving in Waynesboro tomorrow, and there we can re-supply our men."

"That will be a good thing," Hood replied. "We were only able to muster a week's supply. It is so unfair, that we ask so much of these men, and then cannot find the means to feed them."

"The Yankees will have to be held accountable for that," Cheatham smirked.

Patrick Cleburne took a seat upon a hard tree stump, and began eating his meal. Following close to him were Mark P. Lowry, Daniel C. Govan and Hiram B. Granbury, his brigadier generals.

Hood watched Cleburne with careful eyes. He was one of the men who he would rely heavily upon in the next few days. The Irishman was a fierce fighter, and his men followed his suit well. The only unfortunate characteristic about the man, was his affinity with Hardee. Hood had his own deep misgivings about Hardee, especially during his performance at Atlanta. He was convinced that Hardee's jealousy was the root of all that befell this army since he took its command. 'Thank God he is gone', he thought.

With such ill fillings directed towards Hardee, it was hard to look at Cleburne, and swallow the fact that the Irish general had recently been at Hardee's wedding… and was in fact his best man. Did Hardee use that time to fill Cleburne's mind with such blasphemy as to discredit his own personal skills as a general? If so, Cleburne had yet to show any indication of such influence. Still, if Cleburne was close enough to be Hardee's best man this past January, then there was sure to have been a lot of mischievous talk concerning Hood.

The arrival of Generals John C. Brown and William Bate, along with several officers from their staff quickly dissipated

Hood's brooding. All of Cheatham's divisional commanders were now present.

Hood waited till they all had finished eating, then he directed the men to accompany him to the newly constructed tent that would serve as his temporary headquarters. Hood sat in the corner, with his leg propped up on an adjacent chair. His staff seated themselves around him.

"Gentlemen, we have made excellent progress. I salute you and your men," Hood said. "Our cavalry is reported to have the road clear before us, and we should have a hearty welcome tomorrow as we march triumphantly into Waynesboro."

The Confederate high command raised their drinks and toasted their commander. The conversation continued and was centered on the morning march and the continued speed of their offensive. However, as the night crept in, so did the fatigue from a long day's march. Even the sound of the army outside of the tent quickly muted, as soldiers made preparations to sleep for the night. Those outside knew what was to be expected of them in the morning... Marching, marching and still more marching.

"Listen to those boys bunker down for sleep," Brown said. "That is the sound of veteran soldiers knowing what is best for them."

"As should we," Bate said, as he put his hand over his mouth to cover a widening yawn.

"Reminds me of Chickamauga," Cheatham said. "I remember having difficulty sleeping the night before the second day of that battle. That was when the rest of Longstreet's corps arrived. I remember lying down, and just busting at the thought of hitting the Yankees in the morning with everything we had. And boy did we hit them."

"I remember that day fondly," Hood said as he reached for his artificial leg. Perhaps it was the mere mention of the battle that subconsciously caused Hood to twist his artificial limb in the presence of his staff. Some of the men tried to turn away in respect, but some were caught staring at the spectacle.

Patrick Cleburne watched as Hood looked up just in time to witness the looks of the generals faces as they stared at his unnaturalness. Always one to think quickly, the Irishman fought to save Hood's pride.

"Sir, how is it that you continually find the courage to fight and lead with the loss of your limb?" Cleburne asked.

Hood took his hand from his leg, but left both legs propped upon the chair. "It is not the loss of the limbs that can keep one from fighting, but rather the willingness to do so. Will it enough, and it will be so, with or without limbs."

The men in the room nodded in agreement.

"My grandfather, Lucas Hood, was felled in battle with the Miami Indians. He was scalped and left for dead. Most men might have just lain there and hoped to die, figuring death to be a better fate than trying to get back up to fight your way home through hostile territory. But not granddaddy Lucas. He was soon back upon his feet looking for an Indian that could assist him, and he would find one too. The Redskin was armed with a bow when old Lucas charged. The first arrow nicked his thigh, the second missed completely. There was not to be a third. My grandfather felled him with two solid roundhouses, stole his horse, and raced back to friendly lines. That my friends, is the power of will."

Hood took a moment before continuing. "You know, my father wanted me to pursue a career in medicine. Could you imagine? The sad thing is that I may have pursued that course, if it wasn't for Mr. Lucas Hood. I can remember sitting on his lap and listening to him to tell the same Indian stories over and over again. His stories were so exciting, I knew that there was no way that I could follow my father's aspirations."

"Our Irish man has some of that will," Cheatham teased. His red cheeks were once again giving away the contents of his coffee mug. "Tell General Hood about your story concerning your will power."

All of the men eagerly turned from Hood, glad that they could now focus their attention on Cleburne. Hood's history, preceded by the awkward moment with his cork leg, put a solemn mood upon the men. Cheatham's redirection towards Cleburne came as a relief.

"No matter how many times I tell you of this story, you keep on me for more."

"And I won't stop until every man of the Confederacy knows it," Cheatham grinned.

"And from the sounds of it thus far," Brown said, "perhaps we should extend the tale to General Grant and the Union army too."

Cleburne bowed his head, as the laughter filled the tent. When it dwindled, he stood up from his chair.

"I must stand to tell this tale, so that you can fully appreciate it. It happened when I first came into this country, while I was living in New Orleans. Christmas day, I cannot tell you how happy I was being out of Ireland and living on this great American soil. I thought it best to show my joy by attending a party.

"I have never seen so many beautiful women in one place, as I did that night. I must have just stood by the bar and stared for hours. I watched the ladies dance, and thought how I would like to dance with one of them. Instead, I had a few drinks, and continued to watch the men and women dance. I said to myself, Patrick, there is nothing to it. So, I fueled my Irish blood with one last drink, and proceeded to ask a fine woman to join me on the floor.

"Her name escapes me, but not her face. Heaven could not have put a prettier girl in that room. She had long blonde curls that cascaded over her face and fell beside her two ocean blue eyes. My hand simply fell in hers as she led me to the dance.

"I listened to the music and shut my eyes, as I began to move my body in conjunction with the band. I held her hand for a few moments, but when I opened my eyes..." Cleburne deliberately made a dramatic pause. "I can't go on."

"No, you must finish," Cheatham said.

Cleburne was obviously entertained himself at the telling of his story. He waited for a few more of the men to beg him to continue.

"When I opened my eyes, this lady was just standing still staring at me, as were all of the other men and women on the dance floor. I just stood there wondering what had caused their gaze when they all broke out in laughter. They were mocking my dancing skills. There I was, fresh off the boat, and practically being laughed back to Ireland."

The laughter inside of the tent was infectious. Cleburne watched as tears ran down from Bate's face.

"How were you dancing? You must show us," Hood said.

"That is why you are the general," Cheatham added. "I have heard this story a number of times, yet have never thought to ask him to show me the dance."

"Well, if I must," Cleburne said. Then the general started to sway his body in a way akin to a fish floundering once taken out of water.

The roar in the room threatened to wake the entire Confederate camp.

"And how is this tale, a testament to my grandfather Lucas' belief in the power of will?" Hood asked.

"Because General, since that day, I have practiced my dance vigorously until I have become one of the finest dancers in New Orleans. Practice made me excel in that field."

"So now you are a dancer?" Hood asked. His gestures were an obvious indication that he wanted Cleburne to provide a visual of his dancing acumen.

Cleburne proudly demonstrated a few steps.

"So my most feared Divisional commander is nothing more than a glorified ballerina," Hood said. Once again the tent was moved with laughter. "I just must add, that if what you just showed is called dancing, then I am glad I have this cork leg, to keep me away from your ballrooms."

Cleburne was not bothered by the laughter at his expense. He knew he was a fine dancer. The main thing was these men had their spirits returned, and they no longer saw Hood as a broken man.

"Well General Cheatham, I am glad to see that this tale has brought you amusement again," Cleburne said.

"That it has Patrick, but the thing that is funnier is, that is not the story I was referring to. The story I meant for you to tell was about the wound you received at Richmond, Kentucky."

Cleburne rubbed his beard and smiled. Underneath the well-trimmed facial hair, he could feel the long scar along his left jaw. The goatee helped to hide the wound he received during battle in Kentucky. The bullet that caused it smashed through his mouth and took two of his teeth with it. He thought for sure that the wound had been fatal.

For the first time since that incident, he could feel the raised skin and laugh. He looked at Cheatham and realized that the general had finally got one over on him.

He continued to laugh hard into the night, even when he was alone in his bed. All he could think of was his dancing in front of Hood and his staff. He could hear his mother even now, "What a fool you make of yourself Patty... what a fine fool you do make."

Chapter IX
November 23
Waynesboro, Tennessee

The long winding columns of Cheatham's corps entered the city of Waynesboro and immediately scattered through its streets like a pack of hungry wolves. Their ravenous appetites were only part of their malcontent for this day. The other was the rapidly falling Tennessee temperature. The weather had taken an alarming turn for the worse, which could plainly be seen in the beards of many of the men. Frozen secretions from the nose, clung to facial hair like icicles.

Waynesboro was supposed to be a major supply depot. It promised to offer a decent day of rest, as well as food and supplies to help rejuvenate the Southern army on their continued march north. But as the Confederate's neared their destination, the view that opened before them told of something different.

Waynesboro was completely deserted. Not a single civilian from Tennessee was on hand to cheer the arrival of the Confederate army. The condition of the city offered a clear motive as to the vacancy of its inhabitants. There was not a standing structure suitable for any person to reside in. The war had taken its toll here.

Buildings were either torn down or they were burnt. Those that were still standing did so with three walls or less, their sidings no doubt used for materials in the Union war effort. Gardens were ravished, carts lay overturned and strewn about. One hard look at this smoking village of ruin confirmed that there would be no supplies gathered from here. And if that was not bad enough, Cheatham had received word that his supply wagons had broken down several miles in the rear. His men would not have the rest nor the warm meal that they had been promised.

Cheatham sat on his horse and watched in despair as his men fanned through the city, searching for anything to eat. It was pitiful. The cold wind cut into his face, as a cruel reminder as to just how unfortunate this turn of events would be. He tried to raise his collar, but it had no effect. He listened to the sound of the wind howl through the open city. It was pure mockery.

The sound of the hoof steps behind him alerted him to Hood's presence.

"General, a most unfortunate turn of events. This city no longer exists," Cheatham said.

Hood did not turn towards him. He just looked at the carnage through heavy saddened eyes. He spoke more to himself than his general.

"How can this keep happening to me? My plans are well thought out, the goals accomplished, but these circumstances, they are so unforeseen..."

Cheatham looked towards Hood, but did not know how to respond. Not even their worst nightmares could have foreseen this. The reports from Forrest's cavalry spoke of desolation at Waynesboro, but no one thought it would be as severe as this.

"At least the sun is strong," Hood said. It was the only favorable condition he could find, and so he clung to it. "If this wind would subside, I think the weather could actually be tolerable. Let the men find whatever rest they can. Tomorrow, we will take the pike that leads from here to Mt. Pleasant."

"It is a shame that that road is not wider," Cheatham said.

"It is also a shame that the sons of Tennessee are not here to great us with warm homes and warm meals," Hood shot back. "Instruct your men to be ready to march out in the morning. By the looks of that sun, I would imagine tomorrow to be a favorable day for a march. Make it clear to your corps, General, that tomorrow morning marks the beginning of a very crucial race. We must reach Columbia before the Federal army at Pulaski can. If we do, we will have accomplished the major objective of this campaign. The Federal army will be cut in half."

Cheatham saluted Hood, and spurred his horse forward. He understood the task presented to him, and began issuing orders to his officers.

Hood watched him with keen eyes. When Cheatham and his staff disappeared from his view, he softly closed his lids.

'Lord, every obstacle is a challenge. I understand that. But all I ask is this one favor. Allow this army to reach Columbia before General Schofield does.'

*   *   *   *   *   *   *   *

The sound of the galloping cavalry was like a majestic symphony of thunder to the ears of Nathan Bedford Forrest. He clung to his reins and inhaled the cold air with a deep affection. He rode at the head of Chalmers' command. Next to him was his adjutant general Major J.P. Strange. Strange was both a loyal officer and a close friend, but it was moments like now, when Strange felt his loyalty tested most.

Forrest was one of those generals that led from the front, and though Strange heard that cliché before, he did not fully understand what it meant until serving under Forrest's command. Brave and heroic generals were expected to march with the leading elements of their army. Such valor was rewarded with deep conviction and trust from those that were to be led.

But Forrest wanted to give his men something more than that. He didn't just ride within the vanguard of his cavalry, he was the vanguard of its advance. It was his way of showing the men that he would not send them anywhere that he himself would not go. Foolish perhaps, he had lost over twenty horses beneath him since the start of this war. But his men were in awe of him, and the enemy was in dire fear.

Strange galloped slightly behind Forrest and continued to marvel at the general. It was back in '62, during the battle of Shiloh, when Forrest's tenacity had grown into legend.

The Confederacy completely surprised Grant's army at Pittsburg landing. They overwhelmed the Yankee army and pushed them back to the Tennessee River in utter chaos and confusion. The only thing that prevented the total destruction of Grant's army was the disorganization of the Confederate army and those nasty Union gunboats that continued to hurl hell into their lines.

Knowing that there were Federal forces en route to reinforce Grant, Forrest pleaded through out the camp that they needed to follow up the success of the day with an offensive that night. The Confederate high command refused to listen. The next morning, Forrest was condemned to watch his fears come to fruition. General Buell's army had arrived, and with Grant's reorganized army, they combined to sweep the Confederates from the field.

Forrest was given command to serve as the rear guard as the Confederate army retreated towards Corinth... it was a task that did not sit well with him.

He glared at the pursuing cavalry with eyes that were filled with hatred. And it was a hatred that was not directed solely at the enemy. There was no doubt in his mind, had anyone heeded his warning the night before, whose cavalry would be doing the retreating this morning.

With his skin burning with agitation, he could not let the situation change who he was, and Forrest was not one to retreat. Instead, he chose to lead a charge into the pursuing Yankees. His animosity was so intense, it must have infected his mount, for it raced several hundred yards ahead of his closest regiment.

Like a strike of lightning, Forrest crashed into the Federal cavalry, still screaming the order to charge. With his saber slicing, he cut into the bewildered Federal forces. They were completely stunned. It appeared as if there was a single rebel maniac charging into their brigade. The Union officers were the first to regain their composure, shouting orders to kill the rebel.

Forrest quickly found himself surrounded in a sea of blue, with screams to "knock him off his horse" and "kill him" coming from every direction. Forrest blocked out the Yankee chatter and sliced through two of their men, their blood splattering across his chest. He tried in vain to discover a path that would lead him back to his own troops, but it was futile. He realized that there was no escape. Forrest prepared to meet his maker.

It was then that he felt the cold steel of a muzzle against his lower back. It seemed like an eternity, but he soon heard the crack of the rifle. The bullet ripped through his side. The impact of the bullet lifted Forrest from his saddle, and threatened to throw him to the ground below.

That was when the Yanks witnessed first hand the infamous demon red glow that would enter Forrest's eyes.

Like a deranged lunatic who possessed the wit to think clearly, Forrest reached with one hand and grasped his mount's reins. With great agility he was able to bring his airborne body back down into his saddle. This unbelievable feat stunned the Union cavalry. They could not believe what they had just witnessed. Forrest, seeing their delay, was not one to hesitate and lose the initiative.

He spurred his horse around and charged back towards his own troops. The force of his gallop trampled two soldiers in his path. Realizing that bullets from the Federal cavalry were only moments away, he rode directly towards a Union officer. He *slashed two of the soldiers who tried to get in his way. The officer tried to raise his saber, but as Forrest rode by, he ducked to the side of the slash, and grabbed under the man's left armpit. Perhaps it was the momentum of the horse, others would say it was Forrest's adrenaline, but whatever it was, it had a dramatic affect.*

In one foul swoop, Forrest lifted the man from the ground and slung him over his back. The move was accomplished seconds before the Federal cavalry fired into the fleeing rebel. Forrest heard and felt the impact of several bullets as they crashed into the human shield slung over his back.

An officer in the Federal cavalry cried to cease-fire. The spectacle retreating before them was too much to bear. A Confederate general was galloping away with one of their officer's slung over his back like a sack of potatoes. The body of the officer was grotesquely twisted so that he lay almost upside down, his head facing back towards the Union troops with dead eyes that looked as if they were still pleading for help.

When Forrest reached his men, he dropped the body to the ground. It was probable that at that moment, his own soldiers were more afraid of him then the enemy was. They would have to answer as to why they left him alone in the midst of the enemy.

Fortunately for them, Forrest had lost consciousness from the loss of blood.

'And that is why I'll ride at his side,' thought Strange, who would gladly retain his place, than to be on the side of the enemy who had the task of trying to detain Forrest.

"Sir Mt. Pleasant looms ahead," Strange said.

Forrest nodded. He knew what he was charged to do. He had ridden his cavalry well in front of Hood's infantry. He was pushing them so far ahead, he threatened to put his men into an exposed situation. Yet he had no choice. The Confederate army had to reach Columbia before Schofield's army could.

Forrest had chosen to take personal command of Chalmers' division for this all-important push towards Columbia. He had to. The report he received the other day regarding a roadblock set before the 7th Alabama was not acceptable. There were times to deploy your forces and engage the enemy in an orderly fashion. This was not one of them.

Whatever resistance was set before them, it had to be

overrun quickly… No matter the cost, for any delay was not a tolerable one. Chalmers' had reported that several hundred Federal troopers caused his situation. Yet when Forrest surveyed the scene there were not but fifty to sixty horse tracks. Forrest later solved the riddle. They soon caught up with the Federal cavalry that had hampered the 7th Alabama. Forrest was right, there were not but fifty of them. But they were armed with Union issued Spencer repeating carbines. These rifles fired at a rate unequaled by any Confederate weapon. One man armed with such a gun could easily equal seven men armed with muskets. That said, fifty well-concealed men firing these guns, could easily seem like several hundred.

Forrest captured most of the Federal cavalry, and appropriated their Spencer carbines. He distributed them to his own troops. From the prisoners, he learned that there was another Federal brigade to their front, led by a colonel named Horace Capron.

Forrest immediately renewed the pursuit. There could be no Yankee cavalry between Waynesboro and Columbia. The chase led him through Henryville and towards Mt. Pleasant.

"Sir, it is getting dark," Strange said.

Forrest looked up to the sky and noted the setting sun. Reluctantly he called for a halt.

"The enemy is surely looking to make camp," Forrest said. "Get word to Chalmers to meet me here. I want some of his men to scout ahead and report the position of the enemy."

Strange saluted and rode to find General Chalmers.

Forrest dismounted and gave his reins to one of his troopers. There were only twenty of them. Forrest was growing impatient, but he had to wait for Chalmers' division to arrive before he could take any action. He asked his men to stay where they were, and he walked several hundred yards ahead towards a small hill.

He climbed the hill and descended the other side. He sat at the base of the earth, and listened. Not hearing anything, he put his hear to the ground, nothing. The silence confirmed his suspicion… the Federal cavalry was close and resting.

Being from Tennessee, he knew this area well. If he were Capron, and had a brigade at least seven hundred strong, he knew what he would do. Up ahead was Fouche Springs. It was along that road, that Forrest would dig in and brace himself for an expected attack. The position would be a strong one. Several hundred dismounted cavalry entrenched behind fortifications would be a difficult obstacle to overcome.

A charging cavalry trying to take that position could easily be decimated. Yet what choice did he have, for that was the road that led to Columbia? And so the road needed to be opened. Forrest looked at the setting sun again. He thought of Shiloh. They will not suspect an attack in the night he thought. They would not have thought so then, either. Forrest looked down the road towards Fouche Springs and smiled.

"We will take that position," he promised himself.

*　　*　　*　　*　　*　　*　　*　　*

When Forrest returned to the other side of the hill, he was glad to see Chalmers present with the majority of his troopers. The men, eager to finally get some rest, were rapidly dismounting and stretching their legs.

'Not for long,' Forrest gritted.

Chalmers was giving orders to his officers when he noticed the large frame of Forrest approaching. He saluted his general.

"General Forrest, my compliments to your selection of terrain. We can easily bivouac here for the night. That hill up ahead is excellent ground. We can deploy a strong skirmish line, and allow these men and their mounts some much needed rest."

Forrest looked at his surroundings for the first time. He could not have picked a better place to bivouac Chalmers' division. The space they occupied was flat and open. Thick brush enclosed their location, and the road that led out passed the hill that he had already scouted. The hill could be easily defended against Capron's brigade, allowing his troopers to have a solid nights sleep.

However, Forrest's reason for halting at this place was not to bivouac. Capron was not going to attack him, and there would be no sleep this night.

He halted his men here to regroup and coordinate an attack. The look on his face told Chalmers all he needed to know.

"Sir, forgive me for being presumptuous," Chalmers said.

If Forrest was either upset or forgiving, he chose not to

show it. He walked back towards the hill with Chalmers.

"General, assemble your officers here. I strongly believe that Capron has his brigade positioned near Fouche Springs. It is getting dark, and his men must be tired."

Chalmers wanted to add that his men were made of the same sweat and bones as the Yankees. They had not stopped riding and fighting since they left Florence days ago. Fortunately, Chalmers knew better than to externalize those thoughts. He only nodded and looked into the distance at the imaginary lines of Federal troops.

Strange approached the hill, accompanied by Colonel's Edmund Rucker and Jacob Biffle.

"I gather we ain't stopping at this pretty place," Biffle said.

"No colonel," Forrest replied. "We must not allow the Yankees a chance to reach Columbia before us."

Forrest looked at his officers and could read the concern in their eyes. Their troops were hungry and exhausted. Their mounts were dropping off like flies. The frenzied weeklong chase of the Federal cavalry was too much to bear for many of the weaker steeds. And now they faced a well-entrenched Federal brigade over eight hundred strong. If that was not enough, the sun was setting in the west. How on earth was Chalmers' division supposed to move them Yanks?

"Gentlemen," Forrest said, "I do not care how tired this division is. I do not care if every horse and mule were to drop dead in pure exhaustion. If they do, I fully expect every soldier to pick up his mount and continue the charge with it on his back. That is the least they could do for the animal that has carried them thus far. The Yankee brigade we are chasing is fleeing before us. That means they are scared of us. Do not underestimate the power of fear. Right now they are settling in for some much-needed rest. They will deploy a rear guard, but I can guarantee that they do not expect us to bring them the battle this evening."

Forrest took a moment to let his words settle upon his men, "I want to make this very clear… there are no options here. We must clear the path for General Hood. I would rather my entire cavalry be destroyed while securing Columbia for General Hood, than it being intact while the enemy held the city."

And let me remind you how much I love this cavalry," he continued. "I have no intention of allowing the enemy Columbia, nor do I have the intention to let this cavalry be destroyed."

Forrest finished speaking and turned away from Chalmers' division and looked in the direction of Mt. Pleasant. The other men followed suit, all staring ahead. There were many thoughts flowing within their mental images, but only Forrest foresaw the battle.

"What is the plan for attack General?" Chalmers asked.

"Colonel Biffle, is your brigade present?" Forrest said.

Biffle hated to disappoint his General, but he could not deny the facts.

"General, the 10th Tennessee is not present at this time."

"We have not the time to gather them. Colonel Rucker, your brigade will engage the rear guard of the enemy. Approach them headlong, but cautiously. You must occupy their attention and keep their thoughts fixed on your position."

"General, I am not clear as to my objective," Rucker said.

Forrest walked from the group and broke a cold twig from a nearby tree. When he returned, he squatted to the earth and began to sketch the battle plan into the exposed earth. The ground was so frozen that it took significant effort to allow the twig to make any impressions.

"Colonel, your forces will approach Capron's rear guard from this road. You will engage them from a distance. I will take an escort of eighty men wide around their flank. When you hear my charge into their side, that will be your order to mount your whole force and join the assault. I hope that this is clear now."

Rucker nodded, but looked dubious. Chalmers studied the battle plan carved into the earth.

"General, you and eighty men plan to storm a brigade over eight hundred strong," Chalmers said. "Your plan has merit, but why not wait until Biffle's troops arrive. The force of such an attack with their added weight would be devastating."

Forrest stood up and approached Chalmers. He placed himself barely a yard from his general.

"Do you think that Biffle's men could be deployed this night? Because I sure as hell don't. If we wait till the morning, the Yankee cavalry will be gone."

When Forrest finished speaking, he stood glaring at Chalmers for a fraction of a second before taking a few steps back. It was a glare that only Chalmers saw, and the general knew what it meant. 'Do not question me again.' And Chalmers would not.

"The gathering dusk will help conceal my escort's flank attack", Forrest continued. Forrest called for his horse, and a sergeant quickly brought the mount up the hill. Forrest turned the horse to its side, and brandished his rifle.

"We also have these," he said. "This rifle holds a clip that allows them to fire seven bullets without reloading. I think Colonel Rucker and General Chalmers know how effective such a weapon might be. A small detachment of fifty cavalry armed with repeating rifles held your entire division at bay. That is not surprising. When you cannot see an enemy armed with this weapon, but only hear its firepower, its size can easily be misunderstood. I will use that advantage tonight."

"While your brigade occupies the attention of their rear guard, I will crash into their flank. This will stun them. They will have a large enemy to their front, and one of unknown size to their side. That is when you must charge with everything that you have. The element of my surprise will not last long. The enemy will quickly see that my force is a small one. But the hesitation will have cost them. Your brigade in full charge from the front will cause them to fall back in confusion."

When Forrest was finished, he noticed that in his aggressive telling of the battle plan, he had crushed the twig in his hand. He threw the remains to the floor and brushed the debris on his pants. He then began to kick his foot over the dirt, so as to erase his strategy from the carved earth.

"My brigade will charge on your command sir", Rucker said. "You put a lot of faith in the element of surprise, so much that you risk your own self. We will not let you down."

Forrest looked up and patted Rucker's shoulder. He then shook his hand. Turning, he shook each of their hands. Again, he held Chalmers a fraction of a second longer. Chalmers understood it was his general's way of saying that he was forgiven. It was time to move on.

"Let me tell you something about the element of surprise, Colonel," Forrest said. "I learned this lesson many years ago, and not from any fancy military academy I might add. I was a young pup, out riding alone in the woods. I can remember that day as clear as this morning. I heard dogs barking up ahead, several of them. My family had warned me about some rabid dogs that were roaming the countryside. They traveled in packs. I did not doubt that these were the dogs that I heard that day. I was almost home, and decided to rush my course. My horse raced up a hill such as the one we are standing on now. When it leveled out, I picked up the pace. To my surprise, I saw the dogs break from the forest and crowd the path to my front. My horse, startled by the appearance of the dogs came to a complete stop. I was unprepared. The sudden stop of my horse catapulted me into the midst of those rabid canines.

"By all accounts, I should have been shredded to pieces. But I was not. The dogs did not expect to see me get thrown into them. They retreated, some falling over on themselves. For a second, their tenacity was replaced by fear. A pack of wild, crazed and hungry dogs had hesitated at the sight of one unarmed lad being thrust into them. That was the second I regained my mount and rushed home."

"Gentlemen, I have never forgotten that lesson and I do not expect any of you to, either. General Chalmers, have Rucker's brigade ready in the next half-hour. We will attack the Yankee cavalry tonight, and we will clear this road for General Hood."

*   *   *   *   *   *   *   *

A small contingent of Confederate cavalry parted from the main force and set out on a wide arc around the Federal encampment near Fouche Springs. The Federal position was defended exactly as Forrest predicted, Capron's rear guard was holding a strong line blocking the turnpike that led to Mt. Pleasant.

With apprehension, Forrest's escort cantered through the woods, hoping that the dusk would be concealing enough to hide their presence. As they traveled farther and farther from Rucker's command, there was a fear that the Federals would find them out in the open. If that happened, there was no doubt that none of them would make it back alive. Occasionally, the heavy step of one of their horses would bring a hard snap from the numerous twigs that littered the forest floor. Many of the surrounding soldiers would glare at the man whose horse was led so carelessly.

The only comfort that the men found was in the sound of sporadic gunfire that came from the direction of Rucker's brigade. For the present, it meant that some part of the Federal cavalry was too occupied at the moment to concern themselves with anything else.

After riding for several minutes, the company was halted.

Forrest issued orders to a few men. These brave scouts dismounted and took off into the woods towards the Federal lines. After an impatient amount of time, they returned. Words were said to Forrest, and the general looked pleased. It was evident by the rare grin that overtook his face. His mood had an immediate effect on the soldiers around him. The report from the scout must have been a good one. The news was repeated down the line, as was the call for complete silence.

Forrest and Strange then dismounted, and followed four of the scouts back towards the Federal campsite.

"Probably a half hour to forty-five minutes until total darkness," Strange said.

Forrest agreed. "How much further?" he asked one of his scouts.

The scout, a farmer from Tennessee, was eager to impress the general with his knowledge. "Sir, if you keep low, and peer ahead, you will see the two Yankee sentries on duty."

Forrest searched the distance until he found the two Federal pickets. The wicked grin immediately returned to his face. "I can not believe that there are men chosen to command who do so with such irresponsibility." Forrest listened to the gunfire in the distance. It was escalating.

"Colonel Strange, the time is at hand. There are only two men that I can see. We will overcome them and charge straight into the Federal encampment. Instruct the men to dismount, and walk their horses to this point. Remind them that if I hear any one so much as speak before I give the order to charge, I will personally give them the steel myself. We will attack as soon as they are in position."

Strange looked at the open flank and envisioned the havoc Forrest was moments from creating. He saluted his general, and headed back to summon the rest of Forrest's small war party.

As he turned, he wore Forrest's grin. The Yankees liked to refer to his general as the devil himself. 'Well Yanks,' he thought, 'the devil is a coming.'

*   *   *   *   *   *   *   *

Elijah Harrison was tired of standing watch. He was also tired of riding, sitting, fighting and being scared. The confirmation that it was Forrest's cavalry that was after them caused the entire brigade he rode with to turn tail and flee. He had never seen so many adult men ride with such passion. The only thing that allowed them to stop and rest was the arrival of night. Capron had ordered a rear guard set back upon the turnpike and allowed the rest of the men to eat a meal while trying to get some rest. Elijah wished he were one of those eating at this moment instead of freezing in the middle of the woods. He leaned his back up against an old bare tree and sulked.

"What is your problem now Elijah?" his captain asked.

"Sir, this cold is my problem."

"And it will be colder tonight, I already miss the sun. But tell me, there seems to be more than that on your mind. I can see it in your eyes."

"Captain, if I am allowed to speak off the record, I will."

"There is no one here but us. I gave the rest of the men some time to grab some chow before reporting back. So speak your mind. Now is not the time for me to have any disgruntled men in my command."

Elijah looked back towards the camp... his relief was not coming yet. He then peered into the woods ahead. He thought he saw some movement beneath a clump of bramble in the distance. He was too upset to care. It was probably just a deer anyway.

"Captain, I am just tired is all. I am tired of this damn war. When we took Atlanta, I figured we were done. I figured the rebs were done. I was ready to go home and see my family, and see my old lady."

"How old are you boy? You don't look old enough to know nothing about women."

Elijah smiled the first smile he had shown in over a month. "I bet I know far more than one at your age captain. Anyway, I just figured that the war was over after Atlanta. I had no idea that this would happen. Why did General Sherman leave us here if the enemy could still put up a fight?"

It was a question that the captain had often asked himself. "The force that Hood has is not supposed to be one that we need to worry about. General Sherman was convinced of that."

"But it ain't Hood that we are running from captain, is it? It's that devil Forrest. And don't tell me that you ain't as scared as I am. I have never seen so many men ride as swiftly as we did today. And you heard what Forrest did at that Fort Pillow. He killed everyone, even those that surrendered."

Elijah's fears were making his captain uncomfortable. It was like they were two boys sharing ghost tales while camping alone in the woods. Elijah wrapped his arms around himself, trying to keep warm. It was futile.

"Elijah, I understand your concerns. I can't say that I do not share many of them, but that is not the issue. We have a job to do, and we must have the right mindset. This war will be over soon, I promise. All we are asked to do right now is slow Forrest's advance until Schofield's army can secure Columbia. We may be running from Forrest, but we are doing so for good reason. We are impeding his path and preventing him from reaching Columbia before Schofield can. Now, I am going to run back to camp and see what is taking the others so long to report back. I was hoping that giving them some time to eat and rest would warm their morale for picket duty. Is there anything that I can get you?"

"No sir. But thank you for listening."

"Pleasure was mine Elijah, I will be right back."

Elijah watched his captain hurry back towards the camp. 'Damn, it is cold,' he thought. He tried blowing air into his hands, but whatever breath he could muster was ineffective. He looked back into the woods, towards the bramble that caught his eye before. It was undisturbed. It was also harder to see. The darkness was seriously obscuring his vision.

'What use is this,' he thought. 'I can not see a thing anyway.' Again he looked back towards the camp. There was no sign of his captain or of the others. Then he heard a branch snap in the distance. He spun his head and peered into the woods. He could no longer see the bramble patch clearly. The stories of Forrest at Fort Pillow began to haunt him.

Elijah squinted his eyes, towards the noise he had heard but there was silence. He thought of picking up his rifle that leaned against the tree, but his frozen hands said otherwise. The sound of gunfire from the rear reminded him how close the rebels were. Not to worry, his captain had said, there was no way the rebel cavalry could attack down the turnpike and succeed. The position was too well defended.

Elijah was not comforted by the thought. Again he heard a sound from the woods in front of him. This time he thought he saw branches swaying to the sides. Could it be the wind? He did not think it was strong enough to cause such movement.

It was too much to bear. He should not be out here alone anyway, where were the others? He decided that he better pull his hands from his sides and grab his rifle. The gun was freezing.

"I do not believe that I have ever been so cold, nor felt anything as cold as this in my life," he said aloud to himself. He was hoping the sound of his voice would shake the scare that sent goose bumps prickling along his cold flesh.

The sentence was barely out of his mouth, when he heard the command to charge. In the gathering darkness, he had no concept of where the voice came from. For a second, he thought for sure it was an order from one his officers, then he realized his mistake.

The thundering gallop that roared towards him removed any discomforts he might have still had concerning the cold. He remained frozen, but it was not due to the temperature. Like a living statue, Elijah watched the cavalry charge his position. The rebel yell had an effect that would have sent a Banshee fleeing.

Within seconds they rode by him, towards the camp that he was supposed to be protecting. Elijah felt a horse brush by his side, and thought there might be a possibility that he would not be seen in this darkness.

His hopes were short lived. One rebel rider brought his saber down as he passed the Federal sentry. Elijah felt the weapon slash across his forehead and quickly withdrawal. He was left standing there for several minutes as the rest of the host rode by him.

He did not remember kneeling, but he was on his knees clutching his wounded head, the warm blood trickling down his face. 'There weren't many of them,' he thought. 'I have to tell the captain that there was not many of them.'

There was a sound behind him. Very laboriously, Elijah turned upon his knees to tell the captain what he saw. The man holding the saber was not his captain. Elijah tried to raise his hand to defend himself, but the cold steel of the saber slipped through his defenses and pierced his chest, sinking deep into his heart.

Elijah stared at the sword and was in disbelief. He had found something that felt so cold, it made his previous complaints concerning the weather seem absurd.

Then he felt no more.

*　　*　　*　　*　　*　　*　　*　　*

Without warning, Forrest's eighty-man force plunged into the Federal camp. Their captured Spencer repeating rifles had their expected devastating effect. Many of the routed Union troops were gunned down in seconds. Forrest himself had two pistols thundering in hand, adding his own personal carnage to the scene.

The Federal rear guard were busy returning fire towards Rucker's brigade when they heard the explosion of gunfire in their own rear. Many turned to try to see what the situation was. It was at that moment, that Rucker's entire brigade roared forward.

The Yankee rear guard was stunned. With the sound of battle behind them, and the emerging rebel brigade charging their front, the Union soldiers quickly lost their confidence. Not wanting to be cut from their rest of their command, they chose to retire towards the camp.

It was the wrong decision.

Many of the soldiers were shot in the back trying to make their escape. Those that thought they had managed to escape from Rucker's attack quickly discovered the error of their ways. They rode from one battle right into another. Somehow, the enemy had slipped around their flank and had infested the camp. Many officers tried to rally the frightened Federal troops, but it was futile. The Union cavalry rode right through camp, trampling many of their own men, as they stampeded down the turnpike towards Mount Pleasant.

Forrest, knowing his escort too small to block the Yankee escape, ordered his men to the side of the road. He told them to fire at the routed Federals as they rode by. It was easier than duck hunting.

Forrest left the majority of his escort on the side of the road, and took a few men down a side path. He was hoping to find additional ground to fire upon the fleeing Yanks.

"Sir, congratulations," Strange said. "This battle will be for the history books."

"I only wish I had a little more light. I can barely see the road to my front. I think if we take this path here, we can come upon the…"

"Sir, there are cavalry approaching to our left."

"Come on Major, that must be Rucker's boys, if there are enough of them, perhaps we can capture the rest of the Federal host."

The other cavalry emerged from a small cut in the woods, and approached Forrest's men. Forrest rode to greet them, with Strange close behind.

"Halt or we will shoot," shouted the company's captain.

"No need boys, the fight here is done," Forrest said. He rode amongst the cavalry and tried to see which officer he was talking to. In trying to discern the man's face, he noticed the captain still held the revolver aimed at his chest. Forrest focused his eyes, and saw the man's uniform was blue...

'Damn,' he gritted.

In a flash, Strange had barreled his horse in between Forrest and the Union captain, and struck his saber at the revolver just as it fired. The bullet whistled harmlessly past Forrest's ear. Alarmed by the sound of a single gunshot, the rest of Forrest's escort burst upon the scene, causing the Federal company to immediately surrender.

"Major Strange, that was a most honorable service that you have awarded me with."

"General, when I can take the bullet that was meant for you, then you can thank me. Until then, this Confederacy and myself owe you more than we can ever repay."

Forrest shook Strange's hand and together they road into the captured Federal camp. The Confederate cavalry was looting the remains left behind by Capron's brigade. There were guns, ammunition, and most importantly food. Many of the meals being enjoyed were still warming on the fire when the Federals fled. Forrest's cavalry had once again re-supplied themselves without the help of Richmond.

"Why does our President complain about the lack of supplies caused by the Union blockade?" Forrest asked Strange. "The are plenty of supplies available to us already. You just have to know the right way to ask for them."

Strange laughed. "Sir, Chalmers and Rucker are approaching."

"General, you are simply a wizard," Rucker said.

"I believe if old Jeff Davis gave you full command of this war, we would win it within the next year," Chalmers added.

"Dislodging a Yankee brigade is hardly worth that honor. Now, what are the reports?"

"It is too early to be accurate, but we have over fifty prisoners. We have not counted the dead yet, but we can perform that task in the morning," Chalmers said.

"No General, we can leave the clean up to Hood when his men pass through here. We will rest here briefly. Have the men settle down and try to get some sleep. At one in the morning they are expected to be fully awake and ready to pursue the remnants of that Federal brigade."

Chalmers saluted and retired with Rucker into the night.

Forrest returned the salute and turned to face Strange who was talking to one of their captains.

"General, it seems we have also captured a Yankee ambulance, along with many horses that we can appropriate for our men," Strange reported.

"That is excellent, Major. However, what I want most are these repeating rifles. I do not want one left behind. Be sure that we leave a small company behind to search the ground for any that we might have missed."

Strange saluted before departing, leaving Forrest alone in the center of the camp. Forrest casually felt the side of his head, and still could not believe that the Union bullet had missed its mark. Even more surprising was the fact that he managed to get through an encounter without his horse being shot from under him.

He stroked his mount's cold thick mane. Perhaps he had finally found a mount as lucky as he.

Chapter X
November 24
The Road to Columbia

The weather cleared in the morning as Hood had predicted. Though still early, the sun was already a warm flaming ball hanging low in the sky. Finally an intangible had gone his way. Hood thanked the Almighty, then with the assistance of his crutches, labored up a rising knoll so that he could view the leading elements of Cheatham's corps as they resumed their march towards Columbia.

The long lines of gray infantry had an added bounce in their step this morning. Though still hungry, they were wise enough to be grateful for the weather. Seasoned veterans, as they were, they knew that they needed to make the most of such clement conditions. There was no telling how the weather might fare the next day. And though the weather was uncertain, one thing was not... rain or shine, they would still be on the march.

Hood called one of his staff officers to help him mount his horse. He wanted to ride out and meet Cheatham. He had slept a little longer than he wanted, and had not seen the latest dispatch from Forrest's cavalry. The last one he read concerned the rout of Capron's brigade that had occurred late last night. He wanted to know if anything else had occurred since then.

Hood had to admit that any misgivings he had about Forrest were rapidly dissolving into admiration. He originally wanted Wheeler to lead his cavalry. Unfortunately, Beauregard felt that it was more important for Wheeler to harass Sherman's march east. Looking back on that now, Hood had to wonder if that had indeed been a blessing. As good as Wheeler was, he was not sure if he could have performed as magnificently as Forrest had thus far. Thanks to Forrest's cavalry, his infantry was marching unobstructed towards Columbia. There was a strong belief that they were actually closer to that city than Schofield's army.

Hood thanked the officer for helping him to his horse, and then rode towards the long lines of infantry heading down the Mt. Pleasant pike. To his left, he saw a few men talking with Chaplain Charles Quintard. The chaplain looked up as Hood rode by and waved towards him. Hood raised his able hand in return and continued on.

The chaplain was a good man. Hood often enjoyed long talks at night with him. After every conversation with the chaplain, Hood felt a sense of understanding and righteousness. That was the power of God, he thought. Seeing Quintard reminded him that he had not had a long talk with the chaplain in a few days. He made a mental note to set aside some time in the very near future.

Hood saw Cheatham up ahead on the turnpike. A quarreling staff surrounded the general. Several of the officers were pointing down the road at the mass of soldiers congesting the pike. Hood could hear a young officer with an effeminate voice arguing that the road was just not wide enough to allow for the rapid travel of the huge infantry columns.

"Good morning gentlemen, I see we have a congestion problem here," Hood said.

"Morning General Hood. We will have this straightened out in a few moments. We will just need to condense these columns. This road is just so darn narrow," Cheatham said.

"As long as Schofield does not know that we are on it, it can be as narrow as it wants to be. Has there been anything new from Forrest since that last dispatch?"

"Not as of yet."

"How many miles do you reckon till we reach Columbia?"

"I would say less than fifty. We are making excellent progress. And speaking of Forrest, sir, I must be honest, I had my doubts, but he has performed an astonishing job."

"Funny you should say that, I had the same thoughts only a few moments ago. His victory last night is a good omen of things to come."

"I agree. And now we have this wonderful weather to start us on this day. This campaign could not have had a more auspicious start."

Hood and Cheatham continued to ride together through out the remainder of the morning. As they reminisced about things past, they watched the sun ascend the sky in all its radiance. It was moments like this when Hood felt his best, allowing him to keep his worries, like his laudanum, locked away in a special chest.

"General Cheatham, General Hood," a voice called from the road ahead. It was one of Cheatham's staff officers. "A dispatch from General Forrest has just arrived."

When the general reached the officer, Cheatham leaned over on his horse and took the dispatch. Hood instructed him to read it while they rode.

"General Hood, we are in full pursuit of the Yankee cavalry that we were victorious over last night. We have met up with them again today and Chalmers once again routed their remnants by attacking them on both flanks. We have occupied Mt. Pleasant and are but a few miles from Columbia. We have learned that General Schofield is finally aware of his current situation. The Federal army at Pulaski is in full retreat towards Columbia. I have ordered Buford and Jackson to have their divisions race to cut them off and detain their approach. Chalmers will continue to push his division and attempt to occupy Columbia first. If we do, then my fate is in your hands. I will try to hold Columbia with my one division. One division against a whole Federal Corps, those poor Yankees don't stand a chance. The race is now full on General, the rapid march of your infantry columns will be much appreciated. Signed- General Forrest."

"Well General Cheatham, you read the note yourself. Have this army step up the pace."

"Yes sir. You know, I honestly believe that if any one division could hold their ground against a full corps, it would be Forrest's."

"Let's hope so General. Let's hope so."

*　　*　　*　　*　　*　　*　　*　　*

Federal Brigadier General Jacob D. Cox marched through Columbia in a state of pure exhaustion. Hastily awakened several hours before dawn, he had received an urgent dispatch from General Schofield at Pulaski. He was told to immediately mobilize his division and have them in Columbia as soon as possible. It was believed that the Confederate army was already in full motion and headed towards that vital objective.

Cox had originally thought all he had to do was get his men to Columbia and await the rest of Schofield's army. He did not think that the rebels were actually within striking distance as of yet. However, news arrived that the rebel cavalry had defeated the Federal cavalry only miles outside of Columbia. His men were needed at once to assemble on the pike that led into the city and help halt the Federal rout and turn back the rebel attack.

'Well,' Cox thought, 'Someone needs to pay for my loss of sleep'.

As soon as his men entered the Mt. Pleasant pike, Cox could hear the approaching cavalry. His men were still deploying in a defense formation when what was left of Capron's brigade came rushing through them. There was fear in their eyes, so much so, that even the presence of the Federal infantry did little to slow their rout. Like frightened children running from ghosts, they barreled through Cox's men and fled towards the city.

Seconds later, the riders in gray came like unsuspecting hungry wolves. So intent on crushing the Federal cavalry, they failed to notice Cox's division neatly deployed with rifles poised and ready.

'Too bad,' he thought. 'That'll teach you to have me woken up at midnight.'

*   *   *   *   *   *   *   *

General Chalmers pushed his troops forward. A few miles ahead loomed Columbia, and it was theirs for the taking. All that stood in their path was the demoralized Federal command that they had routed twice in two days. Chalmers wasn't sure which victory brought him more pride. And though last night he caught Capron's brigade by total surprise, the plan was put together by Forrest. This morning, however, was the result of a masterful attack which he coordinated. He sent his troops in on both Federal flanks and beat them with their own weapons. Those repeating rifles were truly an unfair advantage, but better he had them than the enemy. Chalmers looked ahead and his pride continued to swell. What could be better than viewing the frightened back of your enemy?

Chalmers kicked his horse in the side. He couldn't help but compare this to chasing a cowherd. Alongside him, his men charged on with reckless abandon. Why shouldn't they? The enemy had their backs to them, and the long awaited goal of Columbia was before them. Every second brought his division a few yards closer to capturing one of the major objectives of Hood's campaign.

Chalmers watched with eager anticipation as his charging

division closed in on the fleeing Yanks. He calculated a full minute until they caught them, then another minute to decimate their scattered units, and a few more minutes to race past what was left and capture the city. Five minutes and Columbia would be in the hands of the Confederacy. The rebel yell went up amongst his men. It was a terrifying scream that meant death for the Yankee cavalry.

*   *   *   *   *   *   *   *

Forrest had left the chase to Chalmers division and ridden with a small escort to the top of a large hill. He looked through his field glasses to survey the situation. He saw Chalmers' men close the gap with the remnants of Capron's brigade. From his vantage point, he could clearly hear the rebel yell. It would only be moments now. He then moved his glasses towards Columbia and almost dropped them to the ground. Assembling before his advancing cavalry were masses of Federal infantry. He needed to get word to Chalmers, but that was impossible. Forrest had to look through his glasses with the nauseous knowledge of what was about to happen to Chalmers' men.

With a loud crack of hundreds of rifles fired in unison, Chalmers' leading units were instantly cut down. It was like watching tomatoes being splattered against a brick wall.

Gun smoke quickly screened his view.

"Damn," he grunted. This time, Forrest did throw his glasses to ground. "Where the hell did that infantry come from? And where the hell are Buford's and Jackson's divisions? They were supposed to prevent any infantry from getting here."

No one in Forrest's escort dared answer the question.

"Major Strange, send word to General Hood. Tell him that I have failed. The enemy has occupied Columbia. I will await further instruction."

Chapter XI
November 26
Vicinity of Columbia, Tennessee

He sat at the end of a finely adorned dining table as the honored guest of President Lincoln. The President sat across from him at the head of the table. To his left were Generals Grant and Sherman. On his right sat Generals Thomas and Schofield.

For John Murphy this occasion was monumental.

By escaping from behind enemy lines and reporting several key positions of the enemy, John Murphy had saved the Union army in Tennessee. General Thomas rewarded his valor with the instant promotion to brigadier general. It was this new rank that allowed him to dine with the President and his generals as a peer. The stars that were sewn onto his coat were his shields that defended him against any intimidation.

John had to admit that he was entirely engulfed in the acclaim he had received. Like Caesar or Napoleon, his entry into the state's capitol had been one of triumph and acclaim. His mother had once told him that there were opportunities for people like themselves in the land of America. John was sorry that she wasn't alive to witness how correct her judgment was.

President Lincoln stood and offered a toast to the new general.

"I just want to take a moment to honor this boy, he sure is a tuff one. Look at his gritted teeth and clenched fists. There is some rage in there. If I had been the rebel guarding him, I sure as hell wouldn't have put down my rifle for a second," Lincoln said.

John was thrilled by the President's use of such strong words to describe his character. They all raised their glasses and clanked them together in cheer. John placed his lips gingerly upon the delicate glass and sipped the rich red wine. It was ice cold. The sensation of it in his mouth almost caused his teeth to shatter. He looked towards the fireplace for warmth. Inside flared a crimson inferno, but when he reached over to warm his hands, he had to immediately withdraw them. The fire sent a chill through his arms, through his body and into his feet. He quickly looked to others at the table to see their reaction to the wine. They consumed the beverage without concern. 'How could that be?' he wondered.

The door to the adjoining kitchen swung open and there appeared a tall servant dressed completely in white. Carried in his out-stretched hand was a large covered silver tray. John felt the rumble in his stomach growl its appreciation of the serving of dinner. The waiter placed the silver tray in the middle of the table and removed the cover. The aroma of the cooked turkey sprang from its containment and raced towards the ceiling.

'A good warm meal, it has been so long,' he thought.

The servant began carving the bird and placing thinly sliced cuts onto all the plates. He then scooped heaping portions of mashed potatoes, steamed squashes, buttery corn and mounds of assorted beans.

John impatiently waited for the server to finish serving all of the men in the room. When it was time to eat, he grasped his fork without hesitation. The metal of the utensil was so cold, he could have been grasping an icicle. John fought the urge to drop the fork, surely the warm meal would warm its metal hide.

He stabbed into the turkey and shoveled the white meat into his mouth. After one bite, he had to spit it back upon his plate. He frantically touched the rest of his food. Though heat clearly rose from his plate, it might well have been snowballs resting on his plate. Everything was ice-cold.

He looked at the other generals. They were all bent over their meals and consuming them with reckless gluttony.

"What is wrong with you all?" he pleaded. "This food is frozen."

If the President or the other generals heard him, they did not show it. They continued to put mouthful after mouthful of food into their mouths.

"Stop eating, this is insane," he yelled.

"He is not going to make it," General Grant said.

"Make what?" John replied. "I will make a fine general. Just because I can't eat food that is frozen doesn't mean I can't command my men."

The others just looked at him. Lincoln reached down into his lap to remove the napkin that was placed there. He thoughtfully wiped the corners of his mouth and then very carefully folded the napkin. He placed it on the table next to his finished meal and rose. The other generals followed his lead and they all departed from the room.

John did not mean to offend anyone, certainly not the President, but this dinner was beyond any measure of acceptability. How could they eat such a cold meal, with wine that was as cold as ice, and in a room that was so frigid that he was able see his own breath?

John just stared at the door expecting them to return. After several minutes he realized that they would not be coming back. A sudden flash of anxiety flashed through his nerves, as he couldn't help to feel that the door that they left through was now locked. He did not know what made him think of such a horror, but he had to find out if it was true.

He rushed to the door and grasped the knob. It would not turn. He began knocking on the door, calling for help. When none came, he began pounding his fists ferociously against the door. He did not know why, but he suddenly felt a strong urgency to get out of the Presidential dining room. With a nervous impulse, he slowly peered over his shoulder like a frightened child. He did so just in time to see a black mist forming in the corner of the room.

The mist swirled in all of its nefarious harmony. It slowly began to creep towards him. As it moved, it completely blackened all of the area behind it. John turned back towards the door and renewed his struggle to escape the room. He did not know what that black cloud was, but he did not want to be caught in its grasp.

As he slammed his fists into the door, he felt cold water begin to trickle on his head. Looking up, it seemed that the ceiling was leaking. When he looked back down, the black mist had entwined itself around his ankles and slowly begun to ascend his legs. The cloud brought fear, but it also brought warmth. His lower limbs finally began to un-thaw as the mist soothed in its crescendo.

'That's not too bad,' he thought. John dropped his hands to his side and let them fall towards the mist. The frostbite was gone. A smile spread across his lips as he welcomed the comfort of the dark vapors. The water that rained from the ceiling no longer concerned him.

Just then the door swung open, and in its portal stood John Murphy's mother.

"Mama. 'How can it be you?" he asked.

"John Murphy, my sweet boy, now is not your time. Stand up like a man and walk through this door with me."

"But it is so cold through there, I can feel the chill even now."

"It will not be so for long my son." She reached towards her son with open arms, and took his hands in hers. She led him through the door and closed it behind them. She helped lay him on the floor and watched him fall asleep. She then kissed his head softly.

"You have made me so proud my son," she said. Then she was gone.

John gingerly opened his eyes. Somehow, he knew that his mother had gone. She left too quickly, there was so much more that he wanted to say to her. He attempted to stand up and run after her, but was completely disoriented by his surroundings.

"I didn't think he would make it, but like I said, he is a strong one. Have the others buried in the morning," a dark shadowy silhouette said.

John tried to focus his sight in the dark. The cold rain that began pelting his head did not help him much. He went to rub his eyes, and realized that he had been shaking feverishly with the chills.

"Damned rebs," he whispered. "Only a dream, a god darned dream." He turned to his side, trying to fall back a sleep and felt the lump of a fellow prisoner. The man's cold stare made him reconsider his dream. The prisoner to his left was also dead. John had been sleeping on the cold wet earth, in the rain, between two fresh corpses.

During some other time of his life, he may have been scared to death to awake to such a visage. But on this night, it was more prudent to pull the corpses close and use their dead flesh as shelter from the cold rain.

"Thank you mother," he prayed. He then closed his eyes in the comfort of knowing that the dream must have been a premonition of his impending escape.

*   *   *   *   *   *   *   *

The rain continued to fall throughout the day in a calm, but steady descent. It was the type of rain that would greatly annoy the man caught plowing his fields. That man could choose to continue plowing or to put his tools down and wait for the weather to clear. He had his options... the soldier of the Army of Tennessee did not. For the men of Hood's Army, the weather did not matter. The rain would be just another part of their long and tedious day.

Cheatham's corps had marched to within six miles of Columbia. Their objective was to reach the city before Schofield's army could. It was a task that they fell a day short upon. The news was not received well by the men who would have to do the fighting. It meant that the enemy would be the ones entrenched behind a fortified position. Earlier in this war, that was not thought of as such a difficult task. However, many of these men were veterans. They had seen what it meant to attack a well-defended position. It was as close to suicide as a man could come.

S.D. Lee's corps and Forrest's cavalry were reported to be in the immediate vicinity of Columbia. They were encircling the south side of the city, waiting for Cheatham and Stewart to come up. By this time tomorrow, all of Hood's army should finally be consolidated outside Columbia.

Consolidated and ready to strike.

As Cheatham's corps funneled down the Mt. Pleasant and Columbia Pike they were welcomed by the delightful bucolic surroundings of an unstained portion of Tennessee. For many miles the pike had stretched north without a single tree closer than twenty feet from the road. But as the men of Hood's army climbed over a slow rolling hill, they were met by an assemblage of the sylvan world. It was almost as if the trees had gathered from afar to watch the parade of Confederates march to reclaim their land. Several trees lined both sides of the pike, their branches twisted and raised as if in cheer. The soldier's spirits were lifted at the sight. They passed in silence as the sounds of the rain tapping against bare branches had a very soothing effect upon their spirits. The sweet sounds of the rain, and the rich foliage that it played upon, was only a prelude to what lay ahead.

For all the carnage that these men had seen, for all the cities and towns that they battled in and through, no one could have guessed that there was any place left in this part of the Confederacy that had seen any peace. They were wrong.

The men of Cheatham's command passed through the Polk plantation in awe. They passed a grand home that sat several hundred yards from the road. A long path led to the front steps of this mansion. George Washington Polk built the home over twenty years earlier. Several soldiers were able to see someone waving to them from the terrace. It was hard to see who the person was, their view was obstructed by the four large pillars that were set across the front of the home. The men waved back, as they continued along the road.

Not far from the grand mansion, the men passed a serenely quiet church. They could not help but to marvel at the craftsmanship of the seraphic structure known as St. John's Episcopal Church. Long strands of ivy, hung heavy with rain, cascaded from the roof upon the rich red brick siding. The steady rhythm of the light rainfall seemed fitting for such a place. The sight of which caused many a man to observe a moment of silence.

Whispers that carried through the entire column told that this was the church of their former General, Leonidas Polk. Polk was not just their commander on the field of battle, but he was also their commander on the field of the Lord. He was a reverend who preached the good word of God at this very place. General Polk had served with these men until the Yankee artillery in northern Georgia decided otherwise. As the men marked the beauty of this place, they remembered their former general with a fond affection.

To counter the solemn mood, Cheatham's staff had instructed one of the regiment's bands to set up opposite the Church, in front of the Ashwood Hall. The band began to play and their music quickly gathered many of the town's residents. The ability of the band to draw such a crowd was a testament to their music.

Cheatham's men turned to the music and raised a cheer. They settled around the town anxious to get as much rest as they could, knowing that there could well be a battle in the next few days. A final look over their shoulders towards the church and its memories of General Polk, reminded them of what they had marched all this way for. Silent promises were made to their fallen commander.

Vengeance would be served.

*   *   *   *   *   *   *   *

General Hood looked towards Ashwood Hall from the window of his headquarters. He was in the home of Colonel Andrew Polk, and Hood thought it the appropriate place to conduct the business at hand. His present view afforded him the luxury of listening to the band as he watched Cheatham's corps fill the plantation.

'One more day and we would have beat them to Columbia,' he thought.

Hood closed the drapes and sat back at the table to await his officers. The recent news from Forrest that the Yankees had occupied Columbia first was initially disheartening. His whole plan was so predicated upon his reaching that city first, that he was at a loss as to what options were now left to him.

Then the reports began to fill his headquarters. His army had captured several mills that would help to re-supply his army. Reading that dispatch helped Hood to realize that had he captured Columbia first, without the appropriation of additional supplies, it would have been a useless accomplishment. His current situation was arguably better. He had his army re-equipped and consolidated. They were on the offensive, and for the first time in many long months, it was the Federal army that was on the defensive.

There was a knock at the door, and an orderly announced the arrival of the officers in Cheatham's staff. Hood smiled and nodded as the men filled the room and took their places along the dining table. The last men to be seated were Brigadier Generals Daniel Govan and Hiram B. Granbury of Cleburne's division. After they were seated, Chaplain Quintard entered the room and shut the door behind him. His chair was adjacent to Hood's.

Hood raised a glass and toasted his men. "Gentlemen, I want to congratulate you on a job well done. The enemy is cowering in Columbia, and by this time tomorrow we will unite with the armies under General S. D. Lee and General Alexander Stewart. I offer a toast in memory of the past and our beloved General Leonidas Polk, whose family grounds we reside upon. I also raise my glass in anticipation of the future. We stand to score a victory that will finally turn the tides of this war. I ask you men, are you with me?"

There was a loud commotion as men raised their glasses and pounded their fists upon the table. When the men had calmed down, Hood called in the dinner. When the plethora of food was placed upon the table, Hood stood again.

"My good sirs, by your reports we know that Schofield has his army entrenched in Columbia. But unfortunately for him, General Thomas has still not come to his aid. What that means is that we still outnumber the enemy. We cannot let such an opportunity escape us. With your permission, I ask that our

Chaplain bless this meal and pray for our success in the days ahead."

Hood seated himself, and touched the chaplain's soft hand. It was his indication to stand and inspire the men gathered with all the grace of the God he represented.

"Lord, I ask that you bless this meal. It is truly a blessing that you have allowed these fine men to dine together in such a sacred haven that we did not know still existed in our homeland. The enemy has taken all that we hold true and they have destroyed it. All we ask is a chance to have our independence. We do not wish to occupy their lands, or harm their countryside as they have done ours. We only want to be left alone. This Lord, I pray to you. Please allow this army of General Hood's, to have glorified success in your name. Allow us to push the enemy from our homes, with the least amount of casualties on both sides. Help us to free our lands, and reestablish our kinship with our brothers to the North. This I ask you in Jesus' name. Amen."

It was several hours after dinner when Hood and the chaplain decided to take an evening stroll around the plantation. With his cork leg fitted, Hood checked the skies for rain. It appeared that the wet weather had finally subsided and would allow for a comfortable evening. He met the chaplain on the steps of Ashwood Hall and together they began to stroll.

"General Hood, I must say that I have not seen you in such favorable spirits in a long time," Quintard said.

Hood smiled at the chaplain with his sunken hallowed eyes. "Nor have I felt this good in such a long time. I have not had a sip of my medicine, and do not feel the need to."

"That is good Sam. That is very good. We must learn to take comfort in the Lord first, and not on these medicines alone. Only then will you find true happiness."

"I believe you are correct in that. You know, if you stay out in this cold wet weather long enough, it fails to be a bother to you."

Quintard simply smiled. The two walked in silence for several minutes. Each was engulfed by the serenity of the plantation. It was hard to think of the war in such a place.

"General, if it is not a bother, let us walk towards those divine magnolia trees."

Hood and Quintard walked onto the Church grounds and

rested with their backs against two closely spaced magnolia tress. Though their robust pink and purple flowers were not in bloom, they were not any less magnificent.

"God's creation is truly a thing to be in awe of."

Hood agreed. "I wish Miss Sally could be here to see this".

"You must miss her terribly, Sam," Quintard said. "I understand that you two are to be married?"

Hood averted his eyes and chose to stare at the ground. Quintard stepped over and placed a gentle hand on Hood's towering shoulder.

"Speak son, there is no one here but you and I and our Lord. And since you and he already know what lies heavy in your heart, I must admit that I feel a bit left out."

Hood's grimace broke into a smile.

"Sometimes she makes me feel like she loves me above all else, and yet sometimes it is as if she does not want anything to do with me."

"Sam, it may seem that way at times, but I am sure Ms. Preston does not mean to make you feel that way."

Hood nodded. He looked up into the midnight blue of the sky and pointed towards a cluster of radiant stars. There was one star that shown with a brilliant hue. Next to it was a smaller star, its light significantly less prominent as compared to the neighboring orb.

"Chaplain, when I am here, and I am with these men, I feel like that bright star up in the heavens. These men look to me for leadership, they respect me. Yet when I am in a room with Miss Sally, I feel that she is the bright star, and I am like that smaller one that resides close by."

Quintard looked up towards the stars and listened to Hood's analogy. "Sam, that may be how you feel around her, but I can assure you that that is not how you appear. You are a grand man, and a rather large man. However, what is important is not that you see yourself or Miss Preston as the brighter star, but rather that you are both bright stars in different ways. One of you might shine at times brighter than the other, and that is just fine. The point is, each one of you must carry enough light to shine most when the other is at its dullest. Do you understand this Sam?"

"Yes chaplain. It is amazing how a few moments of time

with you can help a poor wretch like me understand just how foolish I am."

"Not foolish Sam, just human. We can't help who we are, or how we feel. That is our nature."

"Then it is acceptable for me to still harbor such ill contempt for General Hardee."

"Sam?" Quintard was not expecting such an abrupt change in the conversation and so was not sure he understood what Hood was meaning to imply.

"I am sorry Chaplain," Hood continued. "It is just that I can't help but to think that he had so much to do with the fall of Atlanta."

"Why would General Hardee do such a thing?" Quintard asked.

Hood stepped away from the tree and turned from the chaplain. It was as if he were embarrassed to admit his innermost feelings. However, he felt he needed to tell someone and who better than a man of God?

"He wanted my command, I know that he did. Hardee was so chagrined at my promotion, I believe that he decided to do whatever he could to ensure that I would not succeed."

The chaplain stepped around Hood and faced him. "Sam, that is an unfair statement. I cannot believe that anyone would harbor such feelings as to allow the enemy's success. I can assure you General Hardee's inability to succeed at Atlanta was more because of the Federal army than any work of spite aimed against you."

"Chaplain, we had an excellent opportunity to annihilate over one third of the Yankee army. And not just any part of the Yankee army, but the corps commanded by General Thomas. The same man who now has overall command of all these Yankees that stand in our path to Nashville. My orders were clear and precise, and yet Hardee could not bring his men forward in force."

Quintard was not a man of war. He could not fully understand the implications of what Hood described. It was obvious that Hood felt that Hardee could not have failed in his attack, but somehow he had. Not knowing how to offer military advice, he offered the kind of advice he knew best.

The quiet comforts of silence.

What Quintard learned best from his years of being one in the Lord's service, was that sometimes it was best to let an angered man voice out all his malcontent.

"I lost more then just the battle that day," Hood said. "There was the report that Buck's brother, William, was killed in the battle. I had to send his body back to the home of my fiancée with the thought that I was accountable for his death. I know she must harbor such ill feelings for me. And I had nothing to offer in my defense. I could not say that he died in valor, wrecking the Federal army along Peachtree creek. Instead, I had to draw my army back within Atlanta."

Hood had to pause to collect himself before continuing. "And yet, if that was all Hardee had done, if he only lost me that battle and the life of my fiancé's brother, then I might be able to say it was not his own personal vindictive doings. But there was more. When the Yanks closed around Atlanta like a suffocating snake, there was still a chance for victory. I pulled Stewart, Cheatham and Smith closer to the city, along a front more defendable by our troops. Then I had a plan that was even better than the earlier one aimed at General Thomas. At the time, I still trusted General Hardee to be my most able commander, and so my new plan involved him greatly.

Thomas was still north of the city with his entire command. And that was fine. I intended to leave Thomas alone, choosing to renew the attack against Mcpherson's command to the east of the city. Mcpherson's left flank was reportedly completely open to attack. I only asked that on the morning of the 22nd, General Hardee hit it and hit it hard. Such a strike would roll the Federal army towards the river like an old blanket. As Hardee pushed on, my other corps would join in, making it a complete rout."

Hood finished the sentence, and seemed to become lost in his memories. Quintard waited patiently, until it appeared that the General would offer no more of his pain. The chaplain would not let that happen. He had a deep conviction that Hood needed to let these ghosts out.

"And what happened?" Quintard asked.

Hood rubbed his eyes with the thumb and index finger of his good hand. From behind clenched teeth, he blew out a cold breath that sent a fine mist into the night. It was like watching a dragon preparing to blow his fiery flames from the jowls of his maw.

"Hardee never attacked in the morning. It wasn't until almost noon when he hit the exposed Federal flank. Only when he hit it, it was not longer exposed. It seemed that a Yankee division had appeared out of nowhere. We had some success but not the sort we needed to carry the field. Hardee had failed me for a second time. Two chances for complete victory, both spoiled by one man. And once again my army was forced back within the defenses of Atlanta."

"And there we held for over a month, while General Sherman lay siege upon us. The Yankees bombarded us with reckless abandon, but the greater part of their wrath fell on the civilians of Atlanta instead. How the enemy managed to miss his mark, I will never know... unless that was his cruel intent. My men were over a mile from the inner city... Sherman had to know what he was doing. I even sent a letter personally asking him to stop this type of cruel and inhumane warfare. What part did Atlanta's good people play in this war I asked? And do you know what his response was? He said it was his duty to destroy the enemy's country and that Atlanta was the chief depot of the manufacturing of war for the Confederacy. Just a few days later, a large shell whistled into the city and struck a building at the corner of East Ellis and Ivy Street. When we cleared the rubble, we found the mangled remains of the daintiest little blonde girl I have ever seen... her dead dog was still clutched within her tiny arms. Her lifeless eyes stared back into my own, asking the question why? A question I will never be able to answer."

"Some day, I would like to be face to face with Sherman, so that I can have him explain to me how this little girl helped to manufacture our war effort", Hood continued.

Hood could no longer suppress the flow of hot tears that ran down his face. The chaplain had no idea that his night stroll with the General would come to this. He now began to understand the frustration and the solemn mood he often saw reflected upon the face of Hood. He remembered how earlier in the night he passed several comments on how Hood seemed to be in the best of spirits. He would not retract those comments. What was said on this night would stay forever between them and God.

What would also stay here on this night was the groan of bitterness that swelled deep within the Chaplain's chest. He thought of the crushed form of the innocent little girl with her dog. How could General Sherman order such a cowardly act as the firing of his big guns at civilians? Chaplain Quintard honored God above all else, but if Sherman were to appear before him in this instant, there would be no thoughts of his Bible. It was an emotion that he was not proud to have.

"Yet for all the devastation that Sherman has caused, he is not the one I hold the most contempt for," Hood continued. "If given the chance, Chaplain, I would rather duel with that scoundrel Hardee."

"Sam that is not fair. Your faith in God should give you the power to resists such temptations from the devil."

"Well, it does not," Hood shot back. "Forgive me Chaplain, for I am a believer in His good word. But sometimes I struggle to find the comfort that you have obtained. I know that I should love my fellow man, but with Hardee it is different."

"It is a hard battle Sam, but one that can be overcome through faith and forgiveness. I must admit, what you just told me about Sherman's bombardment of Atlanta, and the death of that little innocent child… well let's just say that I too have a difficult time suppressing my ire. But it must be done. We are God's children first."

Hood's large frame towered for a second, and then it seemed to dwindle as it deflated. His shoulders sank, and his able knee buckled. With a trembling hand, he pointed towards his cork appendage. "Why then would God do this to his children? What have I done to deserve this? I understand that being at battle puts me at risk. I accept that. But to take my leg and the use of one of my arms, that I can not understand."

"General Hood, it was not God's choice for you to fight this war, it was yours."

"I know, I know. But I was close with another man of God back east. Chaplain Davis. It was two winters ago, when times were better for us. I remember how all of us officers sat around the campfire and talked about women, war and the God that allowed both of those to ruin man."

The two shared a brief sputter of laughter from Hood's anecdote.

"But it was sitting there," Hood continued, "fraternizing with excellent soldiers, many of whom are gone now, that I thought that I had really communicated with God. I took Chaplain Davis' Bible and with a simple random gesture, opened it and pointed to the words on the page. And do you know what those words were? It was Psalm 118:17 and it was a message from God that I would never forget. I have since memorized that passage. It read, 'I shall not die, but live.' I was so inspired by the passage that I asked all the officers to do the same, to attain words of inspiration from our God. It was my belief, …no, my conviction that I would not fall in battle. My leg and arm are the curses of that pompous conviction.

"And as for Hardee, well I have not finished my story of him. Like I have said, we were besieged in Atlanta, with only one rail open to bring our supplies. The Yankee cavalry threatened the Macon and Western Railroad, but Wheeler's cavalry successfully repulsed them. This gave me an idea. With the Yankee cavalry temporarily disposed of, I sent Wheeler to circle into Sherman's rear to try and cut off his supply. If the Northerners were cut off from their supply line, they would be forced to pull back or attack my entrenchments. If I remember correctly, it was roughly a month after Wheeler had left, that we started receiving reports that the Federal army was on short rations. It seemed my plan was working. We even sent spies across the lines, and they confirmed these reports. Then the guns stopped shelling the city. It was the most unnatural silence that you could have ever experienced. We were so used to hearing their menacing, whistling, and impacting explosions, that the silence seemed ominous. When we peered out of our entrenchments, General Sherman and his army were gone."

"Chaplain, the bells rang and roared as the news reached the good people of Atlanta. We had saved Atlanta. The dancing and celebrating that went on that night was nothing but pure jubilance." Hood fell quiet for a moment as he reflected upon that brief glimmer of hope. When the mood passed, his head quickly sprang back up. His eyes were aflame.

"But Sherman was not gone," he continued. "With my cavalry out of reach, I had no way of knowing that Sherman simply slipped his army west. I did not fully understand the Yankee position until reports came that two of their raiding divisions were threatening the rail at Jonesborough. Foolishly, I once again called upon the services of Hardee. We had a clear conversation as to what he needed to do. Simply march his command to the area and drive the Federals across the Flint River. And once again, his troops arrived at the battle late, and failed to take the objective. Hardee was himself pushed back and we were cut off. I had to evacuate the city lest we become trapped like General Pemberton at Vicksburg. I had to burn much of the city as

I left. Over eighty rail cars, five locomotives, artillery pieces, not to mention the amount of supplies, all that had to be destroyed. All this so as not to let it fall into the enemy's hands."

"One day I was the savior of Atlanta, and the next I was the cause of its ruin. The Yankees could not have done a better job of destruction than the one that I was forced to do. And all because Hardee had failed me three times. My own personal Peter."

Quintard watched Hood's massive chest exhale when he finished talking. It was like watching a grand balloon deflate into limpness. It appeared that Hood had vented all of his frustration on this night. That was good. Quintard was not one to judge, but if half of what Hood had said was true, then General Hardee should be held accountable. Yet, Quintard was sure that if Hardee were present, he would have some choice words to say in his defense.

"General, I am glad that we have had this talk. I can fully understand your frustrations, but there is a lesson here. God will always provide if you let him. He has taught you a lesson, a valuable lesson… one that you must use in the battle ahead. For isn't your next battle far more important than Atlanta. The enemy is not as strong in numbers as he was then. This is the chance that God has given you, and I believe what he is saying is not so much to harbor hate for General Hardee, but instead to learn from your associations with him, so that you can make better decisions in the days ahead.

"Pray to Him, and he will help you. Ask him to show you who your men in command should be. He will listen Sam, that I promise you."

For the first time since dinner, a warm smile settled upon the face of General Hood. His large frame once again stood proud. He took the chaplain's hand and shook it with a force long forgotten.

They walked into the night towards the church grounds. They had both decided that before retiring for the night, they wanted to pay their respects at the Polk family cemetery. With a careful step, they walked towards St. John's Church. A cold wind met them as they approached the front steps. Like the hand of a jilted lover, it slapped them across the face, reddening their complexions with its touch. The two companions simply turned their collars up and headed towards the cemetery.

*　　*　　*　　*　　*　　*　　*　　*

Patrick Cleburne and his three brigadier generals marveled at the Polk family cemetery in quiet respect. They knew that tomorrow would bring them one day closer to the war that General Hood was seeking. Rather than catching a few extra winks, they unanimously decided to spend a few silent moments in a place that was not and could not be harmed by this bloody war... a cemetery.

Like the war, the season itself seemed to lack the ability to disrupt the confines of the dead. Many of the shrubs and flowers had a color that was an aberration of this time of year. Even in the dark, one could see the rich green colors on the plants that inhabited the cemetery, as well as the ivy that clung to the church's walls.

The four men walked in pairs through the headstones, their boots softly sinking into the damp earth with each passing step. It was as if the ground was inviting them to the place that they all must attend at some point in their future. It had a ghastly effect on the mood.

The night was cold and dark, but the moon shone its light from above and reflected its pale glow on the otherwise non-luminous gravestones. Cleburne paused to take note of the remarkable workmanship that was used in crafting some of these monuments. One in particular was easily over seven feet in height. Carved into the stone was an extremely realistic looking mantle scarf. Written beneath the name of the deceased was the quotation, "And there was no night there." Cleburne was not sure where that saying had originated from, but it seemed fitting for this evening.

When Cleburne spoke, he broke the silence of the dead, and caught his generals off guard. Brigadier General Mark Lowrey actually jumped a step.

"This place is truly remarkable," Cleburne said. "Sorry General Lowrey, I did not mean to frighten you. It is just that, well, I mean, if I close my eyes and reopen them, I could swear that this is the same place that my father is buried back in Ireland. So much so that I am tempted to search for his grave." Cleburne did take a moment to look behind him, towards the side of the church. It was remarkable how similar this church was to the one where his father now rested. He turned back to his right and could make out a large twisted tree several yards behind the church. Gathered around it, like children waiting to hear a story, were several small flat headstones.

"I am sorry for the loss of your father, General", Brigadier

General Govan said.

"Thank you General. He was a good man. His memory is strong in me. I hope to visit him again at some point. He is buried back home, in the Athnowen Churchyard in Ireland. Gentlemen, please make a note to remind me of this night when this war is over. I must visit Athnowen again."

"Was your father in the army as well?" Brigadier General Hiram Granbury asked.

Cleburne laughed. "No sir. In fact, he was against my wish to serve. You must understand...my father was a pharmacist. That was what he wanted for me as well. And I did try, I was an apprentice studying to be all that that my father wanted of me, but I failed the apothecary exam. It is amazing how certain events, or crossroads in your life, can dramatically affect the outcome of your existence. Had I passed that exam, who knows where I would have been now?"

"So how did you get into the military then?" Lowrey asked.

"Let me see, I joined Her Majesties 41st regiment, and served with them for three long years." Cleburne was silent for a long time after that, obviously stuck wrestling thoughts of his past. Before speaking again, he began walking towards the next tombstone. "Then there was America. Simply, I decided that I wanted to live in this country. I came here, and ironically followed in the same footsteps as I did in the old county. I did start out working as a pharmacist. But try as I might, that was not my fate. I later took up the study of law, but when the war broke out, I dropped it all to join my fellow men for the Southern cause."

Cleburne suddenly ended the conversation. The four companions came to a halt in front of one particular tombstone. The name engraved upon the strong granite was that of a Polk descendant. It was not that of Leonidas Polk, one of their own whom was recently felled in battle. Yet, the name on the stone had the same effect on the companions. It instantly brought back memories of the beloved General Polk.

"Gentleman," Cleburne said, "this is why we fight the enemy and this is why we must win."

The others nodded their heads and tipped their hats.

Cleburne took in a deep breath of the night's air. "Yes my good men, this is such a place that I would gladly say... it was worth dying to be placed in such a spot."

The men continued to silently entertain their own thoughts on mortality. For the three brigadier generals their thoughts were on their homes, their families and their lives. With the battle ahead of them, the cemetery was like a foreshadow of things that might come to pass in their very near future.

Cleburne's thoughts were not on his own future. Instead, he meddled in affairs that were far greater. It was no doubt partly the fault of the late Leonidas Polk. Now that Cleburne stood on the church grounds that his commander had once preached at, he was reminded of several wonderful tales that Polk was fond of telling concerning his church. One in particular was more a personal awakening than just another story from the reverend. Polk had often mentioned how he had allowed the Negroes to worship with the white men during his sermons.

He reached towards the tombstone and plucked at some weeds that clung to the base. Without an effort, he ripped the cold and wet leaves from the earth, and threw them to the side. "Death is so final," he whispered. Staring at the grave sight, and reflecting on his fallen friend, he could not help but to be reminded of Shakespeare's play, 'Hamlet.'

Act V scene I was a favorite passage of his. In it Hamlet and Horatio enter a churchyard and observe two gravediggers at work. Hamlet soon discovers the skull of his old court jester Yorick, and it is at this moment that he gains significant insight concerning the meaning of life. Cleburne experienced that same discovery while reading the play for the first time, and understood that it was not what one did in life that mattered. All the skulls and bones in the graveyard were indistinguishable. In their final resting-place, King Caesar's skull could lie next to the skull of a local farmer, without anyone being able to tell them apart. No matter how great or important the person was in life, they eventually would turn to decay in the same fashion as everyone else.

> '*Imperious Caesar, dead and turn's to clay,*
> *Might stop a hole to keep the wind away:*
> *O, that that earth which kept the world in awe*
> *Should patch a wall to expel the winter's flaw*'

Cleburne contained a silent laugh. 'Oh, our greatest folly,' he thought. When this war is over, when thousands of years had passed, would anyone be able to place the skull of Jefferson Davis next to a slave, and be able to tell who was who?

Yet, if that was the case, if the remains of the President of the Confederacy were indistinguishable from that of a Negro slave, then what was to be said of the fundamental beliefs of the aristocratic Southerner?

They were flawed.

The Negro was not a working animal. He was a human being. And yet the South refused to believe this. And by doing so, doomed themselves, for slavery was now an albatross that would eventually drown his country.

It was not that Cleburne chose to fight this war for slavery. It was never an issue with him, he never even owned a Negro. He joined the South because they were the people he was associated with. They had stuck by him through all of his endeavors. The Negro was never the issue.

It was that way for many Southerners. They did not pick up their arms and march to war just to keep the Negro enslaved. They did it to show that the industrialized North could not force their will by invading their homeland.

Union President Abraham Lincoln used the slavery issue very wisely in the course of the war. Knowing that the South needed foreign recognition to help sustain the war, Lincoln issued the Emancipation Proclamation in 1863. In this act of freeing the slaves, Lincoln guaranteed that France and England would never enter the war on the side of the South. Europe had already freed their slaves, and any action aiding the Confederacy would be seen as an act of hypocrisy in their own countries.

'Why do we not just free the Negro?' Cleburne often wondered. Though he fully knew the answer lay in the greed of the rich. They needed the slave population to help maintain and increase their profits. Their belligerent dogmatism would ensure that their profits would never be harmed. Yet the cause of the affluent South was not the same as the rest of her population. The average Southern workingman did not even own a slave. His fight in this war was for another reason... state sovereignty and state pride. And though the wealthy were more belligerent, they easily left the actual fighting to the average workingman. And because the wealthy had more say in politics, the rest of the world incorrectly assumed that the South was at war to defend its institution of slavery.

This made Cleburne irate. If the opulent were so cantankerous with their beliefs, why then were they not the ones doing the fighting? Until the old and obese landowners picked up their rifles and fell in line along his men, he would never respect their prejudices. That being said... free the Negro and let the black man augment the depleted Southern army.

The freedom of the Negro was a thought that he pondered many times, and each time he became more confident in his conviction. That was the only way to turn this war around. There was still time, as long as he could convince others of his belief. Free the Negro. Turn this back into the war it was in the beginning, a war against Northern oppression, not a war against slavery. This would instantly revive the possibility of foreign intervention. It would also extinguish much of the political coal that the North was using to help furnish the war. If it were not a war to free the slaves, then many Northerners would not be fighting or supporting this enduring battle. Added to all of that was the fact that the black population could considerably augment the armies of the South. The huge disparity in numbers between the two armies could be dissolved with one swift decision.

It was so simple it flared the famed Irish ire that resided in the general's soul. By freeing the slaves, they would reduce Northern resolve, regain foreign recognition, and add numbers to their army so that they could meet the enemy on equal terms.

But who would listen, and more importantly who had the power to issue such a claim? Cleburne knew the answer, but there had been a tremendous risk in broaching such a delicate topic. He had already sent a proposal to President Davis, but he never received a reply. Instead, he heard the rumors that many in Richmond considered him to be a Union sympathizer.

Still, Cleburne knew that at some point, he would have to send a second letter to President Davis. One that was more detailed, more convincing. President Davis was the only one in the South with the power to free the slaves. Cleburne hoped that Davis could understand the long-term implications that emancipation would have on the South.

There were other ways to fight this war without the use of men, guns and cannons. It was time that someone else in the South realized it.

Cleburne turned back to his men and began to speak, but a shivery wind blew past them and raced towards the front of the

Church. The men all followed the trailing wiffet until its passing chill was gone. They then turned back towards the tombstone and once again paid their respects.

"Greetings gentleman," General Hood said, as he approached the silent companions. Hood leaned on his crutch with a well-contained limp that failed to camouflage his false leg. Chaplain Quintard was at his side. "I see we are not the only ones enjoying a peaceful cold night."

Cleburne turned around so that he could see the general. "General Hood it is good to see you. Dinner this evening was most excellent," he said. Cleburne tried to peer through Hood and wondered how this fellow Southerner would react if he knew what he had just been contemplating. He couldn't help but shudder at the thought.

Hood stepped closer and read the inscription on the tombstone. "One of the Polk's. Did you know chaplain, it was General Polk who baptized me?"

The chaplain smiled.

"Well gentleman, I will count on you all heavily in the days ahead. The night is already late. Let us part from this sacred place and retire for the night. We all could use a good nights rest."

The officers followed Hood's orders as if they were on the battlefield. They exited the church cemetery and sought their much needed rest.

All except Patrick Cleburne. He sought parchment to write upon. On this night of his Hamlet like revelation, he would begin his letter to the President. This was not the first of such sent. He had written a plea earlier, but it was rejected. This time, he would write a letter that would take an approach that was more stern than the last. A letter that could either save the Confederacy, or cost him his place in it.

Chapter XII

November 27

Columbia Tennessee

General John McAllister Schofield stood sheltered on the terrace of the Athenaeum Rectory and watched as the cold rain continued to fall on yet another day. The Athenaeum Finishing School for Women, which had served as his headquarters since his arrival into Columbia three days ago, stood behind the rectory. And right now, that was exactly were he wanted it. Currently, the school contained far too much commotion caused by the bantering of his own officers. Their actions had grown so tumultuous that he found it unable to hear himself think. After hearing so many of the men talk about the rectory, he decided to steal a few moments and see it for himself. He was glad that he had.

The etymology of the Athenaeum Rectory was derived from the Greek God Athena. The name denoted a place of wisdom. That was good. It was the very type of building that Schofield needed at this time of his life.

The architecture of the two-story building was one that Schofield was not familiar with. The archways over the terrace were of Moorish design, yet the construction had a gothic appeal. The Athenaeum also contained some of the most magnificent décor that he had ever seen. Set before the steps that he had climbed was a beautiful French fountain that had sprayed him with cold mountain water. Inside, the reception room housed an inspiring chandelier made from seven distinct metals. Their different metallic hues blended into a wondrous spectral of opalescence.

If one could manage to gaze away from the illuminating fixture, there was the inspiring craftsmanship of the flashed glass. Brilliant triangles cast in vibrant colors of red, yellow and blue were sectioned to the sides and over the door. When the glass was manufactured actual gold shavings had been added. The hints of gold created a dazzling shine as the sun poured through its glorious hues.

Yet, this finishing school lacked certain aspects that would appeal to its practical use. There was no kitchen in the facility to prepare meals. A separate kitchen was situated a few yards from the rectory making it difficult to attain a quick bite. What was worse, especially in this cold rain, was that there was no internal staircase in the building. For Schofield to get back down stairs, he had to actually step outside and descend a staircase to the main floor. If he had to live here, he would have gladly traded the expensive chandelier for a staircase.

However, he could not help but feel grateful that it was he who occupied this institute for learning and not Confederate General John Bell Hood.

From the reports he had received days ago, it seemed that the rebels had indeed outflanked his position at Pulaski, and were within moments of capturing the city. Had it not been for his order to march General Cox's men to Columbia, he was sure that he would have been cut off from General Thomas in Nashville.

But now that his army had won the race, the question was what to do next?

Schofield was convinced that Hood should have attacked by now. He fully expected the rebel lines to have advanced back on the 25th, but no such attack came. In fact, except for the rebel cavalry, Schofield was uncertain of the whereabouts of Hood's army. Believing that Hood fell back to claim Pulaski, Schofield decided to all but abandon the southern side of the city and move his troops into better defensive positions on the north bank of the Duck River. If Hood wanted to attack over a river and against a well-entrenched enemy, Schofield would be only too happy to oblige.

But that was days ago, and as the sun began to decline, Schofield looked into the distance with worry. He had been so confident with his assessment, that he had sent a telegram to Thomas in Nashville. In writing, he stated his report to his commander. He ended his telegram with the intention of reestablishing any confidence that Thomas may have lost in him since Hood's almost successful flanking march. It read, 'I assure you, General Hood cannot get the start on me again.'

Sent two days ago and already he wished there were some way to get that telegram back.

The rain that crashed from the heavens yesterday must have been similar to that seen by Noah before the flooding of the earth. The Duck River was so swollen it was impossible to get the remainder of his army consolidated on the north bank.

Making matters worse, was the news that the telegraph lines had been severed between Columbia and Nashville. The only instruction that he had received since the late morning of the 25th was the telegram that he currently held in his trembling hand. It was from Thomas, and simply read 'A.J. Smith is expected shortly. If you can hold Hood on the south side of the Duck River, I think we shall be able to drive him back easily after concentrating.'

Schofield raised the telegram to eye level and read it one last time before angrily crushing it between enraged fingers. He stepped back into the large single room and threw the crumpled ball of paper onto the table. All the confidence that emanated from him these past two days was now crumpled within that misshapen ball of paper.

Earlier this morning, one of his captains had reported the chilling news that Schofield was entirely unprepared for.

Hood was back.

He had been so confident that the rebels had fallen back to Pulaski, that he was at a loss when it came time to issue direction to his army. He could not fall back without first giving up a contingent of almost eight thousand men that still guarded the south bank of the Duck. The rain filled river prevented a safe exodus from the city.

"I assure you, General Hood cannot get the start on me again," he had wired Thomas two days ago. Schofield did not like the taste of eating his own words. Hood's whole army was now confirmed to be concentrated on his front and threatening to attack. What was he to do?

The only comforting prospect was that the continuous rainfall had made the Duck River too dangerous to ford. There was no way Hood could cross it at this time. This natural delay would give Schofield the time he needed to strengthen his defenses and await the reinforcements promised by Thomas' last message. 'But how long am I to hold Hood here?' he thought. 'And am I to abandon a part of my army?'

The stoic suggestion to hold the rebels south of the Duck did not state for how long. Did it mean until Schofield thought it was practical, or hold here at all costs? With the telegraph lines severed by the enemy, there was no sure way of knowing.

A sharp knock at the door caused Schofield to lose his train of thought. Wanting to appear professional, he put on his uniform's jacket. The dried candle wax that had dripped from the

143

chandelier in the front parlor still clung to his shoulder like a milky leach. He quickly went to work using his fingernails to remove the dried wax. When he was done, he angrily called for the officer to enter.

"I am sorry to disturb you General, but I have some very important news."

Schofield impatiently indicated to the officer to get on with his report.

"There is a cavalry officer downstairs sent from General Capron. He reports that they have captured three Confederate privates and have successfully interrogated them."

Schofield felt the wave of relaxation settle upon his stomach. Prisoners were a welcome addition to his current state of affairs and he needed some sense of the direction of Hood's army.

"Private, please instruct the officer to enter."

Schofield did not have to wait long to hear the footsteps of the cavalry officer scrambling up the external staircase. He was led into the room by two of Schofield's staff officers. The man was young, in his early twenties, with thick wavy hair that reminded Schofield of how much he missed his own mane of manhood. The officer's hair was matted down by the same rain that claimed his entire uniform. The puddle that was quickly forming beneath him was a clear indication of how recently he had come from the field.

Schofield led him in and did not object as his staff members eagerly followed them into the room. Schofield watched his officers, all warm and dry, as they dispersed to form a circular wall around the general and the wet cavalryman. This was an anxious moment for them all. The peril of being cut off from Nashville and facing a vengeful rebel army was not a pleasant thought in this dreaded weather.

"General," the officer began without any introductions, "we have captured three privates trying to cross the Duck River in a small boat. It was near Davis Ford."

Schofield rested his left arm across his chest, while the elbow of his other arm resided in the palm of his left hand. With purposeful fingers he scratched at his long crinkled beard. "What time was this?"

"This morning. We interrogated them immediately, and I was sent to bring the report to you."

"And what have you found?"

The cavalryman wiped the mixture of sweat and rain from

his brow and deposited it upon his muddied trousers. He looked around the room at Schofield's staff like a frightened puppy. It was not a look that pleased Schofield.

"General, if they speak truly, then we now know that the Confederate right extends to Huey's Mill."

Schofield tried to recollect that location. He failed. "And where is that location?"

"Roughly seven miles to the east."

"Trying to outflank us again," Schofield said rhetorically. He motioned to one of his staff officers and instructed him to depart at once and find General Wilson. He would need his cavalry commander immediately.

"Is there anything more to report?" he asked.

"No sir, just that General Capron is sure that the enemy will cross to the east unless we deter him."

"Thank you, sir, for your advice," Schofield said with a flavor of sarcasm. "But you may tell General Capron that I can guarantee that not even Hood will attempt any such crossing while the river is flooded. Thank him for his report and tell him to expect new orders in the next few hours. You are dismissed." Schofield looked around at all of his officers who stood around the room like ancient Greek statues. "You are all dismissed. And someone get that man into some dry clothes."

Schofield waited till the last officer left and closed the door behind him. He now had the information that he needed in order to direct his army. He would send for his generals in a few moments, but first he wanted to meet with his new cavalry commander, General Wilson.

His first priorities were textbook obvious. He needed Wilson's cavalry to cover all of the fords east of Columbia. If Hood so much as spit over the Duck, he wanted to know about it. After Wilson departed, he would instruct his generals to begin the rapid mobilization of the rest of his army to the north bank of the Duck. This would in effect surrender Columbia to the rebel army, but it would also keep the enemy on the south side of the river, just as Thomas had instructed. From the north banks, they could easily watch the movements of Hood, and be poised to intercept any crossing that the rebels might attempt to make.

Schofield had regained the confidence he needed to lead his army. It was that same confidence that let him write that telegram to Thomas that stated, "I assure you, General Hood cannot get the start on me again."

Schofield was once again committed to his own confidence.

*   *   *   *   *   *   *   *

The sound of someone playing the harp could be heard coming from the front parlor downstairs. The mellifluous sound of the stringed instrument worked instantly to remove the heavy stress that lay deeply in the General's nape. Schofield walked across the wide poplar floorboards back towards the terrace. He liked the way the door opened to allow entrance to the outside balcony. The large window had to be lifted up, and then the two panels below it swung open like the doors in a western saloon.

Schofield stepped back out into the cold night, and rested his tired body against the sturdy balcony made from walnut wood. He stood quietly in the shadows of the recess as he watched his officers pass through the front yard. There were two young men standing around the fountain. He secretly yearned to have their rank. There was no pressure involved. You simply followed the orders of your commander.

Their elevated voices were most likely due to some intoxicating beverage.

"Can you believe that, they teach young women how to be ladies," one of them said.

"Where? At that big old school?" the other asked.

"Yes sir. They get to learn the proper etiquette. Didn't you notice that petticoat mirror in the front room? I think my girl back home needs a lesson here. There is even a dormitory on these grounds for the women who are studying."

The other soldier seemed to stand up straight when he heard this. "Well then, perhaps we need to go and find some of these young ladies. I promise you this, I can teach them all that they need to know about being a woman."

The two officers laughed as they retired from the fountain and made their way across the campus. Schofield was once again left to himself.

He reflected upon his brief respite in the town of Columbia, and regretted having to leave its charms behind. The enemy had not given him a choice.

"Congratulations, my dear old Sam, the city is yours," he said out loud. "But this is as far as your army may go. You will never cross the Duck River."

*   *   *   *   *   *   *   *

All through the day of the 27th, the masses of gray troops settled in around the southern end of Columbia like moths to a flame. The cold rain that splattered thick dark mud against their dilapidated shoes did not bother them. How could it? This army had just completed a march of over sixty miles with all of the elements against them in this, one of the coldest winters that Tennessee had ever seen.

The leading corps commanded by Lieutenant General S. D. Lee formed against the river on the west side of the city. Divisions of Johnson, Stevenson and Clayton triumphantly paraded their men into position on his left flank. Lieutenant General Alexander Stewart's Corps took the center. Loring's, French's and Walthall's divisions falling in place directly to the south of the city. On their right were the divisions of Cleburne, Brown and Bate of Cheatham's Corps. The cavalry under major General Forrest had been rewarded for its excellent performance in screening the movements of the infantry from the enemy. They were temporarily retired to the extreme right flank of the line, next to Cheatham.

For the first time since departing from Florence, Hood's army was consolidated in one compacted area. Consolidated and ready to strike.

A new mood had embraced the Confederate army on this day. It was one best summed up as jubilance. They were tired of retreating from the enemy. Ever since the Union victory at Chattanooga, they had simply given ground to every advance made by the enemy. It became demoralizing. But now General Hood had changed the direction of their step. They were moving forward, and it was the Yankees who were giving up ground. Those same Yankees lay huddled within the city of Columbia at present. Estimates of their strength had filtered down to the level of captains and foot soldiers. It was no secret, not only were they finally pushing the Yankees back, but they actually outnumbered the enemy.

Revenge was long overdue.

Columbia

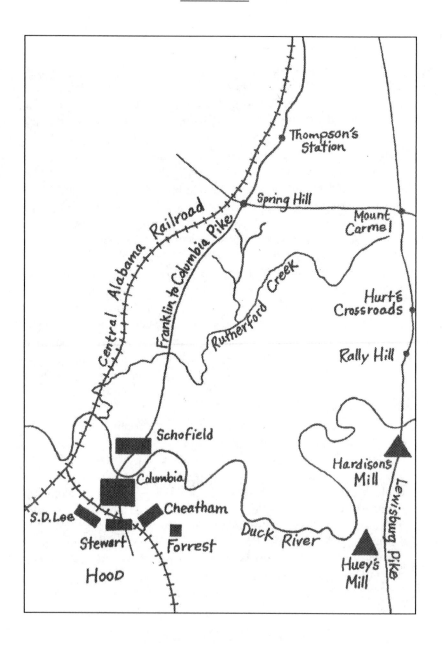

The men who made up Hood's army were ready to strike a blow for every defeat they had suffered since their last victory at Chickamauga back in '63.

With eager rifles and anxious feet, they more than once turned their heads towards the home of a Mrs. Amos Warfield. For that house now served as the headquarters for General Hood. And from that house would come the order that each cold and tired soldier savored more than warmth itself.

The command to attack.

*   *   *   *   *   *   *   *

In a warm and comfortable room that centered on a blazing hearth, were the four most important men in the Army of Tennessee. Sitting around the fire were Generals Hood, Cheatham, Stewart and S.D. Lee. By the looks of the cleared plates that were stacked in the next room, one could easily discern that the dinner provided was one that was well accepted. With dinner consumed, it made way for the men to concentrate on the situation at hand.

Their date with war had once again returned.

"I need to send my compliments to Mrs. Warfield," Hood said. "Her home is most beautiful, and I would like to personally thank her for letting me use it as my personal headquarters."

"I might also add that the lady has a fitting name for the occasion. I mean war-field. If I do not miss the mark, I gather that her name will be exactly what will befall this place in the next day," Stewart said.

Hood agreed. He looked at Stewart and realized that this man had some very large boots to fill. Stewart was promoted to Lieutenant General soon after the untimely death of General Polk in the mountains of Kennesaw. Polk was a preacher turned General who had the love and admiration of all the men he commanded. Stewart would need those same characteristics in the days ahead.

"Do we have any word on the status of the enemy?" Hood asked. "Has General Schofield managed to get all of his forces within Columbia, or have we managed to cut off any of them?"

"I am sorry to report that it appears all of General Schofield's forces are retired within Columbia," S.D. Lee said. "With him are the Fourth Corps and the Twenty-third. Our estimates are fifteen thousand men with the Fourth and another twelve thousand with the Twenty-third. Those figures do not include any of their cavalry detachments, roughly three thousand in all."

Hood could not help looking at his general and seeing a younger Robert E. Lee. Although the two were only distant relatives, they shared a slight resemblance. Both men had the thick facial hair that rested upon a sturdy square jaw line, but there was more than that. Hood felt that Stephen had the same piercing eyes as his relative Robert. They were eyes that exuded a sense of intelligence and understanding that few men possessed. Hood could listen to a report from this man and know that what he was told was reliable information.

"And what are their intentions?" Hood continued. "Do they mean to stay and fight?"

"Well General, that is not exactly clear," S. D. Lee said. "The rain has flooded the Duck River, leaving Schofield very few options at this point. His forces are leaning towards the north side of the city. There were also reports earlier this afternoon, that when the rain ceased for a while, the enemy was seen to be hastily preparing pontoon bridges to cross the river. That can only mean one of two things. General Schofield is either preparing to leave the city at night and move north, or he is ensuring there is an escape route in the event we attack his forces here at Columbia. I myself, being captured at Vicksburg, cannot stress enough the importance of an escape route for troops defending a city that has its back to the river."

"Well gentleman, what is clear is that we can not let General Schofield escape our grasp. He has already done his country a great service by reaching Columbia before us, we can not allow him to do another by reaching Nashville and joining the forces of General Thomas. Someone please bring forth a map."

General Cheatham got up and walked into one of the adjoining rooms. The weight of his heavy steps brought a tired creaking from the hard wood floors. After several minutes of wrestling through papers and various maps, he found the exact map he wanted and returned to the hearth. Stewart pulled a small table that was placed against the window to the center of the room. He carefully removed the various knickknacks that resided on its top and took the map from Cheatham. When opened, the map fit the tabletop as if each was made with the other in mind.

The four men independently spent several moments studying the map in silence.

"The Harpeth River is the only real obstacle that exists between here and Nashville. Perhaps by flanking a march around the Federal left, we can once again interpose our army between those of General Schofield and General Thomas," Stewart said.

Before the other generals could voice their agreement of Stewart's very sound plan, General Hood interjected. "General Stewart, your plan has merit, but it lacks proper thought. You assume that Thomas is just sitting in Nashville doing nothing. According to your plan, we need to reach the Harpeth before Schofield does. If we do as you say, we would have Schofield to our rear, and the river to our front, a perfect obstacle to prevent Thomas from interfering while we destroy General Schofield. That part I do like. But what if Thomas is already at the Harpeth when we get there? We would be caught between two armies and cut off from our supply base. No, what I propose instead is a direct assault against Schofield in the morning. We cannot afford any more delays. Our men are tired of the march. They want to strike now... I want to strike now. It will not take the Federal high command long to realize the jeopardy they are in. Soon Thomas will be united with Schofield and we will lose our advantage in numbers. I will not let that happen. Our men have not marched all this way to be outnumbered."

'Nor slaughtered,' S. D. Lee thought. "General Hood, the enemy is extremely well fortified. If I am correct, he will retire to the north side of the Duck by the morning. We will either attack a well-defended position, or an enemy that is not there. Either of which is not good for this army. And once General Schofield can successfully cross the Duck, then I believe the option for attack is denied. Our men will have to cross a river just to get to their defenses. Their artillery will ensure that whatever men reach their lines will be those that are surrendering. General Hood, I do not mean to object, but I feel strongly against the direct attack."

The red splotches that consumed Hood's face were not from the heat caused by the hearth. "Will these men ever be able to attack? General Johnston seems to have taught them all too well how to maneuver and fall back. I am beginning to seriously wonder about their ability to take the offensive. They must be taught again what it means to attack. It is a lesson lost here."

"General, I can assure that these men know how to attack,

we only want to be sure it is a well prepared attack," said Cheatham.

Hood spun on Cheatham, his eyes as wide as his height was tall. "What do you mean we? Are you all for this flanking move? Have my generals themselves also forgotten how to fight?" Hood reached for his crutch and hobbled towards the window. He peered towards the far distant east, in the direction of Forrest's cavalry.

"Perhaps we all need a lesson from the one man who is never unwilling to fight?" he said. And they all knew whom he meant.

"I am sorry, General," Cheatham said. "I did not mean to make it sound like you would not have my support. If you want to attack the city, only name the hour and my corps will be ready."

S. D. Lee and Stewart both flashed Cheatham a look of contempt. If he wanted to send his men in an attack that was doomed to fail, then he was not acting in the best interests of the Confederacy. To save this army from a frontal annihilation, S. D. Lee chose a different approach with Hood.

"General, I only ask you to think this over, and please keep in mind all of the stories that you have often told concerning Gettysburg. You yourself begged General Longstreet to not attack, but rather move around the flank. He could not convince Lee to see what was so obvious to you. The situation here is not that different. We still have an opportunity to cut the Federal forces off at the Harpeth. I do not believe that Thomas' command is as close to arriving us you may think. General Schofield would not have pulled back to the north end of the city if he had reinforcements en route."

The mention of Gettysburg extinguished Hood's temper quicker than a hot iron submerged into a bucket of water. Perhaps S. D. Lee was correct. A move around the Federal flank would force the Yankees out of their entrenchments. It was what he wanted to do in Gettysburg, and it was what Sherman had repeatedly done to this army until the fall of Atlanta. And hadn't Sherman's tactics worked brilliantly? No matter how strong the position General Johnston fortified, Sherman simply went around it. Perhaps it was time to start using that Yankee strategy against them.

"General, I thank you for your honesty in judgment," Hood said. Cheatham felt ashamed at his own willingness to follow his commander and not his heart. He kept his eyes averted from the other men in the room. "General Cheatham, are your men ready to advance on the right flank?"

"We have made all the preparations to cross the river, but there is a delay in the arrival of the pontoon bridges."

"General, first find those bridges and get them to the front. Secondly, have your men at the ready, as soon as those bridges are in place we will march to outflank the Federals again."

A great weight was lifted from the shoulders of the generals in the room. As much as they wanted to go on the offensive, the current position of the enemy was one that did not warrant an attack.

"And perhaps you are correct about General Thomas," Hood said to S.D. Lee. "He was one of my instructors back at West Point. I was not fond of his practices. During cavalry exercises, I would purposely cause my mount to gallop when Thomas ordered a trot. As our horses raced through the fields, we all would laugh as we heard Thomas shouting from the rear. Slow down, he would say, slow trot...slow trot. He would keep saying that until he could catch up with us. A common joke was to refer to him as slow trot behind his back.

"Well my old friend slow trot, let's hope that you can once again live up to your very fitting name."

*　　*　　*　　*　　*　　*　　*　　*

It was several hours since Hood's corps commanders had left him with his staff at the Warfield home. Hood was very tired and heavy with anticipation of the events that would mark the next few days. He tried to fight the urge for his laudanum, but failed. He took the bottle to the bedroom and there took enough sips to drown all of his concerns away. He was moments from sleeping when there was a soft knock at the door.

The sound reminded him that he had asked Chaplain Quintard to visit him at some point this evening. The chaplain was late, but always welcome. Hood was never ashamed of his physical appearance in front of Quintard. He stood up on one leg and took three unsteady hops to the door. He admitted Quintard into the room.

"I am sorry general, I did not know that you were already asleep."

"No bother chaplain, I was still awake."

The bottle of laudanum on the nightstand next to the bed caught the chaplain's attention. He did not like Hood to rely solely on the contents of the elixir for his comfort. The general needed to put his trust more in God and not in medicine for matters that would heal the heart. However, he was not here to chastise the General. "You asked to see me this evening, Sam?"

Hood hopped back to the bed, and sat upon it. Quintard pulled over a chair from the corner and moved it closer. "Sam, what is on your mind?"

"Chaplain, I have some very confused feelings about my commanders. Tonight after dinner, they all but denounced my plan of attack. I managed to agree with a reassessment, but I can't help feeling a certain lack of trust from them."

"I see, but I am sure that is not what was meant."

Hood continued as if he had not heard Quintard speak. "I really think that a quick strike would catch General Schofield by surprise. If I could find and gather seven hundred men who shared my conviction, I would lead them on one desperate charge against the enemy. And we would take that city... I know it. And at the same time, teach the rest of this army what it means to be an army."

Quintard looked at Hood and wondered if the man he was facing was indeed the general or an apocryphal impostor. How could seven hundred men take that city he thought? Again, the bottle of laudanum caught his attention. That is the work of the devil, he thought. He had seen it so many times before, where a prescribed medicine became abused, making strong men do wicked things. Seven hundred men would do nothing except fill seven hundred graves. Either that or receive the laurel crown to honor a valiant attempt at such an ill-conceived plan. "Sam, I am sorry to say it, but there are not seven hundred men in either army who could be said to be of your caliber."

Hood smiled. "And because of that Chaplain, we will march around Schofield again."

"Sam, I believe that is the right choice, God's choice. I believe that our Lord works in mysterious ways, and He has done so this evening. He has spoken to you through the three men you must trust most. You believe that His hand is in everything. If you see it that way, then your generals were not speaking against your orders, but rather speaking with a divine intervention for the good of the cause."

Hood stared past Quintard for several minutes, and then he began to nod his head in agreement. A smile founds its mark upon his face. "Chaplain, I do believe that you are correct. I will trust that this is God's intervention. It could be not other way. I will pray to Him tonight to continue to give me the strength to follow His plan. And if He does not mind, this army could use a break from this foul weather."

Quintard reached into his jacket and produced his Bible. He opened it and said a prayer out loud to the Lord above. He asked for God's continued blessings over General Hood and the men in his army. He asked that God continue to provide him with sound judgment in the days ahead. When he was finished, he helped Hood into bed and turned to leave. As he turned, Hood, very disoriented from the effects of the drug, reached for the chaplain's arm. He missed miserably.

"Chaplain, a moment with your Bible?" he asked.

Quintard handed Hood the Bible. The general closed his eyes and took a deep breath. He then thumbed through the pages and randomly pointed at a passage. Job 10: 18-22

"Why then have You brought me out of the womb?
Oh, that I had perished before and no eye had seen me!
I would have been as though I had not been.
I would have been carried from the womb to the grave.
Are not my days few?
Cease! Leave me alone, that I may take a little comfort,
Before I go to the place from which I shall not return,
To the land of darkness and the shadow of death,
A land as dark as darkness itself,
As the shadow of death, without any order
Where even the light is like darkness."

When the chaplain finished reading the passage, he was glad to see that Hood was already deep in sleep. There was no way Hood could have read the verse that fast. Judging from the amount of medicine he took, it was also doubtful if he would even remember having opened the Bible.

Quintard quietly closed the good book, then leaned over and kissed the troubled head of General John B. Hood.

Chapter XIII
November 28
Columbia, Tennessee

John Murphy awoke to the sight of a burning yellow sun over his head. Had he known that this morning's weather was the exact prayer that General Hood had asked the Lord the night before, he might have believed that God was for the Southern cause.

He squinted his eyes and turned over upon his side. His legs were an awful mess. They were stiff and cramped and in no condition for another day of marching. Trudging along as a captive to this rebellious army was the worst ordeal he had ever faced in his life. The men captured with him had all died from either hunger or the cold. He himself was barely hanging on in a wraith-like condition. Why were they even dragging him along, he often wondered?

The only thing that kept him willing to live was the thought of his escape. The sentries assigned to him had been very slack since the others had died. They hardly noticed his ghost like form trailing them in the march. That would be their mistake. After gathering as much information as he could, he planned on making his escape at the most opportune time.

As he looked down at his thinning arms, he realized that he did not have much time left to follow through as he planned. He needed to eat something very soon. From behind, he heard the sound of approaching footsteps.

"Hey Yank, morn' to you, this here is your lucky day," the guard said.

John turned over, and shaded his eyes with his hand. The morning sun silhouetted the figure before him. When his eyes were able to focus, he saw the face of the two guards assigned to him.

"You deaf Yank? Anyway, take some of this, compliments of the CSA."

John was handed a large portion of cornbread and a mug full of water. He eagerly consumed both, relishing in the taste of the crumbling stale bread. He thankfully washed it down his throat with the metallic taste of the water. A meal for a king, he thought.

"We also got some company coming for you," the Southerner said. "Several prisoners captured a few days ago are moving down our line. General Hood finally got you blue bellies on the run."

The taste of food had the instantaneous effect of revitalizing John's capacity to think. This soldier was in good spirits and eager to speak, he could not pass up this opportunity.

"Thank you for the breakfast reb. Most kind. But what makes you think we are running from you?"

"Because you only made it into Columbia by the skin of your teeth anyhow."

"And you think your army is large enough to carry the field?" John pried.

The Southerner looked to his fellow soldier and grinned a tooth-depleted smile. "We got over forty thousand Southern men ready to give you Yankees the whooping you deserve."

"Wow that is a large force. Does that include the cavalry?"

The Southerner looked puzzled. "I reckon it does, if not, well General Forrest must have over seven thousand men."

Before John could continue his questioning, the other Federal prisoners had arrived. There were half a dozen of them, led by three armed Confederates. John nodded at each and fell silent.

"Well Yank, I hope these friends of yours can last a bit lot longer than the others. I am truly sorry for that, wish we could have done more for them."

Just then, a tumultuous yell bellowed from the far distant front. It caught momentum as it carried through the camp, finally exploding the rebel yell in the rear. There were loud sounds of whooping and cheering. John stood up and tried to discern the cause. Some event had obviously turned in the rebel's favor. Had they just won a battle?

The Southern sentries looked as confused as their captured Yankee prisoners did, but they raised their hands and cheered all the same. It would not be a long time until they all discovered the answer. They would be moving again very soon.

*   *   *   *   *   *   *   *

In the early morning, the corps of General Steven D. Lee cautiously marched towards the outskirts of Columbia. For a city that was supposed to house an entire Federal army, the place was unnaturally quiet. Upon closer inspection, it became obvious that Schofield had abandoned the place. In the distance, the flames of the burning railroad bridge flickered its glowing hues in confirmation of the enemy's retreat. Stephen Lee said a quiet prayer of thanks, knowing that Hood could not change his mind and order an assault on the city... for the enemy was clearly gone. Schofield must have evacuated late in the night, just as he predicted at dinner. Still, he sent his men into the city in an orderly fashion. He did not want to have his corps caught off guard from any surprise counter attack.

At the first sight of his troops triumphant entrance to the city, the inhabitants were beyond any measure of jubilation. They cheered from their windows, porches, rooftops and the streets. It was the first time in a long time that he and his men were cheered for in victory. It was exulting. Stephen Lee's corps returned the welcoming cheer with the much-famed rebel yell. The yell caught momentum throughout the city, and gathered force as it went. By the time it reached the rest of Hood's army back in camp, it crashed like an enormous tidal wave.

Stephen Lee let his men enjoy the moment, but there was still a Federal army positioned on the northern side of the Duck River. The realization was bittersweet. His men had just liberated Columbia, but the enemy had wisely fallen back to a position that was much more defensible. If Hood did not follow up as he agreed last night, by flanking the Federals out of position, his men would have to cross the river, while being fired upon, reform on the opposite bank and charge a fortified position.

He shuddered at the thought.

He immediately took an account of his surroundings and began issuing orders to his staff. Food and supplies were to be appropriated for the use of Hood's army. There was also the matter of positioning to attend to. He could not let his men just disperse within the city. Order must be kept, his men would have to be ready to attack or march upon a moment's notice.

He needed ground that was advantageous to his corps deployment in the area. He found it opposite the Federal position, on his side of the Duck. The earth there was elevated over the river giving him exactly what he needed. Artillery was quickly placed upon that high ground overlooking the Federals across the river. Perhaps the enemy would risk an attack on his own lines, he fruitlessly hoped.

Stephen Lee sat upon his horse and watched as the first battery of artillery was unlimbering upon the hill. He looked back towards the enemy, hoping to see them forming for an attack, but none came. The Duck River stood between the two combatants like a mother between her two angry sons. Upon closer inspection, Stephen Lee noted that the river had fallen dramatically since the flooding from the day before. Very soon, it would be crossable. Mother would no longer be there to stop her babies from killing each other.

He took one last look across the river before constructing a dispatch that would be sent to Hood.

'Columbia is secured from the enemy. The people of the city are wild with cheer. Will await your orders. P.S. It appears that the level of the river has fallen, perhaps there are some fords now accessible for crossing farther down the flank.'

He handed the letter to his adjutant and watched the officer ride away. Stephen Lee needed some time to think...and to pray. He added that last P.S. as a further reinforcement of his convictions against any form of frontal attack.

"General Hood, please do not assault this position," he whispered. He then turned his mount and rode towards his staff. This morning had been auspicious, but there was plenty of sunlight left to accomplish more. Whatever orders came back from Hood, Stephen Lee's corps would be ready.

He just hoped that they would not call for him to cross the Duck and charge head first into that wall of blue.

*   *   *   *   *   *   *   *

Hood awoke to a pounding clatter in his head. The pain was so intense, that it made his movements dizzied. He saw the bottle of laudanum on the nightstand beside his bed, and realized that he may have had a little too much the night before. The sun had not fully risen. Its light a somber golden glow slipping into his room through drawn drapes.

A hot cup of tea was brought to him, and he sat for several long moments in solitude. He put his hand upon the warm mug, and let the heat filter through his body. He brought the cup closer to his face and inhaled the rich aroma while slowly blowing cooling air upon the surface of his drink. With steady lips he sipped his morning awake.

His head began to clear. He reached to the side of his bed and grabbed his artificial leg. With a melancholic routine he fitted the limb to the stump of his leg and secured it. Hood quickly dismissed his saddened mood. His conversations with Chaplain Quintard were coming to him in bits and pieces. He was remembering his covenant with God. He was not to question him anymore. From this day on, there was a renewed trust between Hood and his Maker. If the Lord had it in His plan to humble Hood with the loss of limbs, then he would have to accept that.

With his head clearing, Hood approached the window and pulled the drapes. He was met by a glorious morning. Hood felt chills populate his back as he remembered his prayer before he went to sleep. It was miraculous. He had asked God for a break in the weather and God had answered his prayer. Hood had never before felt so close to the Lord.

Hood heard noises begin to stir outside his room. There was and excited commotion building amongst his officers. He turned to get dressed when he heard the tumultuous cheers coming from Columbia. At that same moment, two of his staff officers knocked at the door and entered the room. The joy on their faces was one not seen in the army in a long time.

"General Hood, Columbia is ours. General Schofield has fled before us."

Hood let out a cheer to rival the one that came from the liberated Southern city. "Gentleman, this is great news."

"General Lee's corps is positioning in the city now. Initial word is that the enemy had vacated during the night. We are awaiting a dispatch from the city." The officer cautiously presented a dispatch from the fold of his uniform. "We thought this was from General Stephen Lee, but it was not."

Hood eyed the letter with concern. Judging from his officer's presentation of the dispatch, he quickly concluded whom it was from. "Please read it to me."

The two officers looked at each other nervously. The one with the letter was silently pleading to the other to read it. Realizing that since he held the dispatch, he would have to read it, he tried to get it over with as fast as possible.

He quickly opened the letter and kept his eyes upon it. "It is from General Beauregard," he said. "General Sherman is rapidly progressing toward the Atlantic seacoast. His goal is most assuredly to reinforce Grant in his battle against General Lee. It is essential you should take the offensive and crush the enemy's forces in Middle Tennessee as soon as practicable, to relieve Lee."

When the officer finished reading the dispatch, he braced himself for Hood's verbal retaliation and sworn oaths against Beauregard. What he got instead was a full-hearted laugh. The officer looked up from his letter and saw a general that he did not know.

"You can inform General Beauregard that the enemy has evacuated Columbia this morning. Our forces are entering the city triumphantly. The enemy is no doubt in full retreat towards Nashville, and we are in full pursuit."

The officers waited for more, but Hood simply smiled. Feeling awkward, they retired from the room to write Hood's dispatch and send it to Beauregard.

Hood walked back towards the window to think. Now that Schofield had retired from the city, what was he to do? God had granted his prayer by clearing the weather, now it was up to him to make the most of it.

He heard a rider approach the house and watched the officer dismount. He thought he recognized the young man, an officer that served under General Stephen Lee. The man handed one of his staff a dispatch, then returned to his horse to await orders. Hood listened for the footsteps as another one of his officers knocked at his door. Hood called for him to enter and eagerly took the dispatch. He was correct, it was from General Stephen Lee. He read it in silence, then told his officer to relay back to General Lee that he should continue to fortify his position until he received further orders. The officer repeated the message and ran back to the front of the house. Within moments, Hood heard Lee's officer galloping back towards Columbia.

Hood decided that his best course was to call for a council. He wanted his corps commanders present to help him decide the very important next few hours of this day. The same exhilarating thought that swelled his mind last night had resurfaced. He felt the compelling urge to ride to the front and lead a gallant assault upon the Federal forces. "Hit them right here, right now, while we have them outnumbered," he gritted. If his generals were present at this moment, he was sure he would give them the order to attack. But then he remembered the words of his chaplain. It was God who spoke through his generals last night. The frontal attack was not the right command, not this day. The glorious sun that poured through his open window was the proof of that conviction.

God is with me, he thought.

*   *   *   *   *   *   *   *

It was a meeting centered around a breakfast table, but no one was eating. It was still early in the morning, and a sense of urgency suffocated the ambiance within the room. General's S.D. Lee, Cheatham, Stewart and Forrest all stared ahead with a grim sense of determination. Hood had once again assembled his corps commanders.

The situation at hand called for one of two measures. Either Hood advanced his entire army against the Federals entrenched across the Duck, or he moved around them.

Every inch of his body ached for one fantastic assault. He had the enemy pinned down and outnumbered. He would eagerly strap himself to his horse and lead the attack if must be. And deep down, he knew that that was exactly how it would have to be if it were to be done. His generals would not support his attack. They were very clear in their opinion that they should circumvent the Federal force to their front. This would cause the Federals to fall back, or risk being cut off from Nashville.

The more Hood thought on it, it was the less heroic, but more favorable approach to victory. Back east, during the winter of '62, he had witnessed first hand the folly of an ill-supported attack against a fortified position. The Union army led by General Burnside tried to throw their superior numbers against the slopes of the hills at Fredericksburg. The result was a Union massacre. Longstreet stood behind his fortifications and easily broke each wave of Federals that tried to reach his front. Hood could remember Longstreet gloating as he wished Burnside would send his entire army at him. When the carnage had subsided, the Federal dead and wounded covered the slopes like a blanket of torn flesh.

That would not happen to his army here on the slopes of Columbia. Instead, Hood would listen to his Lord's words spoken through his generals. He would choose the circuitous route around the enemy's flank and force them from their position. Once again, he would borrow a page painfully learned from the tactics of General Sherman. If the enemy is dug in, simply move around him.

The concept was easy enough, but the problem he faced was that he needed to keep Schofield in place long enough for him to position his army between Schofield and Nashville. If Schofield got the jump on him, he could easily outpace Hood along interior lines and win the race to Nashville. If he did that, Schofield would augment the size of General Thomas' army and would diminish the superiority in numbers that Hood was counting on.

"General Hood," Forrest said, breaking the silence that captivated the room. "What are your plans? My cavalry is eager to make amends for the lost race to Columbia."

Nathan Bedford Forrest had spent a long few days brooding over his inability to reach Columbia before the Federals. Although it appeared that he narrowly lost the race, being turned back by Cox's brigade at the steps of the city, it was later learned that had he actually been able to capture Columbia, it would have been hell to hold it. At the time, there were more Federal infantry in the area and they were much closer to the city than Hood's. Forrest's cavalry could very well have gained the city, only to be cut off from Hood and annihilated.

Forrest doubted that. If it would have been hell to hold the city, who else but the devil to lead the defense? Forrest did not dwell on the repercussions of being trapped in the city, instead he thought of how he could have held it against the Federals, as Hood arrived and attacked the Yankees from the rear.

For the past three days, Forrest let his men take brief furloughs in reward for their stolen victory. He did not give himself that same luxury. He was savoring the moment when he could attain his retribution. Realizing that the Duck River would offer the enemy a natural obstacle for defense, he instructed his men to find fords that were suitable for a flank crossing. Regardless of Hood's final decision, there was no way he was going to let his men cross the enemy's front.

His inquiry paid off when local citizens of Columbia responded with alacrity. They showed his troopers several fords that could be used to cross the Duck River. With the recent fall of the river level, these fords were now accessible and he readied his cavalry for mobilization.

"My plan, General Forrest, is to march around the Federal flank. Have your men find a ford that can be crossed..."

Forrest was raising his hand to cut the general off. "We have already done so. There are four fords that I feel can now be crossed. I have my command ready at your word."

Hood was impressed. "Excellent. Most excellent. General Lee, your corps is already situated across from the enemy?"

"Yes sir."

"And from your dispatch, I presume that you have your artillery in position overlooking the north side of the Duck?"

"Yes sir, all my batteries are in position," Lee said.

"Excellent work. When the command is given, your artillery will show force to the Yankee front. I need you to convince the enemy that we intend to stay in place, as if in preparation for a frontal assault. We cannot afford to let Schofield slip from us again."

"Won't he be alerted to this move once his cavalry reports that Forrest is attempting to cross his flank?" Stewart asked.

"He will, but that is why I need General Lee's batteries to threaten his front. They must hit the enemy with enough shell so as to convince them that we are preparing for an attack with infantry."

"And you are sure that Schofield will buy into this ploy?" Cheatham asked.

Hood smiled as if he knew a secret that the others did not. "I have faith in the Lord in this General."

Cheatham looked at his commander with a dubious frown. Hood was not kidding. His whole body was never so much alive. He looked like the fighting commander of old, the one that led his men under the command of Longstreet. Perhaps he was possessed by the fever of the Lord, or maybe he was just exalted with battle lust. Whatever it was, this current offensive had reawakened the soul of John Bell Hood.

Forrest agreed with Hood's assumptions, but not because of any theological deity. "General Hood, I do believe you have an excellent point. If I may, I would further add that General Schofield has probably been given the order to hold us below the Duck River. That would explain their retiring to better ground last night. It is also clear that the enemy is in no position to attack us at this point. I would gather General Schofield is probably very frightened at this moment. He must keep us here for as long as he can, possibly until Thomas arrives with reinforcements. He will be afraid to take the initiative. Schofield was tardy in vacating Pulaski when it was apparent we were racing to cut him off, and only by seconds did he beat my boys to this city. General Hood, that will not happen again, I promise you. Schofield will not retire from his position until it is too late. This time, I will cut him at off at any point you choose."

"Thank you General, I will hold you to that. Then it is decided, Forrest will begin by moving the cavalry across the fords. General Lee, have your artillery readied for my command to attack. General Cheatham and Stewart, please investigate where my pontoon bridges are, and have your infantry ready to cross upon their completion over the Duck. Please tell all your men that General Hood congratulates them on their efforts thus far. But I will need them again. The Army of Tennessee is once again moving forward."

Chapter XIV
That Afternoon
Columbia, Tennessee

Schofield had started the day in complete command of the situation. The lines of communication had been reopened between his headquarters and Nashville, prompting him to send a telegram to Thomas, informing his superior that his retiring to the north side of the Duck was on his own initiative and by no means a forced retreat.

Soon after he sent that message, his sturdy foundation began to crack into a thousand tiny pieces. A rebel prisoner had told his officers that Hood was planning to move around his current position. He immediately began to second-guess his decision. He had sent another message to Thomas telling him that he may have to pull back farther, in the event he is outflanked. In the few minutes following the completion of that telegram, Schofield once again changed his mind.

The rebel prisoner may have truly believed that Hood was preparing to march around Columbia, but the constant barrage of artillery that pounded his defenses said otherwise. And as long as the enemy artillery was to his front, then so must Hood. A third telegram was issued, this time to advise Thomas that Schofield would hold the fords nearest to Columbia and prevent any crossing attempted by Hood's army. The Confederate cavalry was fully expected to cross any of the numerous fords, but Schofield assured Thomas that Wilson's troopers would contain the threat.

Since sending those last telegrams to Thomas in Nashville, Schofield already began harboring thoughts of despair-ridden pessimism. He had one of his aid's summon General Wilson. He needed his cavalry commander to get into the field and provide him with the most accurate reports of the enemy's progress.

General James L. Wilson soon entered the headquarters of General Schofield and was befuddled by the greeting he received from his commander. Schofield looked up at him, and gestured for him to enter the room. Then he turned his back to the young officer and began pacing the room.

Wilson was incredulous as he watched Schofield pace the floors of his headquarters. This was a time for action and commanding, not pacing, he thought. It did not take the young cavalry officer long to realize that General Schofield was not a man made from the same substance as General Thomas. He made a mental note to report this to Grant as soon as he could.

It was almost a comical sight to witness, forcing Wilson to exercise great effort in order to resist the urge to laugh. In his hurried pacing throughout the room, the short, balding, and corpulent Schofield looked amorphous. He was anything but the picture perfect general that West Point painted for all its aspiring cadets. There was more sweat glued to his pasty white forehead than there was water in the Duck River.

The only break in this steady rhythm of pacing was the sound of rebel artillery firing from afar. The sound of the blast would cause Schofield's neck to tic. The mental state of this man was obviously not rooted in solid ground.

Schofield had stopped pacing and quickly turned on his cavalry commander. "General Wilson, we need to know more."

Wilson raised a handsome eyebrow. "General, I have reported all I have. The enemy is forming to our front, upon the south bank of the Duck River."

"I know that…, I know that, I can see that. But is it a feint? This is what is so confusing to me. The rebel privates captured yesterday were very convincing in that Hood would circumvent our position. But, I was schooled with General Hood. I know him, he wants to attack us here, on this ground. Hood would like nothing more but to charge us like a maddened bull. The sight of his men deploying openly to our front confirms that. Are the fords still covered?"

"Of course General, you needn't worry about them. If Forrest tries to attempt a crossing, you will be notified immediately."

Schofield finally let out some air. His slumping shoulders regained their posture. "What do you think Hood will do? The fords are no longer flooded. He could attempt a crossing far to our flank, but that is not like him. John Bell Hood once told me how he chased a force of Indians across the open dessert. Those Indians were making for the Mexican border, outnumbering him by almost four to one. That did not deter his pursuit. He did not even send a dispatch for help. He was so adamant on capturing the Indians, he did not give much thought to what he would do once they were attained. Out manned four to one, and he just assumed he could catch up with the enemy and defeat them. That is how that man thinks. Hood is excellent at bringing his men to the field, wherever that may be, but he only knows how to do one thing when he arrives, and that is to simply cock his fists and brawl. With that in mind, let me ask you again, do you think Hood will try to cross the fords?"

Wilson gave the matter the briefest of moments before answering. "General Schofield, I would not be one to attack this position. We are fortified here, and if the enemy tries to circumvent us, well then we are in excellent positions to impede their advance. I was not with you at Pulaski, but I can assure you, Forrest will not get the jump on my command. If Hood acts as you say, then he better be prepared for the defeat of his career. I do not think any army can take our current position."

The color started to reappear in blotches on Schofield's face. "Good. Very good."

The sound of hurried steps approaching from the outside brought their attention to the door. There was a quick knock and Wilson opened the door. It was an officer from Colonel Capron's brigade. The man's eyes were wide with anticipation. That was not a good sign.

"General Schofield, General Wilson, Colonel Capron reports that the enemy's cavalry is forcing their way across the Duck River, north of Huey's Mill at the Lewisburg Pike crossing."

Schofield looked to Wilson, "Where… How far is that?"

Wilson remained calm as counter plans were already forming in his head. "It is roughly eight miles to our left flank. How long ago was this first reported?"

The officer had replied that it was received shortly before noon. This urgent message was already two hours old. Wilson knew he had to act quickly. Was it just the rebel cavalry crossing on a scouting mission, or was it a full mobilization? He needed to get back to his own headquarters and brief his staff. He did not want to alarm the volatile Schofield, but intuition told him that this was not a probe by the enemy. Forrest was attempting to gain the north side of the Duck. The problem with his acting on his intuition was the source of the dispatch. The colonel who sent it was one of the many whose force had been decisively routed several times by Forrest in the preceding weeks. Was the dispatch from a reliable source, or a colonel facing an intimidating foe? Wilson had to find out for himself.

To Wilson's surprise, Schofield remained stoic. "General Wilson, please investigate this report. I fully expected Forrest to cross the fords at some point. He is to be your concern not mine. With the rebel infantry still deployed in our front, I doubt that we are facing a serious threat to our flank, at least for the moment. If the infantry to our front gives any indication that it intends to pull back, I expect to be notified immediately."

Wilson promised to keep Schofield informed, but he was not so sure of Schofield's assumption that this reported crossing was not yet a major concern. He saluted Schofield and took his leave. He followed the officer down the stairs and mounted his horse. The two rode east towards Wilson's headquarters.

The young cavalry commander felt his head swell as he contemplated the best decision for this new turn of events. He galloped through a surrealistic fog of Union gunpowder as he listened to the banter of the futile artillery duel with the forces across the river.

'Someone needs to quiet these batteries,' he thought. 'Some of us need to think.' Unfortunately, none of the Union artillerymen could hear his thoughts and they kept up the slow, but steady exchange of fire.

Wilson succumbed to casual acceptance of the noise, though he still could not understand why both sides accepted a needless waste of ammunition by firing their cannon at ranges that were too far to cause any real damage.

The only real damage that could occur over the next few hours was the damage to his reputation. Wilson was not one of the youngest major generals without reason. He had worked hard at establishing himself amongst some very important people in the Union hierarchy. At the top of that list was General Grant. Grant held him in such high esteem that he sent the young cavalry commander west in order to organize and command all of Sherman's cavalry. Wilson felt a strong sense of loyalty and respect for Grant, and he did not want to let him down.

Until now, Wilson had not had a major impact on the cavalry engagements that had occurred since Hood's advance. All he knew of the command that he now had was that they had spent the past several days disorganized and herded north by their rebel counterparts. Wilson often contemplated what actions he would take the day he was in command and opposed the forces of General Forrest.

It appeared the time had come.

And for all his preparation against various strategies, he was currently at a loss. Schofield was convinced that Hood was still in his front. And he was right. However, there were reports that Forrest's cavalry was attempting a crossing on one of the fords east of Columbia. Would Hood allow his cavalry to cross the Duck and risk it being cut off from the infantry?

To this point of his career, Wilson had been instrumental in the strengthening and effectiveness of the Union cavalry. He saw things like none other, and his thinking was not limited to the battlefield. Logistically, Wilson asserted his obdurate will over the recently created Cavalry Bureau. His reputation as a stubborn, adamant and unlovable negotiator helped remove horse contractors that were suspected of committing shady deals with the Union army. The end result provided the Federal cavalry with more horses for the money.

Yet on the day he needed such fortitude to face the likings of Nathan Bedford Forrest, Wilson found his decision-making skills to be tenebrous.

'General Wilson," Capron's officer riding alongside him said. "That officer riding to us is from my division as well."

Wilson looked ahead and saw several of his staff riding towards them as well. In the middle was the man that the officer referred to. The group was rapidly approaching with a strong sense of urgency.

"General Wilson," one of his staff members said. "This is Captain Johnson. He has another dispatch from Colonel Capron."

The young captain handed Wilson a blood stained dispatch. Wilson avoided the blood by carefully placing his fingers on the dry parchment. He noted that the captain had a severe cut on his right palm.

This dispatch was more recent than the last one he received from Capron, but it was still almost two hours old. It read that Capron was forced to retreat up the Lewisburg Pike as a superior force was pressing him.

"Captain, the name of the ford above the Lewisburg Pike currently escapes me."

"Hardison's Mill, sir," the captain said.

"Please bandage that hand quickly, then with God's speed report back to Colonel Capron and tell him he is to hold his ground at all costs. He is not permitted to fall back and let the enemy gain the north side of the Duck. Reinforcements will be sent to aid him. Is this understood?"

"Yes sir," the captain said. Without giving his bleeding hand much thought, he turned his mount and raced back towards the Lewisburg Pike. The officer carrying the original dispatch accompanied Wilson and his staff towards their headquarters.

Wilson had not realized it, but he had already set the stage for the strategy he would command against this rebel threat. It was not one that he was comfortable with. It was hard for Wilson to believe, but it was only a few months ago, back in September, when he led Sheridan's cavalry across the Opequon in the Shenandoah Valley. Being on the offensive was a much easier task to control. You simply selected a point of attack, and then you attacked it.

Now, in Tennessee, the boot was on the other foot. It was Wilson who had to guess where the enemy would attack, and be able to be in a position to thwart it. Somehow, he needed to anticipate Forrest's next move. Wilson knew that he only needed to contend himself with the immediate threat. Hood's infantry was not his problem, they seemed content to occupy the south bank of the Duck and trade ineffective volleys of cannon fire that did nothing but inflate the vainglorious ego of the artillery corps.

With Hood removed from the equation, Wilson could now focus on Forrest. Wilson had been studying maps of the surrounding area. If Forrest was crossing the Hardison Mill Ford, then he must be trying to get himself in a position between Schofield and Nashville. If Wilson were Forrest, he would be real careful not to expose his unsupported cavalry too close to the Union lines. He would choose to ride past the Yanks at Columbia and occupy a position across the Rutherford Creek. Forrest could then dismount his troopers and establish a strong defensive position. Wilson figured that this is when Hood would launch that offensive attack that Schofield feared. Hood could press from the front, while Forrest threatened the rear.

Or perhaps Forrest planned to use enough force to threaten Schofield's rear and cause him to fall back before Hood attacked. Either way, if the rebel cavalry were allowed to cross the Duck in force, they would have an excellent opportunity to force Schofield out of Columbia. Wilson knew that this would allow Hood to gain the north bank of the Duck, an advance that was not acceptable to General Thomas in Nashville.

If Forrest was pushing across the Duck, then he was hitting Hardison's Mill with everything. Wilson understood that for Forrest's plan to be effective, he must clear the ford, gain the north bank and move on before Union reinforcements could arrive.

Wilson began issuing dogmatic orders to his staff. All cavalry in the area was to be sent to reinforce Capron's brigade. Several officers pointed out that this would remove a substantial force guarding the other three main fords closer to Columbia. Wilson was belligerent.

"Forrest will not divide his force. Even if he were to, it would be to advance past our position and gain our rear. He will not risk exposing his troopers to our infantry. There is a crossing north of the Lewisburg Pike, I believe that it is called Hurt's Crossroads. Instruct Croxton and Hatch to have their cavalry defend that position. Forrest cannot harm us unless he gets around our position. What that devil will find is that he will hit our position and be forced to pull back. We can then swing upon him from the rear and decimate his force. Forrest has finally made the mistake that will cost him. He will be cut off from Hood and destroyed."

Wilson's staff erupted in a frenzy of commotion. Orders were hastily written and messengers were sent to the front. Wilson took a private moment to congratulate himself on such a brilliant strategy. He thought of how proud Grant was going to be when he learned that James L Wilson had destroyed the infamous cavalry of Nathan Forrest.

Wilson was so absorbed with pride in his ability to devise a strategy based on what he would do if he were Forrest, that he neglected one simple fact.

He was not Nathan Bedford Forrest.

*   *   *   *   *   *   *   *

The 5th Iowa cavalry, a contingent of Capron's brigade, watched the ford at Hardison Mill with knowing anticipation. The thought of the enemy crossing the cold waters of the Duck River at this time of the year was enough to make the sturdiest of men shiver. The river, several hundred yards wide, rolled north of Columbia like a massive green slug. Its surface was covered in calm ripples that were caused by the cold wind. The men guarding this ford knew that the waters would not remain calm for much longer. The Confederate cavalry had already tried several attempts to rush the ford, but were repulsed each time. What scared the 5th Iowa was that the numbers of Confederates that made the charge, increased with each attempt. They knew full well that had it not been for the Duck River as an obstacle between them, they would have been routed hours ago.

Several members of the Union cavalry actually felt sorry for the enemy cavalry. Trying to gain the north bank was not any easy task. They had to wade their mounts across a freezing river, before attempting to rush a well-defended position. Those that made it halfway became barn-side targets for Union marksmen.

Still they came, trying to establish a foothold on the north side of the river. The evidence of their previous attempts lay scattered across the battlefield. The lucky ones were killed outright. There were some that were shot and dropped into the river. Their wounds too severe to allow for the opportunity to swim back to the other side, they were forced to endure a drowning death. The only horror more abysmal than actually drowning was having to watch those poor men breathe their last.

It was a sight that made the most hardened Union cavalrymen remorseful. For the Federals guarding the crossing, the melancholic lamentation was a sojourn. As soon as one wave of rebels broke, a new wave would stampede across the ford. The enemy would rush forward with wild determination, knowing that if they did not make it across, their fate would be as their brothers who lay broken before them.

And so the tragedy would repeat itself.

The sound of the rapidly approaching rebel cavalry was muffled by the wet mud, but was still loud enough to alert the Union cavalry guarding the ford. General Buford was sending his gray troops again. Would he never learn?

Capron's brigade watched as the enemy advanced with the same enthusiasm as those that tried earlier. The first few attempts did have the Union cavalry apprehensive. But those attacks had failed miserably for the Confederates. Worse than that, they had given the 5th Iowa the experience to understand that all that was expected from them was to stay put and fire. It was a very reinforcing concept. As long as everyone fired as fast as they could, the rebels would eventually dwindle and fall back.

This time would be no different. Capron went up and down his line, steadying his men. He waited until the rebels were within a range that promoted accurate and effective firing, and gave the command to shoot at will.

In one loud flash, the leading mounts of the attack were rider-less. Those rebels riding behind the first casualties had to avoid crashing into the horses that were no longer under human command. The beasts became frenzied and broke in random directions in search of escape. The chaos cost the momentum of the charge, and Capron eagerly directed his men to keep firing into the enemy.

Another flash of gunfire, more smoke clouding the air, and more rebels lay shattered upon the ground. Capron tried to see through the smoke, to ascertain the enemy's next move. He would have known had he been blind. The rebel yell gave the gray cavalry away. They continued to come. This time, they were advancing closer to his lines. Capron understood he was rapidly approaching the point in a battle, when one lost total command of the situation. When the enemy is at a distance and you have a clear field of fire, it is a battle best led by the officers in command. But when the men become intermingled, and the smoke of gunpowder fills the air, and screams can be heard from every direction, it becomes a battle that is decided by the men who are bleeding. He did not want it to reach that point.

Another strong volley discharged from his lines and the rebel yell was extinguished like a torch dunked into the ocean. When the smoke finally cleared, Buford's men had pulled back across the ford. They would not be coming back today. Though Capron was victorious, he was relieved. The last attack was close. If the rebels managed to make it to his lines, then they would be able to charge in reserves and push his outnumbered cavalry back up the Lewisburg Pike. Capron's losses were light, but he knew if he did not get reinforcements soon, the rebels would eventually succeed.

Capron retired back up the road. As he passed he con-gratulated his officers with much relief. He dismounted towards a nearby tree and put his back against its thick bark before letting his legs collapse. It had been an exhausting day.

With a trembling hand, he wiped his sweaty brow and for

the first time in a long while, was proud of his cavalry's performance. His brigade had spent all morning and afternoon contesting the crossing of the Hardison Mill Ford. This ford represented the eastern most flank of the army. If the Confederates were able to gain this position, they could easily force the entire Union army out of position.

Several times his outnumbered men found the courage to turn back the charging advances of Forrest's cavalry. General Buford had led his Confederates on charge after charge, but he could not avail. This day clearly belonged to Horace Capron and the Union cavalry.

For Capron, the victory was long overdue.

The tide had finally turned, as his brigade was able to stand its ground and drive the enemy from the field. Rectitude was the word that came to mind. Had he had the energy to inflate his chest, he would have popped the buttons from his jacket.

He heard his name being called from behind the tree. Capron stood up and saw three of his staff officers approaching. With them was Captain Johnson, the man he sent with the urgent dispatch to Wilson almost four hours ago.

"Captain, what has General Wilson said?"

The captain closed his eyes as he reported the message from Wilson. It was obvious that he had the details rehearsed somewhere in his cognitive shell.

"General Wilson reports that you are not to fall back, and that the enemy is not permitted to gain this side of the Duck."

Capron gave his officers a look of disbelief. "That is what he said? I need him to tell me that? Captain, my men are holding this ground with their lives, you better have more than that."

The officer was shaken. "Yes sir. Reinforcements are on the way."

That was the message that Capron needed to hear. Knowing fresh troops were on the way, the colonel was able to finally relax. He noticed that the captain's hand was mangled. His curled knuckles revealed a deep purplish clot that oozed and dripped down each of his fingers. "Captain, that is excellent news. It is getting dark, as the days are so short this time of year. Please attend to that wound upon your hand at once."

Captain Johnson smiled and retired to find a surgeon. Capron called for his mount. When an officer brought it over, he quickly hopped into the saddle. Capron stared towards the sky and marked the westward position of the sun. "I am retiring to the rear for the night. Tell Major Young that he has command of this field. The enemy will not try to cross again today, but we are to remain vigilant. Tell the major to expect reinforcements some time this night. If Buford tries to cross this ford in the morning, he will be in for a nasty bite."

The officer shared a grin with Capron before saluting. Capron then stirred his mount north up the Lewisburg Pike in the direction of his reserves. He wanted to have these troops readied for action in the morning.

He had chosen to return to the rear without his staff. He wanted some time to clear his mind from the day's events and assuage his mind in a place that was relaxing as well as very far away. It only took him a moment to transition from this war and place his soul at work on his farm.

If Horace Capron would give up his command for any-thing in the world, it would be to pursue his interests in agriculture and farming management. Capron loved the challenge of developing new ways to produce a better crop. It was providence. With his own hands and with his ingenuity, he had the power to create a farming system that allowed for maximum productivity. The harvest that was collected after a season of caring was his reward. It was exhilarating. Capron was almost enveloped in his contemplation when he once again heard his name being called from behind. Capron brought his mount to a stop to allow his staff to catch up with him. A new dispatch had arrived from General Wilson.

Capron took the letter and opened it. At first, the tremors did not stir his spine as they should have. It was upon his second time through the letter that Capron realized his brigade was in dire jeopardy.

The dispatch had informed him, that he was still to hold the north bank of the Duck, but could fall back up the Lewisburg Pike if necessary. A few miles north of the pike was a point called Hurt's Crossroads. Croxton and Hatch had already been informed to move their troops to that position and fortify the road against any advance of the enemy.

Capron could not have farmed a tomato with a color as red as the hue that saturated his face. "What is General Wilson thinking? These matters of commanding an army are not any different than farming the land. Things must be done with thought.

You cannot plant anywhere you fancy. Every seed must be placed where it will most benefit the other seeds. Too much in one area will strangle out production, while too little would fall victim to the environment. And if you build an irrigation system and build dams at several key intervals, you can prevent the environment, in this case the water, from flowing at will. As long as all the key areas are dammed, you can control the level of irrigation. If you allow some of those damns to be opened, then you allow for a deluge."

The officers were completely lost by their commander's baffling outburst. "Sir, we do not know what the General has written you."

Capron shot a fiery stare at the officer. "The general has ordered Croxton and Hatch to our rear. We are to fall back upon their position."

The officer was not afraid to carry on his questioning. "So we now have reinforcement to fall back upon. Forgive me Colonel, but I do not understand your ire."

Capron looked at his officer, as an officer for the last time. One should learn not to speak at all if they did not understand a situation. "You do not understand my ire? Well let me ask you this. How old is your dispatch?"

"Over an hour."

"So over an hour ago, Croxton and Hatch have been instructed to vacate their positions to our west and retire to our rear. They were protecting the fords on our right flank. They are no longer doing so. For all intents and purposes, there is no one guarding the fords to our right. This means that Forrest can cross the Duck without fail. He has probably done so already. That means that Forrest now stands between our position and the rest of the Union army. We are cut off. So now do you understand my ire?"

The officer's face cast a white glow.

"If you want to keep your rank, you had better report back to Major Young and tell him to be ready. Advise him that I feel that Forrest is already over the river, and may fall upon us at any time. As much as I believe this is true, I cannot allow us to give up the ford at Hardison Mill at this time. Tell the major to fall back at first sign of a flank attack from the enemy. I will gather the reserve force and send orders from there. Now go!"

Capron watched the officer ride into the distance, then he turned to the other members of his staff. "Let us hurry, every second matters here."

The small party raced their horses up the pike. It was not long before they reached his reserves. Capron had just dismounted and begun shouting commands when the enemy burst into the Federal rear. His command was caught completely off guard. They were the reserve force, their position was not supposed to be vulnerable. The emergence of the rebel cavalry this far behind the Union troops guarding the fords caused an immediate panic. Where had they come from, how many were there? And they had come from the west, cutting them off from the main Union force.

Capron mustered enough men to offer a momentary resistance. But too many of his troops chose to drop their guns and turn tail. His command had disintegrated with his cavalry running in the opposite direction from the fords.

Capron hopped back upon his horse. It was once again time for his cavalry to flee.

*   *   *   *   *   *   *   *

Nathan Bedford Forrest led the charge that caught the Federal reserve force completely off guard. With his uniform still wet from the cold dark waters of the Duck River, he moved like a nefarious shadow through the ranks of fleeing Federals. His two hands were stretched out before him, emptying the contents of his pistols with deadly accuracy. An eruption of gunfire would briefly mark the infamous general's presence in the midst of the Yankee troops, but before they could react, he had moved on with the night. When his pistols were out of bullets, he quickly replaced them in his holster and brandished his glimmering saber. With a ferocity that belied a human being, he slashed at whatever blue uniform came across his path.

His goal was to not drive this reserve force from the field, but to annihilate it. The Federals had managed to put up a temporary resistance, but it quickly crumbled. Forrest capriciously continued to race ahead of his regiment undaunted by the sea of Union troops that parted before him. His momentum gained as he heard the sound of Jackson's division rout the Federal force. His pride needed this victory to make amends for his having lost the race to Columbia.

Forrest himself did not know how he could see so well in

the gathering dark, perhaps he was the demon the Yanks claimed him to be. Whatever it was, he could make out the commander of this Union force a scant thirty yards to his front. The man was shouting orders and quickly mounting his steed. This was the prize that Forrest would present to General Hood.

Forrest tightened the grip on his saber and sent his mind into that special place. A place where there was nothing around him except him and his objective. This form of cynosure allowed his to see the colonel with a clarity that was incarnadine. He had chased this elusive colonel for several days, he knew it was none other than Horace Capron. As he closed in on the departing colonel, a Federal soldier crossed his path. With out taking his eyes from his target, he slashed his saber into the exposed neck of the soldier. The force of his swing was so violent that his blade gnawed through soft flesh embedding itself within the man's collarbone. Forrest's momentum stalled as he tried to pull his weapon from the man's flesh. After several aggressively forceful tugs, the saber refused to part from its victim.

Another mounted Union cavalryman witnessed the exposed Confederate general and rode towards him with his own sword drawn. Forrest saw the incoming threat and quickly let go of his saber. The dying soldier quickly fell to the ground like a tree branch dismembered by lightning. With uncanny agility, Forrest caught the wrist of the sword-wielding officer. Forrest forcibly turned the man's wrist in a direction that it was not meant to go. Listening for the snap of bone, Forrest let go of the wrist and caught the falling saber with his left hand. His right hand caught the officer's jaw and sent him off his horse.

With his immediate threat removed, Forrest was able to continue after Capron. Unfortunately, the Federal colonel was long gone, undoubtedly fleeing up the pike with the remnants of his command. Forrest threw the Yankee saber on the floor and dismounted. He bent over the dead soldier whose collarbone held his sword steadily upright, much like the rock that housed Excalibur. Forrest placed his boot upon the dead man's chest, and with one strong pull, made himself king. Forrest remounted and rode back towards his victorious cavalry.

Major Strange saluted him with an obvious excitement to find him alive. "General Forrest, you had me worried again."

Forrest accepted the majors concern like rock taken from one place and put in another. "Where is General Jackson? I need a full accounting of this victory."

"Severe casualties for the enemy," an exuberant Jackson announced as he approached from the rear. "We have a whole company captured intact, the 7th Ohio, I do believe. The Yanks never knew what hit them."

Forrest still withheld any emotion. "We should have had their entire command captured, General. Still, we are over the Duck River and we can concentrate on relieving the pressure to General Buford's front. General Jackson, I do congratulate you and your command. This has been a great victory, but we are not done this day. These Yanks were only the rear guard to the cavalry that is positioned at Hardison's Mill Ford. That Yankee cavalry is now caught between General Buford's division and us. Begin organizing your men to hit that force in its rear as well."

Jackson saluted and aggressively rode off to find his staff officers. Forrest turned to Strange. "This has been a good day."

Strange agreed. It was good in the sense that Forrest had cleared all but one of the fords that crossed the Duck east of Columbia. But it was also a mysterious success. When the assault for the fords began, Forrest had split his cavalry into four attacking arms. Jackson was to force his way across Carr's Mill, Chalmers had to cross Holland's Ford, Forrest riding with Biffle's regiment, had to swim his command over Owen's Ford, and Buford had to penetrate Hardison's Mill, the extreme left flank of the enemy.

While riding with Forrest, Strange was surprised at how easy Biffle's regiment had gained access to the north side of the Duck. The only substantial wounds that the regiment received was that it had to endure the uncomfortable clinging of wet uniforms in this cold air.

Upon gaining the north bank, Forrest was told that Buford was unable to push the Federal cavalry to his front. It was also quickly reported that Jackson and Chalmers had crossed to the north of the Duck with as much ease as Biffle. Forrest quickly gathered Jackson's command and led them east in an effort to attack the Federal force at Hardison's Mill. When he rode with Forrest into this battle, he could not help allowing an ominous ambiance to overwhelm him. Where was the Yankee cavalry that was supposed to be guarding the fords west of the Lewisburg Pike? Strange's fears were put to rest with the rout of Capron's reserve force, but he still questioned the whereabouts of the remainder of the Federal cavalry.

Forrest's Advance

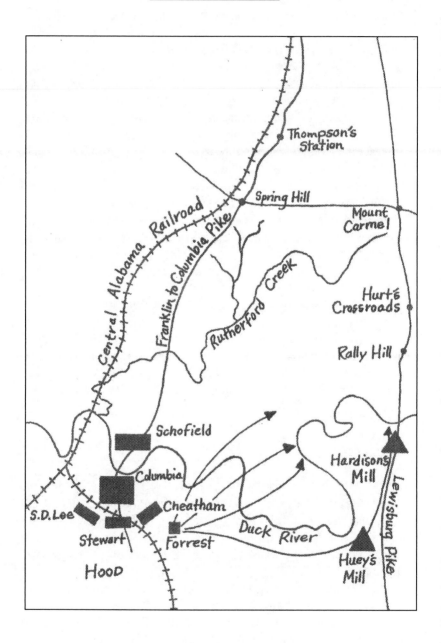

Two of Chalmers officers approached Forrest with a dispatch. Strange assumed that this was the missing piece to the puzzle. The Federals undoubtedly allowed Forrest to cross the Duck so that they would be cut off from the protection of Hood's army. The dispatch would undoubtedly report that Chalmers' command was being assaulted from all sides.

Forrest read the dispatch and smiled. "Major Strange, you may now remove that sickly look that exhibits itself upon your pretty face. Chalmers reports that he has learned that Hood's chief engineer has also successfully forded the Duck within spitting distance of Columbia. Not only is the Confederate cavalry on this soil, but the Confederate infantry as well."

The auspicious dispatch was interrupted by wild stampede of thundering horses. The thumping earth came from the direction of the Hardison Ford, where the Federal cavalry was supposed to be trapped. The Union troopers must have realized their peril and had obviously chosen to disengage Buford to their front and charge through Forrest in their rear. Forrest was more impressed by their bold attack than he was upset at his men for allowing them to ride through them untouched. It happened so quickly that Forrest was actually grateful, for the damage done to his own force was limited.

As Forrest watched the last barrier of the Duck River flee north, he felt the arrival of his own redemption. He would report to Hood that his whole command was over the Duck River and would continue after the fleeing Federal cavalry north up the Lewisburg Pike.

*   *   *   *   *   *   *   *

After a hearty dinner, General John M. Schofield retired to the solitude of his room. He unbuttoned his uniform jacket and sat upon the hard wooden chair that idled next to the desk that it accompanied. Schofield poured himself a tall glass of water and spread out the many dispatches that he had received throughout this day.

There were many. Some reported frantically that the rebel cavalry had crossed the Duck River. When these first came in Schofield was not overly concerned. Surely General Wilson could counter with the Federal cavalry and contest these crossings.

Unfortunately, that was an assumption he should not have made. Later dispatches arrived from his infantry commanders claiming that there was no friendly cavalry in the area to oppose the rebel infantry. This angered Schofield. He did not want Hood to get the start on him again. As a precautionary measure he sent a telegram to General Thomas asking him to ensure that there were bridges suitable for his army to cross at Franklin. In the event he was outflanked, Schofield wanted to be sure there was a viable escape route still open. If there was not, General Wilson would have more to fear than the Confederate army.

According to Grant, General Wilson was supposed to be the Union's answer to Forrest. It was not the first time that the Union charged one man with the responsibility of defeating Forrest. And this was not the first time that elected man had failed miserably.

Schofield lifted and read for the third time tonight, the latest dispatch from General Wilson. It reported that the enemy had seized Rally Hill, a point twelve miles northeast of Columbia. The initial realization that Forrest was so deep in his rear caused an immediate concern. But that subsided with the news that Hood's infantry had not followed. That meant that Forrest and the rebel cavalry was Wilson's problem and that was exactly why the young commander was sent here.

"Deal with him," Schofield cursed.

He began to wonder if Forrest even mattered any longer. He had just received word from Thomas that Grant had reported that Forrest's objective was to fall upon Sherman's rear. Schofield hoped that was Forrest's plan. If anyone deserved the hindrance of Forrest, it was Sherman. After all, it was Sherman who thought it best to leave Atlanta with the majority of the Federal army marching with him. Schofield already had too much on his hands, he did not have the time, nor the energy, to concern himself with a cavalry raid. He had larger tasks.

His main objective was keeping the Confederate infantry on the opposite bank of the Duck. The enemy's cavalry might advance, but the fact remained that Hood's army was still stationary to his front. As long as Hood was in close proximity, Schofield could not send his army chasing an elusive cavalry. That would only open the door for an advance from the rebel infantry.

Schofield took a sip of his water, the condensation on the glass leaving his fingertips wet. He dried them off on his pants before handling the telegram he received from Thomas in Nashville. Thomas' message confirmed his resolve to stay put until Hood's army moved from his front. On December 1, A. J. Smith was expected to arrive in Nashville with his corps fresh from their excursions farther to the west. A few days after their arrival, Schofield was to expect their support for an offensive against the enemy. The arrival of Smith's men would greatly tip the odds of victory in his favor. If Schofield could keep his army separated from Hood's by the Duck for a few more days, then he could consolidate his force with Smith's and strike the enemy such a blow they would be sent reeling back into Georgia.

The general was able to slip out of his uniform in the comfort of knowing that he had made all the correct decisions throughout the course of this day. Admittedly, the Confederate cavalry was on the north side of the Duck, but Hood's army was not. Wilson would have to contend with their cavalry on his own. In just a few more days, his force would be augmented by the reinforcements from Nashville, and then he could take the initiative against his old classmate John Bell Hood.

A knock at the door prevented him from slipping into the embracing bed. Schofield let one of his staff officers in. It was adjutant Mark Stemmons. Stemmons needed a shaving desperately, and a bath would not hurt him either. He handed Schofield the latest dispatch, one that would be added to the pile on his desk.

Schofield took it and read it.

"It is another report from Grant's prodigy, the wonderful general Wilson. He feels the need to inform me that Hood is going to flank us on one side or the other."

Schofield laughed sarcastically as he tossed the message onto his desk. "Is that what they teach in general school, to write messages that contain sentences constructed of ambiguity? Doesn't it make the game of war so much more fun to play? Hood is crossing on one side or the other. What the hell does that mean? Am I to move this army to one side or the other? Or am I to guess?"

Stemmons averted his eyes hoping that Schofield was not asking him the question directly. He scratched the thick shrub that cascaded from his jaw and shrugged his shoulders.

Schofield did not expect an answer. He thanked the adjutant for the report. "If another letter arrives this night from General Wilson, I charge you with the task of reading it first. If it is like this one, I do not expect to have my sleep interrupted. If you feel the need to wake me, it better be that Hood's army is attacking mine. Now enjoy the rest of your night."

Stemmons left Schofield's room feeling extremely unfortunate. Why was he the one that had to deliver that last dispatch to the general? Stemmon's ability to use inference was his greatest foible. What if Wilson sent a letter that he thought was necessary to wake the general? Would he wake him only to be scolded by Schofield? The general was obviously not in good spirits this night, and he did not want to be the one to incur his wrath.

He left Schofield's headquarters praying that there would be no more dispatches until the morning.

Chapter XV
November 29, Early Morning
Nashville, Tennessee

Already 3:30 in the morning, and General George Thomas was still unable to sleep. Thomas took a damp cloth and slowly wiped the clammy night sweat that clung to his brow. He tried several times to reacquaint his body with the bed, but each attempt only brought more restlessness. After an unsuccessful fifth attempt to fall back asleep, Thomas threw his blanket to the floor in disgust, and resolved to prepare himself for this new day. His inability to sleep did not come as any surprise.

Earlier in the evening, he had made every effort to ensure he would have a full night's rest. He had eaten a heavy meal for dinner, and even ended his night with a warm bath. If that wasn't enough to assist Thomas in attaining rest, nothing would.

Lethargic legs carried him towards the washbasin, where he let his hands fall into the cool water. After a few moments he retrieved the saturated washcloth and pressed it flush against his forehead. It was time to leave his room. The St. Cloud Hotel was still quiet. Soon it would be like a beehive, buzzing with officers and aids, all rushing in and out with dispatches. Every officer claimed his dispatch to be the most urgent. It was those damned dispatches that had prevented Thomas from getting any sleep.

He walked into his headquarters and nodded at a few officers that were on duty. Saluting, they seemed surprise to see the general awake. Thomas asked if any new news had arrived. There was none. It seemed that the rebel cavalry had once again managed to sever the telegraph lines that led to Schofield in Columbia. The only way to get any message to Schofield was through the use of couriers and dispatches.

There was that word again, dispatches.

Lately, it seemed everyone from everywhere was sending them to Thomas. The ones that bothered him the most were the telegrams sent from General Grant back East. They spoke of mistrust. Thomas was sure that Grant had little faith in his abilities to deal with Hood. Grant wanted Hood attacked immediately. Thomas thought it funny how easy Grant fit into the role of a

Washington politician. It seemed whoever led the campaign west of Virginia, had to contend with someone from Washington telling them how they should be attacking and driving the enemy before them. Well, Thomas did not care who ordered him to attack, he was in command here, and until he was relieved of duty, he would run this campaign on his own terms. And his own terms were that his army was not yet ready to take the offensive.

With Grant out of his mind, the next dispatches that burdened him were those from his cavalry commander James Wilson. Wilson had apparently been driven up the Lewisburg Pike and allowed Forrest's cavalry to gain the north bank of the Duck. Wilson reassured him that Forrest was held in check, and there was no infantry north of the river.

Though Wilson was confident he could hold Forrest in place, he was still forced back from the fords that denied the rebels access across the Duck. How soon would Hood wait to exploit this? Now more than ever, he wished that the soldiers under A.J. Smith were at his immediate availability. If not them, then he would settle for the arrival of the supplies to outfit the majority of cavalry under Wilson. It still amazed him that there were thousands of troopers who could not be in the field due to a lack of mounts and weaponry. Either of those two options would allow Thomas to seize the initiative. However, Smith's infantry and the re-supplied cavalry were at least two days away from becoming serviceable.

Thomas realized that his options were limited. If Wilson said he had held Forrest in check, he would have to accept that. He could not order Schofield to retire from Columbia. That would give Hood immediate access to Franklin. Thomas wanted the enemy held off as long as possible. He did not want to have to face the Confederate army until he was prepared for it. Time was still needed to outfit his cavalry, and organize the command from A.J. Smith. Once that was accomplished, he could then march out to Franklin and unite with Schofield's army. Once his entire command was consolidated, there was no doubt that the outnumbered Confederates would be crushed.

That was the decision he made earlier. It prompted him to wire Schofield advising the commander to hold Hood at the Duck River until A.J. Smith could arrive. Once Thomas had Smith and his cavalry ready, he would then send the order for Schofield to fall back, allowing Hood over the river. This way, Thomas' combined army could descend upon Hood and drive his army against the Duck, where there would be no escape.

The plan sounded perfect. And that was Thomas' problem. It was too perfect. What if Hood pressed with overwhelming numbers and threatened to outflank Schofield? Should he expect Schofield to remain at Columbia at the risk of loosing his corps? Thomas shook his head in relief. He had realized that this was the insight lacking earlier that had deprived him of his sleep.

The solution was an easy one. He would send word to Schofield to hold the Duck, but if he felt threatened by Hood, he should fall back to Franklin, behind the Harpeth River.

Thomas called to an aid that was still awake and issued the order to send this latest message. The general then retired to his room. He would not be sleeping, that he knew. General Thomas was awake for the remainder of the day.

* * * * * * * *

Columbia, Tennessee

While Thomas was struggling in the predawn with an overwhelming sense of anxiety, Hood was forced from sleep by a deluge of impatient anticipation. This was going to be the day when he, John Bell Hood, saved the Confederacy. Perhaps it would be this heroic deed that would allow Buck Preston's family to finally accept him as the deserving husband for their daughter.

Hood had not thought of Buck in a while. As he lay in bed, he decided now was as a good time as any to indulge in a few fond memories of the woman who was the inspiration behind every move he made. The nostalgia was so overwhelming, Hood swore he could smell her hair as if she were lying next to him in bed.

"Soon my love, I will return to you. And though your parents do not approve of me now, when this is all done, I shall be the hero of the Confederacy. Then they will be honored that I have chosen you to be my bride. Soon my dear Buck, soon."

Hood rose from his bed and reached for his crutches. He quickly dressed himself with the help of his aids and called for the chaplain to enjoy a cup of coffee with him. While waiting for Quintard, he was joined by Governor Harris.

"Good morning, General Hood," Harris said. "I hope the weather holds like yesterday."

"Morning, Governor. I do believe it shall. God has blessed us."

"Now that is what I like to hear at this early hour," Quintard said as he entered the room to join Hood and Harris for some coffee.

"Chaplain, thank you for joining me this morning."

"General Hood, if you call this 'morning', you are sadly mistaken."

Harris and Hood laughed.

"General, if I may ask, what are the plans for this day?" Harris said.

"Well, before I begin, I would like my chief of staff present. Have any of you seen Major Mason this morning?" Hood asked.

"I haven't," Quintard said.

A door opened in the adjoining room and in stepped Mason.

"General, Governor, Chaplain, I am sorry I am a bit tardy," Mason said.

Hood waited for Mason to be seated while he poured himself some coffee. "Major, the governor would like to hear the plan of attack for this day. I have done some very deep thinking this past night, and I want you to be ready to convey my orders to the rest of the staff." Hood's face seemed to glow with excitement as he began detailing his plan to defeat Schofield.

"Gentlemen, I do not exaggerate when I state the claim, this will be a great day for the Confederacy. General Stephen Lee will remain at Columbia with two divisions of infantry and all of the artillery. Even if the artillery could be moved to join my flanking maneuvers, it would be too slow and could spoil my surprise march against Schofield. Instead, they will stay behind and continuously pound the Yankee lines north of the Duck. Their barrage and the presence of Stephen Lee will force Schofield to believe that we are still at his front. General Cheatham and General Stewart will then march their corps over the Davis Road, which is now in our possession. I will be present to personally lead this advance. I will not have another situation like I had in Atlanta. This move will put my forces in the vicinity of Spring Hill. Our objective is to take possession of the town and cut Schofield off from Thomas. We will still have the Harpeth River between Thomas and my army. From there we can fall upon Schofield, who cannot re-cross the Duck. He has already destroyed his own

Hood's Advance

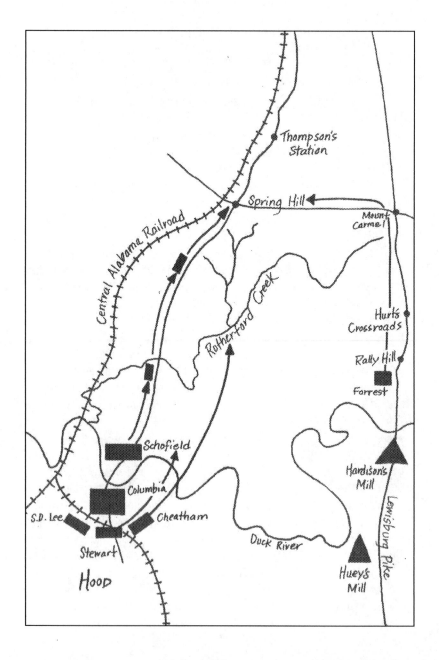

pontoon bridges to prevent us from using them. Or, we can race ahead and strike at Thomas.

Again, by crossing the Harpeth and destroying all bridges, Schofield will be unable to join the battle. General Stephen Lee will not cross the Duck and join the rest of the army until Schofield vacates his position. If Schofield chooses to stay put, we can fall on him from above, while Lee hits him from the front. Like a scampering rabbit, he will be crushed within the jowls of the hungry gray wolf."

"And what of the orders for Forrest off to the east. He is currently engaged with the Federal Cavalry?" Mason said.

"You may tell General Forrest that I am most impressed with his performance. His orders are to drive the Federal cavalry away from Spring Hill and then to converge on the town in conjunction with my infantry. He must ensure that there is no Federal cavalry to impede our march. Gentleman, General Schofield had better realize the situation he is in and leave his line to meet me in battle. The enemy must give me fight, or I will be in Nashville before tomorrow night."

Governor Harris and Major Mason were both impressed with the volition in Hood's strategy. They honestly could place credence that Hood's earlier assessment would be correct. Today would be a great day for the Confederacy. And they were all to play a part in becoming her heroes.

Before they departed from their breakfast, Quintard took a moment to pray. He once again asked for their Lord's blessing and protection of the Army of Tennessee.

As they stepped outside into the brisk air, it appeared that God had already granted them another of their huge requests. Hood's grand strategy, so well thought out, so detailed, was off to an auspicious beginning. It was cold, but the weather looked like it would continue to hold without rain or snow.

*　　*　　*　　*　　*　　*　　*　　*

Lewisburg Pike, Tennessee
Hurt's Crossroads

General James L. Wilson approached the recently constructed barricade like a mouse cautiously peering from its hole.

191

These makeshift earthworks were all that separated him from the enemy. It was not much.

"Where the hell is the reply from Schofield?" he said.

It was shortly after midnight when he sent an urgent message in search of Schofield..., but there had been no reply. That was not good. The situation here had changed dramatically, and Wilson needed his commander to be aware of that.

Tragically, it now appeared that his earlier assessment concerning the enemy's intention was incorrect. It was not too many hours ago, when he was convinced that the threat to his command was only one caused by the rebel cavalry. He countered their offensive by consolidating all of his detached cavalry units at Hurt's Crossroads. There, he would face Forrest with his combined command. Though his counter offensive left numerous fords over the Duck exposed, it did not worry him.

By the sound of the artillery being fired, Hood seemed content with staying on the south side of the Duck. And that was just fine, for it would leave Wilson to deal with Forrest one on one. With Capron's command escaping the overwhelming surge by the Confederates, Wilson had saved almost his entire force... though he had lost the fords to the enemy. At least that was what he wanted Forrest to believe. Once the infamous general led his troopers to the north banks of the Duck, Wilson intended to drive him back against the river with one massive strike. He even had thoughts of requesting Schofield to send infantry sweeping east and then north up the Lewisburg Pike, while he contained Forrest. The combined force of his cavalry to the front and Schofield's infantry to the rear would spell certain annihilation for Forrest's command.

Yet all those plans ended for Wilson when he received the latest reports.

Wilson peered into the night and could not see the ground a few feet from him. His men were half asleep trying to remain on picket duty. "Come on boys, stay alert. You will have plenty of rest soon enough," he ordered.

"They have been hearing that for some time now General... promises lose their luster when they are broken," Capron said.

Wilson was caught off guard. He had not realized that Capron was standing two men down to his left. He responded with words that belied his grim countenance.

"My apologies to these men, Colonel. They have performed admirably. If you do not mind, please walk with me."

Capron and Wilson walked back up the pike, towards the command of Colonel Hatch. "Colonel, my apologies to your men again, but if you ever question my command in the open again, you will find yourself on guard duty in some remote part of this God given country. Is that understood?"

Capron wanted to shoot forth a string of obscenities at his commander, but knew better. He was tired, his men were tired, and he just needed to cool down and get some rest. "General, it will not happen again," he said through clenched teeth.

"Colonel, I have not had a reply from General Schofield. And that makes me hesitant to decide my next move."

Capron did not respond. Wilson's inability to make contact with Schofield was something he should have thought of before calling all of his cavalry this far to the east. What else did the general expect? He chose to isolate himself, and was now questioning why he was isolated?

"Sir, what was your exact message to the general?" Capron said. As much as Capron wanted to string Wilson out on this, he realized that this game of pride would do nothing but cost him the lives of the men in his command. He did not like Wilson, or all of the arrogance that came with him, but he would not sacrifice his troops just to see Wilson crumble.

Wilson pulled out the last report he received as if he meant to read it in the dark. Realizing there was insufficient lighting, he simply shook his head and returned the dispatch back inside his jacket.

"Hatch's men had captured one of Forrest's troopers just after midnight", Wilson said. "The man claimed that Hood intended to cross the fords, following on the heels of Forrest's advance. It was this report that caused me to reconsider my earlier strategy, and instead of asking for Schofield to aid in my offensive, I felt the need to advise the general to withdraw his command to Spring Hill... and to do so immediately while I held the enemy as long as possible. If Hood was over the fords, I feared that Schofield would be in peril.

And now I do not know where the enemy's infantry is, nor do I know if the general has received my message. And without knowing if Schofield has received my warning, I am paralyzed. Earlier, I had assured the general that this situation was under control, and that there was no threat of the Confederate infantry crossing the river. And now, there is strong indication that Hood is already over the river and may very well be between my command and Schofield's."

"General, if Hood is on this side of the river, could he have not intercepted your dispatch?" Capron said. He hoped the question would strike more fear into the heart of his young commander. He always liked to watch the dreadful sweat of doubt mark the clean face of the pompous and vainglorious. He received no such satisfaction from Wilson.

"That is what I fear has happened, but until I know otherwise, I must still cling to hope. The prisoner said Hood was making preparations to cross over, but had not done so yet. Being unsure of Hood's position, my dilemma is whether to hold here or to pull back? Adding to this consternation, the prisoner also stated that it was Forrest's goal to reach Nashville."

"Nashville," Capron replied. "I have men already en route to the Mount Carmel road. If Forrest is truly heading that way, he will need to pass through that town. I can leave now and instruct them to fortify that position while you pull this force back. I seriously doubt that this position can hold Forrest, not to mention Hood's infantry. In the meantime, you can stall here for as long as possible, hopefully until you receive Schofield's reply. If you are still here, then that means the enemy still is and that is good. If you cannot hold here, then I suggest you fall back to my command, while drawing the enemy with you. That should take some pressure off Schofield, and allow us to consolidate with the infantry farther north, closer to Nashville... where we should have been by now anyway."

Wilson did not ponder the thought long. He agreed with Capron's assessment, but for different reasons. His defense was made up of Hatch's and Capron's commands. The units under these two men had done nothing the past two weeks expect flee before the advancing rebel cavalry. The more Wilson thought on it, the more it made sense. There was no way these men could be expected to stand up to Forrest for a third time.

"You may be right there, Colonel. Forrest's command will probably overrun this position in the morning, especially if he had Hood's infantry arriving in support. I can no longer wait for Schofield's reply... I must recapture the initiative. Please find Colonel Hatch and instruct him to have his men ready to move out on my command. Now if you will excuse me Colonel, I need to find another messenger and attempt to resend the same dispatch to General Schofield."

Capron turned from Wilson and went in search of Hatch. Capron marveled that his commander had not even whispered thanks for his advice that had probably saved the Federal cavalry.

Within the next hour, the Federal cavalry was awakened and heading farther north along the pike. Disgruntled troopers shook off another restless night, and on exhausted mounts, began pondering their fate. For Capron and Hatch, this was nothing new. They only hoped to reach Capron's brigade intact. Capron had already sent word up ahead to have his men begin entrenching the area. Both men had realized that by Wilson's command, the eyes and ears of the Federal army were being taken away from Schofield. The amount of time that a deaf and blind army could survive would soon be discovered.

Just as the leading elements of Wilson's command departed for the Mount Carmel Road, an explosion of gunfire announced that the rear guard was under attack from Forrest's cavalry.

*   *   *   *   *   *   *   *

Morning

Schofield awoke at 6:30 in the morning. His sleep had been untroubled, and he immediately felt the rejuvenating effects of a much-needed rest. He stretched his arms into the air and was about to let out a yawn, when a momentary spell of anxiety gripped his esophagus like a rusted guillotine. Had Hood slipped by him in the night? The thought made it difficult for Schofield to breathe. As he reached for the pitcher of water beside his bed, he heard the thunder of the Confederate artillery. Ironically, it was a pleasurable sound. It meant that Hood was still at his front.

Relaxed, he could feel his senses slowly returning to him. There was a chill in the air, but it was not enough to comfort him. He opened the shutters to his window, hoping to see signs of either rain or snow, anything that would delay movement orchestrated by the Confederate army. Instead, he was blinded by the ascending sun in all its morning glory.

Disheartened, he finished dressing and joined his staff for breakfast. Most of the men had eaten much earlier, but they would not hesitate to join their commander for a fresh brew of coffee.

Schofield sipped his morning awake as he filtered through the dispatches that had arrived since last night. Many of them claimed to be urgent, but Schofield knew that they were written by officers who felt the need to report anything and everything. One dispatch simply read, 'Urgent! Several dark shapes were seen to our front. Without the daylight, I must assume that they were rebel pickets.' Well of course they probably were. And that was something Schofield would expect the enemy to do. Thankfully, Stemmons remained true to his word, and did not wake him for any such frivolous messages.

Schofield looked around the room for Stemmons, but the man must have gone to sleep. He reminded himself to thank the man later. Schofield was about to get up and take a ride around his camp. He wanted to see his staff officers, as well as his chief engineer. However, when he slid his chair back, an officer bearing a dispatch ran into the room. The man must have been possessed by the devil, to make such a speedy entry.

"General Schofield, this has just arrived form General Wilson. It reads Important! Trot!"

Schofield took a moment and stared at the dispatch that was trembling in the hands of the officer. He reached out and accepted it. For the second time this morning he could feel a throat closing anxiety wrap itself around his jugular.

'3:00 A.M. Second Sending.

I think it very clear that they are aiming for Franklin, and that you ought to get to Spring Hill by 10:00 a.m. I'll keep on the Lewisburg Pike and hold the enemy all I can. There may be no strong advance of the enemy's cavalry till the infantry has crossed which will be between now and daylight. Get back to Franklin without delay, leaving a small force to detain the enemy. The rebels will move by this road toward that point.' It had been signed by General Wilson.

Schofield felt the palpations in his chest threaten to explode. At first he was angered by Wilson's tone. The message was written more like an order than a report. But it was the content of the letter that consumed his wrath more. With a fury that was misguided, he exploded on the officer.

"Why the hell does this message read the second God damned sending? Where the hell is the first? And why was this second message, which was written at three a.m., just finding its way to me now? If you cannot tell time sir, that is four hours late!"

The officer responded through shaking teeth, "General, I just received that moments ago. The cavalryman who brought it said he had to ride a very round about course in order to avoid the enemy."

Schofield felt displaced, collapsing into his chair, as he looked towards his gathering staff. Helpless blank stares reached for him.

"Wilson had assured me that this would not happen," he said. "The rebel infantry were not to get the start on me. Someone find me General Stanley at once. I want him to send two divisions towards Spring Hill without delay. Without delay! Is that understood? And inform him that the wagon train is to follow. We will not be trapped here."

As Schofield began readying plans for the rapid withdrawal of his army, the room in which he stood violently shook as if it suffered the effects of an earthquake. When the officers in the room regained their footing, they looked to Schofield, asking the question that was also now on his mind.

How could Hood be in two places at once?

The amount of artillery that was shelling his position was evidence that the rebel infantry had not moved. Was Wilson overreacting to his situation... or could his cavalry commander simply be wrong?

"Gentleman, can someone please go and find General Stanley and Major Goodspeed, and have them personally escorted here. Everyone else is dismissed for the time being."

Schofield waited an impatient twenty minutes before the men he summoned arrived. Schofield ordered all of the escorting officers from the room.

"Gentleman, this army is currently at a serious disadvantage," he said without wasting any time on formalities.

"How so, General?" Goodspeed asked.

"Major, you are currently combating the artillery of the Confederate forces. Please give me your evaluation of their force."

"Sir, by the amount of fire they are directing upon my batteries, I would seriously beg you to reconsider any offensive action. The enemy has secured good ground on the southern side of the Duck."

"Rest assured that I do not mean to attack Hood... not yet anyway. Unfortunately, I received this dispatch perhaps an hour ago. It is from Wilson... here, read it. He reports that Forrest has pushed him over the Hardison Mill ford, and that their infantry are close behind. This message was sent at three a.m."

"That cannot be," Stanley fired. "If that were true, then there would not be such a demonstration of artillery to our front. General, I can assure you that Hood is still in place. If you would like, I could take you to the front now and show you several brigades that are in clear view."

Schofield nodded. This was what he was hoping to hear. The sound of a courier arriving in the next room caught their attention. Schofield called for his officer to enter with the latest news. It was from Thomas in Nashville.

It called for Schofield to hold his current position until either General Smith arrived with his command or the cavalry under Wilson could be fully equipped. With the availability of either Smith or the cavalry, Schofield could then retire slowly north, baiting Hood to cross the Duck River in pursuit. Once Hood was over the river, the combined Federal forces could fall upon him with overwhelming numbers and smash the Confederates against the river.

Thomas' message was the confirmation Schofield needed to convince him to hold his current position. As he made preparations to issue new orders, the courier reached into his jacket as if he were unsure of its contents. The look upon his face confirmed that he had forgotten that he had another delivery for the general. Schofield was soon handed a second message. It was also from Thomas, sent shortly after the previous, but this one advised Schofield to fall back to Franklin, if he felt his current position threatened.

"How can anyone command under these chaotic directions?" Schofield fumed. It appears that Thomas would like me to both hold Hood across the Duck and fall back to Franklin at the same time." The ambiguity from Nashville convinced Schofield that it was up to him and none other to take control of the situation. He turned back to his generals.

"Major Goodspeed, instruct your artillery to continue its counter barrage against Hood's positions to your front. General

Stanley, for the time being, we will delay the retreat of this army. Thomas seems to feel strongly in the ability of this command to deny Hood access across this river. It is my intention to prove him correct. Where Wilson is with my cavalry only God may tell? It appears that we cannot depend on his services. And as for the threat Wilson was so worried about, well I believe it is nothing but Forrest. General Thomas informed me that he had word from Grant that Forrest is to disengage from our vicinity and turn east to fall upon Sherman's rear. I believe that to be the case. Again, for the time being, send only two divisions with the wagon train towards Spring Hill. As a precautionary measure."

Stanley saluted Schofield as he departed with Goodspeed.

"General, I will have those divisions on the road shortly. With the absence of our cavalry, I also ask permission to send a division near the fords to better ascertain if the enemy is attempting a crossing."

"That is an excellent idea. Now please hurry, I must inform Thomas of our intent to hold the Duck River. I also need to find the officer responsible for that missing dispatch that necessitated Wilson sending this second one."

The officer was one who would never be found.

*   *   *   *   *   *   *   *

Stemmons listened intently to the ire of his general in the next room. The guilt he felt was so intense, he was confident that even the best poker face would fail to conceal it. With hurried steps he ran out to his tent, which was adjacent to headquarters. He crawled within and grabbed the dispatch from his haversack.

It was from General Wilson and it read Urgent. But that was the problem, they all read urgent. Stemmons had read every report that arrived last night, and this was the only one that caused him any concern. He thought it significant enough to wake his commander, but Schofield seemed so adamant on getting his sleep. He thought of getting the opinion of one of his fellow officers, but he was too embarrassed to ask.

A simple factory worker from New Jersey, he was considered a nobody before the war began. Since then, he had served so well in several campaigns that he was rewarded a place on Schofield's staff. His family was extremely proud of his military accomplishments, and he would not let them down. Rather than risk his reputation, he chose to ignore the arrival of this particular dispatch. He would just pretend it never arrived.

And as he ripped the paper into a thousand pieces... it never had.

*   *   *   *   *   *   *   *

Once the turmoil of the morning began to calm down, Schofield was finally able to begin regaining the confidence needed to face Hood and keep the enemy south of the Duck River. But how quickly that house of cards was to topple. An urgent report arrived from Stanley's command. Upon investigation of the vacant fords, it was learned that elements of Hood's infantry were indeed on the north side of the river. The exact number was not yet confirmed. But the threat was enough for Schofield to chew off what little remained of his fingernails. Assisting in this squall of confusion was a conflicting report that arrived from Wilson. Forrest had driven him up the Lewisburg Pike, but there was no rebel infantry to be reported.

Was there or wasn't there Confederate infantry on the north side of the Duck?

For reasons even Schofield could not explain, he chose to place his trust in Wilson's report. It was after all the most recent of all the dispatches. No matter how inept Wilson may have appeared in the last few days, there was no way Schofield could believe that he would have allowed the rebel infantry access over the river. And since they were not over the river, Hood had not stolen a second march upon him.

The thought did help Schofield realize how close he came to having his army trapped in Columbia. Not wanting to cause an immediate panic by withdrawing his forces in daylight, he called for a retreat of his position in the evening. If the majority of Hood's force was on the south of the Duck, they would be so at least until tomorrow. For the time being, there was no way the enemy could move a force across the river and threaten his current defensive positions.

And so for the remainder of the day, Schofield intended to feign a decision to stay and fight. But tonight, under the cover of darkness, Schofield would send the remainder of his force north, up the Columbia to Franklin Pike, and would not stop until he crossed the Harpeth. He just hoped that if he was forced to march all the way to the Harpeth, that Thomas had put in place a means to access the crossing of the river. He did not want to be trapped again.

Chapter XVI
November 29, Mid Morning
Lewisburg Pike, Tennessee

Forrest rode at the head of Chalmers' division as it hurriedly flanked the retreating Yankee cavalry. Forrest hoped to reach the Mount Carmel road before the enemy could. That was the first part of his plan. The second required Jackson's division to pursue the Federals as they withdrew up the Lewisburg Pike. Forrest had issued Jackson specific instructions not to press the enemy too intently. He did not want their troops to be routed towards his objective and reach it before he was there waiting to receive them. Forrest wanted the Yanks to believe that they could stop and resist Jackson's advance. Each barricade constructed by their rear guard easily detained Jackson's pursuit. But what they did not realize was that it also gave Chalmers' division, the critical time it needed in order to arrive at Mount Carmel first.

There were several times earlier in the morning, when he could hear the sound of battle between Jackson and the Federals. It took much fortitude for him to resist the urge to abandon his objective, and ride through the forest and smash the Federal cavalry on its exposed flank. He knew that this would crush the enemy's cavalry and cause it to flee north. But he also knew that allowing them to flee further north would also mean allowing them to escape. Forrest understood the bigger picture with unprecedented clarity. If he could arrive at the town of Mount Carmel first, he could capture and destroy Wilson's entire command.

The sounds of battle continued, but grew more distant with each galloping stride. It was a positive sign that his plan was coming to fruition. Up ahead, Forrest could see a small company of cavalry approaching. It was the command that he had detached earlier to ascertain the situation in Mount Carmel. Needing his information quickly and accurately, he had instructed Major Strange to lead the scouting party. Now that Strange had returned, he called Chalmers' division to a halt.

"General Forrest," Strange reported, "it appears that the enemy has had some success in arriving at the town before us. I believe that it is Capron's brigade that currently occupies the vicinity, and are in the progress of barricading it with any means they can. There is also a division approaching from the Lewisburg Pike. Apparently Jackson is detaining their rear guard, but the Federals seem to be satisfied with that. They are moving with great speed towards the town. I believe that one of their brigades has a chance of reaching it before we do."

Forrest looked at Strange with that omniscient smirk upon his face. He gave Strange a wink as he turned upon his saddle. With a raised voice, he began to incite his men. "Did you hear that boys, my adjutant here claims that one Yankee brigade can hold a town against this entire division? And not just that, he also claims that another Yankee brigade can ride their horses faster than you can and reach that same town first. Do you believe that?"

There were fiery protests and several wicked glances cast at major Strange. The major was too impressed with Forrest's ability to be resourceful than to let the ire of his fellow men get the better of him. He fully accepted that the end would justify the means.

"General Chalmers," Forrest continued, "are your men ready to prove this man wrong?"

Chalmers shrugged his shoulders, "How about it boys, can we whip them Yankees or not?"

The Confederate division raised their caps and began shouting into the cold air. The cacophony they produced was not intelligible to the civilized man. The entire Southern cavalry sounded more like a legion of screaming, wild Comanchees. With that awful noise resonating with their approach, Chalmers division broke from the concealment of the forest and charged towards the Yankee brigade defending the strategically critical town of Mount Carmel.

*   *   *   *   *   *   *   *

Horace Capron was completely exhausted. He had not slept the night before, choosing instead to retire to Mount Carmel and make plans to barricade the town. This latest plan called for Wilson to consolidate his entire command at this new location. However, it was not long after his departure from Wilson, that he learned that Forrest had initiated the offensive. With a renewed sense of urgency Capron rode into town and immediately gave the orders to begin the construction of earthworks.

That was several hours ago. Now all he had to do was wait for Wilson's lead division to arrive and relieve his men, so that he and they could get some much-needed rest. An aid had ridden in moments ago, announcing that Wilson's rear guard was successful in holding Forrest at bay. Coon's brigade, at the head of the withdrawal, was approaching the town. They were expected any minute.

Capron was thankful. The rebel cavalry was advancing, but in doing so, were separating themselves farther and farther from the support of Hood's army. At the same time, Wilson was continually calling his command to Mount Carmel. Once his forces were consolidated, he could begin to take the initiative against Forrest.

Capron walked towards a few of his men, who were resting against a crudely constructed wooden barricade. Capron was saluted as he settled at the base of a small cedar. He could see General Wilson approaching from the town. Capron was still not sure of the young commander. Part of him thought that his brash decision making process was ruled too much by dogmatism.

He raised a tired hand and waved at the General. Wilson saw the gesture and began riding towards his Colonel. A look of complacency on his face replaced the threatened countenance that was there in the hours before dawn. It said that Wilson was comfortable with the current situation. Capron even thought he could see the general begin to smile, but that visage quickly vanished, as it was slapped from his face by the sound of utter savagery exploding from the woods to the east.

Capron felt his heart rip through his chest as he jumped up and tried to see what was making that feral clamor. His first thought was Indians. But he knew that could not be true. Perhaps it was Coon's brigade trying out a new cheer as they reached town. But that could not be it either, the sound was not coming from that direction.

As the bullets whipped by his head, Capron understood the plight. He raced behind the cedar, as Wilson dismounted and joined him there.

"That damned Forrest. I do not like him Colonel, in fact I can honestly say I hate him, but he is a smart son of a bitch."

Capron agreed as a bullet embedded itself in the tree a few

inches above their heads.

"That he is General. He has sent part of his force around your flank, while the other part led a half-hearted attack at your rearguard. Brilliant. While slowing our withdrawal, he has allowed himself time to reach a point to cut your retreating command off."

Wilson shot Capron a look of admonition. "Colonel, Forrest may have beaten my men to this town, but let me remind you that it is your command that currently occupies it. See to it that Forrest is held at bay until Hatch's division can be sent in to reinforce your line. Is that understood, Colonel?"

Capron understood well enough. He also was fully aware of Wilson's tone when he addressed him as *colonel*. Capron, put back in place, began shouting orders to his men to hold their position at all costs.

Wave after wave of the rebel cavalry stampeded towards Capron's lines, only to be beaten back with considerable ease. Capron wanted to credit his men for such a stellar resistance, but he knew better. These new rifles that were issued to his command deserved all of the acclaim. With a rifle that could fire seven shots before reloading, it was no wonder how his small brigade was able to turn back the advance of an entire division.

Still, the rebels assaulted their barricades with an intensity that complemented their wild screaming. Capron had no doubt that this was Forrest's doing. Surely, the Confederate general understood the importance of occupying this town, and was willing his men in charge after charge to take the position. In past wars, it was said that will alone could win a battle, but with this new type of rifle, Capron knew better. He realized that with this repeating rifle, will had just gone the way of the sword and shield.

It was not long until Coon's brigade arrived to reinforce Capron's command, and together they poured volley after volley at the direction of Forrest's assault. Capron continued to watch in disbelief as the Confederates continued the attack. There was no doubt in his mind that if those were his boys charging these works, he would have called it off a long time ago.

The colonel's attention was pulled back down the Lewisburg Pike as the sound of a thunderous cavalry approached. It was the rest of Hatch's division, the rearguard assigned to detaining the initial Confederate pursuit. A large contingent of the enemy's cavalry was hot in pursuit.

General Wilson could be seen ordering Hatch's men off their mounts as soon as they entered the protective front of his defenses. They were quickly put in line to brace for the attack of this new threat. Artillery was brought forward and unlimbered. For several precious minutes the two sides clashed with shrapnel, bullet and steel. Slowly and defiantly, the rebel cavalry was forced to pull back.

Capron was so excited, he swung his cap and led his men in a cheer. He ran over to General Wilson and hugged him with all earnestness.

"Excellent work, General," he said. "Forrest was whipped pretty badly just now."

Wilson was not so sure. "Perhaps Colonel, or perhaps he wants us to think he is whipped. Just like he wanted us to think he was attacking with his whole force this morning. Forrest should have taken this position. No discredit to your brigade, but how could they have held against a division?"

"General, with these," Capron said, lifting a Spencer carbine rifle in front of him.

"No Colonel, I am not so sure that this rifle could thwart Forrest. He is up to something. And this time, I am sure of what that is. He is disengaging and continuing north. His goal was not this town, but rather to have us delay here, while he continues towards Nashville."

"Nashville," Capron said. "Sir, I still doubt that to be true. Why would he want to go to Nashville and cut himself off farther from Hood? That does not make sense."

"What does not make sense Colonel, is your constant questioning of my command. From this point on it ends, or you can find employment in this army somewhere else. Forrest is marching to Nashville. Do you forget already the words of the prisoner captured last night? Well, I have not. And I intend to have this army racing there before the enemy can get a start. Have word sent to General Schofield, that the enemy had pushed us up the pike, but there is no sign of infantry. That will allow the general some comfort. I can assure you he is one that needs all the good news he can get. Also have General Thomas informed that his position in Nashville may be threatened by the rebel cavalry. Tell him he better look for Forrest at Nashville tomorrow at noon. I will be there before or very soon after he makes his appearance.

Colonel, Forrest can not be allowed to ever get the jump on my command again."

*   *   *   *   *   *   *   *

Forrest pulled his demoralized cavalry back behind the woods that screened him from the enemy. He watched as his men dismounted and shook their heads in disbelief. Asked moments ago if they could take a position guarded by only a brigade, the answer was a unanimous yes. Now, Forrest saw their confidence shaken. He himself was growing frustrated at his inability to reach a position before the enemy could. Time and time again, he fought battles that drove the Federal troops in his path, but yet he always managed to arrive at his objective moments too late.

Forrest was reloading his pistols when he heard the sound of his officers approaching.

"General Forrest, the men are reorganizing, but I fear they are reluctant to try and take that position again," Strange said.

Forrest turned to see Chalmers, Jackson, Rucker, Armstrong, Ross and Strange. He thought it ironic that he was faced with six officers, one for each bullet he placed in his firearm. The men looked at him as he gingerly placed each bullet within the cylinder. They did not need the ability to read minds in order to know what he thought.

"Gentleman, if I order another attack at this position, those men will honor my command or they will be shot. And any general that cannot get his men moving forwards, will also be shot."

None of the men present even offered to challenge Forrest's stare.

"Now, you may inform the men that there will not be an attack as of this moment," he continued. "They did not lose this battle to the Federal cavalry, they lost it to their repeating rifles. It just does not seem fair. Not only is the enemy supplied with a bottomless barrel of infantry that they can put in the field against us, but they also have weapons of this magnitude. If we had the facilities to produce such a gun, we could easily offset the advantages they have in numbers. Ironically, it is they who have this weapon. Combine its awesome ability with an infinity of manpower, it makes for a very unfair playing field."

Forrest's anger visibly swelled within him. He took one of the Spencer rifles that his men had captured earlier and grasped it at its ends.

"We must not only find a way to defeat the enemies superior manpower, but we must also find a way to defeat this weapon." With a sudden flash, he brought the weapon down across his knee, but it did not break, depriving him of the desired effect. Forrest hurled the rifle into the woods.

Several men nearby jumped at the sound of it crashing through the foliage. Thinking the enemy had approached, they fired wildly in its direction. Forrest simply shook his head.

"Well boys, Wilson has the Yankee cavalry entrenched before us. We could not dislodge a brigade, so I doubt we can dislodge his divisions. Yet, we must not be delayed here, General Hood expects us to be in occupation of Spring Hill by this afternoon. Has anyone here any suggestions on how we may accomplish such a feat?"

"Might we not just disengage and ride towards Spring Hill? Once there, it can be us entrenched ready to brace for an attack, instead of the other way around?" Jackson asked.

Forrest gave the matter some thought. "That leaves too much at risk. If the enemy is already in occupation of Spring Hill, we will be hard pressed to take them on, especially as Wilson attacks our rear. And I am sure that there is no need to remind anyone that if there is a force at Spring Hill, hell, any size force, perhaps even a company, and they are armed with those rifles, we would still have a problem removing them."

That statement silenced the gathering. Forrest resolved to write his report to Hood. In it, he informed the general that his force could not be expected to secure Spring Hill. The Federal cavalry had them occupied at Mount Carmel, and there they would remain until further notice. When he finished the report he nonchalantly handed it to an aid.

"Sir, find General Hood and deliver this note at once," he said. He was about to pat the courier's horse on the backside to help it get a jump on its ride, when a very excited General Buford rode towards him. Buford was followed by two of his officers.

"General Forrest, the most unbelievable news," Buford said. "It appears that the Yanks are withdrawing to the north."

Forrest grabbed the reins of the courier's horse and took back his dispatch. A look of hope appeared upon all of their faces.

"To the north?" Forrest questioned. "Nashville? I am not sure I understand. Does the enemy think that we are racing for Nashville?"

Forrest let out a laugh that was cathartic. "Men, have your command ready to move at once. If the enemy thinks we mean to go to Nashville then by all means lets help to reassure him of that. I want this cavalry removed from the presence of the enemy. When he looks for us, I do not want us to be found. If Wilson cannot make contact with us, he will be convinced that we have again moved past his flank. If he continues to withdraw north, then I want him pursued. General Ross, have your men immediately mount and give them a chase, but do not get too close. If the Yankees see that there are fewer than seven hundred cavalry chasing them, they will surely turn with a fury.

The rest of you make preparations to race west. General Wilson has made a huge miscalculation here and we need to make every effort to exploit it. Gentleman, we are heading to Spring Hill, to join up with Hood's army. By its own will, the Federal cavalry has removed itself from the events that will occur this day."

Forrest watched as his generals took off to relay his command to their men. He liked the look in Ross' eyes after he was informed that his small force would chase the whole Federal cavalry. He turned to the parting Strange and grabbed him by the shoulder.

"Major, I think we may have found the only way to defeat the hordes of Yankees, and these weapons that they bare."

Strange waited for the general to elaborate upon his statement.

"We don't do a thing, Major," Forrest continued. "We do not attack, we do not press, we let their own damned stupidity work against them. Them Yankees are the damned, dumbest army that has ever been assembled. And it has taken us almost four years, and we still can't whip them from our soil."

Forrest hopped onto his mount and waited for Strange to follow. In the next few hours, Forrest's cavalry was riding west towards Spring Hill, while Wilson's retreated north towards Nashville. One of those two places was soon to be the sight of a crucial battle that would decide the fate of Tennessee.

Chapter XVII
That same day, late morning into the afternoon
Outskirts of Spring Hill, Tennessee

The Confederate cavalry rode in the direction of Spring Hill with over forty-five hundred troopers. To the small companies of Federal pickets guarding the northern and eastern vicinities of the town, the trembling ground was the harbinger misconstruing the arrival of a force much larger than that. Their only confidence was that which was placed in their repeating rifles. Still, when the rebel horseman charged the defenses, there was a moment of deep apprehension. Union pickets braced against the Confederate charge, and fired... and fired, and fired, and fired, and fired and fired and fired, without having to stop and reload after each shot. With this continued barrage of lead, they were able to throw back the wave of charging rebels.

The gray storm could be seen gathering across the field, and in a few minutes, their line would be tested again. Just as the rebels began to gallop, the Union men assigned to defend this area received a welcoming addition to their defense. Fresh reinforcements were jumping into position along the line to help repel the next Confederate advance. Their mettle fortified, the Federals eagerly replaced the long cylindrical casing that housed the next seven bullets that could fire both rapidly and repeatedly. Rearmed, reinforced and ready, the Federal pickets eagerly anticipated the next headlong charge from the Confederate cavalry.

They did not have to wait long.

The Confederate's rode forward with a wild look glaring in their eyes. From their mouths issued that infernal rebel yell. With a grim determination, the gray cloud climbed the small hill in hopes of breaking the Federals positioned there. The Confederate cavalry may have looked like a great gray cloud as it moved across their front, but it was the entrenched Federal line that had the power to summon thunder and lightning. With a hellacious volley fired at near point blank range, the Confederate charge was once again shattered.

Cheers erupted from the men in blue as they once again reloaded their arms and welcomed the arrival of even more reinforcements. Apparently not all of the Federal cavalry was with Wilson en route towards Nashville. There were some isolated detachments in the vicinity and they were quickly summoned as soon as the rebel host was spotted approaching Spring Hill. The men in blue greeted each other with smiles of security and eagerly awaited the next Confederate charge.

This time it never came.

As soon as Forrest's fist attack was repulsed, he understood his situation. Still, he allowed his command to make a few more attempts to charge the enemy. Each was repulsed. Forrest was correct hours ago, when he told his generals that even that smallest force, when armed with the repeating rifle, could hold off his entire advance. If Wilson had been pressing his rear instead of racing in the opposite direction, the Yanks occupying the position before him would have caused him a great deal of consternation. But by all reports, Wilson had retreated north, and never looked back.

This gave Forrest the time he needed to reorganize his command. It was still not even noon yet. Thus far, he had managed to drive Wilson's command from the area and begun his advance upon Spring Hill. General Hood was supposed to be arriving soon from the south, and together they could easily rout this small force. Forrest looked up at the bright sun as it promised hours of light. There was no reason to fruitlessly charge a position that could be taken in time. Forrest had better ideas. For him, it was time to show these ignominious Northerners how a Southerner learns from his mistakes.

All units were ordered to dismount from their horses. The advantage in numbers lay with the Confederates and vainglorious charges against the Federals would do no good except offer the Yankees some much needed target practice.

Instead, Forrest wanted his men to disregard their horses and forget all they knew about being cavalry. For at this moment, it was the infantry mentality that was needed most.

"Them Yankees know how to put up a quick defense. They must have pulled every available fence from the area and placed it upon the crest of that hill," Chalmers said.

Forrest surveyed their position and turned to Chalmers.

"That is quite all right General, there are not that many of them. Have your division dismount and slowly press around their northern flank. I will instruct Buford to do the same to their middle, while Jackson pushes them from the south. They have not the men to face every front. The pressure from either you or Jackson will force them to turn, that is when Buford will move forward."

"Understood sir," Chalmers said.

Forrest watched his plan unfold. His men moved forward with hesitation. They were all too familiar with the effects of the rapid firing Yankees. Some of his command was armed with the same captured rifles, but not enough. The progress was slow, but it was working. As one of the Federal flanks was turned, the rest of the force had to pull back. However, their rapid fire enabled them to stem any attempted breakthroughs. This meant that the whole advance had to be reorganized and attempted again. Each advance turned the Federal flank, but could not rout it. Slowly, deliberately, the Federal forces were withdrawing to Spring Hill, but they were doing so on their own terms.

It took Forrest's cavalry almost two hours, but they had finally managed to push the stubborn Federals within the outskirts of Spring Hill. Anxious to learn the whereabouts of Hood and his army, Forrest looked for a hill that would be high enough to offer a possible view of the advancing Confederate infantry. He saw such a hill towering towards the south. 'Excellent,' he thought, 'that hill's position would also be ideal for a clear view of the entire battlefield.' Mounting his steed, he called for Major Strange to follow, then rode towards the hill.

He was unconcerned with the possibility of any Federals lurking before him. He was sure that his men had cleansed the area. The sounds of firing ringing in the distance told him that his men were still pressing forward. Eager to survey the situation, he put a great distance between himself and his trailing companion.

He raced up the top of the hill and was greeted by a superb view of the field below him. He could see the Yankees being pushed back by his division, but he could also see that there were fresh Yanks arriving to bolster their lines. Forrest looked for Strange, but it was apparent he had not arrived yet.

"Where are they coming from?" he asked himself. He turned his gaze from the immediate battlefield, past the town of Spring Hill, to the turnpike that led from Columbia to Franklin.

The road was in complete chaos. There were wagons, artillery, troops, horses, and mules all striving to go in different directions. The troops were trying to get to the battlefield, while the wagons were obviously intent on escaping to the north.

Forrest gleamed with the possibilities before him. He quickly tried to see if there were any signs of Hood's arrival, but several tall trees obscured his view. With clenched fists, he thought, 'Where are you General, we have these Yankees where we want them.'

Growing impatient for Hood's arrival, Forrest raced back down the hill towards his men. He flew past Strange on his descent, and waved his hand for the major to follow. Forrest assumed Strange would understand.

The Confederate commander rode into the rear of the battlefield frantically searching for General Buford. A wounded officer pointed him in the correct direction. Forrest rode forward to where his men were exchanging fire with the enemy.

"General Buford," he called.

Buford had somehow managed to hear his commander over the clatter of rifle fire. "Yes, General," he said.

"Can you have a force mounted in the next few moments to assault this stubborn position?"

Buford was hesitant. "Sir, forgive me, but they would not stand a chance. Those Yankees are producing a hailstorm of bullets. The only thing keeping us intact at the moment is the fact that we are not mounted."

"I understand that General. I even agree. But the Yankee rear is in complete turmoil. That is where I want your regiment to strike. If we can rout them, there will be no place for them to reform. These Yankees in your front may very well panic once they realize that we have occupied their rear. Just give me a single attempt with one division, that is all I ask."

A half an hour later, the 21st Tennessee was remounted and sent galloping towards the Union wagon train. They broke from the cover of a cluster of trees and raced through the open field. Forrest watched with a great deal of hope as the 21st closed in on the Federal supply line. If they could take and hold that position, his men would augment the chaos along the pike, as well as force the entrenched Federals to pull back or risk being cut off from Spring Hill. And that was when Forrest would finally advance his entire command.

The 21st were within a few yards of the pike, when a company of Federal cavalry appeared before them. Forrest's sense of hope was quickly replaced with dread. He knew that the Yankees were undoubtedly equipped with their new menacing rifles and that they had purposely withheld their fire till they had his men in desirable range. Forrest also knew that the 21st was aware of that as well. Still they charged, into the murderous volley of the repeating rifles.

Forrest had to look away as his troopers were cut into shreds. A shadow of the force that was sent out returned. The valiant regiment was dismounted and sent to recover in the rear. Once again, he was frustrated by the Yankees and the unfair advantage that they had in firepower. He called for a quick meeting with his commanders and awaited their arrival. The first to show was Major Strange.

"Do you need a lesson on riding, Major?" Forrest asked.

"No sir, but you may need one on the lesson of staying close to your troops. You risk yourself too much, General."

Forrest removed his right boot. He was sure that a twig or small stone had somehow lodged itself between the leather bottom and the sole of his foot. He shook the boot violently, but nothing fell out.

Strange attended to an officer who arrived. Forrest looked at the officer, and realized he was not one under his command. He came from General Hood. This caused him to jump up, with boot in hand, and approach the man.

"Where the hell is the general?" he spat.

"Sir, General Hood reports that he has heard the battle taking place here and he instructs you to hold your position at all hazards. His advancing infantry columns are rapidly approaching this area."

"Well, it's about damned time," Forrest said. He quickly worked to replace his boot. He leaned on Strange as he did so. "You may report to General Hood that we will hold this position, at all hazards. I will work south of the Mount Carmel Road, so that our forces can consolidate all the quicker. Please tell Hood to hurry. My men are tired, but we have the enemy in check."

The officer saluted and rode back towards the direction of Hood's approaching army.

Forrest once again looked to his friend in the sky. The sun

was still shining, but it had started its trek west.

"Major, I understand that General Hood travels on one foot, but I was not aware that his horse did as well."

*   *   *   *   *   *   *   *

It was almost three in the afternoon when General Hood called a halt upon the south side of the Rutherford Creek. The morning had not gone exactly as he had expected, but in the end, he was glad to finally be mounted and riding at the head of his advancing army. Two aids quickly dismounted and helped untie him from his horse. His artificial leg stuck out like an aberration on the human form. With care he was placed on the ground and handed a crutch.

Generals Cheatham and Stewart were quickly at his side. In the distance, they could hear the sounds of a battle waging at Spring Hill. It was easy to tell that this troubled Hood.

"Sir, it is assuredly Forrest occupying the enemy," Cheatham said, trying to quell the anger that was within his commander. Cheatham had seen Hood explode into rage twice already this day, and he was not willing for a third. When Hood's army first crossed the Duck and traveled along David Ford Road, they were under the impression that the distance to Spring Hill was only twelve miles. However, as they meandered up a road that was ill suited for travel, it became obvious that something was awry. A local soldier was found, and he explained that the distance was in fact close to twelve miles, but only if you could travel that in a straight line. The road that they were on twisted and turned, making the twelve-mile distance stretch into seventeen.

When Hood had learned this, he threw his map onto the ground and bellowed about all matters that occurred to him that were beyond his control. Cheatham was embarrassed for him. The men marching past cast a worried look at the tantrum-ridden general. Was this the man who was to lead them into battle? It was Cleburne who diffused the situation. He quickly calmed Hood down and assured him that they still had the jump on Schofield. It appeared that the Yankees were still in Columbia, unaware that two corps of the Confederate army was marching completely east of their position.

For the moment Hood was assuaged. It was not to be that

way for long. Soon after the news that their map was not entirely accurate, came the reports of Federals occupying a position along a creek that intersected the David Ford Road. Hood was once again rattled. It seemed that he was so intent on the perfection of his plan, so completely sure that he would march to Spring Hill unabated, that when he received the news of Yankees to his front, he was momentarily stunned.

Hood was almost ready to call off his plan, complaining that somehow Schofield had anticipated his march and had cut him off. Hood halted the army as he sent a scout to investigate the Yankee presence. The scout quickly returned with promising news. It was only a Federal skirmish party. The report from his scout enabled him to regain his composure. Hood surveyed the landscape and noted several hills that separated his army from the pickets. He cautiously ordered his men to march forward, keeping the hills between them and the Federals. It was the lucky position of those hills that enabled Hood's army to escape the watchful eyes of the enemy.

It was this last thought that allowed Cheatham to comprehend the concern embedded on Hood's brow. Now that the Confederate army rested upon the Rutherford Creek, the sound of battle a few miles ahead at Spring Hill opened the possibility that perhaps they had not slipped past the pickets successfully.

"General Cheatham," Hood said, "that battle that we hear tells me one thing and one thing only... General Forrest is not in occupation of that town. It also tells me that the force that is at his front is obviously large enough to contest his advance. It also makes me unsure of the position of General Schofield's forces. Have the Federals at Columbia withdrawn up the pike towards Spring Hill? Until I have these answers, I must remain cautious. For the time being, we will hold here. Please send one of your messengers to Spring Hill. I want him to get word to General Forrest, that he must hold his position at all hazards, this army is rapidly approaching his position."

"Yes sir," Cheatham said. "In fact, we are within three miles of the town." With that Cheatham turned towards a member of his staff and issued orders for the dispatch to be sent to Forrest.

"I am sure Forrest will have little trouble holding the enemy at bay," Stewart said.

"I do not doubt that claim. It is still hard to believe that he has both driven the Federal cavalry before him and also managed to reach Spring Hill in so little time. It is just most unfortunate that it is there that he must wait, until this army can join him. We should have reached that town hours ago."

"There was no way of knowing that the map was not accurate."

"Perhaps. And perhaps we who are from this country, these men of Tennessee, should not have used a captured Yankee map. I blame myself for that."

"I always said that the Yankees were never good at anything," Stewart smirked.

Hood returned the smile. By now, Hood's senior officers were gathered. Stewart's divisional commanders quickly mingled with their counterparts from Cheatham's corps. The hour for socializing was now past.

It was time for the commander of the Army of Tennessee to take charge.

"General Cheatham, are all your divisions at hand," he asked?

"Sir, Cleburne's is, as you are aware," Cheatham said. "General Bate, please give the status of your command."

"General Hood, my men are not far behind," Bate reported.

"That is fine, please depart at once and bring them forth with all haste. General Cleburne, I want your division to cross this creek and make contact with Forrest at Spring Hill. Once you can link with his left flank, I want your men to assist the cavalry by moving forward to engage the enemy at Spring Hill. General Cheatham, when Bate returns, please instruct him to have his division cross this creek in support of Cleburne."

"Yes sir," Cheatham said.

"General Hood, what of my command?" Stewart asked.

Hood turned his sunken eyes south as he answered. "You are to have your men form in line on this side of the creek."

Stewart and his staff were astounded. "General Hood, I beg to have my men out in line next to Cheatham's," Stewart pleaded. "We have the enemy occupied before us, would not the combined might of two corps overwhelm their position and leave us in occupation of Spring Hill?"

Hood's head shook in agreement, but his words were a different sort.

"That would be my choice as well general, if I were sure

217

of Schofield's force. What if that Federal company we saw earlier reported our position to Schofield? And Schofield in turn has raced his army to this town using quicker interior lines. If that is the case, and we are attacked, Cheatham will need a place to fall back to. A place that is defended by a well prepared command. Stewart, I know you want the battle, and I assure you, if Schofield is at Spring Hill and he is able to push Cheatham back across this creek, it will be your boys who can shell them back."

Stewart's disdain was not comforted by Hood's proposal. "Sir, you are assuming too much and I fear you are overestimating the enemy."

Hood retorted like a striking rattlesnake. "General, this is my army, I am responsible for its fate. I must use great caution here. Two thirds of my army is separated from its cavalry, while my other corps is isolated south of Columbia. I have taken much risk to place us in such scattered positions, and I will not rush these men into a battle in which I am unsure of the enemy's numbers. Perhaps we have beaten Schofield's army to this position, but can you with confidence say that Thomas' command is not present. We can not forget that there is another Yankee army in Nashville as well."

Many of the officers were so intent on chasing Schofield, they had forgotten to consider the fact that the more north they went, the closer they came in proximity to Thomas' army. Stewart and others present thought that these prudent words ironic coming from its source. Was this John Bell Hood... the man who struck first and asked later, the commander who led several frontal charges in the face of a shrapnel infested hell, the general who very recently was willing to give the order to have his men cross the Duck and strike the defenses of Columbia... was this that same John Bell Hood telling his men they needed to be careful? Stewart let his trepidation dissolve in the hopes that this new cautious commander was portending to a new hope for the Army of the Tennessee.

"General, my men will form here. But what are my instructions if Schofield is still in Columbia, as we so hope?" Stewart asked.

"If Schofield is still in Columbia, then I may call upon you to either fall into line next to Cheatham, as you wish now, or better yet, if Cheatham is able to drive the enemy before him, I may have you travel this creek northwest, so that you can arrive south of the

Columbia to Franklin turnpike and cut off the enemy's escape.

"Gentlemen, I hope all is fully understood. Now, please retire to your men and have them readied to move out. Tell them the battle that they have waited for so long is finally upon them. I expect them to show those Yankees no quarter for what they have put the citizens of Atlanta through."

Hood was re-saddled with the assistance of his aids. He started forward to ride with Cheatham, but Cheatham was headed the other way.

"General, the battle is this way," he remarked.

Cheatham smiled. "That it is, but I am going back down the road to make sure that Bate has his men moving forward. I also want to impart to him his need to connect with Cleburne's flank and join the attack for Spring Hill."

Hood agreed and watched Cheatham ride off. After gathering his staff, Hood rode off after the advancing brigades of Cleburne's division. The men were wading through the Rutherford creek with alacrity. The realization that they would finally have the long sought battle with the Northerners was showing in their step. Heads were held high and chests lunged forward. General Hood was never so proud of these men or this army.

As Hood rode by, the Army of Tennessee raised their hats and gave a cheer. Hood smiled and spoke many words of encouragement. As he reached the other side of the Rutherford, he began searching for Cleburne. Being mounted with the other officers, the Irishman was easy to locate. Cleburne was in the middle of reviewing the strategy for the day with his brigade commanders. Hood raced towards them, wanting to be sure that they all understood their part in the unfolding events of this day.

"Generals," he called as he approached.

The officers all turned upon their mounts and greeted their commander.

"General Hood, will you be riding forward with us?" Cleburne asked.

"For now," he said. "I wanted to be sure that my orders were clear. Too many times I have issued commands that were not followed. Or not followed with a sense of urgency and understanding."

"Sir, I can promise you that my division will not falter this day. Your orders were very clear. We will continue to march along the Rally Hill Pike until we deploy into line and make our advance upon Spring Hill. At that time, General Bate's division should be on hand to support our attack. General, I would say that those orders are as clear and precise as they come."

Hood looked at the faces of Cleburne's brigade commanders. They were determined, all of them, that was good. The sounds of battle could still be heard at Spring Hill, but it was dwindling. Eager to know more concerning the situation at Spring Hill, Hood spotted a high hill looming up the pike. He called for his staff to follow as he rode on. He could hear Cleburne in the distance call for him to be careful, as this was still the enemy's territory. Hood thought it ironic how Tennessee could be considered the enemy's territory.

Hood, however, was not concerned with any danger. His army was quickly gathering behind him, and his cavalry could be heard before him. Taking little note of the bucolic countryside, he galloped up the hill with a burning desire to finally see the objective of his grand strategy materialize before his eyes. There were a lot of men who doubted Hood's bold offensive when he first departed from the mountains of northern Georgia. That was something that the giant Texan from Kentucky had to live with every single day. He felt that even the President had lost faith in him after the fall of Atlanta. Why else would Beauregard have been put in command, except for Hood having to report to him? It was Davis' indirect way of saying that Hood still had command of the army, but he needed to confer all his actions with Beauregard.

Though that had hurt him greatly, it was hard for him to lose much sleep over it. Hood needed this victory for other reasons... more specifically to prove his worth to the parents of his beloved Buck. Hood was fully aware that the Preston family felt that he was not good enough for their daughter, and until Hood could win their approval, Buck would forever remain outside of his grasp.

And then there was Sherman. And if Hood needed to prove himself to anyone, it was he.

There were several sound reasons as to why Hood harbored such an intense hatred for the Union Commander. Sherman had committed atrocities against the people of Atlanta, he ordered the bombardment of civilians, and then he ordered all of the inhabitants of Atlanta to flee. But the fall of Atlanta left nowhere for them to go. Amongst the many exiles were women, some pregnant, children and the elderly. Their husbands were all off fighting and dying to prevent the very destruction that had happened to Atlanta. That was enough to make any man hate his enemy, but what happened after Atlanta was the salt that was poured upon his open wound. Sherman simply turned his back upon Hood and marched east. It was the Union generals way of saying that Hood and the Army of Tennessee were no longer a concern. It was the greatest disrespect ever imparted upon John Bell Hood.

His impending conquest in mid Tennessee meant to silence all his critics, have his President's faith restored in him, win the Preston's favor, and most of all, to show General Sherman that he had made the biggest mistake anyone can make when dealing with him.

You do not turn your back on John Bell Hood.

Hood reached the top of the hill and looked before him. The view was magnificent. He could see the battlefield as if it were displayed for his own personal viewing. His staff quickly surrounded him. Hood was handed a pair of field glasses and he carefully studied the scene.

Forrest's cavalry was dismounted to the east of the town. It appeared that they had contained the Federals entrenched there. There was one set of hills that anchored itself along the northern end of the Rally Hill Pike. A large creek cut through these hills as if it meant to divide them in half. The Yankees were in possession of that hill, and were facing off against Forrest's troopers situated on the raised plateau opposite them. Closer to Hood's present location was an elevated ridge. A creek that branched from another creek, the McCutcheon, separated the ridge from the Yankee occupied hills farther to the north. He quickly figured that all of those intersecting creeks combined with the enemy occupying the high ground could present his army with a tactical problem.

The general turned his attention to the west of the enemy position and he saw the town of Spring Hill. The place was in chaos. There was severe congestion bottlenecked in the center of the town. Supply wagons were trying to go one way, while troops were trying to go another. With his glasses, Hood followed the long trail of wagons as its tip rode north, with its long supply chain trailing south down the Columbia to Franklin Turnpike towards Columbia.

Hood felt his heart race.

Those wagons were a clear indication that Schofield was pulling out of Columbia. The inferior amount of Federals defending the town meant that he won the race to Spring Hill. So elated that he had actually accomplished his goal, he began to feel disoriented. It was like trying to court a woman who was not interested in you. You pursue her for months upon months and to no avail. And then one day she turns and says yes. Then what do you do? Hood smiled at the analogy.

"Gentlemen, we have the enemy where I want him," he said. "Now how do I finish him off?"

"Sir, give the order to attack," said an excited officer.

Hood did not seem to hear him. "That turnpike, I fear may be the problem. There are not enough Yankees at Spring Hill to threaten my attack. Yet the position they occupy could very well hold against a single division. I will be forced to commit more men, and if the Federals control that pike that leads into this town, Schofield could very well fall upon our rear and smash us. That cannot be allowed to happen.

Spring Hill is no longer the objective, instead it shall be that road feeding Schofield's army into the town. The only good ground the Yankees can occupy is that which they are on, I do not intend to let any more of them get into that favorable position. We will have Cleburne's division form here and march directly to that turnpike. They will ignore the Yankee presence to their north, their numbers are too insignificant to be a concern as of yet. When Cleburne reaches that pike, his men are to wheel and cut off that road. Schofield will have to get his men through our best division in order to get to this town.

General Bate's orders, however, will remain unchanged. Bate will still march his division in support of Cleburne's flank, only instead of advancing to Spring Hill, he will be advancing towards the turnpike with Cleburne's division."

Hood's staff was struggling with the revised orders. Internally, many of them were questioning their commander. The Federals seemed trapped within the town. Two corps of the Confederate army could be on hand in a few hours to entirely crush their defense and still have time to block the turnpike that led into the town. Yet, it was Hood who was in command and not they, and that was so for a reason. Perhaps the Federal occupied hills east of the town were more formidable than they seemed. They had after all held Forrest's cavalry off for several hours.

As if Hood was reading their minds, he spoke. "We need to make contact with General Forrest and let him know we are on hand. Perhaps he can lend some support to Cleburne's advance?"

An explosion rocked the hill just as Hood finished speaking. Many of the horses reared in fear. The men fought to control their mounts, when more shells began to invite themselves to their location. Hood, with the benefit of one good hand, fought desperately to control his horse. A shell struck far to his right, but the sound caused his mount to take off back down the hill. Hood pulled on the reins with all the might he could muster from his right arm, but the horse jerked back even stronger. The horse's wild descent from the hill, coupled with the awful muddy condition of the road led to a most unfortunate accident for the Texan.

Under normal conditions, a rider could use his legs to help maintain his balance on a wild steed. However, Hood was not riding under normal conditions, besides being handicapped in one arm, he also had the use of only one leg. The wooden peg that was attached to the stump of his thigh was as much use as a walking stick to a deaf man. When his horse took a violent turn to avoid a tree limb that intersected the path, Hood came free from the rope that tied him to his mount and was thrown into the brush and mud.

Luckily, he was not seriously hurt. His men quickly flew to his side to assist him back upon a calmer horse. Hood tried to maintain his dignity by assuring them he was fine. Biting down the swelling he felt in his side, he quickly wiped away the mud that clung to him.

"No one is to hear of this," he said. Hood was obviously shamed by his crippled condition and the inability it caused him. Controlling your horse was considered a right of passage to a Southern man. In front of his staff, he failed in this considerably. He quickly tried to change the subject. "I will need to retire at once to that farm we passed earlier. I need time to think on these new plans."

His officers were not fooled. The general had obviously hurt more than his side... his pride was also damaged. "Yes, sir," one of his staff said. "That was the home of a Mr. Absalom Thompson. Mr. Thompson has already said that he would consider it an honor if you would use his abode as your headquarters."

Once remounted, Hood and his staff rode back down the Rally Hill Pike. From ahead, he could see Cleburne's leading divisions marching towards them. There was never a chance to mistake the men of Patrick Cleburne, for they waved one of the most unique battle flags of the war. Framed in white, it consisted of a large white moon centered upon a blue sky. This one of a kind flag was the perfect complement to its commander.

Riding with Cleburne was General Forrest. The sight of his cavalry commander helped to soothe the pain in Hood's side.

"I regret that your army was not here sooner," Forrest said. "I do believe that at first we faced dismounted cavalry, but their infantry soon arrived and reinforced their positions. However, if I had captured the town earlier, I might not have received this." Forrest shifted his coat to the right and pulled a parchment from his waist. He handed it to Hood.

Hood opened it with much interest. The look on Forrest's face told him it that the dispatch contained something monumental. He was not mistaken. Hood held a captured dispatch sent three thirty this morning from General Thomas to General Schofield. It read, 'I desire you to fall back from Columbia and to take up your position at Franklin, leaving a sufficient force at Spring Hill to contest the enemy's progress.'

Hood stopped reading and looked up at his cavalry commander. "This is wonderful news," he said. "This confirms that the Federals will fall back to this point and proves all the more that this division must block that pike until the rest of our army can be brought up."

Forrest knew that there was more to the dispatch than that. He waited for Hood to figure it out, but grew impatient. "General that is true, but that dispatch provided information far more valuable than even what you have discerned. Have you read it all?"

Hood looked puzzled.

"General, nowhere does it state that Thomas or his army will be on hand once Schofield reaches Franklin. If I can recite the last words of that dispatch, it reads something to the effect that General A.J. Smith's command has still not reached Nashville, but when he does, he plans to make an immediate disposition of his troops. General Hood, this means we have the enemy cut in half, and there is no need to fear the presence of Thomas. Schofield is in this alone."

The words were an awakening to Hood. He looked down at the dispatch and quickly finished reading it. Forrest was absolutely correct. Thomas was still at Nashville. The Confederate army was hours from occupying Spring Hill, and moments from blocking the road the Federals needed to escape. Unknowingly, Schofield was marching into his own coffin.

Hood parted from Cleburne confident in the success of his plan. He went in search of General Bate, and very quickly found him along with his arriving divisions. Hood was upset that Cheatham was not with Bate, apparently his corps commander had just ridden off only a few moments ago. Hood informed Bate of the new objective and apologized for his not being able to ride forward with the men. The pain from his fall was throbbing. He was also quite tired, having had a long day, and his broken body was feeling all of its effects.

With his army marching to its destiny, Hood did not mind the pain his body was in. Besides, there was a half-filled bottle of laudanum waiting for him back at the supply wagon.

Just a few sips of its contents and all his bodily discomforts would be long forgotten.

Chapter XVIII
Late Afternoon
Spring Hill, Tennessee

Initially, General Stanley was not enthusiastic about his march up the Columbia to Franklin Turnpike. As far as he was concerned, his place was back at Columbia with the majority of the Federal army. Though he was Schofield's senior officer, he did not hold his grudge towards him. It was Sherman who made the decision as to who would command this army. And Sherman had not thought well of him since Jonesborough.

So, instead of being at Columbia and preparing the army against the imminent attack from Hood, Stanley was sent to escort three brigades from General Wagner's Second division, along with a plethora of supply wagons towards Franklin.

The noise of the march fell silent upon his ears. So depressed with his charge, he simply guided his mount with a melancholic pace. Sometime around noon he had received word from Schofield that the rebels were north of the Duck, and that he should select a strong position at Spring Hill. The thought of having a purpose this far north of the enemy rekindled his heart. Schofield had wanted the pike protected so the rest of the Federal army could use it later this evening. He also wanted Stanley to send out skirmish parties to guard all roads leading east and southeast of that town.

Stanley was dubious of Schofield's concern. He thought that the general was being too worried about a non-existent threat. But when his men approached Spring Hill, Stanley saw first hand how wrong he was. As much as he hated to admit it, Schofield's earlier order of sending him to Spring Hill now seemed the only thing that could save the Federals from disaster. The rebel cavalry was threatening the town, and with no sign of Wilson, Stanley realized that Schofield's escape route could be cut off at any moment.

The next few hours were as close to pandemonium as he had ever experienced. He and his staff had to clear the road of the lumbering supply wagons to make room for his troops to get through. It was a slow process, but eventually Stanley succeeded.

Opdycke's and Lane's brigades were sent to the north and to the east of the town to hold off the advancing Confederates and to also guard the wagon train.

The last brigade to form was Bradley's. Confident that Forrest could not push past the brigade to the north of the town or the one that occupied the hills to the east, Stanley was on hand to personally deploy Bradley's brigade on a wooded knoll to the south of Lane's position on the hills. There were also two creeks that separated his brigades from supporting one other. Initially that was a concern for Stanley, but as they day wore on, it appeared that Forrest's men were running low on ammo. And when their attacks finally subsided, Stanley worked on entrenching his positions. Fortunately, the terrain he occupied was favorable for the defense. It should allow him to hold off the rebel attack at least until later this evening, when the remainder of Schofield's army should arrive.

His stern gaze followed the sun as it passed over Spring Hill. The sooner the better, he thought. The rebels wouldn't attack in the dark, and they would not see the arrival of Schofield's army. The morning would show just how brave Forrest and his cavalry were.

Taking one last look at the wooded hills towards the east, he turned his mount and rode back towards the town. The threat here had been contained and this sector was now in good hands. Bradley had such ease repulsing Forrest's last advance, Stanley was able to part from his general with a shake of hands, and words of confidence.

The positions that his three brigades now occupied were formidable enough to hold off the rebel cavalry as well as protect Spring Hill from the north, east and west. Bradley only had to keep Forrest at bay until the rest of the Fourth and Twenty-third corps arrived from Columbia later this evening.

*　　*　　*　　*　　*　　*　　*　　*

The men in Bradley's command felt a great deal of relief when they saw the general ride away. No longer having to put on a show for their commander, they slowed down considerably on the construction of the barricade protecting their front. Many of these men were new to the army and obviously did not have an appreciation for the task that was assigned to them. With the Confederate cavalry beaten back, they did not understand why they had to spend the remainder of the day gathering fence railings and whatever else that could be used as a deterrent to the enemy's advance. It was cold and the approaching night meant that it would soon get colder. Having spent the entire day marching on a congested road, many wondered when they were going to be afforded some rest?

Suddenly the entire line became ominously quiet. No one knew from where the silence permeated, but one by one, all of the soldiers in Bradley's brigade peered over the barricade. To their utter disbelief, an entire rebel division had just emerged from a wooded hill into the open field. From the flags that were seen waving with the winds, it was none other than Patrick Cleburne.

And Cleburne meant infantry.

Bradley's men did not know about the situation surrounding the other two brigades in their corps, their concerns were of their own. Defending this knoll against dismounted cavalry was one thing, but were they actually expected to do the same against the Confederate army? And where had Cleburne come from? Wasn't Hood supposed to be contained south of the Duck River?

Men began casting rude remarks concerning the impotence of General Wilson and his cavalry. And if Cleburne was here, might not the entire rebel army be close behind? With thoughts of pulling back to the village, they turned to their commander. Unfortunately, one look at Bradley told them that there was no hint of a retreat. His brigade was going to hold this ground for as long as it could.

What the soldiers of the Federal brigade had not noticed was what separated their military acumen from Bradley's. It appeared that Cleburne's division was oblivious to their position. They were not marching for their knoll, but past it to the west. Cleburne's formation was also spaced awkwardly. Since they were marching towards the turnpike, the rebels were soon to be perpendicular and to the south of his current position. As the enemy marched across the open field, their echelons were stretching north to south. That would give Bradley an excellent opportunity to volley against their exposed right flank as it came in the vicinity of his gunfire.

Many of Bradley's men were raw recruits, but as he observed down his line, he knew that he did not have to tell them what to do. The momentary silence was soon replaced by a susurrus of anticipation. Quietly, the soldiers in Bradley's' brigade began to pile anything they could onto their barricade as they readied themselves for the surprise volley they hoped to score on the enemy.

*　　*　　*　　*　　*　　*　　*　　*

Patrick Cleburne's division marched over the campestral landscape that was to the west of the Rally Hill Pike. Concealed by the woods, over three thousand soldiers rapidly made their way towards the Columbia to Franklin Pike. They were supported on their right by a detachment of cavalry granted from General Forrest. Up ahead, Cleburne could see that his men would have to ascend a hill and emerge through a screen of trees. From that point, they would have to embark on the last part of their march through an open field. He quickly halted his command at the edge of the woods.

"General Cleburne, your men march with as much august-ness as any army I have ever been a witness to," Forrest said.

"General, coming from you, that is a great honor."

"Well sir, you have my Colonel, Tyree Bell's brigade in support, I trust you will take that pike and hold it, while the rest of Cheatham's corps move into position on your flank. I must retire and attend to the needs of the rest of my command. Besides being in desperate need of both a good meal and rest, many of my men have no ammunition left."

"Your men are in good hands, General," Cleburne said as he shook hands with Forrest. He watched the cavalry commander turn and ride back towards the Rally Hill Pike with his staff. Cleburne then reached into a saddlebag and produced his field glasses. He dismounted from his horse, and walked towards the clearing. He could hear his men engage in conversation about the nearness of battle. It brought a smile to his face as he crouched to one knee and viewed the Federal escape route.

The pike looked undefended. Hood's revised plan seemed to make sense. With little casualties, he could get his entire division to that road and cut it off from Spring Hill. With Cheatham's corps denying the remainder of Schofield's army from reaching the town, Stewart could then easily defeat the Federal forces trapped there. Cleburne noted the sun starting to set in the west.

The time for action was upon them.

"Gentlemen," he said as he turned towards his brigade commanders, "You are to march your men to that road which runs into Spring Hill. We are expected to take and hold a position astride it, denying Schofield access to that town. We will march in echelon. General Lowrey, your brigade will occupy our right flank, General Govan, you will take up the middle, and General Granbury will be the left flank. Colonel Bell's brigade of Forrest's command will lend his support on our right flank. Together, this division is expected to march to that road, and then wheel to the south forming a solid line. We will hold that position by ourselves, until General Bate's division arrives in support.

I expect the time that we are alone to be a time of desperation for the Yankees and not us. Once they realize that our division has cut them off from Franklin, I am sure that they will do whatever it takes to remove us from that road. Tell your men that once we are astride that road, that they are not permitted to fall back under any conditions, unless there is an order to do so from me. You may also tell them that I will never give that order."

Cleburne watched as his brigade commanders dispersed to their commands to begin the formation of their lines of battle. Shortly after, the leading division of the Army of Tennessee emerged from the wooded hills and marched with their immutable command over the open fields south of Spring Hill.

As Cleburne rode behind Govan's brigade, he could not help but offer a prayer of thanks to God for giving him such a magnificent division to command. Forrest's comment about his men made him bashful earlier, but it was not something he could deny. The blue flags of his division waved wildly as they guided his troops across the Tennessee hinterland. It was a moment that needed to be captured in a painting.

For months, his men have been on the receiving end of blow after blow from the Federal army. Well, the Yankees gave it all they had, and after the smoke cleared, the Confederates were beaten, but not defeated. They proved that they could handle the best that the Yankees had to offer. General Sherman had come at them with over one hundred and twenty thousand aggressors, and that was their best, the strongest this Yankee army had ever been. And now Sherman was somewhere in southern Georgia with over half of those men. Cleburne liked these new odds a lot better. The Confederates had faced the epic battle against Sherman's overwhelming numbers and had survived to fight another day.

Now, it was their turn to deliver the lead, and Cleburne wondered just how the Yankee mettle would hold.

Cleburne eased his horse, as he surveyed the pike ahead. For some reason the brief respite brought forth the image of his beloved fiancée Susan Tarleton. Her presence at this moment reminded him how important she was to his life. He could not wait for the war's end, so that he could spend his days with his love. He had fallen in love with Miss Tarleton while attending the wedding of his good friend General Hardee. He let his eyes close for a moment as he imagined his hands dancing in her parted hair... her beautiful long eyes staring at him with nothing but love. The feel of her warm lips against his as he lowered his mouth to....

An explosion of gunfire erupted from Cleburne's right. The presence of Federals this close to their position caught the entire division by surprise. Cleburne was furious. The pike was just over one mile away, and his flank was being attacked from the north. There was not supposed to be a Federal threat present until they reached the pike. Cleburne left his finance's lips wanting that kiss, as he galloped towards Lowrey's brigade. Something had gone wrong.

As he rode forward, he could see the smoke of the Federal guns as it clung to the top of a knoll like pogonip indigenous to the Western mountains. Cleburne felt his fury mount as he approached Lowrey's very disorganized brigade.

How could Hood have missed the Federal position upon that knoll? Cleburne agreed with the proposal to march to the Columbia Pike because he was under the impression that there would not be any enemy present to impede his march. He had been instructed by Hood to deploy his men in echelon so that they could wheel to the left and cut off the road into Spring Hill. That ordered formation could be disastrous if there was a significant enemy force to the north.

As Cleburne joined Lowrey's rear, he realized his worst fears were true. The knoll that the Yankees occupied was to the north of his position. With his men marching west, their right flank was completely exposed to enfilade fire. What was worse, the rest of his command was deployed south of this position, also marching west. It would take considerable time to reorganize his formations and bring his other regiments to the point of attack.

He had to make a decision. Was he to hold off this Federal threat with Lowrey's brigade, while his other brigades continued to the turnpike? Or was he to change Hood's battle plans and commit his division to the Yankees on the knoll, and let Bate's brigade have the responsibility of the turnpike?

"General Cleburne, General Cleburne," yelled Lowrey.

Cleburne turned to see his general rapidly approaching.

"They came out of nowhere and delivered a deadly volley onto my men," Lowrey said. "I can't get my other regiments into position fast enough, and those Yanks that we are facing are only the right portion of their line. It continues to stretch farther that way."

"There are more of them?" Cleburne asked. "General, how many Yankees are in occupation of that knoll?"

Lowrey shot a worried glance back over his shoulder. "I would say that there is probably a brigade dug in on our flank. And like I said, we have only engaged their right most regiments. I believe that their units not yet engaged are preparing an attack of their own. Colonel Bell's cavalry are hard pressed as it is. Sir, we are outflanked. If those Yankees attack, I fear we will not be able to hold long enough for our other regiments to wheel into position."

Cleburne studied the line of battle. Lowrey's assessment of the situation was most accurate. It was true that his men were only being attacked by the right portion of the Federal line, but if he could bring Govan's brigade in support, and have them march around Lowrey's engaged men, he could then outflank the Federal right, and force that side to rout. From that position, Govan's brigade could return the favor of enfilading fire on the remainder of the Federal Brigade.

The sound of a wild Yankee cheer blared from the north side of the knoll. One look at Lowrey's widened eyes told Cleburne that was the start of the attack he most feared.

Cleburne kicked his horse and turned it towards his other two brigades. "General Lowrey, you may return to your men and inform them to hold their position. You need not worry about the Yankees charging for I will charge them first."

The two generals galloped off in opposite directions.

Cleburne's Advance

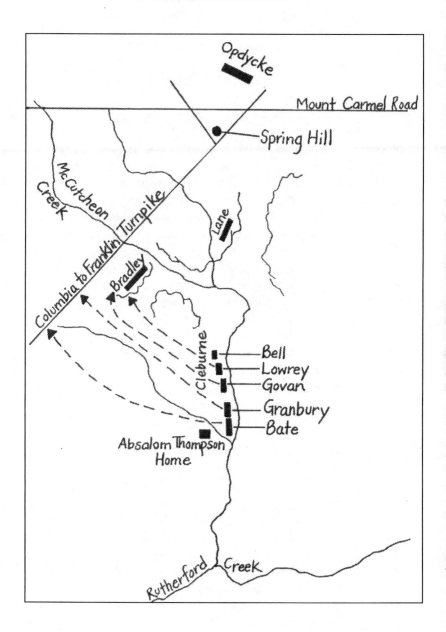

Cleburne's choice was decided for him, the turnpike was no longer the primary objective. What was Hood thinking having his men march unprotected and exposed to a Federal brigade on his flank? He would demand an answer later this evening. Had anyone else in this army made such a mistake, Hood would not be so forgiving. We'll see how he holds up to his own judging?

Cleburne rode in the direction of his second brigade under the command of General Govan. He had to fight against his internal rage and force himself to accept the situation as it was. He was not the one responsible for the predicament, but he was the one responsible for how he would react to the predicament. The problem was that with the enemy to the north and on his flank, his westward marching echelon formations were so out of place on this battlefield. The simple task of bringing supporting divisions to the point of attack would now require great skill.

Cleburne would not trust anyone but himself to the task.

As he approached Govan's men, he could see that there was a unanimous look of concern from the sound of battle to the north. The men marched west with heads that swiveled to the right. Cleburne rode through the Arkansas divisions till he found General Govan. The general was accompanied by his staff, and was conversing with Cleburne's aid Lieutenant L. H. Mangum.

"General Cleburne," Govan said. "My men are continuing west but it sounds as if we are marching away from the battle?"

Cleburne looked past Govan towards the south. His third brigade was still marching for the turnpike. There would be no time to bring those men up at the moment. Perhaps with Granbury's brigade he could still accomplish his initial objective and occupy the pike with his lone brigade.

"Lieutenant," Cleburne said, "please send word to General Cheatham that we cannot afford to move against the turnpike while the enemy is in position upon our right flank. Inform him that I intend to give battle."

Mangum saluted his general and rode off. Cleburne did not want to waste another moment issuing any orders except the ones that got this brigade moving alongside Lowrey's left. The sounds of the battle still could be heard and Cleburne was sure that the Yankees had not braved a charge as of yet.

"General Govan, we have little time," he said. "Lowrey's brigade has been disorganized by the surprised flanking volley delivered by the enemy. The Yankees position atop the grassy knoll is a heavily entrenched one. Fortunately, only the right half of their line is currently engaged with Lowrey. I fear that a Yankee counterattack by their rightmost divisions is imminent unless we can get your brigade there to attack first. I want this brigade to wheel north and march to Lowrey's left flank. From that position you will be beyond the Yankee right. The attack launched by your command must completely flank and rout the Federal brigade. Once your attack is underway, General Lowrey's brigade will then move in support. Since time is of the utmost importance, please allow me to address your men."

Cleburne and Govan rode to the front of the advancing brigade and called it to halt. "Men of Arkansas, you march by my command to the west, but I can tell by the direction of your gazes that your heart is for the battle to the north." With raised hats, the men issued a wild cheer. Cleburne smiled to them as he pulled his saber from its scabbard. "Then let me not be the one that denies a man from Arkansas what his heart demands. The battle is to the north. Let us wheel this brigade immediately so that we may come in support of Lowrey's left flank."

The brigade from Arkansas continued to cheer as they re-formed their lines with amazing speed. In a time too short for Cleburne to appreciate, the men of Govan's brigade turned their determined faces to the north, gritted their teeth, and took a firm hold of their rifles.

The long wait was over. The Army of Tennessee was on the attack.

*   *   *   *   *   *   *   *

General Lowrey looked over his shoulder one last time, but there was still so no sign of Cleburne or the support he was promised. Luckily, he had been able to realign his men so that they faced north in anticipation of the Federals counterattack. The shock of the Yankee presence had finally fizzled, as his men were able to settle down and exchange fire with the Northerners. Lowrey was thankful that his brigade was made up of good southern veterans. A lesser brigade may very well have routed had it been surprised with a similar attack.

Still it took tremendous effort not to commit his men too far forward. He thought he could hold his ground until support arrived, but the Yankee left began to cheer again. If those men attacked while his brigade was pinned down as it was, then even his stubborn veterans would be forced to retire. Lowrey quickly called to an aid and instructed him to have a regiment ready to be thrown into the path of the imminent Yankee advance. The regiment selected was expected to sacrifice itself so that the rest of his brigade could successfully withdraw to safety.

As the officer departed with his command, the Yankee cheer reached a crescendo for a third time. 'The third time's the charm,' Lowrey thought as he peered out to witness the Yankee counterattack. It never came. The explosion of the infamous rebel yell completely swept the Yankee cheer away. Lowrey spun around to see the flags of Govan's brigade, led by none other than General Cleburne, move up in support of his left. The men from Arkansas raised their caps as they marched past his men and towards the right of the Federal knoll. Lowrey's brigade returned the cheer and looked for their commander to give the word to attack.

Realizing he had the support he needed, Lowrey heeded little attention to the Yankee right and sent his men charging the enemy to his front. The Federals poured a meager volley into the stampeding Confederates. Any thought of holding their ground was washed away with the emergence of the second rebel brigade advancing on their right. A brigade that threatened to cut them off from the safety of Spring Hill. Faced with rebels to their front and on their flank, the Yankee right crumbled. The men in blue dropped guns, knapsacks, flags, and anything else that would delay their escape. The shame in seeing the Yanks drop their flags made it easier for the Confederates to fire into their fleeing backs.

The Federal left watched in horror as half of their brigade was routed towards Spring Hill. Not to be left behind, they quickly left their defensive position and raced across the creek after their fleeing comrades. Within minutes, Cleburne's men were in possession of the knoll. The battle was a complete success, but he couldn't help thinking that had his men been in better position prior to that attack, it could have ended much sooner and much worse for the Yankees.

Cleburne took a moment to gather his staff and issue new orders. His men had not stopped advancing after the victory. They were charging close upon the heels of the fleeing Federal brigade. That was something Cleburne liked to see. His men did not have to be told to attack when it was so clear to do so. Cleburne raced towards the action. If his men could catch the Yanks before they could reform, there was an excellent chance of destroying the entire command. With his sword held high above him, he charged ahead.

As he neared the southern perimeter of Spring Hill, he noted that the ground, once filled with corn, was now littered with discarded Federal debris. The only casualties that he passed thus far were men in blue uniforms, fallen with their faces buried in the mud and their backs spotted with bullet holes. His horse began to sink in that same mud, making for an unsteady ride. Not wanting to race too far ahead while mounted, he slowed down to watch his advancing division close in on the Federals.

Complete victory was seconds from his grasp, until a bellowing thunder of a Federal battery roared from the town ahead. He cautiously moved forward as the artillery continued to pour into his men.

"General Cleburne, the enemy has rallied behind a battery upon a ridge to our front."

Cleburne looked to his left to see his aid. Magnum's face was muddied, he must have been riding with the advancing divisions.

"We almost had them, sir," he continued. "There is another creek up ahead and a then another ridge. It seems the enemy has been blessed with an abundance of favorable ground."

Cleburne watched as his men began to withdraw from their assault. These boys have had enough experience with Federal artillery to allow bravado to take over. "Lieutenant, this is strong ground, but it does not belong to the enemy. This is our homeland." Cleburne raised his field glasses in the direction of the ridge to the north. He could see the Yankees reforming around their guns. With a quick glance he also noticed another Federal brigade arriving from the east. Within moments they would have two brigades and a battery of artillery in command of the ridges just south of Spring Hill.

He looked at the faces of the men in his command. Squinted eyes said that though they were turning back from the Federal guns, they were not beaten. There was still a lot of fight left in them. Cleburne would not deny them this battle.

He still had Granbury's brigade not yet engaged. His third brigade had undoubtedly continued west making for the turnpike.

Whatever Hood's prior instructions were, they were no longer relevant. His two brigades were faced with their same number opposite them. The enemy also had the advantage in terrain. Granbury would be needed to offset that advantage. He turned to give Mangum the order when a shell struck a few feet from them.

His horse had been hit, but appeared to be fine.

"Sir, are you hurt, is your horse hurt?" Mangum said as he jumped from his horse and ran to his side. Mangum took a cloth from his pack and began wiping the blood from the mount's side.

There was too much at stake for his lieutenant to be worried about some exploding shrapnel that was lodged in his horse's flesh. No one cared for the beast more than he, but right now, the horse was of little concern.

His two brigades needed support and they needed it quickly.

"No, I am not hurt. Now get back on your horse and do not worry about mine. Go and find Granbury and instruct him to have his brigade on hand immediately. The battle is here, and his support his greatly needed. I will reform our lines from this point and try to renew the attack."

Magnum saluted his commander for a second time this day and rode off. Cleburne rode along the cornfield searching for his brigade and regimental commanders. With the help of his staff, they were soon all safely gathered out of range from the Federal artillery.

There was much frantic talk concerning the events of the battle. They all felt that the Yankees they defeated at the knoll must have been inexperienced troops. They ran too easily, leaving half of their brigade unsupported. If Govan and Lowrey's brigade could be reformed, they were convinced they could take the ridge occupied by the Federals with one strong push. Those Yanks were terrified earlier. If they had to face a second charge, Cleburne was convinced that they were susceptible to a rout again.

Cleburne and his officers began realigning the two brigades in preparation for the attack. General Granbury's men would join the attack once they arrived. As Cleburne was finalizing his plans with Govan and Lowrey, he received an urgent dispatch form General Cheatham.

With his mind so intent on the battle at hand, Cleburne forgot about the dispatch he sent earlier to his corps commander. He quickly read over the message. Apparently Cheatham wanted all actions halted. Cleburne was soon to have the support of more than just Granbury's brigade. The divisions of Bate and Brown were soon to be in place alongside Cleburne's men. Cheatham was planning to consolidate his entire corps to launch an overwhelming attack against the two brigades that defended Spring Hill.

Cleburne reluctantly told the officer that he would instruct his commanders not to attack until Cheatham gave the command. Cheatham's plan was a sound one, but the gathering darkness was an obstacle that was growing with each passing minute. Cleburne looked across the field to the north and watched as the Federals worked feverishly to barricade their front.

"General Cheatham, I hope you can have your men here soon," he said. With darkness approaching, and the Federals reinforcing their lines, the odds were beginning to turn against them. Cleburne contemplated sending his men in before the Federals could fully fortify their position, but his obedience to his commander prevented that. With his heart beating with impatience, he stared past the ranks of his gray clad men, to the Federals gathering on the ridge across the creek.

*   *   *   *   *   *   *   *

General Cheatham rode alongside his staff as they departed from Hood's headquarters towards Spring Hill. The mounting gunfire he heard escalating just a half-hour ago had finally dwindled, thanks to his orders. He looked at his watch and noted the time, it was nearing five. That meant there was still time to order his corps into launching one massive attack at the enemy facing Cleburne.

Roughly an hour ago, his second division, commanded by General Brown, had arrived at the battlefield. Based on an urgent message that he received from Cleburne, Cheatham ordered Brown's men to march to Spring Hill and form in line to the right of Cleburne. Cheatham then located Hood at the Absalom house and told him of his plan to crush the enemy.

Hood was satisfied with his strategy, but Cheatham was not. What was bothering him was Cleburne's predicament. From the reports that he had gathered, Cleburne was in echelon from north to south and marching west towards the turnpike and not towards Spring Hill. Cheatham could not fathom why Cleburne had done this. Had Cleburne been aligned horizontally and proceeding north as planned, his combined division should have easily swarmed the Federal brigade hours ago.

The sound of sporadic gunfire announced that he was nearing the battle scene. Several soldiers helped him by pointing in the direction of General Cleburne. The Irish general was accompanied by several of his officers and was arguing with General Granbury. As Cheatham approached, he tried to decide the proper tone to take in reprimanding Cleburne for his earlier reprehensible echelon formation.

"General," Cleburne was saying to Granbury, "I care little of your concerns, your brigade is a part of my division. That is final. I need you here for this attack."

General Granbury looked like a man wild with despair. He was apparently unaware of the situation that the rest of Cleburne's division corps was in. As they were battling with the Federals on the knoll, he had continued to march his men west as instructed by General Hood. His objective was to occupy the turnpike south of Spring Hill and cut off its access to the town. His men had performed as requested, and when they approached the pike they found the only enemy to confront them was a meager Federal regiment placed on reserve. Captured flags told him that it was the Thirty-sixth Illinois that he had sent scurrying to the north.

Yet Granbury's triumph was to be short lived, for at that moment, he received the order to march to the aid of Cleburne's other two brigades. He understood that Cleburne obviously needed his aid, but if the objective was the turnpike that led into Spring Hill and he occupied that objective, why was he being ordered to abandon it? "General, I am not doubting what you say," Granbury replied. "It is just that my men have just routed the only Yankee regiment in control of that pike. We had the objective sir. The turnpike was mine for the taking."

The debate was silenced when the men noticed that general Cheatham had arrived. Cheatham could not believe what he had just heard. Did Granbury just say that the turnpike was the objective?

"Gentlemen," he said as he waved at the others present. "What is this I hear about the turnpike, who made that the objective? Was it you Patrick, is that why your men marched in a formation that I did not assign?"

Cleburne had just finished arguing with Granbury and had

no patience left for his senior commander. "Why don't you go ask General Hood why my men marched west towards that pike, with my right flank hanging in the air so that a well placed Federal brigade could deliver a deadly volley of enfilading fire?"

Cheatham was stunned. He got off his horse and walked as if in a daze towards Cleburne. "General Hood changed the plan of attack? When, How?"

Cleburne was amazed. How was it Cheatham could have given him a command to halt his actions, while it now seemed that Cheatham had no idea what his actions were? "Earlier, when we crossed the Rutherford Creek, Hood rode ahead with his staff. Upon returning, he said that he saw something that made him revise his plan. He wanted my men to strike for the turnpike instead of the town. He was more concerned with Schofield's army arriving from Columbia. He told me that he was going to send General Bate to my support, then he departed."

"I just came from General Hood's headquarters, he did not even mention this. How could the general change the plans of my corps and not involve me?"

"General, that is something that you will need to take up with him some other time. It is getting late, it is already dark and my men and those of General Brown's are in position to advance upon those Yankees across the way."

Cheatham was handed his field glasses by an aid and he quickly used them to study the Federal position. Across the creek and perpendicular to the turnpike was a battery of Federal artillery. There was also a large contingent of Yankees situated atop a fortified-ridge to the right, obviously placed in support of the guns. The Yanks gathered there looked like men from several different regiments, totaling a little more than three thousand men.

With the combined commands of Cleburne and Brown, Cheatham was putting double that number of Confederates against them. And there was still more Southern might consolidating upon the area. Granbury's command was being hurried forward, as was General Bate's entire division. Cheatham took one last hard look at the Federals. All that stood between him and Spring Hill was half their number of Yanks. Cheatham liked his chances.

"General Cleburne, you are correct about the time," he continued. "We do need to get this attack under way. General Brown will march forward and engage the enemy's left. I wish that we had several hours of light available to us, but unfortunately this is winter. And due to this darkness, your division will have to listen for the sound of Brown's guns as the signal to begin the advance. That means your guns... General Brown, are to signal the commencing of the attack. I have to depart now and ride back towards the pike to try and locate General Bate. I have no doubt that he is also following Hood's revised orders and marching away from where the battle will take place. Had this attack gone as I planned earlier, we would not be in this mess. But be that as it may, we must make do. Expect General Bate's arrival upon Cleburne's left and together your divisions must drive that artillery from its position."

"General Cheatham," Brown asked, "what of my right? It was reported that the Yankees also occupied the positions to the east of Spring Hill. And I would rather have General Gist's brigade with my division as we march forward."

"Your concerns are valid General, but I do believe that the enemy to our front is made up of both the scattered forces that Cleburne defeated, as well as the Yanks that were east of the town earlier today. In any event, I will have General Forrest's cavalry support your right."

"Thank you, sir," was all Brown said.

"General Cheatham," Cleburne interposed. "When I was last with Forrest, he informed me that he was retiring his men from the field. They were exhausted and completely out of ammunition."

Cheatham patted Brown's shoulder. "Thank you Patrick. General Brown, rest assured that I will have Forrest's men sent for. You may begin the attack as soon as possible".

"One last question," Cleburne asked. "What of General Stewart?"

"General Stewart and his corps have been called up from their position astride the creek and are advancing north to cut off the turnpike north of Spring Hill. If we rout the enemy, they will be running right into the open arms of Stewart's boys. The victory is before us, all we need to do is capture it."

Cheatham remounted his horse and departed in search of General Bate's division. He left behind a very worried General Brown. Brown had just been told that Forrest's cavalry would be sent for and that it would advance in support of his right. Yet in the same breath, Cheatham very dogmatically told him to begin the attack without Forrest already there.

Brown took his leave of Cleburne telling him to be sure to advance when he heard the sounds of his guns. His commanding officer may have been confident in the impending attack, but he was not. Brown would have to march his division, less Gist's brigade, in the dark, across the front of a heavily fortified position. To his right, Forrest's cavalry may or may not be on hand to protect his flank. To his left was an arboreal fog separating his men from the support of General Cleburne's division. With a stomach filled with butterflies dancing in ominous delight, General Brown instructed his commanders to commence the attack.

*   *   *   *   *   *   *   *

Cheatham rode with his staff in the direction of the Columbia to Franklin Turnpike. If General Bate were following Hood's orders, then he and his brigade would no doubt be somewhere in that vicinity. As Cheatham rode, he tried to understand why Hood would change the objective from the town to the turnpike. The enemy was clearly before them in the town. Why not completely crush this isolated force, and then worry about the pike later?

As Cheatham rode, he struggled to hear the sounds of battle that should have been waging at Spring Hill. He even stopped his horse several times so he that he could give more attention to his listening. There was nothing.

Torn between searching for Bate's brigade and knowing why General Brown had not started the attack against the town, his intuition chose the latter. He turned his horse in a great circle and raced back towards Spring Hill. Like a well-trained horse show, his staff mimicked his riding abilities and followed. Cheatham had no choice but to follow his instinct. It was already dark and if the attack did not begin soon, it might never.

A rider approached them from the direction of the town. It was one of General Brown's staff officers. Cheatham fervently asked him why the attack had not commenced. The officer reported that as General Brown's brigade went forth, a large Federal contingent appeared on his right flank. Cheatham was disturbed by this latest news. There was not supposed to be any Federals that could threaten Brown on the right. Cheatham's head swam with numerous questions. He knew that the officer would not have the proper answers... he needed to speak with Brown right way. He instructed the officer to lead him to General Brown.

By the time they found the general it was after six. The sun had completely gone for the day, having lost its daily battle with the darkness. Temperatures were also dropping, as evidenced by the soldiers who were now huddling for warmth. Small fires began to sprout like weeds south of the town. Cheatham could see that there would not be an attack made this day.

Surrounded by his staff, Brown was seated beneath a beaten, old, winter-worn tree. He saw Cheatham approaching and was obviously relieved.

"General, what has happened here, why has there not been an attack?" Cheatham asked.

"General Cheatham, I could not in good conscious continue this attack. I sent my men forward as you commanded, but as soon as we got started, a Yankee force of unknown strength appeared on our right. My flank was seriously threatened."

Cheatham took a quick look from right to left. "And where in hell is Forrest?"

"Sir, I do not know. What I do know is that my right was not supported. Not knowing the size of the enemy to my flank, I could not continue to march north. General, that decision is one I will stand behind, even if it means my removal from command. I was at Perryville, I have witnessed first hand the effects of an army hitting the enemy's flank. I was not going to let that happen to my men."

Cheatham could not blame his general. If he were in a similar situation, he was sure that he would have reacted the very same. "General Brown, please do not concern yourself with your removal from command. As long as I command this corps, you shall have a place in it. You did the right thing by not attacking. I have no idea where Forrest is, his men should have been in support."

When Cheatham finished talking, his head bent towards the ground for a long while. He was unsure of what to do next. He had his men ready to attack, but a Federal contingent had emerged to its flank. He thought of revising the plans to take the new threat into account, but the darkness and the sounds of his troops beginning to bivouac prevented that. The situation had grown beyond his capabilities. He needed to confer with his commander.

"General Brown, you may tell your men not to get too comfortable. I will ride back to General Hood's headquarters and seek his advice. There still may yet be an attack this night."

Brown assured Cheatham that if there were to be an attack, his division would be ready. As the general rode towards Hood's headquarters, Brown began to doubt his own words. His men were exhausted. They had marched several miles this day and with the setting of the sun, had assumed that they had earned their share of rest. From the conversation he overhead, the focus was no longer on the enemy. There was talk of the cold night air, hunger and shelter.

Brown hoped that Hood would not expect these men to attack before the morning.

* * * * * * * *

John Bell Hood took his leave of Absalom Thompson's home and stepped out into the cold night air. He turned to admire Mr. Thompson's grand abode, then was helped upon his horse and trotted up the road in the direction of Spring Hill. He took his first few steps slow, not sure if the pain in his side was still there. It was not. Hood was once again thankful for his supply of laudanum. The medicine seemed as if it could heal anything. The only side effect it produced was that it made him extremely lethargic. On some nights, that was just fine, but on others he could do without the sleepiness. This night was one of them.

Cheatham had come by over an hour ago and assured him that he would be attacking soon. From the silence he had heard since Cheatham's departure, the battle was either a success without a casualty, or it had not taken place. The thought of the latter made him nauseous. It was Atlanta all over again.

Hood began to feel dizzy and stopped to rest. While holding on to a small tree that lined the road, he tried to regain his balance. He tried to focus his thoughts but everything began to blur. This effect seemed to always occur if he drank too much of his medicine.

A bright flame kindled up the road and for a moment, Hood thought he was being haunted by an image of the burning Atlanta. The incandescent wraith that stultified his existence beckoned him forward. On one shaky leg, Hood embraced the

245

flames and continued along the road.

Staring into the flames allowed him to relive his failure at Atlanta. He saw the long lines of southern citizens on their exodus from the city. The dancing flames laughed at his inability to stop Sherman's army as it advanced. Hood, like a cornered rattlesnake, struck out three times against his enemy, and three times it was he who received the venomous bite. With sweating palms, he fought to contain the shaking fit that threatened to make itself external.

Sherman should have been beaten. His flanks were left open, and that damned Hardee did not take advantage of it. As he neared the fire, he felt it scorch his soul with the realization that Spring Hill was turning into a second Atlanta. He had once again given his subordinates the orders for victory, and once again they were not being carried out. This did not happen back east when he served under Robert E. Lee. When Lee gave a command, it was followed. Why was he not receiving the same respect here in Tennessee?

When Hood reached the fire, the images of Atlanta gave way to reality. Several of his soldiers were gathered around the flames of a campfire. Hood's presence silenced their social conversations and they waited awkwardly for their commander to make conversation.

"Why is it, that no matter who I give orders to, they are not carried out?" Hood irately asked.

This was not the conversation that the soldiers wanted to engage in.

Hood ignored them and continued. "A simple plan. Take the turnpike. Does that sound like a hard task for this army? I don't think that it does." Hood began violently pacing around the campfire. He noticed a gnarled log protruding from the fire, and threw it into the night. A sparkle of fiery ashes followed the branch from the fire.

The soldiers were embarrassed by Hood's incontrovertible actions. The appearance of General Stewart and his staff was a sight much welcomed.

Hood stopped his tirade when he saw Stewart dismount from his horse and approach.

"General, what is the matter?" Stewart asked.

"What is the matter? It is almost six thirty, and I have still yet to hear General Cheatham's guns. I have no idea of his situation."

"Sir, my men are at hand. If you would like, I can send an officer from my staff to gather some information."

"No thank you General, I have already sent Governor Harris. I am expecting his return shortly."

"Has the situation changed?"

"Not that I know of. Cheatham's corps was instructed to take hold of the turnpike south of town. I am not sure if he has accomplished that as of yet."

"What are the plans for my men? We have been eagerly awaiting our involvement while waiting at the Rutherford creek," Stewart said.

Hood squinted north into the darkness. "General, you and your division may continue along the Rally Hill Pike and take a position beyond Spring Hill. Once at your position, you are to deploy across the turnpike. With Cheatham in position of his end of the pike, you will be in position to seal off the town of Spring Hill as well as corral the fleeing forces of the enemy."

Stewart relayed the orders to his officers and took his leave from his commander. Hood watched as Stewart and his staff disappeared into the darkness. Their horses trudged on tired limbs as they rode back towards the Rally Hill Pike. This had been a long day for them all.

Hood turned from the campfire and began walking back towards his headquarters. He had not had his dinner yet and his officers were planning for a great feast that was to be provided for by the Thompson family later this evening. As he approached the Thompson house he could hear the sounds of verbosity reverberate from inside. He began to dismount and enter the house, when he was called from behind. Hood turned around to see a very pasty looking Cheatham. At first, the sight of his general here and not on the battlefield surprised him. Then his anger exploded through his chest like the impact of twelve-pound cannon ball.

"Why in the name of God have you not attacked the enemy and taken possession of that pike?" he yelled at Cheatham. The sounds from within the Thompson house were silenced like night crickets.

Cheatham handed the reins of his horse to his aid, and very sheepishly approached Hood. "General, I was never informed of your decision to take the pike. I had always thought the objective to be Spring Hill. When I reached the battlefield, General Cleburne was marching west, by your command, and under attack from the north by a Federal brigade. His flank was in serious jeopardy. I have managed to realign his men to face north, and have moved Brown's division in support of his right. With Forrest supporting Brown, they were to move in concert against the Federals defending the ridges south of Spring Hill."

Hood was growing impatient. "And have they? It is already dark, and unless my hearing has gone the way of my crippled arm and severed leg, I have not heard the sound of battle."

Cleburne felt a cold sweat soak through his back. "General Hood, please allow me to explain. Brown commenced his attack as planned. I went in search of General Bate, to have his command support the attack, but when I did not hear the sound of battle, I grew as concerned as you. I rushed back to Brown and the general informed me that as he marched forward, a Federal force was in position on his right flank. Apparently Forrest's cavalry were not in support. Feeling his flank threatened, Brown wisely halted the attack and sought my advice. I in turn rode here to confer with you."

"And what is it you want from me, General? It sounds like your whole command is deployed for battle. A battle that you have failed to launch."

Cheatham took a deep breath. He recognized Hood's condescending attitude. But he failed to see this situation as a fault of his own. He had not been informed that Hood had changed his plans earlier in the day. If this debacle was anyone's fault it was his commanding officers. Not wanting to start an argument with Hood, one that would no doubt lead to his arrest, Cheatham chose to accept the responsibility.

"My men can still march and take that ridge," Cheatham said. "All I need is a flank support to my right."

Hood looked towards the Davis Ford road. "Well, you just may be in luck. General Stewart and his division are just now marching north along the Davis Ford road in an effort to cut off the turnpike north of Spring Hill. I can call them back and have them in support of your flank. Would that allow you to make your attack, General?" Hood asked.

Cheatham nodded his head. "That would be exactly what I would need General."

Before Cheatham could continue, a lone rider approached from the east. The officer was not someone that Hood or

Cheatham had ever seen. Alarmed, they allowed the soldier to approach. The officer was not a young man, as he looked like someone who had seen far too much of this war. The officer halted his horse and dismounted. He quickly tied the horse to the fence rail and with an obvious purpose approached the two generals.

"General Hood?" the stranger asked.

Hood looked at Cheatham, who shrugged back at him. Cheatham's aid had his hand poised over his holster. "Who wants to know?" Hood said.

"That is not important," the officer responded. He then made a quick note of Hood's artificial leg and his limp arm. "General Hood, I am glad to see that I have found you." The officer reached into his coat.

At that moment, two of Hood's officers who were obviously eaves dropping on Hood's conversation with Cheatham, rushed from the porch, with sabers drawn, towards the unknown officer. Cheatham's aid also reacted by whipping out a pistol and taking aim at the man's chest.

The officer was not perturbed. He brought forth a dispatch and handed it to Hood. "My instructions are for you to read this and no one else. I must take my leave now." The officer remounted his horse and was gone. Hood looked at Cheatham, who was still in a state of bewilderment. Hood looked at the dispatch and wondered whom it was from. Had General Beauregard resorted to his old ways of demanding an account of his every action? Or was it Beauregard's favorite watchdog…George Brent? Not liking the source of the dispatch, he dreaded its contents.

Hood walked into the front room of his headquarters so that he could have enough light to read the dispatch. Cheatham was quick to follow. He paid him no notice. With a cautious hand, he opened the message. With eye's that could not be contained within their sockets, Hood fell back into an embracing chair. The officers gathered were inflamed with curiosity. What had just caused their commander such trepidation?

Just then the front door was flung open and in stormed General William Bate. Bate was extremely upset because his division had marched west towards the turnpike as ordered by General Hood. The home of Nathaniel Cheairs was adjacent to the pike, and Bate used it as the converging point for his brigades. There they met and had driven a Federal regiment from the field. The Confederate victory left the turnpike undefended by the Union army. Unfortunately, as had occurred to General Granbury earlier, Bate's command was ordered by General Cheatham to give up the turnpike and march towards Spring Hill.

Bate gave Cheatham a look of contempt as he pushed past him to get to Hood. "General Hood, I know that General Cheatham is the commander of the corps, but he is not the commander of this army. The last I was informed, my orders came from you. If this has changed, I would like to hear so from none other than you."

Cheatham was not intimidated by Bate's temper. If anything, he was taken back by the fact that Bate did not understand how the chain of command worked. He stepped directly in between Bate and Hood and grabbed Bate by the collar of his muddied jacket. "You will do what I say, when I say it. Is that understood? If not, you will be placed under arrest, and a new commander will be assigned immediately."

Bate took hold of Cheatham's hands and very non-combatant like, removed them from his jacket. When he spoke, his tone lost much of its fire. "General Hood, my men were within yards of that turnpike. We had the road completely in our possession… that is until an order arrived from General Cheatham. He called for my men to give up the objective and march to support his brigade to the north. Sir, I refused this order openly. Your instructions were to take possession of the Columbia to Franklin Pike. General Cheatham wanted me to give it up to assist his assault upon Spring Hill. General Hood, you are the overall commander of this army. I chose only to obey your command."

Hood looked into the eyes of Bate and all he could see was the radiance of contempt directed at Cheatham. The two generals stood patiently waiting for his decision on the matter. Normally, he might have used some harsh words against both his generals. Bate was at fault for not following Cheatham's orders, just as Cheatham was at fault for not following his own personal orders. Hood tried to remember if he actually gave the revised plans to Cheatham. The day had been so long, and he had taken quit a bit of his laudanum after his accident on the hilltop. He felt as if he was captivated within a spell of drowsiness.

Hood took a moment to orient himself by silently reading the last sentences of the message one last time. They read, 'for the moment, this matter is between you and I alone. No one is to be involved. All will be explained.'

Hood very carefully folded the dispatch and placed it in his pocket. The answer to all of his problems was now neatly tucked away. His officers looked towards him, begging for some indication of what had just transpired. Hood could not satiate them. Feeling as if a tremendous weight had just been lifted off his shoulders, he stood up and addressed Bate and Cheatham.

"General Bate, you may return to your command. Your hostility stems from the inability of this army to convey orders through proper channels. You were correct to take possession of the turnpike, however, General Cheatham is in command of the battlefield. For now, please follow his orders, and have your division march in support."

Without acknowledging Cheatham, Bate saluted Hood and returned to his men.

"General, you may return to the field of battle as well. I will instruct General Stewart to no longer march north, but to fall in on your right flank."

Cheatham could not find his voice. Before Bate's entry, Hood was consumed with anger. Bate's arrival should have added fuel to the fire. The conflicting opinions of the battle made it painfully apparent that no one in the field knew exactly what was expected of them. Yet Hood seemed to shrug all of that off. Whatever the message contained in that dispatch, it was one that soothed General Hood. Cheatham turned to leave, but was called back by Hood.

"General, you have done well today. You did not know that the plans had been changed, and acted only according to what you had in your knowledge. Stewart will be on your flank, and Bate will be sent in support as well. We have Schofield's army trapped and we shall either defeat him this night or first thing tomorrow."

Cheatham had come to Hood's headquarters for some direction, but he was leaving more confused than when he arrived. He felt like he had just consumed a quart of whiskey. Perhaps that was exactly what was needed. He decided to make one quick stop before returning to his men.

He saw nothing wrong with a brief sojourn that would allow him to wet his lips with some of the south's finest. 'Besides, it would help to combat the chilling night,' he thought.

Chapter XIX
Evening
Spring Hill, Tennessee

The cold and dark night told the Confederate forces gathered around Spring Hill that there was probably not going to be an attack this evening. The tired men of Cheatham's corps began to fall out and make preparations against the chilling night. Many campfires sprang up across the land like anthills and the mood around these burning embers was a positive one. The Confederate army had marched around the Federals at Columbia and had gained control of their rear without much of a fight. Much of the night's conversation centered upon the long awaited attack that would surely begin in the morning.

One person that did not share in much of the night's excitement was Captain English of General Granbury's staff. The battle would not commence until tomorrow, and that was still hours away. His concerns remained on the present. And presently, Granbury's brigade anchored the left of the Confederate line. To his right was the rest of Cheatham's corps. From that direction, English had no apprehension. But towards the west was another story. If at some point this night the enemy was to arrive from Columbia, there would only be one single brigade on hand that could effectively contest their march into Spring Hill... and that would be Granbury's.

Earlier he had been informed that Bate's division was to arrive during the early evening and fall in to his left. So far, there had been no sign of Bate's brigades. Not wanting to waste any more time just sitting around awaiting Bate's arrival, English mounted his horse and prepared to ride in the supposed direction of Bate's command.

"Hey Captain, where you off to?" one of his soldiers asked.

English walked his horse towards the soldier. The man had just finished erecting his tent. Three men behind him were feeding a dying fire with broken fence posts. English could smell coffee brewing as well as a faint aroma of lit tobacco. A small table was being set up, no doubt to allow the men to revel in a few games of poker.

"Son, you and your friends need to get yourselves some rest. You know how General Hood feels about socializing after dark. Tomorrow is going to be one hell of a day. I am just going to ride a bit and see if I can find out what is taking Bate's brigade so long to come up on our left."

The soldier looked back towards his men before saying, "You need me to go with you, captain?"

"No, I should be fine, I will be back in just a few moments anyway."

"Are you sure?" the soldier asked. "You seem a bit worried."

English picked his head up and looked into the west. The night was so dark that it severely hampered his vision. When he turned back to the soldier, he noticed the man had gathered some corn into his haversack.

"No, I am not worried. Who is that corn for?" English asked.

"Oh, this here is just a few rotten pieces I found within that cornfield. It ain't for me anyhow. It's for a few of them prisoners."

English raised an eyebrow. "Prisoners? Captured from today?"

"No sir, the ones we got from Florence and from Forrest's battle near Mount Pleasant."

"What? I thought we were supposed to tend to them as far as Columbia. Why are we still carrying that baggage along?"

The soldier finished wrapping the corn into a neat bundle. "General Forrest's orders sir. There ain't too many of them left anyhow. There is just that skinny Irishman that has lasted with us from the beginning, and another score or so from Forrest's most recent battle."

English had no idea why Forrest wanted to carry these prisoners along with the army. That was something he definitely needed to address with General Granbury later this evening. For right now, his only thoughts were on the arrival of Bate's division.

"You may continue to care for these prisoners. I will be back shortly. Please be sure you get some rest. I assure you, come tomorrow, you will wish you had, and not been so worried about feeding rotten corn to Yankee prisoners. And one more thing, that fellow on the left looks like he is marking his cards."

*   *   *   *   *   *   *   *

John Murphy sat amongst several of the Union prisoners. The ground was as hard as the wind was cold. The chilling wind continued to bite at his exposed skin. More than anything, he wished for a huge woolen blanket. With an animalistic alacrity, he ignored the cold and chewed into the rotten cobs of corn that were fed to him by his captors. No matter what would happen to him, tonight had to be his night to escape.

Murphy figured that he had learned everything he possibly could to help the Federal cause. More importantly, he knew that if he did not make the Federal lines by morning, it would be because either a rebel bullet found his back, or he froze to death in his sleep. His fleeting health no longer left him a choice.

John had managed to make friends with many of the new prisoners. There were two in particular who shared his enthusiasm for an attempted escape. Their names were Stephen Adams and Robert Toombler. Both men were part of Capron's brigade until they were routed near Fouche Springs. For the past several nights, the three men had plotted their escape.

They were not sure why they were being dragged along with these rapid marches conducted by Hood's army, but they were glad they were. John had explained to them, that if any of them made it into Spring Hill, it was vital that General Schofield receive accurate information concerning the enemy.

John had also feigned a decent friendship with the guards that were assigned to him. During the past two weeks, he had managed to learn the size of Hood's army, as well as its position. What John stressed to Robert and Stephen was that General Schofield needed to pull out of Columbia immediately, if he had not done so already. What was also important was that the Federal army had seriously miscalculated its estimates of Forrest's cavalry. General Schofield had been given reports that Forrest had ten thousand troopers in his command, but John had learned differently. Their number was half of that. Another important detail was that Hood had only two of his corps present at Spring Hill. S. D. Lee's corps was still at Columbia with all of the Confederate artillery. Perhaps there was a chance to turn and attack Hood's position at Spring Hill while he was divided and without the use of his cannons.

John Murphy spit a dry hard kernel onto the ground as a

guard approached. That was the signal for them to stop discussing tonight's plan. Stephen and Robert retired to get some sleep. Any amount would be most useful when the time came to run.

John lay where he was. If nothing else, his time in captivity had taught him how to live without the comforts he had grown accustomed to. When you were in dire need of sleep, a cold and hardened muddied earth was just as comfortable as a luxurious bed built for a king. As he stared into the dark heavens, he thought of the reception he would receive from General Schofield. Surely he would be deemed a hero. From how he saw it, General Hood had managed to cut off the Federal army's only hope of escape.

The one thing that could save them now was the information that he had gathered.

With heavy eyelids, John succumbed to the deep sleep that he knew he needed in order to have enough energy later in the night. He also hoped that there was enough life left within him to resist the urge to remain asleep forever. During the past three nights, the darkness that terrorized his dreams had gotten closer and closer to consuming him.

'One last time to shut my eyes,' he prayed. 'That is all I ask my Lord. Please allow me to wake up one more time and at least have my chance for freedom.'

*   *   *   *   *   *   *   *

As English rode towards the open turnpike, he heard the sounds of picket fire coming from ahead. As he raced towards the sporadic gunfight, the pickets seemed to abruptly cease their commotion. Suddenly, the whole countryside became ominously quiet. English would never admit that being alone in the dark would have frightened him, but he could not hide from the reality of his own fears. He had ridden well beyond the range of his brigade. He knew that because he could no longer smell the aromas of tobacco and coffee. For demulcent reasons, the captain reached into his pack and produced his clay pipe. English brought the pipe to his face and slowly brushed it under his nose. The smell of tobacco was faint, but it was there. The comfort allowed him to forget his fears for the moment.

"Now whose pickets have I just heard firing? Were they of General Bate's command? And exactly who were they firing at?" he whispered.

English looked up into the night sky and wished in vain that the moon would make an appearance. Any light shed would be a huge asset to him right now. He began to wonder what he was doing out here anyway. Why hadn't he taken a few of those soldiers with him? At least then he would only be afraid of the Federal army and not this dark night.

English began to ride back to camp, when he heard the sound of a large body of troops marching on the road. He quickly dismounted and tied his horse to a tree. It was about time that Bate arrived to support his flank. He quickly began walking towards the turnpike in order to direct General Bate to his proper position in line. To his left lay a large motionless black object. Thinking it to be a bear, English readied his pistol and approached with caution. As he neared it, he laughed at his own fears. It was only a haystack. It was not even as big as he first fathomed. His gun was re-holstered with much personal embarrassment. When he looked up again, he noticed that the ground was littered with several haystacks. Only some of them were moving towards him.

Before he had time to discern whether or not his fears were playing tricks on him, he found himself surrounded by several Federal soldiers. He immediately raised his hands in surrender. At first, he thought his capture to be foolish on his part, and an awful state of affairs. But the more he thought about it, his own embarrassment would be nothing when compared to that of General Hood's. The large body of men that he heard approaching was not Bate's division... they were Federal soldiers arriving from Columbia. Which meant that the turnpike had not been cut off.

While Hood's army lay sleeping, General Schofield was sending reinforcements from Columbia into Spring Hill.

*   *   *   *   *   *   *   *

Union General John McAllister Schofield approached the vicinity of Spring Hill with his mind heavy with trepidation. In many ways, his march along the Columbia to Franklin turnpike was a fuliginous travel. Not only could he not see more than a few feet in front of him, he was also not sure if Stanley's division was still an effective force. The varied reports he received throughout the day had placed the Confederate army in several different locations at the same time. He did not know which reports to believe.

Most of his cavalry, under the command of General Wilson, had been driven from the Lewisburg Pike sometime this morning. Wilson initially had claimed that Hood's army was preparing to cross the Lewisburg Pike, but later changed his mind, stating that there was only the threat from their cavalry. If his young cavalry commander seemed to be content with his report, Schofield was not. He did not care if it was only Forrest's cavalry that had crossed the Duck River. The fact was, the rebels had crossed over and had gained a foothold on the northern banks of the river. How long would it be until Hood followed? General Thomas had wanted his men to hold Columbia for as long as possible. That option was completely evaporating with each passing hour. It was not long after when Schofield learned that there was a Confederate presence across the Davis Ford Road. This put the enemy much closer to his position than the Lewisburg Pike crossing, as Wilson had reported.

Thankfully, Schofield had not heeded Wilson's latter message. As a precautionary measure, he had sent General Stanley with two divisions, as well as the wagon train, towards Spring Hill. It was not until the enemy was reported at Davis Ford Road that Schofield realized that there was a very real possibility of Hood having crossed the Duck and falling upon his rear at Rutherford Creek. This caused him to alter his orders to Stanley. Kimball's division was to remain at the creek, to protect against his worst fears. That left Stanley with only one division and the army's wagons and artillery marching towards Spring Hill.

Based on his fears that Hood was in the process of cutting him off from Nashville, Schofield decided his position could no longer be held. Preparations were then made for the remainder of his army to evacuate Columbia during the evening. The constant bombardment of Confederate artillery assured him that the majority of Hood's army was still to his front. There was still sufficient time to get his army to safety.

His assumption was wrong. In the late afternoon, Schofield received the worst news possible, the Confederate army was reportedly already at Spring Hill. Hood had left him holding the bag at Columbia, while he marched his army around the open flank and cut off the escape route to Nashville.

Schofield tugged on his beard now, as he did when he first

heard the news. At first, all he could think about was the wrath of William Tecumseh Sherman. If the enemy managed to defeat either Thomas or himself, they could turn the tide in Tennessee. If that happened, Schofield knew that the fault would be his own. Sure he could cast the blame in any direction he chose, but the bottom line was that it was his responsibility not to allow Hood to move around him. If Schofield thought Sherman could forgive him for this, he was mistaken. Perhaps the first near failure at Pulaski would be excusable, but to be outflanked a second time was not.

Still, there was hope. After conferring with several of his officers, Schofield began to realize that perhaps Hood's entire army was not at Spring Hill as first thought. Reports indicated that there was definitely a large contingent of the enemy still visible on the southern side of the Duck River. And if that were true, then the enemy blocking his escape at Spring Hill was not at full strength... and Schofield fully understood that he could ill-afford to wait around until they were.

What was that adage he had first heard at the academy...'the only cure for grief was action.' With as much grief that weighed upon his soul, it was time for him to take action.

He chose to personally lead a march of two brigades from the Twenty-third corps second division. If General Stanley's lone division still held Spring Hill, Schofield meant to reinforce him with these two brigades. If the enemy at Spring Hill was nothing more than a detached division, the combined might of Stanley's division and his two brigades would crush them easily. That thought made him feel better, but he was still troubled.

Even if Hood had not yet fully outflanked him, Schofield realized that it would only be a matter of time for him to do so. He ordered the rest of his command to pull out of Columbia during the cover of darkness. This was done for two reasons. For one, as much as he would have liked to evacuate his entire army at once, there was still a significant Confederate force to his front.

The other reason came from a suggestion by General Cox. If Hood had managed to get the bulk of his army to Spring Hill, then Schofield would find himself in a desperate situation when he got there. Hood may have already defeated Stanley's division. Hood could then turn on Schofield and crush his two brigades. With Schofield's army crippled, the rebels would have complete command of Tennessee. The Union soldiers still at Columbia would be trapped between the two contingents of Hood's army.

The more Schofield reflected on Cox's theory, the more he was thankful for it. It justified his pulling the remainder of his command out at night, ensuring that they would not be too far from him in the event that he needed to fall back from Spring Hill.

Those thoughts were the catalyst for the anxiety he now felt consuming him as he neared Spring Hill. Was the Confederate army at Columbia the main force, or was it just a detachment?

The sound of gunfire erupted from the darkness ahead. The threat of battle caused the column of infantry to halt its march. Schofield could hear Brigadier General Ruger shouting orders forming a skirmish line. He gingerly walked towards the front to get a better understanding of the situation. He had not gone far when Ruger intercepted him.

"General," Ruger said. "We have just a few more miles until we reach Spring Hill. The number of enemy pickets has been increasing with each passing step. So far there has not been a major threat, but I just ordered Colonel Strickland's brigade into ranks for battle. This will delay our arrival, but it will ensure we are able to meet any surprise attacks that the rebels could have in store."

Schofield rubbed his perspiring palms across his legs as he tried to suppress the panic bubbling within. "Very well, please proceed as best you can."

Schofield waited several anxious moments for the brigades to move forward again. Slowly, he followed in their wake. As he passed the long columns of Colonel Moore's brigade, he noted the exhausted look conveyed by the posture of his men. They were tired of marching. It was not hard for Schofield to sympathize with their situation. After the fall of Atlanta, they were all led to believe that the Army of Tennessee was finished. Why else would Sherman take half of his army east, leaving the remainder behind?

For the men in Schofield's command, the war on their front was supposed to be over. As they marched their weary bodies north, it became evident that once again the Federal high command had misled them. The Army of Tennessee was not only still a major threat, it was one victory away from turning the tide of this war. What was worse, General Sherman was miles away with any hope of reinforcements. The eyes that stared at him as he passed told him that these men clearly understood that if Schofield was marching along with them, it meant that it was imperative for them to reach Nashville before the enemy. If they did not, Tennessee would fall back into Confederate hands.

"General Schofield," Ruger called as he approached. "It seems the enemy is in possession of the turnpike up ahead. I have ordered Colonel Orlando Moore to deploy his men in line also."

Schofield watched as the seemingly exhausted troops under Moore's command began to prepare themselves for battle. The time was now at hand for him to take command of the situation. He basically had only three choices. He could battle the rebels that held the pike and hope that they did not detain his advance long enough for the rest of Hood's army to arrive in support. If Hood were truly on hand with two of his corps, his two brigades would not stand a chance.

He could also simply turn his men around and concede that the Confederates had cut off his escape along the Columbia to Franklin turnpike. Such a move would leave General Stanley abandoned if he was still at Spring Hill. It would also incur the temper of Sherman, and Schofield would much rather accept battle with Hood, than have to face the fiery red headed commander.

By default, his third option became his only real choice. If the enemy controlling the pike was, as he hoped, part of the small detachment of Confederates, perhaps his men could bull rush past them into the city beyond. There they could consolidate with General Stanley's command. Even if Hood had his entire army at hand, they could not all be on the turnpike at this moment.

The more he thought on it, the more it made sense. Ruger had to get his two brigades moving forwards at once. "General Ruger, we must reach that town, there is no other choice. Please understand that what I do now is the only chance we have for success."

Schofield turned from Ruger and began riding down the line of men. His beard was waving in the wind like a battle flag. "Boy's there's nothing but cavalry up ahead. Just put your bayonets on and go right through them. General Stanley's division is only a couple of miles ahead."

With Schofield's order, Ruger's two brigades deployed in line and began to push forward. They expected a battle to wage with every step, but it never came. Besides an occasional volley fired by a few pickets, the two brigades reached Spring Hill without a single casualty.

No one was more thankful for this than Schofield. He had

taken a huge gamble by sending his men forward against an unknown enemy. His audacity had paid off. Not only were his men safely reunited with Stanley's brigade, but also there was word that they had captured a Confederate captain just outside of town.

Schofield had always been blessed with talkative prisoners. This captain had better be of that same loquacious mold. He was tired at having to guess Hood's every move. This valuable prisoner and his information would finally allow him to get the rest he so badly needed.

Very soon, Schofield would know just how much of Hood's force had reached Spring Hill ahead of the remainder of his army.

*   *   *   *   *   *   *   *

He had never been more nervous in his entire life. Earlier in the evening he had hoped that the captured Confederate captain could answer his questions concerning Hood's army. As he stared out from the rooftop, he realized just how unnecessary that would be. There must have been hundreds of campfires signaling the size and position of the Confederate army. Schofield's worst fears had come true. The Army of Tennessee was gathered outside of Spring Hill with at least two full corps. The only question that now remained was the hour in which Hood would give the order to attack.

With legs as sturdy as wet noodles, Schofield descended the stairs and entered the brick home that served as his temporary headquarters. Inside Generals Stanley, Wagner and Ruger were the first to greet him. Amongst the other officers present were Colonels Opdycke, Lane and Bradley. One of his aids offered him some late dinner, but he quickly refused. Food was the last thing he needed to add to his upset stomach.

"Gentlemen," he said. "It appears that we are in for a desperate evening. I was actually doubtful that I would find General Stanley and his division still in possession of this town. Can someone please fill me in on what has happened here this day?"

Stanley stepped forward and noted a slight tremble in Schofield's posture. Schofield looked at Stanley and tried to remain demure. 'How could Stanley seem so imperturbable at such a time?' he wondered.

"General, if not for the excellent services of the men of Wagner's division, I am doubtful that we would have held this town for you," Stanley said. "At first, I was convinced that we were only facing Forrest's cavalry. It was not until I saw the rout of Bradley's brigade, did I learn my grave error. General Cleburne's division seemed to appear from nowhere. They overran Bradley's position and advanced towards this town. Luckily, we had artillery near by, I immediately ordered it unlimbered and with the guns, were able to drive the rebels back."

Schofield rubbed perspired hands through his beard as he looked at the faces of all the men gathered in the room. Heavy eyes, with faces grim and dirtied from the day's battle, stared back at him. Schofield was proud of them all. They showed great courage this day. Yet courage could not have been enough to keep the Confederates out of Spring Hill. He still needed to understand why Hood never re-organized his lines to attack again. If Hood had two corps on hand, how could he let just a single division impede his advance?

Additional refreshments were brought into the room and Schofield's need to eat overcame his uneasy stomach. This was going to be a long evening and he realized that he had better consume some form of substance in order to keep his furnace burning. As he nibbled at his meal, he began pacing in front of the windows. He kept nervously peering through the glass fully expecting to see Hood marching at the head of his army through downtown Spring Hill. What was he waiting for?

"General Wagner, I must again commend your division, but I am uneasy as to why the enemy has not reformed and attacked?"

Those gathered in the room cast uneasy glances among themselves. "Sir, as are we," Stanley said. "After we repelled the initial attack, the enemy did reform. This time, another rebel division arrived in support of Cleburne's flank. They began to advance upon us, but it seems that as soon as the attack got under way, it abruptly stopped."

Schofield looked like a man trying to make the last three pieces of a puzzle fit into four vacant spaces.

"General, perhaps Colonel Lane can offer his opinion to your ears?" Stanley asked.

Schofield looked towards Lane and waited to hear his response.

"General Schofield, my men were to the east of this town when Cleburne overran Bradley's position. General Wagner sent the order to have my men fall back in support of the breakthrough. I began sending my troops towards the ridge adjacent to the artillery when I saw an excellent opportunity before me. It seemed that the rebel cavalry to our front had simply retired from the field. They could not have done so at a more opportune time. When the rebel infantry reformed to advance, their cavalry no longer supported by their right flank. In order to make the most of this advantage, I quickly sent a few companies forward with the instruction to deliver a devastating round of oblique fire as the enemy advanced. I only meant to disorganize their initial advance, not stop the whole attack."

General Wagner finished swallowing a glass of wine as he took a step closer to Lane. "Colonel, I will be sure that you receive the due credit for such an heroic action. General Schofield, the only thing that we could come up with, was that the Confederates were surprised to find their flank unprotected. They must have called the attack to confer amongst themselves."

Schofield wanted to believe Wagner's hypothesis, but he knew John Bell Hood all too well. They were friends back in the academy, and even then Hood was one never to back down from a fight. If the Confederates had not attacked yet, it had nothing to do with Federal valor. 'Hood is coming,' he thought. 'He will not let us escape from this place without a battle.' Schofield was thoroughly convinced that at this very moment, Hood was coordinating the movements that would send his two corps at the Union position.

"From what I have heard, it appears that through this division's quick thinking, you have prevented two attacks from an enemy with superior numbers. However, I know General Hood all too well, I will promise you that before this night is over, old Sam will have us face a third assault. I can only hope that the rest of the men now defending this town are as quick to seize the initiative as Colonel Lane has demonstrated already."

Schofield walked past Lane, patting him on the shoulder with acclaim. "General Stanley, please remain," he said. "Everyone else, I thank you for you noble service this day. Please do not stray so far that you are unable to be present in less then a moments need. Have word sent to your men to remain vigilant.

Also, I will need someone to have the captured rebel captain sent for."

When the acquiescent assemblage departed from the room, Schofield turned to see a more artless Stanley. The man, who only a few moments ago stood erect with his wide shoulders and narrow waist, dropped into a cushioned chair with all the grace of a sack of potatoes. Stanley closed his eyes as he pulled at the hair just above his ears. Schofield was relieved to realize that he was not the only one who was finding the air acrimonious to breathe.

"David, what is your honest assessment of our situation?" Schofield asked.

Stanley looked up and removed his hands from his hair, placing them on his lap. "John, I think we are in very serious trouble. We need to get word to General Thomas in Nashville."

"That will be taken care of, but for now, my immediate concern is my army. I know that it appears that the Confederates have gone into bivouac for the evening. Their army must be as exhausted as ours. In fact, I would wager that they need sleep more than we do, but I can tell you right now, Hood will not let them rest. He knows that we are at his mercy."

The silence that ensued after Schofield's statement only obfuscated their thoughts. Stanley was nodding his head in agreement. "Let us first hear what this captain has to say. Then we will do whatever needs to be done."

A sudden knock at the door brought them out of their inner turmoil. Two armed officers escorted the prisoner into the room. The door was shut behind them. The rebel was seated in a comfortable chair, while the guards stood behind each of his shoulders.

"By the looks of your muddied knees, I would say you have been crawling around a bit this evening," Schofield said. "What is your name captain?"

English looked over his shoulder at the two Union officers standing guard over him. With their presence behind him, there was no chance of pushing by this wide-eyed general and exiting the window. Was there any chance that he was just dreaming? It seemed only moments ago that he was safely with his men. Perhaps when he rode off to find Bate's command, he simply fell asleep. He had been up since four in the morning and had spent the remainder of this arduous day marching and counter marching, so this being a surrealistic episode was certainly a possibility. English hoped that in any minute he would open his eyes and see the good face of General Granbury.

"Captain, let me repeat the question one last time. Your name please," Schofield demanded.

English shifted in his chair and confronted the reality of his situation. "R.T. English. My rank is captain. I report to the Brigadier General Hiram Granbury, of Major General Patrick Cleburne's division of Major General Cheatham's corps."

Schofield pulled a chair next to English. He motioned for Stanley to do the same. "Can one of you officers please bring the captain a drink of his choosing as well as something to eat? Captain English, what can we get you to drink?"

"Water would be fine. Perhaps a bit of whisky if I may ask?"

"No problem at all."

One of the officers left the room and returned moments later with a tall glass of water as well as a shot glass and a bottle of whiskey. English moved the tall glass aside and poured the whiskey into the shot glass. He raised his drink to the generals in the room and swallowed it down his dry cottonmouth. He could feel the warm smooth tingle as it burned its way down his throat to make a cordial visit in his stomach. Soon after, three more such visits followed suit. English was able to finally relax.

"I hope that this army has taken care of you since your unfortunate capture," Schofield said. "I am General Schofield, this is General Stanley. We have some very important questions that we need answered from you."

English felt his head swimming as a result of the alcohol he had just consumed. That, coupled with his complete exhaustion, put him in a state that was mildly intoxicating. "General Stanley, I do not know what you want from me, but I can not tell you much more than I have already."

Schofield stood up and walked towards the door. He opened it, and asked the officers to please wait outside. After they left, he locked the door. He was not one to ever resort to such malevolent measures, but under such circumstances, he had no choice. His army and his reputation were strung out along the Columbia to Franklin pike like a fragile strip of glass. If Hood's army struck any part of it, it would shatter into a myriad of abject shards.

English heard the footsteps of Schofield returning, but hesitated to turn. The look upon Stanley's face had said all he needed to know. The sensation of cold steel was then placed against the back of his head.

"I would rather you not turn, captain. You have not answered anything I needed, except the formalities of your rank. Now, simply answer my questions, and you can be assured your stay with us will be most hospitable. If you refuse, there is an excellent chance that you may never see the sun rise in the morning."

English tried to focus through the confusion that swirled in his head. Was the general of the Federal army threatening to kill him? Surely that was not allowed under the rules of war. He looked to Stanley for sympathy, but found none. He slowly brought his hands towards his neck and began to unbutton his coat. If he were going to be forced to speak, he would remain very selective as to what he said.

"General Schofield, you may ask whatever you would like."

English felt the cold metal removed from the back of his neck. Schofield walked around him and settled back in his seat. English noted that the general seemed to be sweating more than he was.

"Captain, tell me about the army that resides just outside this town."

"General Hood has two of his corps deployed for battle."

"Which two?" Stanley interjected. "We know that at least part of Cheatham's corps is here. We have already seen the battle flags of General Patrick Cleburne."

"That is correct. General Cheatham's entire corps is on hand, as is General Stewart's."

Stanley and Schofield then shared a few whispers together. Schofield turned back towards English. "The next time you see General Stephen Lee, please tell the general that I salute the ruse he has performed this day."

Before another question could be asked, there was another sharp knock upon the door. Schofield called for the person to enter, forgetting that the door was still locked. Stanley got out of his seat and opened the door. One of Stanley's staff officers handed him a dispatch. Stanley read it quickly then thanked the officer.

"General Schofield, I think that we should finish our conversation with Captain English at another time."

Schofield looked at the dispatch held in Stanley's hands and understood that something disastrous had just occurred. He took a lesson from the countenance he learned from Stanley earlier. He stood up and offered his hand to the Confederate captain. "Captain English, I thank you for all your help. I look forward to speaking with you again. And please, take the bottle of whiskey with you, it might help you forget about your troubles this day."

Captain English accepted the munificent bottle of whiskey, and then allowed the same two officers who had brought him to this room to escort him out. Schofield waited for them to leave before removing the short iron candlestick from his pocket. He gingerly placed it back upon the corner table.

"I must admit, I was quiet impressed with your little performance with that," Stanley said.

Schofield looked at the iron candlestick and felt ashamed at having to resort to such crude measures. "I can only hope that the bottle of whiskey will let that captain forget what occurred here this evening. I am almost afraid to ask, but what is in that message that you have?"

"John, I must inform you that it is very bad. The enemy has cut off Thompson Station to the north of us." Stanley handed the dispatch for Schofield to read for himself.

"They even managed to intercept a southbound train in the process," Schofield said. "Perhaps we need that bottle of whiskey more than that Southern captain does. So it has come to this, Hood has cut us off from Nashville."

"John, I cannot think of anything else that could be more dreadful than this. Our army is strung out from here back towards Columbia."

"I know. I know. The men at Columbia are probably just making their way now. Our strung out command is facing two consolidated corps of a very avenging Confederate army". Schofield reached for the glass of water that was left untouched by the rebel captain.

"John, I know these men, they will not fight," Stanley said with shameful eyes.

Schofield looked up. "What do you mean they will not fight?"

"Their morale is broken, and not by the enemy. I am not oblivious to the talk around the campfires. They feel, and I am afraid to say rightfully so, that General Sherman lied when he abandoned them. After the fall of Atlanta, we were all convinced that Hood's army was no longer a threat. When Sherman left for the coast, those left behind figured that their part in this war was over. Now, they have had to march back over the country that cost them so much blood. And for what? To face an enemy that thanks to Sherman now outnumbers them? If we are forced to fight Hood here, I am assuring you now that we will sustain more casualties due to deserters than to the enemy's fire. And I can't say that I would blame many of them."

Schofield sat in a stunned silence for a very long time. Very reticently he asked, "David, should we surrender this army?"

Stanley looked at him without an answer.

"If your assessment of morale is accurate, then when Hood attacks, we would suffer the worst rout in the history of warfare. I cannot allow these men, who have been through so much, to be slaughtered just because I have placed them in such a dire situation."

Stanley put two firm hands upon Schofield's shoulders. "John, that might be our only option, but not yet. Hood has still not attacked. There is a small window of opportunity left. Like Colonel Lane performed earlier this day, we must find a way to make the most of it."

Stanley's words seemed to spark an inner fire within Schofield. He remembered something that the prisoner had mentioned earlier. He stood up with a flare and began walking towards the door. "You are correct David. Thank you for being so calm and wise."

"I can assure you that I am far from calm, and as for wise, we shall know that in the morning."

"Very well. I am going to Thompson Station to survey the situation first hand. What is the time?"

"Almost nine."

"Almost nine, that means our men from Columbia should begin arriving and filling this town over the next several hours. We cannot sit here and remain idle. The more troops that congest this town will only add to this death trap set by Hood. I will go first hand to see if we cannot attempt a break though at Thompson Station. That captain said that Hood had two corps on hand. If they are both to the south and east of our position, and General Stephen Lee is at Columbia, who then can be blocking the turnpike north of us?"

"That could only be their cavalry", Stanley said.

"Exactly, and if there is only cavalry at Thompson Station, then this army had better be prepared to fight its way out. And if I hear anyone utter anything about it being Forrest's cavalry, my orders are to have that person shot. Now, please have Ruger's division readied to accompany me north."

They both departed from headquarters filled with the spirit of hope. There was indeed a window of opportunity still open, though it was closing rapidly. Before parting ways at the corner of the street, Schofield made sure that Stanley would have Ruger's divisions ready to be on the move.

"And one last thing," Schofield said. "Also have the men prepared to burn the supply wagons and spike the artillery. I know that the army surplus is needed, but should it fall into the enemy's hands, it would be used against us and whoever else had to battle with Hood's army after we are defeated."

*   *   *   *   *   *   *   *

General Stanley had been sitting idle inside the Federal army's headquarters at Spring Hill for the past hour. He had to look at the time again, was it really just after eleven. He doubted its accuracy. He even went as far as to appropriate another clock. Amazingly, they both told the same time. 'How long must I wait here and contemplate the fate of these men?' he wondered. Those poor souls gathered in defensive positions just outside of the town had no idea how much their lives were hanging by a thread. The more he thought upon it, the less he understood how it was that the Confederate army had not attacked.

Stanley tried to get some sleep earlier, but his mind was troubled with the same plague that infected it now. He made several visits to his men on the battlefield. Part of the reason was to try and exhaust his stress by taking some kind of action, but part of it was also because he fully expected the Confederates to assault the town at any moment.

The wait was horrific.

He could stand upon the ridge and look out into the distance and see nothing but the burning campfires of the enemy. The flames would dance and scatter nefarious shadows across the fields. There were several moments when he would have sworn that a wind cutting through the trees was the sound of the enemy approaching. Long he waited and long he watched, but the attack never came.

As he returned to the headquarters, he observed many of his soldiers collapsed amongst their fortifications. Most of them had been up since before dawn. Perhaps it was these same soldiers who understood best why Hood was not attacking. If the Confederates had marched all day as they had, then surely they were incapable of finding the energy to attack.

Stanley had arrived back at the brick home of William McKissack just over an hour ago. The fine abode was serving as an excellent headquarters. The inside was comfortable and accommodating, perhaps too much so. When he had entered, he was surprised to see many of Schofield's staff officers soundly asleep. The tired men simply contorted into any space that was available to suit their soporous needs. He chose not to disturb any of them. He walked into Schofield's room and hoped to see that the general returned. He had not. Anxious and impatient, Stanley resolved to sit himself at the field desk that was set up in the corner of the room, and there he would simply wait.

He lit the two lamps that rested on each side of the table and stared down at a blank sheet of paper. He reached for the ink well and began sketching the situation as he understood it.

Toward the top of the paper, he marked Thompson's Station. There he drew a colored rectangle to signify General Schofield with Ruger's division. Towards the middle of the parchment, he colored a large dot to represent Spring Hill. There he placed another colored rectangle to signify Wagner's division. He then went to draw Columbia, but remembered General Cox. Cox's division had just arrived from Columbia and was now trapped with his men. A second colored rectangle was placed in Spring Hill. Finally there was Columbia at the bottom of the page. Other rectangles were placed from there towards Spring Hill, representing the rest of Schofield's army.

Schofield's Situation

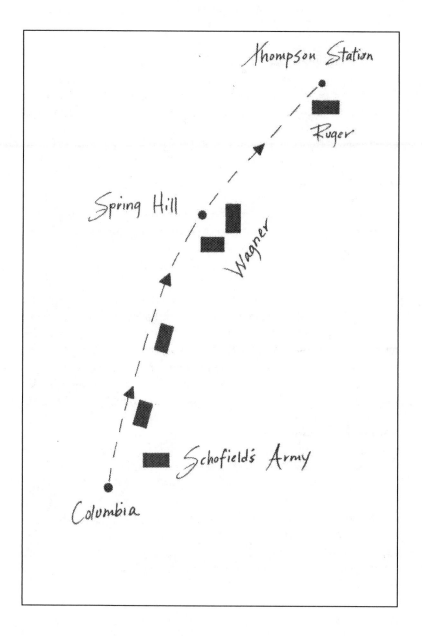

He stared at the piece of paper until his eyes were dried of all moisture. 'We are so spread out,' he thought. He began rubbing his forehead with firm fingers, as a small headache seemed to be taking hold of him. "General Schofield, we are in a bad state," he said out loud to the empty room.

Stanley began wondering what would actually happen if Hood attacked. Earlier, he had told Schofield that he thought the men would simply scatter without a fight. He still believed that. But it was rapidly becoming more convincing that Hood would not be attacking this evening. That bewildered him, but if Hood had not shown himself by now, he was not going to.

The assault at Thompson Station was most likely conducted so as to prevent their escape so that the attack could be ordered at first light. That would give the rebels a full day to hurl their entire army at Spring Hill, a position that Stanley did not want to have to be in. The Federal army was both tired and completely spread out, and there was no river to its front like they had enjoyed at Pulaski and Columbia. Here, Hood could maneuver his army more readily and use their numbers to overwhelm the Federals.

Stanley again looked at the clock. It was now a quarter past the hour. The sound of men working on defensive works resounded from the outside. It was no doubt General Cox's men settling themselves in for the attack that would come in the morning. The arrival of Cox's men meant two things for Stanley, and both were hopeful. The first was that his army preparing for war would now be a bit stronger, though not strong enough to win out in the morning. More importantly was the fact that Cox's boys had made it to Spring Hill. And that meant that the rebels either did not have enough men to completely surround the town, or that they were not vigilant enough to do so.

Thompson Station may be cut off, and Schofield's army may be trapped, but Stanley was not ready to give up hope. Not when he still had choices. And as he saw it, they could either stay and fight this out in the morning, or make their way to Nashville using another route. Stanley did not like either option, but they were both better choices than just surrendering the army as Schofield indicated earlier.

The sound of horses clattering down the street caught his attention. Stanley quickly got up and looked out the window. It was General Schofield accompanied by his staff. Schofield, showing more agility than he possessed, hopped from his mount and raced through the front door of his headquarters. The sight of his staff asleep did not have the same aloof affect on him as it did Stanley.

"Whoever is not up and looking like an officer in the next two minutes is to be thrown out of my command," he roared. Not wasting a glance on any of the sleeping soldiers, he charged into his room and was met by Stanley. The smile on Schofield's face split the thick beard like a piece of brittle wood.

"We have done it David, we have done it," he exclaimed.

"General?"

"It was as I said, a small contingent of cavalry and nothing more. They fled at the approach of General Ruger's division. General Ruger now holds the turnpike open for our escape, but we must move quickly."

Stanley felt as if his body was rejuvenated. "John, that is almost too good of news. Forgive my lack of faith, but I can't believe that the Confederate army is letting us escape like this."

"Nor can I. But we can't waste the rest of the night away contemplating Hood's motives. For whatever they are, the enemy seems to be content right were they are. Most unfortunate for them, but a saving grace for us."

The awakened officers in the next room could be heard scrambling around to catch up with their neglected duties. Schofield stared at the closed door as if he fully expected to see through it. "Can you believe those men, sleeping when their commander is out fighting for their very escape?"

Stanley let the statement remain rhetorical. "Cox has arrived," was all he said.

"Yes, I met him as I entered the town. He has informed me that the remainder of the army is not far behind. There are two regiments left to delay the pursuit of Hood's third corps, but besides that, our entire army could be in and out of this town over the next three hours. General, I do not want to waste another minute in discussion, we have to move this army out, and we have to do it now. My mind is waging a desperate battle that threatens to split my skull. Part of me believes the turnpike is open for escape, and we must take it. But there is another part that believes that it was left open as a trap. Perhaps Hood has spent this time shifting his troops north, so that he can strike at us as we file out of this town."

Stanley shared the same concern. "My vote is for taking that chance."

"As is mine. Instruct General Cox to cease all operations that involve the defense of this town. Have them continue marching towards Franklin. That will be our next position. From there we can cross the Harpeth and consolidate with General Thomas. A.J. Smith's command had better have arrived by now."

"And those pontoons as well," Stanley added. "What do we do if we reach Franklin and there are no bridges available for us to cross?"

Schofield looked at his desk and noticed Stanley's crude map. "Then I guess I had better take some paper and pen and prepare to write a formal surrender to my old friend John Bell Hood. But for the time being, if it is just the same with you, I would rather concentrate on one tragedy at a time."

"It may be difficult to stir our boys to march at this hour," Stanley said.

"Make it a point that all commanders make it known to their men our current situation. They had either get up and march to Franklin, or be prepared to make this place their home for eternity. If we are still here in the morning, Hood will destroy us. You have said that yourself. The only way for these men to revive their morale is to get them united with Thomas' command. Once they can regain their security in numbers, they will be ready to fight again."

"What do we do with the wagons?" Stanley asked.

"Our supply wagons, and probably our artillery will not stand a chance during this escape. I will not have countless wagons alerting the enemy of our march, nor will I have them clogging up the road. They must be destroyed so as not to fall into enemy's hands."

"Sir, I almost feel that we would do more harm to ourselves destroying our supplies and artillery, than by letting the enemy capture them. If we are caught at Franklin and there are no means to cross the Harpeth, we would be in a worse situation than we are in now. Let us at least try to get them out."

Schofield looked long into Stanley's eyes and saw the veracity contained within. "Agreed, but they are not to roll forward until after General Cox has left. And make sure that the men leave their campfires burning throughout the night, I do not want the enemy to know that we are up to something."

Stanley shook Schofield's hand. Both men's palms slid in a thin layer of pasty sweat. "Thank you sir, I will remain behind and ensure that there is no delay in getting our supplies out of here."

Stanley waited alone in the dark as Schofield left the room. He could hear the general shouting orders to his men, as several officers ran from out into the streets with orders to get the army moving north. Stanley took a moment to thank the Lord for this miracle. He also said a second prayer in hopes that this illusion of escape was not because Hood had setting a more severe trap for them somewhere along the turnpike.

*   *   *   *   *   *   *   *

During the next few hours, the Federal army en route from Columbia stumbled into Spring Hill like a flexuous stream of sleepwalkers. Their hopes of finding rest were spoiled by the news that they had to keep marching until they reached Franklin. There were several soldiers who bitterly complained, but in the end, the steady stream continued north along the turnpike as it exited Spring Hill. Weapons, canteens, backpacks, anything that could make a noise to alert the enemy of their march was muffled by the wherewithal of each individual soldier. Slowly, but steadily, the Federal army was marching towards Franklin.

It was not until after four in the morning when the supply wagons could begin the trek to join the rest of the army. Following them went the two regiments that were left behind to impede General Stephen D. Lee's march as well as Wagner's division that had been ordered to serve as a rear guard for the passing army. When the sun made its rise to greet the day, it would find that there were no longer any Federal soldiers left either at Columbia or Spring Hill.

All along the turnpike, column upon column of Union soldiers kept their heads turned to the right, expecting at any moment to hear, either the thunderous charge of Forrest's infamous cavalry, or the chilling cries of the rebel yell. Ominously, there was neither. One captain had even passed the remark that the flight from Spring Hill was one of the most critical moments that he had ever experienced in his entire life.

"If only the enemy would show his usual boldness, I am

sure that he would beat us most disastrously."

The majority of Schofield's army shared that opinion. It was obvious that Hood's whole strategy was to divide the command of Thomas and Schofield and destroy each in part. Yet, in the same breath that attained him that goal, he was also letting it slip away.

The greatest opportunity that the Army of Tennessee had ever been afforded was slipping right past them toward the safety of Franklin. And with it went the fleeting hopes for Southern independence.

Chapter XX
That Same Night
Spring Hill, Tennessee

At roughly the same hour that General Schofield returned from Thompson's Station to begin issuing orders for the evacuation of his army, Patrick Cleburne had called a small council with his brigade commanders. The Irish General was just as bewildered as the Federal army as to why the Army of Tennessee was not attacking. From across the way, he could clearly hear the sounds of the enemy reinforcing and entrenching. What should have been a decisive victory several hours ago was rapidly developing into a difficult task for the morning.

"Well, I still can't figure out why we have not been given the order to attack those Yankees," he fumed.

The high-ranking officers huddled around the fire and stared into its smoldering ashes for an answer. Cleburne listened towards his right, still hoping to hear some sign of General Brown's advance. He then looked back towards Hood's headquarters. The darkness cut his vision a few feet past a tree that was peppered with bullets.

He bent down and picked up a small stone. Without thought he threw it at the tree. The rock tapped against the thick bark and ricocheted in another direction. He had to laugh at the irony. It was much like the coordination of today's attack. General Hood had thrown them in one direction, and then Cheatham redirected them in another. What a complete loss of control.

"Why hadn't General Brown attacked?" he asked again.

Lieutenant Magnum was the first to respond. "General Brown reported his right flank exposed to the enemy. General Forrest's cavalry was not where it was supposed to be in support."

"I know that, I wonder if General Cheatham ever listened to what I said about Forrest needing to re-supply his men." As Cleburne looked at the men present, he noticed that Major General William Bate was not present. "Has anyone heard from General Bate?" he asked.

"He was last reported en route to support my left against

the turnpike. I believe that one of my officers has already ridden out to guide him to his position," Granbury said.

"We did not need General Bate's division to take that position," Lowrey said. The contentious general stood up and pointed to the ridge across the way. "Sir, please forgive my ire, but your command and that of Brown's should have swallowed those Yanks hours ago. One of my sergeants has even informed me that General Brown's right now has the support of his own men. Gist's brigade had arrived hours ago, but still General Brown refused to initiate the attack."

Cleburne was taken back by this news. He took two large strides towards Lowrey. "Are you sure of this report? Then because of General Brown, this army is sitting here motionless, and for no apparent reason."

"General, that is not exactly the entire picture," Govan said. "General Brown would have willingly made the attack, if only General Cheatham had ordered it. General Brown was adamant about not attacking with out the proper orders to do so."

Cleburne shook his head as he tried to rationalize all that he heard. "But he was given the order by General Cheatham earlier, I was there. This situation is beyond my comprehension. General Hood needs to be on hand. There are too many decisions being made by the wrong people. Gentleman, please ensure that your men are getting the proper rest this evening... and that goes for yourselves as well. Lieutenant Mangum, please get my horse."

"Your horse?" Mangum asked.

"Yes, and yours is too. We are going to pay a visit to General Hood's headquarters."

The generals gathered around the fire turned their collars up as they broke off to their separate commands. Mangum handed Cleburne the reins to his horse. As he ran his hands through its mane, Cleburne checked the wound that the horse sustained earlier. The beast was resilient.

When the two were mounted they began riding back towards the home of Mr. Absalom Thompson. Once beyond the hearing range of the camp, Cleburne's demeanor turned stern.

"Lieutenant, we should have attacked today. I can't help but feel that we have lost a great opportunity."

Mangum tried to console his commander. "General, you did all that you could do. After that it is up to men like Cheatham and Hood to take charge. That is the proper order of this army.

You have done your job by obeying that."

Cleburne turned his horse so that he was contiguous with Mangum's. In a very low, but determined tone, he said, "I may have obeyed the command of my superior officers, but I have done a great dishonor to my own spirit. I know in my heart that we should have attacked today. Would it not have been better for me to order the attack... risking arrest, than to not attack and have this army decimated in the morning? Mark my word lieutenant, this is the first time I have ever disobeyed the spirit of my own orders, and if God will forgive me, it shall be the last."

Mangum had no words to utter as he rode silently next to his commander. The sight of General Hood's headquarters could not come soon enough.

*   *   *   *   *   *   *   *

General William Bate returned to Hood's headquarters more enraged than he was when he was there earlier in the day. Hood tried his best to calm his contentious general, but the alcohol that he had consumed during dinner did not seem to be mixing well with his laudanum. He was exhausted and wanted nothing more than to sleep.

"General Bate, I understand your concern about having the opportunity to seize the pike, and in light of today's events, do wish that you had taken it. But General, please do not worry upon this any longer. I have had my fill of generals keeping me up this night, and I am in need of rest. What is done is done this day. Tomorrow will offer us a new chance. Please go back to your men, and assure that they have a quiet sleep this night. In the morning, we will have a Yankee surrender without a fight."

Hood could tell that Bate had much more to say, but he was not going to listen to any more of it. Bate saluted and took his leave of the Thompson residence. Hood waited to hear the general close the front door before removing the secretive dispatch from his jacket. He waited until he was in the bedroom before examining the message for the countless time this evening. The words written on the paper continued to stir his blood as they did the first time he read it.

"General Hood, please expect my appearance at your headquarters some time this morning. I have been riding for

several long and tiring days. For the safety of Richmond, my mission must remain a secret. It has been decided that I will take immediate command of the Army of Tennessee and help you and your noble offensive in driving the Federal forces from the west. I would ask that you suspend all actions until my arrival, unless you deem an attack to be practical. My hope is that you can keep the army consolidated for one more day and together we can drive the Federal army just like we did together against McClellan at Gain's Mill. There is not doubt in my confidence of our united success Your most humble servant. P.S. For the moment, this matter is between you and I alone. None other is to be involved. All will be explained."

Hood placed the letter under his pillow and let his eyelids slide shut. With the pressure of command lifted off his shoulders, he was able to sleep with fond recollections of his past glories serving under the generalship of General Robert E. Lee.

$$* \quad * \quad * \quad * \quad * \quad * \quad * \quad *$$

As Cleburne and Mangum approached headquarters, they noticed a small gathering standing a few feet from the front door. A serious debate seemed to take hold of the conversation. Cleburne tried to make out who was there. The only frame he could make out was the imposing mass that was Bedford Forrest. The gathering halted its discussion when they heard his approach.

"Ah, General Cleburne. As confused as the rest if us, I presume. Please come forward."

Cleburne handed the reins of his horse to Mangum before approaching. He had recognized the voice to be that of General Stewart. "General Stewart, very glad to see you." Now that he was closer, he was able to see the others gathered as well. Next to Stewart was Forrest. Adjacent to Forrest's left was a bitter looking William Bate. All three of them faced General Cheatham.

Cheatham spun on his heels to face Cleburne. "General, you should be resting with your men."

"General Cheatham, please forgive me, but sleeping is the last thing on my mind tonight. Why are you all standing outside in the cold?"

"Because our commander-in-chief seems to be passed out," Forrest said. "Apparently he is the only one who has deemed this day a success. We have been told by Governor Harris, that General Hood was in the best of sprits this evening, and had one too many toasts at dinner. I think the exact words were that he seemed more at ease than ever. I would wager that had a little something to do with either the alcohol or his medicine. Anyway, General Bate was the last to speak to him just over a half hour ago."

"And he could barely keep his eyes open. I know that it is past midnight, but we are all tired, are we not?" Bate said.

Stewart put his hands towards his mouth and blew hot breath upon his chilled fingers. "I just would like to know one simple thing. Where is my corps supposed to be? I came here an hour ago to find out, and honestly I am still unsure. First, General Hood instructed me to march north so as to cut the turnpike as it exits Spring Hill. Following those orders, I continued marching my men along the Davis Ford Road. I stopped for a brief moment to confer with General Forrest, only to find out that my men were being ordered back to support General Brown."

"That was what I was trying to explain," Cheatham said. "I asked General Hood to redirect your men to Brown's right flank. I had General Cleburne and Brown's divisions in position to assault the Federal army at Spring Hill, and only needed your men to support Brown's open flank."

"That is fine, but General Hood told me that by extending that flank, I would still be able to curve my line towards the turnpike. There seems to be some error in that. It is as if he thought your men were in line from north to south. But they were not, your line extends west to east. If I obeyed that order, I would be nowhere near position to block that pike. Under good conscious, I could not march my men again under such conflicting orders. Those boys are tired, and I will not move them one more inch until I can fully understand what has occurred here."

"What did Hood say to you when you reported this?" Bate asked.

"He mentioned something about General Schofield being in for a huge surprise in the morning."

"That is pretty much what he told me," Bate said. "General Cheatham, I understand that our relationship can no longer be the same after this day, but my situation was much like General Stewart's. General Hood himself had ordered my division to cut off the turnpike south of town. I was in the process of accomplishing that task, when your orders came for me to march to General Granbury's flank. This made no sense to me. I came here for an explanation, and was told as much as General Stewart. But all Hood could say was that we can sleep well this night… for we will have the enemy's surrender in the morning."

There was a long silence after Bate and Stewart blew out their steam. Cheatham rubbed a sniffling nose and then casually brushed his hand across his thigh. He looked into the dark farmhouse that sheltered Hood and his officers. Within every shadow, he thought he could see Hood eavesdropping on their conversation. He was sure that Hood was deep in sleep, but just in case, he thought it prudent to disavow himself from the lack of cohesion that had saturated the day's events.

"Gentleman, this whole debacle stems from a change in orders that I was never made aware of. The original objective was Spring Hill. General Hood revised that without consulting with me. Every order that Hood has issued was under the assumption that this army was facing west, when in fact, I had it facing north. That goes to explain a lot of this misdirection on the part of General Bate and General Stewart. When I came here to confer with General Hood, he did not seem to be too concerned with the lost opportunity we had before us. He was reassuringly content that in the morning, the enemy would find himself trapped within Spring Hill, and would be forced to surrender."

"That may be true," Cleburne said, "but we had them to-day like we never have. All we needed was to make one attack and the Yanks would have crumbled. It must fall upon General Brown for refusing to realize that and take that initiative. He must be made accountable."

"That is not his fault. General Hood did not seem to want the attack this late. He did not give me the orders to commence the assault. I in turn, did not order General Brown to attack."

All Cleburne could think about was his inner spirit. No matter what Cheatham could say, there was no convincing him that they should not have attempted one massive assault. They had two corps on hand, against little more than an isolated Federal division. It was not often that the Southerners could enjoy the benefits of having the larger army on the battlefield. It was an opportunity they could ill afford to pass by. Out of respect for Cheatham's rank, he kept these thoughts internal.

Cheatham felt that his actions were justifiable in denouncing his responsibility for all the confusion that occurred earlier in the day. It was extremely late at night, and he realized that there was a big day ahead of them tomorrow. As he looked at his watch, he painfully realized that it was already tomorrow. It was time that he concluded this meeting and sought some much-needed sleep, not to mention a drink from the flask that beckoned from his waist.

"Gentlemen, I am glad that we were able to gather here and talk this out", Cheatham said. "What is important is not what we did not do today, but what we shall do tomorrow. When the dawn breaks, General Schofield will find himself cut off from escape. More than that, General Stephen Lee's corps should be on hand to add its weight to the attack. General Johnson's division is already on hand to support my efforts. Come the morning, this army will triumphantly accept the surrender of Federal command."

Before anyone could respond, a figure emerged from the shadows on the porch of the farmhouse. At first, Cheatham thought his earlier fears were correct, and that Hood had been listening the whole time. But the size of this man did not match Hood's frame or humbled posture. Instead, a wearied man took several slow hesitant steps from the porch and stood before Hood's senior command.

"Come the morning, General Cheatham, that Federal army will be long gone."

If the sound of the voice was not enough to recognize the figure in the dark, there was no mistaking the thick gray beard of the man who had just appeared from seemingly nowhere. The generals parted before him and allowed him to enter the middle of their tight circle. They all looked at each other for some explanation, but there was none available. Somehow, General Robert E. Lee had just arrived at Spring Hill, and the men gathered knew the Army of Tennessee was never to be the same.

"General Lee," Cheatham said through a dried mouth, "How can this be?"

Several soldiers emerged from the side of the house. Cheatham recognized one of them as the messenger whom earlier had delivered Hood that secretive message. Cheatham now understood the enigma. One of Lee's escorts brought forth a heavy woolen blanket and carefully wrapped the general within it. Lee thanked him kindly and then turned his attention back upon Hood's generals.

"I am glad to see that General Hood was able to hold my

arrival as a secret. General Cheatham, how I got here can be explained at a later time. I am far too cold and tired to tell the story at this time."

"Forgive me sir, let me find a warm bed immediately," Cheatham replied.

The normally placid Lee turned austere. "General Cheatham, perhaps you did not understand what I have said only moments ago. The Union army will not be in that town come morning."

Cheatham looked at the other generals gathered, but none of them chose to speak. They were no doubt still stunned by the fact that Lee was now amongst them. "General Lee, forgive me, but I am not sure that you understand the current situation, we have the Federal army trapped inside Spring Hill."

Lee was not one to chastise a general in public, but his old body had been worn down by the arduous travel to Tennessee, and precious time was slipping away. His ire, usually kept reticent, was able to consume his weakened condition. "General Cheatham, I have stood at the side of this home for a long time listening to the bickering that you men call conversation. Let me ask you this one question. What makes you think that the enemy will be in that town in the morning?"

Cheatham had no answer.

"General Cheatham, from what I have heard, General Hood's original plan was to take the town. At some point, he changed this and wanted the turnpike cut off from the arrival of Federal reinforcements from Columbia. Upon your arrival at the battlefield, you had not known that General Hood had changed the plan, and you called for a consolidation of all available troops upon the town. Is that not an accurate assessment?"

"Yes sir, that is an accurate assessment, and that is why we will be in position to strike at the Federals first thing in the morning," Cheatham said.

Lee looked down and in a silent prayer asked the Lord to help him remain calm at this present time. "General Cheatham you have consolidated all available troops to make an attack. That was a decision that was justifiable due to the enemy's position on that ridge. But you never followed through with the offensive. By not attacking, you have stripped the field of all infantry and have left the turnpike open. During the course of this day you have not only failed to engage the enemy, but you have allowed his route of escape to remain open. If I were General Schofield, I would be praising the Lord for this opportunity and have every man in my army marching north in silence as we speak here now."

Cheatham continued to argue in his own defense. "General Lee, I doubt that Schofield will evacuate Spring Hill at this time. General Hood received a captured dispatch sent by Thomas in Nashville to Schofield at Columbia. His instructions were for Schofield to fall back to Franklin with the Twenty-third and the Fourth corps. The same message also stated that Thomas' command was not yet ready to reach him at Franklin, and so he was to delay our force here at Spring Hill, until he can bring his forces from Nashville to Franklin." Cheatham, content that he had said enough to justify his actions during this past day added that Lee could confirm this with General Forrest. It was the cavalry commander that intercepted the letter.

Lee looked at the men and a patient smile spread across the bottom part of his face. "General Cheatham, there will be no need for me to confirm this with General Forrest. I do not question that dispatch. But I will offer this instead. General, you have said that General Forrest has captured this dispatch. If that is so, am I correct to assume that General Schofield has never seen it?" A thoughtful silence from the general was Lee's reply. "Gentlemen, General Schofield does not know that he is supposed to delay this army at this town. Thus he will not do so."

Cleburne and Stewart both cast worried glances in the direction of Spring Hill. Could General Lee be correct in his assessment? Was the Federal army marching past their sleeping army?

"General Lee, I won't bother to ask how you got here," Forrest said, "but I am sure glad to have your company." Forrest walked towards Lee and offered him a firm handshake. His gesture was his way of making it known whom he felt should be in command of this army. Cleburne, Bate and Cheatham did the same. "I have already sent a brigade north of the pike towards Thompson Station," Forrest continued.

"That was wise General, but I am not sure a brigade from even your cavalry could stop the enemy's entire command."

The sound of a horse charging up the road towards Thompson's house caused the men to pause in their conversation. Lee, still needing to conceal the fact that he was in Tennessee, dropped back behind the large frame of Forrest. Forrest, realizing what Lee was doing, took a step out and intercepted the rider.

The solider pulled his horse to an abrupt stop and hopped off. The man was muddied from head to foot. A wild look was captured upon his face as his breathing came in short gasps.

"General Forrest, General Hood must be awakened," the private said.

"Calm down, and collect yourself," Forrest said. "Tell us of your concern and we will advise the general."

The private took a moment to catch his breath before speaking. "I was restless and anxious about the attack that would occur here tomorrow morning. Unable to sleep, I took a walk towards the turnpike to try and tire out my worries. There was a great deal of commotion occurring on the pike, so I went closer to get a better look. It was there that I have seen what I had not expected. I had thought that it was our men marching along our flank, but it was Yankees. They seemed to be in an awful confusion. I did not stay around long enough to discover their intent, but I can assure you that they are up to something, …leaving, if you ask me. All I could think was that General Hood needed to be notified of this immediately."

"You have done this army an excellent service," Stewart said. "We will handle this from here. Please report back to your command."

"But what about General Hood?"

"We will take care of this," Stewart confirmed.

Lee waited until the private had ridden back down the road before emerging from Forrest's shadow. "Gentlemen, that report leaves little doubt in my mind as to Schofield's intent this evening."

"I will wake Hood," Stewart said, as he walked towards the front door.

"I would ask that you do not," Lee said. "Let the general get some rest. Waking him now will only delay precious seconds that we need to organize an offensive."

The generals began assaulting Lee with questions seeking guidance. Lee was overwhelmed. He was also in need of sleep, not to mention that he had not eaten since the afternoon. The last thing he expected upon his arrival was the need for the army to attack. He knew that there was only one source available for the answers he needed. He closed his wearied eyes for a moment to pray to God for guidance and clarity.

"Gentlemen, please spare an old man a few seconds to think," he said. Lee turned his attention to the house behind him and thought of Hood sleeping comfortably somewhere within. How he desired for bed himself.

"Whose home has been appropriated for these headquarters?" Lee asked.

"This residence belongs to a Mr. Absalom Thompson. The Thompson family has been most accommodating to our men," Cheatham said.

Lee carefully hid a soft smile, as his body grew warm with the irony of the situation. 'Lord you are completely magnificent,' he said to himself. Clearly, none of the others had been able see the gift that the Lord had set right before them. One only needed to be well versed in the scriptures to know the name of David's son, Absalom. Lee's standing in front of this house was no coincidence. God was leaving him the foundations for the answers to his questions.

Lee's thoughts were drawn to the stories in Second Samuel, where Absalom's eventual undoing was that his choosing the wisdom of several advisors over that of his God.

Lee brought his hands together and offered God a silent prayer of thanks. The story of Absalom was set right before him here in Tennessee. Gathered around him were general's ready to offer their advice, just as they were for Absalom. Yet, unlike the fate that befell Absalom, Lee knew the lesson from Second Samuel all too well. Trust in no one but the Lord for the direction that you need to take.

"Generals," he said. "If we are to follow Forrest's strike, what forces can we muster at this hour?"

"If you mean to attack at Thompson Station, I would have to say that besides Forrest's cavalry, my corps would be the nearest at hand," Stewart said.

"How many men are available?" Lee asked.

"I can have roughly eight thousand troops on the march in minutes. They are right now already near the Rally Hill Pike."

"I have four thousand troopers that can ride out and hold the enemy at bay until Stewart's men can come up," Forrest said.

"My command is already too far south of the town," Cheatham said. "We can strike them from behind once the attack is made at the railroad station to the north?"

Lee was shaking his head. The advice was freely given to

him just as it was to Absalom. Lee knew that there was only one person who could give him the answers he was looking for. "Can someone please attain for me a Bible?" he asked.

Cleburne motioned for his aid to try and find one. Mangum dismounted and entered Mr. Absalom Thompson's home. A few minutes later, he came out with a leather bound Bible. He handed it to General Lee.

Lee took hold of the Bible with two firm hands. He felt his faith empowered with the Good Book in his possession. He was confident that God had not placed him here without reason. His arrival at this time was due to none other than divine intervention. If he was unsure of that, he only had to take a moment to stare into the face of Absalom Thompson's home. God could not have showed himself any clearer on this night.

With cold fingers, Lee flipped through the Bible to Second Samuel 17. The generals watched him with confused concern. They had no idea about his revelation, and did not understand his intent.

Lee silently and carefully read the first two verses of the passage. "Moreover Ahithophel said to Absalom, Now let me choose twelve thousand men and I will arise and pursue David tonight. I will come upon him while he is weary and weak, and make him afraid. All the people that are with him will flee, and I will strike only the king."

Lee shut the book and considered the passage. Stewart had eight thousand men available, and Forrest offered another four. The comparison was uncanny. Lee could muster the same twelve thousand troops that Absalom failed to do. With them, he could pursue the fleeing Federals and strike them while they were weary. There could be no doubt that Schofield's men must be exhausted from all their marching. One strong push at their demoralized flight from Spring Hill would no doubt do to Schofield's Army just what the Bible said... 'All the people with him will flee.'

Lee had made up his mind. Tonight's actions were to be guided by the direct command of God. Lee looked at the generals who were anxiously awaiting instruction.

"General Cheatham, your men will remain where they are. They have engaged in the battle this afternoon and are the most deserving of rest. And I would ask that they remain in place just in case the enemy is not retreating. I do not want to have your men out of position and exhausted if we do have to make an attack here in the morning. General Forrest, please send your brigade all available support. Stewart will march his men towards Thompson Station and aid you in the attack. You are to either take hold of the pike if the enemy has not yet fled, or attack whatever troops he has marching along it. My assumption is with the latter. Generals, I know that your men are in desperate need of sleep. But they must be made to understand the importance of this attack. The Federal army is more tired than they are, and they are also scared. If they are evacuating the town, they will be strung out in long columns from here to Franklin. With General Forest's cavalry delaying their advance, General Stewart's corps can attack their heavily exposed flank. I cannot stress enough the importance of this attack. If the strike is swift and well coordinated, they will break at the point of impact. What I need now is a way to keep those Federals on the pike until General Stewart can have his corps on hand for the attack."

Forrest looked at Lee and let his lips contort into a sly grin. "General Lee, please leave that to me," he said.

"General Forrest, I am sure that I can trust you to your own devices. From all accounts you have performed most nobly without any schooling from West Point."

Forrest's grin deepened. "General, if I had as much West Point strategy as you have, the Yankees would have licked me every day." With that Forrest quickly turned and departed into the night.

Lee watched the cavalry commander ride towards his men. He tried to compare Forrest to the late J.E.B. Stuart. He quickly realized that there was none to make. Forrest was the antithesis of Stuart and all that the flamboyant cavalryman represented. Forrest cared little for his appearance. There were no fancy plumes in his hat, no cape flowing off his shoulders. Forrest's attire consisted of a uniform, a saber and a pistol. That told Lee that the man's attention was spent on nothing except the battle. That could be both good and bad.

"General Cheatham," Lee said, "your men are to be summoned at four this morning. It is already past midnight and I expect that most of the Union army is already beyond our grasp. Stewart should be able to hit their tail, and rout their force up the pike. The enemy cannot possibly be expected to march to Nashville without rest. General Stewart, your men must keep up the pursuit. If the Federal army is still able to march without sleep, then I expect the same from our men. With your corps present, General Schofield cannot risk flight across the Harpeth River. He will try to form some kind of defense that will allow his army to escape. When they stop to do this, I fully expect General Cheatham's corps to be rested and available for the final push that will drive their disorganized forces into the Harpeth River."

The generals confirmed their understanding of Lee's plan and broke off to find their mounts. Lee quickly reminded them that his presence must remain a secret for as long as possible. Moments later they had dispersed to their respective commands. Cheatham approached Lee and quietly apologized for his earlier confrontation. Lee readily forgave him and told the general that he was probably overly tired and should report back to his corps to get some rest. Cheatham thanked Lee for his understanding and promised that his corps would perform without fail in the morning.

As Cheatham departed, Lee kindly asked Cleburne to remain behind. The Irish general told Mangum to report back to camp and then turned his mount back towards Lee. Lee watched the handsome man step from his horse and approach. There was something in the countenance of these western generals that was very similar. Forrest, Stewart, Cleburne, these men all had the same hard, worn, yet resilient look to them.

It was understandable.

The Confederate army here in Tennessee had not had their fare share of success as compared with his in Virginia. Except for Chickamauga, there were not many rewarding accomplishments for these proud men. The defeats began with the fall of Fort Henry and Fort Donelson. This trend continued with the evacuation of Nashville and the missed opportunity at Shiloh. Soon after, even the impenetrable bastion of Vicksburg was lost to a Federal siege. And even after the transfer of Longstreet's corps west, the victory at Chickamauga was wasted on the ridges east of Chattanooga. Since then, these men had been pursued through Atlanta. By every measure of fortitude, this army should have dissolved through demoralization alone. Amazingly they endured, and for the first time, Lee could understand why.

There was strong leadership out here. Forrest's victory at Brice's Crossroads reminded him of the old heroics often performed by the late J.E.B. Stuart. Different personalities, but similar results. Yet the man that was solely responsible for saving this army from its end was the general now standing before him.

As Grant knocked Bragg's army from Missionary Ridge and sent it fleeing into disaster, Cleburne was able to hold his command together and delay the Federal pursuit. It allowed the Army of Tennessee to escape and live to fight another day.

"Yes, General?" Cleburne said.

"General Cleburne, I just wanted a moment to say it is a pleasure to find you here this evening."

Lee's escorts began to filter back around the house, leaving the two men to talk in privacy.

"General Lee, if the pleasure and gratitude is anyone's it is all mine. If you are correct about the Federal army, you may have just prevented one of the greatest military blunders in history."

"Let us hope so, General. Would you mind if I rode with you back to your camp? I believe that General Forrest and General Stewart are now in command of this situation. They will find a weary Federal army and drive it from the field, or they will block the turnpike north of town. Either way, the battle will occur tomorrow and I am too old to go this night without sleep."

A horse was brought to Lee by one of his escorts. The two generals rode under a veil of blackness towards the direction of Cleburne's bivouacked troops. The company of cavalry that had accompanied Lee on his long westward trip closely followed them.

"General," Lee said, "may I call you Patrick when we are alone?"

"That would be fine, sir."

"Patrick, you are an honored hero back in Richmond." The look on Cleburne's face told Lee that he was doubtful of that statement. "It is true, General. President Davis has called you the Stonewall of the west, like a meteor shining from a clouded sky. That is the greatest compliment anyone in this army could receive. General Jackson was the best commander to serve the Army of Virginia and his loss has been felt on all fronts."

"General, I am appreciative of the compliment. I also feel that I am undeserving of such. General Jackson is a man whose valor one cannot be compared with. However, I am not sure I am convinced of the President's sincerity when he utters such statements."

"Patrick, I am not sure that I understand?" Lee said. "Your services against General Sherman at Chattanooga, and your ability to delay the Federal pursuit at Ringgold Gap, are the sole reason that this army exists now, and has this chance before us to reverse the tide. I can assure you that the President is sincere in his appreciation."

Cleburne remained silent, his eyes fixed on the road ahead. Lee rode along waiting for a response, but then realized why Cleburne was so upset. A man of his accomplishments had undoubtedly deserved more than his role as a divisional commander. Cleburne's response was given in his silence. It was the Irish General's respect for Lee and this army that kept him from forming the words. If he had performed so marvelously in saving this army, then why was he not its commander, or even a corps commander at the very least? Abashed, Lee knew why.

"Patrick, President Davis does hold you in the highest respect. But I am sure you yourself know why you have not been awarded any promotion for your service. The politics of this war cannot be fought by its generals."

Cleburne turned his head in Lee's direction. The twinkle of a cascading tear hung limply in the corner of his eyes. "General Lee, I would not have expected such a response from you of all people."

It was now Lee's turn to be silent. "General, it is the slavery issue alone that defeats this army," Cleburne said. Lee's head hung low and heavy upon slumping shoulders. "And I do not care what rank this army feels that I am deserving of. These men know, and that is all that matters to me. I will fight this war, for the freedom from Northern oppression, but the Negro keeps one hand tied behind our army's back."

"But to ask the President to free the slaves at the height of this conflict may not be the right time," Lee said.

"General, then when would you ask I request it? After we are defeated and the choice is no longer ours to make?" Cleburne realized that the veins on his neck threatened to burst though his skin. Lee was not the person to be bearing the brunt of his repressed aggression. "General Lee, please forgive my outburst."

Lee had been so busy in his defense of Richmond and Petersburg, he had never given what Cleburne said much thought. There was no denying that the slavery issue would soon no longer be an issue for the Confederacy to debate. "General, your feelings are most welcome around me. I only wish more men were as honest as you are. But you must understand the President's decision, if he would even consider your proposal, it would threaten to divide the Confederacy in half."

"What difference would that make? Look at this army, look at our country, we are being split into pieces as it is. Even your army is now under siege, there are not many opportunities left for us. This battle here may very well be the last. We cannot match the manpower of the north. That makes whatever victories we attain shallow ones."

"And freeing the slaves would add to our reserves? Patrick, many of the men in this army do not think like you, they would rather throw their guns down and go home than fight alongside the Negro."

Cleburne looked at the soldiers trailing them. He wanted to make sure that they were far enough ahead so that they could not be heard. "General Lee, those arrogant and ignorant sons of bitches need to understand that there is no longer a choice. We are losing this war. The emancipation of the slaves does a wealth more good than harm. I have just written another letter to the President trying to be clearer than my last. The freedom of the slaves will augment our manpower to face the enemy, yes, but it does so much more. Many of the Yankees fight the war for the sole reason of their freedom. It has become a rallying call in the north. Slavery is fueling their war efforts. By freeing the slaves ourselves, we silence their politicians, and I can even guarantee we rekindle the old flame of foreign recognition. General Lee, I hope that you can see that it is not possible for this victory here in Tennessee to save our country. The enemy will only regroup, muster another hundred thousand troops from its abundant population and drive us back once again. Meanwhile, those we lose cannot be replaced. Our victory will only delay that which is inevitable. What will free us is the emancipation of the Negro."

"Patrick, you have obviously given this matter much thought, I would do you a dishonor to try and convince you otherwise. I happen to agree with every point in your argument, but you do need to understand that men like you and I can only do so much for our country. These troops serve us, but we serve those elected to lead our Confederacy. Our will must be guided by their ability to make the decisions best suited for this country."

Cleburne stopped his horse in its path. Those troops following the two generals respectfully halted in their place. Cleburne took his gloves off his hands and placed them on his lap. The leather was cold and cracked, but had managed to help his hands remain warm. If Cleburne could not convince Lee of his conviction then he knew all hope of its acceptance in Richmond would be extinguished here at Spring Hill.

"General Lee, you speak of our will being guided by those elected officials in Richmond, but let me leave you this. President Davis may be the one who guides your will, but it is the Lord above that guides mine. And what he has taught me is that we should treat others, as we would have them treat ourselves. The Negro may be inferior to us, but he is still our brother. You may forget all my previous arguments for freeing the Negro except one. It is the right thing to do. You know it and I know it. There are some maters in life that require us to break away from the orthodox way in which we do things. I fight this war for the South... not for the ignorance of Richmond. I also am engaged to Suzy Tarelton, who is the love of my life. The thought of her is the only joy that this heart has known during the past few months. General Lee, I must return to her, and if I do not, then I want it to be because I died fighting for something I believed in. I will not pass from this world because of a lost cause."

Lee could only nod. With nothing but the truth, Cleburne had called his faith into question. Cleburne deserved to be reprimanded for his insult, but Lee could not bring himself to it. From deep within his soul, Lee knew that Cleburne was correct. We are all God's children, and by his choosing to place the issue of slavery on the burden of others, he was sinning in negligence to his own Lord.

"General Lee, if someone with authority would just stand up and perform God's will, we could recruit an army of slaves and by guaranteeing their freedom, could arm them for our cause. They can fight, that we know, the Union army already has them employed against us now. But the greater effect these black Confederate soldiers could serve is in the notion that this war is no longer one against slavery, but the war of a people against an oppressive tyranny. And that will turn the ears in France and England.

The two rode back towards camp and spent another hour within Cleburne's tent struggling with the difficulty in trying to get some sleep. Over an hour passed away as the two generals discussed past battles. The losses and victories were both weeded with a myriad of missed opportunities.

As his weary body finally began to feel that sleep was near, Lee turned down the lantern and asked God in a silent prayer to please protect this admirable general. In Cleburne, Lee saw the commander that he had been missing since Jackson's most unfortunate death. In the dark, a surrealistic lethargy helped blend the dark outline of Cleburne's face into that of Jackson. The thought put a rare smile on Lee's face. His eyes heavily drew shut like a fallen oak, but were quickly snapped open when four shots rang out breaking the silence of the night. The shots came from the far west, where Granbury's men were positioned. Lee and Cleburne sat up and shared a look of concern.

Minutes passed by, but there was no more gunfire to be heard.

Chapter XXI
November 30, Before dawn
Spring Hill

At the same hour that Lee and Cleburne had fallen sleep, John Murphy was wide-awake and preparing to make his escape with two fellow prisoners. The three men crowded within a thick cluster of shrubs, huddled closely to share in whatever warmth their consolidated body mass could muster. It was shortly after midnight, the hour planned for their escape from captivity. John had scouted this very spot earlier in the day while the rebel army was settling in their current position. This cluster of bushes was the closest cover available anywhere near the Columbia to Franklin Turnpike. Thankfully, the rebel army had left the turnpike unguarded, thus affording him the escape route he so badly needed.

"Luckily there is no moon, those guards will have much difficulty seeing on this night... and by the way they are leaning on their guns, they will be slow, sluggish. When the time is right, we risk our lives on a sprint for the open pike," John whispered to the others. They would play the odds and hope that one of the three made it to Spring Hill before a bullet found its mark.

Just as John was about to give the signal to flee, several soldiers on horseback came riding up the path. In the still night, they could hear every word that was said amongst the rebels. The captain in charge of the small cavalry company handed his horse to one of his men. The troop dismounted and three of the men led the horses near their place of hiding. The prisoners watched in horror as they approached. Breaths were held, not only to silence their breathing, but to also prevent the cold air from escaping their mouths like smoke from a chimney. The cavalrymen came within three feet of the shrubs before letting go of the reins to let the horses graze for a while. They quickly returned to the gathering.

"You will never believe this," the captain said.

"Believe what?" the guard asked.

"A division of cavalry from General Hampton has just arrived from Virginia. A very large division at that. There are almost five thousand of them. And they brought some artillery as well."

The rebel guards were both stunned. They let out a whoop of joy as they raised their caps and snapped them down upon their knees. "A whole division to join with Forrest, them poor Yankees will be done for in the morn."

The captain shook his head. "No, they don't mean to fight here, they are going to come up this way and ride on towards Franklin. They are going to cross the river and prevent the Yankees from escaping."

John Murphy's head went numb with this news. More than ever, General Schofield needed to be alerted to the danger he was in. When the army woke up, they would be as good as finished. He realized the only chance for the Union Army was if it could reach the Harpeth first. John carefully turned his neck towards the horses. They were not tied down. He tapped the other men on the shoulder to indicate his revised plan. They would leap for the horses and ride out towards the town with a fury. John spotted the horse that he would try for. She was dark brown with a black tail. The darker the horse, the better chance he had at blending in with the night.

Just then the thunderous approach of cavalry could be heard coming through a thick screen of trees. There were hundreds of mounted troops riding past his place of hiding. The long line of cavalry continued down a slow rolling hill that curved towards the right. The procession of troopers continued for what seemed like an eternity, as the three captives tried feverishly to count the passing parade. The captain was correct, there were over five thousand of them, with several batteries as well.

John quickly realized that they were not the only ones staring at the procession of cavalry. The guards were as well. He turned to his companions and shook their hands. "It is now or never. General Schofield needs to hear about his. The brown horse with the black tail is mine. Good luck."

The next few seconds were a blur to him. He rushed from the bushes with a speed that belied his emaciated condition. He threw his body upon the brown horse and turned the wild beast towards the pike. A shot rang out and Richard Toombler dropped at the side of one of the horses. John and Stephen had no time for remorse. They charged towards the rapidly approaching pike as several more shots rang out.

Unable to breathe, John reached the pike and continued towards Spring Hill. The night was so dark, he figured that his distance from the shooters had made him safe now. He heard Stephen approaching and paused a moment to allow him to catch up. The sight of the rider-less horse told him that he was all that was left. The sound of the rebel pursuit grew nearer, forcing John to race up the path towards a temporary safety.

*   *   *   *   *   *   *   *

General David S. Stanley stared numbly into the artfuly burning embers of the vacated Federal campfires. Their burning flames flickered with the wind in the hopes that the rebels situated just outside of this town would believe that the Union army was in bivouac for the night. Stanley had just facilitated the evacuation of the Fourth Army Corps first division, that of General Nathan Kimball. Their departure over a half-hour ago meant that most of Schofield's army was now safely on the road towards Franklin.

Still, there was much work to be done. He had instructed General Wagner to have his three brigades ready to form the rear guard for the Union army's long line of encumbered supply wagons. Earlier in the evening, the command of Wagner's third brigade had to be given to Colonel Joseph Conrad. Bradley's wound suffered earlier in the day would not allow him to serve with his men. With that done, Wagner had told him that as soon as the wagons began to roll north, he would have his three brigades ready to impede any advance attempted by the enemy.

Stanley rubbed his hands together, even though they were gloved. It did not seem to matter how sunny the day may have been, or how it warmed up this winter weather…the night would remain relentless with its chill. With the absence of the sun, the cold was eager to reclaim its rightful hold on the season. Wagner walked towards the soldiers who were preparing the wagons for their departure.

For men who had not had any sleep, they worked with an intensity that inspired him. With careful silence, blankets were fitted over the wagon wheels to help dampen any sound. Items that were worn that had any possibility of making noise were tied carefully to the side of the soldier that faced away from the enemy.

Stanley had to let out a deep sigh and inwardly smile. This was actually going to work. With the dedication that the men were putting into this evacuation, he figured that he could have the rest of this army out of Spring Hill by four thirty a.m., just over two hours from now. That calculated assumption was contingent upon the arrival of the Kentucky regiments who were impeding the advance of Hood's third corps commanded by S.D. Lee. Only when those brave boys from Kentucky returned from keeping an entire corps at Columbia, would Stanley allow himself to leave this Confederate trap.

Stanley headed back towards the Federal headquarters on Main Street. His arrival was greeted with a small meal, which he readily consumed. He then retired from his staff and tried to rest his eyes for a few moments. To his surprise, when they reopened it was three-thirty in the morning. The fact that his sleep was undisturbed meant that the rebels had still not attacked, and were probably never going to. Remembering his early calculation of the army's ability to vacate this town, he was anxious to see the progress that had been made. He left the Main Street residence and began heading north of the town. He had not gone far when he saw General Wagner riding towards him with a host of mounted officers. Stanley swallowed hard. The rebels must have finally realized their mistake and attacked. The thought of his army strung out along the pike and unable to support itself made him dizzy. Wagner saluted Stanley and dismounted from his horse.

"General, is everything ok?" he fearfully asked.

Wagner pulled his cap low around his head for added warmth. "General Stanley, one of our own has escaped the captivity of the enemy. He is one of Hatch's, and by the looks of him, he hasn't had a thing to eat in days."

"Where is he?"

"We have him in one of the houses on Main Street. The pickets that found him said that when they first saw him approaching they tried to shoot him, but he raced his horse so fast he was by them before a second volley could be delivered. He fell at their feet and thankfully he was quickly recognized as one of our own. But he is in awful condition. He keeps shaking uncontrollably and has not stopped crying."

"Most unfortunate. Please see that he is clothed and fed, and as soon as we reach Franklin, get him some medical attention."

Wagner took his cap off and curled it within his fingers. "General, that brave soul did not race here risking his life for his own concern. Before he lost his wits, he was able to tell us some very disturbing information."

Stanley raised his brow in question.

"Apparently, General Hampton has sent an entire division of cavalry from Virginia and they have just arrived tonight. Right now they are riding north to cut us off above the Harpeth."

Stanley rubbed his temples as if he were struck with the most severe headache. He was entirely too tired to have this much to think about. "Why would Hampton send a division here? It does not make sense."

"Neither did Longstreet's being at Chickamauga, but boy did that make difference," Wagner returned.

Stanley was shaking his head vigorously. "This soldier, did he actually see Hampton's cavalry?"

"He estimated over seven thousand of them, with artillery."

"General Wagner, do you know what will happen to this army if it reaches Franklin and cannot gain the northern banks of the Harpeth. Forrest could mount over fourteen thousand troops to our front, while Hood's entire army comes upon our rear. If General Schofield thought that this place was a trap, I would like to hear what he has to say about Franklin."

Stanley could feel the oath he made to those isolated Kentucky regiments shatter like fallen eggs. He could no longer wait for their arrival from Columbia. Those poor heroic men would reach Spring Hill in the next few hours, only to become prisoners of the Confederate army. 'A small price to pay for the survival of Schofield's army,' he thought.

"General Wagner, we have to get this army to Franklin first. Send word to Schofield that his advance elements must reach the north side of the Harpeth and secure it against the enemy. How do we stand with the supply wagons, are they all on their way by now?"

"Just about, the last few should be rolling along now."

"Good. Have your men form a strong rear guard and get them moving at once."

Wagner had confirmed the order when another smaller cluster of officers came riding into the assemblage that was readily turning into a council. This time, there was no mistaking the frantic look that flared from their widened eyes. Somewhere, the enemy had attacked.

"General Wagner, the worst news has just arrived. The

wagon train cannot continue along the pike. The enemy has attacked the head of the wagon train at Thompson Station. From there south, the pike is clogged with impassable wagons."

Wagner threw his crumpled cap to the ground. "Damn them," he spat.

General Stanley wanted to have a tirade as well, but knew that at this moment, this army needed a stable leader more than ever. He had to make a decision here, and what he wanted to do was deploy Kimball and Wood to attack the rebel cavalry. Wagner's division could march at once and support the divisions already engaged. What held him back was the information stolen by the escaped prisoner. If the Confederate cavalry was riding towards the Harpeth, then this attack was nothing more than a ploy meant to delay their march north. Had it not been for such timely news, Stanley knew that Forrest would have easily made him feel like a cuckold.

"Please report back to General Kimball that his division is to deploy and escort the wagons. General Wood should also be at hand to help in this matter. Tell them that it is only a diversionary strike offered by the cavalry that they face. They are to resist them at all cost. The real attack will not occur here. Make sure that they understand this. General Kimball and General Wood are to push by this attack and keep moving. Make sure that this is understood."

The officer saluted and those that rode in with him rode back towards Thompson Station. Stanley turned to Wagner and for a second time ordered his division to form a rear guard immediately. "And General Wagner, that soldier who escaped this night to report his news, what was his name?"

"An Irishman, John Murphy was his name."

Stanley nodded. "To survive as a Confederate prisoner in these winter nights, you can rest assured that the Irish are made of something stronger than blood and bones. Have this Murphy fellow promoted at once."

*   *   *   *   *   *   *   *

John lay in a warm bed as he listened to the sound of horses being ridden with purpose. That put an oneiric smile upon his face. Somehow, he had made it to Spring Hill. Besides the loss of his companions, all else had gone as he had hoped. He was able to warn General Wagner of the arrival of Hampton's division. From the commotion outside, the army was now moving to escape the trap at Franklin.

As he pulled the blankets around himself for a warmness he could never find, he looked at the plate of food that was placed on the small table beside the bed. As hungry as he was, he could not find the appetite to eat. He was able to drink three glasses of water before losing his nerve in front of several of Wagner's officers. He was ashamed of that now, his crying like a frightened child had caused his body to shake in the most embarrassing manner. He hoped that he had not looked too foolish.

John tried to sit up and reach for the food, but found that his legs were marmoreal in response. He slipped a skinny arm under the covers and tried to rejuvenate his lower limbs, but no matter how hard he pressed his hand against his leg, he could not feel a thing. He began feeling other parts of his body to compare with the lack of sensation. That was when he felt the warm spot just above his lower spine. When he pulled his hand up, it was bloodied.

John felt his chest begin to palpitate with fear. He did not recall being hit by the Confederates. He was sure he made it by them safely when he fled. Then the blur of events that followed began to trickle into his consciousness. The Federal pickets had fired at him when he approached their lines. Had one of them hit him?

With a thick sweat coating his decimated body, John tried to call out for help. It sounded like the moans of a dying grimalkin. He looked towards the door in hopes that an officer had heard him, but the only response that he received was the silence of a closed door. His eyes were quickly averted to the one-inch gap between the bottom of the door and the floor. The light that came in through that space was quickly becoming suffocated by the billowing vapors of a thick black mist.

John was all too familiar with the foreboding atramentous fog. The last time it threatened to consume him, he was able to move from its clutches. This time, he was paralyzed from the waist down. John was forced to lay there and watch as the black mist swirled around the floor before slowly climbing around the bed. John could see it twisting around his ankles like a weedy vine choking the earth. As it covered his hips, he realized his abject situation. At this point, his death no longer mattered. He was just glad to have died here with his own men than as a prisoner of the Confederates. He had managed to escape his captivity and alert the Federal army of their danger.

Just then the door was opened and in stepped a dark silhouette. As the figure neared, John could make out the face of his mother. A warm tear escaped from him as he hugged her feverishly.

"Son," she said, "you have made your mother proud."

John wiped the tears from his face. "I only wish I had gotten the promotion that would have made my wife and children proud."

With maternal care, John's mom softly kissed her son's forehead as she led him into the black mist. "John Murphy, you were promoted just this evening by General Stanley himself. When your wife learns of this, she will be told that she has lost a man who has served his country beyond expectation."

It was that thought that allowed John Murphy to pass from this world with a warm smile upon his otherwise cold and stiff body.

*   *   *   *   *   *   *   *

Stanley was not the only general pushing his troops towards Thompson Station. Racing there as well was Nathan Bedford Forrest, followed by his entire command. Though Stanley was afforded the benefit of having to march the shorter distance, the Confederate cavalry had two things that would make their advance move more rapid. One was being cavalry... they were mounted where the enemy was on foot. The other was that they served under Forrest... and he assured that they understood the opportunity set before them.

Earlier Forrest had detached Ross' Brigade of seven hundred troops to the train station. If Lee was correct about the Federal withdrawal from the city, then he wanted Ross to delay their evacuation. That meant that his lone brigade had to keep the Union army occupied until the remainder of his force could be summoned. The attack should have commenced over an hour ago. If not, Forrest warned Ross that he expected to arrive and see his brigade in occupation of the turnpike north of Spring Hill.

However, as he rode north parallel to the Rally Hill Pike, he grew more and more positive that the situation he would find would be of the former.

He had taken a tremendous gamble earlier, when he rode his entire commander towards Granbury's position. The move would seriously delay his arrival at Thompson Station. Had he not first ridden west towards the Columbia Pike, he would have been at his objective already. He was playing the odds and hoping they would roll in his favor. That Irish prisoner had his heart on escaping ever since he was first captured. Forrest wished he had more men like that in his own command.

"What do you think General?" Strange said.

Forrest was so internally absorbed he had completely forgotten that Colonel Strange was riding alongside him. "Think about what?" he said.

"That prisoner. We shot the other two, but it looked like he was going to make it."

Forrest smiled. "That tuff son of a bitch was made of leather, he made it all right." Making it was not his concern. What Forrest hoped was that the prisoner had believed his ruse. It was a tactic that he had used numerous times and its success rate helped convince him to employ it again. Forrest would pick a position that was conducive to his chicanery and then like a great conductor, watch his performance unfold. He would instruct his men to emerge from a position that an observer could not see beyond. From there, they would ride along a selected path and then veer off at a point at which that same observer could no longer see. Once the leading elements turned from the path, they would race along an unobservable route and reform behind the original concealed position. Then they would march the exact same route again. The ploy, if performed to perfection, could make two thousand men seem like five thousand.

That was what he wanted the prisoner to believe and report it as such to the Federal high command. It was the arrival of General Lee that helped inspire Forrest to have one of his trooper's mention that the cavalry was augmented with a division sent from General Hampton. He was hoping that the false report would scare the Federals into making a tactical mistake, or at the very least stall them long enough so that Stewart's corps could be on hand when the attack was made.

The smell of burning wood drifted into his nose, and as he

rode his horse over a rising hill, he was greeted by the glow of several fires flickering from the direction of Thompson Station. He instinctively gripped the pommel of his sheathed saber and raced ahead.

The divisions of Chalmers, Buford, and Jackson were spurred on by Forrest's sudden surge over the hill. At this hour, they looked like a galloping army of gray ghosts as they arrived just east of Thompson Station. From the concealment of the woods they could look down at the pike as it was littered with several burning wagons. Forrest was too astute a commander to think that the debris meant that Ross was successful in his assault. Most of the wagons were still filing through the wreckage and continuing north. On both sides of the long procession was an escort of Federal soldiers. Forrest could understand why Ross had not continued with the attack. He obviously had initial success, but once the Yanks summoned support, the seven hundred men of Ross' brigade were no longer a threat. But now that had changed. Before he could order the attack, he wanted General Ross summoned. He needed to hear a quick statement that was in accordance with his thoughts.

His men peered like jackals over the hill as the slow moving Federal army marched along the pike. Soon, Forrest was surrounded by his highest ranking officers. They all waited impatiently for Ross' arrival. To the right, Ross' men could be heard firing an occasional volley into the flank of the passing enemy. It had little effect except to waste their dwindling ammo.

"General Forrest," Strange said. "we have found General Ross, he is coming now with his officers."

Forrest turned to his left and looked over Strange's shoulder. The dark forms of several riders could be seen approaching. Forrest waited until he could make out the face of Ross before speaking. "General Ross, please keep your response brief but concise. What is your situation?"

Ross went to salute his commander, but knew that when Forrest said to be brief, that all formalities were to be disregarded. "General, we hit the wagons at roughly two a.m. I am sure that we had the head of their procession, the Yanks were most surprised, and for a moment there was a great logjam just ahead on the road. But I had to pull my men out when their infantry appeared. They drove us back up this hill and we have been unable to do anything but watch them file by."

Forrest spat to his left and looked back at the road. The burning wagons cast an eerie glow on the columns of Federal soldiers as they marched by. "Who burnt the wagons?"

"They did sir."

"They would rather burn their belongings than let us get at them," Chalmers said.

"That may be," Forrest said, "but there are a whole lot more of those wagons that have not been touched yet. Do you know whose men those are passing you now?" Forrest asked Ross.

"We saw some flags from Illinois and Ohio. One of my officers has a real knack for identifying regiments and their brigades. He is confident that we are now watching the tail end of the First and Third Divisions of the Fourth Army."

Forrest looked back at the road and the rail station with an intense desire to charge. But something that Ross had said held him back. "Did you say that this was the tail end of two Federal divisions? Are you certain?"

"Yes sir. We have been watching them march by for the better part of two hours. Why?"

Forrest was about to take his second major gamble this night. He could hear himself saying double or nothing as he tossed imaginary dice down the hill towards the fleeing Federals. "Then we will let this mass of troops pass. They are already warned of your presence and are deployed to meet any threat. However, as the day wears along and this procession continues unmolested, these vigilant troops will be too far north to support the attack we make on the next division of troops that traverse our front."

"What if they turn and come upon our rear?" Buford asked.

"That will not matter," Forrest said. "By that time General Stewart had better have his full corps on hand. The way I see it, whatever troops have passed this point already will be the only ones that Hood will face in the morning. Those that are unfortunate enough to still be south of here will soon be cut off from their army."

"General, how can you be so sure?" Chalmers asked.

Forrest winked at Strange as he began issuing orders in preparation for the attack. Strange knew what had made his capricious commander so confident in his assessment of the situation. Forrest was betting everything on the belief that the Federal prisoner that he had allowed to escape had scared the

Union high command into a race for the Harpeth. And if the Union army were racing there, then the troops last to leave Spring Hill would have to be deployed in the most rapidly moving formation. The problem for the Federals was that though the column formation allowed for greater speed, it was also very vulnerable to attack.

*   *   *   *   *   *   *   *

It was almost five in the morning when Colonel Emerson's Opdycke brigade approached Thompson station. Opdcyke's brigade was part of Wagner's division and it represented the last Federal soldiers to vacate Spring Hill. Ahead of them, the long slumbering line of the Union army snaked over twelve miles towards Franklin. What separated Opdycke from the rest of Wagner's division, as well as the rest of the army was the slow moving congestion of the remaining wagon train. Though they were tired, Opdycke made sure that his men remained vigilant. It was only a few hours ago when the rebels hit at Thompson Station. Though, there had not been another attack from the enemy, one could never be too sure. To many of the soldiers, it appeared as if General Schofield would escape one of the best-laid traps in military history. That should have allowed Opdycke some comfort, but it didn't.

Several things aggravated him at the moment. Opdycke twisted the long thin hairs that hung from his chin as he watched his men march along. His brigade seemed to lack a sense of urgency that he knew they might very well need. He wanted to reprimand them, but quickly realized that would be most unfair. If anyone deserved reprimanding it was his superior officers, especially General Wagner.

Why were his men assigned to this rear guard duty anyhow? His brigade, along with Lane and Bradley's made up the first division to arrive at this town. They were the ones who had to dig in just so they could spend the day battling with the enemy. As far as Opdycke was concerned, they had done their fair share of the work already. It should have been their units that were the first to vacate Spring Hill.

Yet, here they were marching dead last. Opdycke vehemently hurled his spit on the road beside him. There was definitely favoritism being played within this army. He had fully expected his division commander General Wagner, to raise some noise against this. To his dismay, Wagner was reticent, or if he had said anything, it had no effect. However, it was plain to all of the other officers in the Fourth corps, as to what was really going on. General Schofield clearly placed his Twenty-third corps in the safest position, while the Fourth corps had to bear the majority of the burden.

The more he thought on it, the more he wanted to stop his men where they were and race off to find Wagner. The only thing that held him back was that he knew what he would say and do if he found him at this hour. It would no doubt lead to his arrest. Opdycke looked towards the east at the thin line of light threatening to break through the darkness. It would be daylight very soon. He hoped that by the time his men marched into Franklin, he could find them a place to bivouac, and he himself could sleep off his aggravations.

The sound of gunfire crackled upon his right flank not far ahead. At first it sounded like the sporadic fire of the few rebel pickets that lined the pike, but it soon escalated. Before Opdycke could issue his first order, the sound of the rebel yell shattered the silence as the Confederate cavalry poured down the hills to the east like a swarm of locusts. Opdycke looked at them in dismay. His orders were to ignore the cavalry pickets. They were supposed to be nothing more then a few isolated companies posted on the hills and nothing more. He tried to spit again, but his mouth was dry. From the way the earth shook as their cavalry thundered forward, Opdycke knew that once again some one high up had made a huge blunder.

Schofield.

Right now, the Twenty-third corps was well on the way towards Franklin, well out of the battle range again. Meanwhile, his men, the same soldiers who spent the entire day fighting with the enemy, had to do so all over again. Unfortunately, this time, they were neatly compacted in long thin columns that were suited for marching. And making matters worse was that they did not have any favorable ground to defend themselves on.

As Opdycke pulled out his revolver, he made sure to visualize General Schofield's face in every rebel he killed.

*   *   *   *   *   *   *   *

There were only two pieces of artillery at his disposal, and Opdycke quickly unlimbered both of them. In minutes they faced the oncoming rebel horsemen and lit up the night with a mammoth volley. The blast unhorsed several of the attackers, unfortunately there were plenty more to renew the charge. Opdycke quickly formed his soldiers into two lines. He instructed the first line to fire and fall back to reload. As the first line withdrew, the second would fire and then fall back behind the first again. They would continue to do this until they could be consolidated with the brigades of Lane and Conrad.

At first the tactic was succeeding. One line would deliver a volley into the charging Confederates, stalling their advance long enough for the second line to step forward to issue a volley of their own. Though it was dark, Opdycke's brigade could barely make out just how well they were doing. Rebel horses were scampering back into the surrounding woods with wild frenzy. Dangling from the stirrups were dead Southerners, their bodies being bounced in the most inhumane manner.

The horrible visage was soon replaced by the haunting realization that they the enemy was coming again. Their undaunted cavalry charged again, and like those that went before them, fell back from the wall of Yankee lead. Yet they still came, and each time, Opdycke had his first line fire then fall behind the second line to reload. It did not take him long to realize that though his brigade had repelled several attacks, overwhelming numbers were forcing his men to fall back several yards. That meant the artillery had to be pulled back as well. Irate at having no option, Opdycke withdrew the battery. Still, his men retired north along the pike in slow, but excellent order. For a brief moment, he even thought that they would escape this assault relatively unharmed, but then the brigade came to a complete and sudden halt. They could not back up any further.

"What the hell is going on?" Opdycke called to one of his officers.

"Colonel, the road up ahead is too congested with the supply wagons. We cannot maneuver our brigade through them without breaking this formation."

"Where are Lane and Conrad?"

The officer tried hard to swallow, "They appear to have broken and fled sir. We have been left to fend for ourselves."

Opdycke growled as he punched at the air. "God damn

this army. Why the hell would they run when we have the situation in control? Couldn't they see that, shouldn't someone have consulted with me? Well damn them, damn them all. Here they come again boys. Have at them. Have at all of them."

Opdycke's staff officer waited for him to finish inspiring his men before continuing. "Colonel, one of Lane's officers risked his life delivering the message. He reported that the other brigades were attacked as well, but not by Confederate cavalry. It appears that one of Hood's corps had hit them on the flank and as they saw it, there really was no option but to run."

"So just leave us here unsupported? There is no excuse for it. None."

"To keep the enemy from pursuing, the rest of the division was instructed to overturn several wagons and set them on fire. Even if we could get through the rebel infantry that hold the pike ahead, we would only find ourselves imprisoned within the clutter of the overturned burning wagons."

Opdycke tired to see behind him, but the darkness and the glowing flames of burning supply wagons hampered his vision. "So all that stands between the entire rebel cavalry and an entire corps of their infantry, is our brigade and those burning wagons?"

The officer did not answer. He was too busy watching Forrest's dismounted cavalry inch closer and closer with every advance.

Opdycke turned to his officer. "Tell the men we must fight our way through this. We cannot give up. Turn these men around and have every man race for Franklin. Select a few regiments to hold the Confederate cavalry in place."

"What of the enemy's corps that lies ahead of us?"

"They are undoubtedly on the pike, so have the men stick to the woods."

Opdycke raced back to the line of defenders. His presence told them how desperate the situation had become. Soon, regiments began to pull out of the line, leaving loaded weapons for those that remained. The loss of these troops allowed the Confederates to come within yards of their position. Sensing that they would not last much longer, Opdycke told the men that remained at his side to prepare bayonets for the charge. This did not surprise the men, they were well aware of their plight.

Opdycke raised his pistol and emptied it at the rebels. 'These bullets would be better suited for Schofield and Wagner', he thought. "Well, damn them," he spat, as his gun no longer had any ammo to expel. Opdycke instinctively turned the weapon in his hand so that he could use its handle as a club. With a bitter rage directed more towards his own commanders who had allowed this debacle, he led a savage charge into the oncoming Confederates.

The rebels were caught off guard, as Opdycke claimed the first causality by splitting the skull of a captain. The battle quickly digressed into a form of medieval combat. Bayonets were impaled through stomachs, shoulders, legs, necks, and any body part that would inflict harm. The rebels quickly gave ground under the fury of this attack. But there were fresh troops behind those that broke, and not hearing the sound of gunfire, they attacked while mounted.

Opdycke squeezed the barrel of his pistol as one of the mounted rebels drew near. He ducked under the swing of his saber and struck him on the back of the head. The rebel fell lifeless. Opdycke could hear firing coming from the pike to the north. Too much was happening too fast for him to think, but he wondered if his escaping regiments had been found. It was then that he noticed that the dawn was breaking, making it much easier to see through the dark with each passing minute, see the faces of the enemy as they massed for one final assault. It also allowed him to see that his command was now reduced to just a few organized companies of resistance. And still, the thought of surrender did not cross his mind.

Opdycke braced himself as a rebel brandishing a raised saber charged towards him. As the rebel drew nearer, he discarded the saber and pulled out a shiny revolver. Opdycke watched the man take steady aim and had to wait an eternity for the result. For Colonel Opdycke, as well as those he commanded, their part in this war was about to end prematurely. Whatever heroic part they might have played in this war's history was snatched from them upon the pike that led into Franklin.

*   *   *   *   *   *   *   *

It took several strong nudges to awaken General Lee. When he finally was able to open his eyes, he mumbled something about Taylor, but then he went back to sleep. Forrest did not know all the details concerning Lee's trip west, but he was sure that if he could not be aroused, then the man needed to be left alone to sleep.

"We should let this man sleep. His arrival could not have come at a better moment than it has," Forrest said. "He was correct in his assumption about the Federal army, when Hood wakes, he will no longer find the enemy at Spring Hill."

"The sun is up, where is General Stewart?" Cheatham asked.

"His corps, as well as my cavalry is in pursuit of the Federal army. We are conforming to General Lee's plan. With our presence, Schofield cannot attempt to ford the Harpeth to safety. He will have to form some sort of defense that will allow his army to escape. That is where and when we expect to find your command General," Forrest said.

Cheatham was nodding his head in agreement. "This corps will be ready at that time. Do you have any estimates from last night's battle?"

Forrest called for Strange to bring forth the report. Forrest held it before him in confidence as he read over the details. "We have routed their rear guard. At a cost of fewer than three hundred casualties, we have captured the first brigade from the second division of the Fourth corps. Colonel Opdycke was identified as one of the dead. Not long after their defeat, two Kentucky regiments stumbled into our rear. They thought we were Yankees. I quickly called for their surrender, and being surrounded by so many of us, they easily complied."

Outside of Cleburne's tent, they were met by several of Cheatham's commanding officers. The long lost smiles of victory resided on all of their faces as they exchanged what they knew of the recent battle.

"General Forrest, excellent work in attaining their surrender," Cheatham said. "And what of their supply wagons?"

"We counted thirty-nine burnt, but one hundred and twenty captured. We even managed to obtain several batteries of their artillery." Forrest looked past Cheatham into the tent where Lee slept. "I have heard a great deal of that man's ability to take control and lead an army to victory. Much of it I attributed to rumor and exaggeration, but after what happened in the early hours of this morning, I will forever hold the highest regard for him. It all went exactly as he predicted, the entire Federal rear guard broke like a stampede of cattle. If we can force them to battle, I think the fight will be easily won."

"What about General Hood?" Cheatham asked.

Forrest shrugged his shoulders. It was clear that he no longer cared for anything concerning Hood. From now on, Forrest would only serve General Lee.

"General Cheatham, if you wish to awaken him that is up to you. I must accompany my men in the pursuit of the Union army. What I need from you is the promise that your men will be on hand when we finally catch up with them. If you waste time to awaken Hood, you will also have to waste time explaining this to Hood. My advice is simple, General Lee is now the commander of this army. He gave us all the instruction we needed last night. The wisest action we can take is to follow the advice of the general with the most wisdom. And I do not think we need a lesson in which one that is. Hood will awaken shortly. Leave an aid behind who can explain what has happened. Hood will find us shortly, that I will guarantee."

Cheatham turned to Cleburne, hoping to get his opinion. "Had we listened to General Hood, the Federal army would have left this town unhampered," Cleburne said. "Thanks to General Lee, we have captured a brigade, a few regiments, as well as some much-needed supplies. I am with Forrest, let's worry about the enemy we have on the run and not the general whose feelings are to be hurt."

Cheatham nodded and then spoke. "Then General Cleburne, as well as General Brown and General Bate, please have your men on the march within the next hour. Also have word sent to General Stephen Lee to comply with Lee's wishes from last night. He is to march towards Franklin with all speed. Let us hope that the Harpeth has risen enough to delay their escape."

"Gentleman, let me remind you all that General Lee's presence is still to remain a secret," Forrest said. "Whoever is unable to hold their tongue, will find me ready to hold it for them. Permanently." Forrest mounted his horse and was accompanied by Strange as they departed from Cheatham's command and rode towards Franklin.

Not long after all of the men gathered had dispersed, leaving Cleburne standing alone outside of his tent. Cleburne knew he needed to get his division moving, but took a moment to step back into the tent. He carefully moved the flap as he quietly stepped towards the sleeping Lee. He bent towards his ear and whispered that last nights attack was a complete success. He was not sure if Lee had heard him, but the sleeping general's lips contorted into a form that did appear to resemble a smile. Cleburne softly placed his blanket upon Lee's chest and kissed his forehead.

"Sleep well, he said, "for I fear we will need you once more this day."

Chapter XXII
November 30 Morning
Spring Hill

Hood was awakened by the intense severity of a pestering itch. Instinctively, he tried to attack it with his left hand, but the arm refused to obey his command. Instead, he had to reach across his face with his right hand so that his numb fingers could burrow beneath his thick beard and rake his chin. With a few hard scratches, his irritation was gone. Hood could now begin his day.

As he sat up against the headboard a strong ray of sunlight slid across his face. Shielding his eyes, he realized that he had slept much longer than intended. Perhaps it was all those toasts he had to swallow the night before, or was it the extra few swallows of laudanum that he consumed closer to bedtime? He kept trying to remind himself that it was not wise to mix the two, but he could not help the relaxed state it put him in. "It's the only way I can enjoy a decent nights rest," he grumbled.

Images of the previous night began filling his head and he could not tell if all them were real or imagined. He could remember feeling as light as a feather as he floated around the dinner table shaking hands with his staff. His euphoria had been so intense, he greatly desired its rapture. But as the night wore on, the more jubilant he became, the less aware he was of his surroundings. It was a far worse intoxication than any drunkenness that he had previously known.

'I do remember toasting my staff', he thought. 'They were well deserving my praise for a job well done.' He also remembered telling them that when they awoke, they would find that the Federal army would discover itself trapped and be forced to surrender without giving battle. Several glasses later, as well as several doses of his opiate, he could vaguely remember his senior commanders arriving. They were all deeply concerned about the enemy's position. Forrest mentioned something about sending a brigade north of the turnpike. He could not remember if Bate was in that conversation, or if he entered later, but Bate was upset about Cheatham changing orders.

Hood shook his head to try and clear his thoughts. That

was when he remembered the letter. Robert E. Lee was supposed to arrive today and take command of this army. If it were anyone else, Hood was not sure if he would give up his command with such alacrity. But with Robert E. Lee as the new commander in chief, Hood knew he could expect to feel a huge burden lifted from his giant shoulders. With that thought, he could not wait to see his old commander and friend.

If only his senior commanders knew about the letter, they would understand why he told Cheatham not to follow through with the attack. Lee did not want the enemy provoked into battle until he was able to arrive and take command. The only thing Lee advised was not to attack unless it were deemed practical. Hood gave that same order to Cheatham. When Cheatham later complained about the enemy's presence on his flank thwarting his offensive, Hood was not overly concerned. He gave orders to General Stephens to have his men move into position upon Cheatham's exposed flank. That was the last he remembered hearing from Cheatham. Well now that he was up and had slept through the night, he assumed that no attack was made. Cheatham must have adhered to his former orders that no attack was to be made unless deemed necessary.

Hood reached behind his head and searched under the pillow for the message from General Lee. There was nothing. Hood knew that it was necessary for the contents of that message to remain a secret. He twisted upon the bed and threw the pillow to the floor. There was no sign of a message ever having been in the bed with him. A tragic thought struck him like a head on locomotive. Was it all a dream? The more he thought about it, the more absurd the thought became. 'Damn that alcohol', he spat. How could Robert E. Lee leave the Eastern theater, currently being pressed by Grant, and travel unassisted to the West?

Hood angrily threw his blankets on the floor and in the process knocked over a small chair that was set beside the bed. Hearing the crash, two of his aids entered the room expecting to see Hood laid upon the floor. Instead they were greeted by the grotesque visage of the stump that was once his leg.

"Don't just stand there looking at me, help me get dressed," Hood said. "Where is my chief of staff this morning?"

The aids hesitantly began helping Hood dress. The younger one with out the mustache answered his question. "He is just outside with Governor Harris. Shall I tell them to come in?"

The other soldier helping dress Hood did not wait for the response he knew that his commander would deliver. "I will bring them right in," he said.

The younger aid fitted the peg to Hood's stump as he listened to the long stream of obscenities mumble from within the general's beard. He had quickly helped Hood to stand and finished dressing him as Governor Harris and Major Mason entered the room. He took this as his leave to escape the awkwardness he felt within the room, closing the door softly behind him.

"Why do I not hear any guns?" Hood roared.

Harris and Mason both exchanged looks that told the other that they did not want to be the one to answer. Although Mason, as the chief in staff, knew that in the end he was the one held accountable.

"General Hood, you do not hear any guns because the enemy is no longer here to receive our attack."

There was a long silence from Hood. Mason wanted to explain that Stewart and Forrest had managed to attack their rear guard as they fled. He was just waiting for the right moment to start to speak, when Hood, with one hand, picked up the chair that he had earlier knocked over and flung it across the room. The chair was hurled with such a venomous tenacity that it caused the other two men in the room to brace themselves for the eventual impact. The wait was not a long one. It shattered the small mirror that hung to the left of the door and sent several large pieces of glass scattering to the floor.

"Do you want to tell me how in the hell an entire army just disengages from a position it is trapped in? I had Schofield right where I wanted him. This army had the enemy where we wanted them. Are you telling me that these men have valiantly outmatched the enemy and successfully cut off his escape route for nothing? Where is General Cheatham? Answer me God damn it, where is Cheatham?"

"Roughly an hour and a half ago, his corps had departed after the Federal army," Harris said. "Sir, if I can have a moment to explain what has occurred here last night."

"With no disrespect to you governor, I must tell you no. There is no explanation that could be given to forgive what my senior commanders have allowed to happen. I had two full corps and part of a third on hand to keep the enemy in place so that this very morning we could gloriously drive them from the state of

Tennessee. Why was I not notified about this immediately?"

"Sir, we ourselves have just found out," Mason said. "I came here right away to confer with you. Apparently there was some attack orders last night by General Stewart and Forrest. They apparently struck too late. The Federal army was all but out of Spring Hill and on their way towards Franklin. Before dawn, General Cheatham had his corps on the road trailing Stewart and Forrest in their pursuit of the enemy."

"And you knew nothing of this?"

"I swear to you General, I knew nothing."

Hood closed his eyes and kept them shut. "General Cheatham should have attacked while he had the opportunity. I clearly told him that he was not to engage the enemy unless he deemed it necessary. I would think that the withdrawal of the enemy's force would constitute a necessary reason to engage the enemy. This damned army either does not want to strike the Federals, or they have forgotten how to strike. If they are not behind trenches, they do not want to fight. You know whom I blame this all upon... General Johnston, that's who. His miserable defensive strategy has destroyed the pride of this army. All he had done during his time as commander was teach these proud boys to be cowards. That must change. Rather, that will change... very, soon. That I can assure you."

It was a long time before Hood reopened his sunken eyes. When he did, his mood changed from animosity to melancholy. "Governor Harris, you see I can not listen to any excuse for what has happened here during my sleep. This was going to be the best move of my career as a soldier and it has all come to naught."

Harris stepped forward and placed a hand upon Hood's chest. "General, it was not all wasted. Stewart and Forrest captured two regiments as well as an entire brigade, not to mention a horde of fully supplied wagons and several batteries of the enemy's artillery. All was not a waste."

Hood's eyes stayed sunken to the floor. "Let us hope you are correct. However, I do not believe that the Federal army will stop short of Nashville. But if they do, I can still whip them with what I have. Where is General Stephen Lee and his corps this morning? I do remember that one of his divisions had arrived last night."

'Yes they did," Mason said. "Johnson was here, but he was instructed to trail Cheatham north. As for General Stephen

Lee, we recently received a message that he should be here by nine. He also reports that he was instructed to follow behind Johnson's Division with all speed."

Hood had to sit on the bed. "Am I still the commander in chief of this army?" he said. "Who is issuing these commands? No doubt it is General Cheatham trying desperately to make up for his letting the army slip from my trap. I must ride out at once. If this continues, Cheatham will have this army destroyed by the end of this day. Johnson's division should never have been allowed to continue north without the rest of Lee's corps present."

Hood was helped out of the room and brought outside to where his horse was already waiting. The governor mounted his own horse and waited in silence for Hood to be tied to his own. He wanted to break the silence by engaging in some form of conversation, but Hood was motionless. He just stared towards Franklin with such a hard look that even the wind seemed to veer off course so as to avoid his wrath. When Mason came over to tell Hood that his staff was ready to accompany them on their ride, Hood answered, but never averted his stern gaze from the north.

"There is going to be a great deal of hell to pay today," was all he said. Hood then kicked his horse hard in the side and took off like a reckless comet. And much like a comet that was out of control, Harris knew that it would eventually lead to an immense collision. One that would shatter General Cheatham much like the chair that had splintered the mirror.

*   *   *   *   *   *   *   *

As Hood was departing to take command of his army, one of his orderlies quickly returned to the General's bedroom to ensure that all of the commander's belongings were gathered before he left. The orderly made a quick survey and did not see that Hood had left anything behind. Remembering the manners his Kentucky mother had taught him, he took a moment to make the bed. He took hold of the blanket and shook it over the bed, before straitening it out so that it could be tuck under the mattress. He then took each pillow and before placing them back against the headboard, fluffed them back into shape. Feeling like he had accomplished a good deed this morning, the orderly had an extra bounce in his step as he went outside to mount and follow after his commander.

He never saw the crinkled letter that was wedged in be-tween the headboard and the mattress. It probably had fallen there at some point during Hood's sleep. And there it would remain, stuck between the headboard and the mattress, for a very long time.

*   *   *   *   *   *   *   *

The morning was unseasonably warm as Hood and his es-cort rode through Spring Hill and continued on the turnpike north to Franklin. Normally, Hood would have greatly enjoyed such a scenic ride. Just outside of Spring Hill the countryside seemed to be a sea of gentle hills covered with trees that had lost their summer colors. Hood did not care to take notice. There was too much weighing upon his mind at the moment.

All he could think about was how easy it would have been to defeat the Federal army at Spring Hill. The victory was all but handed to him, all that it needed was execution. And once again, his senior commanders failed him. This would never have happened with the Army of Northern Virginia. Lee would have gone to bed in confidence, knowing full well that if an opportunity presented itself for attack, commanders like Jackson would not have needed permission to take the initiative.

Since this army did not have men of that caliber, Hood's greatest accomplishment was stolen right out from underneath him. His chance to best his former classmate would have to wait for another time. Hood reflected on Schofield and could only imagine how smug he must be feeling at the moment. Instead of Spring Hill being a disastrous defeat for Schofield, the Federal general was no doubt claiming it as a brilliant tactical retreat.

As Hood rode through Thompson Station, he paused briefly to survey the scene of the battle that had occurred here while he had slept. There were several wagons still burning, their black smoke ascending into the air until a strong enough wind carried them away. There were also several hundred Yankee prisoners corralled on the side of the road. There should have been more.

As they cleared Thompson Station, the ground seemed to be covered with packs, rifles, canteens, and just about any item that a soldier would normally carry. This was no doubt the sign of the Federal rout. The passing Confederate army had emptied most of the packs. Several companies of soldiers were just now collecting the rifles, but Hood rode by them before they could offer any kind of salute.

His attention was focused on the faint sounds of skirmishing that could be heard several miles ahead. For Hood, it was the sound of hope. There was still a chance to catch the enemy. Hood again raced forward with his able hand secured tightly around the reins of his mount. There would not be another riding accident like the one that had occurred yesterday.

It was over an hour before Hood and his staff came upon the trailing regiments of his advancing army. The men seemed to be in high spirits and raised their hats to cheer him as he passed. Hood could only nod as he rode through the path they made for him in the middle of the pike. These were Johnson's men and he wanted to tell them to halt their march and await the rest of their corps, but they seemed so intent on joining the fight, he let them continue.

Hood continued to ride without break as the sun continued its rise into the sky. The day was warming fast, he had to unbutton his jacket and call for one of his officers to bring him some water. The itch returned under his beard forcing him to slow into a trot so that he could scratch through the sweaty hair that clung to his face. With his mount slowed, he could clearly hear Governor Harris conversing about the unseasonable weather of Tennessee with his staff. It was just another example of how his commanders could easily become distracted from the urgency that they were facing.

Hood quickly brought his horse to a halt and turned it toward his staff. "From here on out I do not want to hear anything except that which concerns the battle ahead. Is that understood? I do not care how hot or cold it may be, I do not care which wagon looks the most burnt, and I do not care who is hungry or thirsty. If I happen to hear any such conversation, you may expect the worst of consequences."

Hood turned his horse again and continued his ride. His staff, like scolded children, followed their commander with silent fear. The silence lasted for over an hour as Hood continued to ride past more and more of his marching army. It was near ten in the morning when he came upon General Brown and his staff. Brown saluted Hood as he approached. Hood did not return the salute.

Instead he stopped his procession and strained to listen for the sound of guns. There had not been many more occurrences of the skirmish fire that he had heard earlier. That worried him. Had Schofield already escaped over the Harpeth?

"General Hood, it is good to see you this morning," Brown said.

Hood disdainfully looked at his commander and visibly scowled. "Are you sure about that General Brown? Because I believe if you thought about that for a moment longer, you may wish to recant it. The last I heard from your division was that you were preparing to attack the enemy at Spring Hill. That was what I expected this morning. Instead, I must travel like an ignorant fool hoping to find my goddamned army. And you say it is good to see me this morning?"

Brown was speechless. Had no one thought to notify Hood of the army's situation? He wanted to tell his commander that they were following the orders issued by General Robert E. Lee, but he knew that was highly confidential information. There were many ears that were not given permission to know that Lee was in Tennessee. Brown tried to explain, "General, if you will but ride with me towards that cluster of trees, I can explain…"

"No thank you General. You need not explain that which I can fully understand. The generals in this army refuse to follow my command just as its soldiers adamantly refuse the offensive."

Brown was not going to let his own pride, as well as that of his men, become ridiculed by anyone, even if it was Hood. "General Hood, that claim is most unfair. I can not allow you to speak of these men that way."

Hood raised his eyebrows. "You can't, huh. Let me tell you what you can and can not do. If ever you get the opportunity to trap the Federal army again, you cannot let it escape. Do you understand that, General? You can attack it, you can prevent its escape, but you cannot allow it to simply retire at its own will from the battlefield. This is basic military principal. You nod your head like you understand what I am saying, but I still do not think you are capable of such simplicity. So let me make this much clearer for you. When a pursuing army comes up with the retreating enemy, as we did at Spring Hill, the retreating army must be immediately attacked. If you have a brigade in front as advance guard, order its commander to attack as soon as he comes up with him. If you have a regiment in advance and it comes up with the enemy, give the colonel orders to attack him. If there is but a company in advance, and it overtakes the entire Yankee army, order the captain to attack forthwith, and if anything blocks the road in front of you today, don't stop a minute, but turn out into the fields or woods and move on to the front. I do not want to hear anything about the enemy being on your flank. That excuse had been used once, and that card is no longer in your deck. Good day, General."

Hood left Brown on the side of the pike and continued towards Franklin. He did not feel an ounce of remorse for having scolded Brown in front of so many officers and soldiers. He only wished that he had done more of the same after the fall of Atlanta. Perhaps if he had, the tragedy at Spring Hill would never have occurred.

*　　*　　*　　*　　*　　*　　*　　*

It was almost eleven in the morning when a tremor of anxiety awoke General Schofield from his much-disturbed nap. Schofield quickly sat up in the bed gasping for every breath. His heart was pounding so hard that he could feel it threatening to rip through his chest. He tried to put his two sweaty hands upon his breast in an effort to calm the rapid beatings. His hands shook like thin branches in a hale storm. It would be several minutes before Schofield could successfully get out of bed.

Before leaving the bedroom, he tried to regain his composure by wrapping the sweat-dampened blanket around his body. He did not want any of his officers, nor the residents of this home to see the commander of the Federal army in this way.

A large part of him wished that he could stay wrapped up within the security of his blanket for the rest of the day, but he knew better. He had arrived in Franklin just before daylight. Initially he was astounded that his army had escaped the Confederate trap at Spring Hill. Then one maligned report after another began to pile upon him. The first was the most tragic. The pontoon bridges that he had requested several times from General Thomas had not arrived. That meant that the Harpeth River, which curled north of Franklin, could not be crossed without difficulty.

If he thought Spring Hill was a trap, Franklin was a coffin. At Spring Hill, a break in communication had prevented the

Confederates from sealing their well-constructed trap. But with the Harpeth River blocking his escape out of Franklin, Schofield doubted if anything could prevent the coffin lid from closing upon his army. Simply put, if there were no bridges in place soon, there would be no chance of his army surviving.

Now that he was awake, he began remembering the orders given before he retired for some sleep. The most imperative orders were those centered on getting his army across the Harpeth, both as quickly and safely as possible. All that he had at his disposal was a worn and narrow railroad bridge and the remnants of a wagon bridge that had once traversed the river, but had been destroyed by the war. Schofield had ordered his engineers to have both bridges repaired and suitable for his army's crossing as quickly as possible.

He knew that the work involved to construct and repair both bridges would take several hours. That was fine, it would at least put off one of his logistical problems so he could start to work on the numerous others. He then had ordered Wood's division over the river once the railroad bridge was ready for use. Wood would occupy the north bank of the Harpeth. Following Wood's division would be the artillery of the Twenty-third corps. Schofield's reason for this maneuver was based on his decision to continue with his retreat.

He would need an escape route available once the remainder of his army was on hand. He could have opted to use Wilson's cavalry to cover the army's withdrawal, but the recent exploits of the cavalry had left him too much doubt. He could not afford the cavalry to be brushed aside once again, and allow the enemy to interpose itself between his army and Nashville. If Forrest managed to gain the north banks of the Harpeth before he could get a division in place, it would be disastrous for his army. They would be completely trapped within the confines of Franklin subject to the will of very merciless Confederate artillery.

There were also other motives for sending a division of infantry across the river. Earlier this morning, he received two messages that did not bode well for his army. The first was a message from Stanley. Apparently an escaped prisoner had made it back to Union lines and reported that a division of Confederate cavalry had transferred to the west. If that was true, Forrest could possibly have over twelve thousand troopers at his disposal. If Wilson thought that he had trouble before, he would surely have

Confederates from sealing their well-constructed trap. But with the Harpeth River blocking his escape out of Franklin, Schofield doubted if anything could prevent the coffin lid from closing upon his army. Simply put, if there were no bridges in place soon, there would be no chance of his army surviving.

Now that he was awake, he began remembering the orders given before he retired for some sleep. The most imperative orders were those centered on getting his army across the Harpeth, both as quickly and safely as possible. All that he had at his disposal was a worn and narrow railroad bridge and the remnants of a wagon bridge that had once traversed the river, but had been destroyed by the war. Schofield had ordered his engineers to have both bridges repaired and suitable for his army's crossing as quickly as possible.

He knew that the work involved to construct and repair both bridges would take several hours. That was fine, it would at least put off one of his logistical problems so he could start to work on the numerous others. He then had ordered Wood's division over the river once the railroad bridge was ready for use. Wood would occupy the north bank of the Harpeth. Following Wood's division would be the artillery of the Twenty-third corps. Schofield's reason for this maneuver was based on his decision to continue with his retreat.

He would need an escape route available once the remainder of his army was on hand. He could have opted to use Wilson's cavalry to cover the army's withdrawal, but the recent exploits of the cavalry had left him too much doubt. He could not afford the cavalry to be brushed aside once again, and allow the enemy to interpose itself between his army and Nashville. If Forrest managed to gain the north banks of the Harpeth before he could get a division in place, it would be disastrous for his army. They would be completely trapped within the confines of Franklin subject to the will of very merciless Confederate artillery.

There were also other motives for sending a division of infantry across the river. Earlier this morning, he received two messages that did not bode well for his army. The first was a message from Stanley. Apparently an escaped prisoner had made it back to Union lines and reported that a division of Confederate cavalry had transferred to the west. If that was true, Forrest could possibly have over twelve thousand troopers at his disposal. If Wilson thought that he had trouble before, he would surely have

that a soldier would normally carry. This was no doubt the sign of the Federal rout. The passing Confederate army had emptied most of the packs. Several companies of soldiers were just now collecting the rifles, but Hood rode by them before they could offer any kind of salute.

His attention was focused on the faint sounds of skirmishing that could be heard several miles ahead. For Hood, it was the sound of hope. There was still a chance to catch the enemy. Hood again raced forward with his able hand secured tightly around the reins of his mount. There would not be another riding accident like the one that had occurred yesterday.

It was over an hour before Hood and his staff came upon the trailing regiments of his advancing army. The men seemed to be in high spirits and raised their hats to cheer him as he passed. Hood could only nod as he rode through the path they made for him in the middle of the pike. These were Johnson's men and he wanted to tell them to halt their march and await the rest of their corps, but they seemed so intent on joining the fight, he let them continue.

Hood continued to ride without break as the sun continued its rise into the sky. The day was warming fast, he had to unbutton his jacket and call for one of his officers to bring him some water. The itch returned under his beard forcing him to slow into a trot so that he could scratch through the sweaty hair that clung to his face. With his mount slowed, he could clearly hear Governor Harris conversing about the unseasonable weather of Tennessee with his staff. It was just another example of how his commanders could easily become distracted from the urgency that they were facing.

Hood quickly brought his horse to a halt and turned it toward his staff. "From here on out I do not want to hear anything except that which concerns the battle ahead. Is that understood? I do not care how hot or cold it may be, I do not care which wagon looks the most burnt, and I do not care who is hungry or thirsty. If I happen to hear any such conversation, you may expect the worst of consequences."

Hood turned his horse again and continued his ride. His staff, like scolded children, followed their commander with silent fear. The silence lasted for over an hour as Hood continued to ride past more and more of his marching army. It was near ten in the morning when he came upon General Brown and his staff. Brown saluted Hood as he approached. Hood did not return the salute.

Instead he stopped his procession and strained to listen for the sound of guns. There had not been many more occurrences of the skirmish fire that he had heard earlier. That worried him. Had Schofield already escaped over the Harpeth?

"General Hood, it is good to see you this morning," Brown said.

Hood disdainfully looked at his commander and visibly scowled. "Are you sure about that General Brown? Because I believe if you thought about that for a moment longer, you may wish to recant it. The last I heard from your division was that you were preparing to attack the enemy at Spring Hill. That was what I expected this morning. Instead, I must travel like an ignorant fool hoping to find my goddamned army. And you say it is good to see me this morning?"

Brown was speechless. Had no one thought to notify Hood of the army's situation? He wanted to tell his commander that they were following the orders issued by General Robert E. Lee, but he knew that was highly confidential information. There were many ears that were not given permission to know that Lee was in Tennessee. Brown tried to explain, "General, if you will but ride with me towards that cluster of trees, I can explain…"

"No thank you General. You need not explain that which I can fully understand. The generals in this army refuse to follow my command just as its soldiers adamantly refuse the offensive."

Brown was not going to let his own pride, as well as that of his men, become ridiculed by anyone, even if it was Hood. "General Hood, that claim is most unfair. I can not allow you to speak of these men that way."

Hood raised his eyebrows. "You can't, huh. Let me tell you what you can and can not do. If ever you get the opportunity to trap the Federal army again, you cannot let it escape. Do you understand that, General? You can attack it, you can prevent its escape, but you cannot allow it to simply retire at its own will from the battlefield. This is basic military principal. You nod your head like you understand what I am saying, but I still do not think you are capable of such simplicity. So let me make this much clearer for you. When a pursuing army comes up with the retreating enemy, as we did at Spring Hill, the retreating army must be immediately attacked. If you have a brigade in front as advance guard, order its commander to attack as soon as he comes up with him. If you have a regiment in advance and it comes up

with the enemy, give the colonel orders to attack him. If there is but a company in advance, and it overtakes the entire Yankee army, order the captain to attack forthwith, and if anything blocks the road in front of you today, don't stop a minute, but turn out into the fields or woods and move on to the front. I do not want to hear anything about the enemy being on your flank. That excuse had been used once, and that card is no longer in your deck. Good day, General."

Hood left Brown on the side of the pike and continued towards Franklin. He did not feel an ounce of remorse for having scolded Brown in front of so many officers and soldiers. He only wished that he had done more of the same after the fall of Atlanta. Perhaps if he had, the tragedy at Spring Hill would never have occurred.

*　　*　　*　　*　　*　　*　　*　　*

It was almost eleven in the morning when a tremor of anxiety awoke General Schofield from his much-disturbed nap. Schofield quickly sat up in the bed gasping for every breath. His heart was pounding so hard that he could feel it threatening to rip through his chest. He tried to put his two sweaty hands upon his breast in an effort to calm the rapid beatings. His hands shook like thin branches in a hale storm. It would be several minutes before Schofield could successfully get out of bed.

Before leaving the bedroom, he tried to regain his composure by wrapping the sweat-dampened blanket around his body. He did not want any of his officers, nor the residents of this home, to see the commander of the Federal army in this way.

A large part of him wished that he could stay wrapped up within the security of his blanket for the rest of the day, but he knew better. He had arrived in Franklin just before daylight. Initially he was astounded that his army had escaped the Confederate trap at Spring Hill. Then one maligned report after another began to pile upon him. The first was the most tragic. The pontoon bridges that he had requested several times from General Thomas had not arrived. That meant that the Harpeth River, which curled north of Franklin, could not be crossed without difficulty.

If he thought Spring Hill was a trap, Franklin was a coffin. At Spring Hill, a break in communication had prevented the more than he could handle now.

Fortunately, Fort Granger loomed over the northern side of the Harpeth, overlooking Franklin like a warden. If Forrest was headed to cut him off, Schofield wanted to be sure that he had his army well in defense of the fort before Forrest could make any sort of offensive maneuver. The solid walls of the bastion would easily offset the superior numbers of Forrest's command.

The second message came directly from an officer from General Wagner's staff. It had been Wagner's division that served as the rear guard for the entire Federal army as it retreated towards Franklin. Very early in the morning, Wagner had been attacked while trying to protect the long line of wagons that carried the supplies for Schofield's army.

Schofield did not know the full extent of this disaster, but he did know that two brigades had been routed, leaving the third to fend for themselves. He tried to wait in Franklin for further news, but his body was shutting itself down due to exhaustion. His last orders before departing to his headquarters for some rest called for General Cox to reinforce the preexisting trenches around Franklin. Cox would command the Twenty-third corps as it protected the town until the bridges could be completed. Then, under the cover of darkness, Cox would lead the remainder of the army over the Harpeth to the safety beyond.

Now that he had as much rest as he could afford, it was time to see how his plans had materialized throughout the morning.

From downstairs, Schofield could hear the dependable voice of Stanley greeting the residents of this home. The smells of fresh brewed coffee told him that Dr. Daniel Cliffe and his wife were no doubt offering Stanley some brew. Some food, along with a conference with Stanley was the very elixir that Schofield needed to motivate him to leave the bed. He quickly dressed himself and checked his face in the mirror.

"Just another day. Just make it through one more day and you will have this army safely across that river," he told himself. With a quick tussle of the thinning hair that populated the middle of his head, Schofield left his room to join General Stanley.

Stanley was seated at the table breaking off a piece of cornbread and dunking it in his coffee when Schofield entered the room. "Hope you managed to get some sleep?" he said.

Schofield smiled and gratefully accepted a piece of cornbread from Mrs. Cliffe. "This is most delicious," he said after he consumed the meal in two bites. Mrs. Cliffe blushed as she went to get the General another piece. Her husband poured Schofield a cup of coffee and handed it to him. Schofield thanked him and then kindly asked that he and Stanley be left alone to discuss some urgent matters. The doctor complied by intercepting his wife as she reentered the room with more bread. "Come along dear," he said, as he caught her by the arm and turned her back around.

"Dr. Cliffe, once again I thank you for allowing the Federal army to use your home as its temporary headquarters," Schofield said, "but, I could not let your wife escape with that wonderful smelling bread. Please let me remove that burden from her before you go." Schofield winked at Mrs. Cliffe who bashfully handed the basket of corn bread to the general before departing with her husband.

When Schofield turned around, all of his exuberance was gone. He placed the basket on the table and collapsed into the chair opposite Stanley. "We are sure in another mess today," he said.

Stanley sipped his coffee and carefully placed it back down. He did not want to spill any of it upon the Cliffe's table. "Well, that may be so, but I finally have all of the reports from the attack at Thompson Station. It is not as bad as I first feared."

"Not that bad? We lost an entire brigade."

Stanley reached for another biscuit of corn bread. "Well... yes we did. It was Colonel Opdycke's. A few companies managed to make it out, but for the most part, that brigade is lost to us."

"And you can sit there, eating your corn bread and tell me that is not such bad news?"

Stanley handed Schofield a piece of bread. "John, you need to calm down a bit. Here, take this and eat it. Nourishment does wonders." Schofield took the bread but could not bring himself to eat it. He placed it back in the basket. Stanley took it back out and wrapped it up for later. "John, we lost a brigade, and a few Kentucky regiments..."

"And while you are so content about that, please let us not forget the wagon train and our artillery?"

"John, you are looking at this very pessimistically."

"Are you telling me there is an upside to all this?"

"In a manner of speaking, yes I am. Yesterday, we both

thought that we were trapped in Spring Hill, subject to the mercy of John Hood and his army. When you first arrived at Spring Hill, did you ever think that we would make it out without a fight? Well neither did I, but we did. But as of right now, the remainder of our army and its supplies are within a few miles of this town. By noon, we should have the whole army consolidated again. That means that our whole army has escaped the trap set by the enemy. And all it cost us was the sacrifice of one single brigade and some of our wagon train. If I had told you yesterday that we could make it out of Spring Hill, but we would loose a brigade, how would you have replied?"

Schofield was slow to answer. "I would have said you were crazy."

"Exactly, but that is what has happened. And as for the artillery and the wagon train, well, last night, you told me to destroy it all. I convinced you otherwise, and because of that we still have over five hundred wagons and all of the artillery from the Twenty-third corps. We lost some of the guns from the Fourth, but all in all, our evacuation was a complete success. The enemy is still pressing our rear, they are close in pursuit, but I am confident that the remainder of Wagner's division will reach our lines safely. They have been told to hold the pair of high hills south of this town."

Schofield reached for a piece of bread and dunked it in his lukewarm coffee. "I had not thought of it in that way," he said. "But we still have other problems."

Stanley knew exactly to what Schofield was referring. "The Confederate division sent west from General Hampton? That could be a problem."

"Could be? The last time the Confederate's transferred troops from the east, it resulted in one of their greatest victories of this war. I do not want that history to repeat itself while I am in command. And we both know that General Wilson is completely unqualified for handling such a monstrous task. I consider his performance thus far as a huge failure."

Stanley agreed. "His cavalry has finally reported back. They seem to have misconstrued the rebel intent yesterday. They are now to the east impeding any flanking advance that Forrest may attempt."

"That is most reassuring," Schofield sarcastically muttered as he swallowed a piece of bread. "Is General Wood's division in place?"

"General Wood has secured Fort Granger and has positioned the artillery from the Twenty-third corps with him. His position commands the southern approach to Franklin."

"I knew that it would," Schofield replied. I saw that this morning while conferring with General Cox. From those heights, our artillery should deter Hood from advancing against our position. All we need is one more day, and this army will be free of the rebel threat. To be honest, I am more concerned with their cavalry. I do not believe they will attack us here. They keep trying to flank us... I think Hood will hold the attack until his flanking maneuver finally succeeds. As long as we can keep Forrest from getting the jump on us, the Confederate army will not be a concern."

"Have you sent any word to General Thomas?" Stanley asked. "Is he sending us any support?"

Stanley could tell that he had just struck a sore spot with Schofield. "You know, it is no wonder that Thomas thought so highly of Wilson, the two seem to operate in the same manner. I can't tell what Thomas wants me to do. Every telegram I receive has orders that are not in accordance with the previous ones. The only thing I have asked for during this crucial time, he has been unable to deliver. Because there are no pontoon bridges, our army is forced to wait until we can build our own. In the meantime, there is not much that we can do expect pray that Forrest does not gain our rear.

As for Thomas' other promise, the troops of A. J. Smith, well I was greeted this morning with additional bad news from our commander sitting safely in Nashville. Apparently Smith is with him in Nashville, but his troops are still in the boats on the water. We cannot expect their arrival today. Impossible was the adjective he used. Thomas has instructed me to try and protect our wagon train and get in position around Franklin. Yet, this latest order is in direct conflict with the one I received the night before, when he told me to cross the Harpeth and get to Nashville."

"What have you informed him?"

"I told him that he had better find a way to get Smith's troops to Franklin as fast as possible, or this army would no longer be here to welcome them. I also sent word about Hampton's division. If that cavalry is here in Tennessee, perhaps General Grant can use that to his advantage in Virginia."

"Excellent thinking John."

"Well, it seems that all I have been doing lately is thinking."

"So what is your decision, are we to hold here or fall back?"

"Both. I will comply with Thomas' wishes and hold Franklin, but I will do that for only one more day. I cannot risk this army being cut off again. I am confident that Hood will not attack us here. General Cox has the army digging in the old entrenchments. I have given the orders to defend Franklin at least until we can get the wagons over the Harpeth. Then tonight, under the cover of darkness, and with Wood's division securing our rear, the rest of this army will cross the river. This time, our retirement from the battlefield will not be as chaotic as the one we just completed. We must not lose even a single regiment this time."

"John, I think that the decisions you have made this day far excel any you have made in the past, and I do not mean that in a derogatory way. If I may offer one suggestion?"

"As you will."

"Inform Thomas of this. He may want us to hold Franklin for reasons unknown to us. But those reasons may very well be conducive to the consolidation of our two armies."

"Hold Franklin? General you know as much as I do, that is a task not possible. Hood has many other fords that he can use to gain the northern banks of the Harpeth. The longer we delay here, the more time he has to access them. But you are right, Thomas needs to be informed. I will have one last telegram sent with one clear question. I can only hope it is received back with one clear response. I only want to know if Thomas desires me to hold on to Franklin until compelled to fall back? For the fate of this army, I hope there is no delay in his response."

*   *   *   *   *   *   *   *

General Jacob Cox sat on the back porch of the Carter house carefully examining a battle map that had recently been drawn up for him. General Schofield had given him the responsibility of entrenching the Federal army within Franklin and he wanted to make sure that every position of troops upon the map

Battle at Franklin

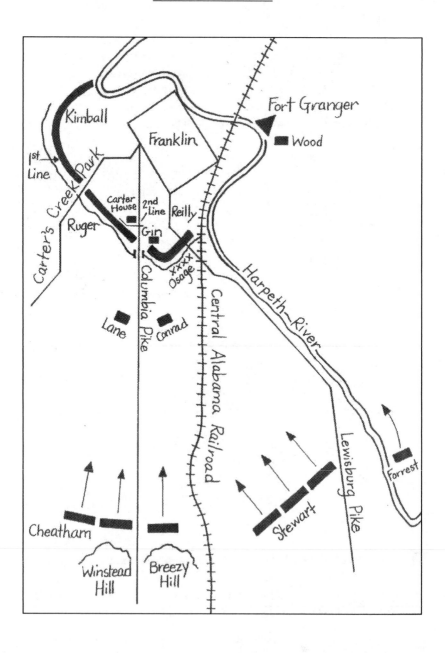

had been placed exactly as he had instructed. Sitting on the steps in front of him were the three brigadier generals of the third division of the United States Twenty-third army corps. Cox glanced at each of his commanders as he placed a finger upon the rectangles that denoted the presence of their troops on his map.

"Gentleman, how is the digging going?" he asked.

Colonel Stiles removed his cap to wipe the sweat from his brow. "It is too damned hot for November, General," he said. "But my men are making the best of it. They have not only dug trenches, but they have found some Osage orange bushes and have cut them down and placed them along their front. If Hood wants to send his men against us, those poor rebels will be caught in some very thick and thorny bramble. It would be like squirrel hunting for our boys behind the line."

Cox made a note to pencil the abatis on his map. As he did, he could remember his father telling him how the Osage Indians used the strong wood to make some very impressive bows. That was fine for natives, but on this day, it was the wood's thorny surface that he was most thankful for. The thought of attacking regiments having to cut through such thick entanglements while being fired upon was one of the few uplifting thoughts that he had had over the past few days.

His men had to feel the same. They had been working at fortifying their defenses since their arrival at Franklin early this morning. To Cox, that seemed like days ago. The lack of sleep that this army was maneuvering on was bound to catch up with them at some time. He still could not believe that his troops were not simply dropping as they fortified their defenses. Many of them had not slept in over twenty-four hours.

Cox stepped back from the stairs as Fountain B. Carter came around the house. The sixty-seven year-old owner of the home was visibly agitated at the appropriation of his property for Federal use. Cox could not blame the man. If it were he who were awakened first thing in the morning and told that his home was to serve as a temporary headquarters for the opposing army, he too would be greatly upset.

Carter was carrying a small box of assorted supplies down into his cellar. Several people were gathered down there already, including one of Carter's sons, a paroled Confederate lieutenant general. Carter had two other sons currently serving the Confederacy, one of which was marching in Hood's army. The boy's name was Theoderick Carter, and Cox had learned that he served as a captain in General Cheatham's corps.

Cox leaned over the staircase and could see Carter placing the box upon the dining room table. Carter made as if he were coming back up the stairs, but when he saw Cox looking down, he simply stopped and closed the door. Cox stared at the shut door for a few seconds, then turned back to his commanders.

"That is one grumpy old man," Colonel Casement said.

"Can you blame him?" General Reilly said. "I mean our troops have swarmed his property like locusts."

"That is his problem for siding with the enemy," Cox said. "We can not feel sorry for these people. And it would be wise if you did not let General Sherman ever hear you mutter as much."

"Do you think Hood will attack us today?" Casement asked.

Cox stepped down the stairs and into the grass. Across from him stood a smokehouse and a small farm office. Stretched around the buildings was the entrenching Federal army. Past them was where Hood would come if he meant to attack. Cox looked up into the sky and still could not believe how unseasonably hot this day was becoming. His commanders wanted to know if he thought that Hood would attack today. Hell, after yesterday, Cox was no longer sure what to think.

Hood should have hit them at Spring Hill, but he had not. The only accomplishment of the rebels well-laid trap was the rout of the rear guard and the loss of several supply wagons. It was General Wagner's brigades that had been routed, one of which was lost to them. But at least the other two had enough sense to overturn several wagons to impede the pursuit of the enemy. From the reports he had read, the Confederate infantry had become very disorganized after their initial assault. The congestion of Federal prisoners and overturned wagons was enough to break apart their formations and delay their pursuit just enough for Wagner to reform his lines.

Since then, the rebels have been nipping at the heals of Wagner's two remaining brigades, but never getting close enough to offer a serious threat. That would cost them. Wagner's troops were right now placed upon the two hills south of Franklin. They had been told to remain there and deny Hood the access of the valley that led into Franklin.

Cox looked back at his map as he reflected upon the question posed by Casement. Would Hood attack here today? The Harpeth River bent around Franklin like a giant horseshoe. Excluding the division of General Wood, the combined forces of the Twenty-third and the Fourth army corps connected both wings of the horseshoe as their defensive line ran a little over a mile and a half east to west just south of Franklin. Cox would have liked to have had his own artillery in place along his well-formed lines, but Schofield had sent the batteries along with Wood's division to Fort Granger. Schofield told Cox that he could have the artillery from the Fourth corps when it arrived, but what Cox found when it actually arrived, was that several guns were lost in the early morning rout at Thompson Station. Even so, with the Twenty-third corps artillery across the river and emplaced at Fort Granger, the Union guns should find it very easy to command the field against any Confederate advance along the Lewisburg or Franklin Pike.

The brigades of Stiles, Casement and Reilly made up the left flank of his army. These men were positioned to deny Hood's march along the Lewisburg Pike. Stiles brigade rested upon the railroad cut that ran parallel to the river. To his front were well dug trenches and parapets, not to mention the Osage bushes that had been cut down and used as a tangling abatis. The line continued west with Casement's brigades and then Reilly's. Due to the Carter cotton gin's location along this front, a salient was constructed for defensive purposes.

Cox thought of the 6th Ohio battery that was placed at the Cotton Gin. After conferring with Schofield, it was decided wiser to limber the battery and place it alongside battery G on the Lewisburg Pike. Schofield was convinced that Hood was not going to attack here today, but rather would try to flank his army again, and those guns needed to be ready to roll.

Cox wished that he too could be so easily convinced. It was bad enough that the Fourth corps had lost several guns during the attack in early this morning, but the fact that he had to strip the center to keep the guns mobile along the flank made matters worse. Not to mention the rumor stirring that a division of cavalry from Virginia had arrived to augment Forrest's force.

Cox could understand why Schofield would want the guns on his flanks and in the rear instead of massed at the center. If Forrest swept around them, the batteries needed to be limbered and moving with great haste. 'I'd still give anything to have just a few placed at the cotton gin,' he thought. However, the loss of

Battery M, as well as several guns from Bridges Illinois battery put harsh limits on where the Federal cannons needed to be placed. One such location that was deemed necessary for battery support was upon the right flank of Reilly's brigade. It was here that a battery of guns was placed, thus bridging the vacant space between the infantry and the Franklin Pike.

Cox knew the guns were needed there because it was the only point of his defense that had a break in the long line of parapets and trenches that ran from one end of the field to the other. It was here, along the Franklin pike, where a gap had to be left open to allow for the passage of wagons and troops into Franklin.

A second line of trenches was constructed seventy yards in the rear as a precautionary measure in the event of a rebel breakthrough. This second line ran across the Carter's garden and continued west until it ran back into the main line as it angled northwest. The most inspiring thing about this second line was that it was constructed without any orders to do so. That made him proud, it was a clear symbol of the transformation of soldiers into veterans.

The main line of earthworks continued past the gap caused by the Franklin Pike and was defended by Twenty-third corps' second division. Commanded by General Ruger, his corps worked as diligently as the third division in using their surrounding resources to their advantage. A grove of locust trees that ran along the southern slope of the hill to their front had been cut down and used in the implementation of earthworks. What was left of the wood was thrown in with the severed stumps to create an abatis to the front of their line.

Cox studied this on his map and hoped to God that Schofield was correct in his assessment concerning Hood's objective for this day. With the Osage abatis on his left and the stumps of the locust trees on his right, the only vulnerable section was a point in between these two. That just happened to be the very spot where there was a looming gap in the line of earthworks.

Cox had appropriated the home of the Carters for his headquarters because it sat upon a hill that offered him a strong command of the field. He now realized its location would also be the key to the battle. 'If there was a battle,' he had to remind himself.

Perhaps he should order Wagner's brigades to fall in at the

Carter House and use them as reserves? He knew that he would have to ask Schofield's permission for such a move, for Wagner was currently ordered to remain at those two hills south of town with intent to dissuade Hood from any kind of advance.

Cox glanced back to his map and studied his defensive line as it continued west past the Carter Creek Pike until it once again touched the Harpeth River on the other side. Kimball's first division of the Fourth army corps defended the extreme right flank and was currently reported to be skirmishing with the rebel cavalry.

Cox took one last look at his map and then rolled it up. His line had only one fault and that was along the line of the Franklin to Columbia Pike. Luckily, his men had seen that for themselves and had constructed a second line to prevent any possible Confederate breakthrough. He only wished that he had all of the artillery at his disposal, or at least more guns massed at the center.

The arrival of Wagner's division and his two brigades should help to ease his concerns. He needed to leave the Carter home and find Schofield so that he could request that Wagner's men be placed at the Carter house as a reserve force. This way, if Hood did attack and break through, Cox could quickly counterattack with two brigades.

With Wagner in reserve, he had a well-entrenched army of over fifteen thousand Union soldiers compacted in a solid defensive line. With the Harpeth bending from one end of his line to the other, Hood could not immediately attack his men except by coming head on, and General Schofield seemed to be convinced that this would not happen. At least not today.

It was believed that Hood would send a smaller force to come up and attempt to hold the Federal army in place, while a larger contingent outflanked the Union position as they had done at Columbia. This time however, Schofield had already given notice to his senior commander that his army was not to wait and see when and where Hood would ford the Harpeth. Tonight under the cover of darkness, it would be Schofield stealing the imitative by having his army retire from the battlefield and marching to Brentwood. There they could consolidate with the forces being gathered by General Thomas at Nashville.

Cox thought about the gap one last time before answering his brigadier generals. "No, I do not think that Hood will attack us here. At least not today. If he did, the guns at Fort Granger would shred his advance. The soldiers that did manage to make it near our lines would be target practice in this clear field of fire. We are too well dug in, even for an army twice our size, to consider attacking."

The three commanders shared a sigh of relief. "I am still going to issue whiskey to the men," Cox said.

"Just in case?" Stiles asked.

"Just in case," Cox confirmed. Cox placed the rolled up map under his arm. "Well men, I need to meet with General Schofield so that I can personally update him as to the position of this army. I trust that I can leave you men alone, I do not expect there to be much danger this day." Cox looked towards the south in the direction of his last brigades to enter Franklin. "General Reilly, please send word to Wagner that his men are to fall back from Winsted Hill and join the main line of defense here closer to Franklin."

Cox left them and waded through the cluster of command tents that littered the grounds around the Carter House. He made his way past the servant cottages that stood behind the house and walked in the direction of the Carter Creek Pike. He could have opted to ride into Franklin on his horse, but he wanted the extra time to help clear the tangled ball of yarn that was contorted in his head.

He opened several buttons on his jacket and felt the sweat sticking to the shirt underneath. This was truly one hot November day. It was hard to believe that it was not so long ago that this area was visited with snowfall. That thought brought his memories to Columbia. That town had been on his mind ever since he had started fortifying the earthworks around Franklin. Had his men not arrived at Columbia when they did, the shoe right now may very well have been on the other foot.

Forrest had routed the Union cavalry and was only minutes from driving them from Columbia. It was at that critical moment when Cox deployed his infantry and repulsed the unsuspecting rebel cavalry. Had Cox arrived an hour later, he knew that it would have been his objective to dislodge Forrest from Columbia before Hood could reinforce him.

Cox looked over his shoulder as his men continued to strengthen their fortifications. The thought of attacking these earthworks was enough to make the most hardened general nauseous. He had no doubt in his mind, that had he not arrived at Columbia first, he would have had to do exactly that.

"Life is a game decided in seconds," he said to himself.

As he neared the Carter Creek Pike he could see a small congregation of officers gathered. There did not appear to be anything impeding their travel along the pike. The last wagons to cross the Harpeth were wheeling smoothly through the town. When Cox realized that General Schofield was one of the men mounted, he hurried his pace. From the direction their horses were facing, it was clear that the general meant to cross the Harpeth behind them. As he drew nearer, he could see that General Stanley was also on hand, conversing with several of the officers. Cox quickly re-buttoned his jacket and called out to get their attention.

"General Schofield, General Stanley," he called.

"Ah, here comes General Cox," Schofield said to Stanley. "General Cox, how are our defenses, almost completed I presume."

"Well, these are the last of the wagons that escaped the early hour attack at Thompson Station. Are you leaving us already?"

"Unfortunately I am. I have a new headquarters across the Harpeth and I was finalizing a few issues before departing. But do not worry, I can guarantee that Hood will not attack us here. Not today, anyway. How are the men? By the looks of things that I have seen already, it appears that all has been carried out as I instructed early this morning. Excellent work sir."

Cox accepted the compliment with stoicism. "As you already know, General Wood is across the Harpeth, and artillery from the Twenty-third is unlimbering at Fort Granger. As for the rest of the army, I have brought you this map, which indicates the position of every regiment in Franklin. General Wagner's two brigades are the only infantry not yet to reach the main line. But, I have given orders to withdraw them from Winstead Hill."

Schofield looked towards Stanley with a countenance of consternation. Before he could speak his troubled mind, an officer came riding from Franklin.

"General Schofield," he said. "Excellent news, the pontoon boats have arrived. We can now more efficiently cross the Harpeth."

The sound of skirmishing gunfire was carried north by a soft wind. It came from Winstead Hill. "Damn," Schofield spat. There were many officers gathered, but he looked directly at Stanley when he spoke. "We can't use those boats. I almost regret to say this, but they will have to be turned around."

Stanley understood. "It is not your fault, you must obey General Thomas."

"I know that, but we are here on the battlefield, not he. The right thing to do is pull Wagner back within our lines and get these men across the Harpeth with God's speed."

"I know and I agree," Stanley said. "However, we have both read Thomas' last telegram. He wants Hood held at Franklin for as long as possible."

Cox meant no disrespect, but he had to cut into this two-person conversation. There was obviously much information that he was not privy too. "How long does General Thomas expect us to hold the town for?" he asked.

Schofield looked down from his horse. "I am not sure."

"What do you mean you are not sure?" Cox asked.

"Apparently neither General A.J. Smith's division, nor the cavalry, is ready for combat."

"General, these men cannot be expected to hold this town after tonight. I mean the whole Confederate army is marching towards us..."

"General Cox, you can be assured that I do not plan for this army to be here in the morning, regardless of what Thomas may desire. I have informed Thomas that we will hold here for as long as possible. I can assure you that we have reached that point and are now beyond it. We are pulling out. However, the rebel army is too close to our position to risk a withdrawal during daylight. For that reason, I cannot afford to use the pontoon boats at this time. And I cannot let them sit around until tonight. If I do that, Hood will know that we plan to evacuate, and there is no telling what he could rush into doing. Hood must be convinced that we mean to stay and fight. If he believes that, he will either spend tomorrow deploying his men to attack, or he will try yet another flanking maneuver. I believe he will choose the latter. And that suites me just fine, because I assure you that we will no longer be here to be flanked come the morning.

The engineers tell me that the bridges are practically re-paired. That being so, the pontoons must go back. Officer, please ride back to the river and ensure that they are sent away. And also, find someone, anyone who has the latest message from General Wilson. His command of this cavalry is as useful as a damn comb upon a bald man's head."

"What if Hood spots the boats as they depart"? Stanley asked. "Right now, Hood thinks that he has our army trapped against the Harpeth. If he were to know that the pontoons were here, then he would understand that we are not in such a desperate situation."

Schofield was shaking his head. "I did not know that November could get this warm. General Cox, have Wagner return his brigades to the hills south of Franklin. He is to delay Hood for as long as possible. Hood is so bull headed, he will concentrate all his attention upon Wagner, and in the meantime we can get the boats clear out of the area".

"I agree," Stanley said. "Our attempt to hold Winstead and Breezy Hill should convince Hood that we mean to stay and fight."

"Let's hope so," Schofield said.

Chapter XXIII
November 30, Afternoon
Franklin, Tennessee

Union Brigadier General George D. Wagner was the acting commander of the second division of the United States Fourth army corps. It was a position he took very seriously and its title he carried with a great deal of pride. Wagner had always had high aspirations within the military hierarchy, hoping to one day command his own corps. With the continuance of this war, he knew that each passing day brought him one step closer to actualizing his dreams. That was until the disaster that had occurred to his command in the hours before dawn.

It was his division that was responsible for the rout at Thompson Station... and that mortified him. Wagner knew all to well how men like Grant and Halleck viewed a commander whose men routed. No matter the circumstances surrounding the defeat, the commanding general was never seen in the same light again.

Wagner watched from Winstead Hill as the last of his men descended into the valley and began the march towards Franklin. The rebel cavalry had been skirmishing with them ever since the predawn battle, but Wagner was able to keep them back, an accomplishment that would count for little when Washington reviewed all of the reports. All they will read, with their beady know it all eyes, would be the loss of Opdycke's brigade.

Wagner bent over and reached for a heavy stone. He tossed it a few times in his hand before hurling it over the hill towards the pursuing Confederate cavalry. It fell way too short. From behind, he could hear the approach of Colonel's Conrad and Lane.

"General Wagner, the men are now well on the way towards the main line of earthworks at Franklin," Lane said.

Wagner turned towards them with an icy glare in his eyes. Part of him wanted to lash out at his commanders for not having the ability to stop the rout before it began. But there was another part of him that was more agitated with General Schofield and General Stanley. His men should not have had the responsibility of performing the rear guard duty for this army when it evacuated from Spring Hill. It was not fair to them. His division was the first to arrive at Spring Hill and had fought valiantly to hold the town open just so Schofield could still have an escape route open for the rest of the army. Yet, the fact that it was his division that held out for the better part of the day against two corps of Hood's army did not seem to be enough to earn them the honors of being the first units to march towards Franklin.

'It should be my boys already at this town,' he fumed. Instead, it was Schofield's own corps, the Twenty-third that was evacuated first. It was a despicable indecency that was not taken well by any of the men in his command. General Opdycke especially complained bitterly, but his words were lost on ears that were impotent at resolving the issue. The order was given, and thus it was General Wagner's very tired and demoralized division that had to endure the nervous wait, while every other regiment cleared out of Spring Hill. Crouched low in the dark night, they had to watch the backs of clean uniforms march along a path that was made possible by the blood of their own men.

Wagner looked back over the hill towards the rebel flags waving with the wind. "We should not be the ones here right now," he said.

His colonels agreed. "Sir, our men have heard that other divisions have already had breakfast and are now napping in this warm sun," Conrad added. "If I may say so sir, that is most unfair to these here boys."

Wagner contained his rage with a gritted growl. "This division will be chastised for its inabilities witnessed this morning. I have lost a very capable commander in General Opdycke and my men are exhausted beyond human comprehension. And now you tell me that the rest of this army, the Twenty-third corps especially I presume, are at breakfast. It is almost noon and we have not stopped fighting with the enemy for over twenty-four hours. Is General Stanley going to ever find his backbone and tell Schofield that enough is enough? Put some damned brigades from the Twenty-third out here. Are we being punished for this morning's rout? I can't understand an ounce of this."

"Not only that, but the brigade that was in support upon Breezy Hill has deserted their position without even notifying us," Lane said.

Wagner quickly placed his field glasses to his face to confirm that the brigade had not returned. "Have you sent the message to Stanley informing him of our need to withdraw?" he asked. With his flanking support gone, he had no choice but to pull his men from Winstead Hill.

"I have, and we have also received orders from Cox to pull within his lines, so we are not doing anything that the high command is not aware of," Lane said.

The three commanders mounted their horses and cantered behind the long columns of their brigades as they vacated Winstead Hill. With the enemy behind them, the road to Franklin was a slow but welcome path. For a long time, they rode in silence, quietly absorbing the heavy footfall of their passing army. With its methodical rhythm, the sound was quite soothing.

"General Wagner," Conrad said, "Perhaps now is the time that we can express our apologies for the actions of our brigades this morning. The men were just too tired."

"And their wills were broken," Lane added. "I mean, they do not understand why they have to take up the rear when it was they who had performed all of the previous day's fighting."

Wagner halted his horse. "Gentleman, that is a matter for men like us to worry about and not them. They're job as infantry is to simply obey whatever order they are given. There can be no excuses, and I will not accept one from either of you."

"I understand sir, but they were able to reorganize with amazing speed. They deployed in line, burned and turned over several wagons to prevent pursuit and were able to retire the rest of the way like the division they once were. I don't know of a single other division that has ever recovered from a rout in such time before," Lane said.

"Retire like the division they once were, you say? If I remember correctly Colonel Lane, we left Spring Hill with three brigades and we now have two. These men were tired and upset, and because of that they left General Opdycke's brigade to fend for themselves. Overturning those wagons was an act of cowardice. It did nothing but ensure that they did not have to march back to save Opdycke. Thanks to such cowardice, all that remains of that brigade is the few companies that managed to escape the same fate as their commander. All of those men are worth more to me than the thousands left in your command."

Lane and Conrad were speechless. Was Wagner mad? His division was strung out in long tired columns when it was hit simultaneously in the rear and flank by the combined might of the

Confederate cavalry and an entire corps of their infantry. By all right, their entire division should have been annihilated. Their presence here was nothing short of a miracle.

"General Wagner, I do not care what it may cost me, but I insist that you not speak such ill of my men."

Wagner turned in his saddle like a voluble wagon wheel. "What it may cost you? Is that what you have the gall to offer me. What about what this will cost me. I will probably be sent to some far away outpost to fend off Indians. I must stand the heat for this, not you. Not either of you. I put my reputation on the line every day that I am in command. This division must learn to reflect that. Do I make myself clear?"

"Perfectly clear sir," Lane said. Like looking into a twisted and very contorted mirror, Conrad and Lane now both clearly understood the cause of Wagner's malcontent. The man was more concerned about his own military acumen than the lives of his own men. His own volition was screening him from how well his division had saved not only themselves, but the entire army from complete destruction.

"General Wagner, if anyone is to be blamed for this morning, it is Colonel Lane and myself, not those brave soldiers," Conrad said. "But I promise you this, these men will never rout again. If given the chance, they will prove themselves and earn back your trust. I stake my name to that."

The contentious conversation was forced to subside due to the arrival of an approaching rider. It was one of Cox's staff officers from Franklin.

"I have a feeling that we shall soon see how well your name holds with these men ... Colonel Conrad," Wagner said.

"General Wagner," the officer said, "General Cox wishes to report that he has new orders and your division is to turn around and hold those hills until nightfall."

Wagner looked incredulously at his two commanders. "Are you sure you are reporting this order accurately?" he asked the officer. "As you can see, my division is already well on its way to Franklin. Does General Cox expect me to simply turn them back around and retake the hill we have just abandoned?"

The officer swallowed hard against the dryness in his throat. He was not prepared to answer any of Wagner's questions. It was obvious that he just expected Cox's command to be obeyed. "Sir, the order comes from General Stanley himself, General Cox is only obeying the command. He wants me to inform you that the entire army plans to cross the Harpeth at some time this night. To help with this, General Schofield wants the enemy to think that we intend to stay. He does not think that Hood intends to fight, but he does want the enemy to have to waste time deploying into battle line, forcing Hood to earn every inch of ground from here to Franklin."

Wagner kept gripping his fist as he turned repeatedly in his saddle to view the hills retreating behind him, and his men advancing before him. "This is madness. My men should not be ordered around like some pack of ignorant dogs. We have not eaten, nor have we slept. Why must we be the ones that are repeatedly thrown into the enemy's path so that the rest of this army can escape? I'd like to know just what in the hell Schofield's army is doing anyway?"

The officer made a feeble attempt to assuage the general. "Sir, I am not sure..."

"Of course you are not sure, I would not expect anything less from an officer from the Twenty-third corps."

"General, this is not the time, nor place," Conrad interceded.

Wagner's eyes narrowed as he peered past the officers towards the earthworks that stood outside of Franklin. "You go back and you tell General Cox that I will turn my men around and march the same damned ground we just crossed. What is left of my division will hold Hood's army until tonight as he requests. Hell, we did it at Spring Hill, I guess we can do it here as well."

The officer's salute was not returned as he turned his mount and rode back to Cox's headquarters. Wagner could do nothing but shake his head in confusion. "Gentleman, please inform your officers to have your men halt and then do an about face. We will march back up those hills and hold the Confederate army at bay once again."

"This is not going to be taken well," Lane said.

Wagner stepped down from his horse and walked towards a large branch that he saw lying alongside the road. He broke off a piece that was the size of a small baton. He began to twirl it around in his hands as he turned his attention back to the hills south of him. He seemed to have completely ignored Lane's statement. With his back to them, he spoke more to himself.

"Then again, if we can hold those hills for one night, this

division's reputation will be restored. That will make two times that we will have single handedly held the entire Confederate army in check."

Conrad listened to his commander's soliloquy with horrid disbelief. He looked to Lane with eyes begging for him to speak up against Wagner's ostentatious mentality. Lane returned his denial with a quick shake of his head. He understood that Wagner's stance was not irrefragable. Wagner saw his situation as one in which he could not lose. General Schofield had ordered him to hold the hills that led into Franklin. If Wagner failed in that, well that was to be expected. Could two beaten brigades really be expected to withstand an entire army? Yet, if his presence were enough to stall Hood's attack for just this night, and allow the Federal army to escape one last time, then Wagner would become a hero. The rout of this morning would be forgotten with a high probability for his promotion.

But as far as Lane was concerned, there was no way Hood would allow two brigades to hold up his army. Not after he had them at his mercy the day before at Spring Hill. 'Hood will definitely be coming through here', he thought. And when he does, something will have to give. The question was, will to be Wagner's division or his reputation?

With all of that at stake, Lane rode back towards his men to begin issuing the orders for a counter march.

*   *   *   *   *   *   *   *

It took some time to convince Wagner's division to turn around and march back towards the same hills that they had just vacated. What the troops saw when they got there proved their concerns all too valid. From their vantage point upon the hills they were afforded a clear view of the Franklin to Columbia Pike running between Winstead and Breezy Hills south towards Columbia. Not far to their left was the Lewisburg Pike running parallel to the Harpeth until it angled across the railroad as it neared Franklin.

Wagner stared at the same view with his men, and what he saw compelled him to agree with their apprehensions. "I should have told Cox that if he wanted these hills held, to do it himself," he told one of his officers.

There was a full corps of gray soldiers rapidly approaching along each pike, their rebel flags waving fearlessly as they deployed into battle formations. Wagner agreed to return to these hills because he hoped their high ground would afford his men a formidable enough defensive position to hold off a single corps until this evening. But one look over his shoulder towards the Lewisburg Pike, and the emergence of a second corps of the enemy, only strengthened his resolve to give the order for the abandonment of these hills for a second time.

Wagner knew there was really no other choice, for the second corps marching along that parallel pike would soon outflank his position and cut him off from the rest of the Federal army. That had already happened once today back at Thompson Station, and he was not going to allow it to happen again. With a great sense of urgency, his cannons were limbered and his men began to march towards the main earthworks at Franklin for the second time today.

It did not take his weary men long to withdraw from the threat and retreat to a small hill known as Privet Knob. That was when Wagner called for his leading regiments to come to a halt. The men were confused at the order, but cautiously complied. They had already seen the large number of Confederates approaching, and did not think they were going to halt until they were safely within the Federal earthworks.

They waited patiently, watching Wagner become surrounded by officers. Behind their commander, they could easily see the strong defensive positions that the rest of the army enjoyed. It tantalized them from a distance of less than eight hundred feet. The men began whispering silent prayers that they might receive the order to continue the march. They had traveled so many miles since leaving Pulaski, and all the distance that was left to secure their safety was a mere few hundred feet.

It would be a distance they would never reach.

The assembly broke up and the officers emerged with orders that rapidly began deploying regiments on both sides of the pike. Many of the soldiers were too delirious from hunger and exhaustion to offer any form of complaint. Like docile zombies they began to fall in alongside the Franklin to Columbia Pike. Many a head stared forward in dreaded anticipation of what was to come. And many a head was also swung upon its shoulder looking at the rest of the Federal army dug in and consolidated a half a mile in their rear.

The question that traveled down the line like a flame upon a fuse was "Why are we being stopped here?" It was an answer only General Wagner had.

*   *   *   *   *   *   *   *

Wagner left his men to entrench their position. It was a task that would not be easy to fulfill. The surrounding area had already been stripped bare so that the main line of earthworks behind them could be constructed. But because they knew the value of even the crudest of earthworks, the second division made the most of an abject situation. Many of them dug with callous hands with the hope that their labor would in the end save their lives from the imminent destruction marching their way.

Wagner gave his division one last look before leaving them as he passed through the only visible gap in Cox's earthworks. He found a captain who pointed to the Carter house as a place where he could find General Cox. Trailing behind Wagner were barely three companies that had survived from Opdycke's brigade. 'These men, they deserve a hard-earned rest', he thought. He would not deny them that. He had instructed them to fall in at the rear of the Carter house to get themselves some food and rest.

'Let my other brigades learn from this,' he thought. Wagner could not help harboring such contempt for the men in Conrad and Lane's command. If they were going to be an asset to his command, then they needed some harsh lessons and they needed them quickly. Leaving them outside of the main works was his first lesson… a lesson in fear.

Schofield had made it known that he did not believe that the rebel army would attack today and when Wagner approached the defenses of Franklin, he could understand why. With the Federal army so well entrenched, and so supported with artillery, any form of frontal attack had to be considered suicide.

No, Hood would definitely not attack here today. Wagner knew that now, but his men did not. They had seen the approach of the Confederate army as they stood upon Winstead and Breezy Hill. They fully expected Hood to come along the pike and advance. And that was good. They needed a lesson on what it meant to stare at the face of danger and not succumb to it. They would shiver in their boots, rifles poised and ready. They would pray that the enemy would not advance, and when their prayers were answered, they would feel an immense amount of relief. Relief that they were not attacked, and relief that they held their ground. That should make it obvious that the enemy was also fearful. That lesson should be a valuable one. Perhaps the next time, they would not rout as they had at Thompson Station. It was simply a matter of discipline.

Wagner also had another reason for halting his division just outside of Cox's line. It was his way of telling the Twenty-third corps that he did not need them. They did not need them at Spring Hill, and they did not need them now. Wagner's unorthodox positioning of his division was done in defiance of the treatment his men had to endure under the command of General Schofield and his favoritism towards his own people.

As Wagner passed the small farm office, he could see General Cox gathered with his staff. Cox saw him approaching and dismissed them all, except for General Reilly. Reilly sat upon a wooden chest and stood up to open it. From within he removed a bottle and brought it with him as he and Cox met Wagner in the Carter yard.

"Compliments from the Twenty-third," Reilly said as he handed Wagner the warm glass bottle that contained a very dark whiskey.

Wagner's pride made him hesitant to accept it, but his thirst for alcohol easily overrode that. He took the bottle with reluctant thanks.

"General," Cox said, "I have not had the time to personally offer my thanks, but I do so now. Your men may have saved this army this morning."

"Thank you sir, but I can't help but feel that they have done this Union a great injustice by routing from Thompson Station."

"But they quickly reformed and regained their composure. I do not think there is another division in either army that could have done the same, especially under such conditions."

Wagner's thoughts began to ease as he could feel the bottle within his hand. He was listening to Cox, but he was thinking about finding a quiet shaded place where he could slip off his boots and pour this whisky down his dry throat. He had not realized when Cox had finished speaking. All he could make out was something about retiring his brigade if he was compelled to do so.

Wagner excused himself from Cox and walked around the Carter house. Once on the other side, he opened the bottle and felt the warm liquid coat his throat as it poured into his stomach like burning lava. He had several more swigs before joining the remnants of Opdycke's brigade for some food. His head swam as he tried to concentrate on tasting the bland food within his mouth. It was not working. Lack of sleep, combined with aching limbs and the alcohol he had just consumed, began to take a disorienting toll upon his worn body.

When an officer from Conrad's brigade reported that Lane wished for his men to fall back, Wagner had to ask the man to repeat the request.

"General Lane reports that the enemy is massing in his front", the officer said. Our skirmishing lines have been driven back."

Wagner tried to focus on the skinny man reporting to him, but his head felt like a great cast iron bell that had just been wrung. From the corner of his eyes he could see a worried General Cox approaching.

"You tell General Conrad that he is not to move from his position. He must stay and fight. There will be no more routs by my division. Inform him that anyone that runs is to be shot. Am I making myself clear to you? Those men are to fix bayonets and hold their ground."

The officer was not daunted by Wagner's dogmatism. He came from the front and he knew exactly what his brigade was facing. If it meant his arrest, then so be it. "General, we can not hold that line, we are facing General Hood's entire army. I do not care what you have been previously told about the enemy, but I can assure you that they mean to attack us here and now."

Just as that was said, the whistle of a passing cannonball was followed by the impact of the projectile somewhere against the Carter house. Gunfire began to erupt from the front, forcing many of the troops from the Twenty-third that had been sleeping, to jump up and begin scrambling for their weapons.

Cox turned from Wagner as he neared to view the destruction wrought by the projectile. He then quickly turned and began moving back towards the Carter house. "General, you may pull your men back now," Cox yelled.

The urgency of his request was evident in his widened eyes. He needed to get back within the main line to ensure his men were braced for the eventual impact of war. But he also knew that he needed Wagner's men in reserve behind the Carter house, not out here dangling like some damned red flag to a charging bull.

He still was not sure if Hood was actually attacking, or performing a ruse with his artillery, yet if he had to choose, his conservatism sided with the former. And if that were true, Hood seemed to be heading straight up the Franklin Pike, right towards the only opening in his entire line of defense... a rebel thrust and breakthrough at that point would have dire results on this army. And the only reserve force available to counter such a threat was Wagner's division.

"General Wagner, do you hear me? The rebel cavalry has also reportedly crossed Hughes's Ford, but they have been checked by Wilson's command. I am not sure of the enemy's intent, to attack or flank, but I need to be ready for anything. So have your men fall into this area immediately," he said. Then trusting his orders to be carried through, took his leave.

Wagner may have heard Cox, but he refused to listen. Upon heels of defiance, he turned back towards Conrad's officer and pulled the man close to his chin. "You tell Colonel Conrad...and Lane for that matter to stay and fight. Fight like hell. Tell Conrad he owes me this, something to the affect that his name is riding on it."

The officer turned and fled with all the speed of one that has just realized that he has been conversing with a madman.

*   *   *   *   *   *   *   *

At the same time that Hood's army was advancing over the low hills south of Franklin, Thomas and General A.J. Smith were in the midst of conducting a private meeting at Thomas' headquarters in Nashville. Thomas had grown more and more apprehensive with Schofield with every passing day. Each telegram or message that he received sounded more alarmingly desperate than the last. He handed the latest telegram to Smith for review.

"This one here is Schofield's response to my request for

him to hold Hood's army at Franklin for just three more days," he said.

Smith took a moment to study the message before handing it back to Thomas. "So General Schofield does not believe that he can. He makes that very clear in his response. What would you have me do?"

Thomas tossed the telegram amongst the cluster of other messages that were piled upon his desk like scattered laundry. "Schofield is planning to retire his army across the Harpeth this evening. He greatly fears that he will be outflanked once again."

Smith was shaking his head in agreement. "His fear of being flanked is a very realistic one. But I doubt that is what is causing him the most concern."

"You mean the supposed division of Hampton's cavalry that was sent west to join Forrest's command?"

Smith folded his hands as if in prayer and then rubbed his fingers against his chin. "That is correct. I do not know how, but I can assure you that this is nothing more than another fantastic theatrical performance conducted by Forrest. He is notorious for such things."

Thomas wanted to believe Smith, but he could not risk that chance. "Until I have more definite information, I must assume the worst. I have sent word to General Grant of the possibility, I am awaiting his reply."

"His reply will be to attack."

Thomas' great shoulders fought to stay erect, but the truth in what Smith had said caused them to sink a few inches. "I know that. He has been pressing me every day to have this army moving against Hood. The capital will not listen to anything unless it is news that we are on the offensive. I wish I could comply with them, but we are still not ready. That was why I asked Schofield for just three more days. My hope was for your entire command to be consolidated and moving forward, joined by a fully equipped cavalry. I keep hearing that their rifles and saddles are due any day."

Smith scratched his head. "I can move what I have now. If that is what you wish? What is the latest from Franklin?"

Thomas gathered a few messages and quickly reviewed them. "The army has fallen in around the earthworks south of Franklin. Wood's division is across the Harpeth, keeping the back door open. Artillery has been placed within Fort Granger to deter

351

Hood from attacking. Schofield is pretty confident in his defenses and is sure that Hood will not attack today. He is more concerned about being flanked by Forrest's cavalry, and whether or not Hampton's division is with them. The rebel cavalry have been nipping at his rear and flanks all morning."

"Where has General Wilson been?" Smith asked.

Thomas stood up to take a deep breath. "Quite honestly, his performance has been a surprise to this entire command. According to these reports, it was his fault that Hood was even allowed to cross the Duck and almost trap our army at Spring Hill. Wilson is either a poor judge of intent, or he is being entirely outwitted by the Confederate cavalry."

"A rebel cavalry led by General Forrest," Smith said. "I know many of our own commanders who would agree with the latter part of what you had just said... Sooy Smith specifically."

Thomas sat back down. "Perhaps you are right. How about what that devil accomplished at Brice's Cross Roads? And to think of him against General Schofield... well let's just say that it makes me very uncomfortable. Between just us two, I sure do wish that Forrest had been born in Ohio."

"General Thomas what can my corps do to relieve you and Schofield of any pressure?" was Smith's only response.

"Take what you have ready and march to Brentwood. Schofield plans to fall back to that point. He thinks your presence is needed at this time if for nothing else but a morale boost to the men of the Twenty-third and Forth corps. If they see that reinforcements are at hand, he believes their attitude will quickly change."

"Consider it done," Smith said.

"I thank you, General," Thomas said. "I must insist that you move your men with great speed. From these reports it does not appear that the army at Franklin is breaking just yet, but it does sound like General Schofield is."

*　　*　　*　　*　　*　　*　　*　　*

At the same moment that General Wagner was sipping his whiskey behind the Carter House, Schofield and Stanley were walking towards Schofield's new headquarters across the Harpeth. Schofield could not help but feel a little more relaxed now that he had a flowing river between him and the rebel army. In a few more hours, the rest of his men would follow him across and would assuredly feel the same pressure relieved from their shoulders.

"How did you wind up responding to Thomas' request that we hold here for three more days?" Stanley was asking.

Schofield's smirk was cynical, "I told him that there was no way we could do so. We are pulling out tonight. I have already heard enough from General Wilson about the rebel's advancing towards Hughes's Ford. I told Wilson that was to be expected. I just do not want Hood crossing a river again without my knowledge."

"Do you believe that Wilson can impede the Confederate advance?"

"Not really. Wilson reported that a division had crossed the river, but he has checked its advance and is driving them back as we speak. But I still lack confidence in him, and that was why I sent two of Wood's brigades to assist him. I have also alerted the artillery at Fort Granger of this possible threat. Even if Hampton's division is with Forrest, there is no way that they can ford a river and attack an entrenched position, one that is defended by two brigades and our cavalry. Besides even if they wanted to, it is already getting late. It is three in the afternoon, a few more hours and it will be dark and then we will be gone from here. If Smith is at Brentwood as I hope, then General Hood will be in for a huge surprise when he catches up with us. There is good reason why I finished ahead of him at the academy."

The two generals entered the home appropriated for Schofield's headquarters. The Truett family knew that they really were not given a choice with the request to turn their abode into a war room. "Come with me General," Stanley said. "The view from the upstairs porch is magnificent. From there, we can see the entire approach to Franklin."

When the two men reached the porch, they were surprised to see a crowd of officers and civilians gathered as they looked through field glasses with concern.

"Make way for the general," a boy said.

Schofield did not recognize the voice. It was Edwin Truett, the son of Alpheus Truett, whose home the Federal army had occupied. Schofield patted the lad upon the head as he took a pair of field glasses from one of the officers and looked towards Franklin.

What he saw turned his legs into spaghetti. He fought to keep himself from being sick.

"Isn't it a grand sight," the boy said?

"It sure is," Schofield said, resisting the urge to vomit over the ledge. "One I am sure that you may never see again. But now that you have, please run along."

Edwin felt as if he were scolded. He turned from the porch and went back into the house. He was heard to mutter, "It's not even your home to tell me where I can and can't go."

Schofield had to look through his field glasses for a second time to confirm the horror of what he had just witnessed. Two entire corps were marching along parallel pikes as they advanced towards Cox's defensive line. This was not supposed to be happening. Hood was not supposed to attack, not just yet. Suddenly, all the confidence he had in his assessment of the enemy's objective was shattered like the broken heart of a jilted lover. "This can not be, this can not be," he said.

The eruption of gunfire told him that it could be and in fact was happening. "General Stanley, that corps marching up the Franklin Pike could shatter our entire line. Send word to General Wood to pull back his brigades from supporting Wilson's cavalry. If Cox's men break, Wood's full division will be needed to cover the escape across the river."

Stanley wished Schofield luck before departing for Franklin. Schofield sent a staff officer to Fort Granger with the order for the artillery to reposition itself so that it could fire into the oncoming ranks of rebel infantry. Schofield's horse was waiting for him outside of the Truett home. He quickly mounted and rode with his officers towards Fort Granger. From there he would have an even better view of the battle, as well as immediate supervision of the artillery barrage he meant to send in Hood's direction. As he reflected upon this, he began to consider Cox's extremely formidable earthworks.

With the combined might of the batteries at Fort Granger and his well entrenched infantry, Hood's army could very well be decimated before it even reached the main line of works. 'No, Hood should not be a problem,' he thought. 'My only fear is that by repositioning the batteries towards Franklin, I have not opened the door for Forrest. But that is not like you John Bell Hood is it? Two separated offensive maneuvers at once is just not your style.'

So putting his hopes in his past relationship with Hood,

Schofield was convinced that if Hood was attempting a frontal assault, than he would not be sending his cavalry on a simultaneous flanking strike.

'I know you all to well. You were always like a big dumb bull... once you decide on your means of attack, you come not only with horns rearing for impact, but you come with all you have. And this time it is going to cost you.'

General Schofield's assessment of Hood's strategy may very well have been an accurate one. And if Hood were leading this army into Franklin, he may have marched his army blindly into the certain death that awaited them. But what Schofield did not know, was that only a few hours ago, the command of the rebel army was no longer Hood's to control. It had been handed over to General Robert E. Lee.

Chapter XXIV
November 30
The Battle for Franklin, Tennessee

It was just after noon when the two Southern corps commanders met under the shade of trees just south of Franklin. For General Stewart, the day had been a long one. His men had been awakened much too early only to be rushed into an attack they were ill prepared for. That coupled with the exhaustion from the previous day's march resulted in a lackluster performance at the battle near Thompson Station. Though they had managed to support Forrest in his attack as well as completely cut off an entire Federal brigade, they were not able to succeed in their primary objective.

Stewart knew that had his men been rested and more prepared, they would have easily decimated the entire rear guard of the Federal army, as well as rout the rest of their command all the way from Thompson Station into the Harpeth River. And he knew that was exactly how Hood would see it, whenever the general arrived.

"Has there been any word concerning General Hood?" Stewart asked.

Cheatham finished gulping his water and then wiped his mouth with his sleeve. "This is November, we should not have to be huddled under these trees to remain cool. You know it's actually very comical, there aren't any leaves left. I think we are all just trained, like animals. When it is hot, find a tree and lay under it... even if that tree is bare. I am sorry, I think that I am delirious from loss of sleep. No, I have not heard from Hood, but I fully expect him at any moment. We should have woken him."

"I was thinking that same thing. But at least we have caught up with the Federal army. The Yankees that were posted upon those two hills are now gone. I know that neither General Lee, nor Hood are present yet, but if they were, they would both agree that those two hills are the gateway to Franklin. We need to occupy them as soon as possible."

Cheatham looked out at the men of their army. Though they were excited to be advancing through Tennessee, inspired by the citizens coming from their homes to cheer them like returning saviors, their bodies were only human. The strength needed in their limbs to keep moving could never match the will in their hearts to do so. The number of men lying down, or sitting, or sleeping, far outweighed the number of men who stood ready for the next command. "I know, but do you think they have it in them today? Our boys are exhausted."

"We have no choice. Besides, the Yankees have to be even more tired. Not to mention, where our men are advancing towards victory, they are retreating in defeat. We must engage that army today, before they can cross the Harpeth."

"You are right," Cheatham admitted. "Since your corps is in the lead, have them continue marching up this pike. I will swing my men around towards the Lewisburg pike and come in on your flank. This way, if there are any Yanks still in possession of those hills, my corps will flank them out of position."

Stewart drank some water and started walking back towards his men. "Excellent, by then, General S. D. Lee's troops should come up and allow my men some rest."

Just before the two generals could depart, the sound of a small escort broke over the knoll south of their position. At the head of the company was none other than John Bell Hood. Stewart and Cheatham both shared a quick look of concern.

"He does not look happy," Stewart said.

"And I thought the day was going to be bright and sunny. Well here comes the storm," Cheatham replied.

With the sight of his generals before him, Hood's trot quickly turned into a full gallop. He did not stop his horse until it practically crushed General Cheatham, who had to move to avoid the impact.

"General Hood, I am glad to report..."

"Do not speak to me at this moment, General," Hood shot back. "I do not know who in the hell you think you are to take my army from me and advance under your own devises. I did not call for this attack, you were told to engage the enemy at Spring Hill, were you not?" Cheatham stood in a petrified silence. "You can answer now, General."

"General Hood, you told me not to attack at Spring Hill. Don't you remember me conferring with you, you were confident that we would find the enemy still in place when we awoke?"

"And is the army still at Spring Hill, is this then another

357

Federal army that we have decided to chase?"

"No sir, this is the same army."

"Exactly. You should not have let them escape from Spring Hill. I know I said that we would find them there in the morning, but that was an obvious miscalculation. Even so, that does not mean that you allow the enemy to simply pack up and leave."

"Well, we did manage to attack them as they withdrew, we even captured an entire brigade as well as some isolated regiments."

"That was your second mistake of this campaign, General. First of all, you should have attacked yesterday when you had the chance."

"I reported the situation to you yesterday. General Brown felt his flank was unsupported."

"Yes, Yes...I know, I have already passed that fallible general this morning and I have since re-educated him on what it means to take the battle to the enemy. That behind us, your first mistake was letting the army get away, your second was giving chase with out first conferring with me. I could discharge you for that General... perhaps even have you shot."

Cheatham looked at the entourage of officers that had accompanied Hood. With him were his chief of staff and the governor of Tennessee. Cheatham could not let them hear what it was that he had to say. He took a step closer to Hood and asked for the general to lean over on his horse. Hood was cautious, but complied. "That order was given by General Lee," he whispered.

Hood quickly retracted and sat straight upon his horse. Though he knew whom his general was referring to, he asked anyway. "Stephen?" was all he said?

Cheatham shook his head from side to side. Stewart was eyeing for him to dismiss his staff. Hood turned to them and asked to be left alone with his commanders. With Governor Harris and Mason leading, the staff rode towards the rest of the Confederate army.

"I had thought that it was all a dream," Hood said. "I had the message that he was coming, but when I awoke, I could not find it. Is he really here, where is he now?"

"General Lee was left behind at Spring Hill. He was in sore need of rest. He plans on joining us here today, but he had instructed us to keep his presence a secret, until he decides the best time to announce himself."

Hood took off his hat and ran his hand through his thick hair. "It is still hard to imagine him here in Tennessee." Hood wanted to tell Cheatham that Lee was the reason why he was not entirely adamant about attacking the enemy at Spring Hill. But he knew that if he did as much, Cheatham would use it as an excuse for not taking the proper initiative and ensuring the enemy could not escape. "When did he arrive?" he asked.

"Late last night, while we were conferring outside your headquarters," Cheatham said.

"And I was not awakened for this?"

"General, I am sorry, but that was something greatly debated. General Bate had just come from seeing you and said that you were not your self. We know that you had a few drinks with dinner…"

"Are you, of all people, the one to tell me that I can not handle my alcohol? And who is General Bate to make that decision. Who else was gathered at this meeting?" Hood said.

Hood placed emphasis on the word meeting as if to suggest it was mutinous. "We were both there, as was Bate, Cleburne and Forrest," Stewart said. "We were collectively confused as to what we should be doing."

"I see," Hood said. "And so it was decided to let the Federal army escape?"

"Please General, that must be put behind us. I apologize for that mishap. As for my corps not initiating the attack yesterday, I can only say that I was not on hand to personally lead them. I left that in the hands of Cleburne and Brown. I will be sure to speak to them about that."

Stewart could not believe what he had just heard. In order for Cheatham to escape Hood's wrath, he was transferring the blame to his division commanders…a blame that could not be responded to because those same men were not here to defend themselves. "General Hood, unlike Cheatham, I will take the full responsibility for not properly coordinating the attack this morning. Had I done so, we would have captured a third of their force."

Hood looked over their heads towards his army as it sat idle a few miles from the town of Franklin. "Well General Stewart, at least your men have done something noble. For the moment General Cheatham, I will agree to put yesterday behind us, what is the situation right now?"

Cheatham turned and pointed towards Winstead and Breezy Hill. "Those two hills mark the entrance into the Franklin valley. The Yanks had a division posted there, but they have since fallen back. We were just preparing to move forward before they might return. General Stewart was going to continue on this pike, while I wheeled towards the Lewisburg Pike to support his flank. This way, if there were any infantry there, we could force them out."

A small black bird fluttered over their heads as it soared towards Franklin. Hood stared at its flight for a moment and thought how it must feel to be able to spread a pair of wings and take to the air. Then he thought of the bird's black wings, they were almost obsidian in hue. There was some kind of ineffable beauty contained within their darkness. Yet somewhere under those dark wings there must have been an even darker shadow, for as they flapped, a devious threnody descended to play a hymn inside his head.

Why should Stewart's corps lead the attack into Franklin, when it was Cheatham's fault for them even having to fight here? It was time that the men in Chatham's command began to understand the responsibility associated with an offensive. If there was still any Federal infantry on those hills, Hood wanted Cheatham's men to be the ones that would receive their fire. Let them earn every step of their advance, and maybe then they could appreciate what it meant to force the enemy from a position.

"Generals, I agree with this plan, but I must insist on one change," he said. "Let General Stewart's men move to the Lewisburg Pike to allow for Cheatham's corps to march for those hills."

Cheatham began to protest. "General, that would require a lot of maneuvering and we would waste valuable time in the process. Stewart's men are already in the advance position and can move forward without delay."

Hood kept the disdain wrapped around his heavily beating heart. He fought back against the urge to tell Cheatham how he really felt. If I gave the command to dig in, your men would be the first to drop their guns and reach for spades. It was time that changed. "General Cheatham, I am sure that Stewart's men are exhausted. They have conducted the only real attack at Spring Hill and have given the enemy chase ever since. I think it only fair that they assume the supporting role in this advance. Don't you agree?"

Cheatham nodded in defeat. If Hood wanted to waste time redeploying men that were already in position, then let it rest on his shoulders. He was not going to be made to feel guilty because of yesterday's misgivings. Besides, General Lee would arrive soon enough to regain command of this army.

"Have Forrest throw his support on Stewart's right until we can occupy those hills. From there I am sure we can get an excellent view of their defenses so that we can decide the next course of action," Hood said.

Hood then trotted off to rejoin his staff and enjoy his first real meal of the day. This time, he would not leave his army for any reason. In a few minutes, his great army would advance towards the hills south of Franklin, and if all went as planned, occupy those heights. From there, it would only be a matter of hours before he could finally sink his teeth, every single one of them, into the very flesh of the Federal army. And the one thing that he was sure of, win or lose, it was to be Cheatham's corps that would take the first bite. This was going to be the day that they learned what would happen if ever again they let a cornered army escape a well-constructed trap.

*   *   *   *   *   *   *   *

It did not take long to brief all of the commanders as to the army's advance. Stewart's corps quickly wheeled towards the Lewisburg Pike and within the hour, began advancing along its path. Cheatham's corps then began its more direct march along the parallel pike towards Winstead and Breezy Hill. A huge scare presented itself as the leading columns reached a few hundred feet from the base of the hills. It seemed as if the Federal division had returned. Cheatham could see their guns being unlimbered, and feared his men would have a serious engagement before they could take the hills.

However, just as quickly as the guns were unlimbered, and the first few cannon fired, they were quickly packed back up and led back down from the hills. The Federal infantry quickly followed in their wake. A quick glance to his right confirmed what he suspected all along. The presence of Stewart's corps marching along his flank was enough of a threat to dislodge the Federals from their defensive position. With the hills now vacated by the Yankees, the Confederates could easily ascend their slopes and see into Franklin.

Cheatham held his army on the southern side of the hills and joined his senior commanders as they climbed towards the top to get a better look at the Federal position. What they saw impressed them greatly. The Harpeth River hugged itself around Franklin like a protective mother. It flowed from the northwest, arching around the town, and then continuing southeast. Due to the ubiquitous river that protected Franklin's flanks, there was only one way to attack such a position, and by the looks of the Yankees across the way, they knew as much, as well. Hood would have to send his men over an open country straight into the waiting mass of Union soldiers.

And the Yanks had not been idle.

The earthworks constructed around them were some of the most formidable that any of the commanders had seen. Cheatham was sure his commanders shared his thoughts... there was no possible way for Hood to continue with this attack today. Hood would most likely have to attempt to flank this army out of position yet again. The only sight that puzzled Cheatham was the presence of a single division that was isolated and deployed outside the main earthworks. Judging by their wavering colors, it appeared to be the same division that had just vacated these hills. He could not understand why Schofield was not pulling them in. Would it really matter anyway? There was no way Hood could send his army against such a position.

One look at his generals confirmed that they came to the same conclusion as he. Cleburne, Brown, and Bate had left him to join their men. Before departing, Cleburne had looked through his field glasses for one last view before saying that the enemy's defenses were very formidable. Cheatham reassured him that he felt the same and did not intend to follow through with Hood's plan. Cleburne responded by tipping his hat and then walking back down the hill.

Cheatham was going to follow, but wanted one more look before reporting to General Hood. The sound of an unnatural step and heavy breathing told him that he would not have to travel very far to make his report. Hood stood beside him, his staff several feet in the rear.

"There is the enemy, General Cheatham. We have finally caught up with them," Hood said.

"That we have, but they are dug in very well. I suppose we can hold them again, and try to cross the Harpeth to outflank them."

Hood quickly dropped the field glasses to his side. He turned towards Cheatham with a look that could have frozen a furnace. "We will make the fight here and now." He then left Cheatham and joined his staff. Hood was helped onto his horse and then rode back down the hill. One of his officers rode back towards Cheatham and informed him that Hood was calling for a council of war immediately at the nearby home of William Harrison.

Cheatham nodded and then sent word for his senior commanders to join him there. He could not help feeling nauseous as he rode back down the hill. The thought of attacking those earthworks was enough to make even the most hardened general sick. How could he give an order to his men, knowing that its execution would result in suicide? He hoped he could find that answer somewhere between here and the Harrison home just south of Winstead Hill.

*　　*　　*　　*　　*　　*　　*　　*

"Come on General, the lad has bet a year of his pay that he can best you in a game of checkers," Mangum said.

Cleburne looked at his old friend and smiled. "The way this army pays, that should equal two potatoes imported all the way from Ireland. That is one wager I would much rather pass on."

Mangum stood up from the stump on which he sat. "Is this the same partner whom I entered law with? It cannot be. The Cleburne I knew would never turn his back on a challenge."

Cleburne could not remove the smile from his face. He stepped over towards the stump that Mangum just vacated and shoved his friend aside before planting his bottom down upon it. "I know," he said.

"Ah...now I have figured it out. Are you dwelling on the lovely Susan Tarleton?"

"Enough, you are treading waters that are hazardous to

363

your well being."

Mangum was perhaps the only man in either army that did not fear Cleburne's wrath. He picked up a long brittle branch and began to poke it at Cleburne's chest. "Look at you, blushing like a lovesick school boy."

Cleburne took the thin branch and snapped it in half.

"If only the enemy could see you now," Mangum said. "If they knew as much, why I think they'd drop their flags and replace them with great portraits of Ms. Tarleton." Mangum then began to laugh uncontrollably.

"All right, enough, you win. I am thinking of her," he said. "I have found that I have been thinking of her more and more these past few days. And I know the reason as well. At some point, our two army's are going to clash with such animosity as never before seen on this earth. I can feel that in our men. It is not like the beginning, when we fought to win the battle, and then thought the war would end. These men here have lived through that, and they know the lie. They have fought battle after battle, have enjoyed a few victories, but for the most part they have experienced defeat. They have been pushed from their homes, from their state, and in effect from the country. When they are next unleashed it will be hell on earth. Many of those Yankees across the way are not the same individuals that these men have faced. Where we have to keep sending the same men to battle, the Yanks enjoy fresh recruits. But that will not matter... to our boys those are men in blue uniforms. And for that they will die."

Magnum's smile was replaced by a blank look. "And this upsets you?" he said.

"No. I want to see the Yankees driven from our land as much as anyone. It is just that when I imagine the battle, I imagine an immense sacrifice on our part to achieve this victory."

"Patrick, I have never heard you speak in such tones before. If you think you are going to die in the battle ahead, rest assured that it is not possible to fell you. I have seen bullets race for your heart, then turn themselves around when they realized who it was they were going to hit."

Cleburne stood up. "I used to feel invincible, but that was when it did not matter."

"And now that you are engaged to Ms. Tarleton, you feel your mortality?"

"No. But for the first time in my life I feel that I matter to someone. The thought of her living a day without me fills my heart with woe."

"And all this time I thought it was I who made you feel so," Mangum said with heavily blinking eyes.

Cleburne smiled and threw a solid punch into his friend's shoulder. "Now, where is that foolish captain that risks his demotion at the hands of my masterful checkers prowess?"

Magnum led Cleburne through his division, until they arrived somewhere in its center. A large circle was already formed in anticipation of Cleburne's acceptance of the challenge. A great cheer erupted with his presence. Cleburne lifted his cap to goad them on.

"Where is the brave captain that risks his reputation against me?" he challenged.

The young captain stepped forth and bowed before Cleburne.

Cleburne looked at Mangum. "He is not even from our division," he said.

The young captain heard what was said. "And does that frighten you," he said. The boyish grin on his face was a sight not seen by Cleburne in a long time.

"I like to know the name of the man before I defeat him," Cleburne returned.

"Theoderick Carter," Mangum said. "And you should not be so confident".

"And why is that?"

"He has you at a disadvantage, you are playing in his own back yard," Mangum replied.

Cleburne was confused. "I am afraid I do not follow, how does that matter in a game of checkers."

"This lad is from Franklin. His father's house sits along this pike as it enters the town."

"I am still not sure I understand how this pertains to checkers. But perhaps that is the strategy... have me try to figure out a riddle that has no answer, while a boy jumps my pieces. Speaking of which, where is the board?"

Theoderick stepped to the side and revealed a large checkerboard dug into the earth. Placed upon it were colored leaves to represent the checker pieces. Theoderick, or Todd as he was called, stepped over to his side and offered Cleburne the first move.

Cleburne admired the ingenious checker set, but deferred the first move. "We will let you make the first step in celebration of your homecoming," he said.

Todd accepted, and the large congregation of soldiers began to crowd around the two combatants. Todd's first move was to place his middle leaf one square forward. The start of the game inspired a cheer from the spectators. Cleburne noted the move and immediately disapproved.

A frontal attack was the way all inexperienced checker players liked to begin the battle. Cleburne had faced such a tactic many a time. He himself liked to use the flanks of the board. He would move his left and right most pieces forward, while retaining his middle in position for as long as possible. His adversary would often extend his own lines too far from his base. Cleburne would then sacrifice a few of his middle pieces, while his flankers moved into the evacuated boxes to cause havoc in the rear. The young Carter's first move told him that he was in for such a game.

Cleburne lifted a rather large leaf on the far right side of the board and moved it up two spaces. "So Todd, is your family still in town."

Todd continued to study the board. "Yes they are. My brother should be with them. He is on parole." Todd moved another of his middle pieces forward.

Cleburne moved to the other side of the board and advanced a leaf on the left flank. He stared at the look of determination on the young captain's face, but it was the thought of his boyish smile earlier that ignited a spark of empathy within. In the past few years, he had witnessed so many bright young smiles cut short by the inhumanity of this war. This Carter boy was only an assistant, and so should not get harmed in any fighting, but Cleburne wanted to be sure. "You know, if there is an attack here in the morning, you should try to not let this battlefield become personal."

"General, this is my father's land. It can be nothing else but personal. There is no power on this earth that can keep me from a battle here at Franklin." A third leaf joined Carter's vanguard as it threatened Cleburne's center.

Cleburne wanted to find the words that would keep this naive boy from harm, but knew that he would not be able to. Perhaps he could use the checkerboard as an instructional device. He began to send another flanking leaf forward when an officer from Cheatham's staff arrived. The officer was so unobservant that his horse trampled their checkerboard. Cleburne wiped his hands upon his pants and waited for the message.

"General Cleburne, General Cheatham has been instructed to gather his offices for a council of war at the Harrison house. Your presence is requested immediately."

As the officer rode off, the crowd of soldiers begged for Cleburne to continue with the game. Cleburne apologized and waited for Mangum to retrieve their horses. "Theoderick, you play a good game. Had it ensued, I think that you would have offered an excellent challenge."

Todd saluted Cleburne as the general mounted. "I was thinking more of offering you defeat," he smirked.

"Perhaps we can continue this another time," Cleburne said as he rode off with a smile upon his face. The thought of the boy sending his leaves straight up the middle was such a move that only the young in heart could admire. Only with the inexperience of youth could one sacrifice so easily his best checkers without giving much thought to the consequences.

That would be a lesson he hoped to teach Theoderick Carter at a more convenient time.

*   *   *   *   *   *   *   *

General Cleburne was one of the last generals to arrive at the home of William Harrison. Harrison's house was now serving as the temporary headquarters for the Confederate Army of Tennessee. Crowded inside were the highest ranking commanders within General Hood's army. All three of Hood's corps commanders were surrounded by their divisional command. Cleburne walked over to Cheatham and shook hands with Brown and Johnson. He also noticed Forrest standing aloof with his back pressed against the wall. Forrest's only motion was to give Cleburne a slight nod. Even his divisional commanders seemed uncomfortable with his statuesque stance. A shift of Forrest's eyes told Cleburne that someone had just entered the room.

"Now that we are all finally gathered, I must bend my will towards the haste needed to finish out this day," Hood said as the officers gathered parted for his entrance. The commanders formed a large ring around Hood so that he could receive their undivided attention. "Thank you," Hood said into the silence. "Before I can even begin, there is a matter that I must bring to light to those of you that are still in the dark. General Robert E. Lee is now with this army."

The wide eyed and open mouthed looks on many of those present told Hood that Lee's secret was well kept. At least this army could do one thing right. "The general arrived late last night, and it was he that conducted General Stewart's attack along the pike. I must assume that once he arrives he will take command of this army. Now, what I have just said is to be shared with your senior commanders and none other. If I find that word has spilled, I will find the person responsible, whoever that might be and will personally shoot them. General Lee's presence here could have a huge impact on how Grant conducts his offensive against the army in Virginia. We must not push Grant into making any attacks, until we can achieve our victory here."

Hood made sure to make eye contact with every person in the room. It was his way of personalizing the order he had just given. Now that he had that out of the way, it was time for him to make the announcement that he knew would not be received well. He could tell that his officers were far too impressed with the enemy's earthworks and much too content to let this day pass with out an attack. He could not allow that to happen.

Hood had finally managed to bring his entire army within reach of the enemy, and he feared the eventual outcome if his army failed to attack today. There was a strong possibility that Schofield would fall back over the Harpeth if allowed the opportunity. And the Harpeth was the last obstacle that stood between Schofield and Thomas. If he did not attack the Federal army now, Hood knew that he would have to attack a larger one later.

But deep in his heart, he knew there was more to it than that. There was his pride. Hood was not offended that Lee had arrived to take command of this army. Lee was probably the only person that he would allow to take over the reins. However, it was his own arduous strategizing that had allowed his army a chance to battle the Yanks without Thomas' interference. If anyone was going to reap the rewards of such a victory it should be him.

With the destruction of Schofield's army, the South would strike a monumental toll for their independence. The Preston family would have no choice but to allow their daughter's hand in marriage to the nation's hero. As far as Hood saw it, there was only one way to ensure that he received the respect and acclamations that he deserved. It had to be he who gave the order to attack. And with Lee not present, the time to do so was now.

"It is just past two o'clock and you have all had sufficient time to survey the position of the enemy. And though it is a strong one, it is also one that we cannot afford not to attack. So, I expect this army to advance within the hour. General Stewart will continue up the Lewisburg Pike and strike from the railroad to the cotton gin. Forrest will split his force, lending support to Stewart's flank as well as to Cheatham's. Bate's division will represent our left most position and will march for the Carter Creek Pike with the afore mentioned division from Forrest in support. Cheatham's other two corps, under Cleburne and Brown, will advance straight up the Franklin Pike towards the enemy's center."

Hood did not like the looks he received in return. Forrest took a step away from the wall and put a hand upon the pommel of his sheathed saber. Hood could feel the confrontation from him brewing within his piercing eyes. Yet, it was Cleburne who was the first to object.

"General Hood, please reconsider. My men will stand no chance making such an attack. Such an assault as you propose will force my command to cross over an open field. Have you not seen the same earthworks as I? Whatever men of mine are able to reach their lines would be slaughtered at such proximity."

Hood figured as much from Cleburne. It was this same attitude that was responsible for the debacle at Spring Hill. Johnston's influence had obviously exceeded the average foot soldier, for even the Irish general was cautious to a fault. It was time that he too received a re-education on how to conduct a military offensive. It was this reason why he had placed Cleburne and Brown in the center of the attack. Why should any but their men bare the brunt of the assault? It was their fault for allowing the Federals to escape Spring Hill and occupy this ground. And so it must be they who lead the attack right into the heart of the enemy's position.

"General Cleburne, there comes a time when you must come to terms with the fact that this is indeed an army, and every once in a while, an army must actually go on the attack." Hood's sarcasm did not go on ignorant ears. "We can not hope to always be the ones behind cover. If we want the enemy to be driven from

369

Tennessee, then we must drive them ourselves. That cannot be done sitting behind walls. Now, there is a break in their line along the Franklin to Columbia Pike. That is where you must get through. For some unknown reason, there is still a division deployed just outside their line. My suggestion would be to engage them rapidly and drive them back. The Yanks won't use their cannon for fear that they will hit their own men. This would be your chance to gain their trenches."

While Hood was busy lecturing Cleburne on how to attack, he had not noticed that Forrest had moved to stand adjacent to Cleburne. Forrest took another step to place himself directly in front of Hood.

"General Hood," he said. "I beg of you not to divide my cavalry. It would be a waste of this army's greatest asset. Instead, lend me one division and in two hours I swear that I will have the enemy outflanked. I have already begun crossing at Hughes Ford. With the combined might of my entire force and a contingent of your infantry, I have no doubt that I can force Schofield from his position. They would have to fall back, or risk being cut off from Nashville."

Hood was rejecting Forrest's plan before he could even finish the proposal. It was more than Forrest could handle. Stemming from yesterday at Spring Hill, Forrest's temperament towards Hood came to a watershed. On the previous day, his cavalry was supposed to meet Hood's infantry at Spring Hill, not wait for them. Without Hood's support, Forrest was forced to spend a large part of the day skirmishing with the enemy, an enemy that was not supposed to be there in force. And instead of receiving an apology from Hood, he was scolded for not supporting his infantry in the attack made later.

Ironic.

Instead of his troopers receiving support, it was he who would had been the one doing the supporting. But by the time Hood's attack began, his men were out of ammunition, tired and had not eaten a thing all day. Forrest had realized that in order for his command to be of any use, he had to have them rested and re-equipped. Besides, at the time, his decision for disengaging them did not seem like a difficult one. If Hood could not defeat a Yankee division with two entire corps, then there was more at issue then the absence of his cavalry upon the infantry's flank.

Enough was finally enough. "General, you shake your

head at me like an old ninny. Let me tell you what will happen if you attack here today. The Federal artillery will rip through Cheatham's men like rocks through glass. And like glass his corps will be shattered. Do you even know that they have mounted artillery at Fort Granger? From there, the field of fire is as clear as day. You must not employ a frontal assault."

Hood often wished that he had the full use of all of his limbs, but at no other time like he did now. 'I would give this all up now, if only I could curl both of these hands into strong and able fists,' he thought.

"General Forrest, you may think that you can conduct a battle better than I, but you are sorely mistaken," Hood said. "I have been in this similar situation before, with men who understood the necessity to attack and responded with alacrity. I trudged through swampy waters to attack the Yankees dug in at Gains Mill. The hill that they occupied there would make Franklin look like an anthill. We were not daunted. Bayonets were fixed and not a gun was fired until we reached their lines. And we drove them from the doorsteps of Richmond until they were across the waters of the James River. And at no time did any of my men complain."

Hood took a step back from Forrest and turned his attention on addressing the others in the room. "Let me explain something that many of you seem not to grasp. You are now facing only a part of the Federal army. Once Schofield crosses the Harpeth, he will consolidate with Thomas' forces around Nashville. The last thing I want is to flank the enemy out of Franklin. Franklin is exactly where I want him to be, with nothing but the river to his back.

We must drive Schofield's army into the Harpeth and destroy it in its entirety. I do not think that you need me to remind you that we currently outnumber the enemy. I will make this choice yours, attack them now with what they have, or wait for them to evacuate Franklin, unite at Nashville and then attack their combined forces. One way or the other, we will be the ones attacking. It is simply a matter of how many of the enemy would you rather face?"

The question hung in the silence like a guillotine over a sweaty neck. A rustle in the far corner preceded the tap of a heavy boot upon the floor.

"It seems that General Hood has an excellent point."

It was General Robert E. Lee, and for many of the men

gathered, his arrival could not come at a better time. Lee walked towards the center of the room with a controlled and steady step. He realized that the battle that he traveled so far to conduct was now upon him. The thought of finally going on the offensive after so many retreats in Virginia filled his veins with vigor that he did not know he still possessed. He said a silent thanks to Longstreet for suggesting this plan. The internal command in the west was in obvious discord. He was sure if they were left to operate on their own, the ending result would be a catastrophic disaster either here, or in some other part of Tennessee. But now that he was here, he would make sure that could not happen.

"Good afternoon gentleman," Lee said. "I understand that many of you gathered here today were unaware of my presence, and that is fine. That was my order to General Hood. First of all, I would like to apologize to the commander in chief for not awaking him last night before the assault at Thompson Station."

Lee faced Hood directly and placed a soft hand upon the general's massive shoulder. "General Hood, if there is any ire in your heart keep it directed towards me. Your men were not given a choice in the matter." Hood nodded his head in acceptance of the apology as Lee turned back toward the group.

"Second, I want everyone to know that I am not here to take command away from General Hood. He will remain as the acting commander of the Army of Tennessee. I will simply assist him here, until the fortunes of this war shift in the west. Then I must return to Virginia to resume command of my own army."

Many of the men gathered were not happy with the announcement. Some were beginning to harbor contempt towards Hood, and the thought of his continued command over this army filled them with dread. To them the debacle at Spring Hill boiled down to one single reason. Their commander should have been on the field directing the battle. Had he been, there could have been no one to blame for the attack not commencing.

Instead, Hood was indisposed with drinking and feasting, only to awaken with fire and brimstone at discovering the Federal army had gotten away. Instead of Hood taking the blame for not being on hand to conduct operations, he chose to blame others for his own misgivings. And it was becoming apparent how Hood would make amends for that mistake. He would send two thirds of his army straight into the fortified position of the enemy.

It was an attack that many knew would be futile.

Lee was not one in agreement with them. Lee had spent four years in the east trying in vain for this very sort of attack... an opportunity where he outnumbered an enemy that was pinned down against a river. If the Army of Tennessee understood how rare such an opportunity was, he was sure that they would not be hesitating in this attack.

Hood knew better, he saw battle back east. The thought made Lee reflect upon the better days of his army of Virginia. It was back at Chancellorsville, when he faced a similar opportunity. The only difference there was that the enemy had outnumbered him. Still, with well-conducted attacks, Lee was able to defeat two separate armies. Unfortunately, by the time he could organize his men to drive the two defeated armies against the Potomac, they had retreated under their own accord. The complete victory was there for him and it slipped from his fingers like sand through a funnel.

But then again, at Chancellorsville he had General Jackson.

At Gettysburg, he had the Federal army once again where he wanted it. And this time, there was no Jackson. Long and hard he had thought on what might have happened if his most brilliant commander was on hand to lead the initial assault that first day. And he knew all to well that Jackson would not have stalled at the footsteps of Cemetery Hill. Jackson would have kept pressing forward until there was no enemy left to press against. That was Jackson's axiom, to always lead, mystify and surprise the enemy. Then when you strike and overcome him, you must never let up in the pursuit. Jackson felt that if a routed army were pursued, it would quickly become panic stricken and then a force half its size could defeat it. That was where the Confederacy erred at Gettysburg, it had not learned well from Jackson. They did not pursue that first day.

Lee understood that here at Franklin the pursuit must be finalized. The Federal army had unknowingly tipped their hand that they were in obvious peril. For if they thought for a second that they could offer battle, they would not have retreated from Pulaski to Franklin. The fact that they had artillery at Fort Granger meant two things.

The first, as Forrest had pointed out was that they could fire directly at any force that approached their defenses. But there was a second fact that was more important to Lee. The guns were across the river so that they could be pulled out in a hurry if the force at Franklin were defeated. Lee knew that with every move Schofield made, defeat was lounging in the back of his mind like an uninvited guest. That needed to be exploited.

However, here at Franklin, just as at Gettysburg, there would be no General Jackson at his side. Lee looked around the room, knowing full well who would have to become his new right arm. Staring back at him from only a few feet away was Patrick Cleburne. The charismatic Irishman had no idea the future Lee had in store for him. But one thing was certain, after the victory in Tennessee, Lee would not return to Virginia alone. Jackson's old corps was going to be led by Cleburne.

"I have listened to General Hood's proposal for attack, and must admit that it is sound," Lee continued. "The enemy will not remain on this side of the river for much longer. Schofield only wants you to believe that he intends to stay and fight, but I can assure you that his position is a mere ruse to allow him some time so that he can fall back at an hour more conducive to his liking. Hood is also correct in that we must expect General Thomas to be gathering forces around Nashville. That city is not far from here. The strength of the two separated Federal armies is in their consolidation. We cannot provoke them into doing that sooner than we want."

Lee turned to Forrest. Lee had a lot of respect and admiration for how the man handled his cavalry in the field. What did not impress him was Forrest's disrespect for authority, and the allegations surrounding his actions at Fort Pillow. Before joining Hood, Forrest had led his men on an attack against Negro and white Union troops at Fort Pillow. When victory seemed apparent to Forrest, he claimed that he offered the Union garrison a chance to surrender. He said that he feared what his men would do to the colored troops. The Yankees foolishly objected and the result was a stain to the Confederacy.

It was said that after Forrest achieved his victory, all of the black troops and the white officers had been butchered. Forrest had since denied the report, and since Forrest meant too much to the south, President Davis had not done much to verify the account. The North did not accept it so lightly. They used the massacre as a rallying cry against the so-called tyranny of the South. It was just as Cleburne had said last night, when he pointed out how the North was rallying behind slavery in order to keep

Europe out of the war… and Fort Pillow was their propaganda. Unfortunately, Fort Pillow was a matter Lee would have to take up with Forrest at some other time, for right now he had to make sure that Forrest would respect his orders. He knew that he could not allow Forrest's tenacious demeanor to dictate how he must treat him. Perhaps it was the fault of many previous commanders who tried to deal with Forrest. They did so with careful attention and that would be the problem. Forrest could not be allowed any such special attention. He had to be ordered just as any other commander in the army.

"Forrest, your plan to flank the enemy would not be a benefit to this army while we are this close to Nashville." Lee waited for a reaction from Forrest that never materialized. That was good. "However, I am in support of you keeping your command together and attacking the enemies flank." A strong exhalation from behind him told him that Hood did not agree.

Lee expected as much, but the analogy that formed in his head at that moment was too perfect to have come from his own subconscious. Surely the Lord had a hand in it, as He did in everything. Lee thanked God for the blessing. "General Hood told you of his battle at Gaines Mill when he led a savage attack up a well fortified hill and broke the enemy. I can testify that it was not an easy feat. Several prior attempts were made and failed miserably. I thank God every day that Hood was there to lead his Texans in that attack.

I have known Hood for a long time and have shared much with him both before this war and now during it. And there is one thing that I have never told him, and I hope he does not mind my saying so now. But there was a time in this war when I had lost a tremendous opportunity by not seeking council and listening to my trusted generals. And at Gettysburg, John, I should have listened to you. If you will remember, that battlefield was defended much like the one we are on today. Only it was I sending my men straight into the enemy, and it was you who suggested flanking the enemy to gain his rear. You may not have known that I knew that, but I did. And I, like a blind fool, adamantly objected. And because of that, this war still wages on over a year later."

Hood fought against the warm tear that was swelling in the corner of his eye. He never knew that Lee had known how much he objected to his plan that called for his attack upon Round Top mountain. Hood saw an opportunity to outflank their position and gain the Union's rear. However, Longstreet told Hood that Lee was in objection to any such maneuver, and that Hood must obey the order. That order cost his men a defeat and him, the use of an arm. And now, only a year later, here Hood was, adamantly objecting to Forrest's flank attack just as Lee did to him at Gettysburg. Would it take the loss of one of Forrest's limbs to show Hood the folly of his ways?

"General Forrest," Lee said. "Take your cavalry and do what you can against the enemy's flank. The division that you request cannot be spared from what this army is being asked to do. My hope lies in the men that make up the Army of Tennessee, that they can march forward and achieve a breakthrough that will allow them to drive the enemy into the river. At the same time, I hope your cavalry might threaten Fort Granger and drive away whatever force the enemy has there. Your presence there should threaten Schofield's only hope of escape."

Lee had to stop for a moment to take a breath. As he thought of the attack that was about to commence, he could not help but become excited with the anticipation of victory. His chest began to pound like a deep drum. A sharp pain ran up his right arm as if there were a loose string within his limb that had just been pulled taught. Cheatham noticed that his face had gone pale and quickly brought him a glass of water.

Lee was visibly embarrassed, but took the water and allowed it to wet his lips. "I am fine now, thank you," he said. "Now please, follow General Hood's orders for this day and deliver your country the victory that will set our people free. Deliver the victory that will allow the men in the army of Virginia the chance to stand up from their trenches and drive the Yankees from Virginia soil for the last time."

One of the generals shouted a cheer and all the men in the room soon took it up. Forrest was the first to approach Lee and gratefully thanked him for allowing his cavalry to remain consolidated. "General Lee, I am eternally in your debt for what you have done for me today," he said.

"General Forrest, you do not need to thank me. You have been nothing but an asset to this army. But one thing I do ask, and I hope that you are not offended. There must not be anything like another Fort Pillow. I am not judging you, only God can judge, I am only telling you that whatever happened there, it's results have hurt our chances of independence."

Forrest's face turned a deep crimson, but not a single word lashed from his lips. Lee was impressed. "Nathan, I only want you to understand that I trust you, and hold you with the most respect."

All of the repressed anger let out of Forrest's face in one massive deluge. A wide grin split his face as he considered what Lee had said. "Then we understand each other General Lee. Now if you will excuse me, I wish to see if I can also gain the respect of the Yanks at Fort Granger." Forrest laughed hard, as he shook hands with Lee and turned to leave. "Again, I thank you for what you have done for my cavalry, and I can assure you that there will never be another Fort Pillow. I was not at fault for that."

Lee nodded and watched him leave. He sincerely hoped that Forrest was telling the truth. Many others of those at the council came over to embrace Lee, including Governor Harris. Lee quickly shook hands with them all, but made his way after Cleburne, who had just exited through the front door.

Lee walked into the warm sun and saw the Irish general standing amongst several of his officers as they prepared to mount and ride to the front. Lee was brought his horse and the chestnut mare reminded him of how much he missed Traveler. He knew that Taylor would take exceptional care of his favorite horse while he was away, but it did little to comfort the great loss he felt without his trusty steed beneath him.

Lee paused in stride as he watched General Hood and General Cheatham approach Cleburne. There was an acute conversation passed between Cheatham and Hood, ending with Cleburne nodding his head with approval. Hood patted Cleburne's shoulder before departing towards General Stewart's corps. Cheatham also said a few words to Cleburne. From the look on Cheatham's face, he knew that the general was not sure if he would see his brigadier commander again.

Cleburne then turned with his staff and began proceeding towards Winstead Hill. Lee cantered towards the general and called to him, as he grew nearer. Cleburne turned a heavy head towards the rear and smiled as he saw Lee approaching. The Irish commander told his men to continue and make preparations for the ensuing assault. He wanted this moment with Lee to be a private one.

"General Lee, I am thankful that you have made it here in time for this battle," he said.

"As am I," Lee returned. Lee looked at the soldiers that

were in proximity and realized that his presence at Franklin was no longer a secret. "It is almost time to reveal to all of this army that I am here. General, I know that you are surprised that I am in agreement with Hood's decision to attack the enemy."

Cleburne did not answer. He did not have to. The thinning of his eyelids said it all.

"Your sash that lays under your belt has magnificent color," Lee said.

Cleburne took a moment to look down and appreciate the sash's red crimson hue. Would his blood be soaked upon it before this day was through? "That is one strong position that the enemy occupies," he said without lifting his eyes from the sash. "But if you believe that the Yanks must be attacked today, then I promise you that my men will give them hell."

Lee placed his horse adjacent to Cleburne's. He placed a warm and concerned hand upon the general's shoulder. "If I did not believe it to be so, I would never have agreed with General Hood. I have prayed long and hard on this, I truly believe that God has put me here at such a time for no other reason. I am ashamed to say this, but I have also asked the Lord to take special care in protecting you today."

Cleburne looked up and let out a deep breath.

"Patrick, please promise that you will be careful. A victory here, with your loss would be a devastation to this army. Chancellorsville has already taught me as much. The Confederacy needs generals such as you, I need a general such as you."

Cleburne nodded his head and the two rode towards his division in melancholic silence. From the southern slopes of Breezy Hill, Lee could see the distinct white moon on the battle flags of Cleburne's division as they were being lifted in arms.

"General, tonight, when the darkness sets upon this battlefield, I expect to see the moon, shining in all its pale glory, over that town of Franklin."

Cleburne looked into the distance trying to imagine what it would be like to survive this day and have his flags hurling over victory. His hopes were evident in his catatonic response. "In less than half an hour, my division is to form to the right of this pike, my left will be overlapped by the right flank of General Brown's division. To our far right, General Stewart's corps will march along the Lewisburg Pike and engage the enemy just west of the railroad line. Once over these hills, my men will march over an open land straight into the muzzles and canister of the enemy. I have orders not to fire until we run their skirmish line from their initial position. We are then to pursue them closely so that we can engage the main works in their rear."

He then reached into a satchel that hung on the side of his horse and produced a small book. He held it in his hands for a few seconds before leaning over towards Lee and handing it to him. Lee accepted it, but was puzzled.

"That is my personal journal of this war," he said. It was his way of telling Lee that he did not think that he was going to be coming back. "I have sworn to take the enemy's works or die trying. General Lee, I can only hope that you have given what I said last night a lot of thought. Hood is proclaiming that Franklin is the key to Nashville and Nashville the key to independence. Well, Hood is in for a surprise. Whether we win or loose here at Franklin does not matter. As long as we retain the Negro as a slave, we will in the end, lose this war. In effect, it is our own dogmatic ignorance, and not any might of the North, that denies us our independence."

The color was quickly returning to Cleburne's face as he began to regain his sense of purpose. He removed a delicate kerchief from inside his jacket and held it tightly before his dry lips. "I have always proclaimed that I have never feared dying in battle, and until very recently that has been true. But now I am engaged to the most magnificent woman in the South. The thought of being separated from her fills my heart with great sadness."

As Lee waited for Cleburne to continue, he noticed a bulbous tear fighting to escape the corner of Cleburne's eye. "General Lee, I fully accept my responsibility in this attack, I just do not want to die without reason," Cleburne said.

Lee placed Cleburne's diary within the breast of his jacket. He watched as Cleburne carefully tucked the kerchief back inside his jacket. The soft linen obviously belonged to his fiancé, and the way that Cleburne took such deliberate effort in resting it against his chest, he must have believed that the love it represented could ward off any bullet intended for him.

Lee wanted to comment on the kerchief, a brief moment to mention its beauty, he also wanted to tell Cleburne that he had been reflecting upon his opinions concerning the slavery issue, but there just was not enough time. Cleburne needed to remain focused on the battle that lay ahead.

"Patrick, what are General Hood's orders once you achieve the breakthrough?" he asked. Cleburne shrugged his shoulders, and then felt a great despair at the realization. Once his men had reached the enemy, they would probably become so entangled with the other divisions that they would be too disorganized to continue. Cleburne looked towards Lee for advice.

Lee had been thinking of this attack since the council back at Hood's headquarters. What he was reminded of was Grant's attack at Spotsylvania a few months ago. Had he observed such an offensive tactic before, he would have employed it at Gettysburg and the fate of that day may have been very different.

"General," he said. "When you break the enemy's line, be sure to contain your men and not let them charge wildly into the rear. Have one brigade wheel to the right and one wheel to the left. Hold that ground, and I will send in General Stephen Lee to exploit the breakthrough."

"What of my third brigade," Cleburne asked?

"Choose your best brigade for this," Lee said. "They must push ahead and make for the bridge in the rear and prevent the enemy from escaping across the Harpeth. They must understand they are not permitted to retire from that position. I do not care if the entire Federal army stands against them, they are not to retire."

Cleburne was about to reply when a loud roar trembled the earth. Lee and Cleburne had both become so entwined in their conversation that they had failed to notice the flock of soldiers gathering around them. The crowd began assembling when a passing soldier said that he thought the man riding with Cleburne was General Robert E. Lee.

The claim was received with skepticism, but the soldier was so convincing, many others ventured for a look of their own. When they all unanimously agreed that it was Lee, the word passed like flame through dry hay. When enough of them surrounded Lee, they began to roar with unexpected hope. The roar quickly turned into the rebel yell, until finally taking on a single recognizable word. With hats raised and hearts filled with a renewed hope, they repeated one name over and over again. "Lee... Lee... Lee..."

Lee was ashamed. He often felt this way when he was received so. Only one person deserved such praise and that was the Almighty. He raised his hat as he leaned close to Cleburne's ear, "These men must be told to keep this a secret from the enemy."

Lee then shook Cleburne's hand and rode off to find General Hood. The men of Cleburne's division kept up the cheer long after he was gone.

Brigadier General Govan approached Cleburne and smiled. "It is good to see these boys this fired up. Look at my brigade, such enthusiasm I have not seen in a very long time. But we have both seen that Yankee position. There will not be many of us left when we get back to Arkansas."

Cleburne stared past Govan hoping to see Lee one last time. Perhaps this was the turning point that Cleburne so desperately sought. Lee was now in command of this army, and tucked neatly under Lee's jacket was the Confederacy's last hope. Cleburne eyes thinned for a second time this day, though he knew it would not be the last.

Cleburne whipped out his saber and flashed it towards Franklin. He then spurred his horse and galloped towards the front with words that Govan would never forget.

"Well Govan, if we are to die, then let us die like men."

*   *   *   *   *   *   *   *

A short while later, the sun had fallen further to the west. As if coming from a dream, the tune of Dixie could be heard. The prideful melody was soon drowned out when Hood's two corps rolled forward and shook the earth. Resplendent with over twenty thousand soldiers, they represented the last best hope for Southern independence.

Chapter XXV
Franklin, Tennessee
Battle of Franklin

Wilson stood before Schofield with all the grace of a delinquent in detention. From outside Fort Granger, they could hear and feel the artillery of the Twenty-third as it began shelling the Confederate advance towards Franklin. Wilson was embarrassed to be here and delivering such a report, but he would never let Schofield know that. He managed to hold his head high, even though he was at Fort Granger to report yet more shortcomings caused by his cavalry.

Earlier, a brigade of rebel cavalry had crossed Hughes Ford, three miles southeast of Franklin. Initially this caused Schofield much concern. His greatest fear was that Forrest would cross the Harpeth and wedge his cavalry in between his army and Nashville. Thus far, Wilson had managed to prevent that from happening, and being this close to Nashville, he did not want to fall short now.

Wilson had replied to that rebel threat by promising to counter the enemy with Hatch's division. Hatch had over twenty-five hundred troopers near the Mathew's house and could quickly move forward and push the rebels back across the river. That was the assurance that Schofield was given when he departed from the Truett house towards Fort Granger. It was also the assurance that allowed him to countermarch Wood's brigade to the north banks of the Harpeth. In the event of a disaster at Franklin, he needed Wood's command in place to support the withdrawal across the river. Schofield had to keep reminding himself that Hood would attack in one place or the other. One attack would be a ruse, and prior to Schofield's arrival at the fort, he thought he knew which was which.

However, when he arrived at Fort Granger, he was quick to discover that Wilson had failed him once again. Hatch's cavalry had been able to push the enemy back over the hills towards Hughes Ford, but that was where the Federal tide was abruptly stopped. Hatch's reports stated that he was outnumbered and being driven back towards Fort Granger by Forrest's entire command.

The question that still hung over Schofield like a swinging pendulum, was whether or not Hampton's brigade was with Forrest?

"General Wilson, my choices here are very limited," Schofield said. He could feel the heat of anger claiming his face.

"As are mine. You can not expect Hatch with fewer than three thousand men to hold off the entire rebel cavalry."

"He has to," Schofield shot back. "Perhaps you need to take command of the field at once. Do you not hear the guns firing around us, we can not be cut off here, and right now the entire Confederate army is advancing on my men at Franklin."

Wilson held firm. "Sir, I can assure you that I hear the guns just fine. But I am not sure how that solves your problem."

"Are you trying to be sarcastic with me?" Schofield fired.

"No at all, I hold your commanding skills in the highest of respect."

The amount of sarcasm that was packed into that statement was almost more than Schofield could swallow. "You must find a way to delay Forrest until tonight. He must be held off so that I can pull this army away from here."

"And how would you suggest I do this? You have already taken Wood's division from my support."

"That was because you told me that Hatch's division could drive the enemy back across the river… or have you forgotten as much already? Listen General, you have not done my army any service of substance since your arrival."

"It could easily be said the same of you General Schofield."

Schofield thought of striking his cavalry commander, but held back. Right now, the Federal army needed him more than ever, and he could not afford to waste any time engaging in a fisticuffs with Wilson. Hood would attack with either the cavalry or the infantry. It would be one or the other, one was a ruse and one was the real thing. The question again, was which was which?

He had to consider both possibilities. The advance of Hood's corps at Franklin was intimidating, but it was also a tactic that had not been demonstrated by Hood at any point of this campaign. Hood's offensive during this campaign had always been to outflank his command. He did this both at Pulaski and at Columbia. Even when Hood had him trapped at Spring Hill, he had still not attacked. Why would he do so now?

On the other hand, Forrest's maneuver complied so well with all that had been done thus far. It was always Forrest's objective to try and gain his rear. Luckily, the Confederates had failed each and every time, but might that be different if now Forrest had an additional brigade from Hampton?

Schofield began to believe that he now understood the rebel attack. It was as he initially thought when this day first began. "General Wilson, the attack by Hood is the ruse. I am sure of that now. The main attack is to be delivered by General Forrest. I will order these guns to be repositioned so that they can fire into the oncoming threat of their cavalry. I will also order General Wood's division back to your support. Would that be enough for you to hold Forrest off?"

Wilson nodded his head in approval. "I will ride now to general Hatch and deliver the order myself," Wilson said. "Forrest will be held south of Fort Granger. And after nightfall, your army will cross the river and my command will comply with the original plans of guarding the wagon trains towards Nashville. But we had better be far from this place come morning," he said.

Schofield turned away from Wilson and held his hand at waist level so that he could see the tremors that vibrated it like a wrung bell. Without turning back around he said, "Please go now and for once do as you promise."

The only response was the sound of the door closing in anger.

*　　*　　*　　*　　*　　*　　*　　*

They peered over their low-lying defenses as their skirmish line sprinted back to them like frightened dear. The word that was spread down the line was that the entire Confederate army was marching towards their position, and to the men that made up Conrad and Lane's brigades, that was all the reason they needed to give up their ludicrous position and retire to the main earthworks that were only a few hundred feet behind them. However, proper military protocol required that they first receive the order to do so.

Many of the men waited nervously and anxiously for the call to fall back. They gripped their rifles all the more when the shells began to fly overhead. Surely that would coax Wagner into giving the order to retreat. Many of the men were too proud to

384

look towards the rear, but just as many were not. They could see the entire Federal army nestled in a consummate defensive position and longed to be with them. Then they heard the drums and the bands playing the tune that many knew would mean their end. Dixie filled their ears with forlorn trepidation.

Upon the heels of the tune followed what looked like an entire corps of Confederates. Many of the Federals could easily see the blue flags of Cleburne's men hurling with the wind. The rebels came to halt a mere five hundred yards from them and began to shift from columns into the well-known two line battle formation. The guns from Fort Granger began to pound their position and as the smoke clouded their vision, many of Wagner's men hoped it would deter the attack. But to their horror, the solid lines of gray mass began to emerge from the smoke and move forward.

Then came the word that must have been delivered by the devil, for it ricocheted along the line spreading panic and despair. General Wagner had denied the request for them to fall back. They had been ordered to hold their position and refuse their ground to the enemy. The men looked amongst each other as if somehow the courier had made a mistake. The size of the enemy force approaching them was indubitable. The guns from Fort Granger continued to deny their advance, and yet they still came. Adding their support to the artillery barrage were the guns unlimbered within the earthworks behind them. As the shells crashed into the Confederate ranks they caused large gaping holes in their formations. Unfortunately for the Federals, it seemed as quickly as the gaps were opened, they were filled with additional troops.

The rebels neared to three hundred feet when a massive crescendo of artillery poured down upon them from every gun that was able to fire. The cloud of smoke that billowed from this impact soared into the sky with such force, many of the Yankees thought that it carried every rebel with it.

But then the guns from Fort Granger fell ominously silent.

And slowly, the smoke began to dissipate revealing the menacing rebel army only a few hundred feet away. Men on both sides were wondering why the guns from the fort had ceased. Many in blue yelled to keep up the fire. A few more rounds of that force would surely send the Confederates reeling back over Winstead Hill.

Then from somewhere within the mass of Confederates

they heard an order yelled to all who could hear. 'Forward men.' The line moved forward again, and this time there were no guns from Fort Granger to stop them. Even the guns from the main line could no longer be fired for risk that they would hit Wagner's isolated division. Conrad and Lane knew that they would now have to hold this position without any support from their artillery.

They began to fire their rifles into the oncoming wave, but their officers ordered them to hold back until the enemy was closer. At one hundred feet, the rebel line paused. Many of Conrad and Lane's men used this time to pray to their God that the rebs' would retire. Then they noted the grim look in the eyes of the enemy. It was reflected on the cold steel of their bayonets. From behind, they heard their officers yell to fire and in that instant a sheet of lead was sent towards the Confederates.

Once again a cloud of gun smoke obscured their view. Instead of reloading their rifles, Conrad's brigade was more concerned with trying to hear any sound that would indicate that the rebels were retiring. Instead, they heard that same voice issuing orders from somewhere deep within their gray ranks. 'Forward men.'

Whoever he was, the officer had a determination in his tone that was unlike anything that they had ever heard before. It was so compelling that many of the Federal soldiers felt the need to obey it and follow his command.

That bewilderment ended abruptly, when the men of Conrad and Lane's brigades heard the rebel yell as it carried the enemy through the smoke, and hurled them at their line. For many of the Federal's present, they had stood their ground long enough. They dropped their guns and sprinted for the safety of the main earthworks to their rear. Their rout was infectious. Soon the whole line had come apart and the entire two brigades were in a chaotic race for Cox's trenches behind them. Many of them never made it there. With their backs to the enemy, they were easy targets for Cleburne's division.

The fleeing Federal division paid no attention to their fallen companions. They were hastened towards Franklin on the momentum of four promising words, "Rally behind the works." For many of the Confederates that heard that, it was a reminder to stay close in their pursuit of the enemy. They watched as the Yankees fought with each other in desperation to climb the parapets of the main line. From this close, they also realized how formidable Cox's defensive position was and reasoned that as long as they could keep themselves close to the force that they had just routed, then the main line could not fire into them. If they did, they would risk hitting many of their own men. It was for this reason that the Yankee rally cry was also taken up by the charging Confederates, "Rally behind their works. Follow them, right into the works with them boys."

*   *   *   *   *   *   *   *

Cleburne rode close to his men as they advanced. He also noted the disadvantage that the enemy had in firing at his men. He also knew that it would not be long before someone within those lines got desperate and ordered their main line to fire at his men even at the risk of hitting their own retreating troops. If he were within those lines, he would have done so already. Cleburne knew this window of opportunity would not remain open much longer. He lifted his hat from his head and with his other hand raised his saber. "Onward men, follow them into their works."

The regiments that made up Cleburne's brigades were now so mixed together it was hard to move them with any sort of cohesion. Yet with the words of their commander pushing them along, they continued forward. Then the guns of the enemy erupted just as Cleburne had assumed. Luckily, there were still many Federals fleeing before them to bear the brunt of the canister. Cleburne could see his men moving forward towards the gap in the earthworks along the Franklin Pike. He still could not believe that Hood's bold frontal assault was actually working. Now that he could see that victory was possible, his spirit was renewed.

With his hat waving wildly, Cleburne led his men through the gap and into Cox's earthworks. The two armies were now fully entwined with all the hatred of hell and earth twice over.

*   *   *   *   *   *   *   *

Through their field glasses, General Lee and General Hood watched the battle unfold from the heights of Winstead Hill. Though standing only a few feet apart, mentally, the two generals were miles apart. For Hood, the spectacle before him was like watching the manifestation of his aggression. Aimed at crushing the Federal army entrenched around Franklin, his two corps swung forward as if they were his own two fists. Clenched deep within these gripped palms was all the hate and fury that they could contain. Hood was jabbing with Stewart as his corps marched along the Lewisburg Pike to tangle themselves with the enemy east of the Carter Cotton Gin. But it was Cleburne and Brown's divisions of Cheatham's corps that would deliver the haymaker as it rapidly changed its formation and began to advance towards the only break in the enemies defenses, the gap left open by the Franklin to Columbia Pike. Flanking this main attack was Bate's division. Hood watched as Bate's men made their way for the Carter Creek Pike. The gap between them and Brown's division was quickly widening to the point that there was no way that they could offer any support.

Hood was reluctant to agree with Forrest and allow his cavalry to rush off like they had, and the widening distance between Bate and rest of his attack was the very reason why. Bate's division was not going to be much of a threat to the Federals if they did not receive additional support.

It did not take the Federal command long to begin using their artillery in an attempt to impede the Confederate advance. As Cleburne and Brown advanced towards the enemy, the guns from Fort Granger began to come alive with lead. Soon the entire field was covered with smoke, making it hard for him to observe the movements of his men. Hood bitterly wondered what Forrest was doing at this time. He should have forced his way across the ford by now.

A steady wind rolled through the valley and helped to clear away much of the smoke caused by the artillery. Hood was able to see his army moving forward again. Hood had to allow himself a moment to appreciate the sight before him. Nearly two thirds of his army, over twenty thousand men strong had just taken a shelling from the enemy and still they held their ranks and moved on. A cheer erupted from the men gathered on the hill, and Hood himself let out a holler. But the cheering soon ended as Cleburne and Brown drew to within a few hundred yards from the enemy's position. In one instant, it seemed as if every piece of enemy artillery erupted at the same time.

The force was so strung that it violently shook the hill that

Hood and Lee stood upon. Once again his view was clouded from the smoke. For a moment, despair set in, he was sure that there was no way his men could remain organized under such conditions. To his right, the scene was just as inauspicious. Stewart's corps, over ten thousand men, seemed to be slowing and congesting due to the hindering Osage hedges to their front. The brambles were so thick that units were completely entangled trying to get through. The roughly five thousand Yankees nestled behind these defenses had the leisure of firing at will at the impeded enemy. Stewart's men were being cut to pieces.

Hood quickly looked back towards the thrust in the center. To his surprise, as soon as the massive volley ended, it grew silent. The guns from Fort Granger were no longer firing. Forrest, he thought. Forrest must have made his way across the fords and was threatening Schofield's flank. Schofield must think Forrest the more serious threat and is countering with his guns.

Hood looked through his field glasses begging for anything that could indicate the condition of his army. He began to see the colors of his army as they rose above the smoke on the battlefield. The blue flags of Cleburne's division were moving forward with terrible speed. A futile volley was fired at them from the defenders in the exposed position outside of the main earthworks, but that was all. The Federals gathered there were quickly fleeing for the safety behind the main line. Cleburne's men were following close behind.

Hood placed his entire future on this one assault and he gladly accepted the responsibility. This attack must be made now, or it would never be. Hood kept his eyes fixed to his field glasses as he willed Cheatham's division into the enemies earthworks.

*   *   *   *   *   *   *   *

For Robert E. Lee, what he saw to this point was nothing short of a catharsis. Watching Hood's army advance across the open fields, he could not help but be reminded of Gettysburg. When he heard the Federal guns began to bellow, he thought of General Picket, and then he thought of all that was lost on that day. Pickets dejected face hung before him, an onus for whatever would happen on this day in Franklin.

Lee had to drop his glasses to his waist as his view became obscured with clouds of gun smoke. Please God, do not let this be another Gettysburg, he silently prayed. Lee instinctively turned to seek the support of Taylor, but his trusty officer could not be found. Taylor was left behind in Virginia with the rest of his army.

The sound of General Hood hollering next to him forced Lee to gaze though his glasses again. The scene was magnificent. It was like the dream he had of Jackson returning to lead his men at Gettysburg. And just like in that dream, the men of Cheatham's corps marched undaunted from the enemy's artillery. They continued marching in the face of peril, until the Federal guns fired once again in perfect unison. This time Lee held his glasses secure to his face. Would that last volley cause his shattered ranks to crawl back to their lines as they had at Gettysburg?

Lee waited patiently for something to happen, but for a few moments nothing did. Not even the Federal artillery were firing anymore. Then he heard a wild sound coming from the center of the line. Lee could not see very well, but he knew the rebel yell enough to know that it was never sounded unless they were advancing.

Lee quickly looked to the left and right of the attack along the Franklin to Columbia Pike. General Bate was swinging too wide, and he had too few men to cause the Federal any real concern. Lee figured that it would not take Schofield long to begin sending regiments from his right flank to support his center. To Lee's right, Stewart's attack had come to an abrupt halt. The defensive position occupied by the Federals proved to be too much for the rebels to overcome. Lee could make out some units trying to march around the railroad cut and gain the enemies rear. That won't work, he thought. This whole attack depends on the center. With that thought, Lee looked again towards the center of the Federal Line. He could see his men pouring through the main Federal earthworks. They had even managed to capture a few guns and were quickly turning them around to face the enemy.

Then he saw the specter that had been haunting him over the past year, seem to materialize upon the field before him. Lee knew that General Armistead personally led his men into the enemy works at Gettysburg. One of his last heroic gestures of that day was placing his hat upon his sword to show his men the way forward. It would be the last service Armistead would perform for his country. Lee thought of Armistead fondly as he watched as an officer below waved his own hat and saber urging his men into the Federal works.

Lee could see the pale moon resting upon the blue flags of Cleburne's division and came to the frightening realization that the man who waved his hat below was indeed Cleburne. Please be careful, God protect him, he thought.

Then he thought of the man who Cleburne reminded him more of. General Jackson. Lee often wondered how Jackson's presence might have made a difference at Gettysburg. He was about to find out.

"General Hood," Lee called, breaking the silence. "I believe that Stephen Lee's corps is ready to enter this battle. If I may suggest, the time is now to send them in."

Hood nodded his head as he rested his field glasses on the saddle before him. He turned around and saw the flags of his last corps arriving up the Franklin to Columbia Pike. The flags of Johnson's division were leading the procession. Hood had to take a moment and thank God for Lee's arrival. Initially, he had intended to have Stephen Lee's corps delay their arrival into Franklin. He thought that Cheatham and Stewart could handle the Federals without the need for him to use his third corps. But now that they were on hand, Hood intended to use them. He looked towards the west, where the sun was making its steady decline in the sky. Lee's corps had plenty of time to carry the battle before the daylight was fully gone.

"I instructed Cleburne to push for the bridges that cross the Harpeth," Lee said. "I believe that Cleburne is on the verge of a breakthrough. I trust he will continue towards the enemy's rear to cut off his escape." Lee said no more, though he wanted to.

Anyone observing the battlefield could ascertain where the three divisions of Stephen Lee's corps needed to be. Stewart's corps on the right was stopped in its tracks. With Cleburne pushing his corps to the rear, Lee could use one of his divisions to move through the break in the line and then wheel to flank the Federals positioned east of the cotton gin. The other division would need to support Cheatham in keeping the breakthrough open. The third division should continue along the pike until it could reinforce Cleburne in preventing the enemy from escaping. But Lee chose not to voice any of this. He did not want Hood to think that he was taking over control of his army.

Hood called for his chief of staff. Mason was nearby and

quickly rode over. "If Cleburne is moving on, then Johnson's division will be needed to outflank those Yanks that are giving Stewart such a hard time. Inform General Stephen Lee to have Johnson's men continue along this pike until they reach the enemy's main line. From there they are to wheel to their right and deliver enfilading fire upon the enemy. Also send word to General Stewart that he is to hold his front, help is on the way. Do you know which division is marching behinds Johnson's?"

"I believe it is Stevenson's," Mason said.

"Excellent, inform Lee that Stevenson will also follow along this pike until they reach the enemy's works, but they will wheel left and prevent the enemy from supporting its left flank. My intention is for the complete destruction of all the Union infantry east of this pike. Make sure that General Stephen Lee understands this. He must understand this, there can be no more mistakes."

Mason waited for Hood's instruction for Lee's last corps, but Hood turned back around on his saddle to view the battle. "Excuse me General, but what about Clayton's division".

Hood did not turn back to face him. "Have Clayton support General Bate's division."

Lee's first impulse begged him to counter that order, but he did not want to offend Hood. Clayton's division could do so much more if it headed straight for the enemy's rear. However, there was also a benefit in assisting General Bate. It may help prevent Schofield's right flank from moving across the field to help his center and left. With Cleburne's division holding the breakthrough open and the combined majority of Cheatham, Stewarts and Lee's corps isolating the Federal left, the battle should quickly turn into the complete victory that Lee failed to achieve against both McClellan at Richmond and Hooker at Chancellorsville. The difference this time was that with Cleburne pushing through the breakthrough, the Confederates would hold the bridges and fords that in the past were left open to allow the Federal army to escape.

Not this time, he thought. God willing, not this time.

*   *   *   *   *   *   *   *

General Jacob Cox raced his horse towards the Carter

House. The battle raging a few hundred yards before him was rapidly turning into a rout by his men. Cox was unsure who he was more mad at, the rebels driving his men from their formidable works, or Wagner for causing this entire debacle. Had Wagner pulled his two brigades back as instructed, the enemy would never have reached his main line. That he was sure of. Every cannon, and every rifle could have delivered volley after volley of lead into the oncoming ranks. The impressive advance of the Confederate army would have stumbled back to General Hood in bits and pieces of scattered regiments and disorganized brigades. But because Wagner's men remained in position in front of all those guns, Cox could not allow the bulk of his guns to fire at the enemy, in fear that they would hit their own men.

Cox pulled on the reins of his mount and found a staff officer trying to rally several soldiers that were trying to hide inside the Carter House. One of the men had actually managed to use his bayonet and cut a hole in the back door. Others were banging on the door that led into the cellar. Cox could not believe it, but even with the sounds of gunfire and men fighting, he could make out Fountain Carter screaming from the cellar to leave him and his family alone.

Cox looked towards his main line in time to see it dissolve under a sea of gray foam. The Fiftieth Ohio and the Seventy-second Illinois were completely overrun and their men were now headed towards the second line of trenches near the Carter Garden. Cox cursed Wagner for a second time this day. A quick look around revealed that the only thing left to stop the rebels besides a section of artillery and a few regiments was the Carter smoke house and small office building that rested behind his line. Instead of being routed, Wagner's division should have been positioned here in reserve, to counter any such breakthrough. By disobeying his order to pull his brigades to the Carter House, Wagner had deprived Cox of his only reserves in this critical section of the battlefield.

The rebel yell almost tore Cox's ears completely from his head. He turned to see his center give way like a weakened dam before a massive deluge. The gray mass of rebels poured over the Federal defenses and was continuing towards the Carter house. In his entire military career, Cox had never felt so helpless.

Then, from behind the Carter House emerged General Stanley riding at the head of what was left of Opdycke's brigade.

They were only a few companies strong, but perhaps they would be enough to stall the enemy's advance in time for General Ruger's regiments to reach the rear. Cox began calling for Ruger to slide his men down the line as soon as he saw that the only threat to his right flank was a single division of Confederate infantry headed for the Carter Creek Pike. Kimball had also been ordered to slide his regiment to the left, allowing for subsequent regiments to continue the slide, until they could form a new line of defense a few streets before the bridges over the Harpeth. Once they secured that position, Cox would order the rest of the army to fall back to that new consolidated position.

"General Cox, I believe my saber may do its best service by finding the breast of General Wagner, and impaling itself there," Stanley roared as he sent his small force into the approaching gray storm. The scene was one to make chaos appear lawful. The small companies from Opdycke's brigade as well as a few other regiments had to wade their way through the rest of the army that was fleeing past them. Once through, they had the task of trying to stop an entire division of infantry.

"General, if those rebels get through and hold that position, I fear that we will have lost the entire Third division of the Twenty-third corps," Cox said. "If this pike is held against us, Reilly, Casement and Stiles will be cut off and I do not know if this army will have enough men, or enough heart to go back in and cut them out."

Stanley gripped his saber all the more tighter. "That may be, but the more important task is ensuring that we hold those bridges open behind us. Forrest is on our flank, and the artillery from Fort Granger is being used to keep him from gaining our rear."

"I have already ordered Kimball and Ruger to send their men this way. The bridges will be held, at least until dark. After sundown, we had better get out of this hell if we ever wish to avenge this day."

Just as Cox finished speaking, Stanley's head was flung backwards in a most unnatural manner. Cox alertly reached over and kept him upon his horse. When he pulled the general forward, he noticed fresh blood dripping down his neck.

"I think I am fine," Stanley said. "It is just a graze."

Seeing that Stanley was not seriously injured he turned back towards the rushing Confederate menace. The rebels seemed unstoppable, as they poured over the second line of Federal earthworks and past the narrow passage between the smokehouse and the office building. But as soon as the first of the rebels emerged, they were met with a savage counterattack led by Opdycke's surviving company.

For a moment, the enemy's assault was stalled. General Stanley told Cox to use this time and do what he could to ensure that the bridges were held open. He then rubbed the blood from his neck and went riding after his routing army. If they could be reorganized, they would give him a substantial force to use against the rebels.

"Make sure that you have the name of every one of those men that are now charging the enemy," he said. "Damn brave men, they are. Damn brave."

Cox saluted Stanley, then turned to watch the effusive display of heroism being performed by a few hundred men against the hatred of several thousand.

Chapter XXVI
Franklin, Tennessee
The Battle Continues

Stray bullets buzzed by his ears like angry yellow jackets. He had to constantly tug on his mount's reins in order to have the horse avoid trampling upon the mass of blue and gray soldiers that blanketed the gentle rise of the earth with their crimson blood. Death was whizzing by him in the form of stinging lead, and the dead were laid before him as a carpet of human flesh. Lifeless eyes staring up at him, begging him to fall from his horse and lay beside them for a while. A normal man, unaccustomed to warfare and placed in this very saddle would probably have lost his stomach at such a sight. But for Patrick Cleburne, there was only one emotion swelling through his veins.

Pride.

Long ago, his mother had taught him that pride was a luxury served to the selfish. God himself punished those that shed their humility and gave way to egotistical arrogance. He knew his mother was right, but as he looked at the Federal trenches less then a hundred yards away, he could not help the strong sentiments that he felt for the men in his division.

He had received word that Stewart's Corps on his right flank had engaged the enemy, but were being repulsed. He knew that if there was going to be any chance for a victory on this day, it would have to come from the men in his and Brown's command. Of his three brigades currently engaged, only Lowry's was having difficulty in its efforts to drive the Federals from their salient around the cotton gin. As for Govan and Granbury's brigades, after the rout of Wagner's division, they had practically stampeded over the next line of Federal works and began driving Cox's next line of defense into the backyard of the Carter house.

Cleburne remembered young Theoderick Carter and quickly took a survey of the field to see if he could spot the vibrant boy. He truly hoped that Todd would not give in to his emotion and would stay far from harm's way.

Brown's division flanking his left had followed his men into the earthworks as well. From there, they had managed to capture several pieces of artillery and had turned them upon the enemy. He saw several of his soldiers running to the rear in an attempt to acquire firing pins. Apparently, some of the Yankees had enough sense to take the firing mechanism with them before they abandoned the line.

Though his losses were mounting, his division was still moving forward. The only set back was when a small counterattack smashed into his assault right in the Carter backyard. His men were initially surprised at the attack, and having been running and fighting for so long, their momentum was easily halted. Fortunately, the Federal counterattack did not have enough punch. Had there been a brigade there, and not a few companies, Cleburne seriously thought his tired men would have been pushed back in defeat. With the battle still hanging in the balance, Cleburne did not have time to wonder why Schofield did not have reserves in place at such a critical juncture in the Federal defensive line.

Cleburne saw Mangum running over to his side. He began to slow his mount so that Mangum could reach him, but his horse buckled underneath him. Mangum and a few other officers rushed over to help Cleburne to his feet.

"They shot my horse," was all he could say as he stood from the ground.

"I would rather it were a thousand horses than you," Mangum said.

Cleburne allowed a small smile. Mangum asked if he wanted another horse, and he did. Cleburne looked towards his right at the cotton gin and saw that, even though this portion of the field was in rout, the Yanks there were still putting up a strong resistance. He also knew that instinct would have his victorious brigades wheeling to the right in order to outflank such a formidable position. Soldiers inherently reacted in such a manner whenever they were able to position themselves around the enemy and force them to fight without the benefits of their trenches before them. He knew his men would be no different, and had General Lee not advised him against such a thing, he would have conceded with his men. But Lee had been very clear in what must be done. He was to continue on with his men and race for the bridges in the Yankee rear. More important than any victory was the possession of southern banks of the Harpeth. The bridges and fords were Schofield's only escape and Lee meant to deny him that.

Cleburne realized how much he had been sweating and unbuttoned his coat. He could see Mangum coming with a new horse, and farther behind him, closer to Winstead Hill than the battlefield, he could make out the flags of General Stephen Lee's corps. Reinforcements were on the way.

A tremendous wave of excitement vibrated down his spine and into his toes, leaving his skin covered in clammy goose bumps. He had witnessed enough battle to realize that something special was on the verge of occurring here. Schofield's entire army was in the process of not just being beaten, but with the capture of the bridges, it would be entirely eliminated from this war.

As soon as Mangum reached him with the new horse, Cleburne intended to ride forward and personally lead his men towards the Harpeth. Again, that pride was swelling within his throat with the knowledge that he was moments away from accomplishing a truly magnificent and monumental task. And that meant nothing to him in comparison to what it would mean to Susan Tarleton. He meant to make her the happiest bride in the South.

He could picture her, standing at the church, embossed in all her ethereal beauty, with her thick hair parted down the middle, just the way he liked it best. The smile on her thin lips would be enough to fill his heart forever with the comfort of knowing that his life had meant so much to her. The ring on her finger would be his simplest thanks for her devoted love.

Mangum brought the horse over to Cleburne and handed him the reins. "Here you are General, please be careful."

With the leather in his hands, Cleburne let the thoughts of his love dissipate. He was still on the field of battle, as there was still a lot to do before the day was done. He put one foot into the stirrup and lifted himself upon the horse. Just as his other leg had swung over the saddle, a small fiery projectile, one he never saw, threw him off the horse. The sight of the cotton gin was the last thing he saw before his back smashed into the ground.

He tried to look up through eyes that seemed to be veiled in a thin layer of water. The sky above him had never seemed so blue. When he tried to lift his hand, he realized something was very wrong. He could barely hear Mangum, who stood right over him, screaming for a doctor. Mangum was now bent over him, fingers seemed to be prodding his chest, just below his heart.

Cleburne tried to tell Mangum to lead the men towards the

rear, but the words would not form on his lips. There were other soldiers now gathered over him. He heard them say that Granbury was shot and that that disorganization and confusion was paralyzing the assault. 'Tell them to push on, tell them to push on' were the only words Cleburne could say, but as simple as they were, he failed to vocalize them.

The men above him had turned into dark shadows, indiscernible to him. The only face he could see now was that of Susan Tarleton. The thought of her having to be in the world without him caused him tremendous grief. The realization that this was to become a fact caused his heart to squeeze as if it were a lemon. Tears wanted to escape from his eyes and run over his face, but that too he was incapable of.

Patrick Cleburne remembered the church he passed on his way to Columbia. 'St. John', he tried to whisper, the words fell silent on dry lips. He thought that such a cemetery would make a fine place for eternal rest.

*   *   *   *   *   *   *   *

Todd Carter stood over the dead body of Patrick Cleburne and was consumed with hate for the enemy. Not only were these Yankee bastards in possession of his hometown, they were literally in his own back yard. Just before him was the home of his family. The Northern men who brought this war here had placed his family, his mother, in peril.

Todd took one more look at Cleburne and thought fondly on the short time he had getting to know the general. He had offered a challenge of checkers and Cleburne had actually accepted. Todd felt that Cleburne was being a bit too fatherly in offering him advice on how to stay away from danger. He appreciated his words of wisdom, but when it was your family that was in peril, there were no words strong enough to keep a man from saving his home.

Todd loaded his rifle and fixed his bayonet. He said a quick prayer over Cleburne's body, though long enough to notice that Cleburne had never released his fingers from its determined grasp of his saber. Todd inhaled that symbolism and followed the charging Confederates over the enemy's earthworks, towards his house a few hundred feet ahead of him.

He took three massive strides before a hail of lead felled him like a weak pine.

*   *   *   *   *   *   *   *

Once the men who made up the brigades of Govan, Granbury, Gordon, Gist and Strahl took possession of the Carter yard, they looked for their commanders for their next course of action. Those crucial orders took a very long time in coming. What many of the men did not know was that Generals Cleburne, Granbury, Gist and Strahl were all no longer on this earth. Officers were scrambling like headless chickens for their next orders.

General Gordon of Browns division sent word that Carter's brigade was held in check near the locust grove, and that a large body of Federal infantry was seen marching from the western portion of the field. Gordon knew that his men were spent and he needed reinforcements against the impending counterattack.

Unfortunately for Gordon, the other brigades were concerned with the resistance near the cotton gin than they were about any new Yankees that were not quite yet upon the field. Instead of looking west, their eyes were fixed in horror to the east, where they were watching rows of Yankee soldiers, some six men deep, delivering volley after punishing volley at the Confederates to their front. The men under Govan and Granbury's command did not need to be given any orders as to what was needed of them. Though many of them were exhausted beyond measure, the sight of Lowry and Walthall's regiments being shredded into confetti filled them with animosity.

Fortunately, it was at this moment when the firing pins found their way to the battery. The mechanisms were fitted into the captured artillery and the guns were rapidly turned towards the direction of the two-story cotton gin. A few moments later, the cotton gin and the Federals around it became victims of a wicked artillery barrage. The attack stunned the Federals for the second part of the assault. With a savage ferocity the Confederates charged headlong into the Federal right flank at the cotton gin and caused a massive rout of blue infantry. From the cotton gin to the railroad cut, the tightly woven yarn of the Federal defense quickly unwound. And once it started, there was no stopping it.

For the victorious Confederates the victory quickly turned into an immense moment of celebration. They waved their hats and fired their rifles into any blue back they could hit. But the victory was about all that these men could accomplish at the moment. Completely overcome with exhaustion, many of the Confederates lacked the energy to keep up the pursuit. It took the arrival of Stephen Lee's corps on the battlefield, for them to reform and renew their cheer.

But what these Confederate soldiers had not realized was that by their flanking maneuver they had allowed the Federal army the critical minutes it needed to reposition their troops from their own right flank towards the rear of Franklin. Kimball's regiments had marched with the speed of knowing that the very fate of their lives depended upon the moment they arrived to their designated position. A new line was constructed and soon the entire right flank of the Federal army was repositioned just south of the Harpeth.

The Federal infantry that were in position to the immediate west of the breakthrough were also able to withdraw from the rebel attack thanks to the thick locust grove to their front. They added their numbers to Cox's new line of defense.

As the sun set over Franklin, the rebel army had taken possession of all the Federal earthworks south of the Carter House. The Third division of the Federal army's Twenty-third corps no longer existed. The majority of it had been captured as the enemy pressed it from its flank and front. Those troops that were not dead or captured had long since routed from this war.

Many of the Confederates in possession of the Union earthworks saw the enemy concentrating and strongly believed that they would counterattack at any moment, but the timely arrival of General Stephen Lee's corps ensured that no such attack would be made. Having secured the breakthrough Stephen Lee sent word to Hood for additional orders. Hood and Robert E. Lee conferred and since Cleburne's division had not secured the bridges, Stephen Lee was told to attempt an assault in the dark. Lee sent Johnson's and Stephen's divisions against the newly formed Federal position, but the darkness kept their attacks uncoordinated. After suffering high causalities, Lee was forced to concede the attack. He would have to be content with the opinions of his senior commanders that the day had been a complete success.

However, the fact that was most critical to General Robert

E. Lee was that the Federal army had managed to regain possession of the bridges and the fords at the Harpeth. He knew all to well that once the sun arose, another Federal army would have escaped from total annihilation. And as the reports began to arrive, Lee also realized that there were far too many of his officers and generals that would not be with this army for the next fight.

There was one name in particular that caused his chest to hurt with such constricting pain that he nearly lost his balance. Lee waited for the tightening to subside and then fell to his knees beside his bed. A cold numbness overpowered his jaw as he closed his hands in prayer. It was the soldiers who fought for those trenches who first brought the news. 'Cleburne has been killed,' they whispered in low respectful voices. The tone was so soft and melancholic, like a child who had just lost their loving father. What are we to do now, was the question that they were really asking.

Lee could only listen to their lamentations for their fallen hero and wonder how it was that such an inspiration to the Confederacy had not attained a higher rank than the one he would now take to his grave?

"God, I am not one to question your decisions, I can only ask that you forgive and accept the soul of Patrick Cleburne into your eternal kingdom."

Lee then stood up and went over to a small chest that was in his corner of his tent. He very carefully lifted the small book that was placed on top of it. He carried Cleburne's personal journal with him as he lay down to sleep. He wanted to spend the entire night reading it, perhaps in doing so, he would have a chance to know better the man whom he would never see alive again. The thought of Cleburne's bright and promising face filled Lee with woe. His eyes watered as he tried to read the words scribed before him. The wind outside had picked up considerably on this cold November night. Lee thought that it must have been the Holy Spirit sent down from Heaven to personally guide Patrick Cleburne up to His kingdom.

Chapter XXVII
December 1
Franklin, Tennessee

While the Confederate army was spending the last night of
November enjoying a hard earned rest in Franklin, what remained
of General Schofield's army marched in solemn silence along the
Franklin Pike towards Nashville. The brave men that endured this
trek north, had to hang on to their positions on the southern banks
of the Harpeth until one thirty in the morning. At that time, they
quietly withdrew across the two bridges that spanned the river. It
was literally seconds after the last soldier touched the northern
banks when both bridges were set ablaze by explosion.

The signal was given to the men of the north. It was time
to once again turn their backs towards the enemy and retreat.

They marched on tired limbs, limbs that were as fed up
with this war as the hearts of the men that they shared. Making
conditions worse was the arrival of inclement weather. The cold
winter wind cut through them like a gleaming carving knife. With
each passing whoosh of freezing air, several of the wounded
soldiers would simply drop to their knees and remain motionless.
The men marching behind them were too cold, too tired and too
scared to stop and offer any assistance to their companions. All
they could offer was a passing glance, a brief look to see if the
fallen was someone that they knew personally.

And as the heads were turned for these few seconds,
scores of stragglers who had enough of this war, simply disappeared into the open country. They would rather take their chances
with the elements than to have to face another battle with the
rebels. At least on their own, they would have some control over
their events, unlike this army where their blood was the price
constantly being paid for the mistakes made by its commanders.
And the one man that collected the largest deposit of such
sanguine currency on this day was General Wagner.

General Schofield rode at the head of his army with several of his senior commanders, at least the ones who had managed
to escape the disaster at Franklin. They had been riding for several
hours and had covered nearly eight miles. It would not be much

longer until he and his men would reach Brentwood and could finally afford to let down their guard and secure a few hours of sleep. Just make it to Brentwood, he repeatedly told himself, and then you can deal with General Wagner's insubordination.

Schofield turned to his side and tried to keep his collar raised to protect his throat against the cutting wind. General Cox, barely awake, rode directly behind him. He knew that after Cox was able to see these boys to Brentwood, his first action would be the call for Wagner's dismissal from command. As Schofield reviewed the final reports in his head, he was in full agreement with Cox' assessment.

Cox's line around Franklin was impenetrable. It's only weakness was the path left open along the Franklin to Columbia Pike. The gap was created to allow the wagon train and the artillery to pass unhindered through the Federal defenses. Cox had realized this, and even though they had all been convinced that Hood could not possibly attempt an attack against such fortifications, Cox still had the prudence to instruct Wagner to pull his division within the main line.

If the enemy attacked, Cox wanted Wagner to have his men fall back to the Carter house on the hill. Why Wagner chose to have his men stay in position outside the main works, against such numbers, was the question that needed answering. Wagner had stated that he never told his commanders to hold their ground, but the soldiers who were there told another tale claiming that they were ordered at bayonet to stay their ground. What a debacle, there was no way those two brigades should have tried to hold against an entire corps, especially when a stronger reinforced line was only a few hundred yards in their rear.

"We could have stopped Hood," he whispered. The breath that escaped his beard hung for a moment around his head, as if a taunt to his thoughts with what might have been. Schofield batted at the air, then blew another cold breath and watched it float harmlessly into the night.

"Are you all right?" Cox said from behind.

Schofield turned to look at Cox, "Besides being exhausted, I would say that I am fine... physically. How is General Stanley?"

"I think the wound just grazed his neck, he should be fine."

"Good." Schofield tugged on his reins and allowed Cox to ride up beside him. "General, it amazes me that these men even follow us at this hour. If I were in their position... I can't even think of how I might react."

Cox rubbed the wanton sleep from under his heavy eyelids. "You know, for all that has occurred this past day, these men performed miraculously in the end. I would wager that as a last effort, Hood's last attack meant to drive us into the river. That corps that attacked us late was relatively fresh, but these boys of ours whipped them pretty bad. I think more than anything else, it was that last portion of the battle, the one in which we were the victors, coupled with the fresh memory of those who we must leave behind here. That is what I believe keeps these men moving. To fall now, would be an insult to those that were left behind."

"Do you truly believe that?"

"I have to."

"Well, at least their spirits should be lifted once we reach Brentwood. The considerate General Thomas has promised that Steedman will be on hand with over five thousand reinforcements, as well as the divisions of the better late than never General Smith."

"Late or not, they will be welcome. Why did you describe Thomas as 'considerate'? Your sarcasm does not speak well of the General."

Schofield felt his inside begin to warm. As far as he was concerned, Thomas' performance thus far had done little except give the enemy an opportunity to destroy half of the Union army in Tennessee. But thanks to Schofield's own cautious and even costly withdrawal, when his men finally reached Brentwood they would be reinforced with the rest of Thomas' command. Thomas would no doubt find himself in position to counter attack the Confederates with overwhelming numbers. Washington would praise Thomas and claim him a hero. The thought made his mouth taste as if it had been sucking upon a fistful of dirty coins. Had Schofield not successfully managed to avoid every trap and flanking maneuver performed by the Confederates, Thomas would be in a very different and much more ominous predicament than the one he would be in now.

"Let me ask you a single question, General," Schofield said. "If this were your army, and your army had been running for its life ever since it left Pulaski, and the fate of Tennessee depended on this army reaching the rest of your forces safely, would you be sitting on your fat ass in some warm hotel in

Nashville? I don't know about you, but I sure as hell would not. I would have been on the first horse that was available to carry me here, with or without the men of Smith's command."

Schofield's tepid banter caught Cox off guard. He had not seen it the way Schofield had, but now that he heard his opinion, it did create some doubt as to Thomas' military acumen.

"We should have won here today," Schofield continued. "Wilson's cavalry and the guns at Fort Granger kept Forrest from threatening our rear. From what I have been told, General Reilly was performing a marvelous job on our left flank. Until Wagner caused the breakthrough in our center, Reilly's divisions were slaughtering the rebels to their front. Had Wagner done as you instructed, I have no doubt that the rebel breakthrough would have been quickly corked up in the Carter's yard. They would have been pinned down there and subject to intense fire from every side."

"General, there is no one more sorry than I," Cox said. "I have lost some very good men back there, my three brigade commanders included. The Twenty-third corps no longer has a third division. God can not forgive me for what I am afraid I will do when I catch up with that rascal Wagner in the morning."

The amount of men that Schofield had lost since Spring Hill caused a cold and thick sweat to permeate on his back. When those in Washington reviewed his performance over the past few weeks, the only thing that they would see would be the number of losses to his forces. He had left Pulaski with more than twenty eight thousand men between the Twenty-third and the Fourth corps. But when his surviving forces marched into Brentwood, he would have to turn over his command of just over sixteen thousand to General Thomas.

He could envision the look of disappointment on Thomas' face now, and that made him want to strike at the cold air for a second time. Thomas would offer a façade of gratitude for his ability to escape from Hood, but in reality, Thomas would wire Washington with the grim reports of casualties. Opdycke's brigade had been smashed at Thompson Station, the rest of Wagner's division had routed at Franklin, leaving the combined brigades of Conrad and Lane with so few survivors that they could no longer form their own regiments. They were assigned to Wood's third division of the Fourth corps. Wagner's debacle in turn caused the complete rout of the third division from his own Twenty-third corps.

The losses were staggering and when taken out of context and read only as numbers on paper, they would look disastrous. But for those that survived the past two weeks of hell, the word they would choose best to describe their current situation would be... miraculous.

Hood had them at Spring Hill and he had them at Franklin. Had it not been for Schofield's ability to outthink his former friend, there is no telling what might have been the fate of this army. Schofield had not sat idle at Spring Hill, but instead risked everything on a nighttime withdrawal. And again at Franklin, his ability to prevent Forrest from gaining his rear may have been the single saving grace of the day. Had Forrest been able to reach those bridges, there would not have been a possibility of a second nighttime withdrawal.

And then once again, the thought of Wagner's obdurate order to his men caused his head to twirl with vertigo. Deep within his heart, he did not doubt for one second, that had Wagner been in a reserved position, the Confederate breakthrough would have been easily repelled. Instead, there were no troops available to plug the hole and the enemy was able to turn to its right and flank Reilly's command from an otherwise impenetrable position. The only good that came from that debacle was that when the enemy redirected its attention towards Reilly, it allowed time for General Kimball to rapidly transfer his regiments from the right flank to the rear center. Kimball constructed make shift earthworks, and aided by the arrival of darkness, was able to repel several furious attacks by the enemy.

Schofield shuddered at the thought of the Confederate attack that was delivered just a few hours earlier in the day. Had they had enough light to see just how few soldiers defended the south banks of the Harpeth, he was sure that Hood would have stopped at nothing to deliver the final blow to Schofield's shattered jaw.

Thanks to Kimball, those that were left at Franklin, were now able to march this long arduous pike into Brentwood. The ground gradually gave way to an inclined slope. Schofield leaned forward and allowed his horse to carry him over the rise. From his elevated position, he was able to see Brentwood before him. The sight caused his beard and mustache to part as his mouth hung open like an unhinged barn door.

"There is no one here," he heard Cox say. His voice was low and depressed as if coming from some surrealistic corner of his worst nightmare. He stopped his horse and those that followed were forced to stop as well. He quickly spun towards Cox as he punched at the air for the third time this night.

"I will ask you once again, would you sit on your fat ass and allow this to happen... What are we to do now? Thomas said that there would be a Federal army here to welcome us, instead there is nothing but a dark and empty town."

Before proceeding, Schofield sent an aid ahead into Brentwood to see if Thomas had left any kind of word as to what might have happened. The aid rode back half an hour later and reported that Thomas had instructed Schofield to continue marching his army another nine miles to Nashville. There would be no sleeping at Brentwood. And for the men that continued to be a part of this army, that meant that there was to be no rest for several more hours. It did not take long for Schofield to alter those instructions, he sent word to his officers that the men were going to be given one hour of rest, then they would have to resume their march until they reached Nashville.

*   *   *   *   *   *   *   *

Dawn had begun to break over the horizon, and for Schofield's army it was just another reminder of their sleep deprivation. Had an hour even passed, many wondered until those with watches confirmed the fact. Without the fortitude to offer any objections, the Federal soldiers succumbed to the march and simply continued marching north. The citizens that were awake at Brentwood stared from their bedroom windows and watched as a walking mass of slumping zombies staggered through their town like some demoralized parade of the macabre.

From behind their windows, they quietly grinned.

*   *   *   *   *   *   *   *

Robert E. Lee had awoken very early in the morning. The sun had still not risen yet when he dressed himself and left his tent. Upon closing the flaps behind him, he was greeted by a ferocious gust of the same cold air that had hindered Schofield's fleeing army. It was the thought of the Federals that turned his attention towards the Harpeth. He found his horse and gingerly climbed upon it. He cantered towards Franklin with the optimistic hope that when the sun rose Schofield's army would still be there.

His wisdom knew better.

As his horse approached what were once the main Federal earthworks, he could smell the remains of the burning bridges. Schofield was gone. Once again, they have escaped me, he thought. Lee continued on towards the Carter house, careful not to have his horse step on any of the Confederate soldiers that were sprawled along the trenches and the Carter hill. These poor men must have been so exhausted to have chosen such a place to sleep through the night.

Not wanting to wake them, Lee stepped from his horse and looked to secure it to something stable. A few yards to the right of the pike, he found a cannon that had lost one wheel, and was leaning on its exposed side. Lee tied the horse's reins to the barrel of the gun and then took a moment to pay his respects to those that had fought and died on this battlefield.

There were several campfires still burning through out town, but there were none on the battlefield. And that was when Lee thought of the numerous Confederates he saw lying upon the earth. They were not sleeping, at least not on this earth. He could not believe that he had not realized that as he rode through them, but there were just so many. He was beginning to understand that he had not been properly informed as to the magnitude of their casualties. Those that fell here, either died from their wounds, or had frozen to death. The end result was that God had chosen to take them on this last day of November.

'Does Hood realize just how many we lost here?' he wondered. Now that he knew that those that resided here were none but the dead, Lee remounted his horse and continued to ride towards the Lewisburg Pike. He could see a large dark shadow a few yards from him and knew that it was the cotton gin. Lee paused and turned his head in all directions. It was somewhere near here that Cleburne had fallen. Lee thought for a moment that he should search those fallen until he could find the Irish general, but there was too much to do and time was once again slipping through the hourglass of the Confederacy.

If Lee thought that there were a lot of dead soldiers

sprawled in the center of the line, he was soon to be mistaken. As Lee passed the cotton gin, he rode out towards the Osage abatis created by the Federals. It was here that his army had encountered the stiffest resistance of the day. And now that Lee was here, he could see why. The branches were so entwined with thorns, it must have taken a monumental amount of will to try to get through them, only to face a well entrenched enemy.

Lee could see a soldier leaning against the bramble a few yards ahead. He cantered towards the man and asked him from what command he belonged. The soldier did not answer. Lee thought he must have been sleeping and decided to let the man rest. But as he passed, the man's eyes were wide open and his mouth was grotesquely twisted as if in the most paramount agony.

Lee once again dismounted and tried to free the man from his hellish prison. Lee's fragile arms pulled and tugged to no avail. When he tried to step back and pull from another angle, he saw a sight more hideous than any other that he had witnessed thus far in the war. The man's hands were clenched in rage as they were wrapped around the perilous brush. The thorns from the Osage had pierced his entire body and literally nailed him in his upright position, a feat that would have been otherwise impossible because the soldiers right leg had been completely blown off below the thigh. It was then that he realized that the Southern soldier had not died trying to escape the bramble. The wound that would prove his mortality was evident in what remained of the severed limb that hung grotesquely from his hip. This man knew he was going to die and this horrific display of struggling futility was the only way he knew that he could leave this earth upon his own terms. He did not struggle to escape his end, he struggled so that he could face it standing... standing like a man.

Lee resolved to step back and offer the man the only thing he possibly could, a prayer to his God. As he continued riding east past the Lewisburg Pike and towards the railroad the carnage was not lessened. Had Cheatham's men not pierced the center and held it, this entire attack could have very well ended like this, he thought.

"General Lee, is that really you," a voice called from somewhere ahead. Lee rode towards the sound and found a young officer, ghastly white, lying beside the fallen. Lee stepped down from his horse again and knelt beside the man.

"General Lee," the man said. "So many of the men have

said that you were with us, that was what gave us the will to attack here. And we did it, we finally licked them Yanks."

Lee put a warm hand on the cold clammy brow of the wounded officer. "Yes you did," he said softly. "Where is your wound, I cannot see it."

The man closed his eyes and whispered, "It is in my heart."

Lee waited for his eyes to reopen but they did not. His breathing had become very slow and deliberate. Lee could not help but see the irony in the man's reply. Surely his heart was wounded in more ways than one. His young life was soon to be over. Like many before him, he would no doubt be leaving a wife, mother, and children to face this world with out him. Lee was reminded of that soldier who froze to death outside his camp back in Virginia. There were too many faces now, too many good men lost to this war.

And for all his accomplishments, what had he really done except extend the duration of the conflict and add more numbers to the fatherless homes of the Confederacy.

The man seemed to take a strong breath, as if he knew it were to be his last. His eyes opened for a brief moment, allowing Lee to see his pupils clearly with the breaking dawn. "But it is better now. With you, my heart has returned."

Lee could almost feel the man's soul ascend towards the rising sun, as if God had sent that glowing orb as this man's personal carriage to his eternal kingdom. Lee took his hand from the man's head and carefully rested it upon the cold hard earth.

There was still much to do this day.

After his survey of the battlefield, Lee rode back towards his tent to formulate his objectives for the day. It was just after eight, when one of Hood's staff arrived and requested for Lee to join Hood at his headquarters. Lee told the officer that he needed a few moments for himself, but would be there shortly.

When Lee left his tent this time, there was more commotion around Franklin than there was earlier in the morning. With the Federal army gone, the Confederates had assumed the task of burying the dead. For the fallen in gray, they tried their best to provide a place of serenity. As for the Union dead, they thought it most fitting to simply pile their bodies in their own trenches, and cover them up with a layer of earth. If these were the trenches they fought so hard to hold, then let them have them for all eternity.

As Lee rode amongst the gravediggers, he realized the sound of their shovels cutting into the earth had stopped. They all were staring at him with shovels slung over their shoulders, or places at their sides. One man gave a holler and soon they all rejoiced. 'Lee…Lee' was the chant.

Lee listened to the men as they called his name. He looked into their faces and he could see it. It was what was missing with his men back in Virginia. Those in Virginia had lost their hope, or as the fallen soldier had said earlier this morning, they had lost their heart. But these men had regained that, and as selfish as it may be, Lee knew that it was because of him. How else could so many men spend the day burying their companions, then stop to cheer the man that was responsible for their deaths?

He suddenly realized that he had the answer to their problem. He remembered that the men were so concerned with the loss of Cleburne, that they were faced with the dismay of finding a leader… one whom they could trust. As they reveled in his presence, he understood and accepted that it would have to be him, and Lee accepted that honor with open arms.

Lee met General Cheatham a few minutes later and asked where he could find the body of Cleburne. Cheatham told him that it was located alongside the other fallen generals, at the Carnton mansion. Lee asked for directions and rode his horse towards the great abode. The Carnton mansion belonged to a Mr. John McGavock and on any other day it would be a most pleasing and welcoming sight to any visitor. Unfortunately, on this first day of December, there was only one visitor that could find the McGavock home welcoming, and that would be Death.

The lawn around the mansion was a crawling field of the wounded. Their bodies were so packed together that many of them lay on top of each other, hoping to be the next to be seen by one of the surgeons. If the screams from inside the mansion were any indication of what awaited them, Lee wondered how they could not have wished for a different end.

Just then, the front door of the mansion swung open and an emotional woman exited the home followed by several servants. Lee noticed that all of their garments were stained with fresh blood. By the way the servants followed close on her heals, he gathered that the genteel woman must be Mrs. McGavock. In her arms she carried a rather large circular bucket, the ladies that followed were pleading with her to return inside. Ignorant to her surroundings, Mrs. McGavock turned on them. As she hoisted the basket, there were tears running down her face.

"I do not mind helping, my husband is doing the right thing, that I know, but must my home have this in every corner? How am I to live here once they are gone?"

Lee stood silently as the frantic procession passed him. He took a brief look at her open basket as she passed and headed towards one of the smaller buildings.

The wooden basket was completely filled with the blood and sawed-off limbs of the injured. Lee watched as Mrs. McGavock opened a weathered wooden door and without entering, emptied her basket inside. Like the hopeless mob that raided the bread store back in Richmond, this war had its effects on more than just the soldiers.

Lee rode around towards the back of the mansion and saw the two-story veranda that Cheatham had told him about. Several officers greeted Lee as he dismounted and approached the lower level of the veranda. The silence here was that of a funeral. There was one man weeping like a child on the other end of the back porch.

Lying side by side, on the veranda's floor were the bodies of Adams, Granbury, Strahl, Gist, Carter and Cleburne. In the infinite night of the Confederacy, they were six shining stars that would glow no longer. Lee hung his head and said a long silent prayer. For all the victory that they achieved yesterday, the only reward that Lee had seen thus far was death.

Lee was given room, and respect, as all of the officers on the veranda stepped off. Lee knelt beside Cleburne and took his cold hand into his own. For all his prayers, God had not saved him. 'No, I cannot think like that, please forgive me my Lord.' He knew that Cleburne's loss would be an immense burden for him to overcome. Lee had such high aspirations for this general, and now they would come to naught.

As Lee gazed at the crimson circle of blood that stained the general's undershirt beneath his unbuttoned jacket, Lee's thoughts were once again changed by his own introspections. He remembered his last moment with Cleburne, when the Irish general had placed his fiancé's handkerchief within his coat before riding off into battle. 'I call your loss tragic because I think only of myself", he thought. The real loss will be to your fiancé. Lee reached into Cleburne's coat and removed the soft linen. Surprisingly, it was stark white, unstained by any of the general's lost blood.

For a moment, Lee thought of how Cleburne considered the handkerchief as a ward against death. Perhaps if he had kept his coat buttoned, it would have saved him? How foolish to even think that, Lee thought. He unfolded the delicate cloth and covered Cleburne's face with it.

Lee sat for several moments in silence. There was something absolutely charismatic about this man that had enabled Lee to grow so fond of him over these two days. Lee could not figure out what that was, but knew that when God wanted to reveal that to him, he would.

"You were an exceptional man," he said. Lee stood up and turned to leave but the man who had been crying now stood right behind him.

"Thank you", the sobbing officer said. "I am Lieutenant Mangum… General Cleburne was my commander… and he was my friend. If you don't mind I have taken his sword for safekeeping?"

Lee watched Mangum's swollen eyes continue to water. He said nothing. He put his hand on the lieutenant's shoulder and hoped that Mangum could find some comfort in that simple gesture. There were times, just as now, when Lee felt that he lacked the effort to offer any consoling. Once in a while, even he needed to be the one who was consoled. That thought made him think of Colonel Taylor. He now wished that there were someway that his colonel could have made this trip with him.

"General Lee, a pleasure," a softer voice said from behind Mangum. Mangum stepped off the veranda and allowed Lee to pass. Lee saw that the man who had just called him was a chaplain. Lee could not help but feel blessed. He welcomed the man like fish would water.

"I needed to see them, before we moved on," was all Lee could say.

"Chaplain Charles Quintard," the chaplain replied offering his hand into Lee's. "And I am glad that you have had your moments with these fine gentlemen, I am here to take their bodies back to the Polk residence. General Lee, are your feeling well?"

Lee hesitated. "Yes, I am fine. I just had not realized how

much loss there was yesterday."

"I don't think Hood does either. Speaking of which, when I left his headquarters this morning, he asked if I saw you, to send you his way."

Lee realized that Chaplain Quintard was someone who was very close to Hood. "How is the general?" he asked.

Quintard looked puzzled. "What do you mean?"

"I have known General Hood a long time, and he does not seem the same to me."

Quintard looked around as an indication that there were too many ears present for such talk. He stepped close to Lee's side and said, "Perhaps when I return we can spend some time discussing this."

Lee assented and was soon back upon his horse. As he departed from the Carnton mansion the screams of the amputees were so horrifyingly dreadful, that he knew they would stay with him for the rest of his life.

*   *   *   *   *   *   *   *

Robert E. Lee was not the only Confederate General to have awoken before dawn. To the south of Winstead Hill, John Bell Hood started his morning within the warm comforts of William Harrison's home. As he stretched himself out of bed, he tried in vain to remember the last time he had slept so sound. He lit a candle and looked towards the nightstand for his medicine, knowing that it would not be there. After yesterday's rout of the Federal army, he did not need any elixirs to help him sleep.

Hood had his aid help him dress and then spent the remainder of the morning gathering all the reports from the battle. He had hoped that the morning light would reveal the Federal army still on the south side of the Harpeth, but the burning bridges told a different tale. If only S.D. Lee's divisions could have punctured their line, he thought. But Hood had been in that position before, and knew that even the best officers would have trouble trying to coordinate their attacks in the dark. It was a lost cause, and for those like Stonewall Jackson, the results usually benefited the enemy that was under attack.

Schofield had withdrawn at some point past midnight and was no doubt moving with great speed towards Nashville. Hood reread the reported losses of the enemy and let a deep smile crescent his jaw. 'You may run my dear friend John, run all you want, but when I catch up with you again, you will find yourself short two entire divisions.' By keeping his focus on the enemy's losses, his own did not seem too great. But deep down, he knew differently.

While Schofield may have lost two divisions since Spring Hill, he would no doubt find their numbers quickly replaced once he reached Nashville. Hood on the other hand was not expecting to have his numbers replaced. Except for Smith's brigade of Cleburne's division, there would not be any additional men in gray to face the reinforced Federal army. As soon as the thought of General Smith appeared in his head, he immediately saw Cleburne's handsome face and he had to extinguish that candle before it threatened to burn him down from the inside.

Patrick Cleburne was no more.

Governor Harris had arrived and joined Hood and his staff for breakfast. Hood had enjoyed his meal of biscuits and bacon, but his mind was on other matters. Though victorious, Franklin had cost him six generals, scores of officers and a large part of his fighting force. The question that remained was where to go from here? He had his own ideas for what to do next, but he wanted to confide with General Lee first. A quick look around the room confirmed that Lee had still not arrived yet.

How he longed for Lee's guidance at this moment.

The enemy was beaten, but not destroyed. And even though his army had been victorious, it was now severely wounded. Stewart's attack on the Federal flank had resulted in nearly two thousand casualties. Cheatham's division, the most successful of the day, had suffered close to a thousand men lost. Then as the night set in, S. D. Lee's corps was sent through Cheatham's breakthrough in an attempt to crush the Federals last stand a few hundred feet from the Harpeth. Aided by the darkness, Schofield's routed command was able to hold their ground and repel S. D. Lee's three desperate advances. All that was gained was an additional loss of almost eleven hundred more Confederates.

His army now amounted to roughly twenty six thousand men. That was not counting Forrest's command. An indignant Forrest had reported to him early this morning, apologizing for his men's inability to gain the Federal rear. Hood told him that his men had done enough so far, and if he could ask for yet another favor, it was to chase the Federals and force them into a fight somewhere between here and Nashville. "Catch them before they unite with Thomas' forces," he pleaded. Forrest's grin was insidious as he departed.

It was somewhere between the time Forrest left his head-quarters and after his meal that he began to realize that the loss of nearly five thousand casualties did not amount to nearly the loss of six of his finest commanders. The names of the six men sang through his conscious like the resonation of a mistuned musical instrument; Adams, Granbury, Gist, Carter, Strahl and Cleburne. If he said the names fast enough they seemed to blend to together into one repugnant word…Death.

He had killed them all.

The thought made him thirst for his laudanum. He got out of his chair and reached for his crutches, refusing to believe that he was responsible. "Has anyone seen General Lee," he irritably asked? He had been so deep in thought that the question startled his staff. It was not too long after that they had all departed searching for the general.

"Are you all right?" Harris asked. "You should be riding the laurels of victory, but you don't look like you are."

Hood stared at Harris. He wanted to open up to this man, to any man, but his guilt would not allow it. He tried to conceal it by telling himself that the attack had to be made and that Cheatham had to force the center. But the truth was that he deliberately sent Cleburne and Brown's divisions in the lead as a means to reprimand their ineptness at Spring Hill the day before. If Harris thought that he did not look well, it was because the nausea of his deeds was now manifested in his swollen jugular.

'What difference would it have been had I let Stewarts' men continue up the pike,' he thought. 'I would only be exchang-ing the fates of one group of men with those of another. I cannot feel guilty for this, the attack had to be made and it was successful. I shall grieve their losses, but I am not the blame. If they are staring down at me now, let them only reflect on Spring Hill. This did not have to be.'

"General Hood, perhaps you need some water?"

Hood had almost forgotten that Governor Harris was still in the room with him. "No, I am well. I only wish that General Lee were here now."

"I remember when you used to feel that way about me," Quintard said as he stepped into the room.

Hood hobbled towards Quintard and firmly shook his hand. It was a gesture that he needed to embrace. There was always comfort with Quintard. His arrival could not have been at a better time.

"General Hood, I congratulate you on your victory, but the day arrives with much loss."

"I know. This army could ill-afford to lose those that have fallen here. I will need to restructure this army immediately if we are to pursue the enemy."

Quintard nodded his head, but his eyes looked disappointed. "General, if I may suggest, perhaps a prayer should be your first action of this day. I think the men that we lost, as well as those left would appreciate that. I only came by to inform you that I would be gone for a few days. We are moving the general's bodies back to St. John's church. We have lost a lot, and I cannot question the Lord as to why. But I am thankful that the enemy is gone."

Hood felt Quintard's hand slip from his. It felt as if his fingers had just lost their grip on the ledge that prevented him from falling into the darkest chasms of his inner self. "Chaplain, if you see General Lee, will you please ask him to come here."

Quintard agreed and then departed. 'He is allowed to grieve', Hood thought, 'but I am not afforded that luxury. They have performed this Confederacy a great service and if I spend my time grieving for them, then I would be doing their heroic services a grave injustice. I must finish what they have started. The Federal army must be driven from the soil of Tennessee by month's end. And if I am to accomplish this, I must hit them before they can reorganize. This will be my oath to their lost souls. But you are right my dear chaplain, those men deserve prayer and I can surely take a few moments to allow them that.'

Hood turned to Governor Harris and politely excused himself. He wanted to be left alone for a while. Hood went back to the bedroom and placed his crutches on the wall next to the door. He then hopped into the bed and lay flat on his back. As he shut his eyes to begin to pray, he inadvertently found himself listening to the sounds outside.

There were none.

In the earlier part of this war, the day following a victory would be one filled with great celebration, but those times were long gone. With each battle, the casualties grew larger and larger. In the distance he thought he could hear the sound of the shovels digging into the earth. This would be a day when his men would give up soldiering and become gravediggers to the carnage that now blanketed Franklin.

He had not ridden out to the battlefield yet, had not seen all that was written in his reports, and he would not do so until Lee arrived. He would not leave these headquarters until he understood how the command structure would work between Lee and himself. He had to laugh at the irony of it all, before yesterday, he had welcomed the thought of handing his command of the army over to Lee. But now that the enemy had been soundly defeated, he was not so eager to step down. But it's Robert E. Lee, he kept telling himself. Had it been anyone else, he would not even consider such a demotion.

He looked at the clock and noted that it was almost noon. He could not imagine what had kept Lee from arriving. Why hadn't he slept here at these headquarters anyway? Hood heard the front door open and quickly rose from the bed. Captain Wigfall knocked at his door and announced that General Cheatham had arrived. Hood reached for his crutches and followed Wigfall into the room where a sunken Cheatham sat with his head hung low.

"General Cheatham," Hood said, "Have you seen General Lee this morning?"

Cheatham did not lift his head. "General Hood, I have not. If I may ask, can you please dismiss the Governor and your aid for a few moments?"

Hood looked to Harris and Wigfall and shrugged with his good shoulder. "Surely, gentleman, please allow me and the general a few private moments. Also see that no one disturbs us until I say otherwise." Hood watched them leave the room and already whished he could take back his adamant order. With his luck, now would be the time that Lee arrived, and Wigfall would no doubt send him away. Perhaps whatever was troubling Cheatham would not take so long. Hood sat opposite his general at the table and rested his crutches beside him.

"You lost some good men yesterday," he said.

This time, Cheatham did lift his head, and Hood could now see why he opted to have his face hidden before. Deep and dry was the riverbed of tears that had recently flowed from his eyes to his chin. Hood tried not to stare.

"General Hood, I can not think of my command without Cleburne, Granbury, Gist, Carter and Strahl not to mention the soldiers that I have lost with them."

"General, your losses are a sadness to us all, but you must think on the victory instead, and what it means to our country. It was not a loss in vain".

"No General, it was not. It was a loss because of my own inability to properly coordinate an attack."

"What are you talking about, was it not your command that I watched through my field glasses from that hill. Did I not see Cheatham's flags smash the Federal center and then roll up its flank against the railroad?"

Cheatham covered his face with hands that shook like rattles. His hands were not large enough to conceal the fresh tears that began to flow once again. "I was not talking about Franklin, my failure was at Spring Hill. I should have done more. I should have personally seen to the execution of the attack."

Hood had to sit back for a second. He had spent the entire morning blaming himself for the loss of Cheatham's Generals. Now here was their corps commander ameliorating him of any responsibility. "General, we can not blame you for Spring Hill, and you certainly can not blame yourself."

Hood could not believe how casual those words sounded once they escaped his mouth. Moments ago, they were the bile that clogged his jugular. And try as he might, he was unable to extract the bitter waste. And now he did not have to. It was being done for him.

"Sir, if I may do you the service of resigning my command…"

Hood stopped Cheatham before he could say another word. "General, there will be no resigning. Like you have just said, we have lost too many good commanders, I cannot afford to lose another. Your place shall remain at my side for as long as I am in command." Hood thought of Lee and wondered himself how long that might be. "Now pick that head of yours up and get your men ready to pursue the enemy. We did well yesterday, but there is more to be done."

Cheatham rubbed the tears from his cheeks and looked up. "My men are in no condition to pursue the enemy. We will need at least another day to finish burying our dead. There is also the

420

matter of replacing the commanders that are now lost to my corps."

"Well, I expect General Lee to arrive here at any minute. Before we announce any promotions, I want to confer with General Lee first. I am not sure what my role will be once Lee takes official command."

Cheatham stood up and straightened his jacket. "General Hood, thank you."

"For what?"

"For your forgiveness of my error. I will ensure my men are ready to pursue the enemy as soon as the dead are properly buried." Cheatham saluted Hood and parted with purpose in his step.

As Hood watched him leave, he tried to remember if during the conversation he ever once said that he had forgiven Cheatham for his debacle at Spring Hill. He was fairly confident that had the battle of Franklin ended with a Confederate loss, Cheatham would have soon found himself without a command in this army. Franklin had only happened because Spring Hill had not. And if Cheatham had not done so yet, he had better take a minute to praise God that Hood's army had routed the Federals towards Nashville.

"General Hood, General Lee is here," Wigfall said as he led Lee into the room.

"At last," Hood said, louder than he intended. He hoped Lee had not heard. "Captain, my orders now are as they were with Cheatham, I need to remain undisturbed with the General." Wigfall offered a polite smile and once again left Hood and his company to themselves.

Hood had never before felt awkward when engaged in conversation with Lee, but then again, he was never in a position where Lee's presence meant that his was being replaced. "General, you should have spent the night here with me. This house does a marvelous job denying this biting wind its ability to discomfort your sleep."

Lee's smile was faint. He looked around the room, at all the bibelot's that made such a place feel so commodious. He thought of his army back in Richmond, how they slept night after cold night in their hollowed trenches. "No thank you General, I have made it a habit to sleep as the men do."

Hood was not comfortable with the tone of Lee's response, but would not show it. "Where have you been this morning?" Hood asked.

"I rode out this morning to the battlefield to see first hand the results of yesterdays battle. A strong position the enemy had. Once you see it, I think that you will agree. I also think that had we had a chance to actually stand in their trenches prior to our attack, that we would never have assaulted their position. I consider it a miracle that we were able to take their ground. From the reports that I have read, Schofield had no reserves placed in the center. And of all the places not to have a reserve, I just do not understand. I can only thank God, for it is He who sees all things before they can happen."

Lee sat in the same chair that Cheatham had vacated only moments ago. He noted that the seat bottom was still warm, unlike the bodies of the generals that he had seen laid upon the back veranda at the Carnton mansion. "I have rode out to the Carnton mansion, to spend a few moments with those generals that have fallen. Their presence will be sorely missed by this army." One of them in particular would be missed more than Hood would ever know. "Have you thought about who will replace them?"

"General Lee, forgive my hesitancy, but I was unsure of my authority in regards to your presence within this army."

"I understand, what do you think your responsibility should be."

Hood was not ready to have answered such a question. "Well, I had assumed that the overall command of this army would fall to you, and I... I am not sure what my role would be."

For the first time, Lee smiled. "General Hood, I have never known you to seem so bashful, and now is not the time for it. You are right... I am here to take command of your army, though only temporarily. The Army of Northern Virginia still needs me, and I must return to them as soon as possible. Their fate depends on how much we can accomplish here and in how little time it takes for us to accomplish it. Yesterday was the start of our tremendous task, we must follow it up immediately."

It was Hood's turn to smile back. "It was how Gettysburg should have been," he said.

Now it was Lee who was caught off guard. Since this morning, he thought of the battle more along the lines of Chancellorsville. Once again, he had the enemy beaten, but did not have enough time to completely crush them. Like sand through his clenched fingers, the enemy had once again escaped.

"We hit their center just like then, only here they broke," Hood said, keeping to the analogy with Gettysburg. "And these men had to march a mile longer than Picket had. And I mean no disrespect to those men that walked down that path at Gettysburg, I only say it to point out how much these men can do when properly led."

Lee knew that Hood was referring to Johnston's constant use of the defensive rather than going on the attack. That was fine, because right now, few knew that it was Johnston who had the over all command of the forces around Richmond and Petersburg. And until Lee returned, that was exactly how he wanted those men to be led... defensively.

Perhaps Hood was right, though. This was the attack aimed at the Federal center that had very different results than in Pennsylvania.

"Have you made preparation to follow the enemy?" Lee asked.

"I have. Forrest's cavalry departed hours ago and General Stephen Lee was given orders to follow. Cheatham was just here and informed me that his men needed time to bury their dead before they could join the rest of the army."

Lee thought of his morning ride near the trenches. "That may take the general more time than he expects. Before we continue, I would like for you to consider my thoughts..."Lee paused in thought as he tried to consider the most appropriate words for his proposal. He decided that bluntness was the best approach, especially when dealing with one such as Hood. "I want you to assume command of Cheatham's corps." He waited for Hood to digest what he had just said.

Hood's eyes seemed to roll deep inside his head as if in search of past memories. There seemed to be a long moment where Hood's still body seemed to be engulfed in some unseen struggle. When the mood subsided, Hood let a deep breath escape his chest. "And what shall become of General Cheatham?"

"I happened to pass General Cheatham on my way in here. When I arrived at Spring Hill, I heard him defending his reasons for not taking the initiative in attacking the enemy..."

"But Spring Hill is behind us now," replied Hood. "Cheatham was just here and he spoke of the very same night. Like an honest Southern man, he has confessed to his errors and has accepted any blame. I think that such a lesson can only benefit him in the future."

Lee looked as if he were not so sure. With initiative went instinct. And no mater how much one tried, you could not learn instinct. It was instinct that separated men like Jackson and Forrest from those like Cheatham. And Lee could ill afford to have the outcome of the next battle decided by a commander who lacked the instinct to seize the initiative.

"Then we let his lesson teach him, but as a brigadier general and not a corps commander," Lee replied. "I will assume the responsibility of informing him. It will only be temporarily, until I am able to return to Virginia. Once I am gone, this army will be returned to your command and you may reassign your generals as you see fit. Now, let's not waste any more time on Cheatham and his feelings. The lives of these men depend on us, and we must do what serves them best. Have you given thought to what our strategy should be?"

"I have. It is rather simple, what other choice do we have but to follow Schofield to Nashville. I understand that Thomas has a force gathering there and will combine it with Schofield's. Consolidated, Thomas will outnumber my command, but that has never stopped this army before. If we turn back now, this army would have accomplished nothing but the loss of a lot of men and six of its best commanders."

Lee rubbed at his bearded chin. "I must admit General Hood, that you must have learned a great deal while you were under my command."

Hood took that as a compliment. He wanted to tell Lee about Atlanta, and how his three failed attacks were also conducted using the same tactics that he learned in Virginia, but now was not the time. Perhaps in the days ahead he could defend his actions that led to the fall of Atlanta. But as for right now, it was a time for looking ahead, a time for optimism.

"If these boys thought that the enemy's position here was one that we should never have tested, wait until they see Nashville," Hood said. "Thomas' position there is one that has been fortifying itself ever since our men were forced to evacuate at the beginning of this war."

"General, we shall see what happens when we get there. What I have to do now is gather this army and announce my presence to them. Many have seen me already, and it can no longer be concealed. I only hope that the news will take a long time before it reaches Thomas, or more importantly, General Grant. Well, I must be going now, and I would like to thank you for all that you have done. You have surprised even me in your ability to take such a command, and that is not intended to be an insult. Please make a list of your personal recommendations as to who should replace our fallen officers and generals."

Lee got up to leave and put a hand on Hood's large shoulder. "If I may ask of you one last request. I only think that it would be fair for you to write the report to President Davis concerning our great victory here at Franklin. The honor is deservingly yours."

If Hood could have stood up and wrapped this patriarchal man in both arms, he would have crushed him. Buck Preston was now assured the honor of being the fiancé of the South's newest hero.

"Thank you General Lee, that means a great deal to me," he said.

Lee smiled and then left Hood to write his letter to the President.

* * * * * * * *

'Honorable Jefferson Davis,

We attacked the enemy at Franklin and drove them from the centerline of temporary works, then from their inner lines, until they were able to reform a new line protecting the bridges crossing the Harpeth. The enemy evacuated at some time past midnight, leaving the dead and wounded in our possession, and retired to Nashville, closely pursued by our cavalry.

The enemy has lost two divisions, one each from the Fourth and Twenty-third corps. We ourselves have sustained a large number of losses to our gallant officers and brave men.

As of this day, I have relinquished my command of this army to General Robert E. Lee. I will take over command of Cheatham's corps. General Cheatham, though not as a demotion, will take command of Cleburne's division. This order of command will continue until General Lee's return to Virginia.

At that time, I have full confidence that we will be in complete repossession of the entire state of Tennessee.'

Very Respectively yours,
John Bell Hood

Chapter XXVIII
December 2
Nashville, Tennessee

To Schofield's dismay, his demoralized army had to not only endure the continued march through Brentwood, but upon their arrival at Nashville, they were given orders to assist Thomas' men in fortifying the pre-existing trenches in preparation for Hood's inevitable assault. Schofield, too exhausted to complain, retired to his room at Thomas' headquarters at the St. Cloud Hotel. Though the roof above his head was impervious to the cold rain that fell from the night sky, his men were not as fortunate. The shattered remains of the Twenty-third and Fourth corps embraced the cold wetness with uncanny stoicism. To them, the rain that pelted their worn uniforms, were the tears of their fallen companions at Franklin.

When Schofield finally awoke, he felt rejuvenated. He quickly dressed himself, had a small breakfast, and then went in search of General Thomas. Thomas' treatment of his men was absolutely disrespectful. What kind of man would have these brave soldiers ordered to help fortify the city's defenses, when they had not slept in over two days. Especially when the reason for their lack of sleep was that they had saved Thomas' army from a disastrous stay in Tennessee.

It was just after seven in the morning when one of Thomas' staff officers informed him that General Thomas was waiting in the dining room. It was there that Thomas planned to conduct his council of war. Already standing outside of the room were General Cox and General Wilson. Schofield greeted the former, but was aloof with the latter. Much of what had occurred since Pulaski he credited to Wilson's inept cavalry.

The three men entered the room and found General Thomas standing over a large wooden table. On the surface of the table was an immense map of Nashville. Gathered around Thomas were Generals A.J. Smith, James Steedman and John Miller. The four men looked up as they entered and Thomas asked the new arrivals to join them around the table.

Schofield found himself standing next to General Steedman. Steedman was in command of a provisional detachment, consisting of five brigades, two of which were colored. The thought of Forrest's reaction to the Negro brigades caused him some concern. Would he be a victim to Forrest's animosity as the other white officers who died at Fort Pillow?

The map on the table focused upon Nashville and the seven forts and redoubts that anchored the cities defenses. The Cumberland River ran its course around Nashville, reminding Schofield of a gigantic upside-down horseshoe. It was strikingly similar to the Harpeth at Franklin. The lay of the vicinity made it very clear that if Hood meant to attack, he would have to do so from the south.

"General Schofield, as you can see by these gunboats placed here and here, Hood will be unable to threaten our flank," Thomas said, as if he had read Schofield's thoughts. "Unlike your situation at Franklin, our navy will be on hand to prevent Forrest from crossing the river and threatening the rear. If Hood wants to make the attack, he will have to advance along these two pikes, the Granny White and the Franklin. From all the accounts that you and General Wilson have provided, I don't believe that Hood has enough manpower to spread his army to these other arteries that lead into Nashville. I am convinced that if Hood chooses to attack us here, his army will suffer a fate far worse than Bragg experienced at Chattanooga."

Schofield continued to study the map, but remained silent. Was this the greeting Thomas was offering for his arrival into Nashville? No thanks for returning his army from the brink of utter destruction? Just a good morning general, and now lets get back to business.

"What if Hood chooses not to attack?" General Cox asked.

"Well that would be an even better scenario for us. General Wilson's cavalry is currently at Edgefield, right here above the city. They are in the process of being reequipped with horses and rifles. The general still has more men than mounts. That will soon change though, and when it does, we will have a substantial force that will allow for me to take the fight to Hood, instead of he to us."

Schofield had to resist the urge to let out an effusively sarcastic giggle. If Thomas depending on the abilities of General Wilson, then they would all find themselves in serious trouble.

"General Schofield, I can not commend you enough for escaping Franklin with the army," Thomas said. "General Stanley arrived here earlier in the day yesterday and we had a long talk before he departed for much needed medical attention. His wound did not appear to be healing well, I hope for all our sakes that it does." Thomas never took his eyes from the map as he commended Schofield. What he dared not ask, not now at least, was why Schofield had chosen to remain on the same side of the Harpeth as the rebels. If only he had crossed over prior to the attack, his army would be two divisions stronger than it currently was, and calculating those numbers, it was a loss he could ill afford.

"General Schofield," he continued, "you will now resume command of your Twenty-third corps, but being as it is only one division, it will remain combined with the Fourth corps. And since Stanley is wounded, you will assume command of his two divisions as well. You will have them placed here and here, denying Hood's approach from the south. General Smith will occupy our lines to your west until his flank touches the Cumberland. General Steedman will continue our lines east until he too touches the river to the east of the city. With General Miller's men included, we can account for over thirty seven thousand men; not counting Wilson's cavalry, which will add another ten thousand troopers to our numbers. From all your reports and calculations, even with Hood's success at Franklin, his numbers are estimated in the high twenty thousands at most. Forrest adds another eight to ten thousand to that total. And much to my own chagrin, General Grant has informed me that there is no evidence that General Hampton detached a division of cavalry to operate in conjunction with Forrest."

Schofield looked towards Wilson with even more reason not to like the man. His cavalry had been whipped by nothing more than ghosts. And where was Thomas going with these numbers? It was not like this was the first time that the Federal army had more men to occupy a battlefield than the rebels had. As far as Schofield could remember, numbers never meant anything to the enemy. If anything, they were harder to beat when they were outnumbered.

Thomas' shadow descended upon the mapped battlefield as his large frame bent over the table. His self-assured index finger traced a line along the placement of his main trenches. He started from Smith's position to the west of Nashville and let his finger slightly meander as it dipped south in a convex fashion. As he

Nashville Defense

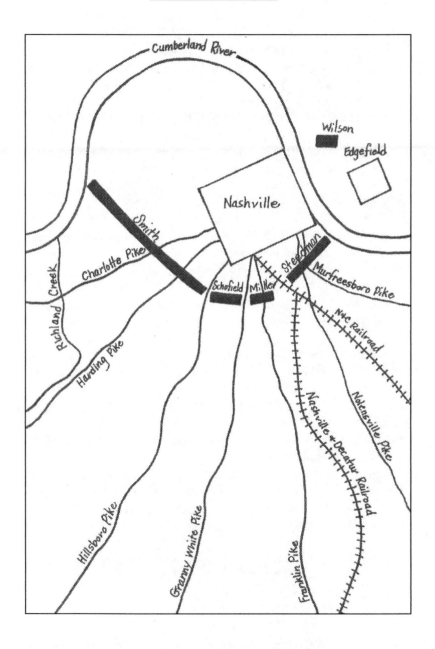

approached the point on the map where the Granny Pike intersected his line, his finger slowed a halt. He then placed his thumb at the point where the Granny Pike touched his defensive line. Without lifting his thumb, he stretched his index finger as far he could, so that it touched the point of his line where a parallel pike, the Franklin, intersected his line a few miles to the east.

"This will be where Hood will make his attack. He has shown his own bull headed mentality at Franklin, and there is no reason to think that he would do otherwise. He will approach Nashville because that is the only option he has." Thomas studied the Cumberland River and made sure that his map depicted the gunboats that patrolled its waters. "He cannot cross this river here, our navy will assure us of that, and Jefferson Davis will ensure that Hood will not leave us in possession of Nashville without offering battle. So when they come, it will be down these two pikes."

The others in the room seemed to be in obvious agreement. If anyone was not, General Smith added the final testimony to Thomas' thinking. "General Thomas, your assessment is most accurate. It would be highly unwise for Hood to attempt to use any of these other pikes. They would cut off his escape route in the event of a failed attack. With the Granny and the Franklin secure behind his offensive, then his path of withdrawal can be held open with minimum use of manpower."

Schofield unconsciously crossed his arms, as he was growing more and more irritated with this council of war. Thomas and Smith appeared to him as arrogant fools, firing their thoughts and observations from the comforts of this room, while he and his men had suffered the past few weeks without such luxuries. Where was Thomas' bold plans and advice when it was needed most? Schofield knew the answer to that was plain enough... it sat in this hotel with Thomas, probably in that chair in the far corner.

"If I may interject," he said, "but what if Hood does not attack?"

"General Schofield, it would be like I said earlier," Thomas answered. "Then we will wait until this cavalry is fully equipped and we will bring the fight to them."

"Then the strength in the numbers that you had also mentioned earlier would surely be negated."

Thomas' head lifted from the table and for the first time his eyes locked with Schofield's like battering rams. "General, we have the strength in the numbers, that can not and will not be negated. When the time draws near, I will disclose the plans that I have made that will sweep John Bell Hood from Nashville like dust in the wind."

The room had grown uncomfortably silent. Except for Smith, all other eyes feared to lift themselves from the battle map. The two rams kept their horns entwined for a few more seconds until Schofield backed down. He knew that he had overstepped his place and now was not the time for such an overt act.

"General Schofield," Thomas said, "if you are now satisfied with our objectives, I will dismiss the council. Please furnish your staffs with their orders and have your men fully prepared to welcome General Hood." Thomas waited for the gathering to break before he slid next to Schofield. "General, if you would not mind, I would ask that you and General Cox remain here. I have sent for General Wagner and would like the four of us to discuss what happened at Franklin behind these closed doors."

Thomas stepped from the room and promised to return shortly. Schofield stared at his back until it was no longer in view. He did not know when Thomas would return, but he wanted to spend every minute that he had rehearsing his answers that would justify his every decision since Pulaski.

*　　*　　*　　*　　*　　*　　*　　*

When Thomas left his war council he was immediately accosted by one of his aids. The young officer had in his hand a newly arrived telegram. Thomas cast a troubled look at the message, but he did not read it. He greatly feared what it would say. Last night, he had sent a telegram of his own to Halleck back in Washington. He had advised the Chief of Staff that he would consolidate his army around the Nashville fortifications and wait for Wilson's cavalry to be fully equipped.

His plans to Halleck were the same as those revealed to his generals moments ago. If Hood chose to attack, he would repel him, and if Hood choose not to attack, then with his cavalry ready he would bring the fight to the enemy. Thomas meant to only glance at the message, but the name printed on the bottom caught him by surprise. It was not sent from Halleck, or even Stanton, this telegram was sent from Grant.

431

The officer looked at Thomas with concern. Thomas simply turned from him without uttering a word and walked towards the front of the hotel. He stepped outside into the brisk air, passing officers and soldiers as he went. Realizing that their general wanted to be left alone, they removed themselves from his path. He waited until his boots could feel the security of the city streets before reading Grant's telegram.

With each completed sentence, Thomas' emotions sank deeper and deeper into despair. Grant was worried about Hood's ability to destroy the railroad links from Nashville to Chattanooga and was ordering Thomas to attack this threat as soon as possible. 'How can he continue to try and control my army in such a fashion,' he thought. Grant is miles from here, has no idea of the condition of the men in my command, and yet he issues these orders which are impossible to accomplish. He is only looking at numbers on paper and not at the intangibles.

Schofield's army did manage to escape from Franklin, but for all intents and purposes it was shattered. The time needed to equip Wilson's cavalry was going to be time well spent in repairing the Twenty-third and Fourth army corps. Now was not the proper moment to use these men on an offensive. Thomas feared that their morale was so low, that it would take little more than a single serious repulse to send them scattering back through Nashville and across the Cumberland River faster than fat rabbits being chased by skinny wolves.

'No General Grant, I can assure you one thing, I will not attack Hood at this time,' he thought. 'And if you would like to remove me from command that would be just fine.'

Thomas thought of the three men that awaited him inside the hotel and how they were all directly responsible for his current situation. The battle of Franklin had no doubt raised the level of concern in the nation's capitol.

He could just imagine how the demagogues in Washington were using Franklin as a catalyst of ammunition against President Lincoln and his ability to conduct this war. Lincoln had no doubt turned to the one man whom he trusted the most and that one man was Grant. There could be no other explanation, except pressure from the President, as to why someone as intelligent as Grant would order an offensive so soon.

It should have meant little that Hood had been victorious at Franklin. The battle was won by the Confederates, but their numbers lost would not be replaced. Hood now had fewer than thirty thousand soldiers. Thomas knew if his government could remain patient, he would be able to augment his own army and overwhelm the enemy. And he also knew if Grant were here he would he say the same thing.

Thomas folded the message and with his hands clenched around it, gnarled a whispered oath, "Just give me a few damned days Grant, you would ask for the same, just enough time to have Wilson ready and the spirits of this army lifted. Then I will completely destroy the army of John Bell Hood."

*   *   *   *   *   *   *   *

Brigadier General George D. Wagner sat next to Generals Cox and Schofield at the long end of the table in the room, but as far as he was concerned, he was in the room by himself. They had just spent the last hour and a half discussing all that had occurred at the battle of Franklin a few days ago and Wagner was not naïve to the onus placed on his command for the army's defeat.

"General Wagner," Thomas said. "You say that you posted your men outside of the enemies earthworks because you were confident that Hood was not going to attack that day?"

Wagner reached for his water, but realized he would probably choke once he attempted to swallow. "Yes sir, that is accurate."

Thomas looked at Wagner as well as Schofield and Cox. To this point, every battle detail that he had heard sounded more absurd than the previous. Had General Stanley not passed through Nashville on his way to seek medical attention, he would have had a struggle believing any word of this explanation. But Stanley had been very clear when he said that every senior officer on the field agreed that there was nothing so improbable as a Confederate assault upon Franklin. Thomas felt he could trust Stanley's conviction. He tried to keep that in the back of his mind as he listened to an obsequious Wagner make a feeble attempt to defend himself.

Unfortunately for Wagner, there was also the testimony of Colonel Conrad, as well as several of his officers, who spoke a different tale. Thomas remembered his father once telling him to believe none of what he heard and only half of what he saw. He would follow that axiom now, and let Wagner himself prove what really happened on that battlefield.

"General, if that is the case, why did you not have your men fall behind Cox's main line once the enemy's advance became apparent? By every account given the flags of the Confederacy emerged from those hills with over twenty thousand men in arms."

Schofield and Cox both turned towards Wagner for his response. They were just as eager to understand why Wagner failed to react to such an obvious circumstance. This time Wagner did drink from his glass, thankful that he did not choke. "General, this feels more like an inquisition than anything else." As soon as the words left his wet lips, Wagner wished he could take them back. In themselves they were an admittance of guilt. No one in the room responded to his audacious statement, they sat idle, awaiting his answer.

The truth was, he had no answer, and by the looks he was receiving, they knew as much. What else was he supposed to say? Could he sit here and admit to General Thomas that he ordered them to stand their ground as a means to teach his men how not to rout? Could he tell Thomas that he was angry with the brigades of Conrad and Lane for abandoning Opdycke the night before at Thompson Station? If he said as much now, how asinine would it all sound after the fact? His own temper had nearly caused the loss of Schofield's entire army. How was he going to absolve himself of this? Wagner knew that many of the men at Franklin all had said one thing in common, that Hood's attack came swift and hard. Perhaps that was his only chance for absolution.

"General Thomas, I have not apologized to General Cox and Schofield yet, and I believe that the time has come for that. I can only hope that my apology is not too late. The men under General Schofield's command performed a most admirable feat by escaping Hood's closing grasp, a grasp that seemed to constrict tighter and tighter with each passing mile from Pulaski to Franklin. It was my own foolishness that placed this army in peril at Franklin, that and nothing else. I fully meant to retire my men behind Cox's line as he had instructed. From that position, we would have dealt the enemy's breakthrough such a blow that it would have crippled their command. I do see that now, and I did give the orders to pull back, but the approach of the enemy was so rapid, I feared a withdrawal in the face of their attack would prove disastrous. I hoped to repel the initial assault, and when they reformed for a second advance, my men would fall back to the Carter house."

When Wagner had finished, he could not believe how candid his testimony had sounded. Surely Thomas would understand his rational and not condemn him for his actions. A soft knock rattled the door and Thomas left his seat to open it. His adjutant general, William Whipple, momentarily stepped into the room and handed Thomas another telegram. Whipple whispered something in Thomas ear, and then departed. Thomas stood by the door reading the message before rejoining the men gathered at the table.

If Thomas intended to handle Wagner's lies with any amount of charity, this latest telegram would change his attitudes for concern. When Thomas once again looked at Wagner his pupils were so thin and piercing they looked reptilian.

"General, I thought if I called you here and treated you like a man, you would respond like one. You have proved me to be incorrect. By every account of the surviving officers that served under your command, they all report the same story. They were ordered to use the bayonet if need be, but they were to hold that position at all costs. Do you understand what that command means to the men forced to obey that order? Because that order came from no one's lips but your own, and that decision has put my army in an extremely perilous position."

Thomas watched as Wagner's head bowed upon his chest. "General Wagner, this may come as no surprise, but you are hereby relieved of your command. No army under my control needs the service of any such as you. If I am being too harsh, I am sorry, but you have no idea how your actions stand to affect this nation that we are trying so desperately to hold together. If you will, please be dismissed. Whipple awaits you outside and will ensure that you are escorted from the city. Where you go, is up to you."

Wagner kept his head low as he pushed his chair from the table and took his leave. The others in the room expected Wagner to be relieved from command, but not in such a fashion. Thomas waited for the door to once again close, before continuing. He did not seem to be affected in the least by the way Wagner was dismissed.

"General Schofield, I understand that Cooper's brigade is

en route to bolster our command?"

"That is correct, I expect his regiments to arrive in a few days."

Thomas would need them sooner than that. Wagner had been removed from command, and would take the blame for Franklin with him. At least that was how it would appear when Thomas made his official report to Washington. Every senior commander that had survived that battle all had said the same thing, that had Wagner's men been in reserve, the Confederate breakthrough would have been easily repulsed. A few small companies managed to stymie the Confederates when they overran the Carter grounds, their numbers were not enough to push the wave back. And yet their sacrifice had not gone in vain. Their brief counterattack managed to give Kimball enough time to swing his command back east so that they could secure the bridges south of the Harpeth.

As he read the reports there was no doubt in Thomas' mind that had the enemy's breakthrough ground to a halt, those same victorious rebels would have been massacred in a savage barrage of fire from every direction. Instead, Cheatham's corps was able to wheel towards the Third division and roll it up like a blanket into the river. Watching his flank crumble before him, General Reilly, God rest his soul, had no choice but to give ground, which allowed Stewart's corps the opportunity to charge his front. Caught between two corps of infantry, Reilly's division never stood a chance.

And that was exactly how Thomas' report would appear once it landed on the Presidents desk. But he still had other concerns that bothered him. One was Spring Hill. How could Schofield risk everything on a night march with Hood's army reported to be only a few feet away? Equally alarming was Schofield's decision to place his army on the south side of the Harpeth River. Why not cross the fords and bridges and use the river too his advantage? Schofield claimed that the pontoon boats had arrived at the same time as the enemy. Thomas was unsure how that mattered? The pontoons were their opportunity to escape, and Schofield should have taken it. If there was time to get Wood's division and the wagons to safety, then time could have been found for the rest of the army to follow.

"General Thomas," Cox said, breaking his thoughts. "I am not questioning your actions, but don't you think that your dismissal of Wagner was a bit harsh. I mean no one would like to see him go more than I…"

Thomas' head snapped up like a rattlesnake. "General Cox, that man has cost us more than you know. General Grant expects me to make an attack no later than tomorrow."

"Tomorrow? My men must be given at least another days rest," Schofield fired.

"I know that, that is why I do not want to comply with Grant's orders. In fact I will politely refuse them. We need to have Wilson's cavalry equipped, no matter what you may think of him, he is needed. But that is not my only reason for being so hard on Wagner." Thomas produced the telegram that had just been delivered by Whipple. He threw it upon the table and watched it slide across and land in Wagner's vacated seat.

"That is our last correspondence from our garrison at Murfreesboro. It has been reported that the rebel cavalry has cut the lines between here and there." The response was silence. "That is over eight thousand men cut off from us."

"Should we send a division to their aid?" Cox asked.

"No, that is exactly what Hood would like us to do. He would welcome any opportunity we give him that will allow his men to strike ours without the benefit of the earthworks that protect this city. I will get word to General Rousseau to hold Murfreesboro against Hood until we are ready to take the offensive. That must be no later than the eleventh."

Thomas stood up and motioned for the others to do the same. "Gentleman, Franklin is now behind us and that is where it must stay. We still outnumber the enemy, and our numbers will grow much faster than Hood's. I cannot find a single reason to be threatened by Hood's approach. They do not even have the numbers to attempt a siege like Chattanooga. Hood cannot cross the river, our boats will prevent that, and he is not strong enough to attack us. Our only undoing will be caused by the provocation of our own leaders back east. I fear that they will try to force this army into making an attack that it is not ready for. So please use these next nine days wisely so that when I give the command, our men will be well rested and ready to comply."

*   *   *   *   *   *   *   *

General Schofield left the St. Cloud Hotel thinking that Thomas was making a grave mistake. If Grant wanted that attack now, then Thomas should do so. By openly disobeying orders, was Thomas not doing the very thing that had just caused Wagner to lose his command? Why was there any difference now?

Perhaps Grant needed to hear a different side of what was now occurring in Nashville.

$$*\quad*\quad*\quad*\quad*\quad*\quad*\quad*$$

Approximately five miles from Nashville there rests a wooden structure referred to by the men in blue as Blockhouse number 2. The blockhouse and the Union troops garrisoned in it had the duty of protecting the railroad trestle bridge that ran close by. For a long time, the only duty for the men stationed there was the occasional cleaning of their cannons and rifles, while at the same time making sure that there was enough time to play a game of poker to win back the wages lost during the previous gamble. The sun came up and the sun went down, and at Mill Creek, the Federal troops simply observed this natural course of events.

That was until the devil himself had planted his cavalry boots upon their soil. Nathan Bedford Forrest had tried with great effort to somehow stop the rapid flight of Schofield's retreating army. Unfortunately, the Yanks had gotten off to a good start, and their men moved with frenzied speed. When Forrest had reached the home of Granny White, along the pike that bore the same name, he could see the remnant of Schofield's army entering the fortifications of Nashville. If Forrest had thought that he had any chance of taking the city, he would have, but if he learned anything during his two-week chase of the Federal army, it was that attacking them behind strong works was useless.

Not far behind Forrest marched the columns of infantry under Stephan Lee. It was just after two in the afternoon when General Stephan Lee met briefly with Forrest at the Granny White house and they both decided that they should not approach any closer with out the rest of the army. They did not want to provoke the Federals into an assault until all of the Army of Tennessee was on hand. Not wanting to remain idle, Forrest sent word that he needed new orders. Surprisingly, his reply came from Hood, not Lee. Hood's response informed him that the remainder of the army would arrive sometime tomorrow, and until then, Forrest was to keep his attention towards the east and ensure that he cut off all communication between the garrison at Murfreesboro and Nashville.

Forrest relished the thought and within moments had Jackson's divisions riding west. They consolidated with Buford's division at the Nolensville Pike and together, the two divisions rode south along the railroad. Any property that existed in their path that was considered an aid to the Federal cause was utterly destroyed. Telegraph lines were severed, blockhouse's were burnt, and the tracks for the railroad were derailed. Until Blockhouse number 2, Forrest had not met a single obstacle worthy of his attention.

"Major Strange," Forrest said as he looked across an adjacent hill at the blockhouse that was now surrounded by his own cavalry. "Can you explain to me once again how it is that any train managed to reach this far, more so how its passengers were allowed to escape and construct earthworks on that slope?"

Strange looked through his own field glasses and watched as Buford's men tried to charge the blockhouse, only to be sent scurrying back followed by a volley of hot lead. He knew that Forrest was enraged at what had occurred here, and was surprised that the general was able to keep his calm. The cavalry had the blockhouse surrounded until a train could be heard approaching from the south. They had been able to stop the train, but in the ensuing chaos, the Yanks that were on board, no doubt headed for Nashville, managed to escape their captors and rush towards the blockhouse. Unfortunately, the wooden structure was not large enough to accommodate them, forcing them to form their own line of defense on the slopes of a hill within support of the blockhouse. Since their arrival, Forrest's cavalry has been kept at a distance from the blockhouse.

"General, I am not sure how it really happened, but I can assure you that the way in which our boys are making this fight, they will never take that stockade."

Forrest looked up towards the sky and was disappointed with the suns descent towards the horizon. "These dammed winter days do not leave us enough light to conduct a decent war with the enemy. Buford and Jackson can answer for this tonight. Advise the men to hold off any further attacks. Our objective was to cut off the telegraph wires from Murfreesboro to Nashville and that has been accomplished."

Forrest stepped off of his horse and sat upon a large rock that rested against a very old and gnarled tree. He slid his hands through his thick hair before resting his elbows upon worn knees. He thought of the Federals that had repelled his latest attacks and felt a sickness swell in his belly. Some of the soldiers that had escaped that train were colored units. 'They are using our own Negroes against us, and still we cannot find the will to over run them.'

The sound of an approaching horse brought him off the rock. Forrest expected to see Buford or Jackson, but was instead greeted by an officer from General Stephen Lee's staff.

"General Forrest, I was told that I could find you here. General Lee has asked that you keep your cavalry in place, but that you return to him at once."

Forrest's look was one of surprise. "Are you telling me that General Lee is now ordering my cavalry? You may go back to your general and advise him that if he expects me to leave my cavalry for a second, he had better consider otherwise."

The officer was waving his hands in apology. "I am sorry General Forrest, I can see how my message could sound confusing. It is General Robert E. Lee who has given the order, not Stephen."

Forrest gave one look over his shoulder towards the blockhouse and the Yankees that defended it. He then turned back towards the officer as he remounted his horse. "Lead on my good sir," was all he said.

*   *   *   *   *   *   *   *

City Point, Virginia

It was approaching midnight and still General Grant found sleep to be the furthest thought from his mind. He sat in the headquarters of his cabin at City Point fearing that any moment he would receive the dreaded news that somehow Hood had defeated the Federal army at Nashville. He knew that an audaciously offensive Hood could never defeat the defensive minded Thomas. Thomas proved his mettle at Chickamauga, Nashville should be no different. And yet, doubt still enshrouded him like a dark secret.

A smooth hand caressed the back of his neck, followed by the warm pressing lips of his loving wife. Julia had come to be with him for a while, hoping that her presence could help relieve some of his stress. Up until this past week, she thought that she had been doing an admirable job. However, when the news of Franklin reached the east, the powers in Washington accosted him with awful taunts of the 'we told you so' sort. They were referring to Grant's support of Sherman's plan to march through Georgia.

Grant knew the risks when he condoned the bold strategy. Sherman was leaving Hood's beaten army behind so that he could march through the heartland of the South in an attempt to bring the war to the Southern people. The strategy was to demoralize their citizens, as well as a means to link the two armies together for a combined final assault against Lee. Sherman had promised that he would leave enough men behind to contend with Hood, and he had. It was just that at Franklin, the unthinkable had occurred, and now there was no way to get word to Sherman. The politicians in the capitol read about Franklin and could draw one simple conclusion. If Hood somehow managed to defeat Thomas at Nashville, the whole West would come undone and this war would take a dramatic turn for the worse.

Grant was not as concerned about Nashville as the politicians were, but the fears of the President were too much for him to bear. Julia knew that her husband's loyalty to Lincoln meant more to him than perhaps even their marriage. She also knew that he would not allow himself to disappoint the President, but ever since the battle at Franklin, Grant felt like he had. Julia wished she could hug his problems away, but knew that her burden would only suffocate him. Still, she tried to console him the best she could.

"Dear, staying up will do you no good."

Grant turned to his wife and set her upon his troubled lap. "My dear, your words have more wisdom than I deserve. I only wish that I could sleep."

"Then talk to me, perhaps by vocalizing your worries, you can release them."

Grant held Julia's hand firmly. "Sit down next to me," he said as he slid the chair out for her. "You know that what I say must stay here, within these walls. I do fully trust that Thomas can withstand an assault from Hood, that is not my worry. Thomas will be slow to attack... I can read that in his telegrams. First he reported that Hampton had somehow managed to send an entire

441

division of cavalry against him, as if I would not see the movement of such a force. Now he needs time to equip his own cavalry, and I support that. Halleck and Stanton want Hood attacked at once, and I agree with them. But Thomas insists that he needs until the eleventh. As hard as I try to reason this, I keep arriving at the same conclusion, there is no reason to delay an attack. Hood's army, though victorious, is still little more than a full sized corps. I cannot understand why Thomas is acting so hesitantly."

Grant fell silent and Julia simply held on to his limp hand. Though she knew the answer, she pressed on, so as not to lose him to his despair. "That is not all that is troubling you, is it?" she softly asked.

Grant's sunken eyes were bloodshot. 'How does this woman know me so well,' he thought. But he knew she was right, perhaps she could hear the same cacophony as the one that possessed his soul. The sounds that continued to echo in his head were of the one hundred-gun salute that was fired from the Confederate lines in honor of their victory at Franklin. Grant took that insult personally. It was he who had fired the first such salute when the news arrived that Atlanta had fallen. And now Lee was throwing that back in his face, perhaps deservingly so. Still, that did not compare to what he now held in his free hand.

"This... I received this telegram from President Lincoln. The President has never questioned anything that I have done, until this...until now. I know that it is Halleck and Stanton who are pressuring him to do so, and the fact that he is succumbing to such pressures tells me that he has lost his confidence in my abilities. The President wants Hood attacked, and in this telegram, he writes that Thomas is acting very McClellan-like by remaining within Nashville's defenses. That may be the greatest insult that I have ever had to endure."

Julia felt the warm tear slide down her cheek and turned from her husband. She did not want him to see her cry... but she could not avoid it. Seeing the man she loved so hurt and yet unable to do anything to comfort him made her feel helpless. She thought for a moment that she had found the words that she needed to say, but Grant was already pulling his hand from hers.

"The man that trusts in me the most, I have let down, and the man whom I trust in the most is nowhere to be found. Sherman is my answer to all of this, and right now, he may as well be in Mexico." Grant dropped his head into his hands and sat motionless.

Julia stood from the chair and walked behind her husband. She bent over his huddled form and wrapped her arms around his shoulders and the two of them remained that way for a very long time.

Chapter XXIX
December 3
Nashville, Tennessee

An unseasonably warm wind cut through the hills surrounding Nashville as if it were searching for a season that was still several months away. Perhaps it was the unusually warm sun hanging quietly over the area that misled the strong gust of air. To many of the local inhabitants, this was the kind of day that could afford them a rare opportunity to catch up on certain duties outside of the home. Perhaps an old barn was in need of repair before the spring thaw. If not, there certainly were mothers who were ready to throw open their front door to let their cooped up, rambunctious, children out of the house. Unfortunately for the local inhabitants, due to circumstances that had little to do with the elements of nature, none of that would occur in Nashville today or any time soon.

The Federal army that was now in occupation of the city had been extremely vigilant ever since the first of the month. The forts and trenches outside of the city were infested with Northerners. News quickly spread that a part of their army had been destroyed at Franklin, and that a great battle would soon be fought here. The citizens hoped that the fate of the Yankees at Nashville would be the same as those at Franklin. The first rays of that hope arrived on this day almost at the same time as those from the sun.

The Southern army had appeared in full force earlier this morning. Their flags could be seen waving triumphantly on the hills south of the city. For the citizens of Nashville those red flags became the beckoning call of hope. Soon John Bell Hood's army would finally expel these Northern aggressors from their beloved soil. It had been a long time since any one of them could truly part a smile, but as they passed the Yankees they noted the anxiousness with which they worked. Those Yankees knew what was coming and they looked scared.

As well they should be.

*   *   *   *   *   *   *   *

"General Lee, I do believe that domed building is the state capitol of Tennessee," an exuberant Hood said.

Robert E. Lee looked through his own field glasses and nodded. Though the proximity of the state capitol was a clear indication of how close they were to driving the Yankees from Tennessee, it was the filled earthworks to the south of the dome that caused him some doubt. A solid line of trenches supported with forts and artillery as well as the protection on both flanks and rear by the Cumberland River seemed an immeasurable task for any army. That was not considering the fact that the Northerners fortifying their strong position outnumbered his own army by almost two to one. Hood was right, the state capital was right before them, but who would dare reach for it? It would be like a child trying to take the dinner from the maw of a starved lion. When those teeth came crashing down, there would be little doubt about the outcome.

Lee turned around on his horse and watched the long procession of Stewart's corps as it marched along the Granny White Pike. The pike ran in between the high hill that he was on and the home of Mrs. Bradford. From his vantage point, Lee could also see the Franklin Pike and on it the arriving columns of Stephen Lee's corps. As much as he tried to remain optimistic, he could not help but look at the men in this army and reflect upon one single thought... there just weren't enough of them.

"General, if this weather continues to hold, we can expect a decisive battle to occur here any day," Hood continued.

Lee remained silent. He watched Hood interact with his staff and wanted to share in their jubilance. From their actions, they must have thought that they had already won this battle just by their presence alone. Again Lee looked towards Nashville and frowned.

Lee noted the time, almost nine in the morning, he expected the other commanders to arrive at any moment. They were going to group on this hill for a brief council on how to conduct this offensive in the days ahead. As Lee surveyed the ubiquitous hills that populated the area, he had to wonder how this army had lost Tennessee to begin with. This state seemed to be filled with an abundance of favorable defensive terrain. Then he thought of men like Grant and Sherman, and easily realized how the Southern army had been pushed through Atlanta. They simply moved around them. Perhaps something he should have done back in

Pennsylvania when he had the opportunity.

A rider ascended the hill and approached Lee and Hood. Lee recognized the man as Captain Wigfall. "General Lee, Generals Stewart and Lee are on their way and should be here momentarily," Wigfall said.

Lee wondered if someone in those forts would see the congregation upon this hill and order some artillery to quickly break it up. "Captain can you please direct the generals to follow after Hood and I, we will move between these two hills."

Wigfall agreed and rode off to direct the approaching generals.

"General, is there something wrong with this ground?" Hood asked.

Lee smiled and then asked for Hood to join him alone. The two rode west where the hill sloped down and then flattened before rising again to join with the adjacent hill. The point where the hills joined was like entwined hands, reminding Lee of an elderly couple that had endured the test of time.

He also felt safer tucked in between these two hills. He looked over his shoulder to see that they were in fact alone. "Thank you, General Hood for making this an easy affair."

"General Lee, if you are referring to my stepping down to give you command of this army, then the honor is all mine. For I have been given one more opportunity to serve under you," Hood said.

Lee went on. "Later this afternoon I will need to ride amongst each of the corps and announce myself to the men. The time for secrecy and rumors has ended. Please have your officers secure an area large enough, yet one that is out of the enemy's view. Now, the question that I face is what do we do with the enemy now that we have them caught."

"My men are eager for the fight," Hood said. "With Nashville before them, they can finally taste their retribution."

"I am sure that they can, but we both have seen their works. The enemy's position here makes Franklin pale in comparison," Lee said. He then took a step forward before abruptly stopping. He seemed to be having a thought to himself and when he spoke, Hood was not sure if he were meant to hear what was said.

"If I had more time, there would be more options. I am afraid that more than anything else... not these trenches, not these hills, not their artillery, nor the size of their force, but time… time will be the deciding factor in the battle here." When he finished talking, he was once again silent. Hood remained silent in respect for his general. Lee remained in a state of reflection for several long seconds before turning his attention towards Hood.

"General, if you do not mind my asking, what would you have done had I remained in Virginia?" Lee said. He was not sure why he asked the question. It was a mere thought that floated through his mind while thinking on this situation. Not sure if God had put the thought there for him to vocalize, he decided to simply ask the question of Hood and see where it might lead.

Hood felt that Lee's question was a genuine one, and not some test of his commanding skills. He did not waste any time in answering. "Well, the lack of our numbers prevents me from having many options. I would extend this army till we enclosed Nashville from the south, dig in, and do my best to convince Thomas into attacking our position. This is the only way that I could see us using our smaller numbers to an advantage. And there is the matter of Murfreesboro to the east. I would imagine I would need to contain that garrison with some of my men. Forrest is already en route as we speak." When Hood said that, he realized that he no longer had the authority to order Forrest to perform such an action.

If Lee was offended, he did not show it. "Actually, I called Forrest back last night," he said. "I made a solemn oath to myself, that I would never conduct another campaign without the full support of cavalry. But still, your chief of staff reported that there are an estimated six thousand Yankees at Murfreesboro. I do agree that we must do what we can to prevent those soldiers from joining the ranks in Nashville. Perhaps a division can be sent to block any attempt they make at reaching the city."

"That could be done," Hood said.

Lee liked that idea better than using his cavalry for the task. "So, you would have been content to simply remain idle on these hills, hoping that the Federal army would give up their strong position and assume the offensive?"

Hood remained confident. "I would have. But I would not remain here idly waiting for the enemy to attack. Forrest has already secured several of the enemy's blockhouses. I would order him to do more of the same, gobbling up the small Federal posts that are in this area, while convincing President Davis to send more troops to reinforce my army.

Lee listened to Hood's strategy and could not help but feel sorry for the general. Hood had not been to Richmond in a while and had not realized how much the situation had deteriorated since his last visit. If Davis could not muster a single division to help reinforce the army in Virginia, there was no chance in the world that Hood could ever expect to receive a single company.

"General, what troops? There are none to spare. I have made several personal visits to Congress begging for the same things you now face. I have pleaded for men, for food, for supplies and all they do is nod their heads and chew their peanuts. There is no hope for additional men any time soon."

"Excuse us for interrupting, but General Lee I would strongly be against this army simply waiting for the attack of the enemy," Stewart said.

Lee and Hood both were caught off guard. They were so focused on their own conversation, they had not heard the approaching footsteps of General Stewart and General Stephen Lee. Hood looked past them, wondering why their staffs did not follow them. Surely they would have heard them if they all had approached together.

"We came alone because Captain Wigfall said that you were alone. We were not sure if this was to be a private council," Stewart said, as if he knew what was behind Hood's narrowed eyes.

"And what would you do then?" Hood vehemently asked Stewart.

"Anything but what I hear you proposing to General Lee," Stewart shot back. "That distance you propose is over eight miles in length. Unless you believe that a five-foot space between each man is acceptable defense, there is no way to cover that amount of ground."

Hood wished that he could walk without the aid of his crutches, so that he could floor Stewart for openly questioning his military acumen. Wait until Lee returns east, he thought, and I regain command of this army. We will see how volatile you will be then.

Lee knew that he should have stepped in between his two generals the moment their words became knives, but a thought flashed within him and though it was already by him, he knew he needed to catch it before it was gone.

Something in what he had said earlier and what Hood had just said seemed to collide and somewhere under the debris of the impact was the answer to his dilemma. He began to carefully shift the rubble in hopes that what lay beneath remained undamaged.

The idea of advancing against the enemy and then inviting him to attack was a concept highly advocated by a general whom Lee held a great deal of confidence in... Longstreet. It was his old warhorse who argued for a similar tactic at Gettysburg, and at that time, it was easy for Lee to find every reason why Longstreet's tactic would not work. It would take the shattered remains of Picket's, Armistead's and Trimble's divisions to convince him otherwise. His lesson was learned the hard way, frontal assaults were no longer a practical strategy. Yet had not the frontal assault succeeded as recently as Franklin?

Lee knew the answer to that riddle well enough. He studied the aftermath of the battle, and realized that the only reason for the victory was Schofield's lack of a reserve force at the most critical position of the battlefield. Had a single reserve brigade been present near the Carter house, Lee was confident that Franklin would have been another Gettysburg. Could the direct assault work a second time? Would the Yankees neglect the placement of reserves again? Lee knew that it was unlikely. Thomas was now in command of the Union army, and Thomas did not make such mistakes. The presence of Thomas, and the reminder of Gettysburg was all the reason he needed to know that no matter how limited his choices were, he could not employ an offensive assault here at Nashville.

But what was he to do? Time was quickly slipping beyond his reach and every day that passed, he feared the dreaded news that Grant had finally achieved the breakthrough he so arduously sought. But time was like a coin hung from a fortuitous string, and Lee needed to use that to his advantage. He knew beyond any doubt that there was no chance of General Thomas taking his army from its secure defensive position and using them to attack the entrenched Confederates. And yet, that was where time could play a critical factor.

How long would President Lincoln, General Grant, and the politicians in Washington allow a Confederate army to sit at the doorsteps of Nashville? If Thomas were left to his own command, Lee knew the attack would never come. But the fact was that Thomas was ruled by men back east. The more Lee considered it, the more it made sense. When Halleck was the commander out west, he was replaced because he let the army at Corinth escape. General Rosencrans was constantly cajoled into taking the offensive and then removed from command the first opportunity allowed. Even McClellan, who Lee considered the north's most able general, was removed for allowing the enemy to escape his grasp.

If the North showed one predictable pattern it was that they did not tolerate any kind of delay once the enemy was before them. And in that, Hood's plan began to make sense. With his army stretched before Nashville, Lincoln would urge Thomas to attack. All that Lee had to do was trust in one of the Lord's highest virtues... patience. Simply remain patient, and allow the North to defeat itself.

But what of Grant? What if he gave the command to attack his army back in Virginia? The only way for Lee to counter that thought was to remember the season. Regardless of how benevolent the weather had been, it was still winter, and sooner or later the cold temperatures would again return. As much as he feared that Grant would attack, he knew that the winter back east would halt his maneuvers until the spring thaw. That would allow Lee the time needed to remain patient and hope that Thomas was pushed into attacking. If the enemy did not attack any time soon, then he could begin to entertain other ideas, perhaps taking this army and marching to Virginia with it? But before he did, he at least wanted to give the Union army an opportunity to commit the blunder that would offset their numerical superiority.

Lee turned his attention back to his feuding generals. "Gentleman, you can have all the fight you want with the enemy just past these hills, but for right now, I need you all to be focused. General Stewart, I understand your concern, but there is merit to what General Hood proposes. We cannot attack their position. Artillery, forts and more soldiers than I dare to count are in support of their lines. Nor can we cross his flank either, we have seen their gunboats, and even if we somehow manage to gain access to the north bank of the Cumberland, we would be cut off from what little supplies we have. And we certainly cannot fall back from here. That would have a most disastrous effect upon the morale of this army as well as negate the victory of all those brave souls who fell at Franklin. Not to mention the fact that the life of my army in Virginia, depends on your victory here, thus drawing

General Sherman and his men back to Tennessee. General Stewart, General Lee, if you have a suggestion that you believe will better benefit this army please say as much now."

"So we will just dig and wait for Thomas to attack?" Stephen Lee asked.

"No general, we dig in and pray that they attack," Lee said. He then unfolded a recently drawn map of the area and laid it upon the ground. The men gathered positioned themselves over it.

"We passed some strong ground just to the north of the White residence, but if we want the enemy to attack, we will need to push on a bit more, closer to their outer works. General Stewart, your corps will secure the army's left flank along the Hillsboro Pike. From there it will run east until it joins Stephen Lee's men at the Granny White Pike. Lee will be the center. General Lee, your line will then continue east from the Granny White Pike as far as it can past the Franklin Pike. At that point, Hood's corps will continue over the Central Alabama railroad bending slightly north and resting on the Nashville and Chattanooga Railroad.

I will have Forrest use the bulk of his cavalry to protect our west flank. That is where the largest gap will be, three to four miles I would guess, but as General Stewart had pointed out, we just do not have enough men to cover the entire southern half of the city."

Lee could see that both generals had been appeased by his strategy. He had managed to commend both men for their observations and opinion about their predicament, and by doing so, he did not appear to take any one's side. Lee then rolled up his map and placed it within the breast of his jacket. "Gentlemen, if you will, please begin positioning your army as we have just discussed and instruct your men to heavily fortify their positions. When the enemy does attack, I fully expect this army to repel their every advance and deliver a staggering casualty list back to their high command."

"General Lee, what of Murfreesboro?" Hood asked.

"Yes, the Federal garrison. Send a division, General Bate's would do. Please be sure that he understands that under no circumstances is he to advance anywhere near the garrison. I do not want the enemy to know Bate's numbers. General Bate is simply expected to deny the Yankees at Murfreesboro any chance of reaching Nashville. This way he might deter their six thousand from interfering in any battle that occurs here. If he is attacked, he

Lee Invests Nashville

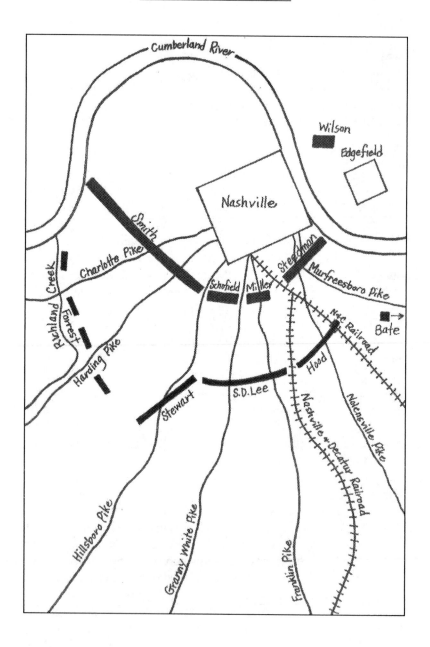

is to hold his position... unless the attack comes from Nashville. If that is the case, General Hood, you must be ready to counterattack and overwhelm those Yankees that stray from their earthworks."

Hood straightened his towering form upon his crutches. "General, if any Yankees leave those trenches, I can assure you they will never have the opportunity to return."

"How are our supplies, do we have enough for the artillery?" Lee asked. He thought of Gettysburg, on how his ammunition had run so low that he could not support the advance of his army. He did not pay enough attention to that detail then, but he would now.

"Thankfully, we have a new supply from the captured Federal wagons at Thomason Station and at Franklin, but we could use more," Hood said. "It would not hurt to send wagons back to re-supply."

Lee seemed content with that answer. "Thank you, gentleman for your time."

Stewart and Stephen Lee remounted and rode back over the hill towards their corps. The day was still early, but there was much work to be done. Lee helped Hood to his horse then mounted his own. Lee placed both hands upon the leather reins, feeling the thick strap secure in his clenched palm. He watched Hood, with his paralyzed arm, and wondered how much such a simple task now burdened him. He then thought upon Jackson, and Cleburne and the thousands of nameless faces who were taken from their loved ones.

"How much more blood will have to be spilled?" Lee said a bit louder than he intended.

Hood turned towards him, with a small fire beginning to escalate in his eyes. He seemed to once again embody the spirited man that he had commanded earlier in this war. "General Lee, we have lost a lot of blood, and I know that I am responsible for much of that, but that will soon change. This will be the fight that we need. With a victory here, the Northern moral will be shaken. They will lose patience with allowing their generals to march around our flanks, we will have proven how little that accomplishes. The tactics that make them so successful, will no longer apply when the next great battle occurs. There will be no more dancing around each other's flanks... I am certain of that. Forced to rectify the loss of Tennessee, be it Sherman or Grant, the

Yankees will be pushed into attacking us as soon as possible. Our two armies will once again clash head on like great rams, and when that happens, it will be the Yanks that are forced into a reckless offensive. And I can promise you this, that when they come, we will be braced for them. To answer your question, there is still a great deal more blood to be spilled, but starting here, the losses will be on the side of the Federal army."

*   *   *   *   *   *   *   *

Lee spent the remainder of the day watching the Confederate army take its position south of Nashville. Fully confident in its ability to repel a Federal attack, he then spent a few moments with General Bate before his division headed east towards Murfreesboro. He felt the need to reinforce to Bate the order not to press the garrison into any attack. Keep your distance, and deny them Nashville, were his last words to the departing divisional commander.

Forrest then reported to Lee and told him that his cavalry would return as soon as Bate's division took their place. Forrest was sincerely grateful for the opportunity that allowed his cavalry to participate in whatever occurred at Nashville. He had not been happy with Hood's orders sending him from the main threat. Lee told Forrest how he wanted his cavalry to protect his exposed flanks, and the cavalry commander assured him it would be done.

Lee then spent over an hour with each corps. He was ashamed of his own pride, but could not help smiling as he recollected how uplifted the men became as he rode amongst them. It was as if his presence alone guaranteed their victory in the days ahead. He told them how proud he was of their accomplishments and how well they performed at Franklin. He also asked that they keep his presence as secret as possible. He knew that soldiers often blurted out more than they intended, but if asking his men to remain silent would help any, he would at least try.

It was dark when Lee finally made his way to the home of Colonel John Overton. Overton considered Lee's presence as a blessing and would not allow Lee to sleep anywhere else in this area except within his own home. Lee reluctantly accepted the offer. He did not want to offend the grateful man. A warm dinner was presented to him, which he consumed with guilt. How could he swallow another morsel, when he knew that there was an army back in Virginia being deprived of such basic necessities?

Lee took his leave immediately after dinner and went into the bedroom. He wanted to spend this quiet time reflecting on his current situation, but as soon as his head hit the bed, he was asleep. A soft tap upon his door stirred him awake. By the quietness of the house, as well as the stillness outside, Lee knew that it must have been very late. As he got out of bed, he shamefully realized that he had never gotten out of his clothes. He lit the candle next to his bed and walked towards the door. He carefully opened it and was surprised at who he saw.

"General Lee, I hope that it is not too late to wake you."

"Chaplain Quintard, I would have been upset if you hadn't," Lee said. "Please come in and have a seat."

Quintard entered the room as Lee lit a few other candles to dispel the darkness. When he turned, he could now see that the chaplain was not the same man whom he met only a few days ago. "Chaplain, are you well?" he asked.

Quintard pulled a chair closer to the bed and sat upon it. He motioned for Lee to sit upon the bed. "General, I serve this army, but my duty is to God first, and though I am ashamed to question, I do not understand how he allows both of our armies to spill so much blood. I have just returned from burying some good men at St. John's Episcopal Church, and seeing their faces, so pale and still, is perhaps the hardest labor my faith has ever had to endure."

Lee knew that Quintard was referring to the generals who were lost at the battle of Franklin. It was such thoughts that had several times brought his own faith into question.

"But I did not come here to discuss that. I did claim that my duty is to God, and that alone is what is allowing me to confide in you now," the chaplain continued. "You asked me earlier about General Hood, and I told you that then was not the time. Since that moment, I have felt compelled to have this talk with you. I came here to tell you this, because I feel that it will benefit our army."

Lee felt uncomfortable with the way the conversation was progressing, and certainly did not want the chaplain to say anything that he did not want to. But before he could stop him, Quintard had continued.

"General Hood means well, but there are strong and destructive demons that he battles within him. He takes his medicine too often and fails to address the real matters that tear at him."

Until today, Lee thought that Hood seemed a different man than the one he once knew. He attributed that to his lost leg and limp arm, but Quintard was alluding to something more. "Chaplain, General Hood seemed to regain a part of himself today, and I took that as a positive step. But from what you are saying, I think that there is more that I do not know."

"There is. And though I should not be telling you this, I cannot let the demons inside General Hood affect how he commands this army. Before he can properly lead this army, he needs to work out two separate yet equally damaging conflicts. First there is his insecurity with Ms. Preston, this damages his confidence greatly. Secondly, he harbors a great animosity towards General Hardee, who he blames, and from all that I have heard, rightfully so, for all his misgivings during the Atlanta campaign. It is my strong belief that he believes the only way to defeat these internal demons is to win on the battlefield. It is in this conflict that he feels forced to push this army beyond its capabilities. I feel that he believes that a complete victory would both guarantee the hand of Buck Preston as well as prove to Hardee who is the better commander. To gain this end, Hood will stop at nothing."

When Quintard finished, he felt very ashamed. He crossed his hands in prayer and hoped for God's forgiveness. "It is just that General Hood needs to put his trust in the Lord. Only then will he find the peace he so desperately needs."

Lee placed his hands over the pastor's in prayer. "I am glad that you have come here and told me this. I am not sure if you are aware that I am now in full command of this army. General Hood has been assigned the temporary command of Cheatham's corps. When I leave to return to Virginia, I intend to place Hood back in overall command. I need to be sure that when I do that, he is once again the man that I once knew. If you had not come here with this, I would not have been able to do that. I think that God would understand that."

When Quintard looked up, his eyes were watered. "General, if you do not mind, I would like to spend a few moments in prayer with you?"

Lee humbly accepted, and sat silently as Quintard thanked

the Lord for His patience and understanding. He then went on to pray for all those lost at Franklin, including the fallen that wore blue. Quintard concluded his prayer naming each of the six Confederate generals that had been mortally wounded, ending with Patrick Cleburne.

Lee's eyes remained closed long after the prayer was over. The bright handsome face of Cleburne refused to dissipate from his conscience. The internal sight of which, brought an issue to the surface... an issue that Lee was trying his best to keep locked in denial.

"Cleburne was a special man," Lee said as he slowly opened the door that was choking his soul. "I intended to take him east with me and give him his own corps to command."

"He would have served you well."

"That he would have, and perhaps he already has. If I may be so bold as to ask... what are your views concerning slavery? I mean in its relation to what God and the Bible teaches?"

Quintard took a moment before answering. "General Lee, let me first ask you this. How do you feel about slavery?"

Lee was not prepared for the question to be turned upon him, but was not surprised to find that he had his answer ready. "I know how Cleburne felt, and there is much to be said concerning his philosophy. I do believe that the Negro, with proper training, can make a highly efficient soldier. The North has already proved that to us. I could see how offering their freedom would benefit our cause. Keeping them enslaved is no longer just... nor is it wise. But those in Richmond would rather concede this war, than accept that reality."

"General Lee, whatever you or I may think that the Bible says about slavery, and how it is interpreted by whoever reads it, is a separate matter. I can only tell you to listen to your heart, for that is the one place that God truly exists in all of us."

*   *   *   *   *   *   *   *

Long after Chaplain Quintard had departed, Lee lay awake in his bed reflecting upon Cleburne and slavery. He spent several hours praying to God for comfort and clarity with this issue, but so far, his prayers remained unanswered. Could slavery be the reason why the South was not winning? Was it God's way of telling them that the only way to achieve victory was to free the Negro first?

Lee got out of bed for the second time this night and walked towards the small dresser that sat against the opposite wall. On its flat surface rested Patrick Cleburne's journal. Lee took it in his hands and brought it back to the chair that was left near the bed by the chaplain. Lee flipped through it, casually reading its contents. As his fingers flipped past the pages, one section seemed to stand out more than the others. It was written with a better handwriting than any previous and was also the greatest in length.

The passage began with a look at the South's current predicament, stating that unless something changed soon, it would be learning its history from a Northern version of the war. The passage then shifted its focus to the hundred thousand Negroes that the United States was training to be used against the South. The enemy that already outnumbered them was soon to grow larger, while the Confederacy's greatest resource was being armed against them.

The paragraph continued, pointing out that this tactic used by the North also allowed other countries to sympathize with their cause and prevent the threat of foreign intervention. The only real way to defeat the North was to defeat the notion of its cause. The United States was using slavery as a facade to wage their true cause… a war of oppression. If the Confederacy could somehow reveal this façade to the rest of the world, the North would be exposed as the military tyrants that they truly were. Tyrants that were using their might to establish a centralized form of government, which would deprive the South of her rights and God given liberties.

Lee stopped reading after that and returned the journal to the dresser. As he walked back towards the bed, he could feel a slight headache begin to swell. He poured himself a warm glass of water and tried to clear his thoughts with a deep swallow, but it did little good. Lee knew that there was too much weighing on his mind this night, and that sleep would come at a hard cost.

Chapter XXX
December 5 – 10
Nashville, Tennessee

Lee spent most of the day facilitating the army's fortifications south of Nashville. By late afternoon, he was fully confident that their entrenched position could repel a Federal advance. Though sporadic gunfire echoed throughout the day, nothing amounted to the full scale offensive that he so desperately hoped for. It seemed that both sides had learned all too well the probable outcome of leaving your works to attack those of the enemy's. Lee just hoped that there was some way that the Federal command could forget that lesson.

Riding along the ranks of his men, he was greeted by soldiers that were in excellent spirits. The warm sun continued to be a blessing as it radiated over the heads of the Confederate army. Many of them took it as a sign of better days to come. One particular regiment put a smile on his face as he rode by. They were whistling Dixie with a jovial spirit as they dug the earth to help construct their entrenchments. It was not too long ago that these same men would have looked down on him for asking them to labor in such an act. What was once deemed cowardly was now cherished on both sides.

The spirit of these men helped to rekindle the flame of hope within him. He wished that there was some way to get this spirit back into the hearts of his own men back east. Grant's massive army had spent the last few months pressing his men back against Petersburg and Richmond. Once Grant had Lee where he wanted him, he began using his overwhelming numbers to move around his flank, forcing the Confederates to stretch a distance that they could not possibly defend. Lee knew that it would only be a matter of time before his stretched army snapped. With one eye facilitating the construction of the earthworks, he kept the other glancing over towards Nashville, hoping that at any moment, he would see the flags of the Union marching out against him.

Lee felt the need to spend most of the day on the western side of the Granny White Pike. It was from this direction that he anticipated the Federal attack to come. Though Forrest's cavalry was posted from here to the Cumberland River, the distance was just too great for the cavalry to cover. Hood had wanted to place his men even closer to the Federal line, but Lee refused and wondered if even now his men were still too close. He did not want his army too close to Nashville, in the event the Yankees could slip around his exposed flank and gain the rear. To guard against this, several redoubts were being constructed a few miles along the Hillsboro Pike, south of Stewart's position. These earthen defenses would help his undermanned army brace against any massive attack that could be sent from that direction, allowing Lee the necessary time to swing support from his center or even his right flank.

Pleased with the alacrity in attitude that assisted the men with their laborious tasks, Lee rode back towards the Overton home. As he passed by a few members of Stephen Lee's staff, he asked if they could summon Hood to his headquarters. The officers replied with a firm salute and then departed. Upon his arrival at his headquarters, Lee found a late lunch waiting for him. He quickly ate the meal in silence. He sincerely wished that there could have been an opportunity for his own staff to accompany him to Tennessee. He had grown so accustomed to many of the familiar faces back east, especially that of Colonel Taylor.

After he was finished eating, Lee decided that the day was too accommodating to spend the remainder of it in doors. He stepped outside and walked towards the railroad tracks. He had not gone far when the sounds of heavy horse steps announced the arrival of General Hood and his staff.

"General Lee, I apologize for the delay, but there has been some news from General Bate's division near Murfreesboro."

Lee looked up at the mounted general and waited for him to continue.

"It appears that Fortress Rosencrans contains more Yanks than we had anticipated. General Bate confirms that there are over ten thousand Union soldiers within the fort. He moved his division within six miles of the fort when attacked by three infantry regiments, supported with cavalry and artillery. Bate easily repelled their advance and from the mouths of captured Yanks, their commander General Milroy, thought he was up against our detached cavalry. It appears that the presence of our infantry so close to Murfreesboro has scared the Yanks into falling back within their defenses. General Bate requests instructions."

"His instructions are the same as when he left. Was I not clear when ordering General Bate not to press too close to the garrison. We must hope that the Federals did not get a good measure of his size. If there are indeed ten thousand Union soldiers there, Bate's division could be easily destroyed."

"Should we send Forrest in support?" Hood asked.

"General Hood, absolutely not. If the Yankees have fallen back to their fort, then let them stay there. Tell Bate that he is not to take another step in the direction of Murfreesboro. If the enemy makes another advance, one that threatens his division, he is to fall back to your flank at once. For the enemy to withdraw from our single division, they must presume that we have more men than we actually do. Let us hope that Bate's presence alone can keep those ten thousand soldiers from adding their weight against us. Now if you will, please join me against this rock for a while."

Hood dismounted with the help of his aids. Realizing that Lee wanted time with him alone, Hood dispatched his staff with the orders for General Bate. He then leaned on his crutches and walked towards Lee who placed his back against a rather large gray rock.

"General, have I done anything wrong?" Hood tentatively asked.

"I can hear from the artillery that we are not firing excessively against the enemy's works."

"No sir, that was as you requested," Hood said.

"Yes, I know. It was General Forrest's plan. He suggested that if we really wanted the Yanks to attack, we needed to make them think that we had a low supply of artillery."

"With the amount of surplus we have gathered from the Yanks as they routed from Spring Hill to Nashville, we have more munitions than I could have ever hoped for. Without those spoils, we may very well have been low on ammunition for our cannon."

Lee nodded in agreement, but stared straight ahead. "I do hope that General Thomas makes his attack before the end of the year."

Hood placed his crutches to the side as he joined Lee against the rock. "General, I have been thinking about a matter I wish to share with you."

"Very well."

"What if we ordered General Price to dispatch a division across the Mississippi? You said yourself that Richmond cannot send us any reinforcements, but perhaps Price can. This way, if Thomas remains still, then the better for us. That would give Price the time needed to arrive here. And if Thomas attacks, then even better. We can use Price for the counter attack."

Lee could see Hood's face brighten as he put his energy in this false hope. Perhaps a few months ago, Hood's plan might have had some credence, but Price's advance had ended in defeat.

As Lee reflected on Price's campaign, he began to consider the folly of the Confederate command structure. How much more devastating might that campaign been if Price's campaign was timed with Hood's bold offensive? Most likely there were Union regiments right now in Nashville that months ago, would have been assigned to resist Price. Had Hood been here then, the Yanks would have had to make a choice as to which threat to face. It was an opportunity missed, but a lesson gained.

'We must begin to think this war differently,' he thought.

"General Hood, you may not know the entire details for General Prices advance, but his army is in no condition to lend us a division at present. If anything, we may need to send him a brigade or two before this is all over."

Hood was visibly deflated. That was not Lee's intention. "It was a fine plan though," he said. Hood cracked a slight smile as he nodded his head. The sound of the Federal guns firing a volley of shells into the Confederate lines could be heard over the hills to the north. The sound reminded Hood of his current duties.

"General, was there something in particular that you needed to discuss with me?" he asked.

Lee had intended to engage Hood in a conversation about the troubles that Chaplain Quintard had mentioned last night. However, Hood had become defensive when he had turned down his plan to appropriate a division from Price. Now was not the time to try and expel Hood's demons.

"I did, but now is not the time. Thank you for the report concerning General Bate. That last round of the enemy artillery was heavier than most. Please return to your men just in case."

Hood's eyebrows bent in complexity. Obviously Lee had something on his mind, he had called him here to discuss it, but now he was being dismissed without ever having broached whatever it was they were supposed to discuss.

"General Lee, if there was a reason for my coming here then I beg to know what that reason was," he pleaded.

Lee stood up and placed his hands upon Hood's shoulders. "Well I can promise you this, it was not to discuss your demerits earned at the academy. Now General, if you would, please attend to that artillery that I hear."

By the time Hood returned to his entrenched corps, the enemy's artillery had subsided. There would be no attack this day. As night began to settle, Hood returned to his headquarters and was helped from his horse by Captain Wigfall. Hood did not say much as he hobbled past Wigfall. He was thinking about General Lee and what he had said in reference to demerits. It was better times, many years ago, when he was enrolled at West Point, and Lee was its superintendent. Hood smiled as he remembered the abundant amount of times that he was called into Lee's office to receive numerous demerits for his misbehavior. Ironic, he thought, how Lee tried to expel me from military school, while Schofield did everything in his power to convince me to remain enrolled. And it is because of Schofield that I stayed on course... and now here I am in Nashville poised to destroy him.

Ironic.

*   *   *   *   *   *   *   *

December 6
Evening
City Point, Virginia

General Grant was once again alone in his headquarters. He had kindly asked his wife to take the children back home until the pressures from Tennessee had found a way to relieve themselves. Though her presence was a comfort, it was also a distraction, and now more than ever, he needed to remain focused.

He had before him a message from General Schofield. Initially he was surprised to see a message from Nashville that was not from Thomas. As he read the sentences, he understood why. Schofield's words were so acrimonious, Grant almost tossed the message into the fire. Apparently Schofield was not happy with the current state of affairs in Nashville. Thomas was being over cautious and allowing the enemy to just sit triumphantly on the hill south of Nashville. Schofield then went on to complain against

Thomas commanding capabilities during the precarious withdrawal from Pulaski. He ended his letter with an image that did not sit well with Grant. Would you have stayed in your warm hotel while your army ran for its life, he asked?

Grant tossed the message on the table before him, as he kicked back upon his chair. He placed two tired hands behind his head and leaned back upon them. "Thomas, what am I to do with you?" he whispered. He began to reach for a cigar when a sharp knock brought him out of his chair.

He began walking towards the door, but it was already opening. Rawlins stepped into his cabin, immediately apologizing for his hasty entry. Grant knew from Rawlins actions that something of immense magnitude had just occurred.

"General Grant, I am very sorry to come in like this," Rawlins said, but before he could finish, a very tall man stepped into the room behind him.

Grant quickly replaced the cigar in his pocket. "President Lincoln, I was not informed that you were intending to visit," he said. "Rawlins, thank you, you may be dismissed."

Lincoln moved to the side to allow Rawlins to exit. The President looked extremely worn, reminding Grant of a very old and bent pine tree. Lincoln had his hat clenched firmly by his two thin hands and waited for Grant to offer him a seat. Grant led him to his table and offered the President something to drink.

"No thank you, General," he said. "I can not stay here long, in fact, my intent is such that no one in Washington will realize that I have left. Halleck and Stanton asked to make this trip here, and I declined them both. I needed to talk to you first, without them. I came here to discuss Nashville. Halleck and Stanton amongst numerous others are very concerned with General Hood's army."

Grant thought of Schofield's letter and began to seriously share in their concern. "I received word from Thomas last night that he intends to attack the rebel army as soon as his cavalry is intact."

"And do you believe him?" Lincoln asked.

Grant smiled. "I guess that I should never play a game of poker against you. I have all the confidence in the world in Thomas ability to repel Hood, but I am not so sure of 'old slow trot' taking the fight to the enemy. I replied back that he must attack Hood at once, but Thomas can be very stubborn."

"Does he realize our fear of Hood crossing the Cumberland and advancing upon Ohio? That event would cause a tremendous outcry throughout the North."

"Mr. President, I have told him that and more, but he still refuses to advance until he is ready."

Lincoln carefully placed his hat upon Grant's desk. He inadvertently covered Schofield's letter with the dark brim. When he looked up, his face was sad, but very intent. "General, I have promised you that I would not interfere with your skills as a general, and believe that I have thus far kept up my part of the bargain. But I must be insistent now. Something must be done."

The only answer that Grant had was to replace Thomas. The notion had crossed his mind several times during the past few days, but the problem was replace Thomas with whom? "I can replace General Thomas with someone more apt to take the offensive."

Lincoln was nodding his head in agreement. "We have discussed that opportunity as well. Only Halleck would put it in a different light. Halleck would have you replace Thomas, but neither he nor Stanton will support your doing so."

Grant unconsciously had his cigar back in his hands. He was rolling it between his fingers, feeling its smooth surface tumble from finger to finger. "So they want me to attack the enemy at Nashville, and when my reply is that Thomas is not the man for the job, their reply is that I should not remove him. This makes no sense to me. The bottom line here is that if Thomas' attack results in success, they will receive their share of credit and acclaim for having the patience of leaving him in command. If I leave him in command and Hood outmaneuvers him from Tennessee, then I am sure that I will incur their wrath. Yet, if Thomas' is replaced, and the new commander attacks and fails, they can say they never condoned such an action on my part. Anyway I look at this, I come out on the bottom. For Halleck and Stanton, I would guess that's politics at its best."

Lincoln stood up and took his hat from the table. Grant saw the letter from Schofield staring up at him like the solution to a complex math equation. Schofield was the next in command.

"Mr. President, I will give General Thomas one last chance to make his attack. If he fails to do so, I will have him replaced with General Schofield."

Lincoln shook Grant's hands with uncertainty. "General

Grant, I will remain faithful to my oath for as long as possible. You must do what you must, and I must trust in all that you do. You have the authority to sign my name to any decision that you feel needs to be made." He then turned from Grant, but paused as he put his hands against the door handle.

"General, if I may ask… how fares General Sherman?"

For the first time in his service to the President, Grant was unable to look him in the eye. Grant had supported Sherman's plan to cut loose from Hood and attack the Southern countryside. Lincoln in turn supported Grant's approval, and with that decision, had to now suffer an intense amount of pressure from those in Washington that thought the whole plan ludicrous. And now those rabble-rousers must be basking in their own pride. There had been no word of Sherman's whereabouts making it almost impossible for Grant to get any word to his general. Lincoln had to only mention the name Sherman and he knew that Grant would understand the question.

The problem was that Grant did not know the answer. Sherman and sixty thousand soldiers of the United Sates Army were somewhere in either Georgia or the Carolina's. The deep brow above Lincoln's eyes said that perhaps those soldiers should have been in Tennessee.

As Lincoln once again took his leave, Grant kept hearing the President's words repeat in his head over and over again. "You must do what you must, and I must trust in all that you do."

* * * * * * * *

General Thomas received Grant's dogmatic telegram at some time past midnight. He held the paper in his angry hands as he paced around his room. This army is just not ready yet, he thought. Why can't you just give me a few more days to have the cavalry fully equipped? I wish I had you here right now General Grant, so that you might explain to me the reason for this rush? Hood cannot get by me, and he has not the manpower to attack me. If you are so concerned, why not order Sherman to fall upon his rear.

Those were the mordant thoughts that danced in his head, but they were not the words that he replied in his telegram. Thomas replied that he would attack Hood at once, even though his army was not yet ready to do so. At least that would get Grant off his back for at least one more day, and hopefully give Wilson the extra few days he needed to mount his troopers.

As soon as the telegram clicked through, Thomas knew that his days as the commander of this army were numbered. What he said in his reply to Grant and what he intended to do were two entirely different things. Thomas would not be cajoled into making an attack that his army was not properly prepared for. The way he saw it, he would rather lose his command, but by doing so, allow his cavalry the necessary time to equip itself so that it could face the enemy on favorable terms, than to remain in command and lead an ill-prepared army into ruination.

Wilson had told him earlier that he would be ready for battle on the tenth. As far as Thomas was concerned that was going to be the day that he would lead his army against Hood's. This battle of wills between he and Grant meant so little when compared to what was at stake. And as far as Thomas was concerned the United States of America meant more to this nation, than his command to this army.

*   *   *   *   *   *   *   *

December 7-10

It was probably very fortunate for the Federal army entrenched at Nashville that Thomas refused to obey Grant's order to attack. The day had begun with a deep red glow that radiated against long sinuous clouds that ominously hovered over the city. The wind that had been cooler the day before had grown bitterly cold by noon. It was as if it knew that it had been cheated during the previous days by the warmer climate and so returned with a fury. Adding to its increasing ferocity was the arrival of rain.

The weather continued to grow inclement as the temperature dropped to normal winter conditions. By the next day, the ground was a frozen slab of ice. Both armies were forced to endure the arriving chill while posted within their entrenchments. This was a more arduous task for the Confederate army who lacked numerous basic supplies such as tents, blankets and shoes. They tried to huddle as close as they could for warmth, but there was only so much you could do when your bare feet rested upon the cold wintered earth.

Just when the Confederates thought that the weather could grow no worse, December ninth came... and with it snow. It was as if God had been watching these two armies and realizing what they were about to do, tried to hide their sin by covering them in an unblemished blanket of whiteness.

The opposing armies sent out small parties to gather anything combustible and began igniting the countryside in hopes of generating as much warmth as possible. For those lucky enough to gather near a kindled fire, the nights became somewhat bearable. But there were many, mostly Confederates, who went to sleep in trenches... within which they would never again wake. At some point of the dark night, the freezing cold simply claimed their souls from this earth.

With the weather so treacherous it became impossible for Thomas to coordinate any offensive operations. The ground was so icy that one had to take each step in careful measured strides. When Thomas informed Grant that he was going to attack on the seventh, and failed to do so, he fully expected a telegram relieving him of command by the ninth. Thomas had not attacked, and yet Grant was ominously silent. Thomas used that extra time to his advantage and had his army ready to move against Hood.

He went over battle plans with all his senior commanders, and carefully outlined the flanking maneuver that would sweep Hood off of the hills south of the city. He planned to attack the rebels on the tenth, hoping for a clear day, but this winter storm remained unyielding. Even the simple task of having Wilson's cavalry cross from the north banks of the Cumberland proved a dangerous task. Several men had their limbs crushed under the weight of their own mounts when the horse's footing gave way to the slippery ground beneath it. As Thomas watched his cavalry suffer the task, it was not hard for him to imagine how disastrous it would be to attempt to have his army march against the fortified Confederate position.

Thomas peered from the windows of the St. Cloud Hotel and watched the ubiquitous snowfall continue its descent to cover the earth. The icy snow that was whipping tent flaps and battle flags and the cold breaths of those outside confirmed the futility of any attack. He sent word to all his commanders that the offensive was postponed. He had a staff officer send a telegram to Halleck in Washington, as well as Grant at City Point, informing them of the current situation. The telegram ended with Thomas promising to resume the offensive once the weather cleared.

Thomas never questioned that his strategy would defeat Hood, his only concern was if those back east would remain patient enough to allow his plans to materialize. As he prepared for his meeting, he kept an ear directed towards the telegram room, fearing that at any moment, he would receive the message that Grant was tired of waiting.

*   *   *   *   *   *   *   *

Grant sat alone in his headquarters gazing at the clock. It was eleven thirty at night, and another day had passed with Hood's Confederate army claiming hold to the hills south of Nashville. As a military tactician, Grant understood that Hood did not pose a serious threat to the west, he could not cross the Cumberland, and he could not attack Thomas's numerically superior army. However, there were those in Washington who saw it differently. The rebels will cross over and move into Ohio, they claimed. It reminded Grant of when the Southern ironclad first emerged in the waters off of Virginia. The papers headlined that the Southern mechanical monster would soon arrive in New York waters and wreak havoc upon the city.

Grant laughed at the thought. Even if the boat reached New York's harbors how much damage could it actually do. How long would it stay afloat with out any base of supplies? In many ways the predicament in the west was the same.

Part of him felt that he should give Thomas the time he needed to defeat Hood, but Thomas had not been honest in his telegrams. He kept promising Grant that he would give the orders to attack, but those orders had never come. And now time was beginning to sway Grant into the opinions of the politicians in the nation's capitol.

There were reports that the Confederate cavalry had indeed crossed the Cumberland River. In addition, the rebels placed artillery west of Nashville at Bell's Mill and had successfully warded off Union boats from attempting to approach the city from that direction. Fort Rosencrans, the garrison at Murfreesboro, was also reported to be cut off from Nashville by a large force of infantry. These were little victories as compared to the loss of

Nashville, but they were enough to keep the telegraph lines from Washington active all day.

However, it was not the communication from Washington that concerned him. What swayed him most on this day were the reports being sent from the telegraph lines out of Nashville. Thomas had already sent word earlier in the afternoon that he intended to attack this day, but the weather had been too awful. Apparently, snow, rain, and sleet were hurling around the city like swarming locusts, forcing him to call off the attack. If that had been all Thomas reported, Grant might have found the sense to leave Thomas in command at least until the weather cleared. If he did not attack after the weather cleared, he would be replaced at that time.

What infuriated Grant was that Thomas did not just send his report to him alone. Thomas had also wired Washington a report... one that carried a much different tone to Halleck... one that Thomas probably did not know had been forwarded to Grant for review.

Thomas had held a council at his headquarters and informed Halleck that his entire senior command agreed with the suspended attack. He also apologized to Halleck for his inability to attack sooner, but had Schofield's army arrived in Nashville with more troops than it had, he may have been able to move sooner. He ended this telegram by stating that he had done all that he could be expected to do, and if need be, that he should be replaced.

Grant held the telegram in his cigar smelling hands for several seconds.

"Done all you could do," he said aloud. He thought of Lincoln's last visit to his headquarters, felt the weight of responsibility placed upon his chest like a sack of cannonballs. 'Do something,' the President had said. Grant's determination began to thicken.

"Done all you could do?" he repeated. "Perhaps had you attacked earlier as I ordered, the storm would not have been a concern. And now you have the audacity to defame General Schofield, the man who did all that he could do to keep his army from being cut off by superior forces, while you sat in your warm hotel doing nothing? No General Thomas, you have not done all that you could have done. And now you do worse by shifting the blame to all but the one that deserves it the most."

Grant thought of Lincoln one more time. 'You must do

what you must, and I must trust in all that you do.' He then threw Thomas' telegram to the table with firm resolve. He began to write a message that was to be telegraphed to Nashville first thing in the morning. Lincoln had asked for him to do something that would remove the Confederate threat from Tennessee. Grant had had enough of Thomas' excuses… it was time for change.

* * * * * * * *

D.C., December 10, 1864

The President orders: I. That Maj. Gen. J.M. Schofield assumes command of all troops in the Departments of the Cumberland, the Ohio, and the Tennessee. II. That Maj. Gen George H. Thomas report to General Schofield for duty and turn over to him all orders and dispatches received by him.

Chapter XXXI
December 11 ‑ 12
Nashville, Tennessee

Colonel Tyree H. Bell led a company of the 21st Tennes-see Cavalry west along the Charlotte Pike towards Bell's Mill. The cold wind cut deeply into his face with each passing stride of his mount. Bell inwardly wished that he could have had this day to himself. He was not feeling too well, and had hoped that a day of rest and warmth would help to recuperate his ill condition. Unfortunately, Forrest had issued revised orders a few days before, and word had come to Bell, that Forrest was not pleased with his performance thus far.

Bell's original task was to have his brigade posted in op-position to General A.J. Smith's Federal entrenchments on the western side of Nashville. It was the responsibility of his brigade, along with the rest of Buford and Chalmers' divisions, to protect the very vulnerable left flank of Hood's army. The distance that Forrest's command stretched was long and thin from the western portion of the Hillsboro Pike all the way to the Cumberland River. But Forrest's orders had been very clear, if the enemy were to attack from this sector, it would fall to the cavalry to impede their advance, while falling back to the Hillsboro Pike. The cavalry was allowed to give ground, as long as it prevented the enemy from sweeping around their flank to gain Hood's rear.

However, as the cold winter days slowly continued, Forrest grew impatient. He did not want to just sit around in the passive defensive waiting for the enemy to make a move. Leaving most of his cavalry in a position where they could inform him of any Yankee advancements, he directed General Chalmers to occupy Bell's Mill along the Cumberland River. From that vantage point, Chalmers was able to position enough artillery on the heights to prevent any Yankee ships from entering the city from the west.

With his rear protected, Forrest then instructed all his gen-erals to send out small companies to harvest the countryside for any possible recruits. Any Southern man found at home, between the ages of fifteen and sixty-five, was to be gathered up and sent to

Lee's line south of Nashville. Bell did not know how the other generals were doing in this assignment, but so far his own efforts produced only ten new Confederate cavalrymen.

That was until Major Strange arrived this morning with a message from a very disappointed Forrest. The general had written that he could not believe that there were only ten available Southerners along the Charlotte Pike. Apparently Chalmers and Buford had successfully recruited almost a thousand men between them. Forrest ended his message by informing Bell that he would arrive as soon as he could to 'help' him in his efforts.

That last line was enough to send the chill of death cascading down his spine. He thanked Strange for the message and told him that he would renew his efforts with a personal vigor. He then gathered nearly twenty of his best troopers and rode out to a small farm just a few miles south of Bell's Mill.

A few days ago, his men had approached the farm and tried to convince the father and his four sons to join the Southern ranks. The father's reply was an adamant refusal, but said he could give the men some blankets and food to help them with the winter. Bell's men accepted the offer and returned with two wagons loaded with much needed supplies. He had thought their ride was a success, but now with Forrest's message in his pocket, he realized that it was not.

As he rode over a small knoll, a well-trodden path broke from the pike and led towards the farmhouse set upon a hill to the north. Bell gripped his reins and kicked his horse in the side, eager to gather these men up before Forrest could arrive. And there was no doubt that Forrest meant to arrive today, he would not have had Strange personally deliver the message had it been otherwise.

When he neared the well-kept front porch, he dismounted and handed the reins to one of his aids. He then approached the front door with three of his biggest soldiers. He purposefully kept his glove on when he knocked at the door. On the inside he could hear the shuffle of footsteps. On the outside, a light snowfall had once again resumed.

"May I help you?" a voice said as the door swung open.

Bell had to lift his head to see the man's eyes. The giant was well over six feet tall and built like an ox. A graying beard hung from his face and indicated that the man had been in the middle of eating a soup of some kind. Bell thought of the three soldiers behind him and wondered if he might not need additional men.

"Are you Mr. Tubler... the owner of this farm?" Bell asked.

"I am, as your soldiers could attest. They were here a few days ago, and I have given them all I could."

"And I thank you for that, let me introduce myself to you. I am Colonel Tyree Bell, and to get to the point..."

Tubler did not let Bell finish. He stepped onto his porch, with only his undershirt on. He closed the door forcefully behind him, never taking his eyes off the four Confederates on his porch.

"I don't give a hell who you are, you are not getting me or my boys to join your army. I have already lost my brother at Shiloh and my three nephews, all at Perryville. And recently I have been informed that William, my oldest son, was found dead at Atlanta. How much more can you ask of me than that?"

Bell was so caught up in this man's argument that he failed to notice that he was now standing at the edge of the porch and his three soldiers were on the stairs behind him. He could empathize with this man's losses, but they were no more than what any other Southerner has had to deal with. He put his left foot forward and began to retake the porch.

"Sir, I understand your loss, but the Southern army needs men like you more now than ever. We have the Yanks pinned up at Nashville, and with one more good push, this state will be free of the Northern aggressors, but to do so, we need more men."

The giant farmer's eyes now widened with frenzy. From under his shirt, Bell could see large muscles tightening with aggression. "For the last time colonel whomever you are, the answer is no. Now take your soldiers and get off my farm before the Confederate army has the Tubler family to fight with, besides all them Yankees. I have already given you all the supplies I could spare, you will get no more."

The door behind Mr. Tubler once again opened, and this time his four sons emerged. Each built from the same mold that created their father. He could see his soldiers already placing their palms on the handles of their pistols. Bell had to react quickly. He needed these men to join his ranks, but not at the cost of a fight that could take the lives of his own soldiers. And yet, he could not simply turn his back from this threat and appear cowardly to his men.

"I will go, and we will leave your farm alone, but to do so, I must insist on another wagon full of supplies. Even if it is just wood so that we keep our fires burning."

Mr. Tubler kept his towering stare fixed on Bell's face. "Boy's, load up a wagon of firewood, plank, anything that will burn and give it to the colonel. I expect the wagon and horses to be retuned, along with the wagons that went yesterday."

Bell nodded his thanks. The gesture was unreturned. After twenty awkward minutes, the barn doors were let open and a large wagon, loaded with combustible materials was ready for the Confederates to appropriate. Just as Bell's men began to climb aboard the wagon, the sound of another mounted company could be heard riding up the path to the farmhouse. Bell looked over his shoulder and was shocked to see General Forrest at the head.

"Colonel Bell, I am glad to have found you so easily," Forrest said. Bell looked up at Forrest, who chose not to dismount. The general had a smile on his face, but his eyes were very intent on surveying the situation. Bell looked at Mr. Tubler and realized that what he thought was intimidation before, was nothing when compared to Nathan Bedford Forrest.

Forrest looked at the well-loaded wagon and turned to the large farmer. "Sir, you are a true Southern gentleman, to furnish your personal belongings, as well as you and your sons to the Southern cause."

Mr. Tubler did not know who this mounted man was, did not know his reputation, but the tone and confidence of his speech was enough to convince him that he was not dealing with someone like Colonel Bell or his other soldiers. "Well, I am sorry to disappoint you, sir, but you can have the supplies, just not me or my family."

Forrest looked down at the farmer, then at his sons. The farmer had a definite defiant look in his eye. His arms were interlocked across his chest in a gesture that indicated that he was on the defensive. His sons however were wide-eyed, possibly with envy at the heroic soldiers that were fighting the battle that they were not allowed to take part in. "Is that what your boys say, or just you?"

"As their father, I speak for them. Now I will tell you the same that I told this fellow here, you can have the wagon, then get off my land."

Forrest's eyes narrowed as his mouth formed an ugly grimace. "First of all, that 'fellow' is a colonel of the Confederate army. Secondly, you call this your land? I was born in Tennessee, these men before you are all from this state. This is not your land, but ours. And for it to remain ours, we must fight for it."

"The Tubler's ain't fighting," the farmer protested, taking an audacious step closer to Forrest's horse.

"Let this be known that this is your last chance. General Robert E. Lee himself has come to Tennessee to lead this battle. Whatever notions or misgivings you have of this army no longer apply. General Lee has come to Nashville for the sake of Tennessee, and so Tennessee must go to Nashville for the sake of General Lee."

Mr. Tubler looked towards his sons with a fire in his eyes that silently told them to get ready to fight these soldiers off their land. The boys looked back towards their father in disbelief. They all knew how important a man Robert E. Lee was, and the fact that he was here in Tennessee, should have been enough to convince their father to finally let them fight along side their fellow countrymen.

Tubler could not believe that his sons were not responding to his silent command. He knew that there was now only one way to get these men off his property. He curled his fingers into tight fists and kept them rigidly at his side. "For the last time, we ain't coming to Nashville. Not for your colonel, not for you, and not for General Lee."

Forrest never took his eyes from the man, or his clenched fists, as he raised his pistol and shot him in the head. The large man slumped over like a sack of potatoes. His four sons began to scream as they ran to their father's aid. There was nothing they could do except hold his head upright as the blood freely flowed from the exit wound in his head.

Forrest put the gun back in his holster. He turned towards Colonel Bell with a very disapproving look. "Have these four boys in your ranks before you leave or shoot them as well. Any man from Tennessee who chooses not to fight for General Lee is Yankee as far as I am concerned, and better he be shot dead on the spot, than have to be dealt with later.

*   *   *   *   *   *   *   *

December 12

The telegram had reached Nashville in the early morning

of the eleventh. Thomas read Grant's demotion and accepted it with stoic callousness. He had known that it would come... he had in fact expected it much sooner. Grant may think that he had won this battle of wills, but Thomas knew better. Even though Grant wanted the army to attack at once, it would take Schofield a few days to acclimate himself to the task. That would mean that the Federal army could not attack Hood until the fourteenth or fifteenth, giving Wilson the extra time that he would need to have his cavalry ready to assist in the offensive.

And so on December eleventh, seven-thirty a.m., Thomas officially abdicated his authority of command. General Schofield seemed eager to assume his responsibility. During a council held at lunch, he announced his plans to attack the enemy, before first light on the fifteenth... weather permitting. There were several objections, but Schofield remained adamant. Grant had put him in charge to conduct the attack that Thomas was hesitant to assume. According to Schofield, there would to be no more delays.

But what Schofield failed to consider was the complexity of his task. It was one thing to change an army's head commander, but it all together foolhardy to do so while trying to conduct an offensive against an enemy that stood only a few hundred feet from view. The result was two frenzied days at attempted reorganization. Headaches spread from staff officer to staff officer like an epidemic. If the enemy knew how hard this army had to fight with the politicians back east, they may very well have stepped aside and let the United States strangle itself with its own chaos.

*   *   *   *   *   *   *   *

While the Union army was experiencing a form of separation within its command, the Confederates were being blessed with a kind of unification. On this day, at the Methodist Meeting House at Brentwood, Major William Clare, of Hood's staff, and his love Mary Hadley were joined in marriage. Chaplain Quintard performed the ceremony and read a glorious sermon from the Good Book. The festive occasion was one of the few events that could take the minds of these men away from their laborious conflict with the enemy.

After the ceremony, those in attendance returned to Colonel Overton's home for a reception dinner honoring the bride and groom. Many of the army's officers were invited to attend, and a large assembly began to gather outside of the Methodist Meeting House. Horses and carriages were lined along the road and were soon loaded with those accompanying the married couple to the banquet.

Captain Wigfall led Lee to his carriage. When Lee had officially assumed command of this army, he had asked Hood to recommend an able officer to serve as his aid-de-camp. Hood had replied that there was none better than his own, and insisted that Wigfall serve under Lee for as long as he had command of the army. Lee found Wigfall to be deserving of Hood's praise, and was thankful for his services.

"General, as soon as the married couple takes to the road, we will follow them in this carriage," Wigfall said.

Lee bent his head from a cold wind that whipped amongst them, and tried to keep his hands warm within his coat pockets. The sight of Wigfall remaining stoic against the cold blast shamed him. Wigfall was busy trying to fasten a loose harness around one of the horses, but he could not complete the task fast enough. It was not getting any warmer, and the thought of General Lee exposed to these awful conditions was not a welcome one.

"General, I am sorry, but it appears that the harness is loose, it should only take another minute or so," he said.

"That is not a problem Captain, perhaps some of these other officers can follow Mr. and Mrs. Clare, so that we will not delay the reception."

Wigfall tried one more time to tighten the harness, but his pull was so forceful it caused the metal buckle to separate from the leather. He was about to utter some harsh words for the apparatus, when an officer not present at the wedding approached to hand him a report. Wigfall quickly read it and then dismissed the officer with a wide smile. "General Lee, this is most grand. The railroad to Alabama is almost repaired… in fact even now supplies are on their way. The quartermaster also reports that our shoe shortage will soon be eliminated. There are several teams of men who are committed to do nothing except produce twenty pair of shoes per day."

Wigfall handed the report to Lee before continuing. "General, if I may add, the land here in this region of the state is the most unaffected that I have seen from this war. There is an abundant bounty to be had once the winter passes. I cannot foresee this army having to leave its present location for any reason except perhaps to enter the sate of Kentucky or even Ohio."

Lee wished that he could share in Wigfall's optimism. The spring thaw was still a long way off, and the enemy to their front was still a very real threat. But he would not voice that to his aid. If Wigfall's spirits were hopeful then that was good. This army needed his attitude to be infectious. Wigfall was again on his way to confer with the men now working on their carriage, when Lee spotted General Hood and his staff preparing to board a carriage of their own. Lee told Wigfall that he preferred to ride with Hood, but would inform Hood's staff to stay behind and ride to the reception in his carriage once it was repaired.

Lee quickly moved through the crowd towards Hood and arrived just as the general was being assisted inside his carriage. The officers present saluted Lee and Lee informed them that he whished to ride with Hood alone. The men parted, with the last officer helping him into the carriage. Another strong wind blew through the crowd and seemed to push Lee inside the buggy. Hood was surprised to see Lee enter the compartment with him. The officer outside closed the door, and the coach was soon rocking forward as the driver led his horses on a slow trot north.

Ever since that night when Quintard arrived to voice his concern about Hood's mental health, Lee had been meaning to have some time alone with the general. The one time that he attempted to broach the conversation, Hood seemed to be on the defensive, and Lee reasoned that the time was not right to discuss such delicate matters as Buck Preston and the failure at Atlanta. But now it seemed that his patience had paid off. The wedding of Major Clare had given Lee the very opening he needed to confront Hood's inner turmoil. This carriage ride alone would be the perfect opportunity.

"A beautiful wedding, wouldn't you agree?" Lee asked.

Hood nodded to the rhetorical question, his thoughts were far away, exactly in the place where Lee knew they would be.

"How is your lovely fiancé, Ms. Preston?" Lee continued.

Hood looked up from his lap and stared blankly outside the carriage window. The winter scene slowly rolled past them like time itself. The cold and gray landscape a reflection of his very soul. As Lee stared at his general, he thought Hood's eyes looked a bit glassy.

"I cannot lie, but I wish it were Buck and I married here today and not Major Clare," Hood said. "I sorely miss her presence, her soft hand in mine. I can only hope that all I have accomplished thus far will make her proud of me."

"How could she not be proud of you?" Lee asked. Lee knew about Sally Preston's flirtatious behaviors, and hoped that her engagement to Hood was serious enough to deny her any carnal thoughts. From Hood's apprehension, it was apparent that there was some mistrust still present. Lee did not like the characteristics that made up Sally Preston, but his hurting general obviously did. And if Hood meant to marry Ms. Preston, Lee would try to support that decision as best he could.

"You are her fiancé, as well as the general who led this offensive north. Your reward was the great victory at Franklin, and there is still one more victory before you. When you return to Richmond, the city bells will be hard pressed at choosing whether to ring for the victory for Southern independence, or for the marriage between John Bell Hood and the lovely Ms. Preston."

Hood tried to turn from the window, but he was anchored with a heavy heart. The feelings that he harbored inside of him were not ones that he shared with many. Chaplain Quintard was perhaps the only man that he had truly confided in since his promotion a few months ago. If there were anyone else whom Hood would open up to, it would be Robert E. Lee. Even though Lee almost had him removed from the academy, he had always been like a father to him. As he stared back at his old friend across from him, he realized that within this carriage, they were not generals or soldiers, but real and genuine friends, if not family.

"I have many times reasoned the same," Hood said. "There are moments when I lie in bed and imagine my return to Virginia. I can envision crowds of people cheering, and standing there is Buck, with arms spread open to welcome me. But as fast as that thought enters my heart and fills it with hope, there are distant memories that follow close behind and destroy my confidence faster than had a bullet entered my chest."

Lee leaned closer to Hood in an effort to gain his full attention.

He wished that Hood would look at him instead of fixing his stare outside, but at least he had gotten him to begin talking. "How is it, that a woman can do to you what the entire Federal army can not?" Lee asked with a compassionate smile.

As Lee waited for Hood to respond, he began to realize why the large Texan kept his head turned from his view. A slow and steady stream of thick tears had finally broken through Hood's tough countenance. Lee made as if he had not even noticed.

"Do you remember my stay in Richmond, after my wound at Chickamauga?" Hood asked.

"I do, you companied with President Davis at that time."

"I did. Many attribute that well spent time to my promotion out west. He did in fact promote me to lieutenant general, and I had never felt more proud. And at the time, I thought I could never feel proud again. Having recently lost my leg, and with the use of only this arm, I was feeling extremely bitter and resentful. But President Davis thought enough of me to look past these bodily hindrances, and offer me a new command. From that moment I made a personal vow to never fail that man for his generous deed. I also believed that such an act would compel Buck Preston to also look past the cripple that I am, and remember the fighter and man that I once was.

"It was Christmas time, and we were having dinner with the President... what a marvelous meal they served. Our ladies had left the room to leave us alone to discuss many things, the war being the most prominent. There were several politicians present, as well as officers from the army. They all had an opinion as to how to handle the war, and fought with each other to get their views expressed. But when I chose to speak up, they all fell silent. It was as if my opinion meant more than anyone else that was in that room, except for the President of course. It was at that moment that I felt the confidence swell within and I knew that I could overcome these physical faults. But in the next breath, that confidence was to be shattered, forever."

"There was a moment of silence, a pause, as I explained how my men drove a wedge in the Federal lines. The men gathered, including the President, listened intently waiting for me to continue, and that was when a giggle was heard from the next room. It was Buck, there was no mistaking her laugh. One of the ladies, perhaps the first lady, had asked her if she and I were engaged. It was at that exact moment when we were all silent. Her reply was her haughty snickering, 'Engaged to that man, never. How absurd to even consider I would. You foolish creatures... to fancy such a thought.' After I heard that, or I should say we all heard that, I was too ashamed to even look up. My story remained

481

unfinished as I reached for my crutches and took my leave."

Lee felt very sorry for Hood. With her inconsideration, Buck had done more harm to Hood than she could ever know. Lee wanted to explain to Hood how his military accomplishment would overshadow anything ridiculed by Ms. Preston, but he knew that he would only be telling Hood things he already knew.

Then a thought struck his mind, a memory of a time long ago, when Lee used to talk to his young students at West Point about matters in life besides war. He would save such lessons for Saturdays when he could invite a few cadets to his front porch for a small reception. There was one particular afternoon that came to him now, and the more he thought about it, the more he was sure that a younger Hood was in attendance.

"Do you remember what I once told you regarding marriage?" Lee asked.

Hood wiped at his eyes, but kept his focus on the passing landscape. "Regarding marriage?" he asked, struggling to find the memory. He was thinking only as far back as the war, and so had no idea as to where Lee was heading.

"Yes, back at the academy. I once told you that when you decide upon a woman to marry, to be sure of one thing."

Hood's face began to brighten at the recollection. "To marry a person so that my child will be proud of us both."

Lee was glad that Hood remembered his advice. "John, I will not tell you whom you should love, but I will ask you to consider my advice. Will Ms. Preston make your children proud? Because there is no question that John Bell Hood has already done so."

The strong and adoring compliment that Lee had just given him was more than even Hood could handle. Years of pent up emotions were unleashed within the confines of the carriage, and they would remain locked there for all time. Lee did not look down upon Hood's open sobbing, nor would he ever mention it to anyone. That confidence was perhaps what had allowed Hood to show his true emotions.

It was several moments before Hood's eyes could begin to dry. Lee hoped that he had somehow broken through to his general. He would need the clear thinking fighter that he once knew in the days ahead. However, he did not want to leave Hood with these thoughts as they joined the banquet.

"You know, that saying goes well beyond the marriage of

two loved ones," Lee continued. "In many ways, that is what holds this nation back from uniting once again. With the Northerners acting as such aggressors, how can we allow our states to once again rejoin their boundaries? Can any Southerner be expected to bring new children into this world under such forced conditions?"

Hood finally swung his head towards Lee and locked eyes with him for the first time. Lee thought he saw an inner spirit resting behind his pupils. "And yet they almost have us beaten," Hood said. "But I truly believe that we are on the verge of something special here. One more victory, and we will once again turn the tide of this war."

Lee was ready to agree, but something held him back. Perhaps it was the careful study of Cleburne's journal, or perhaps it was the years of winning battle after battle, but losing the war, … whatever it was, it was a new thought that was forcing him to think in new directions.

"I hope you are right, but somehow I fear that a victory will be fruitless, unless things begin to change."

"Things will change, we will begin to win the battles again because there will be no more dancing. They will be forced to attack us and we will deliver them one hard blow after the next."

"That may be true, but I think that we have done the Yankees a great injustice by underestimating their will. Lincoln's reelection confirms one great point… they have the will of an entire nation supporting their army. We have the will of an army trying to support our entire nation. It is simply mathematics. The numbers of men that we put on the field are nothing compared to their massive population. That is why we have been losing this war. It has nothing to do with these battles."

"That may be, but there is also much to be said of generals who fail to follow orders," Hood countered. Lee knew that he was referring to Hardee's efforts around Atlanta. Hood would not accept any excuse for the failure of that campaign, except that which put Hardee at fault. The fall of Atlanta made him feel that he had let President Davis down, not to mention his fiancé Buck, whose brother William Preston, had been killed near Peachtree Creek.

"I know that you are disappointed in your efforts around Atlanta, but I have read the reports, your tactics are nothing short of what I would have done had I been in your place," Lee said.

"You replaced Johnston under the condition that you would attack the enemy at once. I would say that you succeeded at that task to your fullest capabilities. You attacked isolated corps in each of your offensives, trying to press your inferior numbers where the enemy was weakest. I have heard that General Hardee holds much of your ire, but I can only tell you that I do not wish to hear any of that. Whatever misgivings exist between Hardee and yourself, I would be ashamed to consider that they would contribute to the fall of our country. The answer is much simpler than that. The enemy simply has too many men.

When Grant crossed into the Wilderness, I held him held in check, allowing Longstreet to march upon his flank. Longstreet's attack went so well, he routed the enemy with more success than Jackson had at Chancellorsville. But this time the enemy did not retreat. They finally have a general smart enough to realize that even a loss such as Chancellorsville meant little when they could just send more soldiers to the front, and that we could not."

"General, I want you to be very clear on my opinion of Atlanta," Lee continued. "You performed most successfully, and did all that could be expected and more. Perhaps the greatest loss that occurred at Atlanta was having you there and not with me in Virginia. I had a tremendous opportunity to crush Grant at North Anna, but failed to have the generals in place that I could trust to deliver the decisive blow. I know in my heart, that had General Hood been in my service, Grant's army would be half of what it is today."

When Lee finished talking, the carriage slowed to a halt. The lights of the party were shining brightly from within Overton's home. Traveler's Rest was a fitting name for such a place. The sound of revelry could be heard from both inside the home and along the front yard. It was hard for Lee to remember that a hard battle had just been fought. His carriage door was then opened from the outside and an officer waited to assist the general in stepping down.

Before vacating the cabby, Hood spoke to Lee and sincerely thanked him for his thoughts. He was then carried down from the carriage and handed his crutches. Lee watched Hood enter the party, and prayed that God would help comfort the man's wounded heart. He followed close behind, with steps saddened by the thoughts of how this war had taken a man once so proud and able, and reduced him to a dejected cripple.

*　　*　　*　　*　　*　　*　　*　　·*

The party inside the army's headquarters was a jovial anomaly. The married couple, as well as the others in attendance, had spent the cold winter night dining and dancing as if the war were a distant memory of a time long forgotten. Harriet Overton floated from table to table bringing with her a warm tray of food and heart felt smile. Earlier she had told Lee that he was God's answer to her prayers. Nashville would once again belong to the Confederacy before too long.

Lee wanted to share in the festive mirth, but found it an arduous task. He stepped very gingerly around the outskirts of the makeshift dance floor as he made his way to his table. Lee did not notice the dancing couples twirling by him in a blur. That was just as well, Lee would not have been able to reciprocate a smile if one was sent his way. As he took his seat, he saw Hood across the room talking with General Stewart, his façade easily concealing the emotional conversation that had occurred on the ride up here. As Lee turned from Hood, he could see the general spread a smile upon his face. That was good. Lee felt better knowing that Hood could still smile. With that worry temporarily out of his mind, he began to focus on another one... the current position of this army.

The day before, he had ridden out towards the front lines and almost had his mount fall from under him. The horse had stepped into the white snow and its front hoof had sunk through the frozen cloud and into a pit below. Before the horse could fully fall in, Lee was able to tug on its reigns and prevent its collapse. Several soldiers nearby quickly ran over and helped Lee and his mount from the pit. The men apologized, but then explained how the pit had gotten there in the first place. The ground was too cold to sleep on, they said. And with the countryside stripped bare of any thing combustible, they had run out of firewood and barn wood to burn for warmth. Realizing that their lives depended more upon their surviving the freezing nights, than fighting the enemy, they adapted to necessity, and let their own ingenuity rescue them from their plight.

The soldiers then went on to uncover the pit and show him how it was used to let four of them sleep comfortably through the night. They had covered the floor with twigs and bramble and then placed a blanket over it. This gave them a warm insulation against the cold earth. Then the four men would pack in the hole and cover themselves with another blanket. In this fashion, two blankets could warm double their number of soldiers, while the closeness of the men generated enough body heat to allow them to sleep safely during these cold Tennessee nights.

Lee thanked the men for their explanation and expressed fondness for their initiative. He then continued to ride a bit farther towards the skirmish line, but the officers and solders nearby forbade him to go any closer. Lee complied and rode back down the Granny White Pike. All he could think of was how his lines were pressed too far forward.

And that was the worry that he could now concentrate upon. As soon as this party ended he wanted to seriously reconsider his extended front. The army was confident, but the fact remained that Thomas still had nearly double the men that he had.

"General Lee, perhaps you could not hear me over this music, so let me ask again. Do you mind if I join you for a moment?"

Lee turned in his chair and warmly accepted Chaplain Quintard's hand.

"Chaplain, I am sorry, there is just too much weighing on my mind to allow me to enjoy these festivities."

Quintard seated himself next to Lee and placed his drink before him. "General, I have felt much the same these past few days, but the Lord has ways of making you remember that there is more to our lives than this war. My spirit was shaken and bent when I had to bury our fallen at Franklin, but my faith did not waiver. That is God's way of testing our mettle. We cannot allow these tests of will to sway us from His path. The rewards are there, if one remains patient. How else can you explain the saddening mass burial of our closest brothers one day, and on the next, my issuing a proclamation to the state? I believe that it was the first one performed since the Yankees drove us from this soil after the fall of Fort Donelson. There can be only one explanation my dear General."

Lee was shaking his head in shame of his own ignorance. "You are so correct, God's hand is in this all. For me it was only weeks ago when I thought that I would never lead an army on the offensive again, and now here we are at the very doorstep of Nashville and the liberation of the entire state of Tennessee."

Quintard was smiling as he stood up. He placed his hand upon Lee's shoulder as he bent over the table to retrieve his drink.

"I must attend the bride, I promised her a few private prayers from the Bible. I trust that smile will remain on your face for at least the remainder of this evening. The war is here, general, and battle will soon come of it, and from that there will be more death. Your part in this is not to ask God why, but to perform your Christian duties the best that you can, and show the Lord that you are ready to accept whatever challenges he may throw upon you."

Lee wanted to tell Quintard that he had spoken with Hood, but felt that now was not the time. There were too many issues cluttering his mind at present, and Quintard was perhaps the only man who could offer him the clarity that he needed. Lee was worried about Hood's infatuation with Buck, it was a harmful distraction for a general in battle. He was also concerned with the army's current position. Should he pull back or not?

He needed more time to reflect on the advantages and repercussions of his position. But he knew that time was not his ally. From somewhere within, he could feel the heavy rhythmic beating reminding him that at any moment Grant might launch the offensive against Richmond while he was still here in Tennessee. And if all that were not enough of a burden, there was this posthumous influence of Cleburne and his sound arguments regarding the existence of slavery in the Confederacy.

He looked at his watch and decided that it was much too late for his liking. Lee knew he desperately needed a full nights rest so that he could attempt to sort out his numerous problems with a clear head. However, he also knew that such an effort would be fruitless, as the room he was provided would not allow him to escape the noises from this reception. Instead, he placed a small silver fork in his hand and stuck in it a piece of roast beef. A casual glance from his meal revealed Governor Harris engaged in an animated conversation with Wigfall across the room. They were putting on their jackets and walking towards the door. Lee quickly got up and followed them out.

When Lee stepped into the cold night, he was relieved to find that the two men had not traveled very far. There were several lanterns illuminating the front yard, and from their light, Harris and Wigfall could be seen across the way, standing close to a large barren tree. Lee buttoned the top of his coat and then walked towards them with his head bent against the wind. As they heard him approach, they ceased their conversation and greeted him with earnest smiles.

"General Lee," Wigfall said, "You should not be out here in this weather, I insist that you return to the warmth at once."

Lee thought that Wigfall was beginning to sound a lot like Taylor. The army needed more of these good men. "Perhaps you are correct, but then the same could be said of you both."

"Well then General, if you must join us, please pardon us if we smoke," Governor Harris said. He then reached into his pocket and produced two cigars, handing one to Wigfall. He took one of the lanterns hanging off a tree limb and used it to light his smoke. When it was lit, he inhaled the tobacco with powerful lungs and then let out a thick bilious cloud of smoke.

"General, I was saving that for the day that Tennessee is liberated from those Yankee tyrants, I know that this is premature, but my confidence in your success is that strong."

"If Thomas does not attack us, I am not sure that this army can attack him," Lee stoically replied. He noted the slight dip in Harris's shoulders, an action he did not mean to produce. "Governor, no one wants those Yankees gone from here more than I, but I fear that the general in command of that army is a very prudent one. He has not attacked us yet, which leads me to believe that he understands our inability to reinforce, while he on the other hand is increasing in numbers.

Thomas is a very cautious commander, and this is such a time in the war where hesitation by the enemy will work to his advantage. My army in Virginia can do nothing but brace itself for the inevitable. This army here, though victorious thus far, simply needs more men to continue in its success…but there are no more men to be had."

"General Lee, that is not true," Wigfall said. "Word of your presence has spread south of here. Part of the reason that we are out here, was that I was telling the Governor that several hundred of his state have arrived late this evening. I just found this out moments ago. They say that more are on the way. Those that previously refused to join our ranks, do so now willingly."

Perhaps as little as a year ago, Lee would have been filled with optimism at such a report. But the fact was, he knew how little a few hundred men meant when compared to the North's ability to replace an entire corps whenever it deemed necessary. He was not about to say as much to them. A few hundred volunteers were still better than none.

"Captain, have these men fitted and added to Stewart's

corps, our left flank is extremely vulnerable to the enemy's attack," Lee said.

He had not meant for Wigfall to carry his orders out at this moment, but the captain took it so, and moved too quickly for Lee to say otherwise. He took one last puff of his cigar then patted it out against his gloved palm. With a thorough salute, he took his leave. Lee watched Wigfall disappear into the Overton's home before turning his attention back to Governor Harris.

"Governor, your state may furnish this army with more men yet, but I am beginning to believe that we should not stay here much longer."

The words came as a shock to the governor. "But General Lee, we are on the very doorsteps of Nashville. Was this not the goal of Hood's entire strategy?"

"It was, and General Hood has succeeded in doing what many, on both sides, would have thought impossible. But the truth is, we can not take their works, and we can not just sit here passively waiting and hoping for an attack that Thomas is too smart to order."

"What of the redoubts being built on Stewart's flank, are we to simply abandon them?" Harris asked. I have ridden there, with you, and we have both witnessed the labor and pride that our boys put into their construction. The men have worked through such harsh weather to make that earth defensible...eagerly anticipating that the reward of their hardships will be paid in full when they repel the eventual Yankee attack. General Lee, those men are prepared to hold those redoubts against Thomas' army, Grant's army, Sherman's army, all three combined if need be. Nashville is right before them, do you truly intend to give the orders to pull away? If so, I beg of you to reconsider."

Lee was already reconsidering as soon as Harris mentioned their ride out to survey the construction of the five redoubts. This army was full of high morale, and he was realizing that his own depression was affecting his better judgment. He was doing now what he had always done in the past... bringing his army against the enemy at both the right time and the right place. He could not forget that the rest lay in God's hands and not his own.

"Governor, perhaps you are correct, let me sleep on this tonight, and decide in the morning as to what is best for this army."

Harris smiled as he brought the cigar to his lips. "Thank

you General, I could ask for little more. I will also continue to do what I can to get more of my countrymen to join your ranks. But General Lee, let me assure you, as I stand here smoking this victory cigar now, that when the battle of Nashville is fought, it will be fairly won."

What then? Lee thought in silence. The enemy will only fall back from its failed attack and fortify itself in the earthworks that surround Nashville. If his estimates were correct, there were over fifty thousand Yanks there now. They could easily afford to lose a battle and then brace against the Confederate counterattack, an attack that would consist of fewer than twenty-five thousand men in gray. Lee was well aware of how high the morale was in this army, but he also knew what would happen if they attacked an enemy that was well entrenched behind fortified lines... an enemy that outnumbered his command by two to one.

It would be Gettysburg all over again.

With that in consideration, there really was not much he could hope for. Even if the Federal attack failed so miserably that they had to retreat across the Cumberland, how long would it take for Lincoln to rebuild their army and have it ready for the counterattack? Images of the empty victories that had occurred at Manassas, Gaines Mill, Fredericksburg, Chancellorsville, and Chickamauga were portraits of confirmation. They helped to convince Lee that if the Federal attack failed, something more powerful than the liberation of Nashville needed to occur in order to change the fate of the South.

"Governor, I have promised to reconsider pulling this army from here, now I ask you to consider a matter that has been weighing on me very heavily as of late."

"Very well, that sounds a fair enough deal," Harris said.

"Please answer as candidly as you can, knowing that God's ears are always in attendance. How do you, as a Southern governor, feel about our population of slaves?"

Harris was in the process of bringing his cigar to his mouth, but stopped half way as Lee finished his question. He twirled the cigar between his fingers, as he carefully tried to form the words to answer Lee's question.

"General, what I say here, I expect to remain here," the governor whispered away from the wind. "Slavery, as you know is essential to the prosperity, wealth, and happiness of our country." Harris paused to make sure that there were was no one around to

490

hear what he said next except for Lee. "However, I also believe there is only one way to decide the state of slavery in our land, and that is the vote. Let the people put the matter to the ballot, and let that alone decide if we are to abandon that institution or to maintain it forever."

Chapter XXXII
December 13,
Nashville, Tennessee

The acrimonious winter wind swirled up and over the contours of northern Tennessee leaving a chill in its wake. The land that it now claimed looked very much like a vast gray desolate waste. Tom Fingle was not used to seeing the country surrounding Nashville look so… dead.

He had spent his entire life living peacefully just a few miles from the city, but gladly gave that up when this war broke out. The Federal army that now occupied Nashville was the very reason why he was now holding a cold musket, instead of the embraces of his wife and three children.

Tom was part of the extended Confederate skirmish line that was assigned the task of reporting any Federal activity. Now that winter had made its full return, his task amounted to little more than sitting in a cold wet ditch. Except for a few daily shouts between his men and the Yankee skirmishers, there was not much to do except trying to find innovative ways to keep warm.

The latest strategy that he devised was to hold his breath for long periods of time. It seemed that the longer he was able to hold his breath within him, the less he would shake from the cold. He passed this on to his friends and it soon developed into a game as to who could hold their breath the longest. Anything that took your mind off the cold was better than nothing.

"Hey Tom, hey Tom," his friend William called from a few feet away. William quickly jogged over, accompanied by a fellow who had a barrel for a chest. "Tom, this man here can beat your record, he can hold his breath for nearly five minutes."

Tom looked the man over, his chest was massive, but he doubted William's assertion. "Are you willing to place a wager on that?" he asked.

"You're darn right I am. If Richard here wins, I get your blanket tonight, and if you win, you can have mine."

William looked the giant over one last time with one thought on his mind. I can take him. "Then let's not waste any more time with this. You count to three, then me and thick chest here hold our breath. First sight of either's cold breath and it is decided."

Richard nodded and waited for William to count.

"Ready, set, one, two, three," William said.

Tom had been practicing this for several days, and knew that the best success lay in exhaling a deep breath first, then inhaling and holding. The large man did not know that, and was relying entirely on the two large lungs that resided in his thick frame. The two stared intently at each other for over a minute, each hoping to see the other give way. Out of the corner of his eye, Tom could see William gleaming with anticipation.

Time seemed to crawl as he could feel his face begin to change color. Come on you big lug, breathe, he thought. Tom realized that he had met his match. There was no way that he could hold out much longer, and his opponent seemed to be content to live without air. He was about to let out his defeated breath, when a loud crack sounded out from across the open field. Before Tom could turn to see exactly from where it came, he saw the impact of the bullet smash into Richard's right temple and then explode out his left. Richard's body crumbled as if his legs were made out of paper.

"Best keep your heads down Johnny Reb." It came from the Yankee line just yards away. Tom and William quickly dropped behind their own works, cursing their own stupidity.

"Damned Yanks ain't shot at us in two days," William said.

Tom nodded. "What's the matter with you dumb folk anyway, I thought we had ourselves a mutual agreement. We don't shoot at you and you don't shoot back," he yelled.

"That was before," the voice carried over. "We got ourselves a new commander now, one that is going to fix you backwards folk real good."

William and Tom exchanged looks of curiosity. "Who you reckon they got in command?" Tom asked.

"It don't matter none," William replied. "We got the best commander in both army's on our side. But we need to find out anyhow. Hey Yank... who is now in command of your army," he shouted.

"Why should I tell you that, Reb?"

William gave Tom a sly wink. Tom knew what William was going to say, he tried to muffle him, but moved too late.

"Because then we can tell you about the new commander in our army," William shouted.

There was no reply from the other side. Tom hoped that there was someway that the Yankees had not heard what William had said. In all his service of his army, there had never been an order given with sterner instruction, nor obeyed so unanimously by the men than the one issued by all of the senior commanders stating that no one was permitted to mention the name Robert E. Lee. Until this very moment, Tom thought that no one in the Confederate army had disobeyed that order.

"That's a deal, reb. We trust you to live up to your bargain, so here it is. General Schofield now has command of this army, and you can expect us to soon be chasing your tails back into Alabama. Now who is commanding your army?"

This time, Tom did not hesitate. He sprang from his crouched position like an agile cat. He landed with both hands smothering William's mouth. He tried with all his might to keep William from replying, but his friend somehow managed to wriggle from his grasp.

"We got Lee in command now, and when you come against us, make sure that you are ready to get the whooping of your life."

Tom could only stare at his friend in disbelief. How could he have yelled this vital secret across the open field for all the Yankee army to hear? William just stared back at him, with a nefarious smile spread across his lower face. He gave Tom another wink as he turned his attention towards Richard's prone corpse.

"And as for you Tom, he ain't let out a breath yet, so I reckon I'll be taking that blanket now."

*   *   *   *   *   *   *   *

A narrow aisle separated the two sides of the church as it led from the large wooden front doors straight towards the magnificent alter that stood directly underneath a massive stained glass window. Lee was kneeling in prayer in his pew that sat on the right side of the church. His hands were clasped in deep conviction to the Lord as his knees rested upon the floor. He could hear the chaplain delivering a sermon, but could not make out the words that he was saying. He looked up from his prayer and noted that the entire church was packed with hundreds of devoted Christians.

The chaplain was a man that he had not met before. He had one wisp of hair thrown across his bald forehead as if it were a tassel. He was very skinny, but his arms were long and they were held up high for the Lord. Lee tried to find someone in the congregation that he knew, but all these people here were strangers to him. As he looked, he could see a few Negroes seated far in the back, in the last two pews. Their heads were also bent in prayer.

Lee turned his attention back upon the chaplain. He was now speaking with more clarity as he read from the book of Psalms.

'For He is coming, for He is coming to judge the earth.
He shall judge the world with his righteousness,
And the peoples with his truth.'

When he finished reading, the chaplain kissed the open Book and placed it carefully upon the altar. He then looked towards his flock and called for any that needed a special prayer to step forward to the altar and bow before it.

A rather large older man that knelt a few feet down from Lee began to stand up. His wife was next to him, and they both fought to hold back the tears that needed to be released. Lee thought they had probably lost their son in this war. Perhaps it was even Lee who was the one that had given the order that sent him to his grave.

Lee kept his head bent in silence and leaned forward as the man tried to make his way past him, but as he did, he stopped in disbelief. Descending down the narrow isle was a limping Negro. The man was tall and thin, and had course black hair that was speckled gray throughout. He kept his eyes averted from the angry scowls that he knew were meant to keep him in his place. When his rickety legs finally brought him before the chaplain, he fell upon his knees and bent his head in hope that he would receive a special prayer.

The chaplain's face reflected the attitude of the entire congregation. How dare this Negro approach the altar from the back of the church, especially when there were several white men on their way to do the same? An ominous silence hung like a noose from the dark recess of the vaulted ceiling.

Lee looked at the faces of all his white brethren and could

see the perplexity of the situation distort their countenances. They wanted to rush the altar to brutally destroy the thoughtless Negro, yet they were kneeling in prayer to a Lord who proclaimed peace. The Negro kept his eyes closed waiting to hear his prayer, but his body began to shake. He had obviously put his faith in God, trusting that he would be allowed to approach His alter and remain unharmed, but that faith was beginning to waver. His neck, once bent for prayer, was now tense from the hot breath of damnation that billowed from the jowls of the white Christians.

Lee knew that something had to be done. Either the chaplain had to deliver his prayer, or the Negro would be taken outside so that the white men could shed their religious façade and give the Negro what he deserved. Lee thought on the last words the chaplain said before this situation evolved.

'He is coming to judge this world with his righteousness.'

It did not take Lee long to search his soul for the righteous action needed at this particular moment. He turned towards the large white man behind him and guided him to kneel back down next to his tearful wife. He then took his leave from the pews and made his way down the aisle.

As he approached the altar, he could hear several women whispering, "That is General Robert E. Lee, he'll know how to handle the nigger." Lee kept his stare focused on the back of the Negro until he stood adjacent to him. With a soft touch, he placed his hand upon the Negro's right shoulder, and then knelt beside him in prayer.

*　　*　　*　　*　　*　　*　　*　　*

When Lee woke up, his entire body was saturated with a thick coat of sweat. He rubbed his eyes and tried desperately to orient himself to his surroundings. The dream had been so real that when he awoke, he fully expected to find the humbled Negro kneeling beside him. Finding no one there, he sat up on the edge of his bed and lit the lantern that stood on the nightstand. It was still very dark outside. He guessed it to be no later than midnight.

He sat that way for many quite comfortable moments, thankful for the opportunity to finally be alone to think. In his dark solitude, for no apparent reason, a poem that he thought had been forgotten surfaced from deep within.

'Soothed with the pleasing calm of solitude,
To lonely valleys, woods, and wilds I stray,
Where naught disturbs my contemplate mood,
And hours, as moment, pass improved away.'

Lee smiled at the recollection of that poem, it had been so many years, he was thankful that he could recite the entire passage.

The poem was written by one of Lee's most influential teachers. He was seventeen when he met the Quaker professor. His name was Benjamin Hallowell, and his academy resided next door to his home in Alexandria. Hallowell had instructed Lee in the years prior to his attendance at West Point, and Lee would never forget those valuable lessons.

"What would you think of me now?" Lee whispered. Lee continued to rub his eyes in an effort to wake. What had made him think of Hallowell anyway? He tried to remember if perhaps he had also been dreaming of the Quaker, but failed to recollect any images. Lee did not need Hallowell around to answer his question. The Quaker's pacifist background made him an advocate against any form of warfare. Lee could envision the look of disapproval that he would receive had he now been face to face with the man.

Lee stood up and walked towards the desk that was set in the other corner of the room. He sat on the hard wood chair and rested his face in the palms of his hands. He began to wonder about many things, including the Army of Northern Virginia, the recent news of the Federal change in command here in Tennessee, and the whereabouts of General Sherman. The last thing he needed was to discover that Sherman had returned and placed sixty thousand Yankee soldiers in his rear. General Forrest had assured him that he had enough scouts posted miles from Nashville to alert him of the first signs of Sherman's return.

He wanted to think about his options should Forrest send word that Sherman had been recalled, but the vividness of his dream hung like a thin veil before him. He took his hands from his face and clasped them together in prayer. He hoped that God would listen to him this evening and guide him and this army in the right direction.

General Schofield was now confirmed to be in command of all forces in Nashville. Lee knew that could only mean one thing, Grant was not pleased with Thomas's lack of initiative.

There was no doubt that the enemy would now be preparing to attack or perhaps maneuver around in such a way as to cut Lee off from his supply lines.

He could not allow that to happen.

Lee spread out the hand drawn map of Nashville upon the desktop so that it was facing north and began to study the position of the two armies. He nonchalantly turned the map around so that it now faced south, giving Lee the view that Schofield was undoubtedly studying as he made his own plans. What would I do if I had your army? he thought. It did not take a military genius to see where Lee was most vulnerable. Lee traced his index finger along the wide arc spanning the Cumberland River to the Hillsboro Pike, his entire left flank.

With the addition of the local recruits as well as the arrival of Colonel Olmstead's brigade from Alabama, his army numbered slightly over twenty seven thousand soldiers. There were also the additional fifteen hundred men serving under General Bate near Murfreesboro. Even if Lee called Bate back, he knew it would do little to offset Schofield's superiority in numbers.

Had Lee had such a numerical advantage, he knew exactly what he would do to this Confederate army. He would have one or two divisions engage his line to the east, holding their attention, while he swung the bulk of his army in a wide arc, driving Forrest's thin cavalry line before him until they crashed into the rebel left flank and rear. Once engaged, the Federal middle could then march forward and in one massive push, the entire rebel line would be swept from their hills and cut off from retreat by the Federal cavalry.

As he studied the map, he was frightened with the realization of how easy it could be for an army to successfully perform such a basic offensive maneuver. Lee noted how close their lines were and wondered if by some remote chance they were able to repel the attack, how much success could they themselves have in a counterattack? If the Yankees were beaten back, with losses as staggering as Fredericksburg, there would still be over fifty thousand Union soldiers entrenched behind their defensive positions around Nashville.

Yet what else could he do? The only defense on his left flank was the five redoubts that Governor Harris had mentioned earlier. But the more Lee studied his map, the more the redoubts became a hindrance and not a defense. Harris was not exaggerating when he said that the men had put a great deal of pride in their work and claimed that they would hold the flank against the entire Federal army. But the redoubts were not yet complete. The cold weather had frozen the earth putting off any construction until a warm thaw could soften the ground. But even when they would be completed, they were not exactly tenable, at least not if Schofield saw the same opportunity that he did. All it would take was for one of those redoubts to fall in the enemy's hands, and the rest would topple.

Lee had seen the earthen defenses first hand, and though each redoubt alone was a formidable obstacle against the enemy, they were not supportable by the surrounding redoubts. If redoubt five fell into enemy hands, Yankee artillery could easily be brought up and used to enfilade redoubts four and three. If redoubt one fell, the same affect would transpire in reverse. Lee could envision the disaster with perfect clarity. The remnants of Pickets division crawling back to his lines kept playing itself in his head like an un-tuned fiddle.

He closed his eyes and fell into a solemn prayer. God, you have been with me during my every effort in this war, and I thank you for such a blessing. But I ask you to please be with me in these next few days. My army in Virginia needs relief and hope, and I feel the only way for that to happen is for you to allow us a victory here in Northern Tennessee. God, what must I do to show you that these boys are worthy of your grace?

He had not meant to question the Lord for his favor, the thought just seemed to reach at him from his subconscious. And before he finished asking it, he knew what the Lord's answer was to be.

'Be righteous for I am coming.'

Lee had heard it said that Abraham Lincoln made a covenant with his same God, asking that if the North were granted a major victory, he would emancipate the slaves of the South. Lee knew that Lincoln had kept his promise, for not long after Antietam, the Northern president issued his proclamation to free the Southern Negroes.

Perhaps that was what God was asking of Lee now. Why else was he given the dream right before he had awoken? Quintard had told him to listen to his heart, for there you will hear God... and right now his heart burned to make a covenant with the Lord. If by His grace, the Confederate army was somehow victorious at

Nashville, he would repay his thanks to the Lord by being righteous and emulating Lincoln's proclamation and free not just the Southern slaves, but all the slaves in all of America.

The very thought of his issuing such a proclamation caused him to break out into another could sweat. Governor Harris had said that the matter needed to be put to the vote. That at least meant that he was not entirely against it. But what would President Davis' reaction be? He knew what Cleburne's and Hallowell's would have been. Yet, what choice did he really have? If Schofield attacked, and lost, he could still fall back to Nashville and remain there until reinforcements arrived. If Schofield attacked and drove the Confederates from Tennessee, the war for all intents and purposes would be over. Sherman would soon come upon Petersburg from the rear and add his weight to Grant's final attack.

Lee thought of Cleburne's journal and his wise intuitions. What if the Irish general was correct? What if the Confederate army, with God's grace, defeated Schofield so soundly and then issued their own emancipation proclamation. Would not the governments of England, France and Russia be compelled to save such a righteous nation? Surely it was the Confederacy's last hope.

Lee finished his thought and gripped his hands tighter together in prayer. God, I humbly come before you to offer this covenant between us both. If you give this army a triumphant victory in the battle ahead, I will take that as a sign of your true intent and will announce to the world that the Southern states renounce slavery from that day forth.

Perhaps it was divine intervention, or simply the fact that Lee needed to spend more time studying the map, but whatever it was, after Lee committed his oath to the Lord, a plan began to take shape as if all on its own. It was one so clever it was reminiscent of the missed opportunity at North Anna.

Staying in this current position did his army little good. He knew that the change in command meant that something had to be happening soon, so why not help the new Federal commander by giving him something to think about.

Lee noted that the main portion of his army currently stretched over four pikes and two railroads. If Schofield did attack, he would have the advantage of using these same pikes to maneuver his army against Lee's thinly held position. Lee continued to study his defensive line, running his fingers down the two pikes that intersected its center, the Granny White and the

Franklin. Perhaps if he pulled the center back between those pikes and curled the flanks around the hills that naturally anchored that position, he could then concentrate his inferior manpower against an army that would have to bunch up in masses in order to get at his front. It would be Gettysburg in reverse.

If he was losing the battle, he could use the two pikes south of his line to keep his rear open in the event that he had to pull his army further south. And if the Yankees refused to make a fight, then why not let them have their way. Their idleness could be used against them. Lee could simply leave Schofield's army in place and slip his own to the east. From there he could rationalize marching his command into the Shenandoah Valley... and from there threaten Washington.

The more he thought of it, the more it made little sense to remain in place. If the Confederate army pulled back, Grant would no doubt want it attacked. They would have to be attacked, Grant would not want to have to deal with the rebel army later, not when they were now right in front of Nashville. Grant would not want the enemy to be given any opportunity to escape, especially one that left the formidable earthworks of Nashville far behind.

If Lee was not totally confident in his ability to think like Grant or Schofield, he needed only to think upon how his own army was maneuvered from position to position during Grant's drive though Virginia.

What Lee liked so much about this new plan was that it opened up a tremendous opportunity for the counterattack. With miles between the Yankees and their earthworks, the Confederate army could inflict heavy casualties on the retreating Yankee army.

That last task would have to be assigned to the one general whom Lee could trust the most. And before he finished rolling his map, another devious plan began to emerge...one that would help Forrest with capturing the entire routing Federal army.

Lee covered his mouth as a large yawn attempted to escape him. He was once again feeling tired, but this time there was an absence of much anxiety. His head had never before been so clear. This time tomorrow, under the cover of darkness, the Confederate army would pull back a few miles in hope that Schofield would take the bate. As he carried himself back to bed, he laid down in the confidence that he was doing what the Lord wanted of him. How else could such a plan have suddenly come to him?

Lee consolidates his line

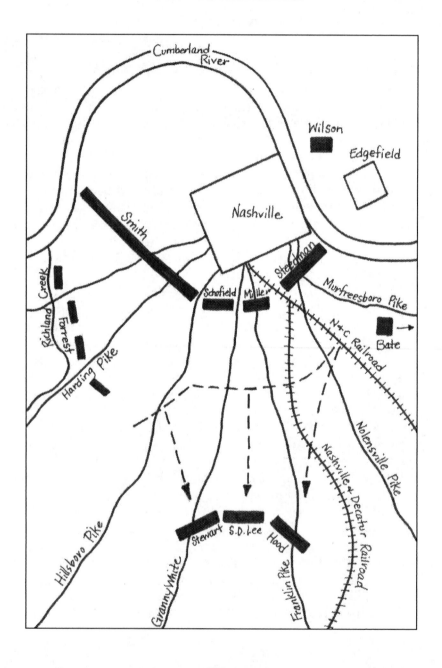

The thought of his covenant with God also made him realize something else. Though he had a lot of respect for President Davis and many other Southern politicians, how could he allow their influences to guide his actions? There was only one being who guided Lee and that was the Lord. And no matter what repercussion would come from his victory, he would know that he had done what the Lord wanted him to do.

That he had remained righteous.

General George Thomas awoke knowing that Schofield's army, his army as far as he was concerned, would undoubtedly be launching its offensive tomorrow morning as planned. There was warmness in the stale air of his hotel room, telling him that the temperature outside had taken a turn for the better. In an attempt to escape the stagnant suffocation that this unseasonable temperature would mean, he donned his uniform, and went for a predawn walk through the streets of downtown Nashville.

An ominous silence hung over the city, almost as if the buildings themselves knew what would soon occur in this vicinity. Schofield had discussed his plans with Thomas the night before and for the most part had chosen to adopt the exact offensive that Thomas was going to use had he been given the necessary time to do so. But what did it matter anyway? The point was, that if all went well, the Confederate army would be swept off the hills south of Nashville and sent scurrying through Tennessee.

As he thought of the coming battle, his foot slipped on a patch of remaining ice. He was able to regain his balance without falling. A quick look over his shoulder assured him that no one had seen him stumble. Thomas rested with his back against a cold street lamp and just took in the serenity of the streets. Looming before him were the awe-inspiring twin towers of the First Presbyterian Church. It was amazing to think how in just a few hours these quiet comforts would be shattered by the mobilization of the entire Federal army as it made its preparations for tomorrow's battle.

Thomas scratched his chin and then let out an uncontrollable sneeze. He took out a kerchief to wipe his nose and then thought that he had better get back to the St. Cloud. This day was definitely warmer than the previous, but it was still winter, and he did not want to agitate his cold. With one last look at the empty street, he took a deep breath of the fresh Nashville air and turned back towards the hotel.

He passed several officers outside the St. Cloud. They saluted as he passed them to reenter the hotel's lobby. General Schofield had called for a early morning council, and Thomas expected to see the other senior commanders arrive through the doors at any moment. A hotel attendant approached him and asked if there was anything that he could do for him. Thomas agreed to a cup of hot tea, and then found a comfortable looking parlor chair in the far corner of the lobby to sit in.

It did not take long for the young man to return with his hot tea, and placed the silver tray on the end table that resided to the right of his chair. Thomas waited for him to leave before engulfing the dainty white cup in his large hands. The warmth of the cup radiated through his fingers and sent slivers of heat up his arms. He had not realized how sick he was getting.

As he sat there sipping the hot tea, he noticed a Nashville newspaper lying on the table before him. With his left hand, he flipped it over and read the headlines. 'Hood Threatens Nashville.' A quick look at the date indicated that the periodical was over a week old. Thomas smiled as he took another sip of tea... so much had changed in just one week. There were confirmed reports from the skirmish line that John Bell Hood was no longer in command of the Southern army. Thomas did not doubt that at all. In fact, it explained so well why the Confederate army simply stopped at the doorsteps of Nashville and pursued no further attack. Thomas knew Hood very well, and was sure that had he remained in command, Nashville would have been attacked already, with heavy losses to Hood and his aggressive nature.

But now the word was that Lee had command of the army. What it was that prompted President Davis to hand over Hood's command to General Lee, remained a mystery to the northern generals. Thomas reasoned that it was probably due to Hood's insistence on some all-out attack that was probably rejected by his subordinates. Davis most likely was called in to intervene and realizing the impossible task of Hood successfully attacking Nashville, placed Lee in command.

The question now was, what would General Lee do with his new authority over the army? Schofield had sent a telegram to City Point and Washington, informing of the change in Confederate command, but as of yet there had not been a reply.

The sounds of an awaking army began to materialize as the morning wore on. Thomas looked up and saw several officers entering and exiting the lobby. They all looked at him with the same apologetic look. They knew that he had lost his command to Schofield, but Thomas felt that what went unsaid was an understood appreciation for all that he had done. Thomas would not allow himself or his army to be cajoled into an attack that they were not ready to commit. The cost of this was the final separation between he and Grant, but it was also time allowed to fully prepare all facets of the army for the attack.

Thomas' head sank back down towards his heated beverage. He reached over and took the small silver spoon set upon a white doily on the tray and methodically began to swirl his tea. It was no longer warm, so he just stared at it instead. There was a thin gold trim that circled around the top of his cup, it reminded him of some of the dishes that his mother used to serve back in Virginia.

'But I have given all of that up for this,' he thought.

Thomas did not look up when he heard the sound of approaching footsteps, he did not have to. He could see the tight shiny black leather gloves and knew at once who stood before him. General Wilson sat on the chair next to him and casually took the newspaper and quickly flipped through it.

"It is old news now," he said. "After tomorrow, the Confederate army will be running back though Nashville as fast, or faster than when they chased us up."

Thomas stopped swirling his tea and placed the cup and the spoon back on the tray. When he looked up, he noted the same look in Wilson's face as he had seen on many of the other officers.

"General," Wilson said. "Before this meeting begins, I would just like to say to you that I, my command, and this entire army are forever grateful for all that you have done. I have seen the rebel defenses first hand, and with the arduous task of maneuvering my cavalry during the horrible weather, I can assure you one thing... those rebels would have easily repelled my men had they been armed with nothing more than brickbats. Prior to today, we would not have stood a chance trying to dislodge the Confederates from their position. But thanks to all that you have done, we will now do so with the most success."

Wilson removed his glove and extended Thomas his hand in thanks. Thomas grasped the cavalry commander's hand with as much enthusiasm as a man drowning at sea. It was the affirmation that he needed to hear voiced by someone other than himself.

"General Wilson, I thank you for your words. I also want you to know that had Grant believed in me, and just allowed me the time I needed, we would not have had to have this awkward moment."

"General Thomas, there is nothing awkward about it. And I am sure, that had Grant been here first hand, he would have agreed with your decisions whole heartedly. Now tell me, what do you think of our new opponent?"

Thomas stood up, indicating that it was almost time to attend Schofield's war council. "I am not sure what it will mean. I don't think it will really matter after tomorrow anyway. It does not matter who commands the Confederate army now, our numbers are too large for them to contend with. So you see, I have not given the change much thought. After tomorrow, the rebel army will no longer be any threat, whether General John Bell Hood commands it... or General Stephen D. Lee."

*   *   *   *   *   *   *   *

Schofield allowed his senior command time to enjoy the breakfast that adorned a very long table that rested against the far wall of the room. When the time came for him to go over the final details of his grand plan, he wanted to be sure that he had their undivided attention. The aroma of hot cakes and coffee, coupled with their consumption was supposed to do just that.

He saw Thomas conversing with Steedman and wondered how Thomas truly felt about his demotion. The smile set upon his face did not show any disappointment, but surely there was some part of him that felt mistreated. Schofield turned from him, not really opting to spend any more time worrying about Thomas' feelings. Thomas had after all deserved everything he had received. He had ample time to conduct the offensive that General Grant had all but begged him to initiate.

As far as Schofield was concerned, it was he who deserved to lead this attack anyway. If it were not for his astute ability to retire his army and the cavalry from Pulaski, there could very well be an absence of twenty-seven thousand soldiers from the defenses of Nashville. Why should Thomas receive the glory for his hardships?

Schofield took one last survey of the men, to ensure that all who were called for were present. He then motioned for General Whipple to close the doors to the room. When the doors were shut, Schofield turned back to the men as they finished quelling their appetites.

"Gentleman, I hope you have enjoyed your breakfast, now if we can get started, I would like to call your attention to this large map that I have prepared to ensure we all understand what is required for the battle tomorrow."

Schofield waited for the generals to gather around the table. Surprisingly, Thomas was the first to take his place before the table, and occupied the center of the map. Steedman stood to his left, followed by Wood and Wilson. Arriving to the table just a few seconds after Thomas was General A. J Smith. Smith stood to Thomas' right, and was followed by Cox, Miller and Donaldson. Schofield moved to the far side of the table, and was joined by Whipple. Whipple handed Schofield a long wooden pointer.

"Gentleman the intent of this meeting is to ensure one last time that each of you understand your role in the battle tomorrow. The plan remains very much like the original one proposed by General Thomas. There are a few differences, and I would like to share those with you now. This long line to the south of the city is our current entrenchment. As you are all aware, our line in continues from the Cumberland above Charlotte Pike all the way to the Cumberland north of the Murfreesboro Pike. The rebel position, on the other hand does not. Except for some part of Forrest's Cavalry, the Confederate left flank is hanging wide open, inviting our attack. So, as you can see, the Confederate infantry is anchored on the left by Montgomery Hill, and on the right by the Nashville and Chattanooga Railroad.

We now know that General Stephen Lee has command of their army, but that will not change our plan. It was Thomas' intent to have his cavalry descend from our right flank, clearing and protecting the infantry's flank as he progressed to this point astride the Hillsboro Pike, at the side of Montgomery Hill. This part of the plan will remain unchanged. Also, as Thomas originally intended, General Smith's divisions will descend in an arc from their current position and aim for the same hill. I have chosen to alter Thomas' original plan by having the second division of the Twenty-third corps fall to Smith's left. I hope no one here will object to General Cox leading the division. With no bias intended, I feel that the Twenty-third deserves to lead this attack more than any other, except perhaps the Fourth Army corps. It was Cox who lost the most at Franklin, and he deserves retribution.

Schofield waited for any objections. He expected Thomas to say something, even if it was just the exhalation of hot breath, but the bearded general was stoic. Thomas just stared at the map, envisioning the battle as Schofield laid it out for them.

"The Confederate army entrenched before us is estimated to be thirty to thirty five thousand strong. There is believed to be another ten thousand, probably from Forrest's command invested at Murfreesboro. The garrison there has been notified to remain on the defensive until our attack dislodges the rebel foothold. Our success will cause those ten thousand Confederates to fall back, and when they do, General Rousseau has been instructed to follow up their withdrawal until he can link with our left.

"It is also prudent for us to distract the enemy from the main attack on their left," Schofield continued, as he turned towards Steedman. "And I believe General Steedman here has come up with a plan to do just that."

"That I have," Steedman said with confidence. Steedman leaned over the table and pointed to the position of his troops along the Federal left. "I have one colonel with a sever itch for the fight. Colonel Morgan came to me yesterday and convinced me that a successful attack could be made on the rebel right. He requested to take his brigade of Coloreds south along the Murfreesboro Pike, past the Rains house, and then wheel like this, so that he can hit their rifle pits from the rear. At the same time, I would have my other brigades hit their front and flank. If given the opportunity to carry out this attack, I can assure you that the attack will result in more than just a feint."

Schofield noted that the other generals were nodding their heads in agreement. That was an excellent indication that they were all on the same page. "Then it has been decided General Steedman. Your six thousand will begin the attack against Cheatham's corps, supported on your right by General Thomas' First and Third division of the Fourth corp. General Thomas, I need your corps to add its pressure against the rebel center. This will keep Stephen Lee's corps in place as well."

"That should place roughly sixteen thousand soldiers advancing on the Confederate right," A. J. Smith said. "Opposing them will be twenty thousand entrenched rebels. No matter how well General Steedman's colonel performs, if the attack against the enemy's left is not quick and decisive, Steedman will himself be exposed to the counterattack. Still, I agree with your plan

Schofield's Offensive

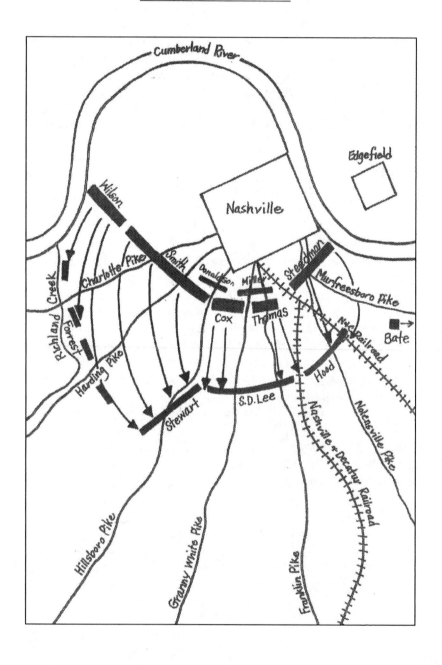

General Schofield. But every officer must understand the importance of turning the rebel left. That must be our priority. It will be difficult to dislodge the enemy from that formidable hill that solidifies their defense. But the combined force of the cavalry, my three divisions and Cox's command should be enough. It will put over thirty thousand soldiers on the enemy's front and flank."

Schofield was following Smith along with the pointer. "That is exactly the brilliance of this plan. Stewart should have no more than ten thousand men under his command. With the rebel center and right engaged in conflict with Steedman and Thomas, Stewart will be left to fend for himself. He will be facing better than three to one odds, and not even with the defense of Montgomery Hill can he stand that much pressure. Here is where we must take advantage of our disparity in numbers. Once Stewart breaks, the center and right will have no choice but to fall back with him."

"What is asked of my command?" Brigadier General James Donaldson asked.

Schofield again used the pointer. "Just as Thomas would have you do, I ask the same. Your men and those under Brigadier Miller will advance from our rear line and occupy the forward entrenchments, to guard against any possible counterattacks, though I doubt this will be necessary. So gentleman, to put it in rough numbers, our ten thousand at Murfreesboro will hold the rebel ten thousand until our attack sweeps them from these hills to the west. The attack itself will put over forty-six thousand of our boys against Hood's... I mean Stephen Lee's, thirty thousand. More specifically, at this point on their left, we will have thirty thousand soldiers to sweep Stewarts ten thousand. I have also requested the Navy to demonstrate against Bells' Mill. If there are no further questions, you have your orders."

"I do have one," Thomas said, raising his hand slightly. "At what time is the attack to begin?"

Schofield's face reddened. So this was how Thomas was going to try to undermine him, by asking a question so innocently... but by voicing it he pointed out that Schofield had forgotten to mention the most important part of the plan. Well what did it matter anyway? After tomorrow, his success will propel him to levels that would ensure that Thomas would never be a factor again.

"The attack will commence at five thirty in the morning.

Every fort will fire its artillery at the Confederate position, softening their defenses for the infantry attack. This concludes our council, you are all to report back to your respective commands and ensure that they are ready for the morning offensive. I will send a telegram to Grant and Halleck, confirming the attack scheduled for the morning." Schofield turned directly to Thomas in an attempt to get back at him for his early comment. "The attack will commence at five-thirty in the morning, and I do not care what the weather has to say about it. This army will advance as promised to General Grant."

*   *   *   *   *   *   *   *

The Confederate army spent the long afternoon laboring in their daily military tasks, all the while filled with anxious uncertainty. For reasons that were not clear to them, an uncertain order had been delivered by high command. At dark tonight, the Army of Tennessee was expected to quietly fall back from their position to occupy the hills two miles in their rear. Many of the men took this as an admission of defeat, that they would not be able to victoriously assault the earthworks around Nashville, nor hold their own line against a Federal attack. The only thought that held their morale was that it was issued by General Robert E. Lee, and if Lee gave the order then there was good reason for doing so.

The advance skirmish line waited patiently for the orders to fall back. They consumed their dinner rations at an early hour, knowing that their real work would begin in a few hours. With nothing to do but wait for the order to withdraw, they just settled down into the warming earth to watch the Yankee lines shift positions. It seemed that the enemy was also getting ready to perform some maneuver. A few men even reported that the Yankee cavalry could be seen crossing the Cumberland with a large force. There was hope that this would mean that the enemy was finally preparing to attack. The report was enthusiastically sent to General Lee. Lee received the news with stoic appreciation, but declined to alter his plans for the army to fall back. Much to the disappointment of his army, he simply stated that all is as He intends it to be.

At midnight, the usual campfires were struck with the intent to convince the Yankees that the Confederate army was

512

bunkering down for yet another cold night. The tune of Dixie was to be played through out the night, so that the instrumental spirit of the South could mask the sound of the army's retreat.

It took only a few hours for the entire defensive line to withdraw over two miles. S. D. Lee's corps was the first to disengage from the line, falling back to occupy the army's new center, a cornfield valley, that was shadowed in between two formidable hills. Stewart's corps followed next, using the Hillsboro Pike to enhance troop movement and took its position on S. D. Lee's left flank. The corps placed its artillery on the top of the steep hill that would anchor the Confederate's new defense. Last to follow was Hood's corps, who used the Franklin Pike to take its new position atop the Peach Orchard Hill, not far from Lee's headquarters at Traveler's Rest.

Hood waited until his entire corps was in place, including Bate's division from Murfreesboro, before taking his leave for the night. Confident that all was as ordered, he rode off in the night. He had not felt well this afternoon and had asked Lee if he could spend the night at his headquarters. Lee amicably agreed, wanting his general to be ready for whatever Schofield would do when he woke and found the Confederate army gone.

As Hood rode anonymously through Cheatham's former corps, he could hear the men whispering in the night. They were clearly upset for having to pull back after they had gained so much. More than once he heard it said that 'if one thing was for sure, it was if General Hood were still in command, there was no way we would have fallen back with out a fight.' The thought shamelessly put a proud smile upon his face. He did not want to be compared to General Lee, but he could not help admitting that his own thoughts were very similar to that of the men.

As the cold night wind began to work its way through his coat, it felt like a thick shivery blanket was being carefully wrapped around his flesh. Just a few more minutes and I will be warm within the Overton home, he thought. An aggravating ache began to swell the remaining stump of his leg with each passing trot of his mount. He reached into his coat and produced a dose of Laudanum to help him deal with the pain. It was not until he could feel the cold bottle in his hand that he realized that he had not been consuming it as much since Lee had taken command. He waited patiently for the drug to assuage the growing pain, but it was not working as well as it should.

He knew that he had to focus his thoughts on something that would take his mind from the pain, luckily that was not hard to do. This was the first night that the army had fallen back since he took them on this offensive. Not even the cold or his nagging aches could keep him from wondering on how things might have been different had Lee not arrived to take command of his army.

For one thing, he would not be falling back without a fight. These men have endured too much retroactive maneuvering under the command of Johnston, and that was damaging enough. But had he had command, what might he have done differently, he wondered?

Hood stopped his mount and turned it back towards the north, towards Nashville. That was supposed to be the city that would mark General Hood as the Southern savior. With its capture, he would have freed Tennessee of all Yankees, enabled President Davis to silence all those that opposed his promotion to command, proved to Hardee just who was the more able general, and above all, guaranteed Sally Preston as his wife forever.

Nashville was to be his destiny.

And in the dark hours of a cold enervating night, Hood slumped upon his horse, staring into the black emptiness of what was supposed to be his fate. For whatever happened from this point on, it would be Lee who would receive all of the acclamations and not he.

I would have not just wasted weeks passively remaining motionless, he thought. Murfreesboro should have been consumed like a man's last meal. He chose not to object to Lee's new strategy, but now wished that he had. What good does this do, to simply fall back? Can you not hear the opinions of this army, as evident in their disgruntled countermarch from our original goal? Schofield will never attack us now, he will see this countermarch as an admission of defeat. Sherman can now freely march on to assist Grant on the final blow that will remove Virginia from the war, and then all of this will have been for nothing.

Franklin would be a scar upon his soul for all eternity. It was now all so clear to him on this dark and cold night. He purposefully placed Cheatham's corps in a position to bear the brunt of that assault for one reason, and that was to teach them a lesson for their failure at Spring Hill. Hood reigned his mount back towards the south and began to ride to Traveler's Rest. Sadly, the only lesson that he learned that day was that men who were as invincible as Patrick Cleburne, would fall like any other under the orders of so selfish a commander.

Nashville was to justify that mistake. He believed that the victory there would somehow make what happened at Franklin acceptable. As the lights of Lee's headquarters illuminated the darkness, he realized that he would have to find that forgiveness elsewhere.

Two officers outside of the Overton's home assisted Hood from his mount. Hood thanked them, and approached the front door, already feeling the warmth of the inside. Before he could reach the door, a figure stepped from the darkness. It was General Cheatham. A slight hint of liquor lingered around his lower lip.

"General Hood," he said. "I came here to find you, I just wanted to report that the entire army is accounted for and in place as General Lee has asked."

Hood frowned. "First of all, General Lee did not ask anything. The general orders, and it is good that this army has done as he has ordered. I would expect nothing less. Second, I would rather you not be here this evening, you would do your division more service by remaining with them until the morning breaks and we see how Schofield has reacted to this maneuver."

Cheatham was already shaking his head apologetically. "I had not intended to remain here this evening, only to inform you so that you could enjoy a night of reassured rest."

'I wish you would have been this concerned at Spring Hill,' Hood thought. "Well thank you, General, now please return to your men, and I will see you in the morning."

Hood leaned on his crutches and moved passed Cheatham. He put his hand upon the door and a thought occurred to him. He turned as quick as his crippled body would allow and called for Cheatham. The general was half way upon his horse and had to stop himself mid mount. He handed the reigns to an aid and quickly returned to Hood's side.

"I have not seen General Forrest?" Hood said.

Cheatham looked bewildered. "General Forrest?" he asked.

"Yes, General Forrest, you were instructed to get word to him to have his cavalry fall back astride the Granny White Pike, in support of Stewart's left and rear."

Cheatham's mouth hung open like the lid of a mason jar. "General Hood, I am sorry, but I was never instructed to deliver any such order."

Hood felt his skin begin to burn with an irate crawling itch. He thought of dropping his crutches and lunging at Cheatham's exposed esophagus. He retained his ire only through clenched teeth.

"Were you not there when Lee asked that we send word to Forrest to fall back with the rest of this army?"

"I was, but I did not know that the order was intended for me."

"General, did I not look at you when the order was given."

"Yes, but how was I to know...?"

"Enough, we will accomplish little by bickering all night. It is almost one thirty in the morning. I want you to find General Forrest and ensure that he is delivered the order that he should have received this morning."

Hood dismissed Cheatham by turning his back to him. He listened for the sound of the general remounting and without turning, sent him off with one last remark.

"And General Cheatham, you can be the one to explain to Forrest why he was not given these orders with ample time to execute them."

Hood then entered Traveler's Rest with the same sinister smile that marked his face hours before the attack at Franklin.

Chapter XXXIV
December 15
City Point, Virginia

It had been a long and sleepless night for General Grant. As he washed his face, he tried to remember if he had slept at all. The dark quietness that waited for him outside his window told him that there would be several more hours until the sun would rise. Grant walked over to a small mirror and casually tugged at his beard. He noted that his eyes appeared more sunken than he wished. He tried splashing more water upon his face in an endeavor to better his countenance, but it was a useless gesture.

His worries had begun the previous day, late in the afternoon. A telegram had arrived from General Schofield informing him that the Confederate army would be attacked at five thirty this morning. Why that should worry him was what had kept him awake throughout the night. Schofield was finally doing what Thomas was incapable of... attacking the enemy. So what was worrying him?

As he donned his coat, placing two cigars inside the breast pocket, he began to understand that it was the enemy that worried him. Apparently, Hood had been replaced by General Stephen D. Lee. Grant would have liked more time to consider what Stephen Lee would do with this new authority. He even went as far as to send a telegram to Schofield asking him to hold off on the attack. He wanted to give Stephen Lee a day or two to show what his intent would be.

Grant took his thoughts from Tennessee and tried to place them on hold. He had spent the whole night worrying about Nashville, he just wanted a brief respite so that he could enjoy a morning ride. As Grant opened the door to the outside, a cold winter wind struck him with almost as much gelidity as the news he had received at five o'clock the evening before.

It was at that time that he was informed from the telegraph office, that the lines to Nashville were down. There was no way for Grant to get word to Schofield ...to hold off the attack against Stephen Lee's army.

Grant tried to find solace in the tobacco of one of his cigars. He bit into the brown stump as he met Rawlins, who had their horses waiting as instructed. Rawlins' paleness was almost glowing against his horse's dark saddle.

"Thank you John, but if you do not mind, I would like to ride by myself this morning."

"General, are you sure? I could ride several feet behind you," Rawlins replied.

"That will not be necessary," Grant said. "This is going to be a fine day, both in weather and in news, and I would just like to have a solitary ride in the open air."

Rawlins knew his commander well enough and understood when to back off. He handed Grant the reigns to his horse.

"Thanks again, John," he softly said. "Although, before I leave I will ask this. If there is any news from Nashville, if the lines are in operation again, then please do find me."

Rawlins saluted in affirmation.

*   *   *   *   *   *   *   *

Grant rode for several miles, his passing mount like a dark silhouette against the dawning sun. Grant tried to admire the glorious hues of red as the sun's nimiety spread across the dwindling night sky, but his dark thoughts denied him even that.

Grant led his horse up a rolling hill until he reached its summit. Once there, he dismounted and walked his horse near the edge of the hill. Looking down the west side, he had not realized how high the elevation was. He made a quick surveillance of the area and noted that the hilltop was barren except for a thin young tree bending with the wind. The stump of what was probably its parent was rooted nearby.

He smiled.

Grant took the soggy cigar from his dry lips and placed it back within his coat pocket. He approached the tree, tying his horse to its thin trunk. He then used his knife to sever one of its branches. With his mount secured, he let the silence comfort him as he seated himself upon the massive stump of what was once undoubtedly a great tree.

Once seated, he began passing the branch from one hand to the other. It did not take him long before he was enjoying one of his favorite hobbies. The knife was soon methodically carving the branch as Grant attempted to whittle his worries away.

Nashville was not the only concern that had been causing him a restless sleep. There were two offensives in his grand strategy that were not progressing as he had hoped.

General Butler was the first. As far as Grant was concerned, Butler was a useless addition to the Federal army. Unfortunately, Grant was handcuffed from doing what he knew was necessary for his army. Butler had strong political influences in Washington, and Grant knew that even he was powerless against such factions. He inwardly hoped that some disaster would occur under his authority that would allow for the removal of his command. Butler had been given just one simple task, to capture Fort Fisher but the general was slow in his expedition, and so the last significant Southern port still remained in operation. But then again, how much anger could he funnel in Butler's direction when Sherman was faring no better?

Sherman was still unaccounted for, and with him were over sixty thousand soldiers, enough men to help Grant deliver the final crushing blow in Virginia. At least Butler's presence was tying up some of Lee's soldiers.

Ironically, it was General Lee who was the person allowing him any reprieve. Thankfully, during this last month, Robert E. Lee remained motionless. The Army of Northern Virginia was no doubt feeling the affects of Grant's war of attrition. The rumors from the advanced line were that Lee was very sick. Grant often contemplated launching an all out offensive while his adversary was bed ridden, but it was his concerns with Nashville, Sherman and Butler that held him back. If just one of those objectives showed the least amount of success, he probably would have given Meade the order to attack. But as he sat on the cold stump, he knew that he only had to remain patient. Lee's army was pinned down and could not maneuver even if they wanted to. There was no longer any need for another disaster like the one at Cold Harbor. The situation here would soon be like it was at Vicksburg. Time will now defeat the Confederacy, not blood.

Grant paused his whittling to stare across the open space between him and the end of the hilltop.

"Besides, Schofield can do the job," he said out loud. The words repeated themselves with each pass of his knife… as if his deliberate shavings would add the much needed conviction to his claim.

Does it really matter who President Davis puts in command, he thought? The rebel army in Tennessee cannot be more than thirty-five thousand strong. Once Lee is defeated here, that force will matter little.

Before Grant could even finish his thought, both the carved branch and his knife fell heavily from his numb fingertips. A soft thud impacted the earth and left a sound similar to one's final heartbeat. Grant felt the sweat begin to paste to his brow as he stood up and walked to the western edge of the hill. He stood in motionless silence, his hands hanging limply at his sides. He tried to see the rebel army entrenched somewhere before him, but knew that he would not be able to.

"You old fox," he whispered. Grant did not know how he knew, but he did. Schofield was correct in saying that Hood had been replaced by General Lee, the problem was that they all had assumed the wrong Lee. Grant felt his knees buckle and unable to resist their momentum, found himself kneeling on the ground. his hand passed grippingly though his hair.

His only thought was that General Schofield would never stand a chance against Robert E. Lee, even if Lee had only ten thousand men under him. He quickly checked the time on his watch. It was almost seven in the morning; Schofield's attack was now well under way. Even if he wanted to race back to his headquarters and call off the attack, he couldn't. The telegraph wires were down.

There was no way to get word to General Schofield. No way to inform him that he was up against the South's greatest general. No way to tell him that if he was attacking, it was because that was what Lee wanted him to do. No way to tell him that he was walking into a trap.

*   *   *   *   *   *   *   *

Nashville, Tennessee

The Federal army awoke from their anxious sleep at four in the morning. They were greeted with the surprising feel of a very comforting spring like breeze. The warm swoops of wind meant that the weather would hold for another day to help support their attack. The soldiers were quick to mold into their battle formations, but as they stood shoulder to shoulder, they realized that a very serious situation had presented itself.

Each man in line could see the soldier to his right and left, but that was as far as could be seen. The rest of the company was concealed behind a shroud of enveloping gray mist. The weather was always one of the intangibles that could alter the outcome of any battle, and as the men strained to get into line, they knew that today's outcome would greatly hinge upon this one critical intangible.

As the men made preparations for the offensive, the dense and suffocating fog continued to rise from seemingly nowhere, and as it did, it blanketed the entire Federal army. As the hour reached five thirty in the morning, the hour designated by Schofield for the army to move forth, not a single regiment was ready to take its first step forward. No soldier dared move forth until they were ordered to do so, and those who had the authority to give the command, were reluctant without the approval from those above them. The silent question that seemed to float with the fog was, 'are we to move forward as planned?'

To the Union army, it had become a disheartening hour. The soldiers had awakened anxious for the battle that once and for all would finally finish the task that Sherman had left behind. After today, the Army of Tennessee would cease to exist.

Unfortunately, a brumous sheet of white mist hung so heavy before them, it threatened to cancel the entire attack. Many began to believe that it was God himself who threw down this misty blanket to prevent the bloodshed that would surely occur. The Southern citizens of Nashville also thought it was God's doing, but for other reasons. It was the Lord offering his protection to the Confederate army across the way.

*   *   *   *   *   *   *   *

General Schofield stood at the edge of the entrenchments pondering what to do. On any other day he would have been able to see the steep slopes of Montgomery Hill rising before Nashville. But as his unfortunate luck would have it, the fog that greeted his morning was so dense, Schofield could not even see Fort Casino behind him. In fact it was so thick, he could not even make out General Cox standing right next to him.

"General Cox, this is awful," he said.

Cox's reply was the only proof that the man was still standing close by. "Should we call off the attack until this fog lifts?"

Schofield had already been thinking the same thoughts. There was no way that he could expect his army to march in such blinding conditions. Perhaps the fog would lift in a few hours, and then he could resume with his orders. He was about to voice his opinion when he heard the galloping arrival of several approaching officers. The fact that they were riding so hard in such a thick fog was concerning enough.

"General Schofield?" a voice searchingly asked. Once Schofield confirmed his presence, the officer continued. "General Thomas requests that we hold off the attack until this fog can be lifted some."

The officer who uttered Thomas' request did not know how fortunate he was that the fog prevented him from seeing Schofield's face contract into a vicious snarl.

'How dare Thomas try to persuade me in this', Schofield thought. Of course he would call off the attack… that was all he knew how to do. That was the very reason why he was replaced as commander. And now he wanted him to call off the attack, there could only be one reason for such a request. If he did as Thomas asked, it would be much to the chagrin of General Grant. Schofield could not allow that to happen. He had promised that if given the chance, he would respond much more enthusiastically than Thomas had. He promised to attack and he promised to do so today. If he did not follow through with that promise, then he would have responded just as Thomas had.

"Well you can ride back to the General and inform him that this army will do nothing of the sort. The attack will be moved to six thirty, and I expect the army to march with or without this hindrance of nature. Do I make myself understood?"

The officer saluted Schofield, and then realized that the General probably could not see his gesture. "Yes, the attack will commence at six- thirty."

Schofield heard the officers depart back to Thomas' command. He tried to visually penetrate the fog, to ensure that they were indeed gone, but could not. He had to place his trust in acoustics. Cox accidentally brushed up to his side, obviously not realizing that he was so close.

"General Schofield, please forgive me for this, but are you sure we should attack as planned?"

Schofield took a step back from Cox. "General, I have never been so sure of anything in my entire military career. Let me ask you one thing, what do you think General Grant's reaction will be when the telegram lines reopen and he learns that this army still has not attacked? I doubt if even Shakespeare himself could write a telegram to describe this detestable fog. Nothing would convince Grant that we were not just making the same excuse as Thomas had. I will not be replaced as he was."

Cox remained so silent that Schofield wondered if he were still standing there. "And besides," he continued, "this fog works both ways. That is the problem with Thomas, he lacks optimism. If we cannot see through this, neither can the enemy. By the time this fog lifts, our army will have marched unabated to the enemy's works. Imagine their surprise when they see over forty five thousand men standing a few feet from their defenses. They will have no time to react, no time to fire their artillery to soften our ranks."

The sound of several mounted men could be heard approaching. For a moment, Schofield thought it was Thomas, come personally to argue against the attack. But the riders were approaching from the west.

"General Schofield, my command awaits your order."

It was his cavalry commander, General Wilson. Thoughts of the army's retreat from Pulaski quickly filled his mind, reminding him of the ineptness of Wilson's cavalry. Wilson had better make amends this time, he thought.

"General Wilson, the attack will commence as planned. The only change is that I have moved the hour to six thirty. I have already informed General Thomas, and will do so to the rest of the senior command as well. Are your men ready?"

Wilson took a moment to imagine trying to conduct an offensive under such uncompromising conditions. Schofield's tone was belligerent and dogmatic, and he knew better than to try and persuade Schofield otherwise. "My cavalry is poised to move forward," he said.

"Very well then, please have them begin their advance as planned. General Steedman's brigades will engage the enemy's right, as you and General Smith swing southeast and meet the Twenty-third at Montgomery Hill. With the enemy worrying about its right, we shall swallow its left more readily than this fog swallows you from my sight. This fog will not last all day, and when it lifts, I expect our army to be right on top of the Confederate earthworks."

Wilson rode back towards his command. He remained silent until he crossed the Hardin Pike, well out of the hearing range of Schofield and any member of his Twenty-thirds corps.

He turned to the two men that followed him and with much audacity said, "Gentleman, I do believe that Schofield has lost his mind. He expects this army to be on top of the rebel works when the fog lifts, and I suspect that part of the army may achieve that goal. The other part may think they have, but once our visibility returns, find that they are somewhere in Ohio instead."

The men that rode behind him were Hatch and Capron. Wilson purposely chose them to lead the flanking maneuver because it was they who had spent the better part of November running from Forrest's cavalry. If anyone had enough vindication burning their souls, it would be these two. They claimed that they were forced to run because Forrest greatly outnumbered their command. Well now that Thomas had bought them enough time to mount the majority of the cavalry, the excuse of being outnumbered was no longer valid.

"General Hatch, Colonel Capron, I know that what Schofield asked this morning sounds like an impossible task. I will not lie to you, it is. But still, I expect this cavalry to accomplish nothing less. It is time we taught Forrest a lesson. I want that general's head served for dinner. I also want to accomplish this for all that General Thomas has done for us. Had it not been for his refusals to Grant, we would have attacked days ago, much less prepared then we are today.

Given the choice, I would rather attack in this fog, with the amount of men I have now, than attack on a clear day, with the amount of men I had then. Today, let's do to Forrest, what he so thoroughly enjoyed doing to us, and drive him so far to the west, that he shall play no part in the complete victory that will occur here in just a few hours."

*   *   *   *   *   *   *   *

If the fog was supposed to lift by six thirty, then it obviously had never gotten Schofield's order to do so. Wilson's cavalry had been poised adjacent to Smith's left for several hours. The restlessness could be heard not just in the men, but also in the heavy neighing of the horses.

Wilson tried for the fifth time in the past twenty minutes to use his field glasses to penetrate the gray thickness that hid the Charlotte Pike from his view. Disappointed, he shoved the glasses back in their case and turned to General Hatch.

"Well, we still can't see a damned thing, but we just have to remember that neither can Forrest. We have to make the most of that. When this fog lifts and Forrest finds us right on top of him, we will have one hell of a fight on our hands."

Hatch replied, "That may be, sir. But the difference is that we will know that we are there, Forrest will not."

Wilson put his hope in Hatch's optimism. "I wonder how Steedman's men are faring against the rebel right. I must admit that I had certain doubts about General Schofield, but the more I reflect on his plan, Thomas' for the most part, I must admit that it is a sound one. If Steedman can grab their attention long enough for my cavalry to unite with Smith and crush their left, then this battle will be over before sundown."

"I do believe that we have the numbers to do so," Hatch said. "I only wish that we knew when this fog would lift. I mean, suppose we reach their defenses and the visibility has still not cleared, it will be utter chaos."

Wilson nodded his head then looked up hoping to see the sun breaking through the shroud. "It will not last much longer," was all he said.

Those were the last words of conversation between the two cavalry commanders as a bellowing roar tore through the fog. It was the artillery from the forts that surrounded Nashville. They had been instructed to unload their deadly hell upon the rebel works so that the enemy's line would be softened by the time the infantry assaulted it.

The heavy cannonade continued with no sign of letting up. Wilson let out a cynical snicker as he kicked his horse forward.

"General Hatch, you may give the command for your division to start the attack. Tell your men to make strong efforts to remain in contact with the divisions to your left. As we swing down in a descending arc, all brigades are to worry about their right. Each brigade must know where its right touches the next, or this fog will swallow us faster than a Mississippi swamp."

Hatch saluted and rode off to his command with alacrity. Wilson took a moment to stretch his tight gloves over his enraged palms. The sound of the cannons roaring filled him with utter grief. Who the hell gave the orders for those cannons to fire, he wondered? I thought the whole reason for allowing this attack to commence under such adverse condition was so that the enemy would not know that we were coming. Now they know that we are coming.

Forrest knows that I am coming.

*   *   *   *   *   *   *   *

His cavalry was being pushed back along all fronts. From the Cumberland River, above the Charlotte Pike, to his far right past Harding Pike, the situation was the same. Early this morning, a blue mass had materialized out of the thick gray haze and like a furious tornado, gobbled up anything that attempted to impede its advance.

Its first victims were a small company of troops from Armstrong's Brigade. Posted astride the Charlotte Pike, the waking cavalrymen had not yet grown accustomed to the thick fog, and so had not even noticed the Federal approach until they were already past them. The Confederate company was forced to give up without a single shot fired.

And the Federal offensive pressed on.

Most other generals finding themselves in such an unfavorable environment would no doubt salvage their command and fall back as rapidly as possible. There were very few who could bring order to such chaos, and thankfully for the Confederate cavalry, their general was one such man.

Forrest knew that this day would not be the same passive day that the two armies had grown accustomed to since confronting each other at Nashville. The ubiquitous fog was his first indication, the blasting cadences of the Federal artillery was the other. The Yankee guns sounded to be focusing upon the Confederate infantry position, specifically Stewart's corps anchored along the Hillsboro Pike.

Forrest's first order was to send a small party to get word

from Stewart. Though the amount of gunfire indicated that this was more than just an exchange of lead, he did not want to abandon his position until he knew for sure that the enemy meant to attack.

Unfortunately, that answer came long before his response from General Stewart.

The initial reports were frantic, the Yankee cavalry was in all places at the same moment. Every dispatch that reached him, whether from Chalmers, Buford or Jackson, read the same. 'Large force of enemy cavalry at my front forcing my command to fall back.' Forrest's reply to all of them was the same, 'you may fall back as much as you please, but the enemy is not allowed to cross Richland Creek, better you surrender your command, than let the enemy across the creek and face the wrath you will incur from me.'

Apparently the point was well taken. Richland Creek was only a few miles in the rear, and once the brigadier commanders received their reply, the Federal drive came to an immediate halt. It did not take a Napoleon to understand the value of the creek's position with regards to the Federal advance. The creek ran vertically from the Cumberland River to just about the Hardin Pike. Its path intersected those two pikes, placing a natural obstacle between the opposing cavalries of Wilson and Forrest. Wilson would need time to coordinate an attack over the waterway, and Forrest meant to use that time as a means to organize his own command.

Forrest had arrived at the west side of the creek moments ago, his horse practically standing in the creek. Intense eyes glared through the fog, waiting impatiently for the remainder of Chalmers retreating division to emerge from the impenetrable mists. His saber was unsheathed and gripped tightly in his gloved hand. The scowl that owned his face bent his brow with a deep creased 'v', jutting his defined jawbone high against his face.

The hard splash of thundering horses could be heard to the south of him, and Forrest's head swung in that direction.

"Is that all of them?" he asked.

Chalmers was quick to reply, "No sir, the last would be the Fifth Mississippi, I would expect them at any moment."

Just as Chalmers finished his reply, gunshots ripped thought the fog and their impact could be heard splintering against the few scattered trees, or thudding into bodies of flesh. Preceding the lead storm raced the Fifth Mississippi. The last of Chalmers division knew that they were supposed to stop once they crossed the creek, and fall in with the rest of their brigade, but this regiment was filled with terror. The regiment routed past the Twelfth and Fourteenth Tennessee, towards the White Bridge Road further west. Shouts of 'the Yankees are coming, thousands of them,' trailed in their wake.

Forrest grabbed Chalmers by the collar and pulled his ear close to his warm lips. "Shoot any God damn man that follows that regiment," he said. Letting go of his subordinate, Forrest raised his saber high above his head and charged after the fleeing Fifth. He raced past the trailing units, who noted his presence with fearful eyes and sunken chests. Forrest dug his spur into his mount in an effort to compel the beast to gallop faster than the lead horses that he pursued. Like his men, the horse knew better than to object. Forrest was soon riding a few feet behind the lead routers. He waited until he was adjacent to one, and then with a flick of his wrist turned his saber so that its edge was to the side, and brought the flat back of the metal down upon the man's shoulder. The trooper fell from his horse instantly. Forrest, without missing a beat, caught up to the next rider and dropped him as well.

The third nearest rider, an officer, seeing the other two men felled, did not need the same persuasion to halt. He quickly reigned his horse half circle and began shouting for them to halt their stampede. Soon other officers followed suit, and the whole command finally stopped running. Forrest led his horse in the middle of the disorganized circle.

"I will not ask what may have caused the proud men of Mississippi to run so. I will only say this, return now to your place behind the Richland Creek, and when the enemy advances against you, show me such a resistance, that will allow me to forget the cowardice that I have seen today."

Forrest moved through the parting regiment and quickly rode back to the rest of Chalmers division. The way the Fifth Mississippi raced through his line, he fully expected to return to the Creek and find Chalmers in a heated battle with Wilson's entire command. Strangely, the area around the creek was silent.

"General, they came through here after them, but they were obviously not expecting us to be here," Chalmers said. "It was like they stuck their hand in a hornets nest. As quick as they came through, was as quick as we sent them back. But I reckon it won't be long till they make another try at it."

Forrest was hesitant to reply. He kept his focus on the fog that was finally beginning to lighten. "General, do we know what we are up against?" he asked.

Chalmers horse tried pulling him back across the creek. He had to tug more than he expected to remain close to Forrest. "Well, right in our front are elements of Wilson's corps, the Sixth division I believe. Buford and Jackson, to our north, are being pushed back as well by Wilson's Fifth and Seventh divisions. Our old friend General Hatch seems to be leading that charge."

"Well, I would say that this confirms that the Yankees are definitely on the attack," Forrest said. "We now know that there are three cavalry divisions operating here against us. Has they're been any word from our right? Has General Stewart reported anything?"

Chalmers shrugged his shoulders and before Forrest could add another comment, the sound of charging Yankees resounded from across the creek.

"Let em' have it boys," Forrest's red face raged.

The dismounted Confederate cavalry shot forth a horrific volley of lead. The sounds of bodies falling in the creek splashed before them. The Confederates fired again and again, until the Richland Creek was swollen with Northern flesh. A loud rebel cheer rose along the line as the Federal threat was finally contained.

The smile on Forrest's face was short lived. One of General Buford's aids came riding amongst Forrest's staff. He brought an urgent message from the cavalry divisions that were defending the Creek at the Charlotte Pike.

"General Forrest," he said. "General Buford begs you to accept his apology, but he insists that if he is forced to hold his position much longer, that his command will no longer exist. The enemy has far too many men pressing, and believes that they have gotten around his right flank. Three regiments from Bells' brigade have been turned to meet this threat, but it seems more of the enemy is pouring in around Bell. Sir, General Buford insists that there is a hole between his division and Chalmers."

Forrest listened to the desperate message while staring into the courier's eyes. He did not remember having ever met this man, but he admired his unwavering report in the face of such peril.

"Sir, you may ride back to General Buford and inform him that I understand his situation. Tell him that he must find a way to locate this hole and plug it up. General Buford is not allowed to fall back, not until I can fully understand the entire situation to my right. Tell Buford to remain in position until further orders."

The aid saluted and rode off, disappearing into the engulfing fog.

"Chalmers, I can not wait for Jackson to find that hole. Send a regiment, the Fifth Mississippi, north of here and instruct them to not stop until they make contact with Buford's right."

Chalmers wanted to question the use of the Fifth for such a task, but knew better. He too rode off into the misty gloom.

"They're coming again," a voice screamed in warning.

This time the blue riders could be seen as the fog continued to dissipate with each passing minute. It looked as if there were thousands of them, all riding low in the saddle with sabers, pistols and rifles drawn and ready. Grim determination carried them as they trudged across the creek leaping over the carcasses of the recently fallen.

The rebel volley fired, but instead of stopping the advance, it seemed to only spur them on. The Confederates fired again and again, and unlike the previous two sorties, this time the Yankees gained their side of the Richland. The sheer numbers of the Federal cavalry were beginning to once again drive Chalmers division farther west.

Forrest realized that if these men were pushed clear of the creek, then they would expose his other two divisions to the north. Buford and Jackson would be outflanked and driven clear out of the state. Even more important than his own cavalry was the thought of what could happen to the left flank of Stewart's infantry corps. Forrest had one reason for being this far west and that was to protect the exposed left flank of the Confederate army. If he allowed Wilson to push him any farther, he would fail in that task.

He was not going to allow that to happen.

Once again his wrist flinched, this time bringing the sharpened edge of his saber back into its correct position. "Tennessee with me," he roared as he rammed his mount into the rushing Federals.

With untamed brutality, the Tennessee native swirled and slashed his severing sword into as much Yankee flesh as he could.

The exhilaration was intoxicating to his furious animosity. Those that tried to challenge him were rewarded with bleeding cuts and punctures. Those that tried to keep their distance were filled with quivering terror. Seconds later, the sudden arrival of the regiments from Bell's brigade smashed into the flank of the Yankee breakthrough and sent them scurrying back across the creek.

Forrest's breathing was heavy and his hand was numb. He looked at his men and saw many hunched over trying to catch their wind. That last attack was close, they will be back again, he thought. Out of the corner of his eye he could see Colonel Bell approaching.

"General Forrest," Bell said. "I just thought you should know that General Buford was correct in his assessment. There is a widening hole between his and Chalmers command. I was sent to fill that void, but the Yankees were so numerous they cut me off from the rest of my division. They then threatened to turn my right, but the Fifth Mississippi appeared out of nowhere and counterattacked most heroically. I must admit that their regiment has temporally saved my command."

Forrest realized that many men of rank, including Chalmers and Bell, now surrounded him. They all had the same questioning look set upon their faces. 'What do we do?' their silence asked.

"Forrest, Forrest," a voice came screaming as a horse charged towards the gathered group. Forrest looked past those to his immediate front and saw that the rider was none other than J. P. Strange. Forrest had dispatched Strange early this morning in an effort to understand the situation on Stewart's front. The man could not have arrived at a better time. Though Forrest was not impressed with the hysterical look upon his friend's face.

"Forrest, the situation is most terrible. There is a division of cavalry crossing your right and driving a wedge between you and the infantry. And what is worse is that the cavalry is flanking the advance of an entire corps of infantry. I believe that is A. J. Smith's men."

For the first time in this war, Forrest felt his head actually spin. Three divisions of cavalry were threatening to cut his command in half, while another division and a corps of Yankee infantry had somehow managed to drive itself in between his right and Stewart's left. Forrest attempted to focus his swelling cognition by trying to convince himself that this was the worse that it could possibly get.

"And there is more," Strange said. "Stewart's corps is gone."

"Excuse me?" Forrest asked.

"Stewart is gone, they are all gone. Lee had the entire army fall back last night. We are defending an army that is no longer here."

Forrest gave Strange a look that steadied his trembling limbs. "Are you sure?" he asked.

Strange looked at the large circle of soldiers and officers that had now congregated around them. "That I am, we encountered some of Cheatham's staff while trying to locate Stewart's left. Apparently we were supposed to receive that order last night, but for whatever reason, it was not carried through. The army fell back two miles to the Peach Orchard Hill. Your orders are to follow with your entire command until your right joins Stewart's left west of the Granny White Pike."

A long thoughtful silence followed Strange's report. They all shared the same thought as their general. If Forrest obeyed that order, then he would join the rest of the army, but he would be without two of his three divisions. Yet if he disobeyed the order, the army's left flank would be in peril. Chalmers, Rucker, Biffle, Bell, Strange, and the others all understood the enormous dilemma that they were faced with.

But Forrest was the only one who knew how to deal with it.

The imposing wizard knew that he had to reach very deep into the bowels of chicanery to overcome this predicament. As he took note of the dwindling fog, a risky plan began to form in his head. He waited until finalizing his last thoughts before addressing the men.

"Everyone listen and listen good. Chalmers, instruct the Fifth to form a screen and they are not to give up a single inch until they are all either captured or killed. The rest of your division is to ride with all haste further west. Have word sent to Jackson that he is to fall back to Bell's Mill, drawing Wilson's two divisions with him, and to hold that position until his entire command is also either captured or killed. Buford must also receive the order to leave a single regiment to screen his front, while the rest of his division retires west to consolidate with your command at a point past the White Bridge Road."

Forrest paused briefly as he menacingly approached Colonel Rucker. "Colonel, I want you to order your most trusted and highest-ranking officer to remain with the Fifth Mississippi. I want him captured with the rest of the regiment when they are compelled to give up the fight."

Rucker looked towards Chalmers with concern.

Forrest wasted no time in boring down upon him. "Colonel, I have no time for you to even consider questioning my command. Do as I say. Your officer will inform Wilson's staff that the majority of my command was sent towards Murfreesboro late last night. All that is currently left to defend this vicinity is Jackson's division near Bells Mill and a few scouting companies."

When Forrest finished imposing himself upon Rucker, he turned to the others. "We can not afford to waste any more time discussing this plan. You all know what to do. I will disclose the rest of the plan once Chalmers' division is united with Buford's. And General Chalmers, be sure that the artillery is with you when I get there."

The gathering crowd was dispersed with a series of salutes and confirmations. Forrest reigned his horse towards the west bearing a heavy burden upon his high shoulders. Strange followed close behind the general with much concern. He had known the man a long time, and had never seen such a rock of fortitude so shaken.

"General, are you okay?" he asked.

Forrest nodded a heavy head. Skirmish fire from across the creek was slowly escalating. Wilson would be coming again soon.

"I don't mean to question your plan," Strange carefully said, "but I have never seen you this way before."

Forrest stopped his horse as he wiped the blood from his saber and sheathed the weapon. "Chalmers and Buford must have their division clear of here before this fog lifts," he said.

Strange cocked his head to the left. "I am not sure I understand sir."

The corners of Forrest's lips curved ever so slightly. "Our army today is not where we thought it was yesterday," he said.

Strange nodded, still not understanding.

"If we did not know of this, then I would gamble that Schofield does not know of this." The curve of his lips started to curl north. "And if Schofield does not know that our army has moved, then his men are marching to a vacant battlefield. Their artillery this morning, would have shelled nothing but vacant entrenchments. When this fog lifts, Schofield will find that Lee's army is two miles farther south than anticipated. But he will have no choice but to press on. Otherwise his army will be outside of the Nashville entrenchments, and exposed to counterattack."

"And with Colonel Rucker's leaving an officer behind, Schofield will be led to believe that you are away at Murfreesboro with two thirds of your command," Strange said, beginning to understand Forrest's plan. "But how does your pulling the cavalry farther west help the army during Schofield's attack."

Forrest took a deep breath as he removed his blood stained gloves. "Strange, I have taken some immense gambles in this war, but none will compare to this. If I fail, it will finally give men like Bragg the validation they need to remove me from this war. But I have always felt that this was my cavalry before it was the cavalry of the Confederacy. And so I feel that these men are mine to gamble with. I will put my trust in them, and in Robert E. Lee."

Forrest pulled his horse closer to Strange's. "When the Yankees attack Lee's new line, do you reckon Lee can hold and perhaps drive them back?"

Strange took a moment. "Well if General Lee can't, then no one can."

Forrest's lips were now completed curved with all the arrogant audacity that made him the man that he was.

"Well sir... that is exactly what I am wagering my entire military career upon."

Chapter XXXV
Nashville, Tennessee
The Battle of Nashville

They precariously stepped through the desolate fog with an overwhelming sense of despondency. Beaded eyes painfully squinted ahead in the hope that at any moment they might yet pierce the brumous veil of gray that enveloped their entire division. Their efforts were wasted. It seemed like an entire day had passed since the surviving division of the Twenty-third corps was given the order to move forward.

The command to move forward was delivered by the officers, but those who were to bear the brunt of the conflict knew it was time when their lethargic morning was suddenly ruptured by the sound of heavy artillery blasting the enemy's lines hidden beyond. As the shelling continued, the Twenty-third corps tensed their shoulders, gripped their rifles and took their first few steps with heavy trepidation. Somewhere, looming before them were the slopes of Montgomery Hill, and on that hill resided the enemy.

The talk that surrounded the camp fires the night before was filled with boasting vengeance, on how the rebels had pushed them as far as they could, and that it was now their turn to push back. But as the men moved forward with a deliberate caution, their mood was rapidly sinking into the softening earth. The notion that they were blindly feeling their way though this fog, while the enemy knelt armed, poised and ready, caused more than one company of men to pause in their advance. Regiments that brought up the rear sent word to the front that Schofield had not been pleased with the artillery that was now sailing above their heads.

The adjective most used to describe his mood was maniacal. The general apparently had whipped his horse towards Fort Negley, parting from General Cox with words that were bilious, 'Wait until I find the person responsible for ordering the firing of our guns. He will no longer serve this army.'

Still Cox pressed his men on, wanting them to focus on the enemy and not their contentious commander. The second division followed as instructed, growing more and more worried as their destination neared. They concluded that if Schofield was upset that the artillery had fired, it was because he meant to use the dense fog as a means to conceal his attack. Under such inauspicious conditions, there could be no other reason for the general having the attack proceed as planned. Yet thanks to some artillery officer who announced their surprise... the Confederates now knew that they were coming.

With eyes that failed them, the men bent their ears east, towards the Nashville and Chattanooga Railroad, where Steedman's Colored corps was supposed to be engaging the rebel right. Pauses in the artillery barrage only revealed an ominous silence. The attack that should have been raging by now, and drawing the rebel attention from this advance, sounded non-existent. Many of the soldiers that made up the Twenty-third whispered curses to Steedman in trusting the Negroes to perform a white man's task.

The only positive report that made it to their ears during this dreary morning was that Wilson's cavalry was successfully flushing the enemy out of the Nashville vicinity. Rumors reported that the Charlotte and Hardin Pikes were now completely open to the Federal army and that Wilson was wheeling southeast in strong support of Smith's corps who were currently marching along the Twenty-third's right flank. Even more revealing was that except for Jackson's division, who was now falling back past Bell's Mill, Forrest's entire command had been sent the day before to Murfreesboro in an attempt to capture Fort Rosencrans.

The thought of a battle without Forrest's presence strengthened the will of many a Federal soldier, and slowly but steadily, the pace of the march increased.

And slowly but steadily the fog began to separate with the long thick sinuous wisps of gray stretching and parting with each passing step. The lead regiments began to stumble, not realizing that they had reached the base of their objective. The artillery had ended a while ago, but many of the men did not take notice. Towering before them was the one hundred and fifty foot menace known as Montgomery Hill. The parting fog seemed to split itself in two as it broke around the sides of the hill and continued to move out of the path of the advancing army.

The lofty hill was littered with the shattered abatis that was meant to deter their advance. A few of the men snickered that the artillery fired better when they were firing blind. But most bent their heads into their chest, expecting at any second the Confederate volley that would rip them apart.

And second by second, nothing happened.

Like a voice that came from another world, General Cox could be heard yelling to his officers, "Keep them moving, keep them moving."

And once again, the Twenty-third moved. At first it was a captain that put his muddied boot upon the slope of the hill, but soon many others followed. Regiment by regiment they ascended the hill like invading ants.

And still the rebels had not fired. Some of the men that were green to the war believed that the artillery had done to the Confederates what it had also done to the abatis, pounded them into ruination. The veterans, however, knew differently. They had been in this situation before, on both sides of it. The worst part of an attack was when the enemy held its fire until you were at point blank range. They prayed against their fears that the Southern army was not waiting until they reached the crest of the hill to unleash its hailstorm.

Then came a yell. A yell so confident and resonant it had to be the infamously terrifying battle cry of the enemy. Many soldiers dropped to the ground and covered themselves against the inevitable. Others dropped to their knees and pointed their loaded guns ahead. But when they tried to take aim at the enemy, they saw only the Stars and Stripes waving defiantly atop the hill.

The yell, that moments ago was so petrifying, instantly became invigorating. Prone men shot up and raced for the hilltop, others took up the chase. In a matter of moments, the arduous three-hour march had finally paid off.

Montgomery Hill had fallen, and there had not been a single Federal casualty.

The smiles that adorned the faces of the Twenty-third remained permanent fixtures. But their wavering eyes begged a question that someone needed to answer.

"Was this a good thing or a bad thing?"

*　　*　　*　　*　　*　　*　　*　　*

The men who wore gray occupied a strong continuous line from the hills west of the Hillsboro Pike to the Peach Orchard Hill east of the Franklin Pike. During the previous night they had conducted a well-organized withdrawal from a defensive line that was much closer to the city. They had only retired a couple miles, but the fact that they had to give up the ground that they had earned in blood, remained a mystery to many. Some even began to question the motives of General Robert E. Lee, but those opinions would never be voiced.

They were instructed to awake before dawn and begin constructing new entrenchments in the event that Schofield proceeded to attack. When the men did wake, they were greeted with the same dense fog that stymied the Federal attack. The men lethargically moved through the heavy mist with tired hearts that lacked the sense of urgency. In their hands hung the tools that were to be used to dig the new defensive line.

Shovels, split canteens, bayonets, all of these implements had as much motion as a snail with no place to go. The men were simply tired of marching, tired of digging, and tired of falling back from the enemy.

Then came the explosion that rocked the earth for several minutes. The fog may have made it hard to see exactly what was occurring, but the men could have been blindfolded and still seen it all with perfect clarity. The old line, which they occupied just the day before, was now being bombarded by Yankee artillery. And from the way that the ground trembled beneath them, that old line was being hit hard. The men also took note of the duration of the shelling. A heavy artillery barrage sustained for that amount of time could only indicate one thing.

Suddenly the sound of swinging shovels, canteens and bayonets could be heard swishing though the air. Hard dirt was torn asunder across the field. Limbs that were exhausted were now revitalized. And many a man said a silent prayer of thanks that they had been ordered to withdraw the night before.

Robert E. Lee worked in mysterious ways.

*   *   *   *   *   *   *   *

Lee continued to look through his field glasses, hoping to see any indication of movement by the enemy, but it was useless. He dropped his arms to his sides and handed the glasses to Wigfall. Part of him wished that he had not pulled back last night. Schofield seemed to finally be giving him the attack that he so desperately desired. As he stared into the gray void, his hands slipped to the mane of his mount. For a moment, he thought that he was on top of Traveler. How he wished that were true.

"Do you think that they mean to attack?" Wigfall said.

"If I were he, I would not. Not in this fog, not with our army pulled back like it is. Yet, if we cannot see them, then they cannot see us. Schofield is most likely attacking our old lines, under the assumption that we are still in occupation of them. The focus of their artillery seems to confirm that."

"Sir, what do you think Schofield will do once he realizes that we are not where he expects us to be?"

"Captain, if you had the command of an army and ordered it to attack in the morning, and once you attacked discovered the enemy had moved beyond your reach, what would you do?"

Wigfall was reluctant to answer Lee's question. He did not want to disappoint him by giving the wrong response. Lee's silence beckoned for an answer.

"General, I would have to say that I would hold off on the attack. Their men would be disorganized. Time would be needed to shift focus and continue the march another two miles. To do so would mean being without support from the artillery. With our army appearing to be withdrawing, why Schofield should just let us go and mount the attack another, more appropriate time."

"Captain Wigfall, that response may earn you a higher place with me in the very near future, but for right now, I pray that you are wrong. Has their been any word from General Forrest?"

"I am sorry, but there has not. Hood has sent several companies out this morning in an effort to contact Forrest, but I have yet to confirm any reply."

Lee did not respond. Even if he wanted too he would not have found the words to do so. A large battle was beginning to materialize through the fog, a battle that might very well seal the fate of the Confederacy. It painfully reminded him of a similar situation that occurred to him two summers ago. Only then it was J.E.B. Stuart, not Forrest who led his cavalry. And though the commanders were different, the result was the same.

Just like it was at Gettysburg, it was now at Nashville, the eyes and ears of his army were nowhere to be found.

God, please let the similarities end there.

Lee departed from Wigfall and returned to his headquarters at Travelers Rest. As he rode south along the Franklin Pike, he could see Colonel Kellar, now in command of Strahl's Brigade, leading three Tennessee regiments north along the pike, towards the Peach Orchard Hill. The men had not noticed his silent passage, and that was good. Lee did not want them to fake any enthusiasm on his part. What he saw convinced him that if Schofield did indeed attack, his men would be ready. The slow step that accompanied these same men the night before was replaced with a steadied determined stride. If the Federals were indeed coming, they fully intended to be ready and waiting.

Lee waited until the last regiment, the Forty-first Tennessee passed along the pike, before continuing to his headquarters. Lee took a moment to reflect upon Strahl, and how the general who had recently fallen at Franklin, would have been so proud to see his men marching so vigorously at the thought of engaging the enemy. The mental picture of Strahl brought forth images of all those fallen at Franklin, including Patrick Cleburne.

Lee knew that the Irish general was the catalyst for his covenant with the Lord. With the severity of the promises exchanged between the two, Lee knew that God would be watching him very closely once the battle occurred. The sight of Quintard standing just outside of the Overton home confirmed his suspicion. The Lord would be with him today.

Lee dismounted from his horse, handing the reigns to an aid. He then made his way to the chaplain. "Chaplain Quintard," he called. "A pleasure to see you this morning."

Quintard returned a very warm smile. "I heard the enemy's guns. At first I thought that it was just a demonstration, but when they did not let up, I was convinced that he meant to attack. I do believe that Schofield will attack us today."

Lee looked back towards Nashville. His line of sight following the central Alabama railroad until it blended into obscurity with the dissipating mist. "I do hope so, but I fear that Schofield will not continue with the attack once the fog lifts and he finds that we are not where we should be."

"General, what Schofield does is beyond our control. The events that will occur today are now in the Lord's hands, and if He wants the enemy to attack us today, then they will. And if He does not, it is because it will benefit us most that they not. A man should not be judged against events that are beyond his control, instead he should be judged by his actions in response to those same events. That is how the Lord tests us."

"Chaplain, I do believe that the Lord's wisdom flows

heavily from your tongue. You are right, God knows what He wants of us this day, and it is only for us to do His will, whether the enemy attacks or stands still. You know, it is rather ironic, when I consider how often I refused to leave Virginia. I felt that the battle had to be won in the East, that a complete victory near the Union's capital would seal the destiny of the South, and win us our independence."

Quintard put his arm around Lee's shoulder as he led him into the Overton home. "You know General, one often meets his destiny on the road he has taken to avoid it."

*   *   *   *   *   *   *   *

General John McAllister Schofield handed the reigns of his mount to one of his aids and moved past his senior commanders as he made his way south on Montgomery Hill. A thick perspiration saturated his pale forehead as he unbuttoned his coat to relieve some of the wrath contained within. This had to be the warmest day that this state had ever experienced during the month of December. After weeks of unrelenting freezing rain, snow and ice, it was as if the fog that descended upon this area early this morning, brought with it a day of warm spring captured from some town along the South Atlantic coast.

He took a moment to inhale the warming air, feeling it rush through his nostrils, down his throat and into the violent turmoil that was now raging within his bowels. When he and the army first began its march, his thoughts were filled with the glorious conquests that would lead to his occupation of Montgomery Hill. His standing in this very spot was supposed to mean that the rebel left had been turned and that the enemy was shattered out of their works and splintering south in an effort to escape their final destruction.

This was not how it was supposed to be. His moment of triumph was stolen by circumstance.

Schofield took one last look towards the south, noted the fog lifting and then returned to his commanders. The way they just stood there waiting for him reminded him of a bunch of lost sheep. General Cox, his three brigade commanders and several captains and colonels, all staring silently. That was all that was left of his beloved Twenty-third corps, just three brigades of six thousand soldiers. This hill was supposed to be their reward for their pains, for all that they had lost, but that glory was taken from them by the cowardice of Stephen D. Lee.

"General Schofield," General Cox said, "I have done as you asked and reconfirmed with Steedman. There is no enemy to his front at the Nashville and Chattanooga Railroad. Thomas has confirmed the same regarding his position, and Smith's flags are now to our right. There can be no doubt that the entire line of the enemy has fallen back. I have word from my skirmish line that Stephen Lee appears to have his entire army just a few miles south of here."

Cox let the statement hang in the air. The question that was on all of their faces was do we continue or fall back? At any moment, he expected to see couriers arriving from the other senior commanders, their dispatches would be asking for direction. Judging by the long creasing wrinkle that split his upper forehead, Schofield was nowhere ready to make a decision.

Schofield tried to mask his true feelings by making a joke that Grant should be notified that the enemy line had been captured with complete success. His commanders all shared a brief chuckle, but when it was done, the seriousness of their situation wiped the smiles from their faces as if slapped by the palm of a very large hand.

"General Cox, are the reports from Wilson also confirmed?" he asked.

"They are. The only cavalry that has opposed him were of Jackson's division. Wilson has part of his force driving the enemy from Bell's Mill, while the rest of his command has fallen to General Smith's right between the Hardin and Hillsboro Pike."

Cox was not prepared for the harsh look that Schofield was casting in his direction after the conclusion of his report. Obviously he had not given his commander the report that he wanted to hear. Realizing what he forgot, he quickly added, "And Wilson has reconfirmed the reports of the captured Confederate officer. General Forrest and his other two divisions were sent east the night before, and are now in operation near Murfreesboro."

Schofield's grim countenance finally faded. "Wilson's report is the only good news that I have heard this morning. I need you to somehow get word to Fortress Rosencrans, and inform those boys to remain within their defenses until we have defeated the Confederate army. I do not want them to needlessly expose themselves to Forrest. Has Steedman's command marched forwards to link with Thomas' left?"

"They have sir," his third brigade commander Colonel John Mehringer replied.

Schofield had to close his eyes in an effort to silence the myriad of voices that reverberated within his skull. They all called for him, beckoning different choices. Like the ghosts of past follies, they chanted to fall back, to stay where you are and attack again in the morning, and to continue as the offensive is already in motion. He desperately tried to consider the rewards and repercussions for each action, but they all seemed to collide and entwine, confusing him all the more. And the more he tried to think, the more knotted the choices became, until he was confronted with a gargantuan ball of yarn that was entirely too immense to be unwound in the time he needed to do so. The bottom line was that he was the acting commander of this army, and this army needed his response now.

His heart weighed heavily with the answer that he knew he should accept. The enemy was two miles south, possibly falling back farther. He should pull the men back and wait to see what the Confederates did. But as solid as that thought seemed, he could also imagine the wrath he would incur from Grant back east. He was not given the command to sit idle. Thomas had done that already and his reward was a demotion.

How could Schofield send the word to Grant that he was letting the enemy escape? How could he wire City Point and inform Grant that he had marched out as planned and finding the enemy withdrawn two miles, decided to wait until the next day so that he could reorganize his attack? And also, what if tomorrow brought with it a return of December's weather with all of its wintry fury? He would be forced to abandon the attack. Or even worse, what if the Confederates used his delay to seize the initiative and attack him while he no longer had the defenses of Nashville to protect him?

It was the latter thought more than any other that convinced him to move forward. Grant would not accept his falling back, and he could not accept sitting idle, exposing his army to a Confederate attack of their own. That left one option, and that was to continue until Stephen Lee's army was engaged.

Schofield's 2nd Advance

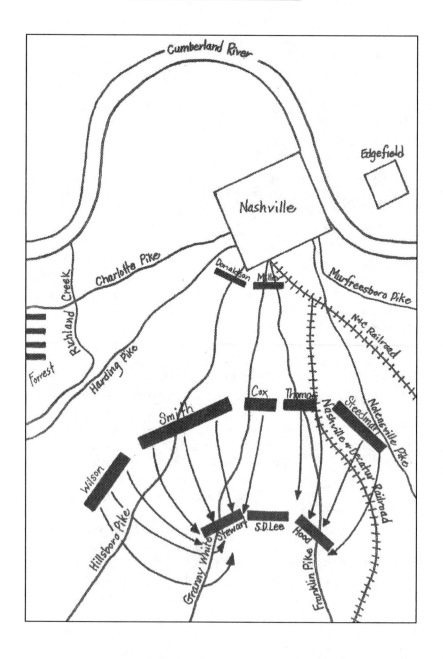

An option that was made more sound by two factors. One was that the new rebel position was hardly a day old. Their defenses could not be as formidable as the one that they had just vacated, having spent several weeks preparing them. The second, and more promising factor was the confirmation of the absence of Forrest's cavalry.

Stephen Lee was probably already calling back his infamous cavalry commander at this very moment. If he waited until the morning to renew the attack, Forrest would add his two divisions to the battle. That was something that Schofield had to prevent if he could.

And he could.

"General Cox, have the men ready to move forward. I want as much detail as I can get regarding the enemy's new position. From what I have already been told, the enemy occupies a similar line, only over a shorter distance. We will march in the same manner as we did this morning. Steedman and Thomas will feint along their front, drawing the Confederate attention from their left. Wilson will continue to support Smith's right flank. Upon Smith engaging the enemy's left, Wilson is to slip around Smith and come upon the Confederate rear. And that is where and when this corps will achieve its place in history. Once their left begins to falter, I expect the men of this Second division to smash a breakthrough on Stewart's front, cleaving one third of the Confederate army. With Wilson in the enemy's rear, he will easily push further east, and cut off the routed rebel army from their only two avenues of escape... the Granny White and the Franklin Pike. The only outcome that has changed because of the Confederate's new position will be the hour in which their army ceases to exist."

Emboldened by his newfound audacious confidence, Schofield gave the order for the army to move forward. And like a giant wave of deep blue, the Federal army was once again set in motion to engage the enemy works.

Though now they would have to march an additional two miles to do so.

*　　*　　*　　*　　*　　*　　*　　*

Accompanied by his staff, General George Thomas rode behind the first brigade of his broken Fourth army corps. His left most regiments rested along on the tracks of the Nashville and Decatur railroad. From there Thomas could see the flags of Steedman's corps closing in from the east. Steedman would offer protection to his left flank, but that did little to compensate for the absence of one third his total strength. But that was the price paid for the retreat from Pulaski roughly one month ago.

As Thomas reflected upon his missing Second division, thoughts of Franklin infected his head like a sickness. He still could not fully comprehend how Schofield allowed Hood's army to slip by him so many times during the Tennessee campaign. As far as the rock of Chickamauga was concerned, Hood's army should have gotten no farther north than Columbia. The fact that they were this close to Nashville was a direct insult to all those that had fallen while driving the enemy through Georgia and out of Atlanta.

And the man that had almost allowed the unthinkable, allowing Hood to cut off thirty thousand Union soldiers from Nashville, was now given the authority to mount the offensive meant to sweep the enemy from Tennessee for the final time. Thomas did not voice a single complaint, choosing instead to remain reticent, at least until the common enemy was destroyed. He would wait until the United States was once again restored before taking carefully aimed blows at men like Schofield and Grant. Men who could not have taken a single step had they been the one wearing his boots.

What helped him accept Schofield's promotion was the promise that Schofield was not going to deviate from his offensive strategy. The only real difference was that Schofield wanted to use his own Twenty-third corps to deliver the breakthrough punch. That changed his battle plan slightly, as Thomas' Fourth corps had to switch places with Schofield's Twenty-third. Thomas knew it was meant as a direct insult, but had enough fortitude to swallow it down like a bitter pill.

Using his thick beard to conceal his true emotions, Thomas led his men through the fog, crossing Brown's Creek and into such places as Thompson Lane and the Nolensville Pike. But as his mount brought him closer to his destination, two emotions consumed his thoughts. The first was his anxiousness to get this battle underway. The second and more alarming emotion was bewilderment. The latter was shared by every member of this advancing army, as the reports were confirmed that the enemy's position had been abandoned the night before.

He knew something was strange when Steedman first reported his front unoccupied. With the thick fog swirling around them, and the enemy gone from the field, Thomas halted his command in anticipation of the order from Schofield that would call for the rapid withdrawal back into the Nashville defenses. He almost fell from his horse when the orders had finally arrived.

Schofield wanted the men to push on.

The Confederate line was confirmed to be two miles ahead, anchored from Peach Orchard Hill on the right to the hills west of the Granny White Pike. Steedman was ordered to have his men march southwest until they made contact with Thomas' left. Once flanking each other, the two commands would continue south until they made contact with the rebel right along the Peach Orchard Hill.

'Make a demonstration along the enemy's front so that you may draw his attention from the main attack which will be delivered on their far left,' was the direct order that Schofield had given.

Thomas fought the urge to disobey the order by focusing his attention to the details of coordinating new formations for his command. The long lines of infantry had been marching southeast since early this morning. They would now have to halt their position and wait for Steedman's command to come along their flank. They then would have to turn west and march yet another two miles. Thomas expected a disheartened response from his men, but was surprised with their alacrity to finish what they set out to do when this day first began. Within the hour, the outer regiments veered from the Nolensville Pike and began swinging down towards the Central Alabama Railroad. The flags of Steedman's command were rapidly coming up on his left, and on his right the flags of Schofield's Twenty-third were now visible.

The attack seemed to be reorganizing much better than Thomas would have thought. As his horse climbed a slight incline along the Franklin Pike, he viewed what would be an immense obstacle in the Peach Orchard Hill. Steep slopes would protect the defenders from any advance to their front and exposed eastern flank. Thick clumps of foliage would add to the arduous task of attempting to charge the hill. Even if the men had enough energy to charge up those slopes, around the thick brush, they would then find themselves facing strong earthworks that looked as if they were erected and fortified months ago, not the previous night.

And that said nothing about the number of rebels that could be seen occupying those works. Compacted in shorter lines, the enemy's numbers looked much larger than yesterday, when they were dispersed over a wider front. Their new lines of defense made the distance between their outer flanks much more accessible to support. Thomas was instantly overcome with apprehension as his leading regiment closed upon the hill.

The whole plan of turning the Confederate left was contingent upon bringing superior numbers to that area and hitting it so fast and hard that the enemy would be unable to reinforce in time. However, the rebel's new position was more consolidated... it would negate that all too important aspect of the Union plan. With a shorter distance to march, Thomas had no doubt in the ability of the enemy to get needed reinforcements to its left in order to repel the main Federal attack. And that would mean that his and Steedman's command would be isolated and exposed to a Confederate counterattack.

Perhaps it was time for him to overstep his authority and demand that Schofield call off the attack. The Confederate's new defensive position begged for a new plan of attack. Thomas began shouting the orders to his officers. He called for them to recall all of his divisions until he could speak personally with Schofield.

Unfortunately, the sound of artillery raking into his front lines told him that it was too late for that.

The battle for Nashville had finally begun.

Chapter XXXVI
Nashville, Tennessee
The Battle of Nashville

He climbed the ascending hill to the east of the Bradford Home and used its elevated vantage point to gain a much wider view of the battle. Below him lay the Franklin Pike, and through his glasses he could follow the long lines of Thomas' corps as it marched into battle. He could hear his staff behind him, yelling for someone to get a message to Smith. He tried to discern exactly what they wanted, but the increasing intensity of musket fire kept drawing his attention towards Peach Orchard Hill.

The hill seemed to rise straight out of the Franklin Pike as the road stretched its way south. As he watched Thomas' men march towards that high ground, his apprehension increased as he noted how that hill formed a natural wall. It would forbid his army any further passage along the pike. And if the hill didn't stop his army, Cheatham's corps entrenched upon it surely would. Schofield tried to strain his eyes as he peered through his glasses. He thought he could see Hood's massive frame in every gray obscuration that entered his view. It was rumored that after Stephen Lee's promotion, Hood had been demoted and given command of Cheatham's corp. Schofield wondered if that were true.

To Thomas' left, he could see the flags of Steedman's command. The closest units to Thomas' flank on that side was Colonel Thomson's Second Colored brigade. The Colored regiments were marching in perfect formation, cutting their angle to link with Thomas' Third division. It would not be much longer until Steedman and Thomas were consolidated on the enemy's right.

He had to admit that the organization and additional marching had gone better than he had hoped. Schofield's only worry now was time. It was already late in the afternoon, as evident by the sun racing west. He did not want to call off this attack because of darkness, and as he scanned his glasses west, he realized he might not have to. On the Confederate left flank the battle was beginning to take form... and from the look of it, things were finally starting to go his way.

A sloping cornfield intersected the Franklin Pike with the Granny White. Nestled in between those two pikes was the Second Confederate corps. The rebels that occupied their center were Stephen Lee's boys, but with the general's promotion, it meant that they were in someone else's command. Perhaps it was Cheatham who now commanded the middle, he thought. Not that it would matter. The attack would not hit the center directly. Thomas' First division under Brigadier General Kimball was positioning itself directly in front of Stephen Lee's command. Schofield allowed the grin to fully widen his jaw.

The plan was so simple, yet so perfect. While the Confederate center and right were being pressed by the combined commands of Thomas and Steedman, their left was being set up for an overwhelming attack by more than two thirds its number. The two corps that occupied their middle and right could hold out all day, but the moment their left crumbled, as he fully intended it to, Stephen Lee's and Hood's corps would have to vacate their defenses and retreat south, where Wilson's cavalry would be waiting to scoop them up.

A very loud explosion sent large fragments of debris scattering across the top of Peach Orchard Hill. Schofield, his glasses directed to his right was compelled to swing his view back towards the east. The sporadic artillery fire that was being shot by his guns was beginning to escalate, forcing the enemy's artillery to do the same. It did not take long for both sides of the battlefield to become befogged with gunpowder. The gun smoke was hindering his ability to see almost as badly as the fog had done earlier this morning. One of the last images he could make out were the flags of the Second Colored brigade as they formed for the attack. But then another volley of artillery was exchanged and once again his view was obscured.

Steedman was probably using the Negroes to put on a show of force, he thought. Good, the better the feint, the more reinforcements Stephen Lee might draw from his left.

"General, sir," a voice said. One of his staff officers had just returned from delivering a message to General Smith. "General Smith has confirmed that his men are in place to attack the enemy's left flank. He reports that the hill is very steep and very formidable, but is confident that with Wilson's cavalry riding around their rear, and your Twenty-third ready to exploit the first opening, his numbers will overcome their defenses."

Not even Schofield's frizzled beard could hide his beaming smile. The gunfire resounding to his left confirmed that two thirds of the rebel army was now fully engaged. They would not be able to assist Stewart's lone corps anchoring their left flank.

His hour had finally come.

"Thank you, you may go back to General Smith and inform him to commence his attack." Schofield watched the staff officer ride down the hill towards the Granny White Pike. The faster that man made it to General Smith, the faster this battle could be won. Eager to see the flags of Smith's corps climbing the hill to the west, he once again raised the field glasses to his eyes and prepared to leave them there until every unfortunate gray soldier in Stewarts' corps was laid out on his back.

While waiting to witness his triumph, he thought of the two hills that anchored the rebel line. Of the two, he was uncertain which was more formidable. The hill that rose to the left of the Granny White was just as imposing as that of Peach Orchard Hill. Schofield did not recall the name of the opposite hill, but since it was Stewart's command that defended it, he just presumed to call it Stewart's hill.

The rebels on Stewart's hill were positioned behind strong earthworks that ran across their entire line. Like Hood's corps anchored on the right, Stewart's men would also benefit from the tactical advantage of a steep slope to their front. Even now as Smith marched his thousands against their position, Stewart's boys were no doubt confident with false hope. Perhaps they believed the steep incline leading to their earthworks would offset the Union's superiority in manpower. And that might be true. But what the enemy did not understand was that as Smith positioned his men to the west and north of the hill, Wilson' cavalry was slipping behind their rear.

Schofield could not imagine why Stephen Lee decided to send Forrest to Murfreesboro with two thirds of the cavalry, but he was thankful. Now it was up to Schofield to make him pay for that mistake. Without Forrest's cavalry to impede Wilson, the Federal cavalry was free to maneuver at will. There were already reports that Wilson's command was in place south of Stewart's hill. He was waiting only for the advance of Smith's corps to occupy Stewart's attention. Once the rebels turned to face the advancing threat, Wilson would explode from their rear and force them to fall out of their position or risk total annihilation.

And if by some chance, they did not fall back as hoped, Schofield had another plan in place. If Stewart weakened his lines enough to stall the attack of both Wilson and Stewart, then that would mean that his immediate front was soft. And that was the very place he intended the Twenty-third corps to strike.

He knew that there was no way for Stewart to meet and repel all three of these attacks. The numbers were just stacked too heavily against him. Stewart would break, of that Schofield was sure. He only hoped that it was at the hands of the men from his own Twenty-third.

Trying to remain patient was now the hardest part of the afternoon. The bleak weather from the morning was long gone, and a warm air had settled upon the area, giving the men an added boost to their march. His entire army was in the exact position that he intended them to be. All he needed to do now was wait for the main attack to announce itself upon the enemy's left. Steedman and Thomas were most likely feeling their own pangs of anxiousness, as they had to hold their commands in place until the eventual rout of the Confederate left. All that he asked of them was to feint a few attacks, something substantial enough to hold the attention of Hood and Stewart.

It was an order that he thought simple enough to execute, until a painfully long cacophony of musket fire volley sounded from the slopes of Peach Orchard Hill.

With field glasses already pressed against his eye sockets, Schofield once again swung his view back to Steedman and Thomas. Thomas' men were still in place, but the flags of Steedman's Second Colored brigade were not. In fact neither were the flags of the First Colored brigade. Scanning the area frantically for their location, it took several long seconds to find them.

A savage howl revealed the Colored regiments charging up the slopes of the hill. To their left, followed Steedman's Third brigade being led by Lieutenant Colonel Grosvenor. Schofield quickly scanned his view trying to find General Thomas, surely this was not an actual attack. Thomas could not be found, but the three lines being formed by his Second brigade indicated that he must have given the order to support the attack.

An attack he did not authorize? Why couldn't they simply follow the damned order? All he asked was for them to hold the enemy in place with their presence. They were not strong enough to take that position, and to do so before Smith was ready could be disastrous.

With a heavy pounding in his chest, he loudly cursed General Steedman for allowing his men to advance.

*　　*　　*　　*　　*　　*　　*　　*

They were former slaves, men who had not wished to be in this country, especially not in the service of the white man. Their family histories were all the same, proud men who had to watch the subjection of their people against their will. They were forced to endure a dehumanizing life, swallowing it down like rotten flesh. Like a man living with starvation, there really was no choice, consume the unacceptable, or die. Until now, there was no other option. To strike back at the white man meant certain death.

Until now.

Their commander, Colonel Charles Thompson had spent the past hour pleading with General Steedman to allow his one chance at the enemy's lines. Steedman, who felt he had his attack stolen from him earlier this morning, was not hard to be convinced. He actually augmented the attacking force by calling for Grosvenor's brigade to march in support of their left. He also sent word to General Thomas to his right. If Post could support his advance, it would be much appreciated.

Several of the Negroes overheard Thompson telling his staff that Steedman was not worried about disobeying Schofield's orders, he fully trusted that the Negroes in his command would carry the enemies works. The darker skinned Federal soldiers felt their chests swell with pride. Steedman was a white man who trusted them. He was also a white man that had just given them the order that many of them prayed for their whole lives. March forward and battle your oppressors.

Generations of slavery were now given their chance to be avenged.

When Colonel Thompson gave the order to move forward, his Negro regiments sprang forward with alacrity. Their dark knuckles gripped their guns with expected hopes as they rushed headlong up the long eastern slopes of the hill. As they charged ahead, they began to separate, the faster soldiers pulling ahead, the slower lagging behind.

Thompson tried to keep pace, but his men were simply too fast. It was not hard for him to understand why they raced ahead so speedily into the hands of certain death. Had his family been forced into a lifetime of servitude to another man, he imagined that he too would have found the speed to carry him up that hill.

A quick glance over his shoulder revealed Morgan's First Colored brigade rushing upon the heels of his own men. The waving flags on his left assured him that Grosvenor's men were also at hand. General Steedman had been true to his word... he was committing his entire efforts to this attack. Everything was progressing as Thompson had hoped. His only concern was that the rebels had still not fired.

With heads now tilted forwards, the Second Colored brigade could make out the tops of the enemy's works. Ferocious speed motivated by years of concealed animosity carried them closer and closer. Unlike their colonel, they moved too fast to ponder why the enemy had not yet fired, too fast to notice the thousands of muskets that rested atop the rebel works.

*   *   *   *   *   *   *   *

General Hood would not dismount. He remained strapped to his horse and glared in disbelief as the Yankees began climbing the hill that he defended. The fact that the Yankees even dared to attack his position was a direct insult to his ability to command. But what was worse was that the Yankees were using Negro troops to lead their attack. There were thousands of them racing up the hill towards him, their white eyes glowing against coal black skin. The hatred in their dark eyes rivaled only by its reflection caught in the unified grimace of his own men.

He moved closer to the front ranks, not caring that his horse exposed him as someone important. He bent over his horse and put his hand upon one of his captains. The flags of the First[l] and Second Florida crowded around them.

"Tell your boys to fire only when I give the word."

Grim Southern eyes took careful aim and waited. The Negro regiment was rapidly closing in on them. It took a great deal of will to hold back itchy fingers from squeezing their triggers. The Negroes were now a few yards from their earthworks, and at the same instant that Hood bellowed the command, the entire front line of his corps issued such an intense volley of piercing lead, that when the smoke cleared, not a single Negro was left standing.

Before the Confederates could let out a cheer, a second brigade of Colored troops came bursting up the hill. Reloaded muskets were once again discharged with similar devastation. Yet still they came. A brigade of white Yankees was now attempting to charge the hill farther to the south. If the color of one's skin was supposed to make any difference, it did not show upon Peach Orchard Hill. The sheet of lead that swiped the two Colored brigades from the field, did the same to the white one. When the hailstorm of lead finally subsided, the Yankees could be seen scrambling back down the hill, with far fewer numbers.

Left behind were the dead and the wounded. Those Negroes that could not get up and follow the rest of the army in retreat were forced to endure the pain of their suffering. Lying motionless, while bleeding to death, their horrific moans wailed of insatiable vengeance.

*   *   *   *   *   *   *   *

Schofield did not stay to watch Thomas' brigades move in to support Steedman's attack. He did not have to. Thomas' men were moving too slowly and would not arrive at the same moment as Steedman's Colored brigade. The sounds of rebel artillery indicated that their guns were already done with Steedman and were turning unanimously towards Thomas. The only chance that the attack ever had was if the two commands struck at the same moment, forcing Hood to direct his firepower in two separate directions.

'What was Thomas thinking', Schofield spat, as he raced across the Granny White and rode with his staff up into the hills to the west. I could not have been any clearer when I ordered the left to simply hold the Confederates in position.

With numbers quickly calculating in his head, Schofield grew more and more concerned with the counterattack that could come at any moment. He had structured the attack so that Thomas and Steedman had enough men between them to force two thirds of the Confederate army to remain in place while his main thrust struck their isolated Third corps.

The fifteen thousand men that made up Steedman's and

Thomas' command were not nearly enough to hold off an attack on their own. And after that feeble and unauthorized attack, their numbers would now be severely decreased. Instead of a strong show of fifteen thousand to his front, Hood was probably now watching the backs of roughly eleven thousand Yankees race down the hill in defeat.

The torrid quake that shook deep in his belly only grew worse as he thought upon his greatest fear... a counterattack upon his own left flank. With more than thirty thousand infantry and cavalry on the far west portion of the battlefield, there were now less than twelve thousand soldiers standing between the Confederate right and Nashville. Even if he wanted to pray for a miracle that would dissuade the rebels from countering, he doubted if even the Lord above had enough power to grant such a request.

The general in command on the Peach Orchard Hill was John Bell Hood. The same man who took over Johnston's command back in July, and since then has ever been on the offensive. That was not a surprise to anyone, especially to Schofield. Hood prided himself in bringing the attack to the enemy, and now he was given an excellent opportunity to do so. Thoughts of Hood's heedless attack upon the fortifications south of Franklin had Schofield listening towards the east for the sounds of the rebel yell.

All the while, he had thought that it would be his right turning the enemy's left, but it was now turning out to be exactly the opposite. It would be the enemy's right who turned his left. That realization sent a thick perspiration rolling down his spine. It then slowly ascended his back until it curled around his throat, before settling upon his pale and clammy face. Moments ago, he could envision his triumphant victory, and now with the threat of Hood's corps marching around his rear and cutting off his army from Nashville... he was tasting disaster.

Schofield realized that the only chance to save this day was with Smith's command on the enemy's left flank. If Smith could complete his attack and rout the enemy, then Hood would not be able to leave his trenches to go on the offensive. Smith's success would keep Hood from attaining the initiative.

Unfortunately, he also realized that if Smith could not do this, it would be Spring Hill all over again. Only this time, he would not be allowed to escape.

*   *   *   *   *   *   *   *

Once he reached the artillery position high opposite Stewart's corps, Schofield hoped to have an immediate conference with General Smith. To his relief, his disappointment quickly melted away as the scene set before him re-kindled his confidence. The Federal artillery was bellowing shot after shot at the Confederate left. With a quick view through his field glasses, Schofield understood why.

Smith's three divisions were steadily advancing towards Stewart's hill like a solid mass of blue will. The enemy's artillery rained heavily upon them, but it did little to deter their momentum. Smith's men were renowned as an excellent combat unit, and from their unwavering advance, Schofield had to agree.

The rebel cannons struck gaping holes in their tight formations, but the soldiers simply closed their lines without missing a step. They did not halt their march to return fire, nor did they utter a single cry. Stoically they accepted their duty, as each stride closed the distance between them and the enemy. Trailing behind, Schofield could see his own Twenty-third corps being led by General Cox. Its three brigades readied themselves to be in a position to force a breakthrough upon Stewart's line.

Although the progression of this advance gave him hope, it took the appearance of Wilson's dismounted cavalry, to resurface the buried smile on Schofield's lower face. Perhaps his plan still had a chance to succeed. The enemy's regiments were shifting to meet this new threat emerging in its rear. From behind, he could hear whispering prayers issued from his staff. He took a moment to close his eyes to add the weight of his own.

It was Smith's First division, McArthur's command, which reached the rebel works first. Like a heavy sledgehammer they struck Stewart's line on the western side of the Granny White, bludgeoning it, but not breaking it. Moments later Garrard's Second division poured over the hill and charged the rebel parapets guarding the northern face of the hill. A savage volley of combined artillery and muskets caused a massive billow of gun smoke to fog Schofield's view. When it began to clear, he could see that the enemy's line still held, but it had bent.

At the same time that Stewart was engaged to the north,

Smith's Third division rose over the hill from the west. Confederate regiments continued to be pulled from the front and sent to face this new threat. They arrived just in time, as Schofield watched another wave of his attack reach their works only to fail in its attempt to pierce their line. That was fine though, Smith's men were not like Thomas' or Steedman's... they would not be retreating down the hill. Instead, the three divisions were remaining in place to exchange rifle fire with the enemy, keeping their attention while Wilson's cavalry emerged to deliver a devastating volley upon their overwhelmed rear.

There is no way you can defend against this attack, he thought. General Stephen Lee will have to pull his left back before it completely collapses. Schofield watched as more and more regiments were pulled from the north side of the hill to meet the Union attack escalating in the rear. Flags from the rebel center were now shifting to the left to reinforce Stewart's crumbling corp.

Now, he thought, now is the time. And at the same moment he silently willed it, his Twenty-third corps moved past the left of Smith's First division and shattered the weakened Confederate works before them. The point of impact put the Federals in command of the Granny White Pike, and completely cut off Stewart's corps from the rest of the rebel army. That same position also outflanked the stone fence that supported their center, rendering the works useless. The gray regiments were already falling back from their exposed position.

His staff was now dismounted and cheering with the artillery crews. The threat of an inevitable disaster had been exhausting. Until now, Stewart's corps was managing to repel not only Smith's divisions from the front and flank, but also Wilson's cavalry in its rear. But now that the Twenty-third corps had penetrated their lines, Stewart was soon to be surrounded. The whole rebel command was visibly disorganized. And most importantly, Hood had not seized the opportunity to attack Thomas and Steedman on the Federal left.

And if he had not done so by now, the situation on Stewart's Hill ensured that he never would.

Chapter XXXVII
Nashville, Tennessee
The Battle of Nashville

After the attack against the eastern portion of Peach Orchard Hill had subsided, Hood rode towards the north to contest a second assault along his front. Two brigades of Thomas' Yankees were advancing from the direction of the Franklin Pike. Thomas' offensive was meant to support the attack that came from the east. The only problem was that the attack they intended to support had already recoiled from its loss.

The two Yankee brigades were marching over virtually open ground towards the elevated parapets that protected the Confederate lines. Thankfully, with the defeat of the Yankees to the east, General Lowrey, in command of Brown's division, had only these two brigades to concentrate every ounce of his fire at. All Hood could say was that it was about time that the war had gotten this easy.

Their attack had not lasted very long. The Federal ranks were cut to pieces in a matter of seconds. Realizing that Steedman's brigades were no longer in support to the east, General Thomas must have given the order to recall the attack. The Federal casualties were high, but Hood knew that they should have suffered much worse.

Watching their backs as they fled down the sloping hill, Hood quickly sought General Cheatham. Cheatham, now in command of Cleburne's old division had been the only part of his corps that had not been engaged thus far. His men would be fresh and ready to leap over the parapets and chase down the disordered Yanks. Perhaps there was still yet a chance for him to achieve the glory that he so desperately sought.

"Find me Cheatham," he snapped at an aid.

The opportunity that presented itself before him would not last long. Thomas' corps was visibly stretched thin. Thomas was trying valiantly to fill the void between Steedman on the far right and the rest of the Federal army that now appeared to the far left. Unfortunately for Thomas, the space between the two was too large an area for his command to cover. Hood knew that a counterattack along the Franklin Pike would sever Thomas and Steedman from the rest of the Union army.

"General Hood," it was Cheatham.

"General, I want your division to march along this pike and engage the enemy. They are fleeing in disorder and are too far from the rest of their army to receive any support. I want two brigades to drive Thomas' reserves west of the pike, while your other two brigades push east and hold the pike open." Memories of Spring Hill caused a wild glare to flare up in his bulbous eyes. "General Cheatham, please confirm that I am being very clear on this matter. I want this pike held and denied to all Yanks that are east of it."

Cheatham was nodding his head in confirmation. The Federal artillery, realizing that the offensive had failed, began to deliver volley after volley into Hood's corps. They obviously had sensed Hood's intentions, and were hoping to deter the inevitable. After one cannonball ripped through the chest of a soldier standing just a few feet from him, Hood was pulled back from the front. The stricken soldier just stood there a moment, gazing in astonishment at the hole that was once his upper body, before falling to the ground in a crumpled heap of flesh.

"We have to move swiftly," Hood continued. "I will send word to General Stephen Lee that we need Clayton's division to support your attack. It is already beginning to darken, so once we cut them in half, there should be little light left for them to counterattack. We will give General Lee an excellent opportunity to cut the enemy from Nashville and devour them in the morning."

Cheatham tried to refrain from bracing as blast after blast of the enemy's artillery tore into the northern face of the Peach Orchard Hill. Stealing a quick glance over his shoulder, he said, "General Hood, they know that we are coming. Steedman's corps is already shifting west to compensate for the distance between him and Thomas.

Hood smiled back. "This time it won't matter. With Cleburne's old division in control of the pike, and reinforcements sent in from Stephen Lee's corps, the enemy will have but two choices. He must either attack you with Thomas' and Steedman's men, men who have been on the march since early this morning and are no doubt exhausted beyond measure, or allow his army to be cut off from Nashville. If he chooses the latter, then we will finish them off in the morning. If on the other hand he pulls the infantry from my front, then I will be allowed to release Bate and Brown's division to move in as well. Either way, I will have the victory that has managed to elude me during this entire campaign."

"General Hood, General Cheatham," a voice was screaming as it approached on a charging mount. It was Hood's aid-de-camp, Wigfall, now serving Robert E. Lee. His face was pale with a whitening horror. "General Hood, General Lee orders that you send reinforcements immediately to Stewart's left. The enemy is pressing Stewart's corps from all sides. Their cavalry has somehow gained our rear and General Forrest's is nowhere to be found. General Lee fears the worst. Godspeed he begs, please General Hood, a division must be sent at once."

Hood sensed that his moment of glory was once again being stolen from him. He wanted to send Wigfall back to Lee, informing the general that if Stewart's corps could hold for just a few more hours, the Yankee army would be split in half and cut off from Nashville. But he also knew Wigfall extremely well. His frantic condition meant that Lee's left was in dire jeopardy. For Hood, it was like old times. Being needed by General Lee quickly brought back those glorious memories of Gaines Mill.

"General Cheatham, I will leave you with command of this corps. Instruct Cleburne's division that they are to follow my lead," he said. If the crisis was as severe as Wigfall had indicated, then Hood meant for no one to handle it but himself. Too many others had failed him in the past, and he could not allow that to happen now.

Within a few minutes, Cleburne's old division was pulled off the Franklin Pike and directed west across the middle of the battlefield... towards the crumbling left flank.

*   *   *   *   *   *   *   *

The Federal artillery was taking careful aim to prevent Cleburne's division from reaching their left flank. Their guns fired at an unprecedented rate, filling the air with the horrible sounds of incoming projectiles. Unfortunately for their gun crews, most of their shot fell short, smashing into the men of Stephen Lee's corps who ducked behind the stonewall to their front. The air became so clouded with smoke that many of the men thought that the fog had once again returned.

Wigfall had instructed Hood to march behind Stephen Lee's command until he crossed the Granny White Pike. From there, Hood would find Robert E. Lee, and Lee would assess what portion of the hill Hood's division was most needed. Wigfall guessed Hood's command would be used to oppose Wilson's cavalry.

As Hood neared the left flank, the more clearly he could see the swarming waves of Yankees pressing upon Stewart's corps. Looking over his right shoulder, past the ducking head of Stephen Lee's corps, he could barely make out the thin skirmish line of the enemy as they fired from the cornfields to the front. From beyond that, the Union artillery continued to hurl its lead into the Confederate lines.

And that was when he understood.

The whole Federal army must be facing Stewart's lone corps, which was why the enemy was so thin towards the middle and right. Schofield had put just enough of his army in place to hold two thirds of Lee's, hoping that his massive numbers could overwhelm their left flank and cut off the rest of the Confederates from the rear. No wonder he was able to repel their attacks so easily.

The sight of Stewart's flags falling back from the hill towards the Granny White caused him to speed up the march. Hood knew that he needed to get Cleburne's division up those slopes before the whole left flank caved. With great speed, he finally brought his command to the Granny White. The question now was, where was Lee?

One look, and he knew he would not get the time needed to locate his commander. The Army of Tennessee was in chaos. Regiments were being pulled from the battle to the north, and sent to impede the advance of the new Federal threat to the rear. Bullets were whizzing from the north, west and south at the same time as Yankee artillery was crashing into anything gray upon the hill. He could see two regiments from Walthall's division being pulled from the northern face of the hill and sent to support Loring's faltering division. Hood thought if they arrived in time, there was a chance at preventing the Yankee cavalry from gaining control of the Granny White farther to the south.

Hood knew that he needed to do something, and he needed to do it now.

"General Govan," he called to the commander of his lead

brigade, "have your men form right here, and have them ready to march forward. I need to find General Lee and …"

Before he could finish a wild cheer broke through the Confederate entrenchments. Hood's head spun towards the north, where the flags of Schofield's Twenty-third corps exploded through the very point were Walthall's two regiments had just vacated. The rest of Walthall's division, already being pressed from their front had to pull back to avoid being outflanked. The Twenty-third's breakthrough extended past Walthall's right, across the Granny White, causing Johnson's division of S.D. Lee's corps to abandon their works. Hood could hear the screams of S. D. Lee as he tried to rally his routing troops.

"General Hood, your orders sir?" Govan said. "French's division is now unsupported and is falling back. Loring will have to do the same."

The time for contemplation was over. Men in gray were rushing past his division with wild fright. The enemy was closing in on the Granny White from both directions, and would soon cut off any chance of escape for Lee's army. Wigfall told Hood that he would find Lee at the Granny White and from there would obtain his orders. Well, Lee was not here, and so Hood would have to act just as Stonewall Jackson would have done.

On his own.

"General Govan, send an officer back to Cheatham and in-struct him to personally lead Brown's division to this side of the battlefield." He then raced past several of Walthall's fleeing soldiers until he reached the color bearer of Cleburne's division. With the use of only one hand, he grabbed the pole and defiantly hoisted the pale moon high into the air, and with a voice that drowned out the sounds of battle, vehemently roared, "Cleburne, with me."

Hood then spun his horse around and raced north along the Granny White towards the thousands of Yankees pouring into their lines.

*   *   *   *   *   *   *   *

A small unit from the Twenty-fifth Michigan saw the wild-eyed general galloping towards them. He represented the only enemy that stood between them and a complete breakthrough.

Repulse at Stewart's Hill

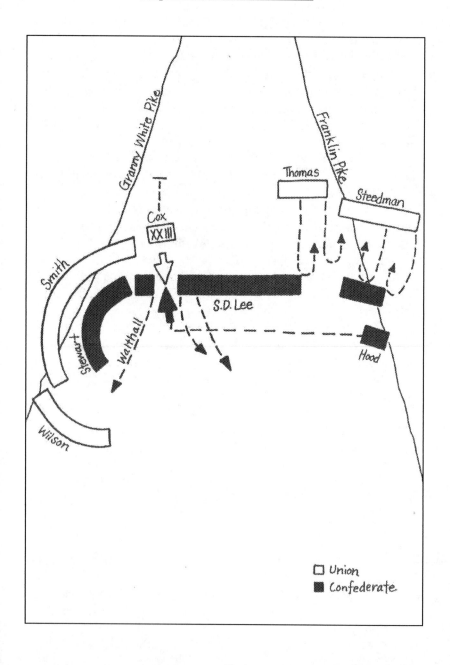

They quickly set their rifles and delivered several shots towards the oncoming menace. They watched in disbelief as his leg seemed to shatter from the impact of their Minnie balls, but the bearded General still came... Cleburne's flag still waving defiantly.

*   *   *   *   *   *   *   *

He felt no pain in his leg as the artificial limb splintered beneath him. Nor did he feel the lead balls that were embedded in his crippled right arm. He took it for what it was, atonement. God was striking him in the very places that had caused him the most hurt. Chaplain Quintard had always said that when unfortunate things occurred, it was God's way of testing your character... His way of revealing the real you. Hood always felt that being the commander of the Army of Tennessee was God's way of testing his perseverance and endurance... God's way of testing his character. His being shot in the very places that could not hurt him was God's way of saying that he had passed His test.

And that carried him forward.

He continued to incite his men by waving the flag and calling upon them to rally... rally for Cleburne. The division responded to the name of their fallen commander by charging with such speed that they rushed past Hood and crashed into the oncoming Yankees. Hood watched his men rush into the battle and longed to be running alongside them. He could vividly remember Gains Mill as if he were there now...his able legs climbing over the wooden fence rail, his saber held high... the steel blade waving his men to take the Federal guns.

Just like then, General Lee needed Hood to save the battle.

The sound of the impact was sickening. Guns were discharged and then swung as clubs. Bayonets were thrust by wild-eyed men. The sound of tearing flesh was rivaled only by numerous gory streams of crimson blood that soiled the earth.

The savage tenacity raged on both sides, as men realized that the victor of this battle would depend on the outcome of this very moment. Hood turned to see General Johnson leading his rallied troops back towards the works that they had just vacated. The Federals were also sending reinforcements to the battle. Theirs were being pulled from Walthall's front, which was good.

It meant a great deal of pressure would be removed from Stewart's corps.

The battle continued for several long moments, both sides swaying their momentum north to south. But Hood knew that it was his men that held the edge. All along the line, color bearers continued to hold Cleburne's flag high above the carnage that was occurring below. Each snap of the peppered blue flags was a reminder that this battle was to avenge Cleburne's honor. It was only fitting that the battle was being contested between this division and what was left of Schofield's Twenty-third corps. They were the ones that started it, and now it would end here.

And it did.

From across the valley, every Yankee battery unleashed its venom at the same instant. The result of which caused the earth to tremble, as Hood was almost shaken from his horse. Had he not been tied down, he doubted his ability to remain mounted. After a quick adjustment in his saddle, Hood's concern was entirely for his men. It was his boys that had just borne the brunt of that assault. Unfortunately, the smoke made it impossible for him to discern the outcome.

Then they came. Their long blue lines seemed to materialize out of the smoky aftermath. There were hundreds of Yankees marching unopposed towards Hood and his staff. Hood quickly turned to see if there were any available troops that he could use to impede their advance, but there were none. The only Confederates that he could find were those that were caving in around him, barely holding off the pressures from both west and south, as Wilson's cavalry tightened the noose around Stewart's corps.

As hope left his soul, Hood relied on the one instinct that had helped him to survive this war… and that was to charge.

He was giving the order for his small escort to charge the Yankees, hoping to at least slow them, when he heard the rebel cheer explode all around him. Hood could not recall every hearing it hollered so… defiantly. Behind the hundreds of Federal soldiers, were scores of Confederates. Their rifles pointed at the herd of blue. Only then did Hood realize that the Yankees were unarmed. Those Yanks were prisoners. The rest of their command was racing back towards their artillery far to the north.

Hood's arm finally gave from the weight of the flag and the long pole slid down his palm until the end of it rested in the dirt. A soldier from Granbury's old brigade was quick to seize the colors and hoist it high into the air. The men around him let out a wild cheer as they began to chant.

It took a moment for Hood to realize what they were saying. When he did, he smiled. The flags waving in the air were done so for Cleburne, but the name that was shouted from their lips was his.

Chapter XXXVIII
Nashville, Tennessee
The battle of Nashville

The rapidly deteriorating situation on his left flank made it impossible for Robert E. Lee to meet Hood's division alongside the Granny White Pike. The mounting pressure was forcing Lee to pull troops from anywhere possible until there were no more reserves to be had. From the looks of Stewart's command, his entire corps was on the verge of collapsing. Followed by his staff, Lee raced atop the hill towards the division that needed him the most. If his presence could do anything to prevent French's division from routing, then he would take that chance and place himself upon that hill with those brave men.

The sight of him riding amongst their lines inspired the soldiers to hold their position, but they also begged him to retire back down the hill. Lee had been in a similar position twice before with the army of Northern Virginia, and in both instances had allowed Traveler to be led away from the fight. That was not to be this time. Never before in this war had he felt the desperation as he did now. A defeat on this slope would mean the end of the Army of Tennessee. And if this army were defeated, it would not be much longer until Grant did the same to his own back in Virginia.

The descending sun made him wish that their offensive had commenced just an hour later. The darkness would have prevented the Federals from attacking, and would have given Lee another day to find his cavalry. Unfortunately that was not the case. The enemy was pouring in from all sides, and Forrest was not around to deter them.

Smith's entire corps seemed poised to toss Stewart's entire command down the hill. And if some miracle prevented that from happening, there was Wilson's dismounted cavalry closing in from the south. With Wilson's presence in his rear, Lee had thought his worst fears materialized, and that Sherman had returned with sixty thousand Union soldiers. The confirmation that it was only Wilson's cavalry did little to relieve his stress. Wilson was not Sherman, but his presence still meant that their rear had been breached. There were not many options left for him. There were just too many Yankees on this side of the Granny White for Stewart to contend with.

And then the thin wall broke. From high on the hill, he could see Walthall's line cave in as several of its regiments routed from the enemy. The breakthrough allowed a massive wave of Federal forces to drive a thickening wedge between Stewart and the rest of the Confederate army. This was Lee's darkest moment. But his despair would last for only that... a moment, until he saw the flags of Cleburne's old division counter the Federal attack with a charge of their own. It was a miracle. No, he knew better than that, it was his covenant spoken with the Lord.

With dried lips, he whispered his thanks to the Almighty above. The Union troops were already pulling back, forcing McArthur's westernmost brigades to follow suit. The Yankee divisions of Garrard and Moore had to comply as well, for their entire left flank was now fleeing up the pike towards Nashville. Lee reigned his mount and raced towards General French.

"General," he said. "As soon as the enemy clears your front, march your division to the west and come behind Wilson's dismounted cavalry. His mounts are no doubt in those hills somewhere, and without the rest of this army to protect him, he is now very vulnerable. You must engage them before they can reach their horses. Cut him off and do not let them escape."

With a conviction that was inspired by Lee's stern tone, French saluted and began issuing orders to his staff. Confident that Wilson's presence in his rear would soon mean the end of the Federal cavalry, Lee rode towards the northern slopes of the hill. The view was magnificent. The entire Yankee army, on all fronts, was routing towards the safety of Nashville. Large numbers of men streamed north along the Granny White and Franklin Pike. Farther west there were additional regiments using the Hillsboro Pike as an avenue to safety. He wondered why the enemy did not choose to hold the hills to the north and retire under cover of darkness?

And then he saw the flags of Cleburne's' division pouring over their own works and understood why. God had promised him a victory and here he was handing it to him. The pale moon wavering upon blue flags was no doubt God's way of reminding Lee that He had fulfilled his end of the covenant. Now it was up to Lee to do the same. Lee thought of the last time he saw Cleburne alive, and softly thanked the memory.

The brief moments that he had shared with Cleburne were

all the vindication that he needed to trust in his heart and do what he knew was right. He went as far as to promise his God that if he succeeded in battle at Nashville that he would labor to all ends to emancipate the Southern slaves. Yet not until God had granted him his victory, did he begin to realize the enormity of such a task. There were Southern commissioners, who swore whether sink or swim, survive or perish, their states would never submit to Black republicanism. Venomous declarations that they would rather see the entire white race burnt in one funeral pyre than subject it to a society where they were on social equality with the Negro...

But then again, for every belligerent commissary that the South produced there was probably an unsung hero like Levi Miller. Levi was the slave of Captain John J. McBride of the Fifth Texan regiment. Lee had to smile at the irony. The Fifth was part of the Texan brigade of Hood's old division. Back in May, near the Spotsylvania courthouse, the Fifth was under severe pressure from Federal forces. Fearing for his master's safety, Levi Miller grabbed a musket and fell in line with the rest of the regiment. Lee had heard that much of the credit of the Fifth that day lay in the tenacious fighting capability of the black servant Levi Miller.

In the end, Lee knew that he would keep his covenant, no matter what the repercussions would be. He may have worried about the consensus of the Southern aristocracy, but he did not fear it. The only thing that Lee feared was God.

The matter was then settled.

Though the victory was not as complete as he would have wished, it was a victory nonetheless. He knew that his army would never catch the routing Yanks. He had seen this too many times before and knew how it would end. The Federal army would escape from the Confederates, just as they had at Malvern Hill, Manassas, Fredericksburg, Chancellorsville and Franklin. The failure to finish the enemy at those past battles was his greatest frustration. It seemed that in every Confederate success, the Union army had somehow managed to escape total destruction.

Nashville, it appeared would not be different.

Through his field glasses he could see the Union army fleeing towards the safety of Montgomery Hill. The Granny White Pike lay just to the east of the hill, with the Franklin Pike running parallel less than a mile to the right. As the two pikes neared the hill, they drew closer in proximity, which would enable the Union command to use that hill as a rallying point for their fleeing soldiers. Lee could already see the dark figures of troop movement upon the southern side of the hill.

It looked as if they were unlimbering artillery. Just a few moments ago, Lee has wished for the arrival of darkness, but as his fortune had changed, he now wished that it were not so late in the day. Lee would have liked to attempt at least one single counterattack upon the Yankee defenses positioned on that hill.

Once the Federal army came under the protection of that reserve force upon Montgomery Hill, their passage behind their works and into Nashville would be secured. He looked one last time at his army as it continued to march after the fleeing Northerners. The Yankees were running on exhausted limbs, but there was ample space between them and the pursuers. There was no hope of catching Schofield in the open. After today, he doubted that there would ever be another chance again… at least not until Grant could rail another thirty thousand Union soldiers into Nashville.

His war in the west had not been any different from the fate that he suffered in the east. Once again, he had won the battle, but in the game of numbers, knew that he would eventually lose the war. Not to let his pessimism diminish his gratitude towards the Lord, Lee once again praised the Almighty for His victory.

When his silent prayer had finished, he instructed his staff to inform all commanders to organize their commands and occupy the positions that they held the day before. It was already too dark to attempt an assault upon their heavily guarded city, and he did not want to waste a single needed soldier on an assault that would end with defeat.

"Instruct my senior commanders that there is to be a council held this evening at my headquarters. I expect to have full reports brought with them." Lee departed from his staff and retired towards the Overton home. He needed to decide the best course of action to take after today's battle. But before he could do that, he knew that he needed time alone to write a very important telegram to President Davis… a telegram that would strengthen the bond between he and his Lord.

He had just crossed over the Granny White Pike when the sound of artillery exploded in the distance. From the burning flashes that lit the dusk, there was no mistaking that it came from the lower slopes of Montgomery Hill… the slopes that the fleeing Federal infantry could not have reached yet.

*　　　*　　　*　　　*　　　*　　　*　　　*　　　*

The Ninety-ninth Ohio was the last regiment in line when the Second division of the Twenty-third corps broke through the Confederate line. Thus they were the first to escape from Hoods timely counterattack. During the battle, they had every intention of holding their ground until the last man was standing, but when their own artillery crashed upon their ranks from the rear, it was too much for them to bargain with.

It was their commander, Lieutenant Colonel John E. Cummins, who gave the initial order to fall back. He had thought that the enemy had somehow gained his rear and he did not want his regiment to be trapped in between. Meaning to fight his way out of the trap, he ordered the Ninety-ninth about face and led a charge with his saber raised high above him. After they raced almost twenty-feet, they realized that there was nothing behind them except the wind.

But by then it was too late. The rest of McArthur's division misconstrued Cummins maneuver as a rout. For those Yankees still stuck in that hornet's nest, they felt that Cummins had the right idea. Soon the entire division was pulling back and racing for the pike. Since Cummins had his regiment already upon the pike, he simply kept them advancing north, back to the safety of Nashville.

His men were tired, he knew that because he himself was. He always prided his stamina in battle, but after marching all those miles from Nashville, fighting the enemy, and now having to march back it was too much for even his conditioned limbs to endure. They continued to run until the sounds of pursuit began to fade in the distance.

The early winter night was descending upon the field, and many of the Yankees that had escaped could not be more grateful. From behind, they could hear small skirmish lines firing at the enemy in an effort to impede their pursuit. The only thing that slowed them from reaching Nashville was the rolling wagons of their own artillery as the guns were pulled out of the hills north of the battle. Cummins just hoped that the wagons would not clog the open pike. Though they were still far behind, the rebel army was still coming, and anything that hindered his escape could be fatal.

Cummins could see the shadows of a large force of infantry gathered upon the hill. It was the most welcoming sight that he had ever seen in his life. Schofield must have ordered a reserve force to occupy the high ground. With the Granny White Pike running so near its base, Montgomery Hill was in a perfect position to protect the retreating army. From that hill, the artillery could support his command as well as the regiments retreating along the Franklin Pike. The reserve force positioned on that hill was the assurance that his regiment, and those that followed, would reach Nashville to fight another day.

He turned to one of his sergeants and gave the order to have the men move faster. "I want our regiment and these wagons past the hill so that the pikes are completely clear for the rest of the army."

The sergeant, a middle aged man with an effeminate countenance told Cummins that he understood. He then raised his hand to salute before departing, but before he could bring his arm back down to his side, a thunderous volley exploded in front of the regiment. Cummins was so startled he had no time to think. Instinctively he ducked, unfortunately his sergeant did not. With a whitening flash, his head was removed from his shoulders as the cannon ball continued past him and tore through the rest of the regiment, severing limbs and shattering bones as it continued down the line, before exploding further down the pike.

Cummins got to his feet and tried to wave his hat at the gunners on the hill. Perhaps they had mistaken them for rebels. "Cease fire," he roared, "For God's sake cease fire."

From behind, a few of his men raised white flags upon their rifles. If they were being mistaken for the enemy, then best let them believe we intend to surrender, they thought.

Cummins could not afford to wait and see if the white flags would work. The cannons were roaring into the men and wagons with reckless abandon. The lead columns of men had already fled from the road, and those that trailed behind were creating a logjam. If they got stuck out here in the open, the pursuing rebels would surely have them mauled. Cummins told his men to keep their flags up, grabbed a half dozen of his soldiers and raced towards the hill. They dodged past hurling missiles, past the obliterated shards of wood that were once wagons. All he could think of was how the Federal artillery had done more harm to their own army today than the enemy had.

He led his soldiers around the burning debris of a broken

cannon and headed up the slopes. With white flags glowing in the dusk, they begged for a cease-fire. Cummins' head tilted forward as he tried to visually locate a single soldier he could reach. More than that, he wanted to speak directly to the artillery officer responsible for ordering that fire.

When they were just a few feet up the lower slopes of the hill, he saw that the reserve force was positioned behind some very recently created earthworks. Their weapons still ominously aimed at his regiment.

"We are not rebels," Cummins shouted. "We are soldiers of the United States Army."

There was no answer. One of his own soldiers, a younger man who stood to his left, held his musket high over his head, the wavering white flag tied around the end of its barrel pleading to be recognized. His other hand was curved around his brow, as he squinted past the earthworks. His words were soft and solemn.

"Colonel, those men are wearing gray."

The entire gray line fired a volley at point blank range. The unsuspecting Cummins, along with his men, did not even have a second to brace themselves for the attack. In a matter of seconds, they simply ceased to exist.

*   *   *   *   *   *   *   *

His guns roared and flashed in the consuming darkness like thunder and lightening. The greatest gamble of his life had paid off as a terrorized Federal army fled from the two pikes and disappeared into the countryside beyond. It was one thing for an army to rout, but when it routed towards safety, only to find that its escape was cut off, the rout quickly degraded in to an all out panic stricken stampede.

When he constructed this plan, it was admittedly the first time in his military career that he was not absolutely sure of its outcome. Perhaps if it were anyone other than Robert E. Lee, he might have been forced to retire his command towards the safety of the infantry. But it was Lee who commanded the Army of Tennessee, and it was Lee who would inspire them to hold their ground at all costs. That was the only part of his plan that he had confidence in.

As far as Forrest was concerned, there was no doubt that

Lee would repel the Yankee army and send them scurrying back towards Nashville. It was that conviction that let him play the last card in his deck... none other than the ace of spades.

It was Wilson's cavalry that first took the bait... once Jackson's division was driven through Bell's Mill, the Federal cavalry simply drove against Lee's left and rear. Forrest had watched them pass, not believing how gullible the Yankee cavalry continued to be. Once the Yankees moved passed his command, Forrest fragmented his command into smaller regiments and instructed his officers to have their troopers re-consolidate on the slopes of Montgomery Hill.

They were to ride low and use the contours of the hilly countryside to mask their approach. 'Make every attempt to remain hidden', he said. 'Your small numbers will not indicate that you are part of a larger force. If the enemy gives you chase, then flee to the west away from the hill. Wilson is to believe that you are nothing more than a small command of scouts.'

As his division began to consolidate upon the hill, all of his regiments were accounted for save two from Crossland's Brigades, the Seventh and Twelfth Kentucky. The rest of the men on the hill were ordered not to show their colors, but to dismount and retire the horses farther up the hill, taking care not to climb too far to the top, lest the Federals still at Nashville view their presence. Forrest finished issuing the last of these orders just in time to witness the failure of the Federal breakthrough.

And that was when his heart began to pump uncontrollably. He had turned to Strange with a trembling jaw that failed to keep from cheering.

"They're coming," he said. "They are coming right into us."

He then turned from his trusted friend and placed himself right beside the raised guns of Morton's Tennessee battery. Together, Forrest and his cavalry waited to hurl over three years of hatred into the very faces of the Northern aggressors.

His patience was rewarded by the explosive chaos that rained upon the unsuspecting Yankees. Forrest's stern face was magnified by the glowing flash of each volley. His eyes never turned away from the pike that ran by his front. He would gladly have traded a hundred victories like Brice's Crossroads for this one triumph.

The Trap has Sprung

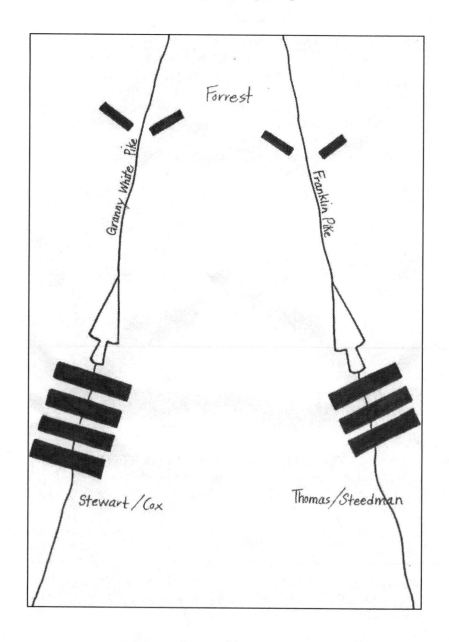

Forrest placed his hand on the barrel of a hot cannon and let its burning metal soak into his veins. Faster, he thought, keep firing this thing faster. He wished that his men had more of those repeating rifles, for his men could not seem to unleash enough lead and canister into the ranks of the passing Federal army. For every company that got past his blockade, one surrendered and another was shredded into human confetti. The amount of prisoners gathered on the hill soon threatened to outnumber all the cavalry he had present. But then again, it was dark, and they would never know that.

So intent on witnessing the passing destruction of the Yankee army, he had not heard the repeated calls from Chalmers. When his general placed a hand upon his shoulder, he spun fluidly upon his heel and gripped Chalmers by the collar. Chalmers could feel Forrest's warm hands as the general began to shake him violently.

"General Chalmers, this makes up for every time those bastards escaped me since Pulaski. Have you ever seen anything so beautiful in your entire life?"

Chalmers decided not to fight Forrest's wild enthusiasm, instead he let his body be handled until the general was done.

"General Forrest, the battle here seems to be over. Smith's corps has managed to rally behind McArthur's brigade and the enemy is moving off the pike to march around McArthur's rear. We have extended our own left flank to allow our boys a chance to fire upon the Yanks fleeing down the Franklin Pike, but many of them are getting by as well. The Yanks will make Nashville, but with a lot fewer men than they would have liked."

Forrest thought of ordering his cavalry to mount and give chase. He turned towards his kneeling boys and noted the intensity that stained their faces with dirt and sweat.

"General, I know what you are thinking," Chalmers said. "But if we do that, we will not be able to control the amount of prisoners that we have. They already outnumbered us, and if you pull even a single brigade from this hill to give chase, they will turn from being the captive to being the captors."

"How much longer until our infantry comes up?" he asked.

"Not soon enough. Hood is leading the chase with Cleburne's old division. Behind him are a few brigades from General S. D. Lee's corp. There is not much more after that. Lee did not know that we were here. Thinking the Yanks had escaped he sent most of Stewart's command south to trap the Federal cavalry. And Cheatham, left behind to command Hood's corps, simply remained behind his breastworks and has allowed Thomas and Steedman to retire unmolested from the field."

Forrest bit his lower lip until he could taste the warm blood flowing across his tongue. Chalmers knew that if he thought he could stop the entire army by himself, Forrest would have already brandished his saber and given chase. "Then let them go," Forrest said. "We must have over four thousand prisoners, and that is not counting those that will never leave these pikes again."

It was now Chalmers turn to take his commander by the shoulder and give him a little shake. "General Forrest, I do believe that this audacious maneuver of yours will scribe your place in military history. Schofield's army may have escaped, but after its losses against Lee, and its losses suffered here against you, I can guarantee that they will not stop running until they cross the Cumberland."

Chalmers took his hand from Forrest's shoulders and extended his right hand forward. Forrest looked down at Chalmers palm and placed his own within it.

"General Forrest, I guarantee that when morning comes, we will find Nashville vacated by the enemy. You have liberated the state capital, and by doing so, have given Tennessee back to the Confederacy."

*   *   *   *   *   *   *   *

Lee knelt by the side of the bed and could not stop shaking as the tears continued to stream down his face. From somewhere outside his contemplations, he could hear the faint echoes of a band as its sounds carried across the Nashville hills and into his bedroom window. He thought of getting up to close the window, but remembered that he had already done so a few hours after his supper. Perhaps he should send Wigfall to instruct the music to be stopped. No, that would not be right, the men had earned this. What he needed to do was to spend less time allowing outside influences to disrupt his prayer, and more time offering the Lord his gratitude.

With two aged hands clenched into one, he bent his brow,

squeezed his already closed lids tighter and thanked the Lord for the miracle that he was granted on this day, for there was no other person more responsible than He. Yet every time his silent lips quivered in gratitude, his overwhelmed emotions broke a deluge of tears down upon his face. Thoughts of his wife and his home in Arlington were like giant rams battering down the wall of self-denial that he himself had so arduously constructed. But he knew that the wall had to be there, and that it had to remain strong before he went to sleep. That wall was all he had left to separate his current tasks from the faces of those that he had lost when trying to accomplish those same tasks.

Like pale ghosts, their faces stared back at him with eyes that were dark and sad, and yet also full of understanding. He tried to count the amount of people that he had placed on the other side of that wall, his wife, his daughters, the fallen soldiers, J.E.B. Stuart...and Thomas Jackson. If there were any one person that he wished to be here today, to share this victory with, it would be Stonewall Jackson. He knew that could never happen, not in this world. Jackson had fallen at Chancellorsville. Ever since that loss, Lee was burdened with a sense of emptiness that he could not fill. It was like losing a son. And he would have so much loved to have his son with him to share in this triumph.

"Thomas Jackson," he whispered, "you would have been so proud of these boys today."

But neither Jackson, his wife, his sons nor daughters could be with him. All he had was the comforts of his wall. It was really the only way that he could properly lead his men without letting his own incompetence interfere. Ever since Grant's army moved through Virginia, occupying his home in the wake, he could feel a growing sense of inadequacy mounting within. Here he was, the person that the South had hung their hopes upon, and yet he could not even protect his own wife in her own home.

Where Mary Custis was now, he could not say. But that did not matter, he fully trusted that God was watching over her with His own divine protection... a protection that Lee as a husband had failed to offer. Since Grant crossed the James River, the only thing that Lee could do was watch as his Army of Northern Virginia was cajoled into a siege. Without the manpower to counterattack the Yankees, all he could do externally was stoically issue orders to a stagnant army.

Internally he had remained hidden behind his wall, hoping

for God to intervene.

Even today, when the Army of Tennessee repulsed the Yanks, it was still not enough to allow him to break down his wall and escape his own captivity. The sight of their thousands retreating back towards Nashville only made his inadequacies more pronounced. Though victorious, he had once again allowed the enemy to escape.

Yet he did not throw down his field glasses in disappointment, nor did he utter a word of complaint… that would not have been a good example for the men. The bottom line was that God had allowed his army a victory, and that he had to be thankful for. And he was, though he had to repress his resentment that the victory was not all that he had hoped for. He knew that God could see through him, knew that God could read his inappreciative thoughts, and so Lee hid further behind the wall.

Then came the sounds of artillery from the hills to the north. Lee understood now that it was God himself firing salvation into his personal confinement and shattering it, like only He can.

Lee had not realized just how absolute the day's victory had been until the reports began making their way to his headquarters. The numbers of Federal casualties on his right, upon the slopes of the Peach Orchard Hill were estimated to be near two thousand. The Confederate middle had not been seriously engaged, but on the hills to the far left, General Stewart had reported another few thousand Federal casualties.

Lee allowed his eyes to open slightly so that he could view the various reports spread uniformly upon his desk. He separated his hands for just a second. Enough time to wipe the thick wetness that helped seal his eyes. He had the pieces of paper arranged so that the reports were placed in their position on the battlefield. It helped him to clearly assess the total picture.

Over four thousand Yankee casualties as compared to fewer than one thousand of his own. The disparity in numbers was impressive, and had this been the first year of the war, Lee would have been comfortable calling the battle a victorious step for Southern independence. But this was not the first year of the war, and if this epic trial had taught him anything about the enemy, it had taught him that the enemy could replace its losses faster than water consumed from a running river. You could fill your cup a million times, but the water would still come. And a bigger container would not help. It would only mean that you had more weight to lift, for the river would still replenish itself. It always would, unless you could somehow remove all of its water at once.

And late this afternoon, through God's grace, General Nathan Bedford Forrest had done just that.

Lee pushed all of the other reports aside and pulled Forrest's closer. He still could not believe the numbers that were written before him. The fleeing Federal army was thrown into total disorder when they realized that their escape route had been cut off. They broke from their command like frenzied cattle.

Thousands upon thousands were herded by Forrest's cavalry and brought upon the hill. There were now over five thousand Union prisoners in Forrest's custody. Roughly another two thousand were estimated to be dead, their bodies would no doubt be found absorbing the morning dew. Forrest had said that the tired Yankees broke because they were fed up. Many of the captured officers complained that they were tired of marching and counter marching... ordered to protect Tennessee, while Sherman had the better part of their army gallivanting through the Carolinas.

Let Sherman do the fighting now, they had had enough of this war. Their attitude was reflected in the last sentence of Forrest's final report.

'Not all of those that escaped fled north.'

.... And still God's work was not done.

Wilson's Yankee cavalry had spent the better part of the day circumventing Lee's left flank so that he could crash upon the Confederate rear. With the initial Federal breakthrough along the Granny White Pike, Wilson was in an excellent position to do just that. With the enemy's cavalry in possession of the Granny White, there would be no route open for Stewart's corps to escape. They would have been completely lost to Lee had the Yankee attack succeeded.

But no matter how much effort and planning Schofield, Wilson and the rest of the Federal army put into their hopes for victory, they were not God. And God's will could not be deterred.

With the Federal breakthrough heavily repulsed, and their army retreating north, Wilson's cavalry was completely cut off from the infantry. Being dismounted, they also did not have their horses close enough to aid them in their escape. The only ally that they were afforded was the early winter darkness. That alone allowed Wilson and most of his command to slip away from the

Confederate counterattack. Still, the Yankee cavalry would be nearly fifteen hundred riders less when they had their next roll call.

Though nearly a third of Schofield's army would return to Nashville, its cavalry would need a few days before completing their circuitous rout around Lee's new left. But that mattered little to Lee, because by the time they reached the city, he meant to have it in Southern possession.

Lee had finally achieved the victory that he so desperately sought, and at a time when his country needed it the most. He did not believe for a moment that such a fact could be coincidence. Since he began this war, it had always been his duty to bring his men to the battlefield and nothing more. Once there, it was up to God to determine the victor.

Lee meant to climb into bed, but shifted towards the nightstand instead. There upon the small wooden table lay the proof of God's will. His carefully written telegram would be wired to Jefferson Davis first thing in the morning. The emancipation was his contract with the Lord, their binding agreement, and their covenant in spirituality. Nashville would be delivered to Lee in the morning... that he was sure of. If it were not, if Schofield attempted to hold the city with his dispirited and defeated army, then Lee would attack at dawn.

He entertained no thoughts that would allow for Schofield to remain behind his entrenchments while Grant railed reinforcements from the north. Nashville was not going to be Chattanooga. God had shown him as much already, and once Lee fulfilled his side of the promise, he knew that there would never be enough Federal soldiers to stop the Confederate cause. His covenant with God assured him of that. After today, there would be no more concerns, no more need to hide from the myriad of faces that existed on the other side of his wall.

The North, without their cries for emancipation would be seen for what they truly were... nothing more than aggressors. From tomorrow on, there would be only one army that could defeat the South, and that army would be their own. Lee understood that for independence to be attained, the Southern states would have to see emancipation with the same righteous eyes as he.

Lee neared the end of his prayer, thanking the Lord for the victory today, and also asking that the Southern people be responsive, especially President Davis. For if they were, and with Nashville liberated, the Confederate army could pass over the Cumberland River, and take the war once again to northern soil.

Pass over the river.

The very words sent chills down his spine, as he felt his soul swell within his chest. Earlier he had whished for one man to be here to share this victory with him, a man that had departed from this world over a year ago. God must have heard Lee's plea, for he realized that that man was with him now at this hour. That man helped Lee to his feet and stepped him over the rubble of his broken wall, over the failure of past incompetence.

Lee stood silently, the sound of the far away band once again entering his room. The tune of Dixie escalating in volume as other bands joined in the melody. Yet all he could hear were the silent words of his fallen friend... the last words Jackson uttered before his death. General Thomas Jackson was in fact here with him now, and his silence echoed in Lee's head.

'Let us pass over the river and rest under the shade of the trees.'

Chapter XXXIX
December 15, Approaching midnight
Washington D.C.

Grant was seated in a chair that had been pulled up close against the Presidents desk. He tried to keep his head raised as a show of self-assurance, but the men on the other side of the desk cared little to take notice. Lincoln, Halleck and Stanton, the three men running this war, all stood over the desk, staring at him with a shared look of disappointment.

And Grant knew that every ounce of it was directed at him. He could feel his cigar pressing against his breast from the inside of his coat pocket, enticing him to strike it with a match. The burning tobacco would probably do much to relieve his mounting stress, but he knew that now was not the time to be smoking a cigar.

He did reach behind his head to massage his stiff neck. The steamboat ride from City Point had not been a pleasant one. He had left his headquarters late last night, after reviewing plans with General Meade for a massive offensive against the Army of the Potomac. If Lee was indeed in Tennessee, as Grant truly believed, then now was the time to strike. That was why he insisted on this meeting at the President's office, so that he could deliver first hand the news that Lee was no longer in Virginia.

At first, Lincoln had doubted him. The President had to call in Stanton and Halleck to see if they would support Grant's claim. Though they too were reluctant to believe that Lee would ever leave Virginia, they did admit to it being a possibility… a very threatening possibility with Sherman's army no longer in Tennessee. How Grant could allow this to happen, to give the South such an opportunity, was the question that wrinkled their foreheads.

They had not left the office since this afternoon. A warm meal was brought in for supper, but the meat was hard to swallow. Their stomachs were left feeling as empty as their hopes. Up until Grant's arrival this afternoon, Lincoln had the utmost confidence that the war was near its end.

Now there was a chance, though remote, that Lee was out

west, drawing Schofield into a trap. With Sherman's army too far to be of any assistance, the fate of Tennessee, and the entire west for that matter, rested upon the shoulders of a general who they all knew was no match for Robert E. Lee. Grant's answer called for an all out attack in Virginia, but with so much in doubt in Tennessee, Lincoln was not ready to make that commitment.

"General," Lincoln said. "We can not allow you to attack the Confederates until we have confirmation that Lee is actually in Tennessee. You must understand that."

Grant reluctantly nodded. His burning gut was all the confirmation that he needed.

Halleck walked past the desk and moved to Grant's side. His voice was loud, directed to the far side of the room. "Anything major?"

"No. Nothing as of yet," Major Thomas T. Eckert replied.

Eckert was operating the telegraph that had recently been moved into the room. Lincoln wanted to be the first to receive any news regarding Nashville. Eckert and his telegram operator had since remained motionless, both being so quiet that Grant had forgotten that they were still in the room with them.

"General Grant, what is the latest report from Sherman?" Stanton asked.

Grant swung back around in his chair. He had to catch himself from retrieving the cigar from his pocket. He made the motion look as if he was scratching his chest. "Yes, General Sherman has reported that he is outside Savannah with over sixty thousand soldiers, and he is ready to take occupation of the city in the next few days. His only opposition is roughly seventeen thousand Confederates commanded by General Hardee."

"Well at least we finally know where a quarter of our army is," Stanton said with obvious disgust.

Grant felt the words press though his spine like sharp nails. Stanton had a right to criticize Sherman's offensive, they all did. He was not going to make any excuses for himself, but there was no way he could have foreseen Lee taking command of Hood's army back in November. At the time, he was apprehensive with Sherman removing half of the army from the western theatre, but decided to let him go. How he wished he could take back that decision, for even his worst possible scenario paled compared to the disaster that was now pending.

Grant did not realize how much he had missed his wife's

presence until now. He could use her soft fingers pressing against his shoulders almost as much as he could use a report that Lee was seen on Traveler somewhere in the vicinity of Petersburg. Perhaps he should offer an immediate trip west, and stay there until Lee's presence could be confirmed. Grant was about to make that suggestion, when Eckert nearly jumped from his seat as his telegraph machine came alive.

"The lines are open," he cheered like a child on Christmas morning. "It is a little past eleven, and the lines are open." The suspense mounted as Eckert's assistant began translating the ciphered message. 'Nashville, Tennessee. December 14. 1864.'

The message was a day old. Halleck quickly moved across the room and seized the rest of the report. He turned towards Stanton and the President and quickly began summarizing the details.

"It says little that we don't already know. The weather had improved, the ice melted. Schofield intends to attack the Confederate army in the morning. There is little else."

"Wait, Mr. Halleck, more is coming now," Eckert's assistant said. This time Lincoln rushed over followed by Stanton and Grant. The five men all anxiously huddled around Eckert's assistant and his machine. They tried to read over his shoulder as he decoded the message, but they could only make out scattered words. That was fine, for there was only one word they looked to see written. And there, towards the end of the message, the specter of their worst fears materialized in written ink. The name Robert E. Lee was on the telegram that had come from Nashville, Tennessee.

Halleck was the only one able to muster the will to respond. He took the telegram from the assistant and read it in its entirety. "This next one was written only an hour ago," he began.

"Our line advanced and engaged the enemy early this morning. A concealing fog obscured the movement of our army. Using this screen to our advantage we marched upon the rebel works only to find that the enemy had vacated the night before. The rebel army was found a few miles farther south, and it was reported that Forrest's cavalry was operating in Murfreesboro.

Not wishing to be caught outside of our entrenchments, the army was ordered to proceed with the attack. Our men fought valiantly to gain their works, and succeeded though briefly at penetrating their line along the Granny White Pike. Except for a *timely counterattack, the breakthrough would have severed an entire corps from General Lee's command.*

I must also add that we have erred in assuming that General Lee meant Stephen Lee, for it does not. From a few prisoners that were taken during the breakthrough, it has been confirmed that Robert. E. Lee is the current commander of the Army of Tennessee.

Our losses were not too severe, but I think it best to withdraw the army across the safety of the Cumberland, allowing the enemy to occupy Nashville for the time being. From our new position we can reorganize our army and prepare to battle General Lee at another time."

Halleck had been shaking so violently that he could no longer read the blurred words. His reddened face turned viciously towards Grant. "This is your damned fault. You should never have relieved Thomas."

"You gave me no choice," Grant was quick to fire back, as he took a step menacingly closer towards Halleck.

Lincoln and Eckert quickly placed themselves in between the two combatants. "Generals, please," Lincoln said. "Schofield reported his losses light, perhaps..."

Halleck threw the telegram at Grant. "Schofield is lying to cover his ass. He would not abandon the forts and trenches of Nashville unless he had been severely whipped. Grant knows that. He also knows that General Smith and General Wilson would never have allowed Nashville lost unless there was no hope of holding it."

Lincoln felt his limbs waver as he took a shaky step backwards. Sad solemn eyes glanced at Grant momentarily before swooping low to the floor. "Could this be?" he whispered.

Grant could not allow the President to feel this way. He stepped past Halleck and moved closer to Lincoln. "Mr. President, please, all is not lost. Now we know that Lee is out west, I already have General Meade in position with the army to launch an offensive in Virginia. Without Lee and his leadership, the Army of Northern Virginia will crumple. I promise you sir, Lee was all that held their hungry and demoralized army together. Let me attack in the morning, then my army and Sherman's will move west to destroy the Army of Tennessee."

Lincoln looked as if he were about to give his approval, but Halleck roared with fury.

"Mr. President, I beg of you to not let this man's twisted tongue compel you into this. How many Cold Harbor's does Grant need before he realizes that his tactics do not work?" Halleck stepped from Lincoln and placed himself directly in front of Grant.

"How many more thousands of our boys must fall because of you. Stanton and I have read over the casualty lists in horror. Your army may have pushed Lee farther than any general before you, but the number of men lost reflect that." He turned back to Lincoln. "Please, reconsider."

"What other choice is there?" the President softly asked.

"Halleck and I have already considered this option," Stanton said. "If it were true that Lee was west, and now we know that he is, and Lee managed to defeat Schofield, as we know that he has done, we devised a plan that would rapidly transfer troops west to secure that part of the country."

"Go on," Lincoln said.

"No… Stanton, please," Grant pleaded. He knew where Stanton was headed with his plan. He knew exactly which troops he meant to send west, and he knew how fatal that would be to the army, and more importantly the situation here in the east.

Halleck blocked Grant off and told Stanton to continue.

"Sheridan's cavalry can leave the Shenandoah valley immediately. They are already in close proximity to the railroads that would carry them to Ohio. General Early's army has been defeated and is no longer the threat they were once to the area. Our other reinforcements would come from General Sherman, and if I might add, had his army been in Tennessee as it should have, this disaster would never have occurred."

"Mr. President, please do not listen to this," Grant said. "This is exactly what Lee is hoping that you will do. Remember what occurred when Jackson was in the Valley and McClellan had troops taken from his army. The same will happen here. Hardee's seventeen thousand will march from Savannah and add to the army of Northern Virginia, their numbers growing, while ours are pulled away. You cannot take Sherman's army and send it back west from where it came. That would have disastrous effects on their morale. Let Sherman capture Savannah, then march to Petersburg to help us defeat the Army of Northern Virginia, and then together we can consolidate our overwhelming numbers against Lee and the Army of Tennessee."

"President Lincoln, I think General Grant finally has it

right," Halleck said much to Grant's surprise. Halleck moved back to his original place on the other side of the desk and began writing something down. When he was finished, he handed it to Eckert to be telegraphed.

"Mr. President," Halleck continued, "As I was saying, General Grant is absolutely correct about one thing. We cannot take General Sherman's army and send them back west. And that is because as of this moment, General Sherman no longer has an army. He is relieved of command, as is General Schofield. I think that we all can agree that Thomas will take command of the army, until Grant can get there. General Grant will once again command the west and we will place Meade back in command in the east. Mr. President, all this needs is your approval."

Grant could not lift his head, could not watch as his President sobbed into trembling hands that failed to cover his face... a face that was nodding its approval of Halleck's new plan.

Epilogue
March 17, 1865

He left his horse tied to the post and looked down the street towards the theatre. He could not wait to enter the theatre house, but it was not to see the play. John Wilkes Booth wished to see the President.

With his tall silk hat set firmly on his head, he took a moment to put on his gloves. What caught his attention were the embedded lines that crossed his palms. What was it that gypsy had said about his crisscrossed lines? Something about him having a bad hand? Booth had to smirk with disbelief. It was years ago when he met a gypsy that had predicted many things concerning his fate. She had said that he was born under an unlucky star, and he would have a short, but fast life... one that would be grand.

Grand indeed.

Booth remembered how her own hands trembled as they held his, as if it took a great effort for her to see into his future. She finally threw back his hands in disgust, saying that she had never seen a worse hand, and whished that she never had seen it.

Oh, that gypsy had no idea.

Booth finished dressing his gloves. He then carefully removed the small derringer from his coat pocket and placed it in his hand. The gun was loaded with a single lead ball... enough to complete his objective. Booth concealed the weapon by draping his overcoat over his arm. His free hand ensured that his bowie knife was still secured inside his pants on the left side.

He was now armed and ready for the task before him.

With a cane in hand, Booth walked stoically down the city street, nodding to many of the faces that recognized him as a well-known actor. Ironic, how his greatest performance would be played out in the theatre.

If there were any doubts concerning what he was about to do, they were lost somewhere in the folds of his dark overcoat. This President was the cause of his country's troubles, and that could not go unpunished. How could these niggers be allowed to roam free in this great country? A country that was formed by the white man... for the white man. That was how God had meant it when he blessed this favored nation. And this President had changed all of that.

Booth's fame allowed him to walk into the theatre and up the stairs towards the President's box. He could hear the play and knew that it would soon come to the scene that would expose the crowd to a very humorous situation. It was at that moment, when the crowd laughed the loudest, that he meant to assassinate the President.

Booth nodded to the two men that stood outside the door that led into the President's box. They nodded back, recognizing the famous actor, and allowed him to freely enter. Booth moved through the door like a malignant shadow. Assured that the President had not noticed his entry, he slowly closed the door behind him. Luckily, the President was currently seated alone, and the scene below was approaching the humorous part. Booth silently exposed his derringer as he softly approached the back of the President. He intended to complete his deed before the President's guests could return.

He slowly raised the pistol at the back of the President's head, carefully resting it behind the left ear. He waited patiently for the crowd below to roar with laughter and then he pulled the trigger.

Just then, the door opened and the President's guests entered the box. Booth was delighted to see the horror in their eyes and heard one of them scream, "The President has been shot." Booth winked at the terrified group and then rushed by them, swinging his cane like a club. Booth was surprised at how easily he slipped by the stunned group. He could hear that the play had been disrupted and many in the crowd below were also screaming as the word of the ill deed quickly spread through the theatre.

Booth quickly descended the stairs, but before he reached the last few steps, his feet became tangled and he crashed awkwardly to the floor. He used the cane to raise himself, but his ankle gave.

"Damn," he spat, "I've sprained my ankle."

Realizing that his escape depended on his ignoring the pain, Booth hobbled towards the exit. With one last look over his shoulder, he could hear the crowd wailing in disbelief.

"The President has been shot... the President has been shot... someone has killed President Jefferson Davis."

Bibliography

Besides the countless articles obtained from the library, and the wealth of information gathered from the internet, field trips, and civil war lectures... the following books were used as references for my work. Without the hard work done by these authors, the two most notably being <u>Civil War</u> Shelby Foote's and Wiley Sword's <u>The Confederacy's Last Hurrah,</u> my work would have been left vastly incomplete.

Foote, Shelby. *Civil War.* 1974.

Frey, Jerry. *In The Woods Before Dawn.* 1994.

Groom, Winston. *Shrouds of Glory.* 1995.

Hood, John, Bell. *Advance and Retreat: Personal Experience in the United States and Confederate States Armies.* 1959.

Hurst, Jack. *Nathan Bedford Forrest.* 1993.

McDonough, James Lee and Connelly, Thomas L. *Five Tragic Hours.* 1983.

McMurry, Richard M. *John Bell Hood and the War for Southern Independence.* 1982

Tucker, Glenn. *Lee and Longstreet at Gettysburg.* 1982

Sword, Wiley. *The Confederacy's Last Hurrah.* 1992.

About The Author

James Cupelli resides in Chambersburg, Pennsylvania. He is an avid Civil War historian who spent over seven years researching and writing this book. The conversations read in this novel are authenticated conjectures, taken from autobiographies, biographies, and a myriad of Civil War literature. When not reading about the Civil War, he enjoys spending time with his wife Heather of 10 years, and two beautiful daughters, Arianna, and Jenna Lee.